SEVEN BRIDES FOR SEVEN TEXAS RANGERS

LONESTAR BROTHERS

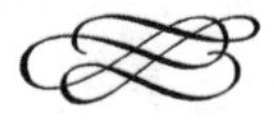

ERICA VETCH GABRIELLE MEYER LORNA SEILSTAD
AMANDA BARRATT KATHLEEN Y'BARBO
SUSAN PAGE DAVIS VICKIE MCDONOUGH

PROLOGUE

Hartville, Texas
January 1, 1886

Hugh Sterling hopped off the train, hand on his sidearm, ready for trouble. He squinted against the sun and the fine grit blown up by a stiff south wind, studying the face of each person on the platform, checking for weapons, on the alert for an ambush.

"We're not in Comanche country, Hugh. Hartville is a perfectly respectable town." Etta, his wife, standing on the top step of the railcar, raised one eyebrow as he reached up to help her. "I doubt any outlaws are lurking behind mercantile windows."

You never could tell. Satisfied that there was no immediate danger, Hugh swung his petite spouse down, smiling as she adjusted her hat and smoothed her skirts. The breeze teased her hair, and though gray now streaked the reddish-brown strands, he still thought her the prettiest gal in Texas or any other state.

"Old habits." Hugh shrugged and took her valise from the conductor. Placing his hand under her elbow, he directed her toward the shade of the depot's overhang. Though it was the first day of the new year, the sun was unseasonably warm even for South-Central Texas.

Etta watched the passengers leave the train, no doubt looking for the men under his command, the ones she considered "my boys." "Whit should be here, shouldn't he?"

"He'll show." Etta would be in nonstop motion until she had everything arranged, including *her boys*, the way she wanted. It was the same every time they came to a new posting. A tornado in petticoats, he'd heard one of his men call her...though not to her face.

"Captain Sterling." Griff Sommer, the youngest of his troop of Texas Rangers, rested his hands on his hips. "Branch and Jesse said they'd wrangle the horses, and Ezra and O'Neal are bringing the baggage. What should I do?"

Griff was the only one of his Rangers who still called him by his full rank and last name. Most of the company called him *Cap*, and some had been with him long enough to call him by his first name, but Griff was new. Hugh hadn't encountered such an eager recruit since...well, since the last new recruit they'd had. What was it about the young ones, so full of energy, and even right out of the chute, ready to whip their weight in wildcats and outlaws? And as with every new man who came under his command, Hugh only hoped Griff would live long enough to get the seasoning he needed.

"Find the telegraph office and see if there's anything waiting for us. I'm expecting a wire from the governor."

Griff frowned for an instant before nodding and smoothing out his expression. No doubt fetching telegrams wasn't quite the assignment he'd been hoping for, but one thing Griff would learn was that a Ranger did the job in front of him, no matter how menial. And when he'd proven himself in the small things, he'd be trusted with bigger and more dangerous assignments.

Whit Murray strolled out of the depot, his strides as long and easy as his personality. "Howdy, Cap. Miss Etta."

"Ah, Whit, did you find us a place?" Etta tilted her cheek up, and Whit dutifully dropped a kiss onto it. She was usually all business, but *her boys* had better take the time to show the proper respect. Which they invariably did.

"Yes, ma'am. Right at the end of Main Street. Not far from the courthouse. Office downstairs, barracks up." Whit pulled a toothpick from his pocket and stuck it into the corner of his mouth. "There's a little house on the street behind that I rented for you and Cap. Far enough away so you can have some privacy, close enough that you can still keep an eye on us." He grinned, familiar with Etta's motherliness.

"Good work." Hugh hitched up the saddlebags he had slung over his shoulder. "Have you met the local sheriff? Is it the same one as when you were here before?" Last week, Hugh had sent Whit on ahead, because Whit had been to Hartville before, and Whit was his best man for procuring things the company needed.

"I did. Same man." Whit pulled off his hat and scrubbed his hand over his wiry blond hair. "Name's Watson, and he's an old-timer. Said he'd appreciate having a company of Texas Rangers stationed in Hartville. Didn't seem to think we were horning in on his territory. I saw my old partner, Chisholm Hart, too. Sure wish he hadn't retired. But he's up to his eyes in ranching and kids now."

"He's a wise man." Etta poked Whit in the shoulder. "It's beyond time all of you boys were thinking along those lines. Not necessarily the retiring, but the finding nice girls and settling down to raise some families."

"Aw, Miss Etta, you know we're all secretly in love with you. No other gal could compare." Whit flashed her a smile, and she rolled her eyes, swatting his forearm.

Several cars back from the passenger platform, a horse whinnied, drawing their attention. A cloud of dust swirled high as a big blood bay clattered down the wooden ramp from the boxcar, wheeling on the end of his lead rope. Branch Kilborn circled with him, one hand on the rope, one hand held high to calm the animal. The horse rose on his hind feet, hooves pawing the air.

"Looks like Charger enjoyed his train ride as much as always." Whit chuckled. "Good thing Branch is dealing with the horses. He's the only one that knot-head will let near him. I don't know why Branch insists on keeping him. He can be more trouble than a wagonload of barbed wire."

Etta smiled. "I think it's because when they get riled, they're so much alike."

Hugh shook his head. "Charger's too stubborn to know when he should quit. I've never seen a horse that can cover more ground."

"As I said—they're very much alike." Etta gave Hugh's elbow a little shake. "We need to move out. I want to be settled before nightfall."

O'Neal Brewster pulled a baggage cart laden with bags and boxes of Ranger equipment and belongings. Ezra Creed, pushing on the other end, called out, "Where to, Cap?"

"Follow Whit. We'll be right behind you."

Heading north, Whit turned onto Main Street, a wide road flanked by businesses. Etta walked quickly, but by the time they got to where they were going, she would be able to name and locate every shop and store and business on either side of the street. She missed very little, and Hugh had come to rely on her powers of observation. It came in especially helpful when dealing with his men.

Hartville was bigger than he'd expected, more settled. Good thing. His job had taken him, and thus Etta because she refused to be left behind, to some pretty rustic places. At least in this posting, she would be able to enjoy some of the benefits of civilization.

They passed a newspaper office and then a dress shop, and for the first time, Etta paused in her march to their new quarters. The front window of the shop held bolts of cloth, draped and billowed and tucked all fussy. There were ribbons and buttons and laces, and hanging dead center of the display area, a pink dress sprinkled with tiny yellow flowers.

"You'd look pretty as a rose in that one, Etta."

She shook her head, giving him a pitying look. "That dress is a few decades too young for me. Can you imagine a woman my age in pink? You're sweet, but you don't know the first thing about women's fashion." She cast a longing eye at the beribboned, beruffled creation before turning away.

"You won't get an argument from me there." Hugh resettled his hat, taking note of the law office and the Hartville Hotel across the street. The hotel boasted a restaurant proclaiming *The Finest Grub North of the Big River*. A good place to eat tonight so Etta didn't have to cook for all of them.

A few doors down, Main Street took a slight curve, and in the bend of the curve, between *Giles Brown: Carpenter* and a stagecoach company, Whit stopped in front of a two-story wooden building. From the looks of it, the place had been a store of some kind with wide windows flanking the double front door. But also from the looks of it, nothing had occupied the space for a good while.

Etta surveyed her new kingdom, a gleam in her brown eyes. "Whit, head to C&H Hardware and get me three galvanized buckets and a pair of washtubs, then go over to Mortenson's Mercantile and get a broom, a mop, some scrub brushes, and soap."

By evening, Etta had the office swept out, the bunks assembled and made up on the second floor, and most of her belongings unpacked in the little house on the street behind their new headquarters. Every man pitched in, following her orders. Branch took charge of the stable, Jesse the arsenal, and Griff ran errands to various shops. The others moved furniture, hauled wood and water, and stowed bags and supplies.

"Men, get cleaned up, and we'll head over to the Hartville Hotel for dinner." Hugh gathered a fat envelope of papers and dug in his saddlebag for a velvet pouch. "Meet us over there in a quarter hour."

He and Etta went ahead, and he was pleased to procure a private dining room for them and his men. Jesse and Branch came in together a moment later, Jesse telling a joke, grinning and talking with his hands, while Branch listened, impassive. Branch's dog, Jack, stuck by Branch, observing the room, lifting his nose to smell the aromas coming from the kitchen next door.

"So I told him, 'That's what you get for aiming at his knee.'" Jesse's laughter filled the room, and Branch's mouth quirked into a brief smile, a rarity that only Jesse Rawlins could coax out of him with any regularity.

Ezra shouldered through the door, with Griff on his heels. O'Neal, Whit, and Micah found their places around the table. Hugh seated Etta at the foot and took his place at the head. Branch sat at his right as his second-in-command, but even he didn't know their assignment just yet. Hugh hadn't told anyone, not even Etta.

A large-boned, aproned woman bustled through the door, her fire-red hair a tangled cloud around her face, though she'd scraped most of it back into a knot atop her head. "Howdy. I'm Tillie, and I'll be serving you. We've got roast, steak, chops, and stew. Everything comes with taters and beans, and there's pie, both apple and sour cream with raisin."

Each man around the table voiced their preference, and Tillie, hands on hips, wrote nothing down. Hugh had doubts about what they would receive, but Tillie surprised him. She was back within five minutes, a large tray on her shoulder. Two other waitresses followed her, carrying their own trays, and before the dust could settle, Tillie had flung their orders onto the table, every man getting exactly what he'd asked for.

"Thank you, ma'am. Could you close the door on your way out? If we need anything more, we'll send someone running." Hugh nodded, and with a final sweep of the room with her bright blue eyes, Tillie herded her wait staff ahead of her and left them alone.

Hugh gave the men time to eat—not that they lingered over their food. Each Ranger tucked in, following the unwritten rule of eating and resting when you could, because you never knew when the next opportunity for either would arise.

When they had their pie and coffee before them, Hugh reached down and picked up the fat envelope and bag from the floor by his chair. "Gentlemen, it's time to get down to brass tacks." He unrolled the thick wad of pages. "We've been reassigned to Hartville by the governor himself. He's given us one task. Rid Texas, through capture or death, of Cass Markham and his gang of outlaws."

Hugh paused as his words sank in. No one spoke, though some of the men looked from one to another.

Cass Markham.

In the annals of American history, some names would be synonymous with villainy. Jesse James, Sam Bass, Billy the Kid, and Cass Markham.

And for the past five years or so, he'd committed his depredations on the citizens of Texas from the Red River to the Rio Grande, eluding capture and mocking peace officers at every chance.

And he had a special fondness for killing Rangers.

More than a decade ago, when the Texas Rangers had been reinstated after Reconstruction, Cass had tried to join up but had been refused, though Hugh never heard why. Cass had born a grudge against Rangers ever since. To Hugh's knowledge, three

Ranger deaths could be attributed directly to the Markham Gang, and probably more.

Hugh handed the bulk of the papers to Branch, nodding for him to look through them and pass them along.

"The governor chose Hartville because this seems to be the area most affected by Markham lately. I'm handing around the *wanted* posters of the outlaws we believe have joined Markham's gang, though we know there are others. He's recruited the best in several fields. Spyder Jackson, safe cracker. Arch Russell, powder man. Bass Tomkins, horse thief. And Markham's got friends all over the state, cronies of his pa, Charlie Markham, who fought in the war with General Hood. He won a lot of regard by stirring things up with the carpetbaggers for a lot of years, and Markham trades on those old friendships for hideouts and supplies."

Pages rustled as the *wanted* posters made their rounds.

Holding up the letter he had retained, Hugh scanned it. "There's extra urgency behind the governor's request. Two weeks ago, near Austin, a rancher was gunned down by some horse thieves trying to make off with his remuda." Hugh paused. "The outlaws terrorized the man's wife, bold enough to tell her who they were and boasting that no one would ever catch the Markham Gang. That woman is the governor's younger sister. The rancher who was killed was his brother-in-law. The governor is understandably riled. He wants regular updates, and he wants results. Until Markham is behind bars or dead, Company B of the Frontier Battalion has no other assignment."

Branch glanced up, holding Hugh's look. They'd been Rangers so long together, Hugh often wondered if Branch could read his mind. The governor being involved in an investigation would be a mixed blessing at best. While he could open doors and bestow powers, he could also delay and hamper their efforts with his interference. Not to mention what the people of Texas might think if and when they found out that catching Cass Markham had only jumped to the top of the governor's agenda when his own family was harmed. Branch raised one eyebrow and stroked his bearded cheek, eyes thoughtful.

"Tomorrow we'll spend some time going over the reports of crimes we know can be attributed to Markham, and we'll put together a battle plan. But for tonight, I have a little gift for you." Hugh picked up the velvet drawstring bag and opened it. "I had these made for us before we left Austin."

He flipped the first one over, read the name, and tossed it down the table to Griff. "Silver Ranger badges. You'll see our name on the front, Company B, Frontier Battalion, and Texas Rangers, but if you look on the back, you'll see your name."

The next one went to Ezra Creed, who caught it deftly. "Thanks, Cap."

Hugh passed out the rest of the badges, noting that while Griff pinned his prominently on his chest, the others held theirs, turning them over in their hands, as if feeling the weight of the responsibility they represented more than the silver coin they were constructed from.

"They're made from Mexican Cinco Pesos. I know it's a fairly new idea for all Rangers to wear badges, but I wanted you each to have one as we set out on this new assignment. And remember..." Hugh looked from one man to the next, brothers by choice and history if not blood. "If you are ever in trouble, all you have to do is send your badge to one of us, and we'll come running."

Hugh tapped his papers together, looking down the table at Etta. She hadn't said anything about this new assignment, but then again, she didn't need to. She knew the danger they were heading into, and that there was a real possibility that some of them might not come out on the other side.

THE RANGER'S REWARD

GABRIELLE MEYER

To Ellis, Maryn, Judah and Asher.
Being your mama is the best adventure of all.

CHAPTER 1

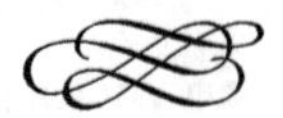

Monday, January 25, 1886

Griffin Sommer sat on his bay gelding at the crossroads outside Hartville, Texas, leaning on the saddle horn and looking long and hard down the road that would lead him away from town. He squinted as he glanced at the setting sun, guessing it to be past suppertime, trusting his growling stomach, which never lied. It had been a hard three-day trip to San Antonio and back. He'd left Ezra and O'Neal there to investigate a burglary that Captain Sterling suspected was tied to the Markham gang. Though Griff had wanted to stay and help, the captain had other ideas. He'd asked Griff to hurry back and check on Widow Prentis, instead.

With a groan, Griff clicked his tongue and pulled on the reins to turn Bolt away from Hartville and all the comforts he'd been longing for. He just wanted a fresh shave, one of Miss Etta's warm meals, and his narrow bunk. But Captain Sterling had asked this favor and he suspected the captain would be disappointed if Griff didn't oblige.

"I thought I'd be doing something that mattered once I joined Captain Sterling's company," Griff groused to Bolt. "Prisoner transfers, checking on old widows, and running a few errands to the post office 'aren't what I had in mind when I planned on becoming a Ranger."

Bolt shook his head and snorted in understanding, twitching his tail for emphasis.

Griff smiled and leaned down to pat Bolt's neck. "I suppose you haven't seen much action, either."

They plodded toward the Prentis farm and Griff's tasteless errand. He'd worked long and hard to finally make it to Texas to learn, once and for all, if his father was the hero his mother proclaimed—or the coward his stepfather despised. But the only man who could answer his question was the man who took Father's life—Charlie Markham. On old-time outlaw who hadn't been seen in nearly a decade, though Captain Sterling believed he was still running with his son, Cass.

It didn't take Griff long to find the Prentis farm. He scanned the property as he made his way up the long driveway, surprised to find it well-maintained and clean. Maybe Old Widow Prentis had a grown son or two looking after the place—but if she did, why would Captain Sterling ask Griff to check on her?

The driveway led to the spacious farmyard, complete with a large white clapboard house on his left and a two-story barn on his right. A pigpen took up space near the barn, with a large sow lying in the mud looking at Griff with deep disinterest. Beyond the red barn, a corral held a pair of beautiful mahogany Morgans, nibbling on the grass, though their ears perked up when Griff and Bolt drew near the house.

From his initial impression, the place looked good—better than good. The paint on the buildings was fresh, all the fences were secure, and the roof of the house and barn were in nice shape. It was one of the finest farms Griff had seen, and he'd seen plenty.

He almost felt foolish coming to check on the widow. What could she possibly need help with?

The screen door opened, and a young woman stepped onto the covered porch. Her blond hair was pulled into a bun at the nape of her neck with soft tendrils of hair dancing in the wind. She wore a white apron over a blue dress, which made her blue eyes sparkle. The sun glinted off a gold band on the ring finger of her left hand, sending a twinge of disappointment through Griff.

"May I help you?" She spoke with a sweet southern drawl, different than the Texas drawl he'd been getting used to since leaving Minnesota behind.

Griff sat a little straighter in his creaking saddle and reached into his vest pocket to remove the badge Captain Sterling had recently given to him and the other members of Company B.

The lady's face became wary when he reached into his vest. She took a step toward the house, reaching for the door.

"No need for alarm, ma'am." He dismounted and held Bolt's reins as he walked toward the house, his badge displayed in his hand. "My name is Griffin Sommer. I'm with the Frontier Battalion of the Texas Rangers, Company B." He slipped the badge back into his vest pocket and took off his Stetson, feeling a bit of pride at the title he'd finally earned. "Captain Hugh Sterling asked me to stop by and check on Old Widow Prentis, see if she's in need of assistance."

The young lady raised her delicate brows. "Old Widow Prentis?"

He didn't like how she said 'old,' but he nodded as he put his hat back on. "Yes, ma'am."

"Mama!" A little boy ran out of the house and let the screen door slam as he stood on the porch, his hands on his hips. "Is this man botherin' you, Mama?"

The boy couldn't be more than five or six years old, yet he glared at Griff with a scowl meant to intimidate. He'd be lucky to scare off a jackrabbit with those big blue eyes and mop of hair. Griff tried to hide his amusement at the boy's greeting, suspecting that he was trying to protect his mama, just as Griff had done a hundred times with his own mother.

"Sorry, ma'am," Griff said to the lady on the porch. "I don't mean to alarm anyone. Just here, doing my job."

"And what is that?" she asked, putting her hands on the boy's shoulders. "I don't believe I asked for Captain Sterling to interfere in my business."

"Your business?" Griff scratched the back of his head, causing his Stetson to tip forward over his brow.

"I am *Old* Widow Prentis, after all."

She was the widow? He suddenly suspected Miss Etta had more to do with this errand than the captain.

"And I'm Harrison Prentis," the boy said, crossing his arms. "And we don't need no help."

"Harrison." His mama shook her head. "Mr. Sommer was misinformed, no harm done." She inspected Griff with the prettiest eyes he'd ever seen. "I'm just setting supper on the table. I'll be happy to offer you something to eat, and then I'll be just as happy to send you on your way." She indicated her farm with a nod of her head. "As you can see, we have everything under control here."

Her tone was confident as she lifted her stubborn jaw.

Griff's stomach rumbled again, and he nodded. "I'm much obliged at the offer, ma'am." He was eager to return to Hartville, but he rarely passed up a home-cooked meal—or an invitation from a nice-looking lady.

Branch Kilborn's warning sounded in Griff's mind. Women and Rangering didn't mix. How many times had he heard the seasoned Ranger tell him that in the short month they'd been in

Hartville? Griff would be smart to head back the way he'd come, yet what was the harm in one meal?

"Harrison," Mrs. Prentis said, "please show Mr. Sommer and his horse to the barn while I finish setting the table." She paused on her way back into the house. "Your horse appears as trail weary as you, Mr. Sommer. Why don't you rub him down and give him some oats, let him rest up a bit before taking him back to Hartville."

"That's mighty generous of you, ma'am."

She didn't respond but stepped into the house and closed the door gently.

"This way," Harrison said, tilting his head toward the barn like a grown-up might do, and shoving his thumbs in his denim trouser pockets.

Griff turned toward the barn and slowed his stride, so the little chap could keep up with him. He wasn't used to walking so slowly. Almost everywhere Griff went, he went with purpose and drive, getting the job done as quickly and efficiently as possible. He sensed things were different with a child underfoot.

"So, it's just you and your ma on the farm?" Griff asked nonchalantly.

"Yep. But we got us a tenant farmer who lives over yonder." Again, he didn't bother to point but simply tilted his head toward the north. "Mr. Griswold's his name."

It was clear the child spent his time with adults. Made Griff think of himself at that age. He'd always wished he had a brother or two, but it had only been him and his ma, then just him and his stepfather. No one else.

Griff unsaddled Bolt and rubbed him down, allowing Harrison to help—though Griff rarely let anyone near his horse. The animal could be temperamental around strangers, but the gelding simply looked at Harrison with curiosity instead of irritation.

After feeding Bolt, they left the barn and returned to the

house. Harrison led Griff inside and his mouth began to water at the aromas wafting out of the kitchen.

A fancy parlor sat to the left and a dining room to the right. Straight ahead was a set of stairs.

Mrs. Prentis came through a swinging door, holding a platter of steaming meat. She must not have heard their arrival, because she paused in surprise on the way to the table, taking Griff in again.

"If you'd like to wash up first," she said, "there's a pitcher of water in the kitch—"

Her words were cut off by the sound of pounding hooves on the road out front.

"Now, who could that be?" She set down the platter and wiped her hands on her apron. "I declare, we've had more visitors in one day than we've had all month."

Griff followed her line of sight out the window, just as a group of riders pulled into her drive. Windblown and dusty, they wore bandanas over the lower half of their faces and looked like trouble.

Lifting his Colt .45 from his holster, he spoke calmly to Mrs. Prentis. "Do you know them?"

She shook her head but didn't answer as she pulled her son to her side.

Four rough-looking men came to a halt in front of the house. One was bent over, almost falling off his horse, while the other three dismounted.

"Stay inside," Griff said to Mrs. Prentis. "And keep the boy with you."

Mrs. Prentis seemed to dither for a moment, as if she wasn't about to let Griff tell her what to do, but then thought better of it and nodded once.

Griff stepped toward the door, but before he could grab the knob, it swung open and one of the men stepped over the threshold. He tugged his bandana off his face, revealing the curled tips of his handlebar mustache. He looked from Griff to Mrs. Prentis in one calculated glance.

"We have an injured man. Where can we put him?"

"Put him?" Mrs. Prentis bristled. "You can put him back on his horse."

Griff lifted his pistol, but before he could aim it, the other man grabbed Harrison with one hand and pulled a gun from his holster and pointed it at Mrs. Prentis with the other. "Hand over your weapon slowly, Farmer," he snarled at Griff, "or your wife and kid die."

"He's not—" Mrs. Prentis began to speak, but Griff shook his head to silence her. The last thing he needed was for them to know he was a Texas Ranger. The longer they believed him to be a simple farmer, the better.

Slowly, he lowered his Colt to the floor, never taking his eyes off the desperado. With a gun pointed at Mrs. Prentis, and Harrison in the stranger's grasp, Griff couldn't start any trouble. Better to do what they wanted for now and find a way to get the widow and her son to safety later.

"Now walk away," the outlaw said. "And stand by your wife."

Two other riders hauled in the injured man. His eyes were closed, and blood dripped from a wound in his left shoulder. One of the men carrying him was also wounded, just beneath his eye on his right cheek, though it didn't look as serious.

"Where should we put Red?" the man with the wounded cheek asked.

The leader looked at Mrs. Prentis. "Well?"

"Turn my son lose and I'll tell you."

He didn't hesitate but pushed Harrison away causing the boy to fall to his knees in front of Mrs. Prentis. She gasped and reached down to pick him up, a scowl on her face as she clutched her son close and started toward the stairs without another word.

"Do what she says," the leader told them. "And keep a gun on her. She looks like a firecracker."

They hauled Red up the stairs and out of sight. The leader kept his gun pointed at Griff while he reached down and lifted Griff's Colt off the floor. He put it in his holster and moved toward the table where the food was still steaming hot. "Looks like we've come to the right place."

Griff clenched his fists as the man dug in his pocket and pulled out a coin.

He tossed it to Griff, a sneer on his face. "Payment for services rendered."

The coin flipped through the air and Griff caught it on instinct.

A cinco peso with a hole shot through the middle.

Griff's insides went cold.

He was holding the calling card of the Cass Markham gang.

~

Evelyn held Harrison tight as she directed the outlaws to put the wounded man in the guest bed. She tried not to think about the bed sheets her grandmother had sewn for her when she had first married, which would now be ruined from the blood. She tried not to think about four dangerous men in her home, one of them on the brink of death. And she tried not to think about the Texas Ranger in her dining room, who had been mistaken for her husband.

All she should think about was how to get Harrison out of the house and to safety.

The outlaws had their back to Evelyn, and she used the opportunity to move toward the door, her son at her side.

"Where do you think you're going, pretty lady?" The only man who wasn't wounded stepped into her path, a half-smile on his wide face. He wasn't very tall, but he was muscular, with a square torso and thick neck, making her think of a prizefighter.

Evelyn didn't say anything as she stared back at the strange man. She didn't owe him an explanation. This was her house.

"You need to take care of Red," he told her. "He's been shot."

It was clear how the man on the bed had gotten his name. Thick, wavy red hair covered his head, with a matching red goatee. He didn't appear much older than Evelyn, at the age of twenty-nine, but at the moment his face was drained of all color, and he lay limp upon her bedding.

"Dusty," the man with the cheek wound pointed at Red's feet. "Take off his boots."

"Who's gonna watch the pretty lady, Willie?" Dusty's smile was still trained on Evelyn.

Willie ran his sleeved arm over his cheek to wipe away the blood. He was a handsome man, with brilliant blue eyes and a baby-face complexion. Under other circumstances, he looked like he would be at the center of every good time—but not now. Worry lined his face. "My pa's not here, so you'll need to take care of Red," he said to Evelyn. "It's real important he don't die."

Evelyn bit the inside of her lip as she surveyed Red's motionless form. Where did she begin? The only experience she had with the sick and dying was during the war when their plantation had become a hospital for the confederate soldiers. But she'd been a child then and she didn't know how to treat a gun wound.

"Now." Willie grabbed her arm and shoved her to the bed. "The man's dying."

Her heart slammed against her ribs as she pulled Harrison closer, almost losing her step.

"I don't much care if I have to hurt you to get what I want," Willie said with steel in his voice. "I won't let Red die."

Harrison began to cry, and she put her hand up to shelter him from the gruesome site. Her son had already lost his father—he couldn't lose his mother, as well.

She gently set her son on his feet and spoke calmly, for his benefit and no other. "I want you to go to your room and stay there, do you hear?"

Fear filled Harrison's beautiful eyes, but his face screwed up in anger and he fisted his hands, turning to the outlaws.

"Go." She spoke in a stern voice before he could stand up to Willie and Dusty.

He hesitated for only a moment before leaving the room, first with a backward glance, and then at a run.

After she heard his bedroom door click shut, she unbuttoned her cuffs and rolled up her sleeves. If she was going to be in charge, then these men would have to listen to her.

She directed her attention to Dusty. "Do as Mr. Willie says and take off Red's boots."

Without waiting to see if he'd comply, she went to the head of the bed to examine the patient. One thing she recalled the surgeon doing when a soldier came in with a gunshot wound was to check if the bullet had gone all the way through. If it hadn't, he'd have to try to remove it, or it would cause infection for sure. Just the thought of trying to extricate a bullet from inside a man made her head swim.

"Here." Willie tore Red's shirt off his arm, revealing a bloody shoulder.

Evelyn grimaced as she put her hand behind his shoulder and felt around for an exit wound. His skin was slippery with blood, and she had to force herself not to gag.

But there! She felt another hole.

Quickly, she pulled away and grabbed a towel from the washbasin, wiping her hand clean.

"Well?" Willie asked as he watched her closely.

"It went through."

The look of relief on Willie's face was plain. "He took the bullet while breaking me out of jail in Bendera."

"You're lucky we got you out before the Rangers heard you were there," Dusty laughed. "They would've been on you like a coyote on a rabbit."

Willie seemed to ignore Dusty as he pushed his wide-awake cowboy hat off his forehead. "I'd hate to see Red lose his life doing something for me."

"He wouldn't be the first." Dusty tossed Red's dirty boot onto Evelyn's clean rug. "Remember Gus? He took a bullet when we broke you out of jail in San Antone a couple years back."

Willie scratched his whiskers. "Gus?"

Evelyn used the towel to wipe the excess blood off Red's chest, trying to ignore the conversation.

"And what about Mitch?" Dusty asked, sitting in the chair, propping his feet up on the bureau, apparently finished with his help. "He died near Waco after we broke you out there."

"Why was I in Waco?" Willie asked, his arms crossed as he seemed to have forgotten about Red.

"A woman, remember?"

"Woman?" Willie leaned against the bureau, wiping at the blood on his cheek again. "What woman?"

"You was dallying with her and her husband caught you. You shot her husband and they was gonna hang you for it—but we got you out in time."

Willie still frowned, but he nodded. "I think I remember that one."

"You always end up in jail when you get too drunk."

Evelyn's pulse ticked higher with each report. These men were dangerous and reckless—and careless with the lives they took. They wouldn't think twice about hurting her or Harrison—and that thought alone made her work faster on the man in the bed.

The sooner she was done, the sooner she could find a way to escape with her son.

The only thing she had in her medicine cabinet was headache powder and cough syrup. She didn't even keep whiskey on hand. All she had to clean the wound was water, so she sent Dusty to get some from the pump outside. She found an old sheet and had Willie tear it into strips, which they used to bandage the shoulder.

The whole while, Red remained unconscious.

When she was done, she washed her hands as best as she could in the basin and walked toward the door.

"Where you goin' now?" Dusty asked her.

"I'm going to speak with that man downstairs and tell him Mr. Red is ready to leave."

"His name's Cass," Willie said, a bit of pride in his voice. "My big brother."

Evelyn stepped into the hallway with Dusty and Willie on her heels. She descended the stairs with as much decorum as she could manage and found Mr. Sommer standing in the dining room with Cass seated at the table, his gun pointed at the Ranger, eating the food Evelyn had prepared for her and Harrison's supper.

She and Mr. Sommer shared a glance, but then she turned her full attention on Willie's brother, who seemed to be the one in charge.

"Mr. Red will live," she said. "I've cleaned and bandaged his wound."

Willie and Dusty went to the table, eating right out of the serving dishes with their hands.

Evelyn tightened her lips as they devoured her food. What gave these men the right to take what wasn't theirs and come into a home they didn't own? She couldn't fathom their behavior.

"I've seen men stronger than Red bleed to death if they're

moved too soon." Cass stood and lifted his Stetson off the table. His eyes were cold and calculating as he looked between Mr. Sommer and Evelyn. "I'm going to leave Willie and Dusty here with you until I get back from Laredo. That should give Red some time to recover so we can move him."

"Leave him here?" Evelyn gripped her apron in her hands. "You can't leave him."

Mr. Sommer walked around the table and put his arm around Evelyn's shoulder, as if he'd done it a hundred times before. She stiffened under his hold. Her first instinct was to pull away from the stranger, but she forced herself to stay in place.

"Don't worry," Mr. Sommer said in a soothing voice. "We'll be fine."

She wanted to protest. How would they be fine?

"Dusty and Willie will guard every step you take," Cass continued. "They won't hesitate to shoot, if you try to escape and warn the authorities."

"Cass heard there's a company of Texas Rangers in Hartville who aim to get him hanged." Willie laughed as he took another slice of roast beef. "I think he's scared."

"Shut your mouth, Willie." Cass narrowed his eyes on his brother. "Or next time you're in jail, I'll leave you there."

Willie's eyes sparkled with humor, but he didn't goad his brother anymore. Instead, respect and maybe a little fear played just under the surface of his countenance.

Cass started toward the door and Dusty turned to him. "When will you be back?"

"I'm heading to Laredo to meet up with Maggie and the others, and then I'll come back and pick up Pa on the way. He'll know if Red's healed enough to move."

Mr. Sommer's arm tightened around Evelyn at the mention of Pa.

"Don't do anything foolish, Farmer." Cass must have noticed Griff tense. "Or you'll end up like Red."

"What's wrong with that?" Dusty asked, eyeing Evelyn from head to toe. "It would be easier if the farmer was out of the way."

Cass leveled a cool gaze on Dusty. "Last time you messed with a woman, you got the governor breathing down our necks."

Prickles of fear ran up the back of Evelyn's arms and neck. What would she have done if Mr. Sommer hadn't shown up when he did? She'd be here alone with the outlaws.

"We don't need more trouble than we already have," Cass said to Willie and Dusty. "Guard the farmer and his wife and make sure they take care of Red. That's the only thing I want, understand?"

Dusty reached for another handful of food. "Yep."

"After you two eat," Cass continued, "one of you take the farmer out to the barn and see to the horses."

"How long we gotta wait?" Willie asked again, shoving a piece of roast beef into his mouth.

"I'll be back in about a week." Cass walked toward the door—but he turned and pointed at Dusty one more time. "No trouble, you got that?"

Dusty didn't even bother to respond this time.

Cass opened the door but addressed his brother. "And take care of that wound. You wouldn't want it to scar."

Willie nodded as he took another piece of beef.

As Cass left the house, Evelyn could feel Mr. Sommer's muscles ripple with tension. No doubt he wanted to ride after the ringleader, but he couldn't very well leave her alone with these two, could he?

As soon as the hoofbeats disappeared into the distance, Dusty gave Evelyn a sickly smile.

How would she ever escape with his watchful eye on her?

Evelyn and Harrison's only hope was in Mr. Sommer now, keeping up the charade that he was her husband.

But how would she convince her five-year-old son to call this stranger Pa?

CHAPTER 2

It took all Griff's willpower to let Cass Markham ride away. After all, Company B had been sent to Hartville to apprehend the man, hadn't they? Yet, Griff knew if he was patient, he could capture Cass Markham, as well as Cass's pa, at the end of the week.

Griff still had his arm around Mrs. Prentis, reminding him that he had more than just himself to worry about for the first time since his ma died. They had so many things they needed to discuss, like her name for starters, but he would be surprised if Dusty and Willie let them alone long enough. "Where is Harrison?"

She kept her eye on the two outlaws sitting at her table, though she spoke to Griff. "He's in his room."

"Why don't you go on up and reassure him that everything is going to be all right?" No doubt the little guy was scared.

"Is it going to be all right?"

He tried to look at her with as much reassurance as he imagined a husband would look at his wife in a time like this. "If we do what these men ask and don't make trouble, all of this will be over within the week."

She swallowed hard before nodding. "I'll do what I can."

"Good." He squeezed her shoulders and let her go.

She started to walk toward the stairs, but Dusty jumped up. "You ain't goin' nowhere without a guard."

Griff hated the idea of this man alone upstairs with Mrs. Prentis, where Griff couldn't protect her and Harrison. There was no telling what he might do.

"If you come with me," he said to Dusty, "my—" He paused, hoping he sounded convincing. "My wife, can see to Willie's wound." If they could bide their time, and play along, he and his fellow Rangers would finally get Cass, Willie, and Charlie Markham.

Willie touched his cheek and grimaced. "Go with the farmer, Dusty."

Mrs. Prentis didn't bother to wait for Willie. She walked out of the dining room and disappeared up the stairs. The outlaw jumped up from the table and followed.

Griff left the house with Dusty close behind. They found the three horses nibbling on a patch of grass near the corral. Griff was thankful he'd already been inside the barn and knew where Mrs. Prentis kept the oats and the currycomb. As he worked to unsaddle the horses and brush them down, Dusty stood by and watched, a piece of hay in his mouth and his pistol always at the ready.

"How long you been married?" Dusty asked.

"How long you been an outlaw?"

"I'm asking the questions, Farmer."

Griff nodded at the pistol. "We gonna have this conversation with the gun pointed at me?"

Dusty put the gun back in his holster, though his hand hovered nearby. "Well?"

Griff's mind worked fast to find a suitable answer. If Harrison was five, then they would have had to been married at least six years, so that's what he said.

"How long you been farming?" Dusty asked.

Griff continued to comb the animal, confident in his answer this time. "Since I was a kid. I grew up farming." It was true. After his father had been killed by Charlie Markham, his mother had taken him to Minnesota where she had grown up. When she married her second husband, she and Griff moved to his farm in southern Minnesota.

He hoped and prayed Dusty wouldn't ask any more questions. Griff didn't want to entangle himself in lies that could easily be disproven or contradicted by Mrs. Prentis. As it was, he needed to get alone with her soon to ask a few questions and work out the details of his plan.

Dusty stepped away from the pole he was leaning against and wandered to the stall where Bolt was standing.

Griff started combing the second horse, keeping his eye on Dusty—when he recalled that his saddle bags were in the stall with Bolt.

The outlaw must have noticed them, because he stooped down.

If Griff acted suspicious, Dusty would start asking questions, so he continued to comb the horse, hoping Dusty wouldn't start rifling around in his saddlebag. If he did, he'd find the prisoner transfer papers Griff needed to deliver to Captain Sterling.

"Just come home from somewhere?" Dusty asked, holding Griff's saddlebag.

"San Antonio." Griff didn't miss a stroke of the brush as he tried to come up with a reason a farmer might need to make such a trip, especially when Hartville was so close. "Just arrived home and was about to sit down to eat when you showed up."

The answer seemed to pacify Dusty. He set the saddlebag down and didn't ask any more questions.

Griff made quick work of feeding the horses and putting them in their stalls, one eye on the outlaw at all times. When he was done, he grabbed his saddlebag and swung it over his shoulder, eager to get back to Mrs. Prentis.

His badge felt heavy and conspicuous in his vest pocket. He recalled the day Captain Sterling gave it to him and told him if he was ever in need of help, to send the badge. Even if Griff knew how to get the badge to the captain, he wasn't sure he wanted assistance just yet. If they captured Dusty, Willie, and Red too soon, then Charlie Markham might not come. The only person alive who knew how Griff's father died was Charlie. Until today, Griff wasn't sure the man was still alive, but now that he knew Charlie was on his way, Griff was willing to wait.

He'd have to keep the widow and her son safe until then, but in the meantime, he'd get Dusty and Willie to talk.

Griff led the way to the house, his hands in his pockets. "I've heard about the Cass Markham gang."

"Yeah? Well, believe what you've heard." Pride rang in Dusty's voice.

"The papers haven't exaggerated the stories?"

"Why would they need to?"

Griff paused. "So it's true, then?"

"What?"

"The Markham gang stole those horses and killed the governor's brother-in-law?"

Dusty's square jaw lifted a notch with pride.

Griff clenched his jaw. If he thought he could take down Willie and Dusty, he'd slap cuffs on Dusty right now and haul him into Hartville. If it was just himself, he might give it a try—but he had Mrs. Prentis and Harrison to worry about.

They walked into the house and heard Willie cry out in pain.

Mrs. Prentis shushed him. "Hold still, or I'll poke your eye."

Griff frowned as he walked through the dining room. Had she gotten the upper hand of the outlaw? He pushed open the kitchen door and found Willie sitting on a chair, his pistol still in his hand, though it was lying in his lap, while Mrs. Prentis sewed his wound closed.

The kitchen was spacious and clean. Sunshine streamed in through the windows, illuminating a shiny black cookstove, a large red pie safe, and a long table with benches on either side.

Harrison sat on one of the benches, an uneaten sugar cookie in one hand, and a look of concern on his face.

"Do you know how to stitch up a man?" Willie asked Mrs. Prentis with a scowl.

"Only those who don't whine." She squinted as she pulled the black thread through the wound. "It can't be much different than mending a seam."

Dusty walked over to Willie and shook his head. "That don't look good."

"Hush up," Willie said.

The other outlaw shrugged. "At least now the ladies'll look at me, instead of you."

Griff relaxed and tried not to smile at Mrs. Prentis's attitude. Though her home had been overrun, she was plucky. He liked that about her. Most women he knew would be cowering in the corner—but not her. She was holding her own. If they were going to get through this week, she'd have to keep that courage.

"Ow!" Willie cried as she pierced his skin again. His hand tightened on the pistol and Griff took a step forward.

Mrs. Prentis halted her ministrations. "Are you going to hold still?"

"How much longer?" Willie groused.

"I'm halfway done."

The skin around the wound was all puckered and swollen, and

Griff was thankful Willie couldn't see what she was doing. It would leave an ugly scar, for sure, and he wondered if she was stitching it that way on purpose—or if she was just poor at sewing.

Willie gritted his teeth and repositioned the gun. "Keep going."

She took a deep breath as she glanced at Griff.

He smiled to reassure her, but she didn't return the gesture.

~

Half an hour later, Evelyn cast a glance over her shoulder at Dusty, who sat on one of the benches in the kitchen. He didn't take his eyes off her as she set the last plate in the cupboard and tossed the dishwater out the back door. It was unnerving to have his gaze follow her every move.

The sun had long since disappeared, and the night stars were hidden by low-lying clouds. She had already seen to Red's needs and found the man still unconscious. She'd have to check on him once or twice during the night, but thankfully his wound had stopped bleeding. Now she would watch for signs of infection and pray he healed fast enough to be moved when Mr. Markham returned.

Harrison was seated on the other side of the kitchen table, his head resting on his folded arms. It was past his bedtime, but Evelyn refused to let him out of her sight, so he had fallen asleep while she cleaned the kitchen.

The door swung open, and Mr. Sommer stepped into the room, Willie close behind. "Are you about ready for bed?"

Her heart did a little flip at the question. Surely, the outlaws would expect them to share the same room—after all, they believed her and Mr. Sommer to be married. Yet, the thought of being alone with him—a complete stranger—was almost as troubling as having the outlaws in her home.

But what choice did she have? She must play the part. "I'm ready."

"I'll get Harrison." He circled the table and lifted the boy into his arms. Harrison stirred, but he didn't wake. Instead, he nestled his head onto Mr. Sommer's shoulder and continued to sleep.

The sight of the big man holding her son did something strange within her. No one had helped her raise Harrison, not since her husband Jake had died when Harrison was six months old. What would it be like to have a husband to help ease her parenting burdens? It was hard to even imagine.

Evelyn led the way upstairs, eager to finally have a private conversation with the Ranger, even if it meant being alone with him in her bedroom.

She entered first, followed by Mr. Sommer.

"This is where you'll stop," the Ranger said to Dusty. "Our bedroom is private."

Evelyn's cheeks grew warm, and she dropped her gaze, lest the outlaw see her embarrassment. No man had been in this room since Jake.

Dusty narrowed his eyes, but Willie nudged him. "You take the first shift here in the hall. I'll get some sleep and take the second shift."

Mr. Sommer stood his ground, staring at Dusty.

"If you try any funny business," Dusty said, his gun still aimed, "your wife and son will pay the price."

A shudder ran through Evelyn as she took several deep breaths.

Mr. Sommer stepped back and closed the door, locking it tight. His shoulders visibly relaxed as he turned to Evelyn, Harrison still in his arms.

"Here." Evelyn went to her bed and pulled back the wedding quilt her grandmother had made for her trousseau.

Mr. Sommer gently laid Harrison on the bed, and then he

stepped back and Evelyn pulled the quilt up to her son's chin. The boy slept peacefully, which was more than she expected for herself. She wouldn't undress him, in case she could think of a way to escape. It would be best to be fully clothed and ready to go at any moment.

"You and I need to have a little chat," Mr. Sommer said just above a whisper.

Anger and frustration started to build within Evelyn. She turned to him, her arms crossed. "Why didn't you do something about all this? Why didn't you stop them? Why don't you get us out of here?"

"Shh." He put his finger to his lips and gently took her by the arm, leading her across the room to stand near the window. A scant amount of moonlight filtered through the clouds and made it easier to see his serious face. "Be quiet, or they'll hear."

She removed her arm from his hold, forcing her voice to quiet. "You're a Ranger, aren't you? Why don't you do something?"

"I'm outnumbered. If I try to overtake them, and I fail, you and Harrison would be at their mercy."

"So, we're to remain this way for a week? I can't possibly do this for that long. There must be a way to escape."

"We don't have much choice." His voice was so low, she had to lean forward to hear him. His brown eyes were serious as he spoke to her. "In a couple of days, Captain Sterling will suspect I'm missing and look for me. Since he asked me to stop here, he'll come this way. When he does, we'll make a plan." His gaze was full confidence. "Until then, you and I will pretend to be married."

She studied him as he spoke, surprised that he wasn't more concerned. Did he think she could actually pull this off? No one had ever put their trust and confidence in Evelyn—no one, except her child. Her parents had always treated her as if she was a disappointment, and rightly so. She wasn't as talented or gifted as her older sister, or as charming and likeable as her younger sister.

She'd always been the one everyone expected to fail—yet, Mr. Sommer treated her the opposite. Could they make-believe for the next week?

"There are some things I need to know," Mr. Sommer continued, his intense gaze on her face. "Like your name."

She couldn't stop the smile that tickled her lips. "I suppose it's only right to know your wife's name."

His eyes softened and he returned the smile. "It might come in handy."

"My name is Evelyn."

"Evelyn." He nodded. "That suits you."

"And you are?" She tried to recall his name from earlier that day when he'd introduced himself—though it felt like a lifetime ago.

"Griffin Sommer, but Griff is just fine." He pointed at the rocker behind her. "Why don't you have a seat...Evelyn? I have a lot of questions to ask. And if I aim to get to know you, this conversation might take a while."

Evelyn's pulse ticked in her wrists at the idea of getting to know this man. She and Jake had never sat across from each other, just to talk. Theirs had been a marriage of convenience. He needed a wife to work the farm and produce heirs. She had wanted to be free of her domineering father and come out from under the shadows of her sisters. The union had seemed ideal—but a loveless marriage turned out to be anything but perfect.

Now, as Griff pulled the stool over from her dressing table on the opposite side of the room, Evelyn lowered herself into the rocker on shaky legs. What would this man like to know? How much would she have to share about her life? She was a private person by nature and made even more so by life's circumstances.

He sat on the delicate chair, and she feared it might not hold his weight. He was a tall man, with thick, muscular arms and shoulders. He looked strong and capable, used to hard work and long days. Knowing he was there to protect her and Harrison gave her a measure of comfort—if comfort was possible.

Removing his Stetson revealed his thick, curly hair. It was dark, just like his eyes and the stubble of a beard on his face.

When he finally settled himself, he glanced up at her and looked a little embarrassed. "I don't rightly know where to begin."

She let out a nervous laugh, conscious of the outlaw sitting in the hallway, but even more conscious of the handsome Ranger within. "I don't know where to start, either."

"I suppose we ought to know how long we've been married. I told Dusty it's been six years."

"That would be about right. I married Mr. Prentis six years ago last June." When she was twenty-three, an old maid by her mother's estimation.

"I'm sorry for your loss."

She bit the inside of her cheek and looked down at her clasped hands. Guilt pricked her conscience, because she wasn't sorry at all. Though she had never celebrated Jake's death, and had been afraid to be alone in the world, she had not mourned her loss like a wife should. What did she have to mourn? They had never loved one another—had barely tolerated each other, if truth be told. Jake had been harsh, demanding, and unsatisfied with her.

Taking a deep breath, she found the courage to look up at Griff again. "He died in a farming accident almost five years ago, so I've had time to get used to being alone."

Griff nodded his understanding, but she didn't think he could possibly understand what it had been like to be alone on a farm, raising a boy by herself.

"How long have you been a Ranger?" she asked, wanting to change the subject.

"A couple of months."

Her eyes grew wide. What did this man know about being a

Ranger in so short a time? Could he protect her and Harrison like she'd hoped?

"My father was a Ranger," he continued. "Killed in the line of duty." He paused and she suspected it was hard for him to talk about his past, as well. "After his death, my mother took me to her family home in Minnesota where she remarried. She died when I was ten and I was raised by my stepfather on his farm. I promised myself I'd redeem my father's death by being a Ranger, but it took a lot longer than I'd hoped to finally get here. I worked at the prison in Stillwater, Minnesota for a year before Captain Sterling invited me to come to Texas."

At least he had some experience with criminals.

"It's a nice spread you've got here," he said, and she suspected he was just as eager to change the subject as she had been.

"This was my husband's farm. He inherited it from his father, and I hope to pass it on to Harrison one day." She glanced at her sleeping son, love welling up in her chest for her boy. "With the Lord's help, a lot of hard work, and a trusted tenant farmer, I've kept it running smoothly. It's all we have in this world."

His gaze also rested on Harrison. "He's a mighty-fine boy. You've done a good job, Evelyn." His face and voice revealed the depth of his praise. "You should be proud."

She didn't know what caught at her emotions more, hearing him use her name, or complimenting her on parenting Harrison.

If she didn't change the subject again, she was afraid she might give in to the tears that had been threatening all day, and that was the last thing she wanted. "What will we do until Captain Sterling comes?"

"We'll pretend to be happily married."

He said it so calmly, she almost believed they could pull it off.

"You should try to get some rest," he said. "It'll be a long day tomorrow."

Evelyn looked at the bed, her cheeks warming at the idea of

sleeping in the same room as this man. Yet, how could she sleep knowing there was an outlaw just outside her room?

"If you can spare a blanket," he continued, "I'll lie on the floor between the door and the bed."

She took a quilt out of the trunk at the foot of her bed, and in a whisper she said, "Will it be enough?"

He accepted it, a smile tilting his lips. "I've slept in a lot worse conditions."

Without another word, he laid on the floor and turned to face the door. "Goodnight, Evelyn," he whispered into the dark room.

"Goodnight." She watched him for a moment, thanking God for sending Mr. Sommer—Griff—when He had, then she climbed into her bed and pulled Harrison close.

She didn't bother taking off her shoes, either, in case she needed to flee.

CHAPTER 3

Something wasn't right.

Griff woke with a start the next morning, trying to get his bearings before he moved a muscle. The sky held the muted colors of predawn, offering a subtle light to fill the bedroom. He felt a presence beside him, and he held his breath. Was it one of the outlaws? What would they think finding him on the floor?

A movement just behind him made him tense. He didn't have his gun, but he kept a knife in his boot.

"Mister?" Harrison lowered his face to within inches of Griff's, his breath warm on Griff's nose. "Are you awake?"

Griff let out a relieved sigh and allowed his muscles to melt back into the hard floor. "I am now."

"Where's my mama?"

Evelyn? Griff sat up straight, looking toward the bed, but it was empty. His heart pounded hard as he stood and scanned the room, but she wasn't anywhere within sight.

Harrison watched Griff, his chin quivering. "Is my mama gone?"

"Stay here." Griff picked Harrison up and placed him on the bed. "Don't move, do you hear me? I'll come back for you—but until then, don't leave this bed." If something happened to Evelyn, Griff would be forced to apprehend the outlaws, and he couldn't risk having Harrison get caught in the cross fire.

The boy began to cry. "I want my mama."

"Shh." Griff put his hand up to quiet the boy. "I'm going to find her."

"Where is she?"

Griff hated to think about the possibilities. Did she leave on her own? She wouldn't escape without her son—so was she taken? Why hadn't Griff been awakened?

He opened the door slowly and looked into the dark hall, but it was empty. Neither Dusty nor Willie were on guard.

Griff prided himself on his courage under pressure, but for the first time in a long time, he felt real fear. What would he do if something had happened to Evelyn, and he had slept through it? He didn't think he could live with himself, especially knowing Harrison would be all alone in the world.

A noise from down the hall caught Griff's attention. It was coming from the sickroom.

He bent and pulled the knife from his boot, then he followed the sound and noticed a light seeping from under the door.

"I don't like how he looks," he heard Evelyn say. "He's burning with fever and won't drink the broth I've been trying to give him."

Griff released the breath he'd been holding and replaced the knife in his boot. She was simply checking on the patient.

He opened the door and entered the room. Dusty was sleeping on a mat in the corner and Willie was standing near the bed with Evelyn. The wound on his left cheek was worse today than yesterday, all red and raw. It had to hurt something fierce.

They both looked up and Willie reached for his pistol, pointing it at Griff in a flash of steel.

Griff lifted his hands, showing Willie he was harmless.

At least for now.

He caught Evelyn's gaze, never more thankful than he was at that moment.

She was safe.

"Why didn't you wake me?" he asked.

Her cheeks filled with color. "You were sleeping so soundly."

A bad habit for a Texas Ranger. If Jesse ever found out, Griff would never live it down, and if Branch found out, he'd be mighty disappointed.

To cover up his embarrassment, his voice turned gruff. "Don't do it again." He couldn't protect her if he didn't know where she was.

The slightest frown wedged between her brows, and he sensed that she didn't like to be told what to do—though she didn't fight his authority. The way she spoke last night about her marriage reminded him of his mother after she married his stepfather. It wasn't so much what she said, but what she hadn't said that had troubled him. Had anyone shown Evelyn unconditional love?

"I'm done in here for now." She stepped away from the patient, not meeting Griff's gaze. "I'll get breakfast started."

"And I'll start the chores," Griff added.

Her frown returned. "I'll see to them."

Griff shook his head. No doubt she usually took care of things around the farm, on top of her other chores, but not while he was there. She shouldn't have to shoulder all the work. It was a husband's job.

Willie stood by Red, his face filled with concern, and for the first time since entering the room, Griff looked at the man lying on the bed. Sweat glistened on his brow as he moaned in his delirium.

"He should be seen by a doctor," Griff told Willie.

Evelyn nodded. "That's what I said."

"No." Willie shook his head adamantly. "They'd put him in jail and Cass would be angrier than a hungry mountain lion." He nodded at Evelyn. "It's your job to make him well again. If he dies, you'll have to face Cass yourself."

Griff's muscles tensed again, and he took a protective step toward Evelyn out of instinct. "You can't expect her to save his life. She's not a doctor."

"It don't matter," Willie said.

Dusty started to move on his pallet, and he opened his eyes. When he saw Evelyn, he gave her the same nauseating smile he'd given her several times yesterday.

She recoiled and took a step closer to Griff, pressing against his side. His instinct was to put his arm around her, which was exactly what he did. If they were going to convince these men that they were man and wife, then they'd need to start acting like it.

"Evelyn will get breakfast ready while I see to the chores," Griff said, wanting to have some sort of authority in this situation. "Dusty, I could use your help."

"Help?" Dusty sat up and scoffed, running his hand down his face. "I don't aim to do chores."

"Go with him," Willie ordered Dusty. "I'll keep an eye on the woman."

It was what Griff had hoped for. He needed to keep Dusty as far away from Evelyn as possible.

Griff was amazed at how good it felt to have Evelyn tucked by his side, though she stood stiff and unnatural. "I'll take Harrison with me," he said.

Her eyes grew wide, and she started to shake her head.

"It'll be okay," he spoke gently, wanting to reassure her. "The fresh air will be good for him, and I promise I won't let him out of my sight."

She took a deep breath and finally nodded. "All right."

They turned toward the door and Evelyn pulled away. She and Griff walked back to her bedroom and stepped inside.

Griff closed the door and spoke quickly. "I don't want you to leave this room without waking me up again."

"Mama!" Harrison said at the same moment.

Griff put his hand on her arm. "I had no idea where you'd gone."

"Shh." Evelyn left his hold and reached for Harrison, who jumped into her arms. "I don't want you scaring him."

"Then don't scare me."

She hugged Harrison close and gave Griff a brief nod.

"Harrison," Evelyn pulled back and met her son's gaze, speaking quietly. "We are going to play a game for a few days."

"What kind of game?" he asked.

She nodded at Griff. "You need to call Mr. Sommer papa until those men leave the house, do you understand?"

Harrison frowned. "But he's not my papa."

"I know, but we need to make-believe. Those men think he's your papa and we need them to keep thinking that." Evelyn smoothed his hair down and placed a kiss on his nose. "Listen and obey Mr. Sommer—and don't forget to call him papa. It's very important."

The little boy nodded slowly, though he didn't seem convinced that this was a good idea.

"Now." She smiled at her son and Griff suspected that it took a great deal of self-control for her to remain calm. "Go with Papa and help with the chores."

Harrison studied her for a moment. "Yes, ma'am."

Evelyn set him on his feet, tucked in his shirt, and straightened his trousers. She also tried to tame his hair one more time.

He stared up at Griff.

"Are you ready?" Griff asked.

Harrison nodded, his blue eyes large in his solemn face.

Griff paused before he opened the door to face the day.

It wouldn't be easy, but this little make-believe family would have to give a convincing performance.

~

Evelyn dipped her hands into the tepid water bucket, washing the starch off from peeling the supper potatoes. She used the opportunity to glance out the window to see if Griff and Harrison were within sight, just as she had done countless times that morning and afternoon.

The pair sat just outside the barn doors, fixing a pitchfork that had recently broken. She suspected Griff chose that spot to work so she could keep her eye on her son. She appreciated his thoughtfulness, though it was of little comfort, since Dusty sat in the shade of the barn, his Stetson tipped forward, and his pistol pointed in the general direction of Griff and Harrison.

Griff had found a piece of wood about the right length for the handle, and he had been working on it for close to an hour now. Harrison sat beside him, his eyes on Griff's every move. From time to time, they would address one another and then discuss what had been brought up.

As she watched, Griff met Evelyn's gaze and offered the slightest smile before going back to his work.

Evelyn sent up a prayer for safety. She had depended on God's protection every day of her life, especially after Jake had died. Surely God wouldn't stop protecting her and Harrison now, would He?

"You plan to check on Red again?" Willie sat at the table in the corner, a cup of coffee in hand, his restless gaze filled with concern. He had spent the day following Evelyn around the house as she went about her work, either pacing the length of the room she was in, or sitting nearby, drumming his fingers against whatever surface he could find. He had a skittish tendency that kept her on edge.

"I don't think much has changed since I checked on him ten minutes ago." She finished washing her hands and dried them on her apron, her attention retuning to Griff and Harrison.

It was clear her son admired the Texas Ranger. Evelyn had been so busy trying to meet Harrison's daily needs these past four and a half years, she hadn't thought much about what he would need in the future. Who would teach him the things Evelyn knew nothing about? How would he learn the necessary skills to be a husband and father? Would there be other men like Griff Sommer who would be willing to step in and help?

Willie pushed away from the table, scraping the bench against the floor. "I'm gonna go crazy sitting here waiting."

Evelyn went to the wood box and took out some kindling to add to the fire in the cookstove. She set the pot of potatoes on to boil, trying to ignore Willie's outburst. He'd had several that day.

He began to pace across the kitchen, and Evelyn was forced to work around him. She tensed each time she almost ran into him, and it set her nerves on end.

How many more days must she endure this madness? She understood why Griff didn't confront them—but surely there was something they could do, some way to escape. It wouldn't take her and Harrison long to get to the tenant farmer's house and ask for help. She could tie some sheets together and climb out her window tonight—but how would she get her five-year-old to climb down knotted bedsheets? And how would she get Griff to agree to the idea? Would he help her escape? Or would she have to try it on her own?

The questions circled around in her mind, just as they had done for most of the day. She needed to speak to Griff soon, or she was afraid she might lose her mind.

A chicken roasted in the oven, and the potatoes wouldn't be

ready for at least twenty minutes. All she needed to prepare was the biscuits, but they could wait until after she spoke to Griff.

She pushed open the kitchen door and stepped onto the back porch.

"Where you going?" Willie asked.

"The necessary."

He didn't seem to want to follow, and she wasn't waiting for his approval, so she let the door close and walked across the barnyard to where Griff and Harrison sat.

Griff smiled at her approach, his brown eyes sparkling in the sunshine and his dimples creasing his cheeks.

The sight of him stole her breath and, for a moment, she couldn't recall why she had come in the first place.

"Hello, Mama." Harrison barely glanced at Evelyn, his focus on the handle. "Papa's been teaching me how to whittle."

Papa. Just hearing her son say the word brought Evelyn out of her stupor.

"Do you need something?" Griff asked. "Harrison and I were just about to finish and come in to wash up for supper."

Dusty sat up straighter and put his Stetson back into place. Thankfully, he was far enough away, he wouldn't be able to hear them if she spoke quietly.

"I'd like to talk to you...in private," she said.

Griff ran his hand along the surface of the handle and spoke just as quietly. "Something wrong?"

"I can't stay here any longer." She squatted in front of Griff and put her fingers on the handle, pretending to admire his work, but speaking with desperation. "I've been thinking of ways to escape."

Griff finally met her gaze, his hand stopping near hers on the handle. "It would be foolish to try to escape. We've already discussed this."

"Why can't we try?" She searched his face, praying for a glimmer of hope.

"They'd come after us—and even if they didn't. . ." He paused and stood, leaning against the handle.

Evelyn also stood, facing him.

"If we run, they'll try to run, too. They wouldn't stay here, knowing we were going for help."

"Who cares if they run?" Her voice had risen a notch, and she forced herself to lower it, so Dusty wouldn't hear.

"I do." His countenance became serious. "My company is supposed to bring these men to justice. If we're patient, we'll have Cass and his father right along with these three. The captain will come soon. He'll help. I promise."

Dusty rose from where he was sitting near the barn and started toward them.

"I'm not convinced." Evelyn put her hand on Harrison's shoulder, pulling him to her side. "I don't care if these men are apprehended—I only care about my son's safety."

Griff gave the slightest shake of his head, indicating that it was time to stop talking.

"What's going on?" Dusty asked as he drew close. "The wife giving you trouble?"

Evelyn held her breath, waiting for Griff to answer. Jake had used every opportunity to belittle and shame her into obedience. Would Griff do the same?

"No trouble," Griff said without taking his eyes off Evelyn, compassion in his gaze. "Just some concerns."

"If you get tired of her..." Dusty let the comment fade away, though his meaning was clear.

Griff's face turned hard, and he took a step toward Evelyn, drawing her close, just as he had done that morning. His jaw tightened as he addressed the outlaw. "You'll keep your distance from my wife, or you'll have me to deal with."

Evelyn stiffened in his hold—but he didn't let her go.

Dusty studied them for a moment, and then he seemed to size

up Griff for competition. Griff stood a full head taller than Dusty, and he was much broader and more muscular. Surely, the outlaw wouldn't stand a chance if he didn't have the pistol pointed at Griff.

Apparently, he thought so, too, because he simply nodded at the house. "Isn't it time to eat?"

Griff's arm was warm and strong around her shoulder, and she didn't want to leave his protection quite yet—but the sooner she fed these men, the sooner she could get to bed, and the sooner this day would be over.

CHAPTER 4

The next morning, Evelyn stood near the clothesline, a basket of wet bedding near her feet. A steady breeze blew across the fields, rippling the sheets and cooling her brow. Willie, Dusty, and Griff had helped her change the bedding in the sickroom and then she had scrubbed the soiled sheets as best as she could. Red was still unconscious for the third day in a row. His fever continued to rage, and Evelyn had been up most of the night with him, putting cold compresses against his forehead and doing everything in her power to make him well. Griff had stayed by her side throughout the long hours, doing all he could to help. She had insisted that he get some sleep, but he had refused to leave her alone.

She was exhausted and no closer to finding a way to escape. As the third day yawned before her, she tried to ignore the urge to run. Griff emptied her washtubs near a lilac bush, Harrison at his side. The boy talked incessantly about the farm and the work he and Griff planned to do on the corral fence after they finished the laundry.

Evelyn had told Griff she didn't need his help with her chores, but he did them anyway. He and Harrison had collected the eggs, milked the milch cow, and hauled the wood.

"You spend an awful lot of time looking at your husband." Dusty moved aside a sheet to stand in front of Evelyn.

She tried to get around him, but he stepped into her path. She walked the other way, but he followed. She stopped and spoke through a clenched jaw. "I need to get on with my work."

"I sure wish I had a pretty lady like you watching me." His beady eyes roamed over her, and she couldn't hide the shudder. "There's just one thing I don't understand," he continued. "Why don't you like when he touches you?"

Evelyn stared at Dusty, her pulse ticking in her wrists. Did he suspect the truth?

"You watch him all day," Dusty said with his eyes narrowed, "but, when he puts his arm around you, you stiffen up."

She took a step back, putting distance between her and the outlaw, and reached into the basket for a pillowcase, trying to ignore him.

"Don't you like your husband?" He put his hand over hers, stopping her from picking up the pillowcase. His hand was hot and sticky against hers. "Or is it men in general you don't like?"

Evelyn tore her hand away from him and backed up, until she was against the clothesline pole.

Dusty came toward her, but the sound of an approaching buggy tore his attention away.

The outlaw pulled his pistol from his holster. "Get rid of whoever it is—and don't breathe a word about us. I won't hesitate to pull the trigger on your guest and then on your son."

Evelyn pushed aside a bedsheet and walked toward the buggy, her heart in her throat, thankful to be free of Dusty.

Where had Griff and Harrison gone?

She shaded her eyes to see who was approaching, hoping it was Captain Sterling and they could be done with all of this.

As the buggy came closer, she saw the silhouette of a single lady driving the vehicle.

Disappointment threatened to bring tears. If it wasn't Captain Sterling, who could it be?

The woman inside the buggy waved, and Evelyn forced herself to wave back. A glance around the yard revealed that Dusty and Willie were out of sight, too—but she knew they were watching her closely. If she gave any hint at trouble, she didn't doubt Dusty would shoot.

Mrs. Longley, the pastor's wife, came within sight and she offered Evelyn a warm smile. "Hello, dear."

Evelyn twisted her hands together, wishing her caller was anyone but this sweet, unassuming woman. She hated to think Mrs. Longley would be in harm's way once she entered Evelyn's yard. She suspected the woman had come for a nice long visit. If it had been any other week, she would have loved the unexpected guest but not today. She needed to make her leave as soon as possible.

Mrs. Longley pulled the buggy to a stop and secured the reins to the dashboard. "I hope I'm not interrupting."

Evelyn forced herself to smile. "Just some laundry."

Mrs. Longley had expressive hazel eyes and smile lines around her mouth. She and Pastor Longley had made Evelyn feel welcomed and loved. After Jake had died, the older woman had stopped by often to see to Evelyn's needs. She had become a surrogate mother, as well as a good friend, and had continued to introduce her to new arrivals. Recently, she'd brought Mrs. Etta Sterling for a visit.

"I'm sorry, I thought you usually washed on Monday. I wouldn't have come, had I known it was washday."

"I usually do wash on Mondays," Evelyn said quickly, "but Harrison had an accident, and I needed to wash the bedding again today." She winced at telling a lie, especially to Mrs. Longley, but she couldn't risk putting this woman in danger with the truth.

The pastor's wife seemed satisfied with the answer, because she turned back to her buggy and took a basket out. "I brought you some preserves that I put up last fall. I've been meaning to give them to you for some time, but my mind isn't as sharp as it used to be."

Evelyn used the opportunity to glance around the yard, but there was no one to be seen.

"Harrison especially loves my peach preserves," Mrs. Longley said, turning back to face Evelyn with a smile.

Evelyn gave her full attention to the pastor's wife once again. "He'll be so happy. Thank you."

"Is he close at hand?"

Evelyn didn't know where Harrison had gone—but how could she tell that to Mrs. Longley? Another lie started to form on Evelyn's lips, but just then Harrison came running to them from the barn.

"There's my boy." Mrs. Longley bent down, opening her arms to receive a hug.

Harrison loved Pastor and Mrs. Longley like grandparents, and he didn't miss the opportunity to get wrapped up in one of their special hugs.

Thankfully, Griff had remained in hiding. Was Willie with him? Were they watching her even now?

Mrs. Longley finished hugging Harrison and then stood again, clutching the basket, an expectant smile on her face. No doubt she wanted an invitation inside—but how could Evelyn entertain her, knowing there was a wounded man upstairs, two outlaws keeping watch, and a handsome Ranger masquerading as her husband?

Yet, how could she be rude and turn away a friend that had come seven miles out of her way?

"Won't you come in?" Evelyn found herself saying.

"If it's no trouble."

"Of course not." But it was bound to be trouble, if Evelyn and Harrison weren't careful.

Harrison! How would she keep the boy from saying something?

The three of them walked into the house and Evelyn cast a look up the stairs. Hopefully Red would stay quiet. He'd been having nightmares in his delirium and had spent most of the night crying out. Thankfully, he'd quieted as the fever went down in the morning, but there was no telling if he might have another episode.

Mrs. Longley followed Evelyn into the kitchen. The pot of coffee was sitting at the back of the stove, so Evelyn pulled it forward and stoked the fire. She had a few biscuits left over from supper the night before and she pulled these out of the pie safe.

As she passed the window, she caught a glimpse of Dusty moving toward the back porch. The screen door allowed a breeze to enter the room. Evelyn was tempted to close the outer door, so Dusty couldn't hear their conversation, but she knew if she wasn't careful, he would make his presence known, and then Mrs. Longley might be forced to stay under guard with them—or worse.

Dusty's footsteps fell on the porch, but Mrs. Longley was so busy talking with Harrison, she didn't appear to notice.

"What's this?" Mrs. Longley frowned at Harrison. "You've been playing a game with Papa?"

Evelyn's heart pounded at the turn in conversation. If she wasn't quick, her son would give away their secret and Dusty would hear.

"It's nothing," Evelyn said with a forced laugh. "You know how Harrison loves to play make-believe."

"Papa taught me how to whittle and he said he'll teach me how to ride a horse and shoot a gun someday."

Mrs. Longley lifted a brow, but Evelyn just smiled. She quickly spread the peach preserve on a biscuit and handed it to her son. "Why don't you go on outside to play?"

Harrison's eyes grew wide at seeing the biscuit. "Can I take one to Papa?"

Evelyn spread more preserves on another biscuit and handed it to him, giving Mrs. Longley a knowing glance. "Of course you can."

Mrs. Longley smiled at Harrison as he stepped out of the kitchen. Evelyn hated that he was out of her sight, but no doubt he'd go back and find Griff again, where he'd be safe.

"How are you doing, Evelyn?" Mrs. Longley asked, concern wedging between her eyebrows. "You seem a little...skittish."

Evelyn glanced toward the door to make sure Dusty hadn't made himself known. Seeing that he was still hiding, she forced herself to calm down, and she took a seat across from her friend. "I'm doing just fine."

She hoped and prayed Mrs. Longley wouldn't say anything that would put her and Griff at risk. The pastor's wife was always trying to convince Evelyn to marry again or take on another widowed woman for companionship, but she had always refused. Now that she was independent and free, she wasn't eager to saddle herself to another domineering man or roommate.

Thoughts of Griff came unbidden. In the past three days, he'd already proven himself to be different than the other men she'd known. He was kind, thoughtful, selfless, and encouraging. He found ways to ease her burdens, and he was quick with a compliment. What would it be like to live with a man who valued her for who she was—and didn't criticize her for who she wasn't?

"I hate knowing you're alone—"

"How have you been?" Evelyn interrupted Mrs. Longley, wanting to divert the questions away from herself. "Has Pastor Longley recovered from that cold? How is everyone?"

Mrs. Longley's entire demeanor changed, and she began to glow as she talked about her husband, children, and grandchildren. She loved to share news about her family.

As long as Evelyn could keep asking the other lady questions, they would be safe.

~

Griff stood near the window in the barn and watched as Mrs. Longley slapped the reins across the horse's back to leave the barnyard. Earlier, when he and Harrison had just finished emptying the laundry tub, he'd noticed her coming down the road. He had taken Harrison into the safety of the barn, not wanting her to see him. He had recognized her immediately and knew she would recognize him, too, since he had met her just the week before at church.

He'd spent the better part of an hour praying as he watched Dusty listen in on their conversation from the porch. In the barn, he had kept busy repairing one of Evelyn's chairs so Willie wouldn't question why he hadn't gone out to visit with their friend.

"Papa?" Harrison spoke to Griff from where he sat on a stool near the worktable, a piece of mesquite in hand. "Can we turn this into a spoon for Mama?"

Griff nodded absentmindedly as he moved toward the barn door to go to Evelyn. "Come, Harrison. Let's go see your mama now."

Harrison jumped off the stool and slipped his hand inside Griff's, admiration in his trusting face. He was the first child who had ever looked up to Griff. The thought was humbling, but he wondered how the boy would feel when Griff had to leave one day.

Willie, Griff, and Harrison walked out of the barn and into the yard.

The dust from Mrs. Longley's buggy billowed in the distance as Dusty came off the porch.

Evelyn hugged her middle and turned toward the house. When she saw her son, she let out a relieved cry. "Harrison."

He pulled Griff toward Evelyn, not letting go, even when Evelyn took him up in her arms to hug him.

"Put your arms around me," Evelyn whispered to Griff.

Griff didn't wait for a second invitation. He wrapped Evelyn and Harrison in his arms, surprised at how well they fit together.

For the first time, Evelyn didn't grow stiff at his touch. Instead, she melted into his embrace.

Concern wrapped around Griff's heart as he held her tight and whispered, "Did something happen?"

"No." She shook her head. "But I need you to be more affectionate with me."

It was Griff's turn to pull away. He studied Evelyn, questioning her with his eyes.

"Dusty made a comment before Mrs. Longley arrived," she whispered, moving closer to him. "We must be more affectionate with one another, or he'll start to suspect."

Griff's pulse turned up a notch as she leaned into him. He could smell the rosewater on her skin and feel the silkiness of her hair against his chin. It wouldn't be hard to pretend—if anything, it was getting harder and harder not to let all this play-acting get to his head.

"I should finish hanging the bedding," she said. "Will you come with me? I don't want to be alone with Dusty, again."

The outlaws slowly made their way across the barnyard toward Griff's make-believe family, and a deep sense of protection came over him. No longer was he thinking in terms of a Ranger doing his duty, suddenly, his need to guard Evelyn and Harrison came from somewhere deeper. If Dusty or Willie laid one unkind hand on either of these two, Griff was certain there was nothing and no one who could stop him from meting out justice.

"Come." Griff took Harrison in his arms, and gently grasped Evelyn's hand. He led them past Dusty and Willie, toward the clothesline, speaking loud enough for the outlaws to hear. "I won't leave your side again."

Evelyn's hand felt small and delicate inside his, but she latched onto him with a force that surprised him. Harrison was light and easy to carry as he wrapped his arms around Griff's neck. Both felt vulnerable and defenseless. What would have happened to these two if he hadn't come along at the right time? Had God orchestrated their meeting so Griff could be there to protect them? But who would protect them when he left?

Griff walked them to the clothesline and set Harrison on his feet. Dusty and Willie were standing in the barnyard, speaking to each other and far enough away not to hear Griff and Evelyn.

Harrison took a handful of clothespins and went to the large oak, lining them up like soldiers going to war.

"What would you like me to do?" Griff asked, still holding Evelyn's hand.

"Just stay with me," she whispered, her eyes large in her pretty face.

"No." He pulled her a little closer, the sheets blowing in the wind and the sunlight making her hair look like liquid honey. "How would you like me to be more affectionate?"

She dropped her gaze and nibbled on her bottom lip before answering. "I don't know. Perhaps—" She paused.

"Perhaps?" he asked gently.

"Perhaps, you could hold my hand more often."

"Like this?" He lifted the hand he held. "What else?"

"I suppose...a-a kiss might not hurt from time to time."

Griff swallowed hard and took a step closer to her. "Like this?" He lifted her hand to his lips and placed a kiss on her knuckle.

Her chest rose and fell with deep, even breaths, but she still didn't meet his eyes. "I suppose."

With the sheets draped all around them, Griff felt a measure of privacy. "What about like this?" He felt bold and almost reckless as he put his free hand under her chin and lifted it for her to look at him. "May I kiss you like this?" He lowered his lips to hers, but he hovered above the kiss until she gave the slightest nod, then he captured her mouth with his.

He intended it to be a quick, light kiss—but when she let out a little gasp and then lifted her hands to his lapels, pulling him tighter as she leaned into his lips, everything else faded.

Griff wrapped his arms around her and deepened the kiss. At first, it had been simply a show—his duty as a Texas Ranger—but as he continued to kiss her, he realized he was no longer pretending. He was kissing Evelyn Prentis because he wanted to kiss her.

It wasn't the first time he'd kissed a woman, but he didn't recall it feeling anything like this. Evelyn's lips were sweet and soft, eagerly accepting his kiss and returning it. For a heartbeat, he almost believed their charade was true.

The startling thought tore him out of the moment, and he forced himself to pull away.

Evelyn looked a bit dazed, but slowly, her eyes began to focus and she stared up at him in surprise.

He cleared his throat and took a step away from her. "I didn't mean for that to happen."

Her cheeks were pink as she slowly bent to pull a pillowcase out of the basket near her feet. He detected the slightest tremor in her hands as she pinned it to the line. "You only did what I asked —nothing more." She took another pillowcase out of the basket and moved aside a bedsheet to get to the next line. "Maybe, next time, don't make it look so believable."

If her kisses continued to make him feel the way they did, there couldn't be a next time.

He forced himself to look away from Evelyn and focus on why he had come to her farm in the first place. He was a Texas Ranger. He'd worked hard to get to this place, and he wasn't about to throw away his dreams just to become a farmer again. Hadn't he celebrated when he got away from his stepfather's farm? His one longstanding goal had been to discover the truth about his father's death and it wasn't about to change now.

He shook his head to clear his thoughts and took another step away from her. It was dangerous to mix his emotions with his work. Branch harped on that all the time. Evelyn and Harrison were under his protection, nothing more. It was risky to start to have real feelings for this woman and her son.

He had a job to do—protect her and Harrison until they could apprehend the Cass Markham gang.

Which was exactly what he planned to do.

CHAPTER 5

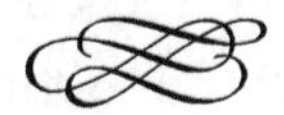

It was long past midnight as Evelyn sat next to Red, placing cold compresses against his feverish brow. The man moaned in his sleep, thrashing about, mumbling incoherently. She was not a healer, didn't know much about infections, wounds, or medicines, and didn't know what she could do to help ease his discomfort. The helplessness of it all made her even more exhausted than before.

"He's in pain," Willie said from his seat in the corner of the room. "Why don't you do something?" His arms were crossed and his face brooding as he watched her work. The wound she'd stitched up on his cheek was red and swollen, and she was afraid it was infected, but she didn't say anything, because she didn't want to draw attention to the horrible sewing job she'd done. He was growing impatient and she felt the tension boiling just beneath the surface of his self-control.

"I'm trying," she said just above a whisper. Memories of Jake's harsh words came back unbidden, and she felt the full weight of her incompetence all over again. She had been a failure to him as a wife. Two miscarriages, one right after the other, had made her feel ashamed and broken. The only time he'd looked at her with a shred of pride was when she'd presented him with a son—her sweet Harrison. But then she could do nothing right as a caregiver and nurturer, and he had continued to find fault in her performance.

Griff stood near the basin of cold water and wrung out a rag, handing it to her to place on Red's head. He took the used one from her and glanced at Willie out of the corner of his eye.

Having Griff close made her breath uneven and her hands tremble. The kiss they had shared near the clothesline had shaken her more than it should.

But his countenance was heavier since their intimate encounter. Something had pulled him away from the kiss and caused him to be more guarded around her. Was he disappointed in her kiss? In her performance pretending to be his wife? In her lack of care for the outlaw?

Red moaned again and without warning, Willie jumped up from the chair and grabbed Evelyn by the arm. He pulled her off the edge of the bed and twisted her arm behind her back, drawing her face close to his.

She whimpered and Griff dropped the rag to rush to her side, but Willie's draw was quick, and he pointed his pistol at Griff while breathing hard against Evelyn's face. "Cass'll be back in a few days, and if Red's not well-enough to travel, I'll personally see that you're the one to blame."

Dusty jumped up from his bedroll on the floor, blinking away sleep, his gun pointed at Griff.

Evelyn's heart pumped hard as tears stung her eyes. "I don't know what else to do."

Griff strained to overtake the outlaw, but the gun pointed at his chest held him back. Her hand started to tingle and her shoulder hurt from being twisted, but she refused to cry out in pain.

"I don't care what it takes," Willie said through a clenched jaw, his breath hot on her face. "Make him well."

He let her go as fast as he'd grabbed her and she stumbled back, falling on the bed.

Willie returned to his chair and Griff finally came to Evelyn. He pulled her into his arms, holding her close as she clung to his shirt.

"Do something," she pleaded.

"Soon," he whispered.

The tears fell down her cheeks unchecked and she took a deep breath, pulling away from his embrace. She hated feeling helpless. When would the nightmare come to an end?

"Papa?" The door creaked open and Harrison stood wiping sleep from his eyes. His face was red, as if he'd been crying for some time.

Evelyn left the bedside and scooped her son into her arms. He cried and reached for Griff.

"I want Papa," he said.

Griff didn't hesitate, but came to Evelyn and took Harrison from her arms.

Part of her felt rejected by her son—but the other part felt a measure of relief that someone was there to help shoulder her burdens. It made her happy to know her son was bonding with a man who was kind, respectable, courageous, and caring. If he was going to reach for someone else, it felt right for it to be Griffin Sommer.

"Let's put him to bed," Griff said to Evelyn. "We'll get some rest and come back to check on Red later."

Willie scowled at them. "No one is getting rest until Red is better."

"My wife needs to sleep." Griff's tone didn't invite a debate. "If she doesn't get rest, she can't care for Red properly."

Evelyn blinked up at Griff. It was an all-together new experience to have someone defend and protect her.

Willie finally stood. "Fine, but only a few hours and then I want her back."

Taking Evelyn's hand, Griff led her out of the sickroom.

Close on their heels, Willie followed until they reached their bedroom. "Three hours," he said. "No more."

Griff closed the door and Evelyn leaned against it. Her legs were weak and she didn't think she could walk across the room without collapsing.

"Papa?" Harrison said as Griff laid him in the bed and pulled the sheets up to his chin.

"Yes?"

"Can we go fishing someday?"

Evelyn finally moved away from the door, wanting to stop her son from making a request that Griff couldn't fulfill. "Harrison—"

"I'd like to take you fishing," Griff said and sat on the bed next to Harrison. "I used to fish all the time when I was a kid in Minnesota. We had our very own lake."

Harrison's eyes grew wide. "A whole lake, all to yourself?"

"Yes, a whole lake. It wasn't very big, but it was deep and held more fish than I could catch in a lifetime."

Harrison put his hands behind his head and sighed. "I like fishing, but Mama doesn't have time to take me to the fishing hole very often. Once, Reverend Longley came to the farm and he took me fishing."

"Reverend Longley sounds like a nice man," Griff said.

"He is, but he's busy being a pastor and all." Harrison yawned and turned onto his side, facing Griff.

"I'm sure he is." Griff moved the hair off Harrison's forehead, a patient smile on his face. "But I imagine he likes spending time with you. I don't know anyone who wouldn't."

Griff's words warmed Evelyn's heart. If she wasn't mistaken, he liked her son just as much as Harrison liked him.

Affection for this strong, handsome man filled Evelyn with surprise and she said quickly, "I think it's time we all get some sleep."

Griff stood. "You're right. I'll sleep by the door again tonight. Wake me up if you need anything."

Harrison yawned again. "Good night, Papa."

With a smile, Griff leaned down and placed a kiss on Harrison's forehead. "Good night."

The little boy burrowed under the covers, but he opened his eyes and reached out for Griff's hand. "Will you keep us safe tonight?"

Griff nodded slowly. "I will always keep you and your mama safe."

Always.

Evelyn knew Griff hadn't meant to say always, as if he planned to stay forever, yet the thought left her yearning for that very thing. What would it be like to have him there forever? To have someone to lean on in good times and bad. Would he continue to be the same, charming man he was now? Or would his true personality start to show, like Jake's had as soon as they were free of her family?

The Texas Ranger took the quilt off the footboard and spread it out on the floor. Whiskers lined his strong jaw, and his curly hair was disheveled, but it only made him look more handsome, if that were possible. He was about to drop into his makeshift bed, but he paused and met her gaze, his brown eyes filled with kindness and strength. "Good night, Evelyn."

Heat filled her cheeks at being caught staring at him, so she dipped her head and mumbled, "Good night."

She slipped into the bed with Harrison and put her arms around him, pulling him close. From where she laid, she had a good look at their protector as he stretched out on the blanket and sighed.

What was happening to her? She'd never met anyone like him —and that's what scared her the most. She thought she'd had men figured out. Told herself she didn't need one in her life—didn't want one, either.

But now?

Now, she wasn't so sure.

~

Griff yawned late the next afternoon as he finished milking Annabelle. The poor cow had missed her morning milking, because Griff and Evelyn had been preoccupied helping Red. The man had started to come around early that morning, his fever finally breaking. For the first time in four days, Evelyn had seemed to relax—as much as she could, given the situation. It was enough to make Griff feel a measure of relief, as well.

Harrison sat beside Griff on a smaller stool, his elbows on his knees, his chin in his hands, watching every move that Griff made. He liked having the little fellow follow him around, even if he did get under his feet from time to time.

"We need to hurry back to the house," Griff said to the boy. "Your mama needs some help in the kitchen."

Dusty stood near the barn door opening, biting his nails and spitting the pieces onto the floor. The only reason Griff had left Evelyn alone to prepare supper was because Dusty planned to guard them and leave Willie in the house.

"Buggy's coming." Dusty snapped to attention, his eyes on the horizon.

Griff stood, his pulse ticking a bit faster. Who could it be this time? Would he have to hide again?

As the buggy drew closer, the two occupants became clearer.

It was the captain and Miss Etta.

"A couple of neighbors," Griff said as nonchalantly as he could. "I'll go send them on their way."

Griff took Harrison's hand, but as he passed Dusty, he felt the cool steel of his pistol in his back.

"I'll be watching your every move, Farmer." Dusty shoved the gun into Griff's ribs. "One wrong move and I'll shoot your son first. After that, I'll kill you." He paused. "You can imagine what will happen to your wife when you're not here to protect her."

Fear snaked through Griff's gut as he gritted his teeth and held Harrison's hand firmly. He didn't bother to acknowledge the outlaw as he stepped out of the barn and into the yard.

Miss Etta waved at Griff with one hand, while she placed the other over her heart in what appeared to be relief. She fretted so about 'her boys.' He hated to think he'd caused her any alarm.

Griff walked away from the barn quickly, needing to communicate the situation as fast as possible to the captain, before he gave something away.

Captain Sterling pulled the buggy into the drive and met Griff in the middle of the dusty yard.

"Whoa," the captain said as he pulled back on the reins. His eyes were shaded under his Stetson, and his large mustache twitched as he surveyed Griff. "Wasn't sure if I'd find you here. O'Neal and Ezra returned today without you and said you'd come back a few days ago."

"Hello." Griff tried to look casual as he and Harrison stopped beside the buggy.

Miss Etta leaned forward, her eyes filled with concern. "We were worried about—"

"Don't say anything," Griff said quickly, cutting her off. "Moments after I arrived here, Cass Markham pulled in with an injured man. He's upstairs, Dusty Dabou is in the barn, and Willie

Markham is in the kitchen with Evelyn." Griff reached out and offered his hand to the captain, as if he was greeting a neighbor. "We're being watched right now."

The captain didn't give away anything. Instead, he smiled and shook Griff's hand, though his eyes were calculating. "Do they know who you are?"

"No." Griff pulled his hand back and nodded at Miss Etta. "They think I'm Griff Prentis, Evelyn's husband. Harrison here has been doing a fine job calling me papa."

Miss Etta smiled down at Harrison, though Griff could see the tension in her eyes. "How are you, Harrison?"

Harrison shied away and stepped behind Griff.

"Is there somewhere we can talk?" Captain Sterling asked.

"Nowhere they won't hear. They'll stay in hiding for now, but I can't stand here for long without them suspecting something. They think you're neighbors and I'm sending you on your way."

Captain Sterling studied Griff for a moment. "What would you like to do, Sommer?"

As the newest recruit, Griff had been tasked with the most menial jobs imaginable. To have the captain ask for advice was an honor. "Cass will be back in a couple of days with his father."

The captain nodded his understanding. He'd been a friend to Griff's father, and he knew that Griff had come to Texas to find answers.

"We have everything under control here for the time being," Griff assured his boss. "So, I'd like to wait to capture the men until after Cass and his father return." He took a deep breath, hoping the captain would go for his plan. "If you could ride into Hartville and gather up the others, you could hideout around the farm and wait for Cass to return. Once he does, the commotion should be great enough for Evelyn and Harrison to escape, and then we can attack."

Captain Sterling was quiet for a moment. "There's a lot of risk in waiting for Cass and his father to return. We could easily overtake the other three tonight, if we want."

Griff was afraid he'd make that suggestion. "If we attack too early, we might miss out on capturing Cass and his pa."

"If we wait, we put Mrs. Prentis and Harrison in more danger."

Griff tightened his hold on Harrison's hand again. "I will do everything in my power to protect them. Knowing you'll be in hiding around the farm will be another line of defense. If I need you at any time, I'll signal for help."

The captain put his foot up on the kickboard of the buggy as he looked down at his dusty boot. His mouth worked for a moment as he thought. "You've done a fine job so far, but I'm not convinced that your plan will work. I'll head back to Hartville and gather up the others. We'll return under the cover of darkness and surprise the outlaws. After we take them into custody, we'll get Mrs. Prentis and Harrison to safety and then we'll lie in wait for Cass and his father to return." He squinted at Griff. "It's the only plan I'm comfortable with."

If Griff knew anything, he knew that the captain's orders were the final say. He took a step away from the buggy and nodded, refusing to let his disappointment show. He forced himself to agree. "I'll be ready."

"Communicate the plan to Mrs. Prentis, as well, and don't do anything foolish in the meantime." The captain turned his serious gaze on Harrison. "And keep this to yourself, young man. We wouldn't want our plan to be ruined."

Harrison stared up at the captain with big eyes.

"He'll do a fine job," Griff assured his commander.

Miss Etta reached across her husband and took Griff's hand, squeezing it tight. "I'll be praying for you."

The captain clicked the reins and turned the buggy around in the yard. He and Miss Etta waved as they pulled down the driveway and turned onto the road, disappearing toward Hartville.

Griff returned the wave and then started walking back to the barn. "We need to keep all that to ourselves, do you understand, Harrison?"

"Yes, Papa."

"That's a good boy." Griff glanced at the house and saw Evelyn looking out the window, though she didn't make a move to come to him. He continued to the barn and met Dusty at the door.

"I was able to send them on their way," he said casually.

"What did they want?" Dusty asked.

"Just paying a neighborly visit."

"What'd you tell him?" Dusty pointed the gun at Griff's chest.

Griff swallowed and tried to think fast. "I told them Mrs. Prentis was ill and asked them to return another day." He reached down and picked up the full bucket of milk. "They offered to look in on her, but I assured them we had everything under control."

Harrison tugged on Griff's hand. "That's not what you said, Papa."

Dusty narrowed his eyes. "What's that?"

Griff forced himself to smile at the boy, though he didn't feel like smiling. "Remember when they asked how mama was doing, and I said she will get better soon?" Griff tried to give the boy a look that would convince him to play along, but he just frowned.

Dusty turned the gun on the boy. "What did your pa tell those people, kid?"

Harrison's eyes grew wide at seeing the gun pointed at him and he tried to hide behind Griff again.

Griff stepped in front of the child, his jaw tight. "Don't point your gun at my son," he said with venom in his voice. "You're scaring him."

Dusty pointed the gun back at Griff. "I'll do a lot more than scare him, if you don't tell me what you said to those people."

"I'm telling the truth." Griff hated to lie, but what choice did he have? He had to protect Evelyn and Harrison at all cost—isn't that what he promised them he would do?

Dusty didn't look away from Griff, but he spoke to Harrison. "Is he telling the truth, kid?"

Griff squeezed Harrison's hand tight, hoping he'd agree. He'd done so well up until now.

"Y-yes, sir," Harrison said quietly.

"Did he tell them your ma's sick?"

"Yes."

Dusty glared at Griff. "If I find out any differently, your son will be the first to suffer."

Without another word, Griff reached down and picked Harrison up with his free arm. He started toward the house, wanting to get Harrison away from Dusty.

The outlaw followed him to the house. Griff went to the kitchen door and Evelyn met him there, concern in her eyes, though she didn't ask any questions. She opened the door to let him in, and he set the bucket on the table.

"Mr. and Mrs. Jones stopped by for a visit," Griff told Evelyn. "But I said you weren't feeling well."

Evelyn swallowed and nodded, going along with his lie. "It's a shame. I haven't had a chance to visit with Mrs. Jones in ages."

Dusty followed Griff into the house. "Willie, keep your eyes open and don't let the farmer out of your sight. He might have tipped off a neighbor."

Willie stood quickly, his gun pointed at Griff.

"I don't want any trouble," Griff said, putting his free hand in the air, trying to sound reasonable. "Red's getting better and you'll be gone in a few days. There's no need to tip anyone off."

Dusty and Willie stared at Griff, but neither one made a move to question him farther.

Maybe he'd convinced them, after all.

CHAPTER 6

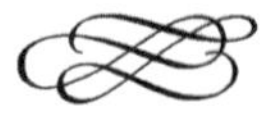

Evelyn put the final dish inside the cupboard and closed the door softly, not wanting to wake Willie who sat in the corner of the kitchen, his chin resting on his chest, snores escaping his mouth. She had found he was a light sleeper and was easily startled.

The evening chores had been done and the first star glimmered on the purple horizon.

Dusty and Willie hadn't let Griff and Evelyn alone since the Sterlings had visited a couple hours before. Evelyn had recognized them immediately, having met them several times at church in Hartville, and entertaining the delightful Mrs. Sterling when the pastor's wife had brought her for a visit. But what had been discussed with Griff? What was the plan?

She tiptoed out of the kitchen onto the back porch where Griff was rocking Harrison. Dusty had been guarding them, but the distasteful man was nowhere to be seen.

Griff tore his gaze from the horizon when she stepped onto the porch, but he didn't stop rocking. Harrison was asleep in his arms, and the tender scene made Evelyn's heart quicken.

She hated to ruin the tranquil moment, but she needed to know what had transpired earlier. "Where's Dusty?" she asked quietly.

"His stomach was unsettled, so he went to the outhouse a while ago. What about Willie?"

"Fell asleep." She paused, her heart racing with hope, but before she could suggest they attempt an escape, she met Griff's steady gaze.

"We would never make it, Evelyn. Dusty will be back any minute and Willie would hear."

She sighed and moved to the rocker beside Griff, sitting down as quietly as possible. "What did the captain have to say?"

A shadow of discouragement passed over Griff's face. "He'll return sometime tonight with the other Rangers." His voice was so low, Evelyn didn't quite catch each word, but was able to piece the sentence together.

Relief washed over her and she bowed her head in thankfulness.

"I wanted them to wait," Griff said.

Evelyn glanced up quickly. "Wait? Why?"

He returned his gaze to the horizon. "I want to catch Charlie Markham, and I'm afraid if we act too soon, we'll miss our chance."

"But don't you want us to be free?" She leaned forward, her voice in a low whisper. "Haven't you had enough of this nightmare?"

"My life's been a nightmare," he said just as quietly, but with more force. He met her gaze with his dark brown eyes. "Charlie Markham killed my father and he's the only man who knows whether my father died as a hero or a coward."

Evelyn sat back in her chair, realization dawning. "So that's what all of this waiting has been about."

"Before my mother died, she told me countless stories of my

father's heroism as a Texas Ranger, but once she married my stepfather, he forbade her to speak of him again." Griff continued to rock, looking down at Harrison. "At night, when she tucked me into bed, she whispered the stories to me, knowing I needed something to cling to. After she died..." He let the words trail away and took a deep breath. "I wrote them down in a journal, but my stepfather found it and burned it. He told me all my mother's stories were a lie, that my father had been shot in the back running away from Charlie Markham." He took a deep breath. "That day, I vowed to find Charlie and discover who was right. My ma or my stepfather."

Evelyn reached across the short distance and put her hand over Griff's. She didn't know what else to do. "I'm sorry."

Griff studied her hand for a moment, and then he turned his over and entwined his fingers with hers. Their palms met and she tried not to sigh. Why did it feel so right and good to be held by Griff?

"I married Jake Prentis when I was twenty-three," she said quietly, suddenly wanting him to know the truth about her. "I was afraid I'd die an old maid, so I said yes, because he was the first man who asked." She couldn't meet his eyes. "I thought anything would be better than living with my parents' disappointment—but I was wrong." She tried to laugh, but it didn't come out right. "Having a disappointed husband is far worse."

Griff stopped rocking and sat up a bit straighter. "How could he be disappointed in you?"

Evelyn frowned, incredulity in her voice. "How could he not? I'm weak, afraid, incompetent. I have no real skills or abilities. My older sister attracted all the admirers and my younger sister had all the talent in the family. I was constantly told I was stubborn, strong-willed, not smart enough, pretty enough, interesting enough..." She'd hoped the time and distance between her and the memories had healed her wounds, but she was wrong. "I once heard my mother say to a friend that I'd be lucky if a man even wanted me. And then—" She choked on the emotion clogging her throat.

He leaned forward, his voice gentle. "And then, what?"

"And then, I had several disappointments before I was able to provide an heir for Jake." She hated revealing her shame. What would he think of her? But what did it matter? If he stayed around, surely he'd see it anyway.

"Evelyn." He ran his thumb over hers until she looked at him. Their chairs were close, close enough for her to smell the masculine fragrance that was all his own. "I've never known a more talented and competent woman in my life. Your strong will has helped you maintain this farm and raise Harrison, all alone, when a weaker woman would have failed." He spoke with no guile or pretense. "You're braver and smarter than you think. You have nothing to be ashamed of and nothing to regret."

It was her turn to take a deep breath.

His touch, his words, the look in his eyes—everything about Griffin Sommer made Evelyn hope, for the first time in a long time, that true love existed. Yet, how could she trust love again? How could she trust her heart to another person, when there had never been anyone who had held it with tenderness and care?

Did she even deserve it?

"I've never met a more interesting woman in my life," he continued, a smile in his voice. "And," his tone became huskier, "you're the prettiest thing I've ever seen." He pulled his hand away from her and reached up to move aside a tendril of hair off her cheek. His skin brushed against hers in a feather-soft touch, and she closed her eyes, inhaling a breath of air.

"Evelyn," he whispered her name as he laid his hand on her cheek.

The pounding of hooves on the road pulled them out of the intimate moment.

Two riders approached, galloping hard toward the farm.

Griff frowned as he dropped his hand from her face and stood.

Evelyn's cheek felt cold and hot, all at the same time. She also stood, wishing he had finished his thoughts, but the visitors made any words they might want to say, forgotten.

"It's Cass," he said under his breath. "And his pa."

A chill ran up Evelyn's back as Griff handed Harrison to her quickly. "Go inside and lock yourself in your room. No matter what, don't open the door to anyone but me, do you understand?"

Harrison woke and began to cry.

"Shh," Evelyn said. "It will be all right."

"Do you understand?" Griff asked again, his voice and face revealing the seriousness of this meeting.

"Yes." She nodded.

He pulled her into his arms for a quick embrace, and then stepped off the porch to meet the riders.

Evelyn clutched Harrison close and ran into the kitchen, where Willie was just coming to his senses.

He jumped up, grabbing his gun out of his holster, pointing it wildly about the room. "What's happening? Where's the farmer?"

She swallowed hard and nodded toward the door. "Your brother just returned."

Willie's eyes grew wide and then he hollered in triumph as he raced out of the kitchen.

Evelyn didn't waste another moment, but rushed up the stairs to her bedroom and locked the door, praying for Harrison, Griff, and a future that seemed so close, yet impossibly far away.

~

Dusty and Willie joined Griff in the yard as Cass and his father pulled to a halt—at least, he assumed it was Cass's father. The man wore a long duster and a bowler hat, with thick white hair sticking out from beneath. His large white mustache was tinged with the yellowed hue of tobacco. He dismounted with a hitch in his movements and a slight limp in his step, then he started digging in his saddle bags, mumbling something under his breath.

This was his father's murderer? The man was old, broken, and looked about as harmless as a pesky fly. Ever since Griff was a child, he'd pictured Charlie Markham to be a monster, larger than life, and menacing.

Charlie Markham was none of these things.

Yet, he knew this was the man who had murdered his father and deprived him of a happy childhood.

Cass dismounted and tossed the reins to Dusty. "Take care of the horses. We've been riding hard to get here."

Dusty scowled but didn't argue.

"How's Red?" Cass paused and grabbed Willie's chin, turning his face one way and then the other. "That wound looks horrible."

Willie touched his puckering skin, but lifted his chin. "I'll heal just fine."

"Once I get some of my salve on it," Charlie said, narrowing his gaze on his younger son.

Cass shook his head, frustration on his face. "I guess that's what you get for landing in jail. Is Red able to ride?"

"His fever just broke today," Griff said.

Cass turned to Griff, his eyes calculating. "Take Pa to Red and then get us something to eat."

Charlie clutched a small satchel and finally turned toward Griff, meeting his eyes for the first time.

Anger and grief waged within Griff's chest. If he wasn't careful, he might give something away, and then where would he be? He needed to keep these men happy until Captain Sterling arrived, which could be several more hours.

"This way," Griff said.

He led them into the house, up the stairs, and to the sickroom.

Red opened his eyes when they entered, a grimace on his face, but he didn't say a word.

Pa went to the bed and pulled aside the bandage Evelyn had placed over Red's wound. He squinted at it, probed around with his fingers, which caused Red to moan in protest, and nodded. "It needs some of my salve, too." He opened his bag and pulled out a dirty jar. The contents looked like lard, which he slathered onto the wound liberally.

Without wiping his hands, he put some on Willie's wound next.

"Is Red able to ride?" Cass asked.

Charlie lifted an oily rag out of his bag and then wiped his hands while shaking his head. "He won't be ready to ride for at least a week, if not longer."

No one said a word as they waited for Cass to respond.

"I can't think on an empty gut," Cass finally said in irritation, turning to Griff. "Where's the wife?"

Griff didn't want to bring Evelyn and Harrison into this mess. "I can prepare something for you to eat."

Cass narrowed his eyes. "Did something happen to her?" He looked at Willie. "Did one of you do something?"

Willie shook his head. "She's been here the whole time."

"Where is she now?" Cass demanded.

If Griff didn't answer, Cass would go looking for her. "She's in our room with our son. I'd prefer to let her stay there."

"Fine." Cass started to walk out of the sickroom. "Just get us something to eat."

A half-hour later, Griff handed large plates of flapjacks to Cass and his pa in the kitchen.

Cass didn't even bother to acknowledge Griff as he started in on his food—but he grimaced after taking the first bite. "What'd you do to these?"

Charlie lifted his plate and sniffed. "They smell fine to me."

"They taste like garbage." Cass doused the flapjacks in syrup. "But I'm too hungry to care."

Griff was the first to admit he wasn't a good cook, but he'd managed to keep himself alive.

"We'll start out at first light," Cass told the others. "Dusty and Willie, you two take turns guarding the farmer and his wife tonight, and then tomorrow, we'll have to risk moving Red."

"He won't make it," Charlie said, matter-of-factly, shoving a forkful of food into his mouth. "That wound will rip open and he'll bleed to death."

"We don't have time to wait. I need all of you for the next job and I've caught word that the Rangers know you're in the area." Cass poured more syrup over his flapjacks. "Pa, we'll move him to your cabin and then meet up with Maggie and the others in Uvalde."

Griff started to clean up the mess he'd made, listening intently, but trying to look disinterested. More than anything, he wanted to corner Charlie and ask about Father's death. It seemed a cruel joke to be so close to the outlaw but not get his questions answered.

Cass met Griff's gaze. He stopped eating his flapjacks and nudged his chin toward the door. "It's time to go to bed, Farmer."

There would be no more talk with him present.

"Follow him, Dusty," Cass said. "Make sure he and his wife stay in that room all night."

"My pleasure," Dusty said with a smirk.

Griff set down the bowl he'd been wiping and left the kitchen.

If he was going to be ready to help the captain tonight, he'd need to spend the next couple of hours preparing. He had enough information to help the captain apprehend the others in Uvalde. For once, they knew where the gang would be before they committed a crime.

Griff walked up the stairs, down the hallway, and knocked on the door. "Evelyn, it's me."

There was a pause and then the lock clicked and the door opened slowly. She looked out, her face pale. "Are they gone?"

Dusty stepped into her line of sight and she had a visible reaction.

"Not yet," Griff said gently, trying to ignore Dusty and continuing to pretend he was the concerned farmer they believed him to be. "But soon. They plan to ride out in the morning."

She closed her eyes briefly.

Griff stepped into the room, closing the door on Dusty's smug face. For good measure, he locked it, too.

Harrison was sleeping in the big bed, his eyelashes lying against his plump cheeks.

"What's happening?" Evelyn asked quietly.

"They're eating now and then they plan to get some rest." He took her hand and pulled her to the other side of the room, to give them even more privacy, but he didn't let go of her hand. "Hopefully they're sleeping when the captain arrives with the others. Our best chance is to catch them unaware."

Her face was shadowed in the dark room, but he could still see her eyes clearly. They shimmered with unshed tears. Her trust in him was unmistakable, and the power of her confidence in his abilities filled him with strength unlike anything he'd ever experienced.

Earlier, as they had sat on the porch, he'd almost declared his heart. Somehow, in just a few short days, he'd fallen in love with Evelyn Prentis. But he hadn't told her how he felt, because he had nothing to offer. He didn't have a home or a normal job. Like Branch said, Rangers weren't meant to have families. Captain and Miss Etta had sacrificed more than they should for one another—but it wasn't the kind of life most women could handle. Did he even have the right to ask Evelyn and Harrison to share that kind of life with him?

Yet, the thought of walking away, and never seeing them again, made him want to believe that anything was possible.

He reached out and drew her closer, wrapping his arms around her.

She set her hands against his chest, though she didn't push away. Instead, she stood, waiting quietly.

He didn't want to make any promises or declarations he couldn't follow through with later. Anything could happen in the next several hours, and the last thing he wanted was for her to be hurt.

Instead, he simply kissed her.

She returned the kiss, lifting her hands to rest on his cheeks.

The feel of her in his arms was exactly what he needed to give him the strength to fight.

With a ragged breath, he pulled away and set his forehead against hers. "No matter what happens, I want you to know that you and Harrison are very special to me, and I will protect you."

"I know you will."

"Try to get some sleep, and when everything begins, stay here with Harrison. I'll return for you. I promise."

He waited until she climbed into bed and then took a seat on the rocker.

The moonlight caressed her face and made her eyes shine. "Aren't you going to sleep?" she asked.

"I can't risk it. I'll stay awake and watched for the captain to arrive." He spoke quietly. "But you should sleep. I'll wake you when the Rangers get here."

She closed her eyes without another word, and soon, her breathing was slow and steady.

He let out a sigh and felt himself relaxing, knowing that she was getting some much-needed rest. The lack of sleep the past four nights was wearing on both of them.

The next thing he knew, he was being pulled out of sleep with the whinny of a horse and Evelyn's scream.

CHAPTER 7

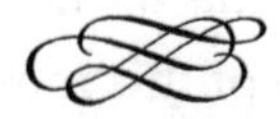

Evelyn frantically felt around the bed, but Harrison was gone. Another scream lodged in her throat as Griff jumped from the rocker, his hair on end and his eyes wild.

"What's happened?"

"It's Harrison," she said, clutching the blankets, panic in her voice. "He's gone."

The whinny of horses seeped into the room and she fell out of the bed trying to get to the window.

There, in the inky darkness, the gang was mounting their horses. She could hardly make out who was who, but one man was leading hers and Griff's horses from the barn.

"Harrison!" She screamed his name when she saw him running across the barnyard toward the outlaws. She tried to pry open the window, to call for him, but it wouldn't budge, so she raced toward the door.

Griff grabbed her as she passed him.

"Let me go!" she screamed.

"What's wrong? Where's Harrison?"

"He's there." She pointed toward the window. "Running toward the gang."

"The gang?" He shook his head to focus.

"They're escaping with our horses," she cried out. "I'm afraid Harrison's trying to stop them."

Alarm registered on his face. He pulled the door open and raced into the hallway. "Stay here," he called over his shoulder. "I don't want you in the middle of this mess."

"I won't stay here while my son's in danger," she yelled back.

He didn't seem to hear her as he rushed down the stairs and out the front door.

"Let go of the ropes, kid." Dusty pulled on the lead rope, knocking Harrison to his feet, but he didn't let go.

"I'm the man of the farm," Harrison said loudly, "and I won't let you steal Mama's horses."

"Stop right there," Griff called.

"Just grab the kid," Cass yelled impatiently. "I want those horses."

"No!" Evelyn screamed as Dusty lifted Harrison off the ground and tossed him over his shoulder.

"If you say so." Dusty mounted his horse with amazing dexterity and spurred it into motion.

Red sat slouched on another horse, tilting from side to side as it went into motion.

"Do something," Evelyn begged Griff as they ran toward the gang.

He reached into his boot and pulled out a knife.

As the gang rushed by, he lunged at Dusty, but the outlaw kicked him in the chest, sending him reeling into the dirt.

"Mama!" Harrison cried, reaching for Evelyn from Dusty's shoulder.

"Come and get him!" Dusty taunted, laughing as Evelyn screamed for her son.

She ran after them, chasing them down the drive and out onto the road.

They moved farther and farther away, and her lungs felt like they would burst. She tripped, and landed hard on her chest, the air knocked out of her. She couldn't breathe, couldn't yell, couldn't fight for her son.

She'd failed him, once and for all, just as Jake had said she would.

Griff appeared at her side, breathless, lifting her to her feet. "They took all the horses," he said quickly. "I'll have to go for help. How far is the closest neighbor?"

She gasped for air, her lungs on fire. "The…tenant…farmer…" she said between gulps. "North." She pointed in the general direction of the tenant's house.

He started to turn away, but she grabbed his arm. "I'm… coming."

"You stay here, in case the captain arrives."

"I can't stay." She put her hands on her knees, fear squeezing out any air she managed to inhale.

"Someone must tell the captain what happened."

Tears pinched her eyes and she tried to blink them away. She needed to stay strong for her son.

Griff grasped her upper arms. "I will get Harrison back. I promise."

She nodded, biting her bottom lip to keep in the sob that wanted to escape.

"But now I must go." He kissed her forehead and then he was gone.

Evelyn walked back toward the house, her legs weak and trembling beneath her. Everything was quiet—too quiet. She felt helpless as she stood in the barnyard, turning in circles, looking for something to cling to. Some shred of hope. But there was nothing.

She'd go mad waiting. How long would it be before the captain came, or Griff returned?

With a cry of frustration, she clasped her hands and pressed them against her lips, falling to her knees in the middle of the dusty yard.

"Please, God," she begged. "Please keep Harrison safe until we can get to him. Please give Griff speed as he goes after new horses—and please," she bent forward and pressed her forehead to the dirt, "bring the Rangers soon."

When her legs began to ache from the awkward position, she sat on her bottom and looked up at the night sky. Millions of stars sparkled overhead. The peacefulness of the moment was in stark contrast to the chaos in her mind and heart.

She didn't know how much time passed before she heard the pounding of hooves coming from the north. She scrambled to her feet and watched as Griff raced toward her with two horses.

"I'm going after them," he said breathlessly as he slowed near her and dropped the reins of the second horse. "Head toward Hartville and give the captain this." He pulled something from his pocket and tossed it to her. "Tell him the gang's headed east and I'm on their trail."

Evelyn clutched Griff's badge and mounted the horse without another word. It felt good to finally have a task.

Griff didn't waste another moment, but left the yard in the direction the gang had gone.

Evelyn went in the opposite direction toward Hartville, hoping she'd meet the Rangers on the way to save time.

She pressed forward, leaning against the horse, willing it to go faster.

Half-way to Hartville, she saw the Rangers riding toward her at a steady gallop, a dog running at their side.

Relief washed over her, knowing they would soon join Griff and give him the help he needed to bring Harrison back to her.

"Whoa," Captain Sterling called, putting his hand in the air to stop the posse. "Mrs. Prentis, what's happened?"

She handed the badge to the captain and pointed behind her. "The gang left with my son and my horses about two hours ago. Griff had to go for more horses, so he just started trailing the gang now. They're headed west." She gripped the reins as her horse pranced beneath her. "Please, Captain, save my son."

He tipped his hat and signaled his men to move forward. "We'll do all we can to save him," he said as he went into motion. "The best place for you is back at your farm, in case your son escapes and makes his way back home."

She couldn't possibly stay at the farm with nothing to do.

As soon as they were around the bend and out of sight, Evelyn began to follow.

~

Griff pushed the horse as fast as it would go. If he had Bolt, he knew he could go faster, but as it was, he was thankful he had any horse at all. The tenant farmer hadn't known who he was and had kept his shotgun pointed at Griff's chest until Griff could convince him he was a Texas Ranger and had come on behalf of Evelyn Prentis. It had taken some coercion to get the horses, but eventually the farmer had agreed, though he looked skeptical that he'd ever see them again.

Sweat dripped into Griff's eyes as he pursued the gang in the predawn hour. It was easy to follow their trail on the main road, but then they veered south about ten miles from Evelyn's farm. The sky turned a dark shade of purple and then faded into a light pink as he squinted to see their marks on the abandoned road he traveled. Overgrown thickets, deep ruts, and washouts made it difficult for him to see if they continued down this way, or veered off again. They couldn't be too far ahead of Griff with a child and injured man in tow.

A half hour passed before he saw their tracks take a sharp left into a stream, and that's when he first noticed the blood. Little drops at first, and then more.

Was Red bleeding? Or had someone else been injured?

"Please, God, not Harrison," he prayed.

Always on guard, listening for sounds and watching to make sure one of the men didn't wait behind to overtake him, he surveyed the opposite bank and finally found their hoof marks and the blood about a quarter mile upstream.

How far would they go? And why had they taken Harrison? Had it been a rash decision on Cass's part, or was it part of a bigger plan? The need to find Harrison pushed him forward with focused determination. He had never been so driven before, not even when he was young and first learned the name of Pa Markham.

The sun had just crested the eastern horizon as Griff came upon a clearing high atop a hill. A quick looked into the valley revealed a rundown cabin and barn. The buildings were surrounded by a high bluff to one side and a stream to the other. Griff dismounted and tethered his horse to a rock, then he crouched to the ground and moved on his belly to the edge of the outcropping.

Movement near the cabin made Griff squint to get a good look. Two men stood near a line of horses, and Griff could easily pick out Bolt's mahogany coat and black mane. One man curried them while the other led the horses to the stream, one at a time.

There was no mistaking the confident set to Dusty's thick shoulders, or the wide-awake cowboy hat Willie wore. But where were the others? Harrison?

The door of the cabin opened and Charlie Markham stepped out, his long duster and bowler cap unmistakable. He led Harrison to a spot next to the door where a log was sitting.

Harrison took a seat, his elbows on his knees.

Griff let out the breath he'd been holding since leaving Evelyn's side.

He was too far away to hear, but Dusty and Willie stopped what they were doing to listen to what Charlie had to say. Willie let the reins go from the horse he was watering and ran toward the cabin. Charlie stepped out of his way, his head low.

What was happening?

Dusty paused a moment, and then went to the side of the cabin and took what looked like a shovel. He walked away from the cabin and began to dig a hole near a large mesquite tree.

"Red." Griff shook his head. Evelyn had worked tirelessly to keep him alive, but the ride must have been too much. It was probably his blood that had helped Griff track them this far.

After a few minutes, Willie and Cass came out of the cabin. Cass's gaze wandered around the property and up the hill to where Griff was lying on his stomach. No doubt he was watching for someone who might be following.

Willie leaned against the cabin wall, his head hanging low, while Cass spoke with Charlie.

Were they planning their next move? With Red gone, they wouldn't need to stay in one place. They could easily leave, and this time it would be harder to track them.

Griff scanned the valley for places the Rangers could hide, working out a plan to attack the cabin, rescue Harrison, and hopefully capture Charlie.

As long as Harrison came away unharmed, Griff didn't care about the rest. Even if he never learned the truth about his father's death, he couldn't live with himself if something happened to the boy.

Where was Company B? No doubt Branch would bring his dog, Jack, who was one of the best trackers in the county. They should have been here by now. He had no way of knowing how long he had before the gang left. Surely, they'd wait until Dusty finished digging the grave, wouldn't they?

No matter what, Griff wouldn't let them leave without attempting to rescue Harrison.

He laid there for at least an hour, watching Dusty dig the grave, stopping from time to time to wipe sweat from his brow.

Harrison didn't move from the log, though he changed positions often.

Charlie and Willie finished currying and watering the horses, while Cass adjusted items from one saddlebag to the other.

Finally, Dusty seemed to be done with his task and the four men went back into the cabin.

Noise behind Griff made him reach for the knife in his boot, but it was the captain who broke through the dense thicket, the whole company behind him.

Silently, the captain motioned for the others to dismount and tie their horses away from the road. Branch gave Jack a hand signal and the dog laid down, watching Branch closely.

Griff kept low, not wanting to skyline and tip off the gang, and then finally came to stand before Captain Sterling.

"Have you located them?" the captain asked.

"They're in a cabin at the bottom of this hill."

"Do you think it's their hideout?"

Griff shook his head. "I think it's Charlie Markham's cabin."

All eyes were on Griff for the first time and he felt the pressure of being the newest member of the company. Branch stood next to the captain, his arms crossed and his serious gaze locked on Griff's face. O'Neal was there, and so were Whit, Jesse, and Ezra. The only one missing was Micah.

Griff admired these men and wanted to do his part to capture the Markham gang, so he stood straight and reported what he knew. "Five men left the Prentis farm," he said. "But they're fixing to bury the wounded man that just died. Everyone needs to be mindful that there's a hostage down there, a five-year old-boy."

Branch pulled out a notepad and jotted down a few things before he addressed Griff. "Have you figured out the best way for us to get close?"

"There's a high bluff behind the cabin to the west and a stream to the east. The only way to approach without being seen would be through the thicket on the north side of the cabin. This road goes down the side of the hill, directly to the cabin."

"Good work, Griff." Captain Sterling took his field glasses from his saddlebag and motioned to Branch. "I want you to take Ezra and Whit to approach from the north. Griff, O'Neal, and I will wait until you're in position." He turned to Jesse. "I want you to stay with the horses and signal if someone approaches."

Several of the men looked Griff's way and he knew they were all thinking the same thing. The menial job of guarding the horses should be Griff's. But the captain was giving him the opportunity to prove himself.

He had a lot to gain if things went well—but a lot more to lose if they didn't. He just prayed he had what it took to make everyone proud.

Branch, Ezra, and Whit mounted their horses and disappeared with Jack on their tail. It would take them awhile to get in place, so Griff and O'Neal joined the captain to spy on the gang from where Griff had been lying before.

They crawled on their bellies to the ledge and the captain looked through his field glasses. "Looks like they're getting ready to bury the dead."

He handed Griff his glasses, but Griff didn't use them to look at the gang, he turned them to Harrison, instead.

The little boy watched with wide eyes as Willie and Dusty left the cabin with a body wrapped in a sheet. He put his face in the crook of his elbow as they passed by and Griff wished he could shelter him from this harsh reality.

"There's Cass Markham," Captain Sterling said with steel in his voice. "We're closer than we've ever been to capturing him. I wish we had Micah and Sheriff Watson with us."

"Where are they?" Griff asked.

The captain's face filled with irritation. "The sheriff fell off his horse right after we left Mrs. Prentis. I was forced to send him back to Hartville with Micah. Looked like he broke his leg."

Just hearing Evelyn's name made nervous energy rush through Griff.

If Branch didn't get in place in time, the gang could start their get-away, and the captain, Griff, and O'Neal would have no chance to stop them from their vantage point, even if O'Neal was one of the best shots in the group. Griff suspected the captain had chosen for him to stay on the ridge for that very reason. If they needed to take a long shot, O'Neal was his man.

Griff handed the field glasses back to the captain and they continued to wait.

"Branch should have had enough time," the captain finally said. "Let's go."

"Who's there?" Jesse pulled his pistol from his holster, causing Griff and the others to point their weapons toward the thicket.

Evelyn appeared on the road, her gaze taking in the scene. Her hair had long since lost its pins and flowed freely to her waist.

"Evelyn," Griff breathed her name.

"Hold her," Captain Sterling demanded to Jesse. "We don't want her anywhere near that cabin."

He grabbed for the horse's reins, but it was too late. She moved past Jesse, and with a fleeting glance at Griff, she continued on the road, along the ridge, and down the hill.

"Evelyn!" Griff called. "Stop!"

"Go after her," Captain Sterling said to Griff. "Stop her before she gets killed." He looked at O'Neal. "Let's go."

Griff ran to his horse and jumped in the saddle.

"Here." Jesse handed Griff his pistol and nodded. "Go get her."

Fear pulsed through Griff's veins. Evelyn would be a prime target for the gang and put them on alert. He spurred the horse to catch up to her, thankful her mare was exhausted from the journey.

"Evelyn!" He rode next to her and swept her off the back of her horse as the first shot rang from near the cabin. Pulling her onto his lap, he tugged on the reins of his horse and came to stop near an ancient mesquite. Bullets rushed past their heads as he hauled her behind the tree and pressed his weight into hers to keep her from bolting.

"No!" she cried as she pounded on his chest. "I need to get to Harrison."

"You've already done enough damage today," he said breathlessly. "You've ruined our surprise attack. We'll be lucky if we can get to Harrison now."

Evelyn's eyes grew large and she stopped struggling.

"I thought I told you to stay at the farm." Frustration burned in his chest. "Do you want to get yourself killed?"

"I just want my son."

"You don't know what you're doing, Evelyn. We have this under control—or, at least we did until you got here."

She grew weak in his hold. "I'm scared," she said through her tears. "He's so young and helpless."

Griff held her shoulders. "Just promise me you'll stay here. I can't risk losing you."

She let out a shaky breath and nodded. "I'll stay."

"Good." He looked around the tree and saw Cass and Willie shooting into the thicket where Branch and the others would be, trying to scramble behind a rock for protection. Dusty fired at Captain Sterling and O'Neal, who were coming down the ridge.

Charlie and Harrison were nowhere to be seen. Had they gone into the cabin?

Griff needed to get in there and find out.

Leaving Evelyn, he hugged the thicket until he was close to the cabin. With Jesse's gun, he approached the back of the cabin, just as Cass, Willie, and Dusty jumped on their horses.

Griff dropped to his knee and fired at the three outlaws, but they disappeared into the thicket between Branch and Captain Sterling.

Branch and his men pursued the gang, but Captain Sterling and O'Neal continued down the ridge toward the cabin.

Griff pressed his back to the cabin wall, walking along it until he got to the front door. With a deep breath, he kicked the door open and poised his gun to defend himself.

Charlie Markham stood in the center of the cabin, his hands raised in the air, defeat on his face. "Those rotten sons of mine left me for dead, didn't they?"

"Papa!" Harrison sat in the corner, covering his ears.

He started to stand, but Griff lifted his hand and shook his head. "Stay there, Harrison." Sweet relief filled him at seeing the boy. "You're safe, but don't move until I take care of some business."

Griff turned his full attention to Charlie. "You don't know me," he said, taking a step toward the old man. "But you will soon."

It was time to get some answers.

CHAPTER 8

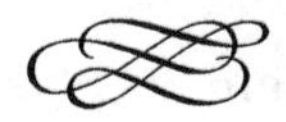

Griff stood in a semicircle with the other Rangers while Captain Sterling barked orders.

Evelyn and Harrison clung together near the cabin and Charlie stood by O'Neal in handcuffs, a scowl on his face.

"O'Neal, you'll come with me back to Hartville to press charges against Mr. Markham. I'll need my best gunman, in case the Markhams try to free their father. Jesse, you'll escort the Prentis's back to their farm."

Griff wished he could take Evelyn back. There were things they needed to discuss and work that needed to be done, yet he'd been waiting to confront Charlie Markham all his life and wasn't prepared to leave him now.

The captain turned to Griff, understanding in his face. "I'd like for you to come with us to Hartville to deal with some unfinished business."

Evelyn didn't meet Griff's gaze. Her hair was still in a mass of tangled curls down her back, and her face was pale. She hadn't spoken to him since being reunited with her son, and Griff didn't blame her. He'd been harsh during the gunfight, though he couldn't have handled it any differently. She'd put everyone in danger and there had only been one way to deal with her.

"Ma'am." Jesse tipped his hat at Evelyn. "If you're ready, we'll see that you get home safely."

"Griff?" Captain Sterling had mounted his horses and was watching him.

Griff nodded once and helped O'Neal get Charlie onto a horse. O'Neal took the lead rein and indicated that Griff should follow.

He had wanted to say goodbye to Evelyn and Harrison before heading to Hartville, but when he turned, they were already on the road up the side of the hill.

Harrison sat in front of Evelyn and he waved.

Griff returned the wave, hoping Evelyn would look his way, but she kept her back straight and focused on the road ahead.

With a heavy sigh, Griff mounted Bolt and touched his flanks to catch up to Captain Sterling and their prisoner.

The trip to Hartville was longer than Griff had imagined. It had been a hard day and he'd had little sleep the night before.

He stared at Charlie's back the whole way, wanting to be done with the man for good. He was tempted to confront the outlaw now and demand answers, but that would have to wait. If Charlie revealed that Griff's father had been a coward, he didn't want anyone else to hear. He'd wait until they could be alone in the Hartville jail before he'd ask his question.

The town was quiet as they finally led Charlie into the jail.

Micah stood when they entered the building. "Did you get Cass?" he asked.

"Not this time," Captain Sterling said, laying his saddlebag on the sheriff's desk. "But we got his pa."

"How's Sheriff Watson?" O'Neal asked. "Things didn't look good."

"They're not." Micah grimaced. "Doc Hart said it's a bad break.

The sheriff's recovering at home. Could be months before he'd able to get back to work."

Captain Sterling motioned for Griff to lead Charlie into the adjoining room where the cells were kept. "We'll have to man the jail until the sheriff's able to get back to work."

Griff walked Charlie into his cell and unlocked his handcuffs, surprised that he felt so calm standing so close to his father's killer.

"Since the Markhams are infamous for their jailbreaks," the captain said. "I'll put extra guards on duty until we can get a trial for Charlie."

Griff walked out of the cell and waited for Captain Sterling to lock the door. After he did, he spoke to Griff. "I'll give you a minute before we deal with the paperwork. I think there are a few things you'd like to discuss with Mr. Markham."

"I ain't discussing nothing." Charlie lowered himself onto the cot and laid down on his back. He hadn't said a word since Griff had apprehended him at the cabin.

Captain Sterling patted Griff's shoulder as he walked back to the sheriff's office. "Take your time, son."

Griff had imagined this moment his whole life, yet now that he stood here, he didn't know where to begin. He couldn't force Charlie to talk about the past—yet, everything in Griff wanted to demand it. After all, he deserved answers, didn't he?

"My name is Griffin Sommer—"

"Never heard of you."

Griff took a step closer to the cell to get a better look at the man he'd despised for as long as he could remember.

"Maybe you never heard of me, but you knew my father, Texas Ranger Aaron Sommer."

Charlie was silent for a moment and then he slowly sat up, his piercing eyes focused on Griff. "I haven't heard that name in twenty years."

"I've waited a long time to meet you," Griff continued. "Worked for years to make it to Texas to join the Rangers for one reason."

"To find the man who shot your pa." The older man said it as casually as if he'd just told Griff what he'd had for supper.

"I know you killed my father." He still marveled at the calm he felt. He'd always thought this moment would be rife with emotion, yet he felt numb. "What I don't know is how you did it."

Charlie took off his bowler and set it on the cot next to him. He took his time, running his hands over his balding head, not looking at Griff.

"I hate to admit it, kid, but I killed more men than I can count. Some, I don't even remember."

The first glimmer of hatred stirred within Griff and it felt red hot in the pit of his stomach. How could this man be so callous?

"But," Charlie looked up at Griff. "I remember your father better than anyone else."

Griff swallowed hard. "What happened?"

Charlie stood, wincing at the strain it took to get out of the cot, but then he walked over to Griff and met him eye to eye. "Your father spent an entire year tracking me, and I knew if I didn't kill him, he'd kill me. So, I laid a trap for him." Charlie shook his head. "But he caught on to what I was doing. Knew me too well after following me for so long. I thought I had him, but all along, he had me. We met behind the alley of a saloon way out in El Paso. It was only him and me." Charlie took another step toward Griff, his face lined with years of hardship. "I'm old and I know when I'm beat. My sons and daughter are probably happy to be rid of me. This here jail cell will be my home until I'm hanged, so I'll tell you something I've never told another living soul."

Griff held his breath, waiting to finally hear the truth.

"I've never been more scared of someone in my life. I knew I'd met my match, so I played dirty. I didn't have the courage to face him, so I hid like a yellow dog between two buildings, and when he passed me, I shot him in the back." He shook his head. "My cowardice is one of my many regrets."

It took Griff a moment to process what he'd just heard. "How'd everyone know who killed him?"

"I was a proud man back in the day. I told everyone that I killed him, because I figured if I could take down Aaron Sommer, there'd be a lot more respect for me—and there was."

Griff stood for a minute, letting all the information seep into his mind and heart.

He didn't bother to say anything else to Charlie as he turned to leave.

"Sommer."

Griff paused and took a deep breath before he looked back at Charlie Markham one last time.

Charlie clutched the bars of his cell. "I know it won't make no difference," he let out a sigh, "but I'm sorry you lost your father."

Griff had held on to his anger for so long, he didn't know how he'd live without it, but he also knew he needed to forgive this man. It was the only way he could live free.

"It does make a difference." It was all he could say before he stepped out of the cell room and returned to the office.

~

A cool breeze tousled the loose tendrils of Evelyn's hair as she pinned another wet sheet on the clothesline. For the hundredth time that day, she looked for Harrison to make sure he was safe. He was sitting near the big oak tree at the edge of the barnyard, whittling a piece of wood, just like he'd been doing since they came outside.

It had been two days since they'd returned from the outlaw's cabin, and she'd kept him by her side day and night. He hadn't complained, and she sensed both needed the reassurance that they were together again.

"Mama," Harrison called to her.

"Yes?" She picked up one of the pillowcases Red had used while in her home.

"When's Papa coming back?"

Evelyn held the clothesline for a moment and searched the road leading to Hartville, emotion clogging her throat. He'd already asked her that question a dozen times that day, and she had given him the same answer each time. "I don't know if he will, Harrison."

"He has to come back," Harrison said matter-of-factly. "He said he'd teach me how to whittle a toy horse and we got lots of things to fix."

"Have a lot of things," she corrected.

Harrison went on to list all the things he felt they needed to fix, and with each item he listed, Evelyn's heart felt heavier and heavier.

"He said he'd take me fishing," Harrison continued. "And teach me how to shoot a gun and ride a big horse like Bolt..." he rambled on, but Evelyn was lost in her own thoughts.

She hadn't realized it before, but in her heart she'd also made plans with Griff. But hers included things like sitting in the parlor together at the end of a long day, drinking a cup of coffee as they'd watch the sun rise, long rides in the country, Sunday picnics after church, conversations at the dinner table...maybe a brother or sister for Harrison.

She looked down, her cheeks warming at the thought.

Those things had seemed out of reach and unrealistic just a week ago—but after getting to know Griff and seeing how much he cared for Harrison, she'd begun to hope.

Now...now, the farm felt empty, the house felt cold, and her heart felt broken.

She had no one to blame but herself. She'd proven to him that she was a failure, had almost gotten them killed, and had caused the Rangers to lose Cass Markham. If he never spoke to her again, she'd understand why. She's been so embarrassed, she couldn't even look at him before they left the cabin two days ago.

"Mama?"

Evelyn sighed and put another clothespin on the pillowcase. "Yes, Harrison?"

"Is that Papa?"

She looked up, her heart pounding hard. "What did you say?"

"There." Harrison stood and pointed toward the road.

A rider was a long distance off, approaching at a steady pace.

Disappointment filled her and she took another pillowcase out of the basket near her feet. "It could be anyone, sweetheart."

Her son watched the rider for a little while, then went back to his whittling.

She pinned the pillowcase in place and couldn't help but sneak a peek at the rider. Every time someone passed, she'd hold her breath, until they rode on by.

How long would she pine after him before she accepted that he wasn't coming back?

Her thoughts paused as she squinted to look at the rider a little closer. It was a single man on a dark mahogany bay. Nervous bubbles formed in her stomach as she watched him come closer and closer.

He wore a red plaid shirt with a dark leather vest, just like the one Griff wore, and he had on denim trousers.

Could it be?

"It's Papa!" Harrison yelled as he jumped up and started running toward the road. "He's back! He's back!"

"Harrison!" Evelyn called to her son, not wanting him to run to the road and be trampled by the horse, but her son didn't hear as his little legs carried him at full speed.

The closer the rider came, the more convinced Evelyn was that Griff had returned.

She ran her trembling hand over her hair and smoothed down her apron. She wanted to run across the yard like Harrison, but she refrained, unsure why Griff had returned. Was it to deal with unfinished business? Perhaps gather the few things he'd left behind?

Griff slowed his horse and turned down their drive. She knew the moment he saw Harrison, because he pulled his horse to a stop and jumped out of the saddle, scooping her son into his arms and throwing him high in the air. They both grinned as they wrapped each other in a tight embrace.

Harrison's sweet laughter filled the barnyard as Griff started to walk toward Evelyn.

Their gazes met and Griff paused, as if he didn't know how she'd respond to his appearance.

She wanted to let him know he was welcome—more than welcome—but she didn't think she could stomach his rejection if he didn't feel the same way she felt, so she held back.

He came closer and she drank in the sight of him. His hair, his eyes, the dimples in his cheeks, the way he walked...and the way he looked at her.

It was the look in his eyes that pulled down the last of her self-defense. She couldn't mistake that look, even if she wanted to.

Griffin Sommer seemed to take her in, just like she had him. His eyes were filled with relief, joy—and love.

He stopped a little way off, his eyes questioning.

"Mama," Harrison said as he turned and looked at her. "Papa came back."

"Evelyn." Griff spoke her name just once, but it was all he needed to say.

Her feet took flight and carried her the final distance.

He wrapped her and Harrison in his powerful arms and she

rested her cheek against his chest, listening to the steady beat of his heart, smiling up at Harrison who grinned from ear to ear.

In all her life, she'd never known this feeling of complete and utter happiness. Love burst inside her and she felt protected, cherished, and accepted.

"I didn't think you'd want to return after what I did at the cabin," she whispered.

"I don't know a mother alive who wouldn't have done exactly what you did." He smiled and shook his head. "It was reckless, and maybe a little foolish, but completely understandable."

He wasn't going to shame her or chastise her for her foolishness? "I wasn't thinking."

"You were thinking." He bounced Harrison in his arm, making the boy giggle. "You were thinking about your son." He returned his gaze to her. "I'm proud of your bravery, Evelyn." He smiled. "I just don't want you to do that again."

She returned his smile, her heart glowing with the love she felt for him. "I promise to leave the rescuing to you."

Harrison wiggled to get out of Griff's arms. "Should I get the fishing poles, Papa?"

Griff laughed. "Maybe a little later. There are things I need to discuss with your mama first."

Harrison wrinkled his nose in disappointment, but then he ran off on his next adventure—and for the first time in two days, Evelyn didn't feel the need to watch where he went. Having Griff there had relieved so many of her concerns.

Griff wrapped his other arm around Evelyn, pulling her closer.

She willingly went.

"I have to admit, Evelyn Prentis, I liked pretending to be married to you."

Her cheeks warmed, but she held his gaze. "I liked pretending to be married to you, too."

"There's only one problem," he said slowly.

"What's that?"

"I don't want to pretend anymore."

"What do you have in mind?"

He kneaded the small of her back with his strong hands. "I was thinking we could take a little trip into Hartville and talk to Pastor Longley about making this marriage legal." He leaned forward and placed a gentle kiss on her forehead. "What do you think about that?"

A breathless sigh escaped her lips. "I think that's a marvelous idea."

He smiled. "Since I don't have to pretend anymore, may I kiss you for real this time?"

She ran her hands up to the back of his neck and pulled him down, not wanting to waste another moment. "You may."

Griff lifted her off her feet and kissed her soundly, when he set her down again, his face had grown serious. "I spoke to Charlie Markham."

"Did he tell you what happened?"

After a moment, Griff nodded. "But I realize now it didn't matter. All along, I knew my father was a hero. I knew because of the way my mother spoke about him."

"The way I'll speak about you," she said softly.

He still held her close as he smiled down at her. "I also learned there's a reward for Charlie's capture."

"Will you accept it?"

Griff shook his head. "You and Harrison are the only reward I'll ever need."

Evelyn couldn't stop herself from smiling. This handsome Ranger had stolen her heart, yet she had no intentions of taking it back.

ABOUT THE AUTHOR

Gabrielle Meyer lives in central Minnesota on the banks of the upper Mississippi River with her husband and four children. As an employee of the Minnesota Historical Society, she fell in love with the rich history of her state and enjoys writing fictional stories inspired by real people, places, and events. You can learn more about Gabrielle and her books at www.gabriellemeyer.com.

Cover design by: Wild Heart Books

MORE PRECIOUS THAN RUBIES

LORNA SEILSTAD

She is more precious than rubies: and all the things
thou canst desire are not to be compared
unto her.

— PROVERBS 3:15

CHAPTER 1

March 1886

The safe's thick metal door closed, and the clang reverberated inside the railroad mail car.

Violet bit her lip, her stomach knotting. "And you're sure they're secure?"

The young man in charge of the postal express car pushed the door's handle downward and spun the combination lock before standing. He pulled out his pocket watch. "Yes, miss. No one will touch your pretty jewels."

"It's just that my father's business—" Steam hissed, and the train released a shrill whistle. She sighed. "Oh, never mind. I don't mean to go on and on. Maybe if I remain here with you. . ."

He opened the door. "You best get to your seat, miss. Passengers aren't allowed in the express car once we're moving. But don't worry about a thing. No one is getting into that safe without the combination, and I'm the only one on the train who knows what it is. Your precious jewels are safe."

~

Whit Murray shifted from foot to foot. Why didn't the elderly woman in front of him just pay the clerk for a ticket without having to complain for a solid ten minutes about the price? If he missed this train, his commanding officer would have his hide. He'd wired ahead to say he'd be back in town today, and for Captain Hugh Sterling, there was nothing worse than a Texas Ranger not keeping his word. At least he was rid of the no-accounts he'd captured and delivered to the Austin jail. Having those two around put a Texas-sized burr under his saddle. Even a good-natured fellow like himself could only take so much.

Now, if Mrs. Slow-as-a-One-Legged-Dog would fork over the money for her ticket, he could be on his way.

"Ma'am, allow me." Whit placed a bill on the counter. "My treat."

She turned, and her gaze landed on the Ranger's star pinned to his vest. "I couldn't do that, young man."

He nudged the money toward the clerk. "Please, I insist."

The clerk yanked up the cash and passed the woman a ticket with the railroad's name emblazoned across the top in arching letters.

"Well, thank you, Ranger." She clutched the ticket to her chest. "You have made an old lady's day."

He touched his hat brim and nodded. "My pleasure, ma'am."

Slapping down another bill, he smiled to himself. He'd done the right thing, and it wasn't her fault he'd hung around the café for a second—and a third—cup of coffee. Some days it was simply hard for a man to get a move on.

With his purchased ticket in hand, he raced to the platform. The train started moving, but he hooked the handrail and landed with a thud on the steps. He made a less-than- graceful entrance into the passenger car. The conductor, who was busy punching tickets, scowled at him, but when he saw the star on Whit's chest, he nodded his approval.

Whit dropped into the first empty seat and sighed. Without making eye contact with any fellow passengers, he slouched down and pulled his hat lower. *Don't look at them. Don't talk to anyone. Just sleep.* His ma always said he could sleep anywhere, and after the short night he'd had, sleep was exactly what he needed.

Perfume. Before he could drift off, the sweet smell of chamomile and orange blossoms drifted to his nose. The scent snaked its way through his thoughts, reaching for some memory. He didn't open his eyes but drew in another whiff. The memory took the shape of a face. Violet? He'd not seen her in a long spell, but she did live in Austin. Why would she be on a train to Hartville?

"Whit? Whit Murray?" Her voice broke the silence between them. "Is that you?"

Should he confirm or deny it? Who was he kidding? He could never deny Violet Tatienne anything—except the one thing she'd wanted most.

He cocked one eye open and glanced to his left. Yep, it was her, and boy howdy, she was even prettier than she'd been eight years ago. Tea-colored curls framed her heart- shaped face, and her hazel-and-honey eyes sparkled like the jewels in her father's store.

He pushed back in his seat, then lifted his hat into place. "Violet. Now, this is a pleasant surprise."

She blinked, and her tongue darted out to lick her pink lips. She drew in a breath and offered a tremulous smile. "Is it, Whit?"

CHAPTER 2

Violet picked at a thread on the trim of her navy traveling skirt, waiting for Whit to answer her question. When he said nothing, she finally lifted her gaze. "Is it a pleasant surprise?"

A slow smile broke across Whit's face, and his blue eyes crinkled at the corners. One corner of his mouth hiked a smidgeon higher than the other, making him some- how even warmer and more charismatic. Some things never changed.

"I guess the verdict is still out on that, Violet." His easy, slow drawl quickened her pulse. He let the words hang for a minute. "So are you off to visit friends?"

"No, I'm on my way home."

"Home? You've moved."

"My father is the only jeweler in Hartville now." She clasped her hands in her lap. "And you?"

He swallowed. "Well, Violet, you're not going to believe this, but I'm in the Ranger regiment that's stationed in Hartville. Guess you could say we're neighbors once again."

She sucked in her breath. Neighbors? Surely not. "How long will you be assigned there?"

"Hard to tell." He glanced out the window. "It might be time for me to move on from the Rangers. You know me."

She certainly did. "An eternally restless spirit."

"Can't help it. Besides, I can't see where I'm making much of a difference. Thought I could change the world, but outlaws just keep coming." He gave her a half smile and patted the badge on his chest made from a cinco peso coin. "I'll be around for a while yet. Texas owns me for the rest of the month."

A month. She could resist Whit Murray's charms for a month. She'd have to.

He leaned forward and propped his elbows on his knees. She noticed his perusal of her left hand, and she instinctively covered it with her right. Whit never missed anything, which surely made him an excellent lawman.

"How's your pa, Violet?"

"He was in a horrible carriage accident which left him badly injured, but he'll recover in time." She let the tension from her shoulders evaporate as the neutral conversation took over. Between stops on the route, she explained how she and her father had come to move to Hartville and provided Whit with the details of her father's accident. "That's why I was in Austin. I had to pick up a shipment of unset gemstones and loose diamonds from my uncle Lucas for my father. My uncle placed an order for his store and my father's."

Whit eyed her handbag. "You aren't carrying the jewels in there, are you?"

"Heavens, no." She laughed, then lowered her voice. "They're in a little velvet pouch in the express car's safe."

He nodded. "Good."

"With my father's injury, things have been more difficult." Tears stung her eyes, but she blinked them away. "I drew some new designs, and I've already secured orders for three pieces. Once I get these jewels back, I can complete the custom pieces. The new sales will help us pay the mortgage until my father recovers."

"And then?"

"I will continue to work beside him as I've been doing." The train slowed. "I love my work, and I'm not like you. I have no desire to run amok through the world in search of adventure."

"Everyone deserves a little fun, Violet." He winked. "Even you."

Before she could offer a retort, brakes squealed and the train's forward momentum came to an unexpected halt. Maybe there was a cow on the tracks, or perhaps there was a mechanical problem.

Whit glanced out the window, and his casual demeanor switched to all business. "It looks like we're in for some trouble." He yanked off his badge and tucked it in his shirt pocket, then unbuckled his holster. He stuck the barrel of his gun inside his boot before tugging his trouser leg back in place. After stuffing the empty holster under his seat, he leaned close, his voice barely above a whisper. "Whatever happens, Violet, do what I say. Understand?"

"My jewels?"

"They're just rocks. You're worth more than rubies."

"But—"

Two men burst through the door to the passenger car with their guns drawn. Kerchiefs hid their noses and mouths. Whit was on his feet in a fraction of a second, placing himself between them and Violet.

"No heroics." The shorter of the two pointed the gun at Whit's chest. "We're in charge now. Listen up and no one will get hurt."

A gunshot split the air. Violet screamed.

The shorter man glanced in the direction from which the shot had come and laughed. "Well, no one will get hurt except the poor buzzard in the express car." He motioned toward the door. "Now everybody off."

Violet looked at Whit, who gave her a slow nod. He wanted her to do as they asked, but what about her father's jewels?

~

Whit watched the passengers file off the train, measuring each of them as they passed by Violet and him. He noted several businessmen, apparently unarmed, four elderly ladies, two younger ladies, and a mother with two small children—all with blanched white faces. He itched to do something, but he had to bide his time. Impatience, he'd learned long ago, got a lawman killed.

"You two get a move on." The broad-shouldered man prodded Whit with his pistol. A scar snaked down the man's cheek and disappeared beneath the bandana masking his nose and mouth. Where had he seen that face? A *wanted* poster?

"Take it easy." Whit offered his hand to Violet. "We're going."

They stepped off the train, and Whit studied the area. From the familiar landmarks, he reckoned they were about twenty miles from their scheduled stop in Hartville.

The shortest of the train robbers directed the scarred one to go down the line demanding the billfolds from the men and jewelry from the ladies. He seemed to take extra pleasure in taunting the ladies. He'd take their treasures and make some comment about the piece before dropping it into a gunnysack.

"Well, lookee here." He tossed a ring to a third man who now stood on the platform of the express car. "I think that gal of yours might even kiss your ugly mug if you give her this sparkly doodad."

The third man pocketed the ring, then waved goodbye with a stick of dynamite and disappeared inside the express car. A figure moved behind the robber. Whit blinked. Was there a fourth thief inside the express car?

"Whit, he's going to blow the safe," Violet hissed. "Do something."

"Shh." Whit pulled her close. "Trust me."

"No, please!" The older woman for whom Whit had purchased a ticket at the train station clutched her hand to her chest. "This ring is all I have left of my husband."

"Why don't you let her keep it?" Whit stepped forward before the woman had a chance to reveal his identity. "You've got enough."

A mind-crushing blow landed on the back of his head. Ladies shrieked. Pain exploded at the base of his skull. He fell to his knees, dazed. He pressed his hand to the goose egg forming there and waited. His head cleared, but he feigned more dizziness.

He eased his hand up his boot, reaching for his hidden weapon, and thanked God for putting him in the perfect position. One Ranger could handle four men, but timing was everything.

He glanced upward, checking on Violet. He didn't want her in any line of fire when the moment came for him to make his move, but where was she?

His heart thudded to a stop. Where had she gone?

CHAPTER 3

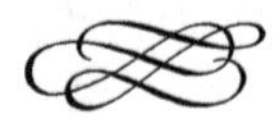

Violet could not let them take her father's jewels. Without them, they could lose everything, and Whit didn't seem to care a lick about stopping these thugs. He'd even taken off his badge and hidden his gun.

The blow to Whit's head dropped her old friend to his knees. He'd said to trust him, but how could he do anything now? With everyone's attention on Whit, Violet took a deep breath and inched backward until she could feel the cold metal of the train's steps behind her. She moved slowly up the stairs, keeping her footfalls as soft as a kitten's. When no one seemed to notice her absence, she made her way inside and hurried to the rear door.

She climbed onto the platform and hiked up her skirt. She'd have to hop over the coupling to reach the express car. Her pulse hammered, and her heart raced. What if someone spotted her?

An explosion sent her flying back through the door. She fell hard against one seat, then landed on the passenger car floor. Acrid smoke filled the air. She coughed and pressed her hands to her ringing ears. Her thoughts were jumbled. What had happened?

"Violet!" Whit's baritone voice carried across the passenger car. "Violet, are you in here?"

She tried to answer, but the words refused to form. Images flickered in her mind. The robbery. Whit getting hit. The explosion.

Hot tears trailed down her cheeks as realization seeped into every corner of her mind. The jewels were gone. How would she ever tell her father?

~

"Violet Tatienne, I ought to wring your pretty little neck." Whit dabbed the blood from a scratch on her temple with his handkerchief. Didn't she realize she'd almost gotten her head blown off over a sack of rocks?

She clutched the armrest of the passenger car. "Wring my neck? At least I was trying to do something, Mr. Texas Ranger."

"What are you talking about? I told you to trust me. I had a plan."

She winced when he touched a new injury. "Then why didn't you do something?"

He forced the anger and irritation warring inside him to still. "Because when the moment came for me to act, you were nowhere to be found."

She yanked the cloth from his hand. "So?"

He pushed to his feet and drew in a deep breath. "So I couldn't start shooting without knowing where you were." He turned to the older lady he'd helped earlier, who he'd learned was Miss Ivy. She and some of the other passengers had returned to the railcar to wait for some sort of transportation into town. "Please, keep an eye on her for me. While the men are clearing the track ahead, I'm going to see if there are any clues in the express car's wreckage."

"I'm going with you." Violet jumped up a little too quickly and wobbled on her feet.

Whit steadied her.

He wanted to insist she sit back down and wait, but when he looked into her hazel eyes, he saw fierce determination. He saw something else too. Something he remembered seeing in her eyes all those years ago. Sadness.

"Let me help." Her milky-soft words touched him. "I need to do something."

And once again, he found he couldn't refuse Violet Tatienne anything. "Stay close to me and watch where you step."

Once they reached the shambles, Violet sucked in a breath. Someone had covered the body of the express man with a sheet. Since he needed to think clearly, he resisted the urge to look at her. He surveyed the split timbers and scattered papers. The express car carried the mail.

They should try to gather up as many pieces as possible. Folks would appreciate even getting a partial missive after this fiasco.

The safe sat cockeyed in the rubble with the door ajar. He took Violet's elbow and led her toward the empty remains that had once held her valuables.

"They're really gone." Her voice broke. "How do you do this all the time? Face this danger? Why doesn't it paralyze you?"

"I learned early on that courage is feeling the fear yet choosing to act." He squatted in front of the safe. He examined the door and the hinges. "That's odd." He moved the door back and forth easily. "This safe hasn't been blown open. See?" He pointed to the locking mechanism. "It's all still intact."

"You mean someone opened it?"

Whit stood. "Looks like it."

"The only person on the train who knew the combination was the express man, and they killed him."

"Maybe they forced him to open the safe first." Whit wiped his hands on his trousers. "But that shot came awfully fast for that. Maybe the fourth robber is a safe cracker."

"Fourth?" Violet bent to run her hand along the empty shelves. "I only saw three."

"I spotted another one inside the car."

"But if they could open the safe, why would they blow up the express car?"

He shrugged. "Gave them the chance to get away, or maybe they like making a point."

"Or maybe they just like explosions." She grabbed Whit's sleeve. "I have to get those gemstones back."

"No." Whit covered her hand. "*I* have to get them back. That's my job. Not yours."

"But I want to help."

"Ranger? Ranger Murray?" Miss Ivy waved something in the air. "I almost forgot to give you this."

Violet and Whit traversed the debris to reach the elderly woman.

"The man who tried to take my ring gave me this." She fished a coin from her pocket. "He said I should give it to you after they were gone." She dropped the silver coin into Whit's outstretched hand. "Do you think it means anything?"

"Unfortunately, yes." Whit stared at the cinco peso with a gunshot hole in its center and swallowed hard. "This is the calling card for the Markham Gang, the meanest bunch of yahoos around. So for the record, Violet, you are definitely not helping me find those jewels."

CHAPTER 4

"I think you're going to need the lady's help after you find those jewels." Captain Hugh Sterling motioned Whit to a chair in his office. "She's the only one who knows what was in that pouch and can identify the gemstones."

An annoying wave of protectiveness washed over him. As long as Violet understood she could identify the jewels after he found them and not try to help him locate them, that would be all right. He didn't want her near the Markham Gang.

Miss Etta stepped away from a small side table with a steaming cup of coffee and plate of shortbread cookies. She set both on the desk in front of Whit.

"Thank you, Miss Etta." Whit rubbed the back of his neck. Boy howdy, was he tuckered.

"I've got to take care of my boys." She smiled and retrieved the pot to fill her husband's cup.

Whit took a swig and immediately felt the brew's restorative powers. "Cap," he began, "I'm sure Vio. . .I mean Miss Tatienne will be more than happy to identify her jewels."

"Did you say her name was Violet?" Miss Etta's eyes lit up, her interest clearly piqued.

"Yes, we knew one another in our youth."

"Honey, you're still in your youth." A slow smile spread across Miss Etta's face. "I do believe I've seen that jewelry store owner's daughter. She's a pretty thing. Tall, but then again, so are you, Whit." She handed her husband his coffee and tapped her finger against her chin. "Now that I think of it, Hugh, remember that brooch I purchased from the gentleman in town the other day?"

"Which one, dear?"

"The genuine ruby one he said his aunt had left him in her will. The clasp broke the first time I wore it, so I do need to have it repaired. After you two finish talking about the train robbery, perhaps Whit would escort me to the jeweler's tomorrow, and he could tell the young lady he'll require her assistance in identifying the jewels when he finds them."

"Etta, don't you think the girl knows that already?" The captain's scowl deepened.

She turned to him and feigned innocence. "But with the Markham Gang lurking about, I'd feel much safer with one of your men by my side. You don't mind, do you, Whit?"

Whit coughed on the cookie in his mouth. Miss Etta no more needed an escort than he needed a wife, but he felt as cornered as a cat in a room full of rocking chairs. "I reckon that would be all right if the captain agrees."

"That's fine." Captain Sterling pushed back from his desk. "I'm sure the young lady needs to rest after this ordeal. And I'm sure you"—the captain's stern gaze met Whit's—"are fixin' to scout the area again this afternoon and see if you missed anything earlier. You know these Markhams are making a laughingstock of us."

"Yes, sir. I know. I'll get right on it."

"Take Griff and O'Neal just in case."

Whit agreed and left the office. He paused outside, expecting the usual thrill of a new case to jolt through him, but it didn't come. Sure, he wanted to retrieve Violet's jewels and catch the Markham Gang members responsible for the train robbery, but right now, what he wanted most was some quality time on his bunk.

Maybe he'd been a Ranger too long. Maybe it wasn't the same without being partnered with Chisholm Hart. Maybe God was trying to tell him it was time to move on. And maybe he simply needed some sleep.

~

Violet sat beside her papa's bed in the small rocking chair the seat cushion of which sported her *maman's* fine embroidery work. Oh, how she wished her maman were here now.

Violet watched the steady rise and fall of her papa's chest. His right leg, still plastered in a cast from his toes almost to his hip, lay propped on two feather pillows. Dr. Travis Hart had said it would take another four weeks to heal. The pain from his injured ribs had ebbed, but even from the confines of their upstairs quarters, her father still tired easily. Would her news today set back his recovery?

He opened his eyes and stretched. "Violet, you're home. I expected you much earlier in the day."

She smiled, his telltale French accent warming her. "I know, and I apologize for my delay. Annie says you've been the perfect patient, doing exactly what her husband ordered."

"As if I had a choice." He glanced down at his cast. "Help me sit up, *mon bijou*."

Her papa's usual nickname for her of "my jewel" stabbed her heart, and her vision blurred behind a curtain of tears. He often told her she was his greatest treasure, but some treasure she'd turned out to be. Because of her, they might lose the whole business. If only she'd kept the jewels on her person or done something to stop the theft. She swallowed the ache and propped two additional fluffy pillows behind her father's back before returning to her chair.

"Now." Her papa took her hand. "Tell me about your trip. Did you get the jewels? Was your uncle Lucas surprised when you arrived instead of me?"

More hot tears burned behind Violet's eyes. Her papa had put his faith in her, and she'd let him down. As she sent up a prayer asking for the right words to say, the droplets escaped. She quickly dashed them away with the back of her finger.

"Violet, what is wrong? Was someone cruel to you?" He squeezed her hand. "I know your uncle Lucas can be crusty, but I'm sure he meant no harm."

"Uncle Lucas was extremely kind, and he sends his wishes for your speedy recovery." She fished a handkerchief from her pocket and dabbed her cheeks. "Papa, I put the jewels in the train's safe, and the express man assured me they'd be secure, but the train was held up and the jewels were stolen."

His face paled. "You were in a robbery?"

She nodded. "And all of the jewels are gone."

"Were you hurt in any way?" He twisted to see her better.

"No, Papa." She pressed him back into the pillows. "But did you hear me? The jewels are gone. I am so sorry. This is my fault."

He frowned, deep crevices forming around his lips. "Yours? How could that be? Did you take the jewels and hide them?"

"No, of course not."

"Did you sell them?"

"I'd never do that."

"Then, tell me, how is it your fault, Violet, that the gemstones are gone?"

"Papa, you trusted me to bring them home."

"And I trusted the railroad to deliver you and the jewels safely." He patted her hand. "But when others choose to do evil against us, we are not to blame for the results. As I said, I trusted the railroad to deliver you on time today, but they could not do that. It is no more their fault for the delay than is it your fault for our jewels being stolen."

"But the jewels..."

"You are the only jewel I truly care about." He drew in a deep breath, winced, and pressed his hand to his ribs. "God will take care of us. We will take refuge under His feathers."

"Some refuge." She swallowed the bitterness on her tongue. "First, Maman died, then you have an accident, and now this. Where is God when all this is happening?"

"He says He'll be our refuge when the storms come."

"But Papa, how will we survive? We have a mortgage to pay, and even if you could get up, you can't fill the orders we have without those gems."

"I, too, am concerned, mon bijou. I should have never sent you to retrieve those jewels. I blame only myself."

His words knifed through her. Did they belie his true feelings? Did he regret trusting her with such an important task despite what he'd said only moments ago?

He yawned, and his eyelids drooped. "We will figure out something, but I'm afraid I can't keep my eyes open at the moment."

"Of course, Papa." Violet slipped the extra pillow out from beneath his head, then pulled the quilt up to his chest.

"Violet." He caught her hand. "The storms will come. They always do. But we must remember where our shelter can be found."

But that shelter may not be in this house if we don't find a way to pay the mortgage. She kissed her father's forehead, stepped toward the door, and placed her hand on the knob. "I'll find the jewels, Papa. You can count on me."

~

Whit offered his elbow to Miss Etta and waited for her to slip her hand into the crook of his arm. Together they headed down the boardwalk of Hartville's Main Street. He nodded a greeting at a couple coming out of the Ritz Hotel and paused to let Miss Etta take a gander at the dresses in Miss Spanner's Seamstress Shop.

He slowed his natural pace so Miss Etta didn't have to get winded as they neared the now-vacant sheriff 's office. His long strides made it difficult for most ladies to keep up—except for Violet. She'd never had any trouble walking at his side.

"Do you like it here, Whit?" Miss Etta smiled up at him.

Whit cleared his throat. "Here? As in, Hartville?"

"No, I mean here on the earth." Miss Etta's eyes twinkled. "Of course, I mean Hartville."

He chuckled. "Yes, ma'am. I reckon I do. It's a fine place."

"All y'all boys need to think about settlin' down, and I think this would be a wonderful town to do it in. Don't you agree?" She patted his arm.

He cleared his throat. "I guess I hadn't thought of it."

"Well, I do believe you should." Miss Etta paused in front of Dr. Travis Hart's office and turned toward Tatienne's Jewelry Company across the street. "It would be a lovely place to put down roots."

"I'm not much for stayin' in one place very long, Miss Etta. I like adventure, and I'm starting to itch for a change." He glanced both directions before stepping onto the hard-packed dirt street.

"Change doesn't have to come from moving on to a new place." She waited while Whit reached for the door's handle and held it open for her. "Sometimes the Lord sends adventures to us right where we are—and in the most delightful forms." She waved to Violet across the store. "Oh, look, there's Miss Tatienne now."

Behind Miss Etta's back, Whit rolled his eyes. If—and he meant a mighty big *if*—there'd ever been a chance with Violet, he'd ruined it long ago by joining the Rangers. They'd only been schoolyard sweethearts, but even then, Violet knew she wanted a man who'd come home to her every night. Whit would never be that man—then or now.

Violet greeted them at the door, then moved behind a glass display case. She wore an ivory dress dotted with tiny pink flowers. Dark circles beneath her eyes told him she hadn't slept well.

"What brings you both in today? Please tell me you have good news."

"I'm afraid not, dear." Miss Etta set her handbag on top of the case. "But with Whit on the job, I'm certain your treasures will soon be found."

Whit studied Violet, but she didn't meet his gaze. Was she disappointed in the situation or in him?

Miss Etta searched inside her handbag and produced a gold brooch with a shimmering red center. "I bought this piece of jewelry from a man in town the other day who said it belonged to his aunt. He said he wanted to sell it as he had no wife or daughters, and that he, frankly, needed the cash." She turned the brooch over in her gloved hand. "As you can see, the clasp has since broken on the back. I do so love the color. Can you repair it?"

"I believe so." Violet took the piece of jewelry and looked at it closely. A furrow formed between her eyebrows. "Miss Etta, did he tell you anything about this piece?"

"As I recall, he assured me his aunt had been quite wealthy. He said that the brooch was gold and the stone in the middle was a ruby and the stones around it were tiny diamonds. Why? Is there a problem?"

"Let me get my loupe and take a closer look." Violet slipped into the back room and returned with a small black cone-shaped eyepiece. She held the cone against her eye and studied the brooch. After a few moments, she set the eyepiece down and frowned. "Miss Etta, I'm afraid the jewels in this piece are not real. They are made of cut glass. We call this paste jewelry. The glass was placed on a metallic foil base to give it the glitter of gemstones. Actual rubies are quite rare."

"You mean the man lied to her?" Whit held out his hand for the offensive piece.

Violet dropped the brooch in his hand. "Perhaps, or maybe he simply told you what he believed to be true."

Miss Etta huffed an exasperated sigh. "I feel so foolish. I should have known better."

Violet touched the woman's arm. "Don't feel too badly, Miss Etta. This is the third piece of paste jewelry someone has brought in to me in the last few weeks."

Whit held the brooch up to the light and angled it back and forth. "You think someone is passing off fake jewelry in Hartville?"

"It's probably a coincidence, but it's a possibility." Violet turned to Miss Etta. "I don't mean to pry or be offensive, but may I ask how much you paid for the piece?"

Whit didn't know much about fine jewelry or about how much a genuine brooch like this would cost, but by the look on Violet's face, he could tell that his commanding officer's wife had been taken advantage of. A red-hot poker of anger sank into him. How dare someone exploit Miss Etta? There wasn't a kinder soul on earth.

The pulse in Whit's jaw ticked. "Did the others tell you the same story about who sold them the fakes?"

"No, not exactly. They'd all purchased the pieces from a man. That's all I recall." Violet brushed a curl from her cheek. "It's still very pretty, Miss Etta, and paste pieces are part of nearly every tasteful lady's jewelry collection. If you want to wear it, I can repair the clasp on the back right now."

"Sorry. That won't be possible." Whit dropped the brooch in

his shirt pocket. "I think we could have a con artist here, and until we find out the truth, this might be evidence."

Disappointment flitted across Violet's face. He should have thought about her losing some much-needed business. He could return the brooch and let her fix it, but as a Ranger, he had a job to do, and if he'd learned anything from his former partner, Chisholm Hart, it was the importance of doing one's duty.

Miss Etta scowled at him. "I think you have your hands full with finding a pouch of true gemstones, not worrying about me foolishly buying a fake from a stranger."

"Begging your pardon, ma'am, but I can handle both situations." He drew in a deep breath and softened his tone when he next spoke. "How's your father, Violet? How'd he take the news of the robbery?"

"Better than I." Violet's eyes glistened. "Now if you'll excuse me, I have to try to balance my father's books."

"Wait." Miss Etta put her hand on Violet's arm. "It seems I'm suddenly in need of a new brooch. Can you recommend one to wear with this dress?"

Violet's lashes lowered. "Ma'am, you don't have to do that."

"Oh, but I do. I need a change." She glanced at Whit. "On the way here, I was just telling Whit that change can take on the loveliest forms." She waved her hand dismissively in his direction. "Why don't you start your little investigation while Miss Tatienne and I spend some time together discussing sparkly things and this lovely town?"

Whit rubbed the back of his neck. Miss Etta was a force to be reckoned with when she had a plan in mind. Since she was his commanding officer's wife, he couldn't insist she not interfere. Miss Etta was spinning a web, but Whit had no desire to be caught —even by a pretty lady with tea-colored curls and a heart-shaped face.

CHAPTER 5

Arch Russell watched his fellow gang members file into their hideout. The cabin, while rustic, was better than some of the places they'd holed up, and with over half of the gang doing another job in Rock Springs, the space was almost roomy.

Good thing too. He didn't like enclosed places. Not since his mining days.

He glanced at young Lane, then dropped his hat on the table and pulled the pouch from his pocket. After snagging a chipped red-rimmed enamelware bowl from a stack by the washtub, he set it on the table and slowly poured the contents of the pouch into the basin. The tiny stones clinked and danced as they hit the metal.

Willie Markham came near and looked over his shoulder. The young gang member let out a low whistle. "Those sure are purty."

Willie's acrid breath fanned the back of Arch's neck. He fired his elbow into Willie's midsection.

Willie doubled over with a grunt. "What was that for?"

"You don't need to stand on top of me, you fool."

Face red, Willie clenched his fists at his side. "I'll show you who's a fool."

"Enough!" Maggie Markham, Willie's older sister, stepped between the two of them and faced her brother. "I'm in charge of this here outfit, and I'm not lettin' anyone, including my snot-nosed kid brother, make a mess of this operation. If Pa were here—"

"Well, he ain't."

"You better be praying that Cass comes up with a way to get him out of Huntsville before they hang him." She gave him a solid shove. "And stop your fightin' about these rocks."

Willie stumbled back. "I just wanted to look at 'em. Besides, without me, there wouldn't be any jewels."

"You think?" Arch laughed and smoothed the sides of his mustache. He jingled the gemstones. "I could have gotten them out."

"And blew them to smithereens." Willie tugged his vest back into place.

Maggie yanked the basin from Arch, and the jewels rattled. "We got them. That's all that matters." She pushed the jewels around with her index finger. "Willie, you start making some vittles while I see what we have here."

"Me? Why me?"

"'Cause I said so." Maggie sent him a steely glare that silenced any further protests.

Arch grinned. Brother or not, they all knew not to cross Maggie. The only person who could stand up to her was Cass himself. Willie, the youngest Markham, tried to measure up, but he didn't have a chance.

"They sure are small, aren't they?" Maggie pinched an emerald between her fingers and held it up to the light.

Arch dropped into a chair and crossed his ankle over his knee.

"Yeah, and who's going to buy those pretty rocks? They're not even set in anything."

"Heard tell, they're worth a fortune." Willie turned the bacon he had sizzling in the pan. "And I bet that jewelry store owner will offer a reward to get 'em back. Lots of stores do that."

"Probably, but I got a buyer lined up. He'll pay hard cash to get his hands on these gems come May. He said he'll take all we can get." Maggie passed the bowl back to Arch. "Put those jewels away, real careful like."

Arch opened the pouch and dribbled the rocks inside. His stomach growled. "Willie, you about got supper cooked?"

"Hold yer horses." Willie carried a tin plate of bacon to the table along with a crusty loaf of bread. He pulled up a chair and snagged the bread. He broke off a chunk and stuffed it into his mouth. He spoke, but the words came out garbled.

Maggie smacked the back of his head. "Don't talk with your mouth full."

He swallowed. "I was saying that if there's any more jewels expected to be shipped, I'm sure my special lady friend will tell me just like she told me about the bank money being shipped to Medina." He rubbed his knuckles on his vest. "I've got her so charmed, I think I could get that filly to do just about anything for me."

"Charmed, huh?" Arch stuffed several slabs of bacon into a hunk of bread. "Not the brightest star in the night sky, is she?"

Willie lurched for Arch's neck, but Maggie stabbed her knife into the table. "I've had enough of you two. Next one of you that talks while I'm eating will see this here knife up close and personal."

The mimicked caw of a crow came from outside. It was a prearranged signal, but Arch moved to the window, hand on his sidearm, to check. "It's Paul."

"Good thing." Maggie polished off her last bite. "I'm mighty ready for some civilized conversation."

Paul Carey, who looked more like a schoolteacher than an outlaw, tied off his horse and strode into the cabin. He immediately took out a leather wallet and withdrew several large bills. He handed them to Maggie.

"What do you think? Not bad for a few days' work. All that plus a robbery." Maggie thumbed through the bills. "No, not bad at all."

"This town's ripe for the picking, but one of those Rangers seems to be nosing around today, asking questions about fake jewelry." Paul snagged a piece of bacon and took a bite.

Arch's muscles bunched. Cass had declared war on Texas Ranger Company B, and since then, they'd had more than one run-in with a member of the unit. "What's the lawman's name?"

"I'm not sure." Paul went to the stove and poured himself a cup of coffee. "But he was on the train yesterday. Glad I didn't let anyone see my face. What are we going to do if he gets too close?"

Maggie picked up her rifle and sighted it. "If he does, I'll take care of him." She lowered the rifle and grinned. "Or maybe I'll let Arch do it. That ought to let them know not to mess with us."

Arch's lips curled beneath his mustache. Yep, dynamite made a mighty big impression.

CHAPTER 6

After heaping a lump of mashed potatoes on his plate, Whit scanned the table to see who was holding up the gravy. Branch. It figured. Thankfully, Miss Etta always made plenty for her boys.

She fed six of the Rangers in Company B in her home. Since the seventh Ranger in Company B, Griff, was married, he dined with his wife on the Prentis farm. Miss Etta expected the boys to say grace before they ate and to display good manners. He had no problem with either. Getting the gravy, on the other hand, seemed to be an issue tonight. At last, the gravy boat reached him. He tipped it up, but only a small blob came out.

He sighed. Too little, too late. It fit with the rest of his week. "Whit." Miss Etta stood. "Pass that to me, and I'll go fill it."

"Much obliged, Miss Etta." When she returned, he drenched his mashed potatoes with the rich beef gravy. His mouth watered.

Captain Sterling didn't give him a chance to take a bite. "Whit, Etta said you think we've got someone trying to pass off fake jewelry for the real thing?"

"Yes, Cap. I asked around today, and all three of the people Violet mentioned buying the fake stuff describe the same man."

"The one who sold the brooch to Miss Etta?" Jesse slathered a bun with butter.

Whit nodded and hurried a forkful of potatoes into his mouth.

O'Neal reached across the table for the meat platter, and Miss Etta swatted his hand. He looked dutifully corrected.

"Do you think this situation could be related to the jewelry theft on the train?"

"I doubt it." Whit washed down his pot roast with a swig of coffee. "The man they described didn't exactly sound like a Markham Gang member."

Miss Etta dabbed her mouth with a napkin. "If it's the man who sold me the brooch, then I'd say he was more schoolteacher or undertaker than outlaw."

Ezra scratched his head. "Too bad we can't get a rendering of the man. Do you know anyone who can draw a lick?"

"I do. Violet showed me her design drawings for new jewelry pieces while I was at the shop. I'm sure she could make a likeness of him if I describe him well enough." Miss Etta looked at Whit. "Can we go there in the morning?"

"Whit needs to work on getting those jewels back." Captain Sterling pointed at her with his fork. "Let him be, Etta. One of the other men can take you."

Miss Etta mashed her lips together, apparently trying to hold her tongue.

"It's all right, sir," Whit said. "I can take Miss Etta, but we'll have to go later in the day. I have plans to search the robbery area again."

"You need some help?" Branch asked.

"I should be okay. It's a scouting trip. I'll try to use some of the tracking skills Chisholm taught me."

"Maybe you could ask him for a hand."

Whit laughed. "He'd probably jump at the chance, given his spitfire of a wife is about to have another young'un. But he wasn't there when his five daughters came into the world, and I'm not about to suffer Caro's wrath if he misses this one's entrance."

"Is he hoping for a son?"

Whit sucked in the sides of his cheeks and bit back a chuckle. "Wouldn't you be?"

"There's nothing wrong with a nest full of girls." Miss Etta began to gather the empty plates. "Especially if they are as strong as Caro Hart."

"True, Miss Etta." Whit downed the last bite from his plate.

Captain Sterling cleared his throat. "Branch, I want you to go with Whit. Your dog has a good nose for tracking. And take Ezra along too. He can do some questioning of the railroaders. If you need any more help—"

"I'll send word." Whit gave his commander a firm nod.

Captain Sterling looked around at his men. "I know I don't have to tell you how dangerous these Markhams are. No telling what they'd do if you caught them unaware. Be on your guard."

~

After securing her favorite horse from the livery for the early-morning excursion, Violet rode out of town toward the site of the train robbery. She had a keen eye, so maybe she could find something Whit had missed.

Guilt nudged her. If someone came to the jewelry store to make a purchase, her absence meant she'd be losing money. Hopefully, the person would read the note she'd left on the door that said she'd be back in the afternoon. Besides, if she didn't find those gemstones, there wouldn't be a store in a few months.

Even though the reason for her trip was unsettling, the ride over the rolling terrain of the Texas Hill Country was peaceful.

The warm spring sun brought joy to her heart. Budding burr oaks and cedar elms lined the path, and the Texas redbud, with its showy rose-purple blooms, stole her breath. Warm March temperatures meant bluebonnets and Indian paintbrush flowers should dot the landscape in early April.

Nearing the area where the train had been held up, she and Sassafras crested a hill. Debris still littered the area from the decimated postal car. However, the safe had been hauled away. No doubt the railroad would come to clean up the rest in time, but their first priority had most likely been clearing the tracks, reclaiming what they could still use, and restoring service.

Violet slowed Sassafras and circled the area. What was she looking for? She reined in the horse and dismounted. All kinds of footprints marred the ground, but the thieves had to leave in some direction. If she could find that, perhaps she could follow their trail. Whit wouldn't like her heading out on her own, but she wouldn't do anything irresponsible.

After nearly half an hour, she came across an odd set of hoofprints snaking their way through a narrow slit between two hills. The trail led toward the Sabinal River, but after she reached the water, the path seemed to disappear. Which way would she go if she were the thieves?

She directed Sassafras to follow the river. If she found nothing, she'd still enjoy the view of the rushing water.

Behind her, a flurry of flight made her jump. Wild turkeys flapped their broad wings and lifted a few feet from the earth. Violet pressed her hand to her thundering heart. Had something frightened them?

Don't spook yourself. She drew in a deep, calming breath. She was in no danger. Even if the gang members found her, they'd have no reason to harm her. As far as they knew, she was simply lost.

She spotted a series of rocks in the river causing the water to fall over them in sparkling curtains. This must be the area the locals called Indian Springs. If it was, there was a cave nearby too.

Fear crawled up her spine. A cave would be an excellent place for the Markham Gang to hide out.

Maybe she should turn back, after all.

~

How odd. Whit squatted next to the footprints he'd discovered on a narrow path nestled between two hills. The prints were fresh and had been made by small boots. The depth told him the person didn't weigh a lot. Leading away from the footprints were hoofprints. One set was new and another a few days old, so both could have been made by the same horse.

Whit stood and thought about the Markham Gang members who'd held up the train. There'd been the man he'd not got a good look at, and the man on the express car who'd caught the ring. One of the two who corralled the passengers was a broad- shouldered man around six feet tall, but the other was much shorter. The shorter one had barked the orders, and the others complied. But the short one had a strange voice. It was as if he'd tried to make his voice sound deeper to make it more authoritative or tougher. Whit scratched his temple and pushed back his cowboy hat as a thought began to take shape in his mind. Maybe the reason he sounded so strange was because he was a *she*. He recalled hearing Cass Markham's sister was part of the gang. Would gang members listen to a woman? Maybe they would if she was half as tough as Cass Markham.

Was she the mastermind behind the train robbery? And if so, had she returned to this area for some reason?

Maybe he should signal the other Rangers. He glanced toward Branch. His dog, Jack, seemed to have caught a scent and was headed off in the opposite direction of Whit's location. Ezra was talking to some of the railroad men and jotting down notes in a little book. No, he might be way off base about the short one being a woman. He could check these prints out on his own and report back to them.

He mounted his pinto, Shakespeare, and directed the stallion to follow the path. A shadow blotted out the sun, and Whit glanced skyward. Gray clouds were moving in. Hopefully, rain would hold off until he'd finished scouting this area.

The older set of tracks seemed to end at the river, but the newer set continued along the shore. Whoever made these tracks hadn't tried to cover them. Either the person wasn't worried about being found or they figured no one would be looking for them.

Excitement surged through him. His breath quickened. This could be the break they needed to find the Markham Gang's hideout.

Dark clouds were gathering, and the air hung heavy. He nudged Shakespeare's sides with the heel of his boots, and the horse responded by picking up speed. He did not want to lose this trail to a rainstorm.

A male gobbler strutted on the path up ahead, so Whit slowed his mount. He looked past the turkey and spotted a dappled gray horse with a woman on it. Then she turned the horse around, and he could see the lady's face.

His stomach clenched. What was Violet doing out here in the woods alone? Didn't she realize how dangerous this could be?

He eased Shakespeare off the path, behind a grove of trees. It was time to teach Violet a lesson.

CHAPTER 7

Sassafras needed a drink, so Violet led her to the water's edge. Violet sat down on a rock and let the sweet mare have her fill before the trip back. Sight of the heavy clouds caused a nudge of worry. If they didn't hasten along, both she and Sassafras would return to town a sopping mess.

"Come on, girl. We'd better get a move on." She stood up and tugged on the reins.

A leather-clad hand clamped over her mouth, and a man's arm wrapped around her waist.

She froze. Her body didn't know how to react. Fear took hold of her every muscle. She wanted to scream. She wanted to fight. Instead, she stood there with her heart thumping so hard, she could hear the blood rush in her ears.

Then, all at once, her courage returned with a vengeance. She kicked and clawed at her captor's hands.

"It's me, Violet." The man released her. "Take it easy."

She whirled. "Whit Murray! You scared the life out of me!"

"Good." He crossed his arms over his chest. "You have no business being out here all by your lonesome. What do you think you're doing?"

"Trying to do what you've obviously not been able to do—find the Markhams and recover my jewels."

He tapped his boot in the dirt. "And exactly what were you going to do if you found the Markhams?"

She scowled. "I don't know, but I'd have thought of something."

"Sure you would. If I remember correctly, courage hasn't exactly been your strong suit." Thunder rumbled, and he looked upward. "We best head to the caves."

"The caves?" Her voice trembled a little. "Do you think they're inside?"

He took hold of Sassafras's bridle and motioned for her to mount. "I've already checked this area, Violet. The Markhams are not living in the caves."

She stepped onto the rock, put her foot in the stirrup, and then climbed onto the saddle. "What if they've moved?"

He chuckled. "Then maybe we'll find your jewels, after all."

Before they reached his horse, it started to sprinkle. Violet followed his lead as he wound his way along the water's edge and through the trees. When the cave entrance came into view, the rain began to fall harder. Whit picked up the pace. A crack of lightning split the sky. He reined his horse to an abrupt halt and jumped off. He reached for Violet's waist and swung her to the ground. "Go. I'll see to the horses."

Rain pelted Violet's face, and the wind whipped her hair. Still, she stood there.

"Go on, Violet. Get out of the rain."

She hiked up her skirt and petticoat and darted for the cave, only to stop at the entrance. What if Whit was wrong? What if the Markham Gang members were inside? And if not them, then surely, this was the home to any number of creatures she had no intention of meeting.

A bolt of lightning struck the top of a tall burr oak. The wood splintered, and the top of the tree tumbled down with a whoosh. Violet shrieked.

Whit grabbed her arm and dragged her inside the cave. He dropped the saddlebags and canteen he was carrying, then shrugged out of his heavy duster. He draped it around her shoulders and rubbed her arms. "Why were you just standing there? Now you're soaked to the bone."

Something scurried in the shadows, and she jumped. "What was that?"

"Some critter." He turned her toward him and seemed to study her face in the dim light. "You're scared." He cupped her cheek. "Hey, think of this as a bold adventure."

"I know you like adventures, but if you recall, I do not." Her voice cracked, and she cleared her throat. "How long do you think the storm will last?"

"A long time, if we're lucky." A clap of thunder rumbled deep and low, making it difficult to hear Whit's words. He released her and squatted beside his pack. Did he want to remain here in this cave?

"I'm worried about my papa. I hope Annie checked on him as she said she would."

"I'm sure she will." He pulled out a tin and struck a match. The tiny flame illuminated the cave. "Looks as though someone left us some wood." When the first match went out, he squatted next to the area where a fire had previously been built and set a few pieces of wood on it. He struck another match and soon had a small fire going.

Shivering beneath Whit's heavy duster, Violet didn't wait to be invited to join him. She sat down on the cold cave floor and held her hands, palms out, toward the flame. Heat kissed her fingertips.

Another rustle of activity made her tense. "What kind of things do you think live in here?"

The glow of the fire lit Whit's face. "All kinds."

"Such as...?"

"Violet, you really don't want to know. Let me tell you about my horse." He grinned. "Shakespeare is a—"

"You named your horse after the Bard?"

"Sure did." He rubbed his knuckles against his vest. "On account that he's poetry in motion."

"Miss Williams would be proud that you recalled her lessons." She fluffed her damp skirt. "Your Shakespeare did have a certain air about him."

"He's a perfect gentleman, but he believes he 'lets' me ride him."

"So he's the boss?"

"He certainly thinks so." Whit put another stick on the fire.

"I like to rent Sassafras from the livery whenever I want to ride. She's such a sweet little mare."

"Speaking of the horses, I'd better check on them." He pushed to his feet and went to the entrance. "It's a real gully washer out there, but they're fine. Shakespeare just gave me a look that says he's not happy with this arrangement."

She sighed. "So what breed is Shakespeare?"

Whit leaned against the stone doorway. "Shakespeare is a piebald, tobiano."

"Bald pie?"

Whit laughed. "Piebald. It means he's black and white. Tobiano is the pattern of my pinto's spots. It was the pattern when he was born, and it'll never change. Hey, are you hungry?" He didn't wait for an answer but crossed to his saddlebag and pulled out a cloth napkin with something wrapped in it. He folded back the corners of the napkin and revealed two biscuits. He handed one to Violet. "Miss Etta sent them with me. They have her famous wild persimmon jelly in them."

A snippet of guilt pricked her for eating Whit's lunch, but since she'd not partaken of anything since daybreak, she accepted the offering and thanked him. While Whit dug in his saddlebag once again, she took a bite. The flaky biscuit melted on her tongue, mingling with the honeyed taste of the persimmon jelly. She moaned. "This is delicious."

"Here." He'd filled a tin cup with water from a canteen. "Sorry, I know you're partial to tea."

"And if I recall, you think coffee is more important than breathing." She sipped from the cup. "You've liked it for as long as I remember. Did your mother give it to you in a bottle when you were a baby?"

"Maybe so. A warm cup would sure feel good right now."

"Oh, dear, you're cold too." Violet scrambled to her feet and started to shrug from beneath the duster.

Whit was on his feet in seconds, holding the coat firmly in place. "Violet, I'm fine. It's just damp. That's all."

An eerie screech echoed in the cave, and something swooped above them. Violet screamed and ducked her head. She clutched Whit's shirt. "What was that?"

He pulled her close. "A bat."

She shouldn't lean into the warmth and safety of his arms, but her traitorous body did as it pleased. Her pulse galloped. "Are there more?"

"Again, you don't really want to know."

She wrapped her arms around him more tightly.

"Our fire probably interrupted his sleep." Whit kept a hold of her but seemed to study the area behind her. "It would be fun to explore these caves someday. Who knows what treasures they have deeper in their caverns?"

"Like more bats?" She shivered.

He rubbed her back. "Or fossils or Indian paintings. Not everything outside of Hartville is scary."

Her nerves tingled at his touch. "We're outside of Hartville."

"Are you scared?"

"Of the storm? Yes. Of the bats? Yes."

"Of me?" he asked, his voice a husky whisper.

She licked her lips. Her heart drummed. Her mind spun. She liked everything about Whit—his charm, his sense of humor, the way he took care of others—but he had no intention of staying in Hartville, and she could never leave her father.

Drawing a deep breath, she pushed away from him. "I think the rain has stopped."

He took her hand. "You didn't answer my question. Are you scared of me?"

"No. I'm scared of being hurt *by* you." Violet slipped the duster from her shoulders and passed it to him. Her stomach churned, the biscuit now a lead ball inside her. "There's an undeniable fire between us. There always has been. But you told me earlier on the train that you were ready to leave the Rangers and move on to something new." Hot tears burned behind her eyes. "I'm not a girl anymore. I've always known what I wanted, and I know that if I let anything happen between us, I'm the one who will get hurt."

"But—"

Tears clouded her vision, and she rushed from the cave. When her boot hit the wet stone outside, it slid. She gasped and reached for something to stop her fall. Arms windmilling, she fought to remain upright, but it was no use. She was going to hit hard.

CHAPTER 8

Following only a yard or so behind Violet, Whit saw her foot slip and arms flail. He sprang forward and caught her.

She filled her lungs with air.

"It's okay. I've got you." He kept a firm hold on her upper arms, waiting for her to steady. His chest heaved. If she had fallen on this rock, she could have hit her head or broken a limb.

She yanked away from him. "Thank you. I'm fine now."

He gently took her elbow in case her steps faltered.

"I said I'm fine." She attempted to pull free.

"I know, but you might as well face it. I don't plan to let go."

And he meant every word. She wasn't willing to open her heart to him again, and he would do his best to respect that. His past choices had cost him dearly. Over a decade ago, he'd chosen the Rangers over staying with her. He'd chosen adventure over security. But now, until these jewels were found, he was choosing security—Violet's security—over everything else, whether she liked it or not.

Time stretched long and lonely as they rode back to town with only birdsong between them. The crisp air, freshened by the rain, warmed in the sunlight but did nothing to lighten the mood. Branch and Ezra, who waited out the storm with the railroad men, led the way with Whit and Violet trailing behind. Whit empathized with Shakespeare, slogging through the mud on the dirt road.

He glanced at Violet, then called to the men in the lead. "Branch, I'll meet you two back at the camp. I'm sure Violet is anxious to check on her father. I'll see her home, then take her horse back to the livery."

"Sounds good." Branch and Ezra nudged their horses and trotted away.

"Thank you." She gave him a weak smile, but her lip quivered. Was she shivering or emotionally spent?

As they neared the jewelry store, a woman stood up from a bench on the boardwalk, and Whit immediately recognized her—Miss Etta. He sighed. He was supposed to escort her here. How had he forgotten? Why hadn't he asked Cap to assign someone else to take her to the jewelers? Now his goose was not only cooked—it was charred to a crisp.

Miss Etta moved to the edge of the boardwalk and barely waited until they were near to begin her lecture. "Where have you two been? And why do you look as though you were dunked in a hog trough?" She eyed Violet. "Whit, you get that girl down off that horse and take her inside. She looks plumb tuckered out."

"We got caught in the rainstorm."

"I guessed as much." She shooed him forward with a swish of her hand.

Whit dismounted, then moved to help Violet. His chest tightened when he saw Violet's pale face. He'd scared her, the bats had scared her, and her near fall had scared her. But what frightened her most? Being near him. Still, she didn't resist when he offered to lift her down. Nor did she fight him when he took the key from her hand and unlocked the door. She must be exhausted.

Miss Etta stepped between Violet and him. She pressed her hand to his chest. "I'll take it from here, Whit. And I'll send for you if you're needed." With that, Miss Etta firmly closed the door in his face.

It was just as well. He had to solve this case so he could move on and then get as far away from Violet Tatienne as possible.

~

"I need to open the store, Miss Etta." Violet reached for the sign hanging on the door.

Miss Etta held it in place. "Not yet, dear. Right now, you head upstairs and get out of your wet things. You check on your father, and I'll draw you a bath." She held up her hand when Violet started to protest. "You won't be any good to your father or Whit or me if you make yourself ill. Besides, who would buy jewels from a bedraggled mess?"

Violet surveyed her clothes and smiled. "I imagine that I do look a fright."

"I think you would scare children." Miss Etta laughed and pressed her hand to Violet's back.

After a quick peek in on her father, who was sleeping, Violet hurried to her room to shed her damp clothes. She heard Miss Etta filling the tub in the water closet and sent up a prayer of thanks for the kind woman's ministrations. Her eyes misted. She hadn't felt this cared for since her mother was alive. First Whit and now her mother. Why were all of these old feelings surfacing today?

She put on a robe and padded into the water closet. After tying her hair in a knot on top of her head, she slipped into the tub and let the hot water envelop her. It eased the tension from her muscles but did little to soothe the ache in her heart. The image of Whit's face, so hurt and disheartened, filled her thoughts, making tears slither down her cheeks and mix with the bathwater.

She'd done the right thing concerning Whit. He wasn't a stay-in-one-place man, and it wasn't fair for her to ask him to become one. When they were younger, she'd done exactly that while sitting at her parents' house on the front porch swing. "It's not as if I'll be gone forever," he'd said. "I'll come back for you."

"Don't." She remembered how bitter the word tasted on her tongue. "If you go, you'll have made your choice."

She'd not seen him again until earlier this week on the train. He had no idea how many tears she'd cried or how every suitor she'd had couldn't compare to him. He didn't know how long it had taken her to stop wishing for him to return and tell her he chose her, after all. The girl she'd been wanted her way. The woman she was today knew she couldn't have it. Maybe he'd choose her this time if she gave him a chance, but he'd eventually resent being tied down.

Or maybe not.

Chisholm had left the Rangers to be with Caro and his girls, and he seemed to be making the transition fine. Then again, from what she knew of the former Ranger, his devotion to family ran even deeper than his devotion to Texas. Where did Whit's devotion lie? If he was willing to throw his Ranger career away, did it mean that much to him?

Miss Etta cracked open the door. "I have more hot water."

A bit of remorse prodded Violet. She should be down in the jewelry store, not bathing in the middle of the day, but it felt divine. Surely, between bats and bad guys, she deserved a little refuge.

It was time to let go of Whit forever. She needed time to fortify the walls around her heart. For Whit's own good, until the jewels were found, she had to keep their relationship on a purely professional level. After that, she'd have no reason to see him ever again.

But why did it hurt so much?

~

Arch Russell didn't flinch. Across from him, Maggie Markham held her knife aloft, waiting for the moment to strike. Then, like a copperhead, she thrust the knife downward.

"Got it." She bent close to the table and examined the fly she'd split in two.

"Impressive, sis." Willie Markham crossed the room and sat down in the chair. "Maggie, I've been thinking."

"There's a first." Arch cracked open his gun and removed the bullets in the chamber.

Willie pinned him with a glare, then turned back to Maggie. "You think it's time for me to go to Austin again? Maybe they ordered more jewels or the railroad could be sending a payroll. I could find out, but if I go, I'm goin' ta need some money for a shave and haircut. Maybe some new duds too."

Arch knocked Willie's hat off. "You don't need new clothes."

"I can't go meeting a girl like Miss Susannah lookin' like this." Willie pinched the front of his worn shirt.

"It wouldn't look half bad if you'd wash the thing." Arch scooped up Willie's hat and swatted his head with it.

Willie jumped to his feet, fists drawn back, a split second after Maggie's knife pressed against the bottom of Arch's chin. "Leave Willie alone."

"I was only funnin'." Arch waited until Maggie lowered her weapon, then returned to his chair and stuffed cotton batting down the barrel of his Colt. "Maggie, I know he's your kid brother, but you can't baby him forever. New clothes? Is he serious?"

"It's an investment." Willie touched the scar under his right eye, wincing. "Maggie knows I can get my little filly to tell me anything."

"Why would she want an ugly mug like yours? And what's she going to say when she learns what it is you do for a living?"

"She knows." Willie polished his knuckles on his chest. "And she likes it."

Arch's brows rose. "She likes that you're an outlaw?"

"She likes bad guys. She wants adventure." He rubbed the back of his neck. "Well, Maggie, what do you say?"

"You seem to get yourself in a lot of trouble when you're out of my sight, but you did come through last time." She leaned back in her chair, tipped her hat over her eyes, and crossed her arms. "Let me think on it a spell."

"But—"

He clearly didn't see the knife coming, but it sunk deep in the chair between his legs.

Maggie met Willie's gaze. "Don't sass me, boy."

He swallowed hard. "Yes, ma'am."

Arch bit back a chuckle. For once, the boy almost got what he deserved.

~

Never had Whit seen a horse look happier to be back in her stall. Big Joe, the liveryman, quickly saw to Sassafras's every need while Whit borrowed a curry comb and brush to give Shakespeare a much-needed and well-deserved rubdown. He purchased a bucket of oats for his majesty, too, hoping Shakespeare would forgive him for the rough morning. "Now that's a fine horse," barrel-chested Big Joe said, his deep voice echoing in the barn. "Interested in letting him be a stud for my Sassafras?"

Whit coughed. "Uh, I'll think on it." He smoothed his hand

over Shakespeare's withers. "Mind if I leave him here while I go get a bite to eat?"

Big Joe rubbed Shakespeare's muzzle. "No problem. I'll keep an eye on him, Ranger."

Whit nodded. "Much obliged."

Outside, the sun made Whit squint. With the livery south of town, he had a ways to trek to the Hartville Hotel. As he passed Dr. Hart's medical practice, he glanced across the street to Tatienne's Jewelry Company. Concern pressed down on him. How was Violet faring?

He quickened his pace. He needed to focus on this case, not on her. He passed Mortenson's Mercantile, and Meribeth Mortenson waved at him through the window. Distracted by his growling stomach, Whit didn't see the editor of the *Hartville Herald* coming across the street until it was too late.

"Ranger Murray. Just the man I wanted to speak to." Francis Barth fell in step beside Whit. He had a slight limp, as if one leg were shorter than the other.

"What can I do for you?"

The man whipped out a small pad of paper and a pencil. "I need a quote about how the train robbery investigation is going. Any leads?"

"If we had any, do you think I'd want them plastered on the front page?"

"Maybe not, but the public has a right to know."

Whit stopped and turned toward Francis. The top of the editor's head glistened in the sunlight. "Tell them that Company B is devoted to serving and protecting the citizens of Hartville and all of Texas."

"From the Markham Gang?"

"From any threats to their safety or property."

"Including the Markham Gang."

"And we won't give up until all threats are extinguished."

"Perfect." The editor tapped his pencil on the pad. "Can I quote you on that?"

"Sure, if you'll let me go eat."

"I'll even buy."

They made a beeline for the Hartville Hotel Restaurant. Whit could already taste the tamales and apple pie. Strange. Why, then, did he feel like he'd just sold his birthright for a bowl of stew?

CHAPTER 9

With a flick of her wrist, Violet turned the sign on the door to say OPEN. She then grabbed the hem of her apron and rubbed the fingerprints off the glass. Everything in a jewelry store should sparkle, her father said, including those who worked there.

Unfortunately, she lacked any luster this morning. She'd worked on the store's books late into the night, trying to balance them without the necessary funds. Then sleep had eluded her until well after midnight, and when she finally dozed off, Whit seemed to plague her dreams. In a little while, he'd infect her morning as well. According to Miss Etta, she and Whit would be returning today in hopes that Violet could take Miss Etta's description and produce a likeness of the man selling the paste jewelry. Miss Etta might be gravely disappointed in Violet's artistic abilities or lack thereof.

Aware of her lack of gratitude for God's blessings, Violet said a prayer of thanks as she went into the office to retrieve her sketchbook. The financial fears and worries about dealing with Whit crept back into her thoughts.

She drew in a deep breath. "'God is our refuge and strength, a very present help in trouble. Therefore will not we fear.'" She quoted Psalm 46:1–2—a Scripture her maman had taught her—aloud. She needed to cling to that verse, believe it, and breathe it.

The bell over the door jingled, and Violet looked up, expecting to see Miss Etta. Instead, Mrs. Palmer, the banker's wife, strode inside.

Violet's chest grew tight. "Good morning, Mrs. Palmer. I'm sorry, but I don't have your necklace ready for pickup."

Mrs. Palmer waved her hand dismissively. "Of course, you don't, Violet. Your father is laid up, and I heard about that unfortunate train robbery. But I do trust you will get it completed before next month. That's when I'm planning my trip to Paris."

"Paris? *Parlez-vous français*?"

"Excuse me?"

"I asked if you speak French."

"Obviously, I do not." Mrs. Palmer's lips lifted in a smile. "Would you be willing to teach me some key phrases? I'd like to know if I'm eating frog legs or snails."

"Escargot."

"What's that?"

"Snails." Violet chuckled at Mrs. Palmer's expression. "Of course, I'll teach you. Is that why you came in?"

"No, but now I've forgotten why." Mrs. Palmer drummed her fingers on Violet's newly cleaned glass case. "What was the reason?"

"Perhaps you have a piece of jewelry which needs repaired, or maybe you wanted to take a second look at the design for your necklace?"

"A second look? Oh, you're brilliant. I recall the reason now." She walked directly to the eyepiece section. "I need a lorg-net. I read about them in the *Ladies' Home Journal*. It said nearly every smartly dressed woman wears one."

"You mean you want a lorgnette." Violet was careful to pronounce the word correctly. She opened a sliding door in the back of the display case and removed a velvet-lined box that held a small selection of handled spectacles.

Mrs. Palmer picked up a silver one that sported tiny cherubs on the handle. She unfolded the glasses from the case. "Lorn-yet? Is that how you say it?"

"Yes, ma'am." Violet held out her hand. "May I show you how the lenses fit back into the case?" She pointed out the spring on the nosepiece that allowed the spectacles to fold in half. "As you can see, we have lorgnettes that hang on a chain and others that can be worn as a brooch."

Mrs. Palmer set down her first choice and examined a gold one. The handle was inlaid with blue enamel and set with tiny diamonds in the shape of a flower. "Oh, look at that. This one even has a timepiece in it. It's expensive, isn't it?"

"If you're looking for something more discreet, perhaps this one would be to your liking."

"Discreet? Heavens, no. I want breathtaking, Violet. I want extravagant. I want to be noticed on the streets of Paris."

"And in Hartville?"

"Absolutely. I'm no shrinking violet, mind you." She clapped her hand over her mouth. "I'm sorry. I don't mean that you're a shrinking violet. You aren't adventurous, but you aren't shy either."

"It's fine, ma'am." Violet bit back a chuckle. "Perhaps I could show you my favorite lorgnette." She reached below the case into a drawer, pulled out a black box, and lifted its lid to reveal a solid gold piece with floral filigree. Set in the center was a small dazzling emerald. "See? When the glasses are folded, it looks like a pendant, and the gold slide chain completes the ensemble."

Mrs. Palmer gasped. "That's stunning."

"I think the emerald would bring out the green in your eyes." She passed the piece to Mrs. Palmer. Her papa often reminded her that once a piece of jewelry was in the hands of a customer, it had a much better chance of going home with them. "You could easily wear this piece during the day or to the opera."

The banker's wife opened the glasses and held them up to her eyes, then looked off into the distance. She folded them back into the case, lifted the brooch to her chest, and stared in the mirror. "I do believe this is the perfect lorgnette, Violet."

"Would you like to know the price?"

Mrs. Palmer set the piece back in the box. "No, that's not necessary. Just wrap it and send the bill to Mr. Palmer. He forgot my birthday yesterday, so he'll buy me anything to make peace."

"Happy belated birthday, Mrs. Palmer." Violet withdrew a pink satin ribbon and tied it around the black box before passing it to the banker's wife. "And thank you for your purchase."

Mrs. Palmer walked to the door and wiggled her fingers in a goodbye wave. "Thank Mr. Palmer. He's the one who's paying for it."

Violet giggled, but as soon as the door closed, her smile fell. Familiar worry churned inside Violet. While significant, this purchase would hardly solve their financial woes. If only they could sell a half dozen lorgnettes, they could meet their mortgage. *Be grateful.* God had heard her prayer and had brought Mrs. Palmer to their store. God had provided financially, but had He heard her other prayer? *Lord, how long will it take to get Whit out of my heart?*

Since the store was devoid of customers, Violet went upstairs to check on her father. She told him about her sale, quickly served him a bowl of oatmeal, and helped him find a new comfortable spot. When the store's bell jingled, she hurried downstairs. Miss Etta stood waiting. Violet expected Whit to follow, but he was nowhere to be found.

"Whit is coming later." Miss Etta removed her gloves and

raised her brows. "I saw you looking for him. He was meeting with Hugh, so he sent me ahead and said he'll join us shortly."

Her pulse quickened. "Is everything all right?"

"I have no idea." Miss Etta sat down on the settee in the corner of the store. "Shall we get started?"

Violet nodded and retrieved her sketchbook. They worked for nearly an hour reproducing the image of the man from Miss Etta's recollection.

"Something is still not quite right." Miss Etta studied the sketch. "The receding hairline you've drawn is exactly right, and I don't know how you captured his protruding ears so well. I can see the schoolteacher look I tried to explain, but there was something a little dangerous about him too."

"Close your eyes, Miss Etta." Violet kept her voice calm. "Take a deep breath and try to see him again. Look at his lips. At his nose. At his eyes."

"That's it!" Miss Etta sat up straight. "They were deep-set because of his prominent forehead, and he had thick brows that always seemed stern."

Violet erased the brows and eyes she'd drawn and replaced them as best she could with the qualities Miss Etta had suggested. Before she was finished, Reverend Longley entered the store, bearing a basket. With sketchbook still in hand, Violet rose. "Hello, Reverend. What can I do for you?"

"I came to visit your father." He lifted the basket. "Sarah sent lunch. I can see myself up. You can go back to whatever you were working on with Miss Etta."

"I was simply sketching a picture." She motioned to her pad. "I'm almost done."

The reverend slipped the pad from Violet's hands and studied the image. "I just saw this fellow. Why are you drawing him?"

Miss Etta stood. "Where did you see him?"

"At the mercantile. Why? Is something amiss?"

"I think Ranger Murray would like to question him." Violet didn't want to alarm the reverend. Besides, they really didn't know who this man was or what he was guilty of.

Reverend Longley rubbed his graying temple. "Then Miss Etta, you'll tell Whit where I saw that fellow?"

She agreed, but as soon as the reverend had ascended the stairs and was out of earshot, Miss Etta turned toward Violet. "I'm going after him and confront him face-to-face. Tell Whit when he comes where I've gone."

Violet took hold of her arm. "Miss Etta, you can't. We don't know anything about this man. If he's willing to take advantage of someone like you, he might be willing to do something drastic if he's cornered. You could spook him, and he'd bolt without us getting to the bottom of the whole situation."

"But we can't let him go on taking advantage of the citizens of Hartville."

Violet's stomach lurched, but she could not let this opportunity pass. "He knows you, but he doesn't know me. You stay here and watch the store. I'll go."

"Whit won't like that."

"Probably not." She grabbed her wrap from a hook in the office.

"Do be careful, dear." Miss Etta held out a derringer. "Take this. Whit would never forgive me if something happened to you."

Violet held up her hand. "First of all, I've never shot a gun before. Second, he's not that kind of criminal." She tore the page from her sketchbook. "Give this to Whit and tell him where I went. And don't worry. I'll be fine."

Nerves taut, heart racing, she rushed out of the jewelry store and turned toward the mercantile only to see the man in her drawing walk down the boardwalk in her direction.

CHAPTER 10

"What in the blazes is this?"

Whit's commanding officer's deep voice filled the small Ranger office as he threw a folded newspaper down on his desk. Whit read the headline, and the heat of anger began to rise inside him. How could that editor write something like this? "*Ranger claims he'll extinguish Markham Gang.*"

Captain Sterling's glare bored through Whit. "What were you thinking? When the Markhams hear about this, your name is going to go to the top of their list. You might as well have drawn a target on your back."

Whit picked up the copy of the *Hartville Herald* and scanned the article. "I didn't say this stuff. The only thing I told that editor was Company B is devoted to serving and protecting the citizens of Hartville and all of Texas from all threats to their safety or property. I know that's what I said. I worded it carefully. He's the one who kept throwing the Markhams into it."

Captain Sterling ripped the paper from Whit's hand. "Apparently, that wasn't what the editor heard."

"Or he made up what he wanted to hear."

The commanding officer released an exasperated sigh. "I wish you could get out of town before they come gunnin' for you, but that isn't exactly an option for you. Who am I kidding? We're all marked men. We've already lost two of our own trying to take them down, but Whit, I don't intend for you to be the next."

"Neither do I, Cap. I'll be extra careful. I think we're getting close. You said yourself that the robbery near Medina sounded like the same group. The only difference being they didn't blow up the mail car."

"But again, they were able to open the safe."

"Exactly." Whit rubbed the back of his neck. "Sir, I've got to find those jewels, or the Tatiennes will be ruined."

Captain Sterling rubbed his temple as if a headache was coming on. He grabbed his hat from a hook on the wall and put on his holster. "Walk with me, Whit. We'll come up with a plan."

"Yes, sir." Whit followed his commanding officer out of the Ranger office. "Cap, why haven't the Markhams attempted anything else lately?"

The captain hiked his shoulder. "The Markham Gang is unpredictable at best. Heard there was trouble in Rock Springs. Since Griff reported they've split up, maybe that's slowing them down, or they're waiting to regroup." Captain Sterling took the boardwalk south. "Branch went to see what he could find out. He's planning to send word today."

"Split up, they can do more jobs." Whit tipped his hat in greeting to several ladies entering Miss Spanner's Seamstress Shop. "It seems the four that are around here have a plan of their own."

Neither man spoke again until Captain Sterling stopped at the telegraph office. "I need to see if Branch sent word yet. Wait here."

"Yes, sir." On high alert, Whit scanned the streets for any possible threats but saw only familiar folks going in and out of the establishments across the way from him. A wagon rumbled down the street. Whit jumped and instinctively put his hand on his Colt. The driver waved, and Whit drew in a long breath. He needed to calm down. If the Markhams were going to gun him down, they wouldn't do it in broad daylight in the middle of town.

Captain Sterling came out of the office with a frown on his face. "It looks as though you'll be leaving town, after all." He tapped the telegram in his hand with his forefinger. "And before you protest, hear me out."

Whit squared his shoulders. "I will, sir, but I'm not running away from them."

The captain rubbed his whiskered chin. "No, if things go as I think they might, I believe you will be running into the Markhams, not running away from them."

Whit's throat tightened. "Is Branch in trouble?"

"Not that I know. This isn't from him." Captain Sterling motioned Whit closer. "It's from the railroad."

Whit didn't want to press his commanding officer, but his curiosity was piqued. "And?"

"Let's just say that the day after tomorrow, you need to be on the return train from Austin."

After receiving additional details, Whit reminded Captain Sterling he was supposed to see the sketch Violet had drawn and escort Miss Etta home.

"In that case, Whit, you'd better hurry along. My wife doesn't like to be kept waiting." Whit crossed the street, sidestepping a pile of horse manure, and passed Houston's Hardware Store. A few doors down, he entered Tatienne's jewelry store. He stopped short at the sight of Miss Etta behind the display case. "Where's Violet?"

"She drew this." Miss Etta passed him the sketch. "Then Reverend Longley came in and saw it. He told us he'd seen this man only a short while ago."

Why would she go after this man alone? The protruding ears

reminded him of someone, but who? "Please tell me she is not out there looking for him."

"I'm afraid I can't do that." Miss Etta hugged her waist. "I was going to go myself, Whit, and confront him, but she said he knew me already."

He glanced down at the drawing again and recalled where he'd seen those ears. They belonged to the man in the shadows on the express car—the fourth member of the Markham Gang. Fear gripped Whit's heart.

"Where was she headed?" His voice was harsh, demanding.

"Mortenson's, but that was half an hour ago."

"If she comes back, keep her here." With that, he bolted for the door. Concern and anger mingled in his gut, twisting like a cyclone in May.

Some days a man ought to just stay in bed.

~

In order to avoid the man in her drawing, Violet quickly stepped inside the undertaker's. She needed time to think about what she'd say or ask. She shivered. Which was worse—the live man she was following or the dead man in here?

Bartholomew Rickets hurried to greet her. "Miss Violet, can I help you? It's not your pa, is it?"

"Oh, no. He's fine." She cracked open the door and peered out. The man she'd drawn was crossing the street toward the depot. "It was nice to see you, Mr. Rickets."

She departed as quickly as she'd come, leaving the dumbfounded undertaker staring after her. Since she had a good idea where the man was headed, she kept her distance. She crossed the street and turned toward the train station. He entered the depot, so she slowed her pace.

What if he had plans to leave town? Would she try to prevent his departure until Whit arrived?

Her heart thundered against her ribs. She hiked up her skirt and hurried along the boardwalk, her boots beating out a rapid rhythm. How would she stop him from getting on a train? What if he was armed?

Maybe she should wait for Whit. No, she didn't dare. Miss Etta deserved justice. Drawing in a deep breath, she pressed her sweaty palm to the depot door and whispered, "I will not fear. I will not fear. I will not fear."

But her breath came fast, and her knees trembled. Surely, God expected her to be a little afraid if she was facing a crook.

~

Clutching the drawing in his gloved hand, Whit raced out of the jewelry store and turned north, the direction Miss Etta had indicated Violet had gone.

For a woman who liked security, Violet was sure putting herself into some scary situations.

But where was she now? He paused on the boardwalk. She wasn't in the establishment next to the jewelry story. Unsure where to go, he popped into the undertaker's.

"Well, well, well." Mr. Rickets moved from his desk. "Looks like folks are dying to get in here today." He laughed at his own pun. "It's my day for guests."

"Guests? Have you seen Miss Tatienne?"

"Yes, Ranger, she was in here a few minutes ago." He scratched his head. "She didn't say why. Is she in some kind of trouble, or are y'all quarrelin'?"

Mr. Rickets's slow drawl only added to Whit's impatience. "Which way did she go?"

"Ranger, I don't go spying on the folk of this town."

"Mr. Rickets, which way?"

"Toward the depot." He followed Whit to the door. "I reckon you won't be needin' my services, then?"

"Maybe. I'm fixin' to wring her pretty little neck." The undertaker probably wouldn't hear Whit's words spoken as he raced across the street. How could Violet care more about her jewels than her safety?

"Don't be ugly, son," Mr. Rickets called. "You catch more flies with honey."

He had to catch this man before Violet got hurt, and he sorely doubted honey would do the trick.

Coming to a halt in front of the depot, he paused. He needed to keep everything in perspective. This man might not be guilty of anything except believing an old aunt about the quality of her jewelry. And large ears could hardly link him to the train robbery. Then again, Whit's gut said the man was guilty of something, and right now, he needed to make sure Violet hadn't tipped her hand.

He pushed open the door and strode inside. A few people waited in line at the ticket clerk's booth. He checked the schedule. No departures for fifteen minutes. On one of the benches where families and friends waited for the next train to arrive, Violet sat talking with the man in her drawing. The man's back was to Whit, but Violet could easily see Whit. He started toward her, but she shot him a *stay-away* look. What was she up to?

Whit slipped behind a support pole, which was still close enough to keep Violet in his sight. The man pulled out what appeared to be a piece of jewelry from his coat pocket and held it out to her on his palm. Violet picked up the item and seemed to take great interest in the man's story. Was he telling her about his deceased aunt?

Whit casually made his way to the bench behind where the two of them were speaking. He picked up a discarded newspaper and snapped it open.

"Are you certain this is a diamond, Mr. Carey?" Violet asked.

"Absolutely. My dear old grandmother wouldn't have lied to me."

Good for Violet. She'd gotten his name.

"Sir..." Violet paused. "I think you've made a mistake. This brooch is paste jewelry."

"And how would you know?" This Mr. Carey sounded as if he was placating her.

"I'm the daughter of the town's jeweler. I know a real diamond from a piece of glass."

"So I made a mistake. Are you going to tell the Rangers?" The man's genial voice turned cold.

"That's up to you." Her voice trembled a bit. "I'm hoping we can help one another. You see, I'm looking for some jewels that were stolen from me in a train robbery."

"So?"

"I'd like them back, and I'm willing to pay." Tension made her voice higher, thinner. She paused, and Whit imagined her drawing a deep breath, as she so often did, to steel herself. "If someone were to help me secure the return of my gemstones, I might be willing to compensate him or her and not say anything about said someone who is committing fraud by passing off paste jewelry for the real thing. Do you understand, Mr. Carey?"

The man released a wry laugh. "And how would I know where your jewels are?"

"I am guessing a man such as yourself may have connections."

"Miss." Carey's voice rose, and Whit tensed. "I'm a schoolteacher trying to sell my grandmother's jewelry. That's all. And if you know what's good for you, you'll forget you met me."

The veiled threat made heat build inside Whit. Everything in his heart said he needed to get Violet out of here, but his head said she was making progress in a case that was otherwise at a standstill.

"If you happen to find my lost gemstones," Violet said calmly, "you can find me at Tatienne's. You have two days."

Whit's jaw dropped. A deadline? She gave a possible member of the Markham Gang a deadline? His gut cinched tight. *Lord, help us both.*

Unable to resist getting a visual on what was happening, Whit set aside the newspaper and stood. He kept his movements slow and natural as he turned. Even though the man had shifted to the side, he didn't seem to notice him.

"Listen, lady..." Carey grabbed Violet's arm.

Whit hurried over to her, wrapped his arm around her waist, and kissed her cheek. "There you are, sweetheart. I've been looking for you."

The man dropped his hand and dipped his head. "Ranger."

"Sweetheart, we'd better get out to the platform. The train's just arrived, and you don't want to miss your grandfather." He flashed a smile at the man. "If you'll excuse us, Mr.—"

"Carey." Violet looked up at Whit. "Mr. Paul Carey."

"Well, I'm obliged to you for keeping my girl entertained till I got here." He took Violet's elbow. "Shall we git a move on, sweetheart?"

"Yes." She took a couple of steps, then stopped and held out the paste brooch. "Oh, Mr. Carey. I believe this is yours." She pressed it into the man's hand. "See you in a couple of days."

Carey gave Violet a glare that would shrivel the most seasoned lawman. Violet simply smiled sweetly. When had she discovered that kind of nerve? He didn't know whether to applaud her or throttle her.

Whit propelled her forward. It was time to get Violet out of here before the man shot her on the spot. Then his next step was to figure out where Mr. Carey was headed.

CHAPTER 11

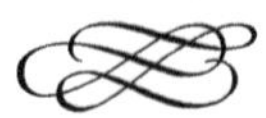

Never had Violet seen this side of happy-go-lucky Whit Murray. She stood off to the left of the platform watching Whit pace. His reddened face scared her more than Paul Carey ever had. She inhaled the sooty, coal-scented air surrounding the depot.

He glared at her. “I’m so mad I could spit and so proud, I could kiss you.”

Her eyes widened. “Oh.”

“That’s all you have to say?” He marched to stand in front of her. “I believe that man is a member of the Markham Gang, and you not only called him out, you gave him a deadline.”

“You were listening?”

“To every word.” His chest heaved. “For a woman who is scared of her shadow, you sure put on a brave front.”

“I was shaking on the inside.” And right now, her body was trembling on the outside. “Why do you think he’s one of the Markhams?”

“Remember that fourth man I only saw in the shadows? He had those ears that stuck out like Carey’s.”

"Is that all?"

"If I had more, I'd have arrested him."

"But you could have, anyway, since he's been hoodwinking ladies with the paste jewelry."

He heaved a sigh. "I know, but I wanted to see if he does bring your jewels back."

"Whit, what do you think will happen?"

"He'll either meet your demands or try to kill you."

Her mouth grew dry, her knees weak. She clasped his arm. "And what about you?"

"Don't worry about me. I can take care of myself, but what are you going to do if they try to shoot you? Blind them with diamonds?"

Now there was the Whit she recognized. Was humor his way of dealing with the stress of situations like this? She'd taken his leisurely attitude for a lack of seriousness, but had she read her friend all wrong? The man before her today was not the same person she'd grown up with any more than she was the same woman. Could he have changed?

Whit rubbed the back of his neck. "Miss Etta said you refused her derringer. If you'd taken it, at least you'd have been armed."

"I don't know how to shoot." She dropped her gaze to the platform and smoothed the gooseflesh on her arms. Her mind whirled from all of the events and the barrage of thoughts about Whit. "Did you say you were proud of me?"

"I believe I said I was 'so proud I could kiss you.'" He lifted her chin with his knuckle, his gaze intense.

A spark shot through her, but this time. she welcomed the fire. She needed the refuge of his touch to still the storm inside her. She lowered her lashes.

It was all the encouragement Whit seemed to need. He dipped his head and kissed her until she forgot about the Markhams, paste jewelry, train robberies, and her desperate need to find those gemstones.

A shrill train whistle broke the trance. She pulled back, her eyes wide. "Shouldn't we be following Paul Carey? He might lead us to my jewels."

"Apparently, I'm losing my touch." He chuckled. "If I thought that would work, I'd leave you here and get on my horse right now. He'll probably circle for hours before he heads back, or he'd double back and shoot me."

She swayed, and Whit caught her arm. "I think your adventure is over for today."

"It just hit me how real this all is."

"Yeah, bullets can do that." He tucked her hand in the crook of his arm. "But with a handsome rogue like me by your side, what could possibly happen to you?"

~

Arch heard a ruckus inside the cabin after Paul arrived. He motioned for Lane to finish counting the dynamite and then hurried inside. He did not want to miss this. He perched on a stool in the corner. No one wanted to be in the way when Maggie was in one of her moods.

"How could you be so stupid?" Maggie swatted the back of Paul's head with her open palm. She moved to the front of the table. "You let the girl identify you, and she's already got you pegged as connected to us."

"It's that Ranger Murray from the newspaper. He's sweet on her. He must have put the pieces together."

Maggie said some unladylike things under her breath. "That settles it." She kicked the foot of Willie's bed. Her brother snorted and ignored her. She grabbed the straw-stuffed mattress and dumped him on the floor. "Git up."

"What'd ya do that for?" Willie stood and rubbed his backside.

Arch chuckled. It served the kid right. He ought to know better than to ignore Maggie.

"Paul's going with you to Austin. He's a liability, and Cass will be furious if we ruin this operation." She went to her leather pouch and withdrew some bills. "Go git yourself spruced up and talk to your railroad gal. We need to make a haul. Then we can lie low until Cass gets back."

Arch crossed the room. "When you sending them?"

"Today." Eyes mica-hard, she looked at Paul. "You'll have to ride to the next town to board the train. Most likely, the Ranger will be looking for you."

"I could take care of him and the girl."

Arch held up a piece of fuse he was carrying. "That'd only bring us more trouble right now, but I'll keep it in mind."

Willie stretched and released another loud yawn. "My stomach is rubbin' on my spine. What's there to eat?"

"Nothing. Quit your bellyachin' and git moving." Maggie gave him a shove. She turned to Paul. "And take those gems and find someone to buy 'em."

Willie chomped into an apple. "I thought you had a buyer all lined up, Mags."

"Not until May, and they're too hot to hold on to. Cass would rather have the

money than jewels lying around, anyway." She paused and crossed her arms over her chest. "And Paul, you'd better earn your keep in Austin, or Cass can deal with you when he gits back."

hit leaned against Chisholm Hart's fence post and watched his former partner put salve on a calf 's sore leg. Chisholm let the calf spring away while he wiped his hands on his kerchief.

"So when is Captain Sterling sending you to Austin?"

"Tomorrow." Whit chewed on a piece of grass, enjoying the breeze. "The railroad let us know they're sending payroll out the following day. I'm to be on the train with that money and make sure it gets here."

Chisholm lifted his Stetson, ran his hand through his hair, and settled the hat back in place. "Want company?"

"And suffer the wrath of your wife? I don't think so." Whit laughed. "I'd rather face the Markhams alone, but don't worry. Captain Sterling came up with a plan. I'll get on in Austin, but at each stop, another Ranger or two will be boarding. By the time we get close to Hartville where we think the Markhams will strike, the passenger car will be plumb full of Texas's best and bravest." Whit paused, then cleared his throat. "I do need you to do something for me. Can you keep an eye on Violet Tatienne while I'm gone?"

Chisholm started toward his buckskin stallion and paused to glance at a silent Whit before mounting. "Sure."

"Thanks. I know you won't let her get hurt."

"You're sweet on her." Chisholm's voice held a hint of teasing as he climbed into the saddle. "Never thought I'd see the day you'd settle down."

Whit swung onto Shakespeare. "Who said anything about settling down?"

Chisholm sighed. "It's not like you think it is. The adventure doesn't end when you get married."

"Says the man who is no longer a Ranger and has five daughters and probably another on the way." Whit chuckled. "Besides, every day is most likely an adventure with Caro."

"That's not what I mean." Chisholm seemed to be considering his words carefully. "I thought I'd hate being tied down, but I learned that it doesn't feel that way when you're tied to someone you love."

"And you think I'd be happy living in one place?" Whit found it hard to believe his best friend could picture that any more than he could.

Chisholm kept his gaze trained on the path ahead. "Your pa left you when you were a kid. Every town we went to, I saw you searching the faces of the menfolk, hoping to find him. I reckon you know by now you aren't going to find him."

A jab of pain knifed Whit's gut. He didn't realize Chisholm had seen him looking for his pa. He'd only been seven when his pa had packed his horse with plans on heading to Colorado to make it rich in gold. Whit could still feel the brush of his whiskers on his face as they hugged goodbye. His pa had promised to come back, but it hadn't happened. Not that year. Or the next. Or the next.

"Maybe"—Chisholm's baritone voice broke through Whit's thoughts—"it's time for you to stop searching for what you lost and start finding who God's given you."

Whit sucked in his breath, then laughed aloud. "Since when did you become the sage old man?"

"Just promise me you'll think on it."

Whit nodded. "All the way to Austin."

They neared Chisholm's expansive home, reined in their horses, and tied them to the hitching post.

Five little raven-haired girls of varying ages tumbled out of the house and raced down the stairs, all calling to their pa.

"Whoah." Chisholm scooped up the youngest. "What's all this excitement about?"

"Our baby is coming!"

Perla, the Harts' cook and a personal friend of Caro and her mother, stepped onto the porch. "Señor Chisholm, go for your brother's wife. The baby is coming fast!"

"I'll go get Annie." Whit swung up onto Shakespeare. "You stay here with your family."

Without waiting for an answer, Whit bolted away. His nerves zinged. After delivering five babies, Caro should have this delivery thing down. Then again, everyone in Texas knew anything could go wrong when it came to a birth.

CHAPTER 12

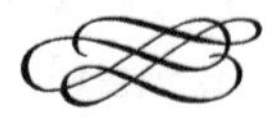

When Whit returned with Annie Hart, they found Chisholm in the parlor holding a bundle in his arms. His former partner looked up and smiled.

Annie nodded. "Congratulations, Chisholm. I'll go on up and check on Caro."

Whit stood at a distance, unsure of what he should do next. In the kitchen, he could hear Perla rattling pans and the girls chattering away about seeing the baby. He caught a whiff of something cinnamon scented, and soon the girls hushed. If he had to guess, Perla had quieted them with some of her delicious churros.

Whit crossed the parlor. "Well?"

Chisholm turned in his direction, a wide grin deepening his dimples. "I have a son, Whit."

Whit let out a whoop.

With a clamor, the girls fought their way into the parlor. "I'm sorry, señor." Perla followed and pinned Whit with a glare. "I couldn't keep them in there any longer after Señor Murray's—"

"That's okay, Perla."

"We want to see our brother." Six-year-old Maria stuck out her bottom lip in a pout.

The oldest daughter leaned over the back of her father's chair. "What's his name?"

"I wanna name him Bluebonnet." The youngest Hart girl, who'd been named after the family's cook, stomped her foot.

Chisholm cupped her cheek. "Perla pie, I don't think he'd make much of a Ranger if we named him Bluebonnet."

"What about Churro?" She wiped her hand across her cinnamon-sugar-dusted lips. "We love churros."

He chuckled. "Your ma and I decided to name him Mateo. It means 'God's gift,' and we'll call him Matt."

Whit felt like an intruder on this intimate family time. He stuffed his hands in his pockets. "That's a fine name."

"What's his second name?" Maria asked.

"You mean his middle name?" Chisholm looked up at Whit. "His whole name is Mateo Murray Hart. Murray after the best friend and partner I ever had—next to your ma, of course." He lifted the bundle toward Whit. "You want to hold your namesake?"

Whit could count on one hand the number of times he'd held a baby, and he'd never held one this—uh—fresh.

Perla wrangled the girls back toward the kitchen as Whit stepped forward and took the baby into his arms. A strange warmth swelled inside Whit's chest as he took in Mateo Murray Hart's face. His dark hair rivaled that of his sisters'. His tiny fist had escaped the blanket and now rested against his cheek.

"It's crazy how much you love 'em right from the start." Chisholm stood and took the baby back into his own arms. His eyes clouded.

Was strong, tough former Ranger Chisholm Hart fixin' to cry? He'd taken down some of the worst miscreants in Texas without batting an eye, but this sweet little baby was his undoing?

A tear slid down Chisholm's cheek. "You want real adventure, Whit? Try being a pa."

~

Violet had had enough adventure to last a lifetime, but she had one more to face.

She settled her father in a chair in the parlor and placed a tray with bacon, eggs, and toast on it next to him. "Are you sure you'll be all right while I'm gone?"

"Of course. Now that Dr. Hart is letting me get up, I'm getting around fine on the crutches he brought over."

Violet drew on her gloves. "The reverend's daughter, Hope, is coming over to check on you today, and her mother will come tomorrow." She pointed to a stack of reading materials. "That should keep you entertained."

He frowned. "I'd be better entertained if you'd let me go down to the store."

"I'm sorry, Papa. You aren't ready to navigate that staircase." She kissed his cheek. "Miss Etta offered to mind the store for us. She enjoyed being there the other day."

"Does she know what's she's doing?"

"She'll come up and ask you if she has any questions." Violet picked up her valise. "I'll be back tomorrow. Thank you for giving me a second chance."

"Be careful, mon bijou."

She started down the staircase. "I'll be fine, Papa. After all, lightning never strikes twice in the same spot, right?"

CHAPTER 13

Whit scanned the interior of the passenger car for an empty seat. He preferred the window. Only one window seat remained, and it appeared to be next to a lady. That would work.

"Ma'am, is this seat—" He sucked in his breath. "Violet, what are you doing here?"

"I'm on my way to Austin. My uncle telegraphed us and said he could loan us the jewels to complete the special orders. I'm going to pick them up and return tomorrow." She patted the seat beside her. "Go ahead and sit down."

Worry spread through him like a wildfire. This couldn't be happening. Not again.

He tossed his knapsack on the floor, then settled on the velvet upholstery. "You're not coming back tomorrow."

"Oh, but I am. With my uncle's loose gems, I'll be able to finish those orders." A smile lit her face. "Isn't it wonderful how God takes care of us? We'll be able to make our mortgage payment on time."

The Tatiennes surely needed this income right now, but his

first concern was Violet's safety. He leaned close and whispered in her ear, "The railroad is sending a payroll here from Austin tomorrow. That's why I'm on this train. I'm supposed to make sure it gets where it's intended."

"You think the Markhams will hit the train?" She breathed out the question.

"Possibly." He caught a whiff of her orange and chamomile perfume. He pulled away a bit but kept his voice low. "That's why you need to stay in Austin an extra day."

"I can't do that, Whit. I need to get home to my papa. I only arranged care for him for today and tomorrow. Besides, there's no way to know for sure what's going to happen. I won't put my, uh—things—in the safe this time." She patted her skirt and whispered, "I've sewn a secret pocket in my petticoat."

He grinned at the thought of her lacy underpinnings, then cleared his throat. "That's a good idea, but I still think you should wait a day."

"I'll be with you." She covered his hand with her own. "You'll keep me safe."

"Where did my little shrinking Violet go?"

"She's getting stronger, the same way that rubies do. Years of pressure." She giggled. "Most of it since you've reappeared in my life."

He lifted her hand to his lips. "You're more precious to me than rubies, Violet, and I don't want you to be hurt."

She inhaled a quick breath, and her cheeks bloomed a pretty shade of pink. She bit her lip and turned to him. "Then I have an idea. When we get to Austin, teach me to shoot. I have Miss Etta's derringer with me, and I want to be able to use it if need be."

His mouth gaped. Her words hit him with the force of a bullet. If she had sprouted horns right then and there, he'd have been less surprised. Then again, there were a lot worse ways to spend a day than spending it alone with Violet teaching her how to fire a derringer. And if he handled it right, he could use Violet's desire to settle this ridiculous idea of her taking the train home tomorrow once and for all.

"All right, Violet." He smiled. "Here's the deal. I'll teach you how to shoot the thing, and at the end of the day, if you can hit even one target, you can take the train home tomorrow. If not, then you wait a day. Deal?"

She cocked her head to the side, clearly contemplating the option he'd presented. Finally, she nodded. "Agreed."

He released the breath he'd been holding. Good. At least she'd be safe in Austin if the Markham Gang stopped the return train tomorrow.

~

After they had lunch together at one of the nearby restaurants, Violet said goodbye to Whit, checked into a hotel room, and then headed toward her uncle's jewelry store while Whit went to the stationmaster's office. She planned to meet him there after she spoke to her uncle.

Her uncle's jewelry store was less than a ten-minute walk from the depot. While the temperature was already climbing beneath the Texas sun, it felt good to stretch her legs after the train ride.

She crossed the street, sidestepping a puddle. She paused to watch a heavily loaded freight wagon pulled by a hulking team of draft horses rumble by. After doing a bit of window shopping, she entered her uncle's jewelry store.

She found Uncle Lucas helping a customer, so she waited until he was finished to greet him.

"Violet, I am so glad you've come." He kissed her cheeks in greeting, then stepped behind his display case. "I have a surprise for you."

"Oh?"

"A man was in here earlier today. He had some loose gemstones to sell, and I offered to take a look at them."

"Were they real?"

"*Oui*, and they were the ones I sent with you."

"The stolen gems?" Violet laid her hands on the display case to steady herself. "Are you certain?"

He nodded and fished a pouch from a drawer. "The large ruby is unmistakable. I did not want to frighten the man away, so I offered him a paltry sum. We dickered back and forth, and I finally purchased the collection well below their value. I believe my brother can still make a significant profit on them once they are set, especially if you continue to create such beautiful pieces." He handed her the velvet pouch.

"But Uncle Lucas, we can't repay you for buying them back."

He shook his head. "We are family. My brother will pay me back when he can. If he never can, that is all right too. God has been good to the Tatiennes, no?"

Tears pricked her eyes as she felt the weight of the pouch in her hand. "Yes, He has." She withdrew a paper from her handbag and unfolded the picture she'd drawn of Paul Carey, then handed it over the case. "Was this the man?"

Uncle Lucas's eyes grew wide as saucers. "It was." He traced his finger under the five-hundred-dollar sum. "This makes me wish I'd have tied him up and kept him in the back room."

Violet swiped a finger under her eye and smiled. "I'm glad you didn't try. The Ranger who is working this case may want to speak to you. Do you mind?"

"Not at all." He folded the paper and passed it back to her. The two of them spoke for a while longer before Violet explained she needed to go meet the Ranger. She asked to use her uncle's office for a minute to hide the gemstones in the secret pocket she'd attached to the skirt of her petticoat. When she returned, she thanked her uncle again for his generosity.

He clasped her hands at the door. "Be careful with those treasures, Violet. We might not be so lucky to retrieve them again."

She kissed her uncle's cheek. "I promise. I will not let these jewels out of my possession."

~

Whit had everything he needed for tomorrow's train trip back to Hartville. After meeting the stationmaster's daughter who was visiting her father, Whit had been provided with times, a ticket, and the name of the man who would be working the express car. The safe, he said, was brand new, delivered just yesterday. It was supposedly impossible to crack. Only he and the express man knew the combination.

The payroll amount, however, had gone up. Just thinking about it made Whit's skin itch as though he'd rolled in poison ivy. Not only would it include money to pay workers in Hartville, but it would now also have payrolls for Uvalde, Brackettville, and Del Rio.

Whit stopped and scratched his temple. How had the Markhams known about the jewels and payrolls? Did they have someone on the inside? He should have considered this earlier because if they did and they learned of the significant payroll sum, it would make this train a mark for sure.

He stepped out of the office and instinctively checked his sidearm. He'd always tried to settle things peaceful-like, finding a little humor often turned a situation his direction. But this time, weapons would most likely be needed.

Still, a grin split his face when he spotted Violet walking toward him. Her eyes seemed bright and alive, and her lips curled in a broad smile. Did she have good news?

She refused to tell him what was going on until they found a secluded location, but then the words seemed to cartwheel from her lips. She relayed the story of how her uncle came to possess the stolen jewels and how he'd identified Paul Carey as the man who'd sold them to him.

Her excitement was contagious, but his thoughts about a possible inside person at the railroad kept rubbing at him. She dragged him to visit her uncle, and once he heard the story for himself, he decided it was time for the shooting lesson. He didn't want to alarm Violet, but if he was right about Carey, and the man had been in her uncle's jewelry store, then the rest of the Markham Gang was most likely not far behind. The shooting lesson guise allowed him to get her and her jewels safely out of town.

Even though Violet didn't mind riding, he secured a carriage at the livery for the two of them and directed the vehichle out of town. Growing up in Austin had its advantages. He knew the perfect spot to take her to practice shooting.

"Whit, I've been thinking." Violet pressed a hand to her ivy-green hat when they hit a bump. "There were three outlaws who held up the train. How are you going to handle all of them by yourself?"

"Four, if we include Carey. Are you doubting my Ranger talents, Miss Tatienne?"

She swatted his arm. "I'm serious. What's your plan?"

"There are Rangers stationed at every stop to board the train. If something happens, we'll be ready." He turned the rig to the right, leaving a dust cloud on the main road. The sound of rushing waters told him he was on the right path. "And for the record, I've been in situations before where I was outnumbered."

"And you came out fine?"

"I'm here, aren't I?"

It wasn't easy, but he managed to steer the conversation away from the odds he might be facing tomorrow. A strange disquiet settled in his gut. Sure, he'd faced some tough assignments, but this one was different. Maybe it was because they'd already lost two Rangers to the Markham Gang. He glanced at Violet, and his heart swelled. Maybe it was because he finally had a real reason to want to make it back.

He neared the area he sought where the mighty Onion Creek fought its way through the rocks. He and Chisholm had helped the man who now owned the property, so he knew he'd have no problems. A previous trip had given up a breathtaking view he wanted to show Violet.

After stopping the carriage at one end of a shaded area, he tied the horse along the tree line. His hands spanned Violet's waist as he lifted her down. He held on a little too long, and crimson apples formed on her cheeks.

Violet glanced around the area. "Is this where we're going to shoot?"

"I want to show you something first." He took her hand and led her through the trees toward the sound of the rushing water. A little family of deer leapt away on their right. A gasp from Violet told him the moment she caught sight of the water tumbling over the rocks. For thousands of years, the force of the spring water had cut cascading trails in various places through the limestone. The curtain of water pounded the rocks beneath it and quieted in a large pool below. He led her as close as he dared to the view.

"Whit, this is amazing. I could watch waterfalls all day."

While the falls were stunning, it was Violet who took his breath away. He wrapped his arms around her waist and pulled her against his chest. Together they stood, mesmerized by the water, both beautiful and brutal.

"Violet." The hiss of the water threatened to drown his quiet words, so he lowered his lips to her ear. "I've fallen for you, and I can't stop myself."

Her silence made his chest heave.

"Please, say something."

CHAPTER 14

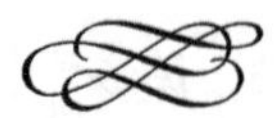

Whit's warm breath tickled Violet's ear and made gooseflesh rise on the back of her neck. His words both thrilled and terrified her, much like the falls before her.

Words jumbled in her mind, crashing into one another and fighting to reach the surface. Deep inside, she knew the truth. Like the water had cut through this limestone, Whit had cut through her walls, but she wasn't ready to give her feelings a voice. It made them too real, too permanent. And while she loved Whit, she still didn't know if she could love him like he deserved without wanting to hold him back from the exciting journeys God intended to take him on.

She turned in his arms. "I'm still scared, Whit. I don't know—"

He trailed his fingers down her arm. "We've got all the time in the world. We don't need to rush."

Her stomach spiraled. Did they have all the time in the world? What if something happened to Whit tomorrow and he died never knowing she loved him?

Whit lowered his arms and gave her one of his cockeyed grins. "Ready to learn how to shoot that little pistol?"

She released the breath she was holding and nodded. "And I haven't forgotten our agreement either." Afraid or not, she would keep shooting today until dark in order to hit the target he selected. At least that way. she'd be with him tomorrow where she could personally make sure the man she loved didn't face the Markham Gang alone.

~

Whit led them back to the clearing and selected an area well away from the horse to begin their lesson. He reckoned they'd practice for a half hour or so if Violet's wrist could handle the recoil that long. It would be long enough for her to understand you didn't become a crack shot overnight and long enough for him to win his side of the arrangement and secure her safety.

Violet withdrew Miss Etta's Remington double-barreled derringer from her handbag and held it out in her hand. "What do you think?"

He picked up the palm pistol, examined it, and weighed it in his hand. "Doesn't amount to much, does it?"

"No, thank goodness." She pointed out the ivory handle and the engraved barrel. "But for a gun, it's certainly pretty."

"Sure, beauty is important in a gun." Whit chuckled. "Makes them shoot straighter, I bet."

"Beauty"—she took back the gun—"is always important. Take it from a jeweler's daughter."

"I stand corrected." Whit explained the parts of the gun and showed her how to flip the lever on the side before opening the weapon to load it. "This is a rimfire, meaning this firing pin crushes the base of the bullet to ignite the primer. Speaking of bullets, where are your bullets?"

"Bullets?" Violet voice grew airy. "I hadn't thought about those."

"Well, you need bullets if you want to shoot the gun. Guess this lesson is over."

Violet's face broke into a smile, and a laugh escaped her lips. "Not so fast, mister. Of course, I have bullets. Miss Etta insisted." She fished in the beaded handbag and withdrew a handful of .41-caliber short bullets. She flipped the lever Whit had shown her moments before, cracked open the gun, and slipped two bullets into the barrels. She snapped it shut and looked up to find Whit's brows lifted high.

"What can I say? I'm a fast learner." She held the weapon out as if she were prepared to fire it. "Now, give me a target."

"Not so fast, Annie Oakley." He pushed the weapon downward, so it was aimed at the earth. "Never point at anything you don't intend to shoot."

He told her to expect the recoil in her hands and arms when she fired. "Now keep that thing pointed at the ground, and I'm going to find you some kind of target." A few minutes later, he set a rusted tin can on a log.

"That's awfully small." Violet squinted into the setting sun. "Are you trying to make sure I don't hit it?"

"You'll have a fair chance. You can't fire that little gun from that far away. You need to move in. It's designed for close contact." He drew a line in the dirt with his boot. "Try it from here."

She stepped up to the line. "How do I stand?"

"Move your feet apart. Put your weight on the balls of your feet." He moved to stand behind her and lifted her arm. "Support your shooting hand with your other. Lift your gun so you can sight down the barrel."

He supported her hands as she complied. "Now use just the tip of your finger to fire. Take a breath, hold it, and squeeze the trigger slowly."

"I would do better if you weren't so close."

"Am I distracting you?" He placed his hands on her shoulders.

She lowered her gun. "Move it, Murray, before my first shot is in you."

He stepped back and laughed. "Give a girl a gun and she becomes a killer."

Violet raised the derringer and fired. Her first shot went high. She shook her hand and lifted the gun again. Whit leaned against a tree, crossed his arms over his chest, and pulled his hat down over his eyes. At least he could stop worrying about Violet being on tomorrow's train.

Ping! He jolted and opened his eyes in time to see the tin can vault into the air.

"I did it!" Violet whirled toward him. "Did you see that? I'm going on that train with you tomorrow."

"Violet..." He spoke her name low.

"We had a deal. If God didn't want me on that train, I would have missed."

Whit sighed. Who was he to argue?

~

Violet descended the stairs to the lobby of her hotel and found Whit waiting for her.

"Morning," he murmured, his voice gravelly. He took her valise and nodded toward the door.

Whit had never been a morning person, so she wasn't surprised he said nothing else as they made their way to the café for breakfast. Still, she worried his mood was an extension of last evening. After the shooting lesson, he'd grown quiet. He'd tried once again to persuade her to remain in Austin an additional day, but between her concern over her father and over Whit, she simply had to be on that train.

She couldn't help but think his silence was also related to her response to his declaration. Expressing serious things wasn't easy for Whit. Did he really understand her reticence to move forward? Life had always seemed like a game for him, and she'd always been the practical one, but in the last few weeks, she'd seen a different side to her old friend. Sure, like a big kid, he handled most situations with a joke, but he'd also grown comfortable with his adult side.

He held the door to the café for her, and her heart swelled when she brushed his arm as they passed.

A heavyset waitress crossed to their table, but before she could ask for their order, Whit spoke up. "Bring a whole pot of coffee, black, for me, and a cup of tea for the lady, please."

"Anything to eat?" the waitress asked.

"Oh, yeah." He rubbed his fist against his eyes and glanced at the menu written on a chalkboard. "I'll take the biscuits and gravy. Violet?"

"Sounds good to me."

The waitress shuffled away and returned a few minutes later with the coffee and tea. She promised to bring the food out shortly.

Whit downed a cup of coffee and sighed. "Best medicine there is."

Violet smiled. "I wonder how my papa is doing, and I'm sure you're curious about whether Caro and Chisholm have had their baby."

He smacked his forehead with his palm. "I forgot to tell you. They had a boy the night before we left. I happened to be out there and went after Annie for them, but by the time we returned, he'd made his entrance into the world."

"What did they name him?"

Whit grinned broadly. "Mateo Murray Hart."

"After you? What an honor." Violet sipped from her cup. "How did that make you feel?"

She didn't get an answer because the waitress delivered their plates. Violet's stomach growled at the sight and smell of the biscuits and gravy. They both ate for several minutes in silence.

Whit chugged another cup of coffee, then leaned back in his chair. "I held him."

"Pardon?"

"Matt, the baby."

"You did?" The idea of Whit holding a baby warmed her. Oh, she'd seen him with children, and they all seemed to love him, but a baby? That was something she'd never imagined before.

"I like kids. Do you want a family?"

Heat climbed Violet's neck. "You know I do."

"Just not with me."

"I didn't say that." Sated, she pushed back her half-finished plate.

His eyes crinkled in the corners. "Well, maybe if we survive the day, we can talk about a future full of babies."

She swatted his arm. "Whit Murray, you oughtn't tease."

"I'm not." He wolfed down his last couple of bites, stood, and dropped a few coins on the table to pay for their breakfast. He held out his hand. "Ready to go take on the world with me, Violet?"

Her heart stumbled. It was simply a question, and he'd said it with his normal nonchalance, but the look in his eyes made her think his words asked for so much more. Fear fought for control of her response, but what had Whit told her the other day? Courage was feeling the fear yet choosing to act. *Dear Lord, what do You want me to do?*

Then the answer came. If she loved this man, she needed to act. With a tremulous smile, she lifted her hand and placed it in his.

~

Whit selected a strategic position in an aisle seat and stepped aside for Violet to sit by the window. If bullets started to fly, he wanted to be between them and Violet. She settled beside him and adjusted her skirt. Did the jewels she carried in the secret pocket make the garment heavy?

She rested her hand on her handbag. He knew it contained Miss Etta's gun, but he prayed Violet would have no reason to use it. Leaning close, he reminded her that hitting a can one time did not make her a markswoman.

The rest of the passengers filed on. He pegged the men as a few businessmen, some salesmen, and a couple of cowboys. The rest of the group was made up of women—two elderly women who chatted like magpies, a mother with her daughter, and a sprinkling of young ladies traveling without escorts. One fellow was already sound asleep in the last seat. He had his hat pulled low over his eyes, and his head was propped against the wood paneling. Probably enjoyed a little too much Austin hospitality.

Another young lady entered the passenger car. She smiled in Whit's direction, and he tipped his hat to her.

"Do you know her?" Violet asked.

"Maybe she finds me irresistible." He chuckled. "Jealous?"

"Not likely." Violet opened the book she brought. "But perhaps I should warn her about your character and wandering eyes."

"I only have eyes for you, Violet." He squeezed her hand. "She's the stationmaster's daughter. I met her yesterday."

The whistle blew and the train gave a grunt. It chugged away from the depot and slowly picked up speed. Whit willed the tension in his shoulders to ebb. If anything was to happen, Captain Sterling figured it would be after they'd reached San Antonio. From that point on, his fellow Rangers were positioned along that route, ready to help when needed.

Violet twisted in her seat and looked back to where the stationmaster's daughter had taken a seat.

"Something wrong?"

"Did you look at the brooch the stationmaster's daughter was wearing? It's the same one Paul Carey tried to sell me."

He quirked a brow. "Similar or the same?"

"Same. I'm certain of it." She forced a smile. "Maybe I can speak to her at one of the stops."

"Not that it'll make a difference. She probably got duped like all of the others."

"Doesn't she seem familiar?"

He nodded. "Well, I did meet her yesterday."

"No, I feel like I've seen her before." She leaned back in her seat and picked up her book. "I'm sure it's a coincidence."

Whit pulled his hat down over his eyes. He'd spent the night at his mother's house in Austin, and the two of them had sat up talking about his father for hours. His mother told him that he and his father were alike in that they both liked to try the impossible, but that was where the similarities ended. "You are not him," she'd said. "You'd move heaven and earth to get back to those you loved. Your sense of right and wrong runs deep." She admitted something might have happened to her husband that didn't allow him to return, but she didn't think that was the case. Apparently, he'd sent money to them once in a while until Whit was about fifteen.

"I died a little every day he didn't come home," she'd admitted. "Promise me you'll never make the woman you love wait on you for months. If you want a family, be part of it. They deserve that, and so do you."

He'd mulled over that for hours, and even now, her words burrowed into his soul. He couldn't ask Violet to become his wife if he wasn't willing to give up his position as a Texas Ranger. He'd also seen Chisholm's life, and he wanted it. He wanted a home and family of his own. So why was this decision so difficult? He'd been ready to quit and move on before this case. Why did it matter so much now? He'd given Texas nearly fourteen years of service. He had scars to show for it. But could he live without the adventure, without the thrill of the chase?

"Whit, are you sleeping?" Violet closed her book.

He cracked one eye open. "Not a chance."

"What if they plan to stop the train between Austin and San Antonio, not after?"

He pushed his hat back in place. "You make a good point." He glanced out the window. If the Markham Gang struck before San Antonio, he and Violet were completely on their own.

"One other thing keeps bothering me. Remember how we found the safe after the explosion? You said no one had blown it open."

"Right, and according to what Captain Sterling was told, the safe on the second job wasn't blown either."

"Then how are they getting it open?" She bit her lower lip. "They killed the express man both times. Did they force him to open it before they shot him? There just didn't seem to be enough time for that."

Whit pinched the bridge of his nose. "More questions than answers, I'm afraid."

Pinpricks of anxiety kept Whit on high alert. He patted the silver star in his vest pocket. Company B had a prearranged signal. If a Ranger required assistance, all they needed to do was send that star back to their headquarters.

He considered doing that, but it would arrive too late. If this train was attacked early on their journey, he'd be on his own.

CHAPTER 15

Violet's head bobbed as they pulled into the San Marcos station, the only stop before San Antonio. The *clickety-clack* rhythm and the gentle sway of the railcar had lulled her to sleep. She blinked her eyes and sat up straight when the train screeched to a stop.

Whit stood and stretched. "I want to take a look around."

"I think I'll get off for a bit too." She set her book aside and gathered her handbag. "I'd like to speak to the young woman about that brooch."

Before they had a chance to leave, the train took on a few new passengers—a man dressed in a suit with a sharp bowler and a woman in trousers. Both found seats in the back of the train.

Whit stepped aside to allow Violet to move into the aisle.

A pistol clicked.

Whit clutched her arm.

Violet whirled and gasped. How had they missed seeing Paul Carey? Had he been the sleeping man in the rear of the car?

He pressed the gun into Whit's back. "You won't be needing this." Carey lifted Whit's sidearm and slid it into the waistband of his pants. "Move on off the train, Ranger. You, too, Miss Tatienne."

As she followed his directions, a familiar voice ordered the rest of the passengers to follow suit. The woman in trousers—the leader of the first robbery—said, "Don't do anything stupid, and no one will get hurt."

As before, they lined the passengers up and demanded their money and jewelry. Since they'd exited first, they were at the far end of the line. Violet let her handbag slide down the length of her skirt. Once it lay on the ground, she nudged the purse beneath her skirt with the toe of her boot.

A shot rang out from the direction of the express car, and Violet's stomach roiled.

Not another victim.

When the youngest broad-shouldered gang member got to the stationmaster's daughter, she put up a fuss about relinquishing the brooch and her gold ring.

This roguishly handsome outlaw with a distinct scar on his left cheek lifted the girl's hand and kissed it. Odd behavior for a thief. Violet's eyes widened. Was this the same young lady who'd been on the train with them before? Is that why she seemed so familiar? Surely, it could not be coincidental.

Violet focused on the unique ring the stationmaster's daughter was wearing on her middle finger. The ornate gold band sported a cameo set on a thick, raised base. Something tried to surface from the corners of her mind. What was significant about this ring? Then it hit her. It was a secret compartment ring. Perfect for hiding a drop of poison, a snippet of a loved one's hair, or a slip of paper—such as one bearing the combination to the safe! Whit said she'd been in her father's office that morning. Why couldn't she be supplying the Markhams with the information?

If Violet hadn't been watching, she'd have missed the outlaw flip the stone cover open and remove something from the ring.

The young lady's eyes held no fear. In fact, admiration flickered across them. Good grief. The girl was smitten with the outlaw.

Violet sucked in her breath. "Whit, I know how they're doing it."

"No talking, you two." Carey loomed over her. "Now where are those jewels? I was watching that store, and I saw you go in and get 'em. I want 'em back. I know you didn't put 'em in the safe. Are they in your bag?"

"The jewels aren't in here."

"Cough 'em up before I start a hands-on search of my own."

The air squeezed from her lungs. She glanced at Whit for direction, and he tipped his chin upward in a *go-ahead* motion. She lifted her skirt and found the pocket in the hem of her petticoat. After unbuttoning the flap, she retrieved the pouch and lowered her skirt. Hot tears filled her eyes. How could she relinquish these treasures again?

"You're more precious than rubies, Violet," Whit said softly.

Carey cackled as she set the pouch in his hand. He tucked it in the pocket of his suit coat. "It's only fair. You've caused me more than enough trouble." He turned to the woman outlaw. "Maggie, can I take these two on a walk now?"

Maggie nodded. "I think we got things handled here."

He pressed the pistol into Whit's side. "Get a move on. You, too, Miss Tatienne, or I'll shoot him on the spot."

Violet's mind whirled. She had to do something. Fear threatened to paralyze her, but if she didn't move, Carey would shoot Whit for sure. She took a couple of steps, fell to the ground, and feigned a twisted ankle. "Ow, it hurts." She clutched her boot. "Please, give me a second to get up. Don't hurt him."

Carey yanked her to her feet by the upper arm, but not before she'd collected her handbag.

"I'm okay now." She shook loose from his hold. "I promise I'll follow. Just don't hurt him."

~

Whit's heart pounded. Being led away from the group at gunpoint wasn't Whit's idea of the best way to handle this robbery, but he could work with it. He sensed Violet making a plan of her own, and he needed to take control before she decided to use that little palm pistol in her handbag.

Carey directed them to a siding. "Lady, get up here where I can see you."

"I'm sorry." She whined. "I can't keep up. My ankle hurts."

Whit bit back a chuckle at her exaggerated limp, but apparently, Carey bought the injury act. A plan took shape in Whit's head. Instead of working against Violet, he'd work with her. Carey directed Whit behind a railcar. Nice of the man not to shoot a Ranger in front of the other passengers. Carey glanced back to make sure Violet was following.

"You can stop here, Ranger."

Whit turned so that he could face the outlaw and flicked a glance at Violet as she drew close. He needed to keep the man talking. "We figured you were part of the Markham Gang even though you don't exactly look the type."

"Looks can be deceiving."

"They certainly can." Violet pressed the derringer into Carey's back. "I've got a gun, and I know how to use it. Please, drop your weapon, Mr. Carey."

Whit sucked in a breath. "You don't have to be polite to outlaws, Violet."

"Truly? I think one should always show a modicum of decorum."

Carey looked befuddled, but it was all the distraction Whit needed. He grabbed the barrel of the gun with his right hand and pushed Carey's arm skyward. Violet jumped back. He prayed she wouldn't try to help.

With all of his might, Whit wrestled with Carey, trying to gain control of the weapon. He pushed the outlaw against the railcar and, over and over, banged his hand against the door hinge. Finally, Carey let loose of the pistol. Whit dropped, rolled, and came up with Carey's gun in his hand.

In a split second, Carey grabbed Whit's gun from his waistband and took aim, not at Whit but at Violet.

A shot rent the air. Violet screamed.

The outlaw fell to the ground with a bullet hole the size of Texas in his chest.

Whit gathered Violet in his arms. Tremors coursed through her, her tears soaking his shirt. He stroked her hair. The passengers needed him, but so did the woman he loved.

"Whit, you need to get back to the train." Her voice was shaky.

"I do." He stepped back and ran his hands down her arms, as if he needed to feel she was all right. "You stay here."

"With him?" She glanced toward Carey's body. "Not likely."

"And I thought you'd become so brave." He picked up her handbag and the little derringer from the ground. He flipped the lever and checked the gun's chamber. "This isn't even loaded."

"I didn't have time." She took the gun and dropped two bullets inside. "Just in case I need it now."

"You won't." Whit retrieved his own Colt and fired it into the distance.

Violet's eyes widened. "Why'd you do that?"

"Carey took two people out here to kill. The others will expect two gunshots." Whit took her hand.

"Wait. My jewels."

Whit lifted them from the dead man's coat. Blood had soaked the outside of the pouch. He stuffed them in his pocket. "I'll hold on to them this time."

Gunfire echoed from the depot. Whit and Violet broke into a run. He pulled Violet to a stop behind a shed. He spotted the three

Markham Gang members mounting up. One pulled out what appeared to be a stick of dynamite. Was he going to throw it toward the train where the passengers still stood outside? No wonder the gang members didn't bother hiding their faces this time.

The outlaw struck a match.

Whit stepped out and fired, splitting the dynamite. The outlaw returned fire, and the bullet whizzed by Whit's ear. He ducked back behind the shed.

"Git out of here!" the woman shouted to her cohorts. She fired a volley of shots toward the shed. By the time Whit could return fire, it was too late. His heart sank as the three Markham Gang members rode away. With no horse, he'd never be able to follow right now.

Company B would get them—just not today.

~

Violet stood with the other weary passengers inside the depot. They'd all been told to wait here until Whit could take down their names, but first, he wired for the other Rangers to join him. Perhaps with the help of his Ranger brothers, Whit could track the Markham Gang before their trail grew cold.

The strain of today's ordeal showed on the faces of all the passengers, but where was the young lady she suspected of providing the combination for the safe?

Stepping outside, Violet glanced around the now-peaceful depot. Things were returning to normal. Baggage was being loaded as another train prepared to depart. It was hard to imagine what had transpired only a short while ago. Passengers sat on the train staring out the windows. Were they concerned about their journey?

The whistle blew, and Violet gasped. The young woman was boarding the departing train.

Violet hiked up her skirt and raced toward the platform where the conductor stood checking his pocket watch. "You've got to stop this train!"

"Miss, I'm sorry if you're running late, but—"

Violet couldn't wait for the man to understand. She bolted up the stairs. "You!" She pointed to the girl. "Come with me."

The conductor came up behind Violet and grabbed her arms. "We can't have you accosting a stationmaster's daughter."

Violet struggled in his grasp. "Go get the Ranger. This girl helped with the robbery. The blood of three express men is on her hands."

Whit bounded inside the passenger car. He scowled when he saw Violet in the conductor's grip, standing over the young woman from the train.

"Ranger, this woman is crazy." The stationmaster's daughter patted her hair. "Please take her away."

"Unhand Miss Tatienne, conductor." Whit dug something from his pocket, then dangled a slip of paper from his fingertips. "And miss, you'll need to come with us. That lady you called crazy figured out how you helped the Markham Gang rob three trains."

The conductor gaped. "But she's the daughter of the Austin stationmaster."

Whit motioned for the girl to precede them down the aisle. "Who better to steal a combination?"

On the platform, an undertaker carried the express man's body away. Whit made the girl watch before he handed her over to the local sheriff. Finally, he returned to Violet's side. He lifted his cowboy hat and smoothed his disheveled waves. "I wonder where her parents went wrong."

"I think she just fell in love with the wrong person."

"How could you tell that?"

"I saw it in her eyes. She loved that handsome outlaw." Violet sighed. "It's easy to fall in love with the wrong person."

Whit turned to face her, his face pale. "Have you fallen in love with the wrong person?"

She took his hands. "I'll be honest. Loving you scares me."

"But Violet, once we catch the Markham Gang, I'm ready to leave the Rangers. I want to build a family with—"

She pressed her finger to his lips as he'd once done to her. "Let me finish. Today, when I almost lost you, I realized something else. Losing you scares me even more." She met his gaze and smiled. "You're a great Ranger, and if that's the adventure God has put in your heart, I'll support you."

He drew her into his arms, his heartbeat thundering beneath her cheek. "The day I saw you again on the train, I knew the truth. You're all the adventure I need. You are my treasure." He traced his finger down her neck until it rested in the little hollow of her collarbone. "Do you have the courage to start a life with me?"

She closed her eyes and drew in a deep breath. "I do." Her heart swelled with love for the man before her. There would be storms, but she could now face them. Together she and Whit were stronger.

Whit's lips curled in his lopsided smile, and then he dipped his head and kissed her with an urgency that made her dizzy. Unafraid, she melted into his embrace, consumed by the fire between them.

Her heart—cut, polished, and shaped like a precious stone—now shone with brilliance in the arms of the man she loved.

ABOUT THE AUTHOR

Lorna Seilstad brings history back to life using a generous dash of humor. She is a Carol Award finalist and the author of the Lake Manawa Summers series and the Gregory Sisters series. When she isn't eating chocolate, she teaches women's Bible classes, runs a toy store, and is a 4-H leader in her home state of Iowa. She has three adult children and a Pyredoodle named Honey. Learn more about Lorna at www.lornaseilstad.com.

Unless otherwise indicated, all Scripture quotations are taken from the Holy Bible, Kings James Version.

Cover design by: Wild Heart Books

JESSE'S SPARROW

AMANDA BARRATT

For those who have felt forgotten by God.
May you know—you are always remembered
and are of more value than many sparrows.

Soli Deo Gloria.

CHAPTER 1

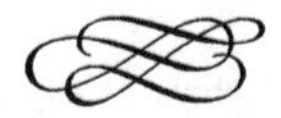

The rope wrapped her waist like a hangman's noose around the neck of an executed criminal. Yet as Sara dangled and inched lower, life, not death, grasped her in its arms.

The first taste of a *real* life in nine years.

Candlelight illuminated the painted faces of the three girls peering down at her, their thin arms clutching the rope. Aiding her toward freedom.

Almost there. The rope swung, jarring her shoulder against the side of the building. Splintering pain arced down her arm, but she didn't dare cry out.

She had plenty of practice at that. Stifling her cries was a thing she and the girls watching her had mastered. Better to stifle now and escape punishment later. A mantra of sorts, told to her the first day she'd been inducted into the second-floor world of Avery's Drugstore.

At last her feet found purchase upon solid ground, the rope coiling and dropping around her as she landed on her backside. With trembling fingers, she worked to undo the knots securing the cord to her waist, darkness obscuring most of her movements.

Good. Better an inky sky than a moonlit one. At least when escape was within reach, so near she could almost taste it.

Her fingers fumbled. Drawing in a shaky breath, she forced herself to stay calm, though her heart beat double time in her chest.

Three sets of kohl-darkened eyes traced her every move.

Just one more pull and...there.

Free at last. She found her feet, humid night air creeping beneath the folds of her scanty dress, slicking her skin with a film of perspiration.

She looked up at the three sisters—her friends. Her rescuers. The thought pierced her again—would the girls be punished when her absence was discovered? How?

There was no end to the punishments thought up by the man who ran this place. *Sir*, they all called him, though Sara supposed he went by something else in the outside world.

How much would Lacey, Dalia, and Addie suffer?

She squeezed her eyes shut, throat tightening. They'd refused to join her, driven by the terror of being hunted down. Not an unreasonable fear, but a real one, as real as the licentious men who came to their doors night after endless night.

But there wasn't time for this. She needed to go. Now.

Once more, she glanced up, conveying with her gaze the one sentence that mattered most of all, the one she'd whispered to each of them in the final moments before she'd been lowered.

I promise I'll come back for you.

Lacey, ever the serious one, nodded slowly. Dalia gave a little smile. Addie, a wave.

They understood—her friends. And Sara knew the promise she had made would feed their hope until she could make good on it.

With a breaking heart, Sara turned away, the street still and silent, save for a night bird trilling in some tree.

"Help me, Papa God," she whispered, willing the prayer to carry heavenward and reach the ears of her greatest friend and only protector. Knowing it would.

And then…she ran.

~

One Year Later
May 1886
Waco, Texas

Fingers trailing the small photograph resting on the mantel, Sara Byrne let her eyes slide shut. The last vestiges of the memories faded, dissipating. Almost. They'd never slip away altogether, had been much too embedded for that. And now, on the cusp of fulfilling the promise she'd made to Lacey, Dalia, and Addie, she needed to keep them fresh in her remembrance.

She opened her eyes, gaze touching the faces in the photograph. The two dearest people she'd ever known, their bodies now in the grave, souls in heaven. All she had left of them was this picture.

And the love they'd shown her.

"You'll always be in my heart, Matthias and Gloria Lawson," she whispered, slipping the frame into the depths of the carpetbag resting at her feet. "I know God has you close right now, and He's rewarding you for what you did for the girl who found her way to your door all those months ago."

She clasped the carpetbag closed, swallowing past the sudden knot gathering in her throat.

With a tremulous smile to the empty room, she let herself look one last time. Bare walls where Gloria's watercolors had once hung. Gleaming wood floors that had been covered with braided rugs.

Spaces where furniture had rested—the easy chair Matthias always sat in to smoke his pipe, filling the room with the musk and tang of tobacco. The ottoman where Sara curled up, always with some new book. The rocker where Gloria busied her hands with knitting, a song ready on her lips, keeping time with each creak of the chair.

> Jesus, Jesus, how I trust Him!
> How I've proved Him o'er and o'er.
> Jesus, Jesus, precious Jesus!
> O for grace to trust Him more!

Sara started, the words ringing through her memory so true and clear, it was as if Gloria sang them near her ear. But the space remained empty.

And her heart full.

She walked quickly from the room, her boots clicking on the floor. Past the homey kitchen, with its sunlit windows and countertop that had seen more freshly baked loaves of bread and berry tarts than one could count. Past Matthias's study, where he'd pored over patient files and taught her how to cipher long division. She tenderly brushed the doorknob, the metal worn but gleaming.

Straight ahead—the door.

Lifting her chin, she walked toward it with determined steps. The new occupants would take possession of the house within the hour, a large and lively family who would fill it with the sounds of busy children and the warmth only a family of seven could bring.

Yes. This was no longer her home. Her future lay on the other side of the door, away from Waco and back to San Antonio. The Lawsons' legacy, she would carry with her always.

But she had a future apart from theirs to begin now.

Outside, the late-morning sun warmed her face, wind riffling her skirt and fluttering the ties of her bonnet. Mr. Garfield, the new owner of the house, stood on the sidewalk, an impatient furrow in his brow, as if she'd overstayed her welcome.

She passed the key into his hands, said a few words. Then, clutching both carpetbags, one large and one small, made her way down the street in the direction of the center of town, where the stagecoach would soon arrive.

Working for a doctor had given her plenty of practice in running parcels all over town, so she was at no loss as to the streets to take. Few acknowledged her, a fact for which she was thankful. She'd had enough of that at the funeral three days prior. Friends and acquaintances, Matthias's patients, had all come to pay their respects. Everyone probably wondered what would become of her, a servant that had become more like a daughter to the elderly doctor and his wife, but she dodged any hints or questions. It was her business, not theirs.

The stage squatted in the middle of the dusty square, men working to unload passengers and luggage, the horses exchanged for fresh animals.

Sara reached into the small carpetbag and pulled out the money for her fare, already counted and secured within a sheet of folded paper. The remainder of her funds had been secreted within the bag's lining. Two hundred and fifty dollars, to be precise. Her gift from the Lawsons. Some for living expenses.

Most would be used to keep her promise to Lacey and the others.

Also, resting heavy in the bottom of the small carpetbag lay the cool, deadly metal of a revolver. She had Matthias to thank for the ability to use it.

Skirt brushing the dust of the street, she opened the door of the stage office.

A middle-aged man, whom she recognized as a frequent patient of Matthias's due to chronic lumbago, sat behind the tall counter. On one wall, advertisements and posters splayed across a wooden board, each detailing some service.

Or offering a bounty for the locating of a criminal.

A shiver curled up her spine. She was no stranger to men in need of justice. Yet for the past year, the Lawsons had sheltered her, given her a cocoon in which to heal and mend. Taught her more about the Jesus she'd served since her mama's death. But the Lawsons' discipleship had added depth, texture to her childhood lessons.

It had been wonderful, a fairy tale that had ended with the passing of first Gloria, then Matthias mere hours later. A fever Matthias had aided many a patient in beating, yet one he himself had not survived. Nor his wife, the sweetest woman in all of Texas.

"I'd like passage to San Antonio, please." She held out the money.

The man took and counted it. "Here you are, miss." He handed her a ticket. Then recognition entered his eyes. "Aren't you that gal who worked for Doc Lawson?"

Sara nodded.

"Thought I recognized you. You were at the office that day I had a real bad spell with my lumbago." The man winced a little, as if remembering. "So you're fixing to leave Waco, now that the doc and his wife have passed on?"

She gave another nod. Though the man was friendly enough, she didn't discuss her doings with strangers. Instinct, her habit of not trusting people. No matter how friendly they seemed. Not even the Lawsons, at first, though eventually she'd made an exception for them. But no one else. It didn't bode well, women who trusted.

He watched her, as if expecting her to elaborate.

"Thank you for the ticket," she said, and walked out.

A wiry kid took her large carpetbag and added it to the luggage secured on top of the stage. The smaller one, she pressed close to her side as she entered the conveyance. The scent of stale smoke and sweat made her wrinkle her nose.

Across from her, a bonneted woman in widow's weeds gave a smile. "Appears we're the only passengers. Thank providence!"

"Appears we are." Sara returned the smile. For the time being, at least, they'd each have a seat to themselves and a more comfortable ride. Though, of course, other passengers could be picked up on the various stops made before they reached San Antonio.

"I'm Elmira Thompson." The woman's double chin waggled beneath the confining strings of her bonnet. At least her fellow traveling companion seemed harmless enough. And thankfully, female.

"Sara Byrne." Her soft reply was muffled by voices sounding from outside, mingled with the snorts and stamps of fresh horses being settled. Sara shifted, trying to find a more comfortable position on the wood-backed, threadbare-cushioned seat. No doubt she'd be a mass of bruises by the time they reached San Antonio.

The carriage jerked. The elderly woman on the opposite seat released a little sigh. Sara leaned toward the window as close as she could without pressing her nose against the glass. The wheels ate up the distance, Waco passing from view.

This town had ceased to be her home.

Now, she had none, a woman bent on returning the favor to the three sisters who'd given her freedom.

CHAPTER 2

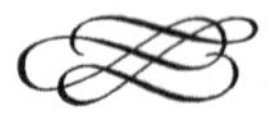

Shots rang out.

Sara jolted, the crick in the back of her neck protesting. She'd been sleeping, or at least trying to.

Mrs. Thompson let out a scream. The stagecoach jerked, hurtling onward. Horses squealed.

Grabbing the edge of her seat, Sara clung to it as the stage pitched forward.

More shots.

She squeezed her eyes shut. Her heart pounded.

"What's happening?" Worry emanated from Mrs. Thompson's eyes.

"Get down. Low."

With shocking agility, Mrs. Thompson dropped to the floor, peering up at Sara with a terror-filled expression.

Sara fell to her hands and knees, scooching closer to the window, her teeth clattering together from the breakneck speed. Who was shooting? She needed to try to look out the window.

Her elbow slammed against the edge of the seat. Pain sparked up her arm.

Help us, Papa God.

The stage thundered to a halt.

Blessed stillness ensued. Hands shaking, Sara gestured for Mrs. Thompson to remain low. A dull throbbing reverberated up her elbow.

Male voices. Footsteps.

Her mouth went dry.

The door jerked open. A man filled the space with his bulk. A kerchief obscured all but his eyes, a Stetson pulled low over his forehead. In his hand glittered the metal and menace of a revolver.

Mrs. Thompson whimpered.

No fear. Show them no fear.

The words had helped Sara through situations much worse. Even if this man hauled them out and shot them down, it wouldn't be a worse fate than what she'd already endured.

The thought was enough to embolden her, make her meet the robber's gaze with a measure of cool detachment. Her mind scrambled. Where was her small carpetbag? If she could only reach for it, she'd have her own weapon. The man would prove an easy target. Not that she'd ever shot anything other than an old stump of wood, but Matthias had trained her well, should she ever need to defend herself.

"Get out. The both of ya."

Sara made a move to raise herself. The man's finger inched toward the trigger.

"Not so fast now. Nice and slow like."

Mrs. Thompson curled into a ball, blubbering. Deeming it best to set the example, Sara clambered out of the carriage, keeping her movements even. Prickles danced up her numb legs and feet. She tripped over her hem and would've landed face-first in the dust had the man not grabbed her arm with a punishing grip. His eyes—one of which seemed fixed in a perpetual squint—speared into her with a look of disgust.

"Put yer hands in the air, missy, an' keep 'em up."

Sara obeyed, the sight of their driver lying in the dust, blood pooling around his leg, prompting her to do so. One of the men kept his gun trained on the driver while two others unloaded the top of the stagecoach.

Perspiration trickled along her spine, the hot, dry air beating on her back.

Mrs. Thompson stood beside her now, the man who had ordered them out of the stagecoach keeping his gun on them while watching the two men paw through the bags and trunk. Tears trickled down Mrs. Thompson's doughy cheeks as one of them pocketed several pieces of jewelry from within the trunk's depths. Dresses, books, and underclothes sprawled in the dust, as if a crazed woman had scattered them. The robbers moved at lightning speed, fingering, tossing aside. Barely moving a muscle, Sara watched as they opened the small carpetbag. She'd stitched her money within the lining.

Did she dare hope they'd discard the bag, as they'd done Mrs. Thompson's wardrobe?

Please, don't let them take it...

The metal of her prized revolver winked in the harsh sunlight. The man wearing the gray bandanna palmed the weapon before dumping it and a coin purse into her carpetbag. He stood, brushing the dust off his trousers.

Everything inside her screamed out to push past and take hold of the carpetbag. The skunk holding it didn't even know its value. But drawing attention to it or herself in any way could prove disastrous. So she remained where she was, hands in the air. Helpless.

A hateful feeling, being helpless.

"Nothin's left." The man with her carpetbag addressed the tall man guarding the driver.

"Help the boys with the horses, then." He seemed almost

bored as he watched the driver groaning and writhing, blood oozing from his left leg. The sour taste of bile rose in her throat.

The robbers struck the horses' flanks, sending them whinnying and stampeding down the road in a choking cloud of dust. One of the fellers laughed, slapping his thigh as he watched the frightened animals gallop off.

"Shut yer trap." The man nearest made a sound of disgust.

They mounted their own horses, all but the one guarding Sara and Mrs. Thompson. He approached, lifting her chin with the muzzle of his pistol.

A thud. Mrs. Thompson no longer stood beside her.

Her blood chilled.

An exhale slipped out as she glanced out of the corner of her eye. Fainted. Nothing worse.

"Pleasure makin' yer acquaintance, missy. Pity we can't stay and chat." Though she couldn't see his mouth, Sara could tell the man smirked.

She pressed her lips together, refusing to flinch.

With a harsh chuckle, he lowered his gun and crossed to where the driver lay.

"Thank you kindly, fine sir. Much obliged." He gave a swift kick, the toe of his boot meeting the driver's shin.

The driver's eyes rolled back in their sockets.

He flicked something onto the ground—something that landed on the dirt beside the driver and glittered in the blazing sun.

Sara remained rigid as the man mounted up.

"Yah!"

The men rode off in a storm of dust, their whoops and hollers echoing through the still, hot air.

For a long moment, Sara stood, staring at the strewn belongings. Mrs. Thompson's frilly pantalets grimy with dust. A bag of mail littering the ground in a jumbled collection of the written word. The stage, squatting on the road, sullen and desolate.

The driver emitted another low moan. Mrs. Thompson stirred.

The sounds roused Sara to action. Yanking up her skirts, she rushed to the driver's side, falling to her knees.

Pressing her hand against the side of his neck, she felt for a pulse. Slow, but at least it was there. She dashed to the pile of clothes and snatched up a petticoat. A rip rent the air as she tore the garment into strips. Spying a canteen of water, she grabbed that, too, and knelt beside the man, next to his injured leg, sticky redness soaking through her traveling dress.

Inwardly thanking Matthias for the medical knowledge he'd imparted, she tore the man's pant leg near the hole caused by the bullet's entrance.

She poured water over the weeping, puckered wound and then probed it.

"Thank you, Papa God," she breathed, swiping a damp strand of hair from her eyes. The bullet had gone clean through.

She wrapped makeshift bandages around the limb until deeming them tight enough to stop the blood flow. Though it could have been worse, doubtless the man would find himself in a world of pain once he came to. Hopefully, that wouldn't be for some time, since she'd no laudanum or even whiskey to ease his agony.

Assured that the driver wouldn't bleed to death, she moved to tend to Mrs. Thompson. Blood and dust still streaked Sara's hands, so she swiped them across her skirt before reaching to unfasten the woman's bonnet strings and collar.

If there was one thing Texas always possessed, besides ranches and cowboys, it was heat. Today, the air baked, a furnace if ever there was one.

"Hey." She slapped the woman on the side of her face, not hard enough to harm but enough to rouse. Doubtful she'd find smelling salts among the scattered belongings. "Mrs. Thompson."

The woman opened her eyes and blinked.

"Are you hurt anywhere?"

"My head...aches some."

Not surprising. Sara removed the bonnet and fingered the woman's skull, finding a bump the size of an acorn but nothing more. Placing her hands around the woman's shoulders, she helped her to a sitting position.

"Drink something." She held out the canteen.

Mrs. Thompson took a swallow. Some of the color returned to her face. Sara sat back on her heels.

"Those horrid men..." The lady's words trailed off in a sob. "Wicked, evil, scurrilous villains."

Sara could add a few more choice descriptors to the list, most of which would singe the woman's ladylike ears. So she simply nodded, a throb brewing in her temples. She could use a drink of water herself, but not yet. No telling how long they'd have to survive on the remainder in the canteen. And as Matthias had always said, patients came first.

"What are we to do?" Though the woman probably exceeded Sara's age by two score, her words came out like a frightened child's.

"They took the horses. And we can't move the driver by ourselves." Not to mention she hadn't the faintest idea where they were, except that it was a deserted road, sparsely tree-lined and miserably lacking in covering from the heat. Falling asleep had been foolishness. Had she stayed awake, she'd be better able to ascertain if they'd passed any signs of civilization within walking distance.

"So we just sit here and die?" Tears gathering in her eyes, Mrs. Thompson looked as if she were trying—and failing—to put on a martyr's expression.

"Don't cry." Sara's tone came out a bit sharp. "You'll get dehydrated."

Mrs. Thompson nodded meekly, rubbing her sleeve over her cheeks.

"I'll think of something." She picked up the canteen, allowing herself the slightest trickle of water. As the only person among them able to form a rational thought at the moment, she needed the strength.

Yet as she wrapped her arms around her knees, the sun high and blistering overhead, she couldn't quell the fear clamping clammy fingers around her heart.

Much as she tried.

~

Even the most stalwart of Rangers needed an occasional rest.

Jesse Rawlings swiped a sheen of perspiration from his brow, his other hand holding fast to Arion's reins. It had been another long, hot day in the saddle. And he, for one, couldn't wait to get back to Hartville and the comforts of a real bed and clean duds.

Beside him on the trail, atop his sleek bay horse, Griff rolled his shoulders, his face set in familiar lines, ones Jesse knew almost as well as his own, having spent almost every day with the man since he'd joined Captain Sterling's company of Rangers.

"Reckon we'll make it to Hartville by sundown?"

"Reckon we will," Jesse replied, keeping his gaze on the dusty, snaking road. "Don't know about you, but a bellyful of chicken and dumplings would hit the spot right about now."

"I'm hoping for warm apple pie. Evelyn makes the best a man's ever tasted." Griff grinned.

Jesse's mouth watered. Fortunate guy, Griff was. Though new to their company, Griff had already proved himself to be a first-class Ranger. Now he'd added to his load of good fortune a beautiful wife and stepson.

Whereas Jesse...

Griff was still talking about food. And Evelyn, probably.

"Bacon and beans don't even compare, do they?" He gave a look of disgust.

"They surely do not. Least the way you cook 'em." Jesse grimaced. Griff Sommer might be one of the finest Rangers he'd ever had the privilege to meet, but a cook he most surely was not.

Jesse returned his attention to the road, scanning it more out of habit than anything else. Tracking outlaws, renegades, or stolen cattle, for that matter, gave one a constant attunement to one's surroundings. Not much passed his notice. Sometimes he rued his inability to simply meander. But no. Always searching. Always aware.

The hair on the back of his neck prickled, like a sixth sense warning him of trouble ahead.

Eyes fixated off in the distance, he confirmed it.

A stagecoach. Common enough on these roads. Most had horses attached and rolled along at full speed.

This one didn't. It sat on the edge of the road, like a great felled bear ready to be gutted and skinned. A bunch of stuff lay strewn all over the place.

And people. Two of them. In skirts.

A Ranger would have to be blind to remain unaware of the trouble they were riding into. Trouble that, the closer they got, hit Jesse deep in the gut.

He sensed Griff noticed everything, too, though the man didn't say anything. When one was a Ranger, communicating could be done in a variety of ways, mostly nonverbal. It suited the type of fella who chose the profession—one had to shoot, ride, and track better than the best but didn't need to know two straws about fancy elocution.

Which was good because Jesse didn't much cotton to fancy elocution.

They neared, giving him a better gander at the scene. The sprawled belongings had come from an open trunk. One of the women was older and garbed completely in black. A man lay propped up against some rolled material, his leg stretched out in front of him and obviously recently wounded.

Jesse dismounted first, Griff right behind him.

The other woman—not the older one—rose from where she'd knelt beside the injured man. Hair the color of chestnuts straggled around her face, which was flushed compared to the pale color of her lips. Brownish stains marked her skirt.

How long had the three of them been out here in this condition?

"Jesse Rawlings, ma'am. This here's Griff Sommer. Texas Rangers, the both of us." He didn't exactly know why such a formal greeting came out. Not that he didn't believe in calling ladies *ma'am* and all that, but usually, he got right down to business.

Griff hastened toward the injured man's side and knelt in the dirt, uncorking his canteen as he did so. The older woman made a beeline toward Griff, picking her way around the disaster of strewn clothing.

"Thank providence help has arrived! Miss Byrne and I have been quite despairing, but I told her someone must surely come along. And I was right too. We would not be forsaken forever, though truly, it's a sorry state we find ourselves in. Ah well, we must take the good along with the bad. At least we can take comfort in knowing we won't turn to corpses here on the road." The woman finished her monologue in the space of time it took Jesse to draw two decent lungfuls of air.

Thank goodness the whole speech had been addressed to Griff. Leaving Jesse to turn his attention to the other lady, the one who seemed most likely to have two rational answers to rub together.

"We were robbed at gunpoint about five hours ago. The driver was shot in the left leg, as you can see." He had to hand it to the lady. Giving him information before he could even ask his questions.

"How many men?"

The woman paused. Despite her measured tone, she looked more wilted than a vase of week-old daisies. He grabbed his canteen from within one of his saddlebags and approached, holding it out to her.

She didn't reach to take it, as he would've done if he'd been hotter than a boiling pot and just as thirsty. He took a few more steps, until they stood less than six inches apart. Up close, her pallor looked even pastier. This gal needed something to drink before she collapsed onto the dirt.

She fidgeted, hands knotted at her waist.

"You'd best drink this before you pass out. I'm not in a female-carrying mood. Leastwise, not today." Blame it on the heat or the long morning riding, but his patience was wearing threadbare.

Those pale eyes turned a darker shade, enigmatic emotion in their depths. She jerked the canteen from his grasp, stinging his hand with her speed. He stood there, arms folded, watching as she gulped down a sizable quantity.

She wiped her mouth with the back of her hand and passed the canteen to him.

"Much obliged." Already, she began to look a little less like keeling over.

Before she could say more, he turned the conversation around to business. "So back to the men. How many were there?"

"Four. Two...contributed to the state of things you see here." She gestured to the luggage and strewn mail. "One kept watch over me and Mrs. Thompson. The other guarded the poor man yonder, who must have been shot when the stage was overtaken. Only"—the slightest flicker of fear entered her eyes, turning their lake-blue depths wide and vulnerable—"he wasn't content just to keep him from taking action. Before he left, he kicked the driver as if he were no more than a dog. Seemed to enjoy it, in fact."

Pieces came together in his mind. Of course, even a rookie could've fit them into place, seeing as their company had been following one trail since the beginning of the year.

One trail. One group of outlaws.

The Cass Markham Gang. A no-good bunch of skunks if ever there was one. Robbing. Kidnapping. Cattle rustling. They'd done it all, and then some.

He jerked his head in Griff's direction. The Ranger stood, in all his Colt-armed glory, looking positively helpless, caught in the barrage of Mrs. Thompson's endless gabbing.

Griff managed to get a word in edgewise with Mrs. Thompson before heading over. He held out his palm. Within lay Cass Markham's idea of a farewell gift. A cinco peso badge—the emblem of the Texas Rangers.

A bullet hole through the silver—dead center.

No words were needed.

"Figures." Jesse toed his boot through the dust. "Markham sure gets around."

The young woman stared between them, as if placing the name with the gang of criminals that had so recently shattered her civilized stage trip.

Since she didn't ask any questions, Jesse didn't bother to enlighten her. The less time spent talking, the sooner he and Griff could get on the trail. For, much as they both salivated for a hot meal, they surely wouldn't get one. Not after all that had happened.

"Let's head out." Jesse directed the words to Griff. "Get these people to Hartville. The sooner Doc Hart can tend that man, the better."

Griff glanced at the driver. Lying on the ground, covered in his own dried blood, the man stared at them, obviously in shock, despite Griff's attempts to hydrate him and prop up the injured limb.

"Mrs. Thompson can ride with you. I'll take the driver." His gaze landed on the young woman. It wouldn't work for three to ride on a horse, even one as strong as Arion. And the injured driver took priority over the other two. As did, apparently, Mrs. Thompson, who had quit talking and dabbed her eyes with a lace hanky. Of all the times for a female to start weeping.

Best leave her to Griff. No way in Dodge did that woman possess the stamina to remain behind.

This one—Jesse swept his gaze over the brown-haired lady's face—likely did.

"Ma'am?" He tried to add a civilized note to his tone. Though there was nothing civilized about what he was two seconds away from asking her to do.

"Yes?"

"I hate to ask, but would you be willing to stay behind while we get the others to town? I'll come back for you just as fast as I can. It'll get dark, though, I'm afraid. But I just don't see any other way." He shut his mouth. It wasn't necessary to say more.

She didn't say anything. Not at first, at least. More than any female he'd ever met, she seemed the sort to measure her words, weigh them out before letting them fly. A peculiar trait. He should know, having grown up with five gabby sisters.

Finally, she gave a little nod. It was all the answer Jesse had time for.

He and Griff worked to help the driver and Mrs. Thompson onto the horses. Griff led the way, Mrs. Thompson hanging on as if for dear life. Jesse followed, keeping one arm secure around the driver, who, in his pained state, had no qualms about lolling his head back on Jesse's chest.

They moved down the road.

And, for some reason he couldn't explain, Jesse turned and watched the young woman standing beside the abandoned stagecoach for as long as he possibly could. Until she became no more than a speck, finally fading altogether from view.

No doubt she was scared. Though she needn't be.

A Texas Ranger came back for those he left behind. Always.

CHAPTER 3

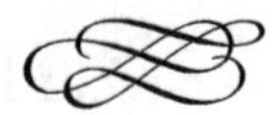

The Ranger had told Sara to wait, that he'd come back for her.

She'd done so for the past two hours. Waited and tried not to think about the twist of worry tightening through her as darkness shrouded the sky.

Worry. Fear. Anxiety. Companions all too familiar in the eighteen years she'd dwelt upon this earth. Why should a reoccurrence of the same occasion more than a twinge? Nothing worse could happen to her than what had already happened.

But it did not comfort.

She'd kept busy, piling the mail, putting everything back into Mrs. Thompson's trunk. Fortunate woman. She'd only lost a few valuables. Whereas Sara...

There was no way to put it gently. She'd lost every cent of the money she needed. Money set aside to rescue Lacey, Dalia, and Addie. No doubt the robbers were smart enough to have discovered she'd sewn it into the lining. Men with such morals were clever at things like that.

Swelling anger rose within her, trumping fear for the moment.

Anger at a world where vicious men committed vicious crimes. Murdered, and thieved coins, valuables.

And the innocence of little girls too young to fight them off. Too powerless to do anything but try to survive. Forget.

A knot worked its way into her throat, but she chalked it up to having not consumed enough liquids, though the Ranger had left his canteen with her.

Because she didn't cry over what had happened in her past. Once, a few weeks after arriving at the Lawsons, she'd wept a little. But the tears had burned too raw, hurt too much. They hadn't been able to bring Lacey, Dalia, and Addie to her side. Hadn't given her back the innocence stolen from her by the depravity of lustful men.

She hadn't cried again.

Somewhere, a bird made an eerie hooting sound. She squinted in the darkness, trying to make herself as small as possible hunched against the wheel of the stagecoach. If only she had her pistol. But the robbers had taken that, too, leaving her woefully unarmed against attack, either by man or by animal.

Was the Ranger still coming? Not that he was anyone she could trust, but at least he could help her get back to civilization. If he didn't do something worse to her first.

His was an imposing face. Hard. All planes and angles. Sharp eyes that missed nothing. The scruff of a beard in shades of golden brown darkening his strong jaw. Sinew and muscle rippling beneath that loose greatcoat—one that opened enough to reveal the pistols at his belt.

Rangers. A powerful lot. Men who shot first and asked questions later. Who defended law and order, at any cost. Men who could see themselves through any situation, capture any criminal.

One couldn't trust what such a man would do next. Even in such a simple matter as coming back for her. He might've found some other lawbreaker to chase and forgotten all about the young woman he'd left by the side of the road.

She tucked her lower lip between her teeth to keep a yawn from escaping. At least thoughts of him had diverted her from dwelling on the darkness of the night.

Fatigue weighted down her eyelids. Mercy, it had been a wearisome few days. From yesterday morning, leaving Waco and embarking on the stage. The long hours being bumped and jostled. One wouldn't think that just sitting could give one an exhaustion that drove straight to the bones. But it was true.

Her head drooped, resting against her knees.

She'd not sleep. It wouldn't be wise to give herself that luxury, alone and in the dark.

Just rest.

For a moment only, she'd rest.

~

He was no stranger to the dark. Even if it sometimes seemed to wrap him in a cloying black shroud. And his horse was smarter than most. Could find the way, even without Jesse's help.

Night sounds enveloped him as he rode in the direction of the abandoned stagecoach and the waiting woman. The rustle of an animal. The mournful hooting of an owl. The wind's whoosh and whisper. Mostly, the silence. A friend and an enemy on a night like this.

It had been quite the afternoon. Riding back to Hartville. Seeing the driver to Doc Hart's office while Griff made arrangements for Mrs. Thompson, who, come to find out, had actually been traveling to that very town to stay with relatives. Jesse doubted the woman had so much as paused for breath during the entire ride. So much chatter, his ears stung from it.

Leaving Griff to make a report to Captain Sterling, Jesse had set off again. And was almost there, by his reckoning.

What sort of state would he find a woman left alone for hours on a deserted road, beside a pillaged stagecoach, with dark creeping fast overhead? Had it been Mrs. Thompson or one of his sisters, she'd either be fuming mad or fainted from terror. He sensed, however, that Miss Byrne was made of different stuff.

He was about to find out. Even in the darkness, he made out the hulking form of the stagecoach. He dismounted, moving with the quiet stealth that was a Texas Ranger's trademark.

Beside the stage, huddled next to one wheel, sat Miss Byrne—from the looks of things, fast asleep.

There hadn't been much to smile about today, but one found its way onto his lips now. Imagine that. Alone, in danger, yet she'd fallen asleep. Either bravery or plumb foolishness would prompt such an action. Or possibly, flat-out exhaustion.

He crouched beside her. The stars, pinholes of bright in the ebony sky, illuminated her delicate features, chestnut curls wisping over her forehead, the sweep of long, dark lashes against her fair skin.

By Jim Dandy, that had been some idiotic thought.

"Miss?" He gave her shoulder a little shake.

No opening of the eyes, no mumbled reply, no indication at all that she'd heard him.

"Hey." He shook a bit harder. "Come on. We have to get going."

Still nothing.

All righty then. Short of using more force than was appropriate with a lady, or dumping cold water over her head, there was nothing more he could do.

A niggle of reluctance poked him, but he squashed it. Squashed it and hefted her into his arms. Such an action would have woken *him* up, but it didn't so much as faze her. She settled against his chest as he returned to Arion's side. Settled there in such a way, her curls tickling his cheek, her body all too warm and soft and feminine.

An unwelcome memory shoved its way to the forefront. Louella. Holding her. Cradling her, her blood wet against his shirt on that day born of perdition itself.

The day his world, his dreams had ended.

A black word sizzled from his lips and out onto the night.

Just as Miss Byrne opened her eyes and screamed.

One minute he was holding a woman lost in sweet sleep, the next, a wildcat thrashed in his arms. Her yells could've woken every corpse in every graveyard from here to Austin. She pummeled his chest with her fists, legs kicking. One of her boots made contact with his shoulder in a mighty whack. He grimaced and set her down faster than if he'd held a flaming firecracker.

Which he very well did.

She took three paces back and stood there, eyes large and full of horror, chest heaving with quick gulps of air. He watched her, mystified. What had made her react so? He hadn't been doing anything more than carrying her to his horse. Okay, perhaps she'd be justified in being a little scared. But the gal had been halfway to killing him and looked as if she still just might.

He should try for an explanation, but at a safe distance. Right now he didn't even want to think about getting her on a horse and riding all the way back to Hartville. Unless she somehow lost consciousness first.

"I tried to wake you. Twice. But you were out cold. My apologies if I scared you."

She regarded him, five feet and sundry inches of fire-breathing fury. But slowly, her breathing evened, her raised fists lowered. No more the peaceful girl who'd slept, but at least she'd graduated down from furious to just plain mad. Though he still couldn't cipher why he warranted displeasure of any sort.

"Why didn't you keep trying?" Her voice shook, but it was better than a scream.

He rubbed the back of his neck, a grin tugging on his lips. "You'd rather I'd dumped a bucket of cold water over your head? For one thing, we don't have any. For another, I didn't think a lady would appreciate the gesture. But I promise, here and now, to remember for next time."

"You think this is funny?" Her words issued from gritted teeth. Warning him that humor probably hadn't been the best approach.

Honesty, then. "No, but I think you overreacted. Not to mention, you ought to have tried to stay awake."

Her shoulders slumped, as if she'd fought enough and was weary of it. "Can we go now?"

"Yeah. We can." He mounted, then moved to assist her atop the horse, but she beat him to it, swinging up in a flurry of skirts and lace-trimmed petticoats. He took the reins and turned them in the direction of the road.

As they rode onward, she didn't—not once, no matter how bumpy the journey—put her arms around him for support.

What people did revealed a lot. What they didn't do told more.

And the fact that Miss Byrne preferred the risk of falling from the horse's back to touching him told him something more lay beneath the angry surface of her reaction.

Something that went deep.

Something darker than the night around them.

CHAPTER 4

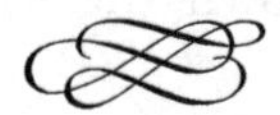

They arrived in Hartville later that night. The Ranger—Mr. Rawlings—saw her to a place called the Hartville Hotel. She slept, which was surprising considering the multitude of thoughts clamoring for precedence in her mind, and awoke the next morning to sunshine streaming through the window.

Though goodness knew there was little sunny about her circumstances.

The instant that thought filled her mind, her conscience chastened her.

Forgive me, Papa God. I have much to be thankful for.

She ate a hurried breakfast, scarcely taking time to savor the delicious meal of scrambled eggs, cornbread, and fried potatoes seasoned with spices. Finding Mr. Rawlings was more important than lingering over her food.

Letting the hotel door swing shut behind her, she stood in front of the building. A wagon drove past, some youngsters in the back, a couple up front. A fashionably dressed woman of late middle-age twirled a parasol that looked ridiculously out of place for the early-morning hour. She cast a curious glance in Sara's direction before turning her attention to the portly, suit-dressed man at her side.

All very interesting sights, to be sure, but how ought she go about finding Mr. Rawlings?

A young man with the garb of one straight off the ranch—blue shirt, brown vest, hair the unique color of freshly ground cinnamon, stopped his stride down the street and grinned an easy smile.

"Something I can help you with, ma'am?"

She forced an answering smile on her lips. It was broad daylight, and the young man looked friendly, not threatening. "I'm looking for Mr. Jesse Rawlings. Do you know where I might find him?"

The grin widened across his freckled face. "You're in luck, because, as a matter of fact, I do."

She inclined a brow, waiting.

"He's down at my pa's clinic. I can take you there myself, if you don't mind the walk."

A nod as her answer, she fell into step beside him as they moved down the street. They didn't move quite as fast as she'd have wanted, though. Everyone had a wave or a howdy for the young man, several making inquiries about a variety of people with the last name of Hart. All of which he answered with a friendly reply, a nod and grin to the young ladies—many of which seemed to want to linger in conversation.

Was everyone in this town so friendly?

A sudden wave of homesickness for Waco and the Lawsons filled her. Not that the people there had shown this degree of amiability, but it had been the closest thing to home she'd ever had. The Lawsons had made it so, with their loving warmth, their kindness.

Oh how her heart ached with missing them.

"Sorry for not introducing myself proper-like. Ma would say

that's rude of me." The young man's words returned her to the present. "I'm Robbie Hart."

One of the Harts. That, at least, explained why everyone asked him about them. There seemed to be quite the multitude of that particular family. Of course, since the town was probably named after them, that wasn't surprising.

"Pleasure to meet you, Robbie Hart. I'm Sara Byrne."

"Nice to meet you, too, Miss Byrne." They'd stopped beside a tiny wood-sided building with an OPEN sign on the door.

WILLIAM TRAVIS HART, M.D., read the neatly painted shingle hanging above.

"Well, this is it. You'll find Jesse inside. And now that you're here, I'd best get on with my errands, so's I can get back to the ranch in time for lunch."

"Thank you for helping me find my way." Her smile came easier now, less forced.

"Happy to be of service, ma'am." With a jaunty nod, Robbie Hart turned and strode down the street, whistling as he went.

The bell above the entrance jangled as she stepped in. Male voices emerged from a half-open door in the back. Deeming it best to wait until someone emerged, Sara seated herself on one of the chairs, the familiar scents of soap mingling with the pungent aroma of herbal remedies, smells she recognized well from her days helping Matthias at his office. How she'd enjoyed tidying the clinic, sweeping the floors, washing the windows. Poking her nose into one of his anatomy textbooks or peering into the cabinet where he kept his tinctures and salves.

There had been such peace there, worlds away from the horrors of San Antonio.

Which was why she must do everything in her power to return. For the girls' sake.

Footsteps sounded. Two men stepped into the front room—

Mr. Rawlings and a man who looked to be William Travis Hart, M.D., based on the bandage roll in his hand.

"Miss Byrne." While the doctor seemed at ease in the small waiting room, the Texas Ranger looked much too large for the space. He held a Stetson in one hand and wore a similar set of clothes to what he'd had on yesterday. She didn't much care for his charcoal greatcoat. It looked far too much like the garb of a gunslinger, a breed of man she'd had the ill fortune of meeting a time or two.

"I'm glad I found you, Mr. Rawlings." Her tongue suddenly felt too large for her mouth. Or perhaps it was simply fear over what she intended to tell him. "May I have a word?"

"'Course," Mr. Rawlings replied. "Thanks for all you did for Mr. Paige, Doc."

"Anytime, Jesse." The doctor gave a smile that matched his son's in friendly ease. "Ma'am." He nodded in her direction, brown eyes kind.

Mr. Rawlings held the door for her to exit and closed it behind them. The sun held full sway over the horizon, heralding another day of blistering heat. Somewhere, a school bell rang, signaling woe to every youngster who longed for the great outdoors instead of their desk.

If only her own childhood had been that simple.

"I was coming over to the hotel to find you, soon as I finished talking to the driver. I asked him some questions about what happened yesterday, the little he could remember, anyway. His leg will pull through fine, in case you were worried."

She hadn't really thought of him, unfortunately, though she'd fretted over Matthias's patients often enough.

"I'm glad to hear it. What was it you were coming to see me about?"

"To make sure you were all right. See what you planned to do now. If there was anything I could do to help before I leave in a couple of hours."

"Where are you going?" She hoped against hope he was heading after the men who'd robbed the stagecoach. She'd rather state her case to him than to some other Ranger.

"To track down the guys who robbed the stage. Griff's already on the trail. So I'll be leaving just as soon as I grab some stuff and get my horse."

She raised her chin. "I'm glad to hear it." Drawing in a deep breath, she loosed a silent prayer. "I'd like to come with you."

"You what?" His eyebrows rose sky high.

"I want to come with you. That way, the sooner we find those men, the sooner I can reclaim what's mine and be on my way to San Antonio. You see, they took my carpetbag to carry away some of the things they stole. What they didn't know is that inside the carpetbag is over two hundred dollars. The way I figure, if I go with you, I can get the money as soon as you arrest the men."

"No." A whole lot of unsaid words went into that single one. None of which Sara wanted to hear. Nor would accept.

"Why not?"

"I'd think that would be obvious. I'm a Ranger, going out to do a Ranger's job. Regular people, especially ladies, don't just come along for the ride." The look in his eyes declared he thought what he said made perfect sense, and wasn't to be meddled with.

Perhaps this man's word had always been obeyed without question.

But that was before he'd met her. She wasn't about to give up without a fight.

"I'm not *regular people*. I was there when the robbery took place. I know what the men look like and could spot them on sight. I can be of help."

He heaved a long-suffering sigh. "I already know what they look like. I've seen most of 'em plastered all over the place on

WANTED posters. Besides, I'd have to ask my superior officer. He gives our orders. And I'm sure he'd have a heap to say about one of us traveling with a lady like yourself."

Lady like yourself. The words burned through her. He hadn't meant them that way, of course. He didn't know her, couldn't know her past. All he'd meant was that she was of the feminine persuasion. But they still felt like a label. Like the fallen woman she'd been, would always be.

The mere fact that she was having this conversation ought to have made her question her sanity. She, a woman who had sworn off all voluntary contact with men, was offering to travel with one, alone, across Texas. If Mr. Rawlings thought it absurd, well, so did she. Though not for the same reasons. But she needed that money to live on. And to keep her promise.

Even if it meant a few days of discomfort on her part, it would be worth it. The moment she hugged Lacey, Dalia, and Addie again, everything would be worth it.

"Then ask him. Or better yet, let me ask your superior." Surely, if she couldn't make this hardheaded Ranger see her way of things, she could convince someone else. Could she not?

"You'd be wasting your time." He rubbed his hand across the back of his neck, like an animal itching to be free of its trap. Or in Mr. Rawlings's case, a disagreeable conversation.

It wasn't working out how she'd thought it would. Desperation wove its way through her, knotting the threads of her confidence, of the bravado that had gotten her onto the stagecoach in Waco and given her the strength to ask a favor from a man like this one.

"I need the money. It's my whole livelihood. Without it, I'm destitute. And...and there are people besides myself counting on it even more." Perhaps tears would move this Ranger's heart? But she wouldn't force any, even if she possessed the ability to do so. Crying wasn't for her, even if desperate times called for equally desperate measures.

The urgency of her tone seemed to soften the flint of his resolve. His moss-green eyes radiated a trace of...could it be... understanding?

"You say you've got family depending on you?"

"In a manner of speaking." No need to elaborate on that. There were some ties that bonded tighter than blood.

A touch of regret filtered through his gaze. "I still can't let you, miss. I'm sorry."

Her mind scrabbled for a solution. A rational one that this ox of a man couldn't refute.

Think, Sara.

She crossed her arms over her chest. "All right, so you can't let me ride with you.But there's no law about me following behind, providing I can keep up."

He chuckled, low, the sound almost of admiration that a woman would have so much gumption. "You ain't gonna give up, are you?"

She shook her head, doing her level best to keep all traces of eagerness from her eyes.

"Tracking a gang of outlaws is dangerous. And I won't be held responsible if something happens. When I'm on the job, the job comes first. Even before you." His tone was level, honest. A trait to appreciate in a man, honesty. "And it ain't easy. It'll be long days, short nights, stopping only for the horses. You'll need one, by the way. A horse. Provisions for the journey."

All things that cost money she didn't have. A sigh fell from her lips. There was nothing to do about that. She didn't have the money, nor did she have time to earn it before he left.

The faces of the girls she'd promised to come back for echoed through her memory.

How could she sleep again at night knowing she'd failed them? Knowing that, while she was free, they still remained prisoners?

Before today, she'd never asked anything of anyone—especially not a man. The Lawsons had given without her even needing to ask.

Asking put one under obligation. Something she did not, ever, want to be when a man was involved. Men, even ones that seemed honorable like Robbie Hart or Jesse Rawlings, were all the same deep down. Matthias had been different. But she'd been like a daughter to him. This Ranger could not only overpower criminals—he could take advantage of her. Easily.

She regarded him—six feet of raw maleness, a Stetson on his head, pistols at his belt, powerful enough to control her. A shiver prickled her spine. He studied her in return, as if witnessing the debate inside her mind.

Her inhale seemed to choke her. "To lay hold of the items you mentioned, I'll need cash. At present, I don't have any. Would you consider a loan?" She swallowed, trying to moisten her dry throat. If he dared make one mention of collateral, she'd forget the whole thing and run. After she let him feel the full impact of her fist.

An eternity passed before he nodded, slow. "I reckon so. Seeing as it was the Markham Gang that stole from you."

"Thank you." For an instant, she lifted her gaze heavenward.

Papa God, don't let this be a mistake. Please.

~

If he'd the sense the Good Lord gave a pump handle, Jesse would've let a resounding *no* be the end of his conversation with Miss Byrne. Instead, he'd let himself listen, really listen. Absorb the desperation in her words. Wonder the true meaning behind why she'd set herself so on coming with him. Now he was stuck like a fly in a trap, taking a woman on a journey suited only to men.

What a dad-gummed idiot he was.

Jesse shifted, standing in front of the livery where she'd promised to meet him when she finished getting ready.

She'd got her kit together remarkably fast, though she'd used his dime to do it. Blame it on his mama, teaching him how to treat a lady, giving to her if she had a need. Not that he was concerned about the money. She could've spent more, for all he cared. But the whole notion of her coming along stuck him like a burr under a bobcat's tail.

Probably that's why he and Branch Kilborn—second-in-command to Captain Sterling, and Jesse's close friend—got on so well. Women were best avoided, the plague to be preferred above romance. Good ole Branch. What would he do if faced with Jesse's current situation?

Footsteps came up behind him—hers. Soft, yet determined. Yep. Hers, all right. He didn't even have to look.

"You all set?" He turned.

Stared. And kept on staring.

What in tarnation did she have on?

Oh, he knew what she was wearing, all right. He'd seen it on countless bodies before. Male ones.

Yes, indeed. Sara Byrne stood in front of him wearing... trousers. Though where in the blazes she'd managed to find a pair that fit her tiny waist, he wasn't sure. A cream-colored shirt tucked into the waistband, a felt hat atop her head. She looked like a lady ranch hand.

She looked—his throat went dry—well, there was good reason ladies didn't wear trousers. These showed off her slim waist and curvy hips in a way no dress could ever do.

He yanked his gaze away.

"What?" Her petite nose scrunched. "These aren't appropriate?"

"Yeah. They're fine." Actually, quite a smart idea. Her saddle was small, but it wasn't a ladies' version. And dresses always got in the way whenever his sisters rode.

"Good." She looked relieved.

"I'm gonna head out now, so whenever you're ready, you can follow behind me." He moved to head into the stable, but she blocked his path.

"There's just one more thing." Shaded by the hat, a flicker of telltale determination lit her eyes, turning them a deeper shade of lake blue.

Jesse toed his boot through the dirt, waiting for her to speak her piece. They needed to get going. He'd promised to meet up with Griff, and every second wasted was a precious, needed one.

She didn't say anything.

Impatience ate at him. "Go ahead."

What he expected her to say, he wasn't sure. What he didn't expect was for her to pull a revolver from her saddlebag with lightning speed and hold it, business end aimed at the ground, in his line of vision.

His pulse leapt. "What are you doing with that?" Mama would *not* have approved of the tone he used to issue those words.

She didn't flinch. In fact, the flint of determination only sparked sharper in her eyes. He'd seen men wear that look before but never a lady. It was a look that said they meant business, were not to be trifled with, and knew the power of the weapon they held and their skill in using it. The look the kind of men wore that he and the other Rangers were famous for dealing with.

A look that seemed at variance on the face of a gentle lady.

"You know what this is, Ranger?" An outsider might not have noticed it, but he caught a hint of a waver in her voice.

"A Colt double action revolver."

A curt nod. "Right. I'm good with using it. Had one just like it in my carpetbag. I've had practice. Enough to spill your guts from here to New York State if you so much as lay a finger on me without my permission. Understood?"

His throat worked in a swallow. He wasn't afraid of her. Even if she were a good shot, which hadn't yet been determined. He'd outgunned many good shots, and the Markham Gang would soon be added to that number, if he had his way. No, her skill didn't worry him a bit. It was the motive behind it, the reason she felt the need to glare at him with a deadly mixture of fire and ice in those stormy eyes.

"I didn't hear you. Understood, Ranger?"

A small number of female outlaws, as well as male ones, populated the West, including one in the Markham Gang. Miss Byrne had too much of an air of gentility about her to be an outlaw. Yet she had been...something. Something that had put fear inside of her, enough to make her lash out at him that night on the road and now today.

Until he learned the truth, he'd do his best to tread carefully.

If he ever learned the truth. Which he probably wouldn't. The second Miss Byrne had her money in hand, he'd have no reason to cross paths with her again.

Something to look forward to. Pistol-toting women in trousers weren't exactly his idea of pleasant companions.

"I understand. And I'd appreciate it if you'd call me either Jesse or Rawlings. Not 'Ranger.' Not in that tone." He leveled her gaze with a hard stare of his own.

She gave a nod, secreting the gun in a holster at her belt. "All right, then." Some of the steel left her eyes. Standing there in the yard of the livery stable, dressed in those absurd trousers, she looked suddenly...fragile. The way one of his sisters did when they were scared of something. Sadie always wore that look before school recitals. Joy Ellen whenever she had to go to the doctor.

And he, without fail, always drew them close, as if, by his touch, he could face down whatever enemies thwarted them.

His chest tightened. Why did looking at Sara Byrne make him, strangely, suddenly, want to do the same? It shouldn't.

But it did.

CHAPTER 5

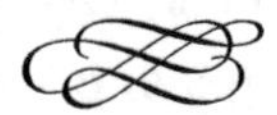

I will not complain. I will not complain.

Not that she could complain to anyone in particular, seeing as Jesse rode several yards ahead and there was no one else in sight. But at that moment, she certainly wanted to. The sun's rays were a whip upon her back, hot and beating down. Her backside throbbed from the hours of riding without stops. Though she'd gulped down half of a canteen, her throat cried out for water.

Only by keeping Lacey's face foremost in her mind could she find the determination to firm her jaw and keep going.

She kept her focus fixed on the horse ahead and Jesse's broad back. Her own mount did her level best to keep a canter, as weary as Sara.

Surely, the heat of the day should have passed by late afternoon.

Best think of something other than heat. Or her muscles. Or her thirst.

The day she'd met the Lawsons, then. She'd managed to stow away in the back of a farmer's wagon from San Antonio to Waco.

The long hours of jostling, hidden under burlap, pressed against crates of vegetables, had seemed like paradise compared to what she was leaving. She'd snuck off whenever he stopped, to relieve her aching bladder and eat and drink whatever she could find—mostly nothing. Then she'd climb back on, mercifully undetected. Once in Waco, she hopped off a final time. For three long days, she wandered the streets. Oh, the misery of those days. Nothing to eat, save the scraps she scrounged from the garbage pile of a saloon. Scarcely seventeen and without any skills but one.

Matthias—Dr. Lawson—had come upon her and brought her home in a gesture of kindness she could never hope to repay. God had sent him down that street on that day. Hours before he'd died, he told her so. She hadn't needed to be told, though. She already knew.

The sun seemed warmer and less boiling. She drank in a breath of sweet-smelling air.

Something moved on the path, like a coiled rope come to life. A snake. Her horse reared upward, surging and twisting. Sara scrambled for a hold, clinging to the saddle.

But she couldn't grasp it. In the next instant, she was flying. Suspended in midair before her body met ground, the breath whooshing from her lungs.

Dust clogged her throat. She coughed.

She had to get up.

Her vision swam, turning one image into two. She blinked, trying to force the dizziness away. The blurry form of her horse, lying like a felled log several feet away.

Through the haze, she made out Jesse, still riding. He hadn't seen.

He would ride away and leave her.

The snake slithered. Toward her.

A chokehold of fear added to the dust in her mouth. She

screamed. Her "help!" didn't emerge very loud, vocal cords as frozen as her limbs.

But it was enough. Jesse turned his horse around and cantered toward her, hoofbeats pounding, his body tall and controlled in the saddle. The way a fairy tale hero rushed to the rescue of his fair damsel… Oh, she must've hit her head hard to have such a thought.

He dismounted, and in a fluid motion, whipped a knife from his belt. It soared in an arc of silver, piercing the snake in milliseconds.

Gracious, that must've taken practice.

In the next instant, he raced toward her. Dropped to his knees at her side.

She looked up at him, into his worry-lined face, into the mossy swirls of his eyes. For some ridiculous reason, a hazy smile turned up her lips.

"Are you okay?" He reached out a hand, as if to probe for injuries, but stopped, fingers midair.

No doubt, remembering the promise she'd made him give. Not that she'd have shot him over helping her to her feet, but the fact that he remembered—and honored it—sent a measure of something through her heart. Something she just as quickly tamped down and stomped on. Something far too dangerous to feel.

Trust.

Though her lower back screamed with the effort, she pushed herself into a sitting position, a lovely grimace, no doubt, contorting her face.

"I'm fine…mostly. One minute we were riding along. Then… the snake…and the horse reared. I flew off." Couldn't she stop rambling? Not one word of her explanation sounded very intelligent. "Maybe you'd better go see if she's all right." Sara motioned weakly to where the animal lay in the middle of the road, whinnies panicked as she attempted to rise.

He stood, then strode through the dust until he reached the animal's side. Pulling her hat from her head, Sara ran her hand through her sweat-dampened hair and repositioned a few hairpins, while Jesse examined the horse. As he did so, his forehead furrowed, eyebrows knitting together.

Since she'd have to stand sometime, she might as well go see what the matter was. The act of rising to her feet wasn't as painful as she'd thought it would be. At least, she wasn't as injured as she could've been, though there'd be bruises aplenty come tomorrow.

Thank You for keeping me safe, Papa God.

"What's wrong?" A gust of wind washed over her face in a swoosh of blessed cool.

He looked up at her, ran his hand over his bearded jaw. A breath blew from his lips.

"Shattered foreleg. Poor girl." He nudged his fingers across the horse's quivering forelock.

"Can anything be done?" She bit her lower lip, cracked from the dryness and the dust.

He looked away, fast. Shook his head, a slump to his broad shoulders. "I'm...I'm gonna have to shoot her, Sara. It's the merciful thing to do. It's broken too bad to be mended, even if we'd the time, or a way to get her to shelter."

She blinked, the moisture in her eyes no doubt caused by the heat, a speck of grit. "All right."

"I want you to go and stand beside Arion."

She turned and did as he bid. Busied herself with pulling a canteen from his saddlebag. Overhead, a few clouds scattered the sky, mounds of fluffy white. If one could reach and touch them, they'd surely be softer than eiderdown. Soft enough for a good, long nap...

Take a drink. Stay distracted. Don't think.

A single shot rang out.

She winced, squeezing her eyes shut. Pressed her cheek against Arion's side, rubbing circles along his silken black coat.

Then silence. A silence much too loud, all too full.

Footsteps. Jesse came toward her, greatcoat over one arm, his Stetson pulled low.

"It's over." She'd expected a tougher-than-rawhide Texas Ranger to be unfazed by the loss of a mere animal. Yet the weariness on his face and lines around his eyes said the opposite.

"I'm sorry," she whispered. "It's my fault."

He shook his head. "Don't talk foolishness."

"What do we do now?" For an instant, she feared he'd take her back to Hartville. After all, she no longer had a mount. She stared off into the distance, not wanting to look at him when he told her to leave. In a single day—hours, actually—she'd already cost him the expense for her traveling gear, and now a horse.

"Well, for starters, you'll be riding with me, not behind me. If you've a problem with that, I suggest you start walking thataway." He jerked his finger in the direction they'd come.

"No." She shook her head. "I don't have a problem with that."

"Riding with me will mean putting yourself in even more danger."

"I'm not afraid. Not with my revolver." *And God*, she almost added but didn't. She didn't know this man's views on faith and wasn't about to bring up such a touchy subject today.

"If you say so. It's good to be afraid, though, a little." He rubbed his hand near Arion's nose. The horse sniffed his palm and whickered, as if expecting some treat. "Keeps you sharp. It's plumb stupidity to be entirely without fear. But I won't argue with you."

"Why? Don't you Texas Rangers like a good debate?" Though foolish, considering all that had just happened, a tiny smile begged to show itself on her lips.

"Sometimes." He smiled back, the tension in his face loosening. A handsome smile, on a handsome, sun-browned face. But an easy one, as if he was used to smiling often, and enjoyed doing so.

And she was an unimaginably stupid woman for noticing any of this.

"But not tonight. We'll go on a little farther, away from...her." Sara didn't need to look to know he gestured toward the fallen horse. "Then we'll make camp. Think you can help build a fire and cook something for supper?"

She gave a nod, wanting to appear confident when she was anything but. She knew how to cook—quite well, in fact—but over a fire? Still, she'd do her best.

Overhead, the sky turned purple and gray, the sun loosed from its stifling hold at last, leaving lukewarm air in its place. Falling dusk with night fast on its heels.

A night she'd spend out in the open, exposing herself to all sorts of dangers.

She darted a glance at Jesse, the thought coming unbidden...

Not least of which were human ones.

~

She couldn't have scooted that blanket any farther away from the dwindling coals—and him—even if she'd wanted to.

Adjusting his bedroll, Jesse blew out a sigh. Why in the blazes did Sara Byrne persist on being so wary? Hadn't he already proven himself, keeping his bargain and not touching her, even to offer a hand up when she lay sprawled on the trail? For a few minutes, she'd seemed to relax. Teased him, almost, asking if he enjoyed a good debate. She'd fixed supper, beans and salt pork, managing only to partially burn the meal. She hadn't spoken much as they cleaned their tin plates, quenched their thirst from the canteens.

Seemed almost chary, in a way, sneaking glances at him, as if he'd bite her. Like a scared colt.

Or a sparrow.

Fear ye not therefore, ye are of more value than many sparrows.

The Scripture verse from Matthew 10:31 sunk into him, deep. Fear seemed to be a constant companion of hers. He could sense it as surely as he knew how fresh a track was or whether someone spoke truth.

One didn't acquire that kind of fear without life—people—teaching it to them. Sara Byrne's past ought not to have occupied this much of his thoughts. But it did. In a way he'd not wondered about another soul, he wondered about her.

Lord, show me. If this is just me being curious, help me to stop. But if this is from You, lead me as to what I ought to do.

She'd wrapped herself in her bedroll until only the top of her head peeked out. He lay down, rolling onto his side, and pulled the blanket around him. Insects chirped. Few stars shone overhead tonight, the moon naught but a thumbnail in the sky. The fire glowed, only embers now.

"You gonna be all right?" he called, loud enough for her to hear, miles away as she was. A prick of worry jabbed him, along with a twig poking through his bedroll. Would he be able to hear, sense, if something happened?

He'd rest a mite easier if she lay closer. But he wouldn't ask it. Not after she'd acted so skittish toward him.

She didn't answer. His pulse sped. Was she already asleep? Or lying motionless with terror while staring into the face of some animal?

He should just go to sleep and forget about worrying. Leave her alone, since that's what she wanted.

"Answer me if you're all right. If you don't, I'm gonna come over." He spoke louder this time, his frustration mounting.

A huff. "I heard you the first time. And I'm fine."

Dad-blamed woman. She'd no right to sound miffed. Didn't she realize the dangers that existed out here? Didn't she know he was only trying to keep watch over her?

Or did she fear him more than she feared whatever lay out in the wilds?

He hoped not.

"You answer me next time, when I call you. All right?" He wanted to punch himself. That had sounded much too dictatorial, like a commanding officer ordering his men. Not a gentleman speaking to a lady.

Since when had he thought of himself as a gentleman in regards to ladies? Consciously, not in a long time. Approximately how long?

Since Louella.

He slammed the door closed on those thoughts, her name. Not tonight. He couldn't take thinking of her tonight.

"All right." Her voice floated across to him, all too feminine despite the revolver she carried and the trousers she dressed herself in.

"Good night," he called in reply.

She didn't answer.

But then, he hadn't expected her to.

CHAPTER 6

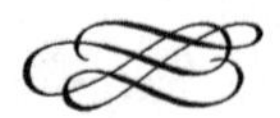

Hours passed by, marked only by the varying countryside. The ceaseless, rhythmic movements of the horse. The heat—so harsh and sticky—making her shirt cling to her back, her body long for a dunk into a lake. Dust and scrubby trees. Hills.

Jesse. Sitting behind her, his chest brushing her back, his thighs bumping hers.

Her pragmatic side forced her to accept that one couldn't ride double on a horse and continue to avoid all physical contact. Yet the scared little girl buried beneath layers of reality had huddled into a ball, struggled, screamed for the first few hours, every time she'd felt Jesse's hand against her waist.

Calm had permeated somewhat as early morning bled into afternoon. Perhaps the heat lulled her into numbness. Or perhaps...she'd begun to realize, to distinguish Jesse from the men at the brothel. Transfer him from that part of her brain to the space Matthias had occupied. That of safety. A measure of trust.

Her head itched beneath the broad-brimmed hat. No doubt about it—she smelled worse than a wet dog. What she wouldn't give for a refreshing bath and a break from being glued to the back of a horse.

Soon. Soon those crisp bills would press her fingers again. Soon she'd see the girls...free them. Together, they'd go someplace safe, where no man could harm them, where they'd rely on each other and the Good Lord's provision.

Ah, the promise of that *soon*.

"That'll be Griff." The low rumble of Jesse's voice thrummed through her. Made her look up and make out with a squint the speck of a rider in the distance, heading their way.

"Who?"

"Griff Sommer. We'll be going on together. Safer that way."

Another man. One that couldn't be given the trust she'd begun to allow Jesse. She'd seen him briefly, after the stagecoach robbery, but hadn't paid him much heed. A big man, like Jesse. Big men overpowered, brutalized. Big men broke spirits, wills. Big men thought only of themselves and their depraved pleasures.

Her throat closed tight. She had her revolver, after all. Helplessness shouldn't dog her, not with her own weapon. But fears formed in childhood were not easily reasoned against. Like a pair of hands that had clutched around an object for an eternity, it took effort to pry them away.

Help me not to fear if there's no cause for it. Give me wisdom. It seems nothing about this journey is meant to be easy.

The horse and rider came closer. When they were within a few feet, the two men dismounted. Sara fingered the reins, unwilling to move from her spot, even if she did long to stretch her legs.

"Figured we'd be catching up with you today." Friendly ease saturated Jesse's tone and smile. Proof that he trusted his fellow Ranger. Not that such knowledge would make her do the same. Men could be brilliant in their career, charming with their friends, yet blacker than soot when it came to their character.

Griff nodded. But he didn't answer. Instead, his gaze swung in her direction. His eyes narrowed. With confusion. And disapproval.

"Miss Byrne?" He had an incomparable memory to have remembered her, especially as she looked now, a dusty lady cowgirl. Yet the question, coupled with her name, told her he doubted her identity and wondered why she was sitting atop Jesse's horse.

"Mr. Sommer." She gave a nod, the leather reins biting into her skin.

"Miss Byrne is after a large sum of money that was sewn into the lining of her carpetbag. She was supposed to ride behind me, but a few hours after we headed out, her horse had an accident, and we had to put her down." Jesse's tone was matter-of-fact. As if he'd accepted her joining him and no longer questioned it. The realization would have made her grateful, if not for the addition of this third party.

"I see." Griff looked as if the only thing he saw was the urge to send her back to Hartville. "Can I talk to you for a minute, Jesse?"

Jesse nodded and followed Griff a distance away. Though Sara couldn't make out the words they spoke, the gist of their conversation was clear. Griff was none too happy about her presence, and he had no qualms about telling Jesse so. They spoke for several minutes—two men standing in the middle of an empty road, debating their course of action without giving her, the reason for their caucus, the least particle of say.

It was a situation all too familiar. Men had decided her life since the day of her mother's death and continued to decide it until the day in her seventeenth year when she'd taken her future into her own hands and risked everything by escape. Not that she'd had much to risk. Death would have been better than continued existence at the brothel.

She shifted, mounting pressure forcing her off the horse's back. Best head behind that yonder tree before the men finished their argument and returned. Lengthening her strides and stretching her aching muscles, she reached her destination.

By the time she returned, the two men stood near the horses. Both wore expressions of grim resignation. Sara ignored them and reached for her canteen. With the gazes of both upon her, she gulped the drink, droplets trickling down her chin. She wiped her mouth with the back of her hand, and returned the canteen to Jesse's saddlebag.

"You ready?" Jesse's voice.

Ready to return to Hartville? Not until she had what was hers. These Rangers may have never tangled with a woman who made mules look tractable, but they were about to.

"It should take us a few hours to reach Calvert's Creek. Griff says he saw suspicious tracks heading that way."

So they weren't going to send one of them with her back to civilization? The mental fists she'd raised and clenched lowered. They'd ride to Calvert's Creek, where the Markham Gang might be even now. Tonight might lead to their discovery. The law and order of the Texas Rangers would prevail.

"I'm ready." She swung atop Arion, ignoring the protests of her bruised backside. These men would have no cause to complain about her. Griff watched her, and the look in his eyes was not entirely convinced. Jesse must have said something, spoken up in her defense.

Not that the nature of their conversation, or Jesse's words, ought to interest her in the least.

Calvert's Creek lay ahead of them.

And the sooner her life no longer intertwined with these Texas lawmen, the better.

~

"*What will Captain Sterling say when he finds out you've taken a lady along on a job she has no business being a part of? You've been spending hours together. Alone. And not only that, we're tracking the Markham Gang! Doesn't that concern you?"*

"This isn't a tea party. Miss Byrne knows full well what she's gotten herself into. She's armed. And she's agreed to the risks."

Finally, after neither making progress in turning the other's mind to a point of view they both agreed with, Griff simply gave up and rode along in silence. Though the rift between them stung, Jesse wouldn't press it. They had a job to do. Griff knew that. Miss Byrne knew that.

The man had brought up a point, though. One that nagged at the back of his mind with the tenacity of a stubborn burr refusing to be plucked and tossed away.

Miss Byrne is a lady. You're a man. Things happen when members of the opposite sex are alone.

Griff should know, seeing as he'd so recently gone and lost his heart to Evelyn Prentis. Still, the notion had hit Jesse like a back-handed slap. The only thing he'd been thinking of in regard to Miss Byrne was her insistence on maintaining boundaries he'd never had any intention of breaching. He'd been the marrying kind, once. With Louella, he'd been that type of man gladly. After the suddenness of her death, he'd vowed never again to involve himself in a romantic relationship.

He'd been able to maintain that promise year after long year. The Texas Rangers had kept him busy enough, and during his time off, visits to his family and an occasional trip to see Louella's parents in Nevada made the days pass. Women were seen only in regards to his duty as a Ranger to protect the citizens of Texas. He'd once overheard a lovestruck female call Branch "permanently wedded to his job," after her attempts to cajole him into taking her to the barn dance had been spurned. Jesse thought the lady's statement something to be commended in a man, something he wanted for himself. Branch—smart man that he was—had wholeheartedly agreed.

And since Jesse had begun this trip with Miss Byrne two days ago, he'd ridden with her for hours without any measure of *anything*, save frustration at her stubborn nature.

But after Griff's words, he couldn't chase the developing awareness. The creamy expanse of the back of her neck, brown tendrils wisping against her skin. The soft curves of her waist and hips. How they brushed against him, an action unintended, yet all the more startling. Louella had been beautiful. Like a china doll, honey hair coiffed, blue-eyed, and pale-skinned. So beautiful she'd seemed almost like an alabaster statue, meant to be admired but not touched. He'd never done more than hold her hand, even after the announcement of their engagement.

Yet, since talking with Griff, he hadn't been able to stop staring at those renegade curls playing at the base of Sara's neck. How soft would they be, wrapped around his finger?

Riding at his side, Griff watched him. And undoubtedly knew that Jesse knew he did so. Texas Rangers were experts at sensing those subtle things.

What was Griff looking for? Jesse with his arms around Miss Byrne's waist? A flicker of something to prove his point? Some sign of weakness in Miss Byrne to confirm her unsuitability to be with them? He'd be disappointed on all counts. Miss Byrne had sat in stoic silence, a feat his sisters would never have been able to achieve for so long a stretch.

They'd reach Calvert's Creek by nightfall. He and Griff would scout around, after he installed Miss Byrne in a hotel. If her clothes felt as grimy as his, she'd be itching for a bath, even though they'd only spent one night under the stars.

"How you holding up?" He hadn't heard the sound of her voice in three hours, hence the question. Hoofbeats and Arion's snorts and the wind were fine sounds. But they could prove a tad monotonous.

"Fair enough." She glanced behind, treating him to the first glimpse of her face in what seemed like an unreasonably long time.

"Hungry?" At the hotel, he'd see to it she had a decent dinner, along with a room.

"Some."

Had she used up all of her words confronting him yesterday morning? Most females had an inexhaustible well. Hers seemed to have run dry. Was it Griff? She wasn't stupid. She had to know what they'd been talking about.

Something had to be done to defuse the tension before they reached Calvert's Creek.

"Think I'll sing for a while. There's no one around, and it'll help pass the time. Do you mind?" He had taken to, on occasion, regaling himself with a tune during solitary rides. But never had the urge struck him when in the company of his fellow Rangers or anyone else. A secret pastime, if ever he'd had one.

Griff raised a brow.

"I guess not." Miss Byrne sounded as if she didn't quite know what to think.

"Do you mind, Sommer?"

Griff shrugged. Jesse would take that as permission, then.

He started off with "Oh! Susanna," hoping to garner smiles. He probably sounded ridiculous, unaccompanied by an instrument, his voice what his mother had once kindly described as twangy. Arion carried them onward, the heat lifted its oppressive hand, and the tune filled the air with a carefree sound.

> I come from Alabama with my banjo on my knee—
> I'm goin' to Louisiana, my true love for to see.

It rained all night the day I left, the weather it
    was dry;
The sun so hot I froze to death—Susanna, don't
    you cry.

He finished the song and opened his mouth to launch into another.

"I liked that." Three words from Sara Byrne's lips shouldn't have this effect—making warmth fill him, a smile tug his lips. A cadre of emotions stampeded through him as her head turned and their gazes met. Beneath the brim of her hat, her eyes were twin seas of the palest blue.

An inanely poetic thought for a man anything but.

"Thank you," he answered.

"It was a happy sort of song." She gave a little smile. "I'd like to learn it."

"I'll teach it to you, then. We've nothing else to do." He started by repeating the first stanza, before they sang it together, their words blending, melding.

And there, riding along a dusty trail toward Calvert's Creek, he learned that a trousers-wearing, mule-stubborn woman could fill the air with an angelic voice. A sound that burrowed deep inside his mind in a way not soon forgotten.

CHAPTER 7

The rooming house at Calvert's Creek proved to be a modest establishment...and a dirty one. Enough to make Sara wish the stars had been her ceiling instead of the cracked and peeling boards. At least vermin had not dwelt inside her bedroll, as they had in the bed she'd spent last night in. She rubbed her arms and shivered, though sun streamed through the dining room's cracked windows.

The serving girl paused by the table to offer a coffee refill, a curl in her lip and an askance glance at Sara's garb of trousers, the revolver at her belt. Not that she could've changed into anything else, or would have simply to please the slovenly woman with faded calico and a greasy apron. Jesse had seen to her request of warm water, and she'd been able to wash the dust and perspiration from her skin with the bar of lavender-scented soap she'd brought. So at least she smelled some better.

Forking another bite of gravy-soaked biscuit, she chewed slowly. She had to, after all. The biscuit could've been used for target practice and the bullet would not have so much as dented the brick-hard pastry. Sara washed the piece down with a gulp of scalding, black-as-tar coffee, and stood. She was to meet Jesse and Griff in front of the rooming house in a few minutes. They'd most likely spent the night outside with the horses and risen early this morning to ask around town about the Markham Gang.

Sara slipped her hat atop her head the moment she stepped out of doors. Though the trousers revealed her feminine hips, the baggy shirt concealed the curves above. She'd never had many of those, anyway. And with the hat hiding her pinned-up hair and obscuring most of her face, any passerby would've never guessed her to be a female.

An anonymity to be thankful for.

She stood beneath the awning of the rooming house. An apron-wearing man swept the space in front of a building called Brody's Dry Goods. A sun-bonneted woman held the hands of two youngsters and ushered them through the doors of a building bearing a red-and-white striped pole.

Two men crossed the street. Instinctively, Sara took a step away. She waited for them to pass, but they stopped beside the rooming house. One of the men spat a stream of brownish saliva into the dust. The other man pulled off his hat and slapped it against the side of his leg.

Her heart kicked. The man carrying his hat angled his face her way, though he didn't appear to have seen her. Good. For if he hadn't seen, he wouldn't recognize. Though she recognized him as the squinty-eyed man who had hauled her and Mrs. Thompson from the stage and held them at gunpoint while his partner riffled through Mrs. Thompson's trunk.

A participant in Cass Markham's infamy—no doubt about it.

She stood, unable to force her legs into movement. What should she do? Griff and Jesse hadn't told her where they would be, only that they'd meet her in front of the rooming house. They should arrive any minute, could pull weapons on the man and discover the whereabouts of the rest.

She could almost taste the sweet victory of justice. The first real justice her life had ever known.

The men still stood, chawing tobacco and talking. Marshaling her every sense into listening to what they said, she made out the words "we'll head to Dinah's in San Antone."

No. They couldn't leave. Not until Jesse arrived. She had to stop them. Detain them, somehow.

Sucking in a deep breath, she strode to where they stood. Her brain scrambled for what to say. She stopped, a few inches before plowing into them.

Both gazes turned in her direction.

"Yes?" drawled the man who'd robbed them.

"I happened to overhear your conversation, when I heard you mention the name Dinah. Is she, by any chance, Dinah Jones, the cousin of the man who owns the dry goods store? I've been looking for her all morning."

For the space of seconds, the men looked her up and down. At first, only curiosity expressed itself in their gazes. Sara clenched and unclenched the hand at her side.

The men continued to stare.

And then it hit her. Her male disguise hadn't changed, but her voice decidedly didn't match it.

Of all the ignorant things to have done.

"We ain't goin' to see no Dinah Jones." The other man spat the last of his tobacco and took a step closer. "The Dinah we're after is a sportin' gal in San Antone."

Heart thudding all too loud, she gave a nod and turned on her heel.

The man grabbed her arm before her feet could take more than a step. He jerked her to face him.

"But I'm a thinkin' we've found ourselves somethin' even more entertainin'." His lips parted, revealing a yellowed leer and engulfing her in sour breath. With a chuckle, he yanked her hat from her head. Her hastily pinned hair fell around her shoulders.

"Looks like you need a new hat, mister. Or should I say, *missy*?" He tossed the hat with one hand, his other holding her captive. "Somethin' pretty, for a pretty gal like yourself. One that looks awful familiar." He squinted. "Have we met before?"

No, no, no.

Memories bombarded her.

That small dark room. Huddling on her cot, arms around her knees. Cheap, silky material on her skin. The creak of the door. The thump of boots. Alcohol-scented breath. That face, those muscled arms above her, while inwardly, a little girl of nine died.

An otherworldly strength took over her limbs. Sara yanked from his grasp with a swift kick. Spun, her boots eating up the ground as she ran. Her arms pumped. Her legs burned. Air choked through her lungs. She didn't stop. She wouldn't stop. Faster. Faster.

She could never, ever run far or fast enough to outrun the horror, the—

"Sara!"

She flashed a glance behind her. Jesse. He dashed toward her—the Texas Ranger who could mete out justice.

Then why couldn't she stop fleeing?

"Please, hold up." He sounded a little breathless.

She skidded to a halt, facing him. With a shaking hand, she swiped her tangled hair over one shoulder. They stood on the outskirts of town, sun blazing in the cloudless sky.

"You all right?" He looked cleaner, rested, a different shirt beneath his charcoal coat, beard trimmed and face washed. Strange things for her to notice, now, of all times.

"I saw...one of the men...who robbed the stage." She gasped for air.

"Where?" His gaze swung this way and that, as if he expected the Markham Gang in its entirety to come charging toward them.

"Back by the rooming house. I was outside, waiting for you, when he showed up. I knew it was him when he took off his hat." She hugged her arms across her chest.

"And?" He wanted answers. To know what had happened next. For her to tell him, so he could go and do his job as a Ranger.

She pressed her lips together. Scuffed her boot through a trail of pebbles. Gaze fixed on the ground, she opened her mouth. "I thought to distract them, keep them there until you arrived. So I went over and made up some story. But in my haste, I forgot to maintain my disguise..."

She couldn't continue. The words wouldn't come. No matter that she squeezed her eyes shut and wet her lips, the memories still lingered. Speaking what had happened would only make them worse. She opened her eyes, seeing Jesse and the rolling hills dotted with hardy trees. But inside, all she saw was that man's face and the endless men at her door, and the scared child she still was.

Jesse took a step closer. Tension and impatience traced itself on his face. "Then what?"

She shook her head.

His hand lifted.

He was going to hit her! As the brothel owner had done whenever she'd pleaded or cried or displeased a customer. In an instant, she'd feel the stinging slap, the bruising pain. Hear his raised voice, the loud cursing.

She fled again, speeding across the uneven ground. Needing only to get away from men and the torture they inflicted upon helpless women. Running was safe. Would keep her safe.

Her feet flew out from under her. She hit the ground, breath leaving her lungs, tasting grit. Dirt and pebbles scratched her face.

Get up, her mind screamed.

But the fight had left her. She was weary. Let him strike her if he wanted. It didn't matter. Nothing mattered. The security she'd known at the Lawsons had vanished the moment she stepped into that stage. It wouldn't return. And she was too dead tired to fight whatever happened next.

The crunch of boots. A soft thud, like knees hitting ground.

She turned her face, slowly.

"Let me help you." Gentle words. Spoken low. An outstretched hand, meant to help, not harm. Jesse's face, kindness in his eyes. Not anger, kindness.

It was enough to make her nod. His hand grasped hers, strength enough in it to pull her to a sitting position but nothing more. His callused fingers closed around her smaller ones, his hand strong and slightly dusty. He knelt at eye level with her, and in his eyes, she read more of that quiet kindness.

It undid her. The way Matthias's soft words had, the day she'd asked in a hunger-weak tone if he had any need of a servant. The way Gloria's embrace had, as Sara whispered the truth about her life before she'd arrived in their home.

The truth.

She looked again at Jesse's face, so different from the men who'd taken her innocence and left jagged scars across her heart. Honor lived in those eyes, in that rugged face. She sensed it, as surely as she sensed the Markham Gang's greed.

Was it enough for her to trust him, not only on their journey, but in this moment, with her past as well?

He said nothing, gaze on her, a sort of sadness in his expression. He could have filled the silence with more questions, empty words to put pressure on her that would only serve to lock everything away for good. But he didn't. He just waited, crouched on the ground, giving her space, allowing her time.

This wasn't what a Ranger did. He ought to have forced the story from her, demanded an explanation for the good of the case. He hadn't, though.

She needed to tell him. How much, she didn't yet know.

But it would be a start. A something. Enough for now.

~

A jagged scrape marked her right cheekbone. A mass of chestnut curls tumbled down her slim shoulders—curls he'd never seen styled any way but up. Dust had turned her cream-colored shirt a dingy brown.

But what Jesse noticed most, shifting to sit beside Sara on the outskirts of Calvert's Creek, was the brokenness in her eyes. A swirl of emotions owned them now—indecision, fear, pain. A glimpse behind the mask she always wore.

She loosed a shuddery breath.

Lord, show me what to do.

Never had a prayer come so truly from his heart. He needed more wisdom than Solomon to know what he ought to say or do where the woman with the shadowed past and stubborn resilience was concerned.

"I recognized the one man as being complicit in the stage robbery. I...I recognized the other man too. And he recognized me." She trailed her finger through the dirt, looking at it rather than him.

He didn't say anything, biding his time. She'd continue her story when she was good and ready. Call it intuition or maybe the Holy Spirit, but he sensed that what she was about to tell him would alter the way he looked at her. And in no small way.

"Don't you want to ask where he knew me from?" She looked up at him, an eternity of suffering warring in her gaze. So much vulnerability, it made his heart ache with an almost physical force.

"I figured you'll tell me when you're ready," he said quietly. "I'll not rush you."

A bird circled overhead—a lark sparrow. Sara lifted her face toward the sky, her chest rising and then falling in a long exhale.

"He knew me from when I was...forcibly employed as a prostitute. I was eight years old. Seventeen when I escaped."

The mere voicing of words couldn't rock a person's world. They were only words, after all. Comprised of syllables, letters. They could only be spoken onto the air, oft-times forgotten.

The emotions, images evoked by them could never.

And in that moment, Jesse had plenty.

Eight years old. The same age as Joy Ellen when he'd bought her that fancy china doll for Christmas. It was what every little girl ought to be doing then—playing with dolls, going to school. Living for the Fourth of July and trips to the store for penny candy.

No, please, no. The world couldn't be that cruel. Men that steeped in depravity.

But it could be. They could be. Darkness ruled this sinful world, as well as light. Evil existed—thrived, even. Often because the good were ignorant. Or closed their eyes and dwelt in denial.

As a Texas Ranger, he'd witnessed plenty of horrors. Men killed in cold blood. Injuries, fatalities, all inflicted due to violence. Yet none of these experiences, not a single one of them, could ever have prepared him for Sara's words.

He struggled to meet her gaze. Not out of any change of feeling toward her but out of shame. As a Ranger, his job was to protect the defenseless. Defend the honor of the citizens who dwelt in their great state and see to it justice prevailed.

All the while, the grossest injustice was inflicted upon eight-year-old girls. Others, too, not just Sara.

Scars still marked her soul, though she'd hidden them well.

"Say something." Her voice emerged as no more than a whisper.

He swallowed hard. "What can I say? 'I'm sorry' is weak.

Calloused. It doesn't even begin to sum up what I think or feel." Lame words. But in that instant, he could find no others.

"Gloria said the same."

"Gloria?"

The faintest of smiles softened her lips. He stared at it, awestruck. How could she smile, after the life she'd lived for nine years? The years a child became a woman. When little girls most needed their mothers. When life should be at its simplest, easiest.

It astonished, transfixed him, her smile.

"Mrs. Lawson. After I managed to escape, I hopped a wagon to Waco. I'd have starved, if not for the Lawsons. They took me in, treated me like the daughter I'd never been. They are the reason I'm alive today. They, and Lacey, Dalia, and Addie." She said the final three names with a kind of reverence.

"They are?" It seemed right to ask questions, now that she'd opened up herself to tell him this much.

"My friends. The only friends I had until the Lawsons. The money in that carpetbag...it was for them. I'm going back for them. It's a promise I made to myself when I escaped. They helped me at great risk to themselves. I can do no less." She spoke the words with more resolve than he'd ever heard from anyone. Even himself. Revenge upon the men responsible for Louella's death had been the catalyst in his joining the Texas Rangers. Though he'd since surrendered that to God, he well remembered the way it burned through his blood, making everything dark and hazy. His resolve had been strong. Hers was stronger.

Hers was for freedom.

"You intended to use the money for...?"

"You can't grow up where I did without learning the way of corruption. Anything can be bought for the right price. Whether that *thing* is a person makes no difference. I had enough in that carpetbag to purchase Lacey and the others. They were sold once before. I'll buy them back, buy their freedom." Her eyes shone with determination. Though brokenness still hovered at the edges, a greater light eclipsed it.

He could have sat with her for hours while the passage of time turned the sky to dusk. But they didn't have hours. The Markham Gang and Sara's money still awaited capture. Both had taken on an even greater significance in the wake of the hour's revelations.

"Griff will be looking for us. Calvert's Creek is a stopping point, before folks head on to San Antone. My guess is, they're headed there. Are you... that is, you still aiming to join us?"

She nodded. He stood.

Though he assumed she wouldn't take it, he offered her his hand. With a dip of her head, she placed hers in it. The joining of their hands sent a fresh wave of sorrow through him. No wonder she'd put such stipulations on their distance. She'd undoubtedly, other than that Mr. Lawson, never known what it was to have a man touch her in any way other than for his own pleasure.

Guilt speared him at the direction his own thoughts toward her had taken only yesterday.

He released her hand, the lack of her fingers in his with his leaving him somehow bereft. Wordlessly, they turned in the direction of Calvert's Creek.

Jesse looked up, toward the sky.

Three other sparrows had joined the first, soaring onward together, none of which went unnoticed by a God who saw them, as surely as He saw the little ones whom the world had abused or forgotten.

CHAPTER 8

Dusk fell like a heavy hand by the time they reached San Antonio, the town she'd not seen since the night she fled from it. Though the nightmare of her existence had only been enacted within the walls of a single building, the aura of oppression seemed to permeate the entire city. That made her grateful that she rode, not alone, but with Jesse Rawlings. A man unlike any that had come before. A man she trusted, though everything in her life had prepared her to do the opposite.

Griff had parted ways with them a few streets back, so it was just her and Jesse. Jesse stopped upon occasion and entered a building, mostly gaming houses and saloons. At the first one, he'd asked if she'd prefer to wait outside. She'd shook her head, fear of being left alone greater than the fear of what anyone in those buildings would do to her with Jesse at her side. Disguised by her trousers and Jesse's greatcoat, she was safe, as long as she said nothing. The men who saw her would think her a lad, albeit a short one.

She prayed she would not recognize any of their faces. Many

she did not remember, but there were a few who had etched themselves on her memory in the worst of ways.

Papa God, keep us safe.

They left one building without any sign or news of the Markham Gang. Jesse swung into the saddle and pulled her up behind him. Then they rode down a street dimly lit and little populated.

The tension knotting her stomach increased tenfold, prompting her to fist her hands into the fabric of Jesse's shirt, something she'd instinctively refrained from doing even when the terrain became especially rocky.

He turned, his eyes finding hers and probing deep, even in the semidarkness. Concern radiated from his expression. Since her confession earlier that afternoon, he'd gone from treating her with civility to gentle care. Like a friend. Like she held a value that outweighed her past.

"You all right?"

Her throat went dry. She wasn't.

They continued down the street. And as she looked up at the edifice in front of her, she knew why.

Avery's Drugstore.

It was a building unnoticed by many, nothing remarkable about the simple wood exterior and plain-lettered sign. On the first floor were counters and bottles, medicines to serve the citizens of San Antonio six days a week, ten to five. She'd only been downstairs three or four times. Ten to five were the quiet hours upstairs. No one talked above a whisper. Mostly, everyone slept. Everyone on the second story, at least.

As clear as if they stood before her now, she saw them. Lacey and Dalia and Addie. Were they upstairs? Of course, they were. Curtains covered the upper windows, letting out only the faintest streams of light. Only a privileged few knew the secrets of the upper floor. By invitation only, was the rule.

She shuddered.

Jesse must've sensed it as he pulled them to a halt.

Her hands shook. Her eyes burned with tears unshed. Everything inside of her cried out to go to them, free them. Fulfill a promise long overdue.

"This is... ?" His eyes dawned with understanding.

She nodded.

Urgency radiated from him as he dismounted and lifted her down.

"Sara... I have some money." He placed one hand on Arion's saddle, speaking fast. "Not your two hundred dollars, but it'll be enough. If you tell me what I need to know, I can get in there. You remember how you said you escaped, right?" She'd told him a few more details when Griff had gone to refill their canteens with water.

Another nod.

"I know of a place where the girls can be safe. If you'll help me, together we can do this."

"Are you sure? Tonight?" It was what she wanted, more than anything else, but there was risk. The owner took care of his property, guarded it well. Although...if Jesse managed to gain entrance by pretending to be a customer, he could get the girls alone for an hour. But would it be enough to get far away before they were missed?

"I'm a Texas Ranger. I know how to think fast when the situation calls for it. I want to help you, Sara. I want to help these girls." His eyes, his voice, everything about him emanated utter truth. Escape could become more than a possibility—it could be a reality.

And all because her stagecoach had been robbed and a Texas Ranger had come to her rescue.

It wasn't without pain, to search her mind and dredge up every detail she remembered from those nine years. How the customers behaved. How they "requested" certain girls. The layout of the rooms, each with locked windows and doors. The latter was only open to admit the men, the former never. It was only by picking the window lock Sara had managed to pry it open enough to let the rope down. God, not luck, had brought her a customer one night who'd pulled a few housebreaking jobs and liked to boast about his exploits.

But she needed to tell Jesse everything if she was to prepare him for what he'd encounter when he stepped inside those doors. Needful if they were to free Lacey, Dalia, and Addie.

She drew a deep breath. "All right. I can tell you what you'll need to know to make a plan. But some of it may shock you."

He gave a nod of understanding.

And there, beside Arion, night wrapping San Antonio in a shroud of ink, Sara held nothing back. Descriptions of the owners, of the girls. What Jesse must say and how he must act if they had any chance of success. She and Arion were to wait in the back alley with a covered lantern to guide them once they'd all escaped, and, if needed, distract any passerby.

He absorbed all of this in his silent way. But tension still marked his features as he handed her Arion's reins and checked the hiding places of his weapons.

Despite it all, a swell of anticipation filled her chest as he strode across the street, his strong frame and even steps giving her a measure of confidence. If anyone could give freedom to the prisoners who dwelt above Avery's Drugstore, it would be a man like Jesse Rawlings.

On the threshold, he paused, glancing back at her. A lone man standing at the gates of perdition, bravery in his eyes and honor in his heart.

And in a gesture that resurrected a part of her she'd long thought consigned to the grave, the Texas Ranger she'd trusted with so much tipped his Stetson in a nod.

~

Shadows could conceal a lot of things, most of which weren't good. And as Jesse waited for his knock to be answered, he craned his neck toward the window in an attempt to see past them.

The door opened. A tall man, wiry with muscles, peered out.

"Yes?" Distrust entered his bloodshot eyes. Obviously, he didn't recognize Jesse as a regular customer.

"Jace Avery told me there was an evening's entertainment to be had," Jesse drawled. Everything about the role he would play revolted him, but it was the only way to break into this den of iniquity. So he'd act his part to the best of his ability.

"Jace Avery, you say?" The door opened a smidgen wider.

Jesse nodded

"You got cash?"

In a slick motion, Jesse pulled out the bills and fanned them in front of the man's face. "This enough?" He kept his voice low, gruff.

The money had obviously done its job in showing the man Jesse meant business. The door opened, and he stepped aside to allow Jesse entrance.

A click. The grind of a bolt, locking them in.

They stood inside a room that, true to Sara's description, looked the part of a modest medicinal shop. Bottles lined the wall behind the counter. Signs decorated the walls, proclaiming the benefits of this or that remedy. Jesse took everything in with a sweep of a glance, taking care to school his expression into utter boredom. A man of the character he portrayed wouldn't give two dimes about anything on this level of the building.

"What sort of company you looking for, mister?"

"I'll only pay if you can meet my requirements." The smirk unfurling across his face was almost physically painful to achieve.

The heart of any man who stooped to partake of these types of services must be colder than a Minnesota winter.

"Avery prides himself on the services we offer." The man puffed his chest out like a banty rooster. "State your pleasure, mister, and we'll make sure it's to your liking."

He spoke the words Sara had told him, keeping his tone matter-of-fact. Sickeningly so.

The man didn't bat an eye. "It'll cost you for all three."

"I'll pay."

The man stated a price. Jesse handed over the bills.

"If you'll wait here..." The man crossed the room and opened an inconspicuous door. He disappeared from view, the only sounds his weighty footfalls.

Cautiously, Jesse crept around the room's exterior, checking windows and the bolt on the door, committing every detail to memory, as he'd done every word Sara had spoken about the descriptions of the girls and what he must do to bring them to safety. Tonight was for Sara. Her friends would be granted their freedom. But he'd come back. With a court of law behind him. The need to obliterate this place burned deep through him, put there by God, who defended His sparrows.

He breathed a prayer, just as footfalls announced the man's return.

"Right this way." The man jerked his hand toward the secret door.

Jesse ducked through the opening, keeping close behind as they climbed the narrow, creaking stairs. Wall sconces lit the hallway above to a hallway consisting of a row of closed doors. Seven.

Behind each one lived a woman, a soul. One deserving of freedom, worthy of more than this.

"Inside there." The man nodded to the second door on the right. "You've got an hour. No more."

Jesse said nothing. He waited until the man disappeared down the stairs before rapping on the door.

"Enter."

He turned the knob. The dimly lit room was small, exactly as Sara described it. No luxuries—none were needed for the purpose of these rooms. Just a small washstand and basin. And a bed, rumpled and unmade.

Three girls sat on it. Girls in scanty dresses with kohl-lined eyes. Each face wearing a dull look of resignation.

Of more value than many sparrows, each of them.

And tonight would be theirs to soar. Theirs for freedom.

No one moved. Each regarded him, wariness in their gazes. He read hatred in the eyes of the one nearest, fear in the eyes of the one in the middle. The other looked as if she'd mildly intoxicated herself. And who could blame her? Not Jesse, certainly.

"You've an hour, sir." With lifted chin, the girl with anger in her eyes crossed to him. "So you'd best tell us what you want."

"Hello, Lacey, Dalia, and Addie. Those are your names, aren't they?" He took a step closer, keeping his voice quiet.

The girls started, their eyes sharpening. Sara's friends, there could be no doubt about it.

"I reckon you can call us anything you want." The eldest girl crossed her arms over her chest. Yet a spark of something had entered her eyes.

"We don't have much time, but I've been sent here by Sara Byrne. I'm sure you remember her. I'm a Texas Ranger, and I'm here to help you escape. All of you."

"You know Sara?" Addie, he thought, came to stand by her sister. A stream of hope glimmered in her eyes.

"Shut up, Addie." The other girl grasped her sister's arm, voice cut low. "This is a trick. We can't trust him."

"I know you can't be expected to believe much about honor, miss, but on my honor, this is no trick. The night she escaped, Sara

Byrne made a promise to the three of you. I'm helping her make good on it." There wasn't time to say more. He crossed to the window and took in the bolt, grabbed tools from his left pocket. It would be easy enough to pick the lock and open the window. But he needed to work fast.

Frowning with concentration, he set to his task. Seconds, minutes passed. His arm ached with the tension of holding it still. There...almost. One more turn and...

Success!

He looked up. The three girls stood together, arms around each other, wide-eyed.

"You're for real, ain't you?" Addie whispered, the spark of hope in her eyes flaming brighter. "Sara really did send you."

Jesse nodded. "She's outside. The both of us are gonna help you get somewhere safe." He pulled off his loose coat where he'd concealed the coil of rope around one shoulder, slipped off the rope, and proceeded to secure it to the bedpost. Assured that it was secure, he opened the window and let the remainder down.

"But what about Avery?" Lacey faced him. "He's always said that if we escape, he's comin' after us. He does what he says."

"He doesn't have the authority of the Rangers behind him, miss." He added a reassuring smile to the words. "Who's first?"

"You go first, Lace." Dalia pushed her older sister forward.

Lord, give me strength. Give us safety tonight.

Over and over, he repeated the prayer as Lacey climbed onto his back. Thankfully, all of the girls were petite. It made it easier to climb, hand over hand down the rope. Back up again.

Lord, give me strength.

Down with Dalia, her thin arms tight around his neck. He stifled a groan as a muscle in his shoulder pulled. Focus. Always focus, or risk death. Captain Sterling had trained his Rangers well.

Addie was the lightest burden of all, and they reached the ground with little difficulty. Though the girls stiffened at his touch, he grabbed Dalia's and Addie's hands, leaving Lacey to follow. They skulked away from the building, the girls casting anxious glances behind them, as if expecting a horde of angry pursuers. Jesse urged them onward to the next alley, where Sara waited. It would be a joyful reunion for the four of them, but first, they needed to get to safety.

They turned the corner. Jesse peered into the night-black stretch between the two buildings.

No lantern. No nicker from Arion.

"Sara." His hoarse whisper echoed all too loudly into the darkness.

No soft reply.

Lacey turned a gaze seething with betrayal on him, but he didn't heed it. His heart thudded a drumbeat against his ribs, racing with one howling refrain.

Sara was gone.

CHAPTER 9

Pain shot through the back of her head. Bricks seemed to weight her eyelids. She didn't want to open them. Better to stay in this state of swirling darkness.

Warning niggled through the haze of consciousness. She needed to wake up.

Clawing through the fog enveloping her mind, Sara forced herself to open her eyes.

She stared down at her hands and feet. Bound with ropes. Her head leaned against a cold, damp wall. Across the room, a solitary lamp sat on a chair, illuminating the dirt floor and windowless walls. Where was she?

What had happened to her?

Papa God. . .help me.

Shards of memory returned, slurred as a drunkard's speech. Waiting in the alley with Arion for Jesse and the girls. Footsteps. A man's voice. A rough demand that she hand over the horse. Her refusal. Then sickening pain reverberating through her skull... blackness...

She swallowed back the dryness in her throat. Whoever had

taken her had no good in store. The extent of the danger was yet to be determined, but danger it was. If she screamed, someone who could help might hear.

She let out a yell.

"Help! Someone. Please! I've been—"

"Shut yer mouth, or I'll shut it for ya." The words were more like a growl, spoken by a man who appeared, drawing Sara's attention to a ladder of sorts where he'd descended. So she was underground. A cellar, maybe.

He dangled a length of dirty cloth in one hand as he drew closer, his hulking frame filling the cramped, low-ceilinged room. A gag. Sara pressed her lips together. He stumped closer, set down the lantern he carried, and crouched at her side, holding the cloth in one hand, fingers of the other reaching for her mouth.

"Please. I won't scream again." She'd beg if need be. The last thing she needed was to be even more trapped.

"See to it you don't." Filling the space with light, he held up the lamp, staring at her.

She gasped. The man she'd seen at Calvert's Creek. And once before...when she'd stood beside Mrs. Thompson, held at gunpoint for the first time in her life.

A member of the Markham Gang. There could be no doubt.

"Well, well, if you ain't the little lady we saw the other day. You ran off before we could be better acquainted." He chuckled, his tobacco-stained teeth and lips glistening with saliva. "From the look of things, you ain't gonna be doin' much runnin' anytime soon." He leered.

Her heart thudded.

I will say of the Lord, He is my refuge and my fortress: my God; in Him will I trust.

Matthias's favorite verse, Psalm 91:2, filled her memory, as surely as if he'd been at her side at the breakfast table, reciting the day's passage. He always ended with that particular psalm, the words so familiar he'd not needed to read from the Book. Just closed his eyes, the syllables rolling off his tongue like a stream spilling over rocks.

Matthias would tell her to be brave.

I will say of the Lord...

"Why did you take me?"

The man chuckled, as if her sharp words had been a congenial jest. "Well, now. One of my friends had his horse shot out from under him. Seein' you holding the reins of that fine beast, well, the temptation was too great to resist. Would've given you no trouble, had you handed him over nice and quiet like. That's a good lesson to remember, lady. You ain't strong enough to win. So you'd best give up without a fight."

"You're mistaken. The horse you stole was not mine, but that of a Ranger. One who's been looking for you and the rest of the Markham Gang. He'll have his entire company on your trail, if I don't miss my guess." The words shot from her lips before she could question their logic.

The man's slivered eye narrowed. "He won't find us. We'll be outta here come daybreak, as soon as Avery delivers the supplies he promised. Those Rangers may be the greatest in the state, but they've met their match this time. They ain't tangled with the likes of Cass Markham yet, and when they do, they'll be beat. Sure as the devil has a pitchfork, they'll be squashed."

"What about me?" Another question she probably shouldn't have asked.

The man stood, knees popping. "I ain't decided yet. Maybe we'll take you to Cass, let him be the judge. Out of them britches, you'd be a pretty dish. And then, I might decide to keep you for myself." With another raking glance, the man stood, taking the lantern with him. His boots clumped up the ladder, leaving her in darkness. And solitude.

He is my refuge and my fortress...

She wiggled her hands, trying to extricate them from the ropes, but they were bound too tightly. And without a way of getting to the knife in her boot, she was trapped.

Again. Just as she had been before, a little girl on the streets of San Antonio, cheeks fresh with tears after watching her mother loaded onto a wagon, her beautiful face and form locked away forever in a coffin. Hands had grabbed her then, arms. No matter how she'd kicked and fought and screamed, they'd suppressed her. And it had taken nine long years to escape.

She'd clung to her faith in Papa God, despite it all. A Man Mama said would always love and take care of her, even more than her earthly daddy, whom she'd never known. She'd done her best to stay strong.

But she couldn't do it again. It would be too much. Her body had been her own since the day she fled to freedom, and she couldn't let it be taken again. She'd sooner die and go up to heaven where Mama was.

Tears scalded her eyes. Where was the hope in any of this? There was none. Unless Jesse came, which, he might try. But how would he find her before daybreak?

It would take a miracle, but she'd been given one before.

My God; in Him will I trust...

She bowed her head, her neck aching. An earthly father would seek to rescue her. Would a heavenly one not do the same and ten times more?

Please. I need help. Don't let that man take me tomorrow. I'd rather die first. Anything but being at the mercy of lust again. Guide Jesse. Give me wisdom. And thank You for hearing this.

She lifted her head. And though no mighty thunderclap or heavenly voice boomed, an idea took root. If she could but get the man to free her, the knife in her boot could be put to good purpose.

But how could she convince a criminal bent on taking her captive to loosen her bonds?

The how came to her slowly. It was the last thing she'd want to try...but the only thing that might work.

~

Griff had done his job, following a lead on the Markham Gang in the San Antonio area. According to one of the girls at Dinah's, a member of the band they'd been tracking since the start of the year was holed up somewhere on the outskirts of town, waiting for a supply delivery.

The tracks left by Sara's captors seemed to be heading in the same direction that the girl at Dinah's told Griff to go. After flashing his badge and convincing a townsman to lend him a horse, Jesse set off with Griff.

They rode out of San Antonio in silence, two Rangers intent on their job.

Yet, for Jesse, it had become so much more than a routine task. He'd taken the girls from the brothel to safety at the home of his reverend friend.

That hadn't quelled the torturous thoughts filling him when he turned his mind to Sara's fate. Which he hadn't stopped doing since the second he discovered she was missing.

Once before, he'd let himself care about a woman. Louella had died, killed by a stray bullet in a gunfight he should've been able to stop. He'd failed his fiancée.

How could he ever look himself in the face again and feel proud to be a man, a Ranger, if anything happened to Sara Byrne? A woman who, though he'd only known her for a short time, had evoked something within him. Something that touched a place in his barricaded heart and made him wonder what it would be like to break down those walls.

Please, God. You've helped me through difficult jobs in the past. Guide me in this one. I want to stop the Markham Gang. But more than that, I want to keep Sara safe.

"This is the place, Jesse." Signals, not words, were the main means of Ranger communication. Apparently, he hadn't been paying close enough attention to Griff's nonverbal cues.

A dilapidated ranch house, so run down that even scavengers wouldn't find much worth taking. It sat on the crest of the hill, moonlight slanting down over the crumbling frame and weedy yard. A cesspool for criminal activities, if ever there was one. But perhaps the Markham Gang had better sense than to hole up at such a dwelling.

Was the information Griff had obtained truth? Or would this rotting hogshead of a house reveal a dead end that would only delay his search for Sara?

In total silence, the men dismounted and checked their weapons. Jesse scarcely dared to draw breath as they crept around the exterior, checking for matted grass, fresh animal droppings, or other signs of recent occupants.

A sound caught his ear. It could be said a mother knew her child's cry among a hundred babies. Branch liked to say a Ranger knew his horse's nicker almost as well.

The noise came again. Forcing himself to take silent, even steps, Jesse scanned the surrounding area. And there, Arion stood, tied to a tree, moonlight illuminating his familiar black body, Jesse's saddle still tied to his back.

Jesse's pulse roared through his brain. If Arion was here, that meant Sara must be too. Sara...and the Markham Gang. At least some of them, anyway.

No words were needed as he and Griff retraced their steps around the front of the house. Just a glance. A nod. Nothing more.

They drew revolvers. Jesse tried the door. The knob turned, hinges groaning mightily.

Tiny feet scuttled into corners. Rats. Once, the place had been a fine establishment, but the walls had been stripped, leaving nothing but bare white where fine wood and wallpaper had hung.

Jesse took the lead, Griff on his heels. Boot prints spotted the dust-coated floor, recent ones. A dead giveaway that they were on the right trail. In the center of the third room, a gleam of moonlight illuminated a trap door.

Was someone down there? Could it be Sara? Her face filled his vision in an overwhelming image.

He'd see her safe. It was what Rangers did best. But never had a job come with this much feeling attached. So much, it scared him.

He pulled open the trap door, slow as molasses dripping from a jar. Slow enough that the hinges made no sound. He eased it down to the ground.

Justice forever.

The words drummed through his brain like marching footsteps, a battle cry from the best of the Rangers. It emboldened him as he climbed down the ladder, noiseless as a panther.

Sara. In the corner, framed by slants of lantern light. Her shirt discarded, wearing only a chemise. Beside her was Oren Killarney, just as he'd looked in every WANTED poster Jesse had seen. Neither glanced his way.

For the space of a second, Jesse stood frozen. He should've shot. Should've kept his aim true and brought Oren Killarney down.

But he hesitated, mind roaring with too many memories of all that had gone wrong on that fateful day when his beautiful Louella Wade had—

Griff landed beside Jesse, the thud of his boots hitting the cellar floor.

Oren turned, gaze pouncing on them, on his feet in an instant, dragging Sara with him. And in a movement slick and fast whipped a revolver from his belt and pressed it against Sara's temple.

"Well, well. Lookie here. If it ain't the Texas Rangers." A sneer curled his lip.

The barrel of the revolver pressed into Sara's skull. She watched him, gaze pleading. As if waiting for him to save the day. Him, a man who'd failed to save Louella. Him, the last man she ought to trust.

But trust him she did.

And that knowledge gave him courage.

"Drop the gun." Jesse held his own weapon steady, aimed at Oren's chest. Griff's weapon clicked, also trained on the man.

A hideous chuckle barked from Oren's lips. "You shoot, boy, and wherever you send me, she'll be a'goin' along for the ride."

Perspiration beaded on Jesse's brow. "Let her go, Killarney."

Oren only jerked Sara closer, his beefy arm around her slender shoulders. "Seems to me we each have somethin' the other wants. You Rangers want the girl. And I"—he paused—"want to drag your law-abiding carcasses back to Cass. After I fill you full of lead."

"Let her go, and we'll do whatever you want." Jesse kept his jaw firm, his tone steely.

Griff glanced at Jesse, uncertainty in his gaze. Jesse gave a nod, willing his friend and fellow Ranger to trust him.

It's a mistake. The words screamed through his mind. Who did he think he was? What if he failed Griff, failed Sara, just as he had Louella?

He'd trained with Captain Sterling since, but...what if it wasn't enough?

I trust You, God. I've got to.

"Music to my ears, Ranger Boy. Music to my ears. Drop your guns. All of 'em."

Jesse let his revolvers fall to the floor, praying Griff would trust him and follow suit. The younger Ranger did, though questions shouted from his eyes.

Once the men stood empty-handed, Oren shifted his hold on Sara and slowly turned the revolver, pointing it at Jesse. "Now, both of you turn around, nice an' slow like." Oren drawled the words. "I've always had a fancy to shoot a law-holdin' piece of scum in the back."

Jesse pivoted slowly. Out of the corner of his eye, he caught Griff's gaze, drawing it to Jesse's sleeve where he kept his knife. Griff gave a barely perceptible nod.

"You're a real smart man for an outlaw, Killarney." Jesse kept his tone lazy, almost bored, buying time. "Never thought this would be the way I'd go. Shot in the back by you of all people. The man I've been hunting. What a story for you to write home about, eh?"

Lord, let my instincts be right this time. If not, I guess I'll be seeing You real soon. But the thought of failing Griff when he's so recently found love. Never knowing love again myself...

Oren laughed almost jovially. "A real story."

Jesse's fingers inched toward the knife, closing around the handle. Once he moved, he'd have only seconds. Any deviation from his aim and he'd hit Sara, not Oren. He couldn't miss. Failure wasn't a possibility.

Guide me, Father God.

One. Two.

Three...and now.

Jesse spun, the knife flying like a flash of lightning bent on annihilation. Oren's eyes widened, and his pistol discharged—just as the knife hit true, lodged in Oren's neck.

Griff and Jesse lunged for their revolvers, a round of shots finishing off another member of the Markham Gang.

In an instant, Sara was on her feet. Coming to him. He holstered his revolver and met her halfway. Time, everything, slid to a halt as she flung herself into his arms. He wrapped his around her, cheek pressed against her hair, breathing in the lingering scent of lavender. He'd found her. She was unharmed.

And nothing had ever felt as perfect as holding her in his arms.

"Oh, Jesse," she whispered against his shirtfront. "I was so afraid."

He stepped back, hands on her shoulders. Her hair fell in a tangled mess around her face. Dirt and scratches marred her porcelain cheeks. Her chemise had a rip in one shoulder. Never, in a million years, had he imagined there could be a sight so unutterably beautiful.

"I know." Looking into her wide eyes made him long to pull her close again. Show her she was safe and would always be so. "But God was watching out for you. He always takes care of His sparrows, darlin'. He was there, with you, keeping you safe, helping me find you."

She gave a shaky nod, glancing behind her at Oren's prone body. Griff crouched beside the man, checking his pockets and weapons. She turned back, gaze finding his again. "What did you just call me?"

Of all the times for such a word to slip out. For them to have such a conversation. Jesse flicked a glance at Griff, but the man headed up the ladder, not even looking in their direction.

"Darlin'." A swath of heat crept up his neck. "Sorry, it just sort of slipped out."

Oh, that smile of hers. He hadn't seen it much, but if anything had the power to slay him, it was the way her lips curved upward in that perfect shape. The way a dimple peeked from each side of her mouth. He let himself bask in it, fill himself to brimming with staring at it, as her smile unfurled.

"Don't say that." She took a step closer and placed a hand

against his chest. His heart pounded against her fingers. "It's a lovely term. When it's said by the right man."

He shouldn't ask. They scarcely knew each other. And the wounds of her past needed time to mend, to heal. But he had to know. And the insistent nudge in his mind told him the Almighty was giving him the go-ahead.

"Sara...do you think...that is...could I ever be such a man? To you?"

She bit her lip. He waited, the course his life would take hanging in interminable seconds of suspense. In the days they'd spent together, he'd grown to care, to feel, so much. Enough to imagine, somewhere in the distance, a future with her lay waiting for him. For them.

She nodded, giving him a little smile. "Yes, Jesse Rawlings. I'd say there's a fair chance." A tiny giggle escaped.

"That's fine, then." He couldn't help his broadening grin. "Real fine."

He glanced up as Griff descended the ladder.

"Is this what you've been looking for, Miss Byrne?" He held up a small carpetbag. "I found it in a pile upstairs."

Sara rushed toward him, grabbing the bag. She ran her fingers over the inner lining. "It's there!" In the dimly lit cellar, her face filled with enough joy to light a thousand candles. "The money's there, Jesse." She held it out for his inspection.

"I'm glad." He smiled softly, so grateful to have met Sara Byrne. God had a way of turning bad situations into something far beyond all imagination. Jesse prayed the same would be said of the three girls waiting at the reverend's. And he trusted their lives would be, with him and Sara giving their all, and the Lord guiding their steps. "But I have a feeling there are greater kinds of treasure in store for the both of us."

She slipped her hand into his, leaning against him. "Me, too, Jesse Rawlings. Me too."

~

A MONTH LATER
HARTVILLE, TEXAS

If she had her pick from a million companions, she'd choose the one beside her every time. Especially when Jesse said, a twinkle in his eyes, that he had something to show her.

They'd driven along in silence down sun-dappled roads, much as they had during those endless hours atop Arion. Only this time, she wore a summer dress of the palest yellow and he a gray suit and string tie. Finer than she'd ever seen him dress. The clothes accentuated his handsome looks, sending flushes into her face and flutters through her heart she knew not how to reckon with. For they did not stem from fear, but another kind of emotion altogether. One she longed to voice aloud with every beat of her heart. Let the word slip from her lips, a refrain. A benediction.

But did she dare? Dare to tell this Texas Ranger who had changed her life so much, she'd fallen unbelievably, incredibly, in love with him?

Her heart cried *yes*. The hours kneeling in prayer, pouring out her feelings before her heavenly Father revealed the same.

He pulled the buckboard to a halt and glanced at her. A mischievous smile played around the corners of his mouth.

"Close your eyes."

A heady stir of anticipation swelled through her, an almost little-girl excitement over what he had planned. Foreign feelings—anticipation and excitement. Yet altogether *right* ones.

She squeezed her eyes shut as they started down the road. She hadn't been paying much attention to their route, in any case. Sneaking glances at Jesse's broad shoulders and bearded jawline had occupied far too much of her concentration.

Finally, after what felt like several hours, but was in reality probably less than one, they stopped again. She was half a second from letting her eyes pop open when his chuckle stopped her.

"Wait just a minute there, Miss Impatience. No peeking." She heard him get out of the buckboard, the sound of his footsteps coming around to her side. His strong hands grasped round her waist as he lifted her down. The scent of soap and something spicy and masculine wafted over her, giving her the absurd longing to press her face against his chest and drink in the fragrance. Or was it so absurd?

He placed his hand against the small of her back and guided her several steps. The Sara Byrne who had boarded the stage to San Antonio would never have given a man such liberties. But a month in Hartville, staying in a spare room with Lacey, Dalia, and Addie at the massive El Regalo ranch, surrounded by love and laughter, had changed much inside her she once thought would never alter.

"All right." His whisper tickled against her ear. "You can go ahead and look now."

Her eyes opened wide.

They stood in front of a two-story house—white-sided and green-shuttered. Framing the house sprawled gentle, rolling hills, so much green it took her breath away. Steps led up to a spacious front porch. A nearby corral held a horse she recognized as the faithful Arion.

She turned to Jesse. He watched her, a hopeful expression in his eyes. The same look she'd worn as a little girl of five, presenting her mother with a handkerchief hemmed by her own hand.

But Jesse couldn't have...this house couldn't be a gift for *her*.

"What is this place?" Just gazing at it told her exactly what it was perfect for. What she had always dreamed of having. She'd shared her dream with Jesse, but he couldn't have truly realized it... Could he?

"Sparrow House," he said softly.

She repeated the name, her heart full to aching. "Oh, Jesse."

"It's your dream, isn't it? A place for all those girls you're...we're gonna rescue. It'll be a place where they can get an education, be taken care of. Plant gardens and ride horses. A place for healing. A place where they can feel safe."

Tears filled her eyes, but they were cleansing, joyous ones. Brought forth from a heart overflowing with gratitude to her heavenly Father and love for this kind, good man before her. A man she'd come to care for so very much.

"You're crying. Don't you like it?" He looked a little alarmed.

"I love it! Words can't express my thanks. But I can't run this big place all by myself." She smiled, swiping a hand across her cheeks. "I'll need someone to help me. Someone with enough kindness in his heart to rescue girls in need of so much. Someone brave enough to fight for them. For me, if I've ever a need of it. You know of anyone, Jesse Rawlings?"

The sun began its descent in the horizon, washing the sky in brilliant sweeps of gold and pink. A masterpiece, painted by the Master Artist. The Giver of all gifts. The God over all creation.

"I just might know of someone." The corners of his eyes crinkled. One hand reached up and cupped around her cheek, his touch so full of gentleness.

"Do you think he could be persuaded?" She reached her hand up and placed hers over his.

"I think so." He nodded, slow. "If the right woman asked him."

"Then will you?"

"Help you run Sparrow House? 'Course I will. After the rest of the Markham Gang is brought to justice, I've decided to leave the Rangers. That life was right for me once, but things have changed. In many ways."

"And will you...marry me?" This man would stand beside her and rescue the girls the Savior loved so much. Girls like she had been. Like Lacey and Dalia and Addie. But there were more...so many more in such great need. And nothing had ever felt so right as asking this man to walk this journey with her.

Nothing except...his answering *yes* and the tender kiss he pressed against her lips.

She wrapped her arms around his neck and let the pleasure of being held, being loved, wash over her like the brilliance of the setting sun.

Life would not always be easy. But love would knit their hearts together in a bond that no man could put asunder.

And their lives, and those of every girl they'd work to save, would always remain in the hands of a God who cherished them. Reminding them of their worth.

That each of them was priceless, more valuable than many sparrows.

> Are not two sparrows sold for a farthing? and one
> of them
> shall not fall on the ground without your Father.
>
> — *MATTHEW 10:29*

AUTHOR'S NOTE

While the spark of this story was lit by the heroic adventures of the Texas Rangers, as I plotted and wrote, a deeper thread wove itself into the fabric of *Jesse's Sparrow*. Though my characters and events are fictitious, the grim truth of human trafficking and enslavement in our world today is all too real. According to the International Justice Mission, an estimated forty-five million people are trapped in various forms of slavery, be it forced labor in quarries or mines in India or prostitution in the United States. The reality of these facts breaks my heart. And I know it breaks our Savior's, too—a Father who values each and every one of us, regardless of the worth assigned to us by the world.

Organizations that work to eradicate this evil and rescue those caught in its trap desperately need the support of individuals who care. And it's because of this that I'm donating a portion of the proceeds from my novella to this cause. Freedom fighters (like Jesse and Sara) can't succeed in bringing about change alone. I'd highly recommend visiting www.ijm.org, the website for the International Justice Mission, for more information and to find out how you can get involved.

The time to take action—today. The voices to speak out for those who cannot speak for themselves—ours.

Blessings,
Amanda

ABOUT THE AUTHOR

Amanda Barratt is the bestselling author of numerous historical novels and novellas including The Warsaw Sisters, Within These Walls of Sorrow, and The White Rose Resists. Her work has been the recipient of the Christy Award and the Carol Award, as well as an Honorable Mention in the Foreword INDIES Book of the Year Awards.

Amanda is passionate about illuminating oft-forgotten facets of history through a fictional narrative. She lives in Michigan and can often be found researching her next novel, catching up on her to-be-read stack, or savoring a slice of her favorite lemon cake.

To connect with Amanda, visit: www.amandabarratt.net.

Cover design by: Wild Heart Books

THE COUNTESS AND THE COWBOY

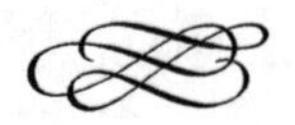

KATHLEEN Y'BARBO

Jesus Christ the same yesterday, and to day, and for ever.

— *HEBREWS 13:8*

For those who put on the uniform,
be it in the service of our country
or in putting on a badge and keeping us safe—
Thank you.
So very, very much.
Thank you.

John 15:13

CHAPTER 1

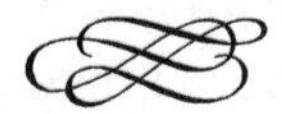

Becker Ranch near Hartville, Texas
August 1886

Opening the door was the hardest part. Not that she expected to find it locked, because no one out here in this part of Texas ever locked anything.

Instead, it was her pride that kept Countess Ava of Saarburg, formerly known as simply Ava Becker, standing out on the porch with her hand on the doorknob. When Papa insisted she be shipped off to marry a count she barely knew, instead of the Ranger she loved, foolish words were spoken.

Words that placed a distance between her and her family that went beyond the

many thousands of miles between them.

Owing to his scholarly interests in geology and natural sciences, Ava Becker's father gave up his royal Prussian title in exchange for ownership to a Central Texas land grant along the Sabinal River where he could further his scholarly pursuits. Though William Becker, formerly Wilhelm von Becker the Count of Trier, had been a proud Texan and a commoner since 1844, he never stopped treating his only daughter like royalty.

Her tutor taught her German and all the math and sciences she needed to learn, and Mama taught her how to act like a proper lady, despite the fact that the nearest city was Hartville, some fifteen miles away. Thanks in great part to Ava's brother, Gus, and his best friend, Texas Ranger Ezra Creed, Ava also learned to ride and shoot—much to her father's horror.

Once her father got wind of her love of donning boys' clothes to ride her favorite pony with her red braids flying, he threatened to have Ava sent back to the Prussian homeland where Uncle Johan and Aunt Hilde, who became Count and Countess of Trier after Papa abdicated, would see that she did no further harm to the family's reputation.

Then somehow Papa found out about her plans to elope with Ezra. Though she tried not to think of that awful time, of the way Papa turned his back as she begged him to reconsider, the images rose all the same.

Of slipping out of her bedroom window under a starlit sky with only the few precious things she could carry in a small bag. Of hurrying down a well-worn path toward the felled log where she and Ezra had agreed to meet. Of finding Papa waiting for her instead of Ezra.

"Mr. Creed wishes me to deliver the message," Papa had said. "He regrets that the farce he carried on with you got this far and wishes you to forgive him for deceiving you as to any affection he pretended to have."

Affection he pretended to have.

Words that were seared into her brain and carved on her heart. Even now, she could feel the pain that sliced through her that night.

What happened next was a blur. Somehow she went from

standing next to that log to being locked in a cabin aboard a steamship bound for Europe.

When she arrived at Papa's family home, Ava found wedding preparations in progress—for her and the Count of Saarburg, a neighboring Prussian nobleman whose health was only slightly worse than his sense of humor.

Ava had run away three times only to be hauled back and put under lock and key. It quickly became apparent she had no choice. Either she remained living in a gilded prison—for Papa had declared her no longer trustworthy enough to return to Texas—or accept the marriage that had been arranged for her.

She agreed but only if she was granted an unsupervised meeting with her future groom. "I request three things," she told him. "My own allowance, the ability to travel freely, and that my parents are sent back to Texas immediately after the ceremony."

Not only had the count agreed, but he had also drawn up papers on the spot attesting to his agreement of the two requests. He also gave instructions to his staff to have the Beckers' things ready the morning of the wedding, for they would be departing directly from the church.

Ava left the room still wishing to remain unwed but knowing of all the grooms Papa might have chosen, at least he had found someone kind. That knowledge softened her anger, although only slightly. She still wanted Mama and Papa sent away, but she did entertain the thought that perhaps someday she might visit them while on her travels. If only her brother had been there. He might have helped her escape. Perhaps that was why Papa conveniently had him busy with family business elsewhere and unable to attend.

At the time, Ava expected that day would not arrive for a very long while.

When her wedding day came, she refused to speak to Papa or Mama and wore bitter tears and Mama's pearls as she nodded her agreement during the ceremony. Ava, now Dowager Countess of Saarburg, and her groom spent their wedding night in separate rooms of Saarburg Castle.

The next morning, there was only one royal left in residence as the count had gained his heavenly promise during the night. In the span of just a few hours, Ava had become first a bride and then a widow.

Wading her way through the multitude of responsibilities that came with her husband's estate and the search for the next heir took the better part of a year. Just last month, the new Count and Countess of Saarburg were installed in the drafty castle and Ava was finally released from her duties.

Unfortunately, she'd also been released from use of the Saarburg fortune, although the new count did deign to continue her allowance for the remainder of the year.

The funds were not enough to continue her travels, so now she was home. Back in Hartville ready to beg forgiveness and ask to be taken back in.

Ava turned the knob and walked inside. And found complete silence.

No boisterous chatting in the kitchen, no loud conversations between the menfolk. Just an eerie silence.

She walked back to the porch where her trunks had been deposited by the hired driver and looked around. Becker land stretched out as far as she could see, and the Creed property, the Three C Ranch, began just over the hill. Every inch of this place was as familiar as the back of her hand.

And nothing had changed in the year since she'd been gone.

One year, one month, and three days, to be exact.

Ava shrugged off the thought and walked back inside, through the parlor Mama furnished with items from the old country and down a hallway that ended at the door that opened onto the back of the house. Heat shimmered and danced along the horizon where trees barely moved in the balmy breeze.

Horses nickered in the western pasture while Papa's beloved cattle grazed in grasslands to the east. The door to the barn opened abruptly, and three ranch hands spilled out. Henry, the ranch foreman, followed closely behind.

"Well would you look at that," Henry called as he hurried toward her. "It's Miss Ava." He shook his head. "Guess I can't call you that anymore, can I?"

As the elderly man closed the distance between them, Ava landed in his arms with a grin. "You've known me since before I could climb up onto a horse. Of course, you can call me that."

"Well, then," he said when he released Ava to hold her at arm's length. "It's real good to see you again. We were awful sorry to hear about your husband. My condolences."

She held his gaze a moment longer and then nodded. "I appreciate that. Now tell me what I've missed this past year."

Henry waved away the question. "Not so much to tell other than your papa hired a few new men. Tiny there is brother to Rowdy. He's not the smartest feller I've got, but he sure is strong, and he's loyal to a fault. I believe he's going to work out just fine."

"Loyalty is important," she said, allowing the sting of knowing she'd been disloyal and had amends to make.

He nodded toward the three fellows heading for the bunkhouse. "Your brother decided it would take three of them to replace one of me, so I'm training them to do what I do. Not that I'm ready for the scrap heap just yet."

"I hope not for a very long time. Where is my brother?" she asked. "And my parents?"

"Well, now, your brother's off to drive cattle to market. Ought to be back in the next couple of weeks." He took off his cowboy hat and scratched his nearly bald head. "Now your mama and papa, that's a funny story, actually."

She gave him a sideways look. "How so?"

"Well, your mama convinced your papa it was time for him to take her gallivanting all over Europe." He paused. "I believe they were planning to surprise you."

"They did." She shook her head. "I don't suppose there's a way to contact them to let them know I'm here. I had intended to surprise *them*."

"You will," he said with a chuckle. "I'd suggest you post a letter to them. Your papa left a list on his desk in the library of where they'll be staying. By now they're probably in England."

"I will do that." She paused. "So is there nothing else going on I need to know about?"

"Got a man coming tomorrow to pick up a horse he's buying from your papa. Just so you know, last I heard, Gus had made the deal with Ezra Creed."

Ava kept her expression neutral as her heart lurched.

Henry shrugged. "Don't suspect that'll involve you, but just in case I'm not back from running fences when he gets here, I'll leave the papers downstairs on your daddy's desk, and the horse'll be in stall number one. The paint with the star on his forehead." He paused. "But I'll try real hard to get back, so you don't have to worry about it."

"Thank you. Anything else?"

"Had some trouble with the Cass Markham Gang lately. Rangers been hunting them, but ain't nobody going to rest easy until they're all put behind bars."

"Nothing that directly affects the ranch, I hope."

He gave what Ava had come to know as his serious expression. When Henry looked at her like that, he meant her to take notice.

"No, and I pray there won't be." He shifted positions and glanced down at her, his blue eyes kind but worried. "Still, you stay close here on the ranch, Miss Ava, especially with your menfolk gone, and even while you're out on Becker land, have your pistol handy. Can't have you putting yourself in harm's way."

Ava stifled a yawn. It seemed as though she had been traveling for months rather than weeks.

"I promise, though I doubt I'll be leaving the ranch anytime soon. Right now, I'd like nothing more than a bath, a bite to eat, and to sleep in my own bed."

Henry chuckled. "I'll see that your bed is fluffed and your bath drawn. As to vittles, I have it on good authority that Rosemary is making fried chicken tonight, so you're in luck."

She smiled. "If it means Rosemary's fried chicken, I'll do my best to stay awake."

Although she tried, however, Ava fell asleep almost immediately after she finished bathing with mama's lavender bath soap. She vaguely recalled the scent of frying chicken mixed with the lavender and awoke the next morning to a cold plate of last night's dinner on the bedside table and the sun streaming through the lace curtains that covered the eastern-facing windows of her bedroom.

Beginning her day was so much simpler on the ranch. Ava tamed her hair into a braid that she let hang down her back and then donned riding attire and boots. She grabbed her straw hat off the peg on the wall and then snatched up the cold plate to take it into the kitchen.

Today might be the day she would see Ezra Creed for the first time in more than a year, but she refused to allow him to think she'd made any special preparations for their reunion. Not after the way he had treated her.

After depositing the plate in the kitchen, minus one chicken leg, she wandered out to watch three of the Becker Ranch cowboys try to tame a wild stallion. Though comical, the process of settling a wild horse into a state where he could be saddled and bridled could also be dangerous.

So engrossed was she in the process as it unfolded, Ava did not hear the rider until his horse was almost upon her. Instinct took over, and before the stranger could rein in his mount, he was looking down the barrel of her gun.

"Hold on there, little lady," he told her as he held his hands out where she could see them. "I mean no trouble. Augustus Becker and I have an agreement that I am to purchase a paint from him. Might he be about?"

"I was under the impression a different man would be purchasing the horse."

The stranger held up a bag and shook it, making it plain coins were inside. "I was quoted a price, and I've brought it. I fail to understand how anyone other than me could be expected when Mr. Becker and I have already made complete our negotiations."

"How much is in that bag?"

When he told her, Ava lowered her gun and looked over to where the cowboys were now watching them. She waved for the men to join her. One remained behind to hold the rope they'd managed to get around the horse, but the others hurried toward her.

"Where's Henry?" she asked when the first cowboy, a fellow named Rowdy, arrived.

"Still riding fences." Rowdy watched the stranger warily. "Want me to go look for him?"

She returned her attention to the rider. "What's your name, sir?"

"Simon Temple, Esquire, from Austin, Texas, at your service. And to whom do I have the pleasure of speaking?"

"Don't matter, sir," Rowdy told him as he slanted a look at Ava. "Why don't you come back when Henry or Mr. Gus can help you?"

"That's not necessary," she said. "Tell me how you and Gus came to talk about this sale."

Mr. Temple sent a broad grin in her direction as he removed a handkerchief from his pocket and mopped his brow. "It's a funny story, actually. I spoke with him in regard to purchasing a few hundred head of his cattle. When I heard he had this paint, well, I am aware of the horse's parentage and had to have it."

"And?" she said.

"And although I have a reputation as a man who can argue a point in court, Mr. Becker has earned a reputation with me as a man who can drive up the price of a horse." He shrugged. "I had to have the horse, so I did what I had to do. And here I am."

"Yes," she said slowly, "here you are. I was told there would be another buyer."

"And perhaps there was to be, but I assure you the final award of that horse goes to me. Why else would I bring the agreed-upon price all the way out here?"

He did have a point. Hartville was several days' ride from Austin, so it was likely the fellow told the truth. Perhaps Henry hadn't been informed of the change in buyer.

Knowing what went into preparing to take cattle to market, that was the most likely answer. Gus had merely forgotten to mention it to Henry.

Ava returned her pistol to its hiding place in her pocket. "I'll just go get the papers." She looked up at the rider. "Might as well get down and go take a look at what you're buying."

"Yes, I would very much like that." He climbed off his horse and straightened his lapels.

"Stall number one," she told Rowdy. "The paint."

"I know the horse," he told Ava before looking at Mr. Temple. "You come on with me."

"Lead on, my boy," he said.

Rowdy met Ava's gaze. "I'll just take him while you and Tiny fetch the papers, all right?"

His meaning was clear. Owing to whatever trouble the Markham Gang had stirred up, Ava would be accompanied by a man named Tiny—who was the exact opposite—so as not to be surprised by an intruder inside the house.

"All right." She gave an almost imperceptible nod. "We won't be a minute."

True to Henry's word, she found the documents on the corner of Papa's desk. Had she not pressing business to attend to, she might have lingered. Unlike any other room of the sprawling ranch house, this room held the essence of her father.

Standing here with the painting of her stern-looking Becker grandparents hung over the fireplace beside a smiling painting of her mother in her wedding dress, Ava felt keenly the loss of their loving relationship.

This was a thought for another time, as was any attempt to repair what had been lost. She snatched up the papers and hurried back out to the barn, her oversized cowboy bodyguard in tow.

Ava found Mr. Temple admiring the paint. "Everything appears in order," she said.

Rowdy offered her a bag of coins. "Mr. Gus told me last week what he was asking for the paint, and I counted the money this fellow brought. It's all here."

"Thank you," she told him before handing Mr. Temple the documents, and he stowed them in his saddlebag. Then she turned to the cowboys who now stood together still watching the new owner of the paint as he went about tying up the horse. "And thank you as well."

They might have been thanked, but neither of them apparently thought they were dismissed. Rowdy leaned against the stall door watching Mr. Temple's every move while Tiny took over and secured the horse.

"Where are my manners?" she said as she realized her lack of hospitality. "Mr. Temple, I haven't offered you anything cold to drink, and it's hot as blazes outside."

Likely due to the hulking figure of Tiny leaning in just a bit too close, Mr. Temple quickly shook his head. "I am well provisioned and anxious to be back on the trail to my law practice in Austin tomorrow, but tonight I will stay in Hartville. I do offer my thanks for the kind hospitality."

Ava was tempted to thank Mr. Temple for preventing her from enduring a visit from Ezra Creed. Instead, she merely smiled and waved as he rode away.

CHAPTER 2

Ezra Creed slowed his horse to a trot as the boundary between Creed and Becker lands approached. Ever since Ava Becker—or whatever she called herself now—had stepped off the train in Hartville, speculation had begun as to when the two of them would meet again.

He'd worked hard to give the impression that there never had been anything between the two of them. Gus probably suspected, but as far as he knew, Ava never told anyone either.

So when she hadn't shown up at their meeting place on the night they were to elope, Ezra had no choice but to pretend to ignore the whole thing and wish her well. After all, most folks around Hartville had no idea Ava was anything to him other than his best friend's sister.

His job as a Ranger kept him busy enough to do that most days, especially now with the Markham Gang terrorizing these parts. But the nights, when he put his head on his pillow but his mind wouldn't slow down? Those were the times that feisty redhead he'd fallen in love with—the little tagalong who'd grown up to steal his heart—would plague his dreams.

He shrugged off the thought and considered the horse he'd paid Gus Becker for a few weeks ago. Ezra and Gus had kept his purchase of William Becker's paint quiet until the last minute.

Once word got out that the paint horse was for sale, everyone within fifty miles of Hartville would want in on the rare opportunity to bid. For, as much as the elder Becker loved his horses, Ezra could only count on one hand the number of times a sale of one of the magnificent beasts had happened.

He urged his horse to a trot toward the hill that divided the Triple C Ranch from the edge of the Becker Ranch. Without pausing at the top of the rise, he rode all the way down to the ranch house praying he wouldn't have to see Ava just yet.

He continued that prayer until he spied the ranch hand he knew as Rowdy. Knowing Gus was still out on the trail, he asked for Henry and then went out to the barn to wait for him.

Wandering through the barn, he didn't see the paint with the star on its forehead. Henry must have him out in the field.

Ezra whirled around to head for the pasture and then stopped short when he saw Ava watching him from the door from beneath the brim of a straw cowboy hat that appeared to have once belonged to Gus.

She leaned against the barn door, her fingers nervously toying with the end of her braid just like she used to do when she was trying to talk her way into whatever adventure he and Gus were planning.

"Hello, Countess," he said evenly.

"Just Ava will do," she said, with an equal lack of warmth. "Why are you here?"

They faced each other as if preparing for a duel. In a way, that was true. "I came to speak to Henry."

"He's out in the pasture. I've sent Rowdy after him." She remained where she stood, barely blinking. "You can wait outside."

"Tell Henry I'll be out at the spring watering my horse." He walked toward her, his heart pounding harder with every footstep. When he was close enough to touch her, he paused just for a moment to look into those jade-green eyes. "Your majesty," he said with a tip of his hat.

Without sparing her another glance, he walked past her and stepped out into the sunshine to retrieve his horse and lead it to the spring that ran behind the barn. By the time Henry joined him, Ezra had watered the horse and begun to pace.

"I hear you spoke with Miss Ava," Henry said after they'd said their greetings.

"Briefly," he said. "But I've come for the paint. I didn't see it in the barn."

Henry stood with his hands on his hips, an old man and yet still in the prime of his life. "That's because the new owner took it yesterday."

"I paid Gus for that horse before he left." Ezra's voice rose with his temper. "How could someone else leave with it?"

"You'd have to ask Miss Ava. She handled the transaction, though Rowdy said he counted the money to be sure it was all there."

Ezra reached up to touch the peace medal his Comanche grandmother had given him. Strung on beads made by her people, the medal had been given to his grandmother by President Lincoln himself and was the last connection to his Comanche heritage other than his reputed resemblance to his warrior great-grandfather.

The feel of the silver beneath his fingers generally calmed him but not today. A horse was pretty much a horse to his way of thinking, but that paint was special. He and Gus had looked all over for a horse with a lineage like that one's sire, and Ezra had picked the dam from among the best horseflesh in three counties.

No, that paint was his, and he would not allow it to be sold out from under him. Especially since he'd already paid for it.

"Mr. Gus is likely two weeks from returning," Henry said, as if reading Ezra's mind. "Maybe three depending on the weather."

Ezra gave Henry a curt nod. "Then I'll handle this without him."

He pressed past the ranch foreman and stalked back to the barn. When he didn't find Ava there, he headed toward the ranch house where a ranch hand named Tiny intercepted him.

"I can't let you go in the house," Tiny told him. "Mr. Henry's charged me with protecting Miss Ava, and it looks like you're up to no good."

Ezra reached into his pocket to pull out the Ranger badge the captain had given the men under his command and held it up to show the oversized ranch hand. "I am investigating a possible horse theft, and I need to speak to her."

Tiny seemed confused and then concerned. Finally, he looked past Ezra to nod. "There's Mr. Henry coming up the path. I do what he says, and I won't lose my job over the loss of a horse. You have him tell me what I ought to do, and I'll do it."

"There's no need." Ava stepped around her bodyguard. "I'll speak to the Ranger, Tiny. Won't you go and let Henry know everything is fine?"

Tiny looked down at his employer, his expression showing worry. "But he don't look happy, Miss Ava. You sure about this?"

"He has every right to look unhappy," she told Tiny. "So yes, I am sure."

Tiny begrudgingly nodded and walked toward Henry, but not before purposely nudging Ezra and giving him a look that said he could easily be torn limb from limb if Miss Ava changed her mind.

"Come on inside, and let's talk about this." Ava turned her back on him to disappear inside the ranch house, not bothering to check and see if he would follow.

He found her in her father's library giving Henry's wife, Rosemary, instructions to bring refreshments. Though tea and cookies wouldn't improve the situation, Ezra kept his mouth shut until the cook was gone.

The former love of his life was sitting in the chair her papa used to favor, her copper-colored braid slung over her right shoulder and the morning sun shining down through the window beside her. In profile, she looked so much like her mama at that age that Ezra quickly shifted his attention to the painting of Anne Becker over the fireplace.

"I'm listening, Ezra," Ava said, causing him to return his attention to her.

He wanted to ask her other questions such as where she was the night she should have eloped with him. Why she chose to cut off all contact with him. And though he could have questioned her like he did the criminals he came into contact with, he refrained.

For now.

"Where is my horse?" he said instead through clenched jaw.

She shifted positions but kept her gaze squarely on Ezra. "I am curious why you believe it is yours."

"Because I paid your brother for that horse several weeks ago."

"Then I'm sure you won't mind showing me your proof for that purchase," she said.

Ezra bit back on the words he wanted to say and forced a smile. "Now that's funny, Ava. I know you've been gone a while, but since when did Gus and I need more than a handshake to transact business?"

She looked away, allowing sunshine to wash over a stubborn profile he knew all too well. Silence fell between them despite the fact that Ava looked as though she had plenty to say.

Ezra shifted positions, his patience at an end. "All right, Ava. It looks like our business here is done. Just so you know, I will be reporting a horse theft to the captain, and the Rangers will be investigating this further."

That got her attention. Ava sprung to her feet. "Horse theft? Just who are you accusing of theft?"

His gaze swept the length of her then returned to her eyes. "I'd say it's either you or that man who rode off with my paint."

Her eyes narrowed. "Are you calling me a horse thief, Ezra Creed?"

"I am calling you a potential suspect. And in my official capacity as a Ranger, I am advising you not to leave town without my permission until this case is settled."

Ava opened her mouth as if to respond and then shook her head instead. "This is ridiculous. How long have you known me, Ezra? In all those years, have I ever stolen anything?"

My heart. "I don't think you want me to base an investigation on my opinion of your character, Ava."

"And I do not think you want to have a conversation about my opinion of your character right now, Ezra," she said, anger vibrating in her voice, "so please just leave."

"You made it perfectly clear what your opinion of me was," he snapped. "As a Ranger, I have to look past your behavior then to evaluate your behavior now."

She gripped the back of the chair beside her. "Get. Out."

Ezra turned his back on Ava and stalked back out into the sunshine with the words he wanted to have said chasing him. Listening to the woman who let him believe she loved him and then ran off to marry someone else talk about character was more than he could bear.

Ignoring the stares of Rowdy and the oversized bodyguard, Ezra climbed into the saddle and took off toward the Triple C. By the time he had cooled down enough to realize he better get his emotions under control, he was halfway home.

Since he was a little boy, his pop made sure he understood no matter how low the other person went, Ezra was called to a higher standard. Someday he would answer for his behavior on this earth, and the Lord wouldn't listen to excuses.

Ezra pulled back on the reins and paused at the ridge. Taking a deep breath, he let it out slowly as he glanced back over his shoulder. Ava Becker, or whatever she went by now, might have stomped on his heart but she absolutely would not get away with stealing his horse.

No matter what, he had some apologizing to do. This was not the way to get any information out of Ava on where that horse was now.

He retraced his path to the Becker Ranch and found Henry waiting for him outside the barn. "She ain't here," he said before Ezra could say a word.

"How'd you know?" He climbed off the horse.

Henry ducked his head and chuckled, then looked back up at Ezra. "Same way I always knew when one of you three young 'uns had a spat, be it you, her, or Gus. The one who took offense would light out toward the horizon on whatever horse could be saddled up the fastest."

Ezra clutched the horse's reins as he looked past Henry toward the west. "We did do that, didn't we?"

"Sure did. Some things never change." He nodded westward. "She went that way."

"Thank you kindly." Ezra climbed back up into the saddle. Something caught his eye as it moved over the horizon.

Henry followed Ezra's gaze. "That just might be her now."

"It might," Ezra said slowly as he squinted to get a better look, "but I don't see a rider on that horse."

He took off toward the horse before Henry could respond, urging the sure-footed pony to practically fly. Sure enough, the horse's saddle was empty.

"Go find Miss Ava, son," Henry called as he headed toward

them on one of the Becker geldings. "This one'll find the barn on its own. I'll take to the hill, and you go that way down by the river."

Ezra chuckled despite the gravity of the situation. Even though he was a Texas Ranger and had been ordering men around for quite some time, old Henry still saw him as the boy he used to be.

"And watch for snakes," Henry added. "Cottonmouth's been thick down there lately."

"Yes, sir," Ezra called as he veered off toward the old familiar trail that ran alongside the banks of the Sabinal River. He and Gus had spent uncounted hours of their boyhood here fishing, swimming, and generally trying to hide from Gus's pesky sister.

She almost always found them, however. Such were Ava's tracking skills. Skills he'd taught her, much to Gus's chagrin.

He continued following the trail, looking out for any sign that Ava had passed through here. As he found the evidence—a broken twig here, tracks there—he would call her name, thus far without any response.

Then Ezra rounded a bend in the river and found Ava sitting on a log—their log where they were supposed to meet that last night before she disappeared—looking as if she hadn't a care in the world. Once again his temper spiked.

"At some point did you not hear me calling you, Ava?"

"I did," she said as she stared up at him.

"And you didn't think to answer?" He paused. "Maybe I should call you 'Countess.' Then would you respond?"

She ignored his jab. "I was hoping Henry would find me." She looked past him toward the trail he'd just traveled down. "He is with you, isn't he?"

His horse stomped at the ground, and Ezra quieted him. "No. Henry took off toward the hills."

"Well, that's strange." She shook her head. "He saw me head toward this trail. Even told me to watch for snakes."

CHAPTER 3

Where in the world was Henry? Surely, he didn't send Ezra Creed after her.

Ava shifted positions on the old log, reluctant to stand and acknowledge the fact that she'd be sporting a collection of bruises by bedtime. Instead, she shrugged as the Ranger climbed down from his horse.

"You've found me, and I'm fine," she said as casually as she could manage. "Just let Henry know I'm here, and he can come and get me."

"What happened?" he asked, ignoring her statement completely.

She sighed. Ezra always was nosy. The skill that served him well as a Ranger certainly made him annoying as a would-be rescuer.

"A snake spooked the horse. I should have been paying better attention. I guess I'm out of practice. We didn't have this problem in..."

Ava clamped down on her lips. What was wrong with her?

"No, I don't suppose you did." Ezra glanced around. "Did you see which direction the snake went?"

"Look down." When the big bad Ranger jumped at the sight of the headless black cottonmouth just inches from the tips of his boots, she giggled in spite of herself. "I buried the head just like you taught me."

The fact that a poisonous snake's head could bite and inject venom for a lengthy period after being removed from the body was just one of the lessons the Ranger had taught her and Gus. Thanks to Ezra, she could also identify all sorts of tracks, respond to a bobwhite's call and have it answer, and navigate her way home at night using the North Star as a guide.

He'd also taught her to shoot, and she'd turned out to be more accurate than either Ezra or Gus. The dead snake was testament to that.

"I'm surprised Henry didn't hear the shot," Ezra said.

"He might have." She pressed her palms against the rough bark on either side of the spot where she sat. "The ranch hands have been getting rid of wild hogs this morning. I heard a few shots before I surprised this cottonmouth trying to cross the path."

Ezra just stood there, a dark-haired Ranger with one foot in the world of the Texas settlers on his father's side and the other foot squarely with his Comanche ancestors. Her fingers curled at the thought of how they once ran through his thick shock of black hair. Today that hair was tied back with a length of leather beneath his hat. A silver star glistened just above his shirt pocket, matching the Comanche beads and medal around his neck.

She had to look away from the eyes that always watched her so carefully. Even then, Ava could still feel his cool stare.

"Why did you come back?" Ezra broke the silence that had fallen between them.

Ava returned her attention to him. "Why do you care?" The

question was needlessly cruel, despite the things Ezra had said about her to Papa. "I guess you haven't heard, then."

"A man in my line of work doesn't give credence to rumors, Ava. I prefer hearing anything you've got to say firsthand." He paused, the reins still in his right hand. "I always did."

Those words appeared to be loaded with emotion, but what he meant by the statement eluded her. If anything, she should be telling him that.

"My husband died." She studied the grass stain on her skirt. "Now that the new count has assumed his role, my assistance in his transition was no longer needed."

"So you're not the countess anymore? I guess you must miss that," he said, sarcasm evident.

"I was married to the man for less than twenty-four hours, Ezra," she snapped. "But he was a nice man. What I missed more was Texas."

And you, she refused to add. Not when he obviously had not missed her.

"Texas would be difficult to leave, I'd think." He still studied her with those unforgettable eyes. "Apparently not for you."

"I had no choice," she said as she gave way to her rising temper.

"You had at least two." Ezra shifted positions and lifted up two fingers on his free hand. "Run away to become a countess or stay here and marry me."

Silence crackled between them.

Ava rose slowly. "'He regrets that the farce he carried on with you got this far and wishes you to forgive him for deceiving you as to any affection he pretended to have.' Do those words sound familiar, Ezra? Because they are words I will never forget."

Ezra released the reins. "Who said that to you? If it was that husband of yours..."

"It was you, Ezra," she snapped. "You told my father and he

told me. I've held those words in my heart for so long that I have memorized them. How dare you act like you didn't say them?"

"Because I didn't." His voice was low and rough. A sliver of sunlight slashed his features as he turned toward her. "I never said any of that."

"But my father told me..."

Her father. Papa had been furious that night. So angry, in fact, that she'd feared for what he might do.

Emotion sunk her, and Ava could only return to her place on the log to gather her hands around her knees and duck her head. Had all that happened in the past year been built on lies?

The sound of leaves rustling caused her to lift her head. Ezra settled on the log beside her, his expression unreadable.

"I waited all night right here," he said softly. "I thought something happened to you. At first light, I went to the ranch house intent on making sure you were safe. Rosemary was at the creek getting water. She told me you and your father were gone to Galveston."

"I suppose by first light we were already headed for the coast." She shrugged. "I remember very little of that night other than being told it was all a big joke you had played on me. For a while I blamed Gus too. You two were always teasing me."

"It was never a joke to me."

She smiled. "I believe you."

"Gus didn't believe you would leave like that unless you were forced."

Tears threatened, but she refused to allow them to fall. "Gus was right."

"I wish I'd let him try to find that out. I told him to let it go." Ezra swung a pained look in her direction as the silver badge pinned to his shirt glistened in the sun. "My pride wouldn't let me chase down a woman who didn't want me."

"If only I could tell you how many times I tried to—"

A shrill whistle cut through the rest of her response. Ezra jumped to his feet and answered with a similar response. "Over here, Branch," he called.

A dark-haired man rode up the trail toward them. Ezra bounded off in his direction without a backward glance at Ava. She watched as the man dismounted and handed something to Ezra.

They seemed to be having a serious discussion about something, but she could only hear snippets of the conversation. Something about the Markham Gang and a horse. The older man handed Ezra a note, and then they both looked back in her direction.

~

"I heard Will Becker's daughter was back," Branch Kilborn said. "Is she the reason your horse got stolen?"

"I haven't decided if she's a suspect or a witness," he told the other Ranger. "Either way, she's the only one who knows what the man who took off with the paint looks like."

"Other than at least two ranch hands who said he presented himself as a lawyer from Austin to the lady over yonder." His gaze never left Ezra's face. "I took the time to ask before I headed this way. Rowdy and Tiny both interacted with him. They gave me a description, but it didn't fit any of the known members of the Markham Gang. Either we're dealing with someone new to the gang or a completely unrelated perpetrator," he said as he consulted his notebook.

"I see. I haven't spoken to the other witnesses because I was waiting for word from the captain."

"Well, you've got it now. And here's a word from me." He nodded toward Ava and then looked back at Ezra with a serious expression. "When you signed up with the Rangers, you made a promise to give your all to every investigation. Allowing yourself to be distracted by a woman is not the way to do that."

Ezra's temper rose. "I'm neither distracted nor giving anything but my all. I'll handle this my way. Let the captain know I got his message, would you?"

"I will," Branch said as he climbed back into the saddle. "But did you get my message? Romance and Rangering don't mix. Keep your wits about you, Creed, or you might as well decide now that you'll never get that horse back, understand?"

He tucked the note into his pocket and turned his back on Branch. "Got it," he said as he walked away. "Tell the captain I'll check in when I've got news."

Branch's response was hooves thundering as he rode away. Ezra straightened his spine and marched back to Ava with renewed purpose. No matter what Branch Kilborn thought, he was not going to be sidetracked by the fact that the woman he loved did not run off without him.

"All right, Ava," he said as she rose to walk toward him. "I've got work to do. Time to go." He glanced down at the remains of the cottonmouth. "Unless you'd rather stay here with your friend."

"No, I think I'm ready to go," she said, although she seemed more than a little reluctant to climb up in front of him to ride back to the ranch house.

To keep himself from thinking about the fact that Ava Becker was practically in his arms as they followed the trail out of the thicket, Ezra considered the possibility that the Markham Gang had added a new member. It was certainly possible.

"Ezra?" Ava said, cutting through his thoughts. "About that paint..."

"What about it?" he said as he tried not to breathe in the lavender scent of her hair.

"I hope you know I will return whatever money you've paid to Gus. Just tell me the amount, and I will see that you leave with it."

"I don't want your money, Ava." He paused to guide the horse around a bend in the trail. "I want that paint back. I've been watching that horse since it was born. There's not a finer pedigree in Texas right now than the one that paint has. I reckon the man who convinced you the horse was supposed to go to him knew this."

"I'm sorry about that," she told him. "His story seemed true enough and, well, I wanted him to be right."

Ezra slowed the horse. "Why would you want that?"

She shrugged. "Because if the horse was his, then I wouldn't have to see you. See, Henry told me you'd be coming by for the paint, but when Mr. Temple arrived, I considered the problem solved."

He spurred the horse on and then had to catch Ava before she toppled off. "Steady there," Ezra said against her ear. "I'll need my witness alive."

"Witness? So I'm no longer a suspect?"

"Not unless you convince me to change my mind," he said as the ranch house came into view. "But being a witness means I'll need you to identify the man who rode off with my horse."

She tried to look over her shoulder but only succeeded in nearly sliding off again. He caught her and this time held her tight against him. "You never did listen to me. Sit still."

"Mr. Temple was staying at the hotel in town. It's possible he's still there, although he did tell me he wanted to get back on the trail to Austin."

"All right. Then you and I will take a buggy to town and see if we can find him."

A few minutes later, Ezra helped Ava down off the horse.

Henry came out to meet them with a grin on his face. "I see you've found Miss Ava."

"Yeah, funny how she was exactly where you sent me," Ezra said. "I need her to come with me into Hartville to identify a suspect. I'll also need Rowdy or Tiny to come along unless you saw the man, then I want you to join us instead. And if you've a mind to let us borrow a wagon or buggy, I'd be much obliged."

The old ranch manager shook his head. "You'll need one of those two, I'm afraid. I missed all the excitement. Believe I was running fences then. I'll have a buggy hitched up and ready in a few minutes."

"Much obliged," he said to Henry as he hurried back into the barn. When he turned around to speak to Ava, she was gone.

Ezra headed for the closed door but found Rosemary blocking his entrance. "You stay out here. I don't know what happened to her out there, but I better not find out you had anything to do with it."

He shook his head as the tiny woman stared up at him in a manner that was more intimidating than the meanest outlaw he'd come across. Just like that, he was the kid who'd been caught pulling her laundry off the line and using it for sails on the boat he and Gus were building.

"No," Ezra insisted. "I found her like that. Her horse spooked and she fell off. Killed a snake and had to hitch a ride back to the ranch on my horse, but she's not hurt as far as I know."

Rosemary rested her fists on her hips. "If her story matches yours, then no harm will come to you, Ranger. Either way, I will be scrubbing grass stains off her dress for far longer than I intend to contemplate right now. So you just go on over to the wagon my Henry's bringing up, and I'll see that Miss Ava doesn't tarry too long in freshening up."

"Yes ma'am," he said as he did exactly as he was told.

CHAPTER 4

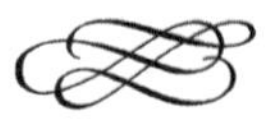

Ezra stepped out into the sunshine and put his hat back on. According to Big Joe at the livery stable, the lawyer who had his horse had been in Hartville until shortly after sunrise this morning. Apparently, Simon Temple, or whatever his name was, had taken his time leaving town.

Folks who were breaking the law tended to make themselves scarce. That told Ezra it was possible the man had nothing to hide.

Possible but not proven.

"He's got a head start." Ezra looked past Ava in the direction of the train station behind the livery.

"I can't believe we missed him."

He shrugged. "We did, but we've got a train leaving in a few hours that'll beat him there."

"You're joking." Her pretty eyes widened, and it appeared Ava was ready to steal the wagon and leave him in the street. Tiny, for all his size, just stood by quietly and appeared to be waiting for instructions.

Ezra curled his fingers to keep from touching her sleeve to get her attention. "Ava, listen to me. I'm completely serious. Wouldn't you rather take a train than try to follow on horseback, sleep on a bedroll, and risk having him beat us there?"

Ava seemed to be studying him. Then, slowly, she nodded. "Yes, we would definitely get to Austin well before Mr. Temple. And I certainly prefer trains to sleeping under the stars."

"Tiny, you go with Ava to gather up whatever she needs for our trip to Austin."

"But there's no time to go back to the ranch," she protested.

"That's true, and I wasn't talking about going back there. I'm sure you can find what you need here in town. Put whatever you buy on my account."

"Oh, I don't think so." She shook her head. "Can you imagine the talk if I buy night clothes and a new dress, put it on your bill, and then leave town with you?"

"Good point. I suppose you'll have to let me pay you back, then."

"How long do you think we'll be gone?" she asked rather than acknowledge his statement.

"If everything goes well, we should be back tomorrow."

Ava nodded. "All right, then."

"All right. Tiny, help Miss Ava get what she needs and I'll buy our tickets."

The oversized ranch hand took a step closer to Ezra. "I don't go anywhere until Miss Ava says I do." He turned his attention to Ava. "And, Miss Ava, I don't like the sound of this. I don't think Mr. Henry or your brother would approve."

She craned her neck to look up at Tiny. "While I appreciate your dedication to keeping me safe, neither my brother nor Henry have any say in what I do anymore."

"That won't stop 'em from asking me why I let you do what they wouldn't have let you do," he said, his voice pleading.

"I believe they would want us to help the Ranger solve this case, don't you think?"

"I think they would want you back home at the ranch." He looked past Ava, presumably for help from Ezra.

"And I *think* since neither of them bothered to tell my father that when he hauled me off to Europe to marry the count, they forfeit any opportunity to say that now," she snapped, pink rising in her cheeks.

Ezra stifled a smile. She sure was pretty when her temper was up.

"Truly, Miss Ava," the ranch hand said, "thinking isn't my job. Keeping you safe is."

Her expression softened. Gradually, the beginnings of a smile lifted the corners of her lips.

"Then you and I are going to Austin." Ava rested her hand on Tiny's arm and gave him a smile, then slipped past him to turn her attention to Ezra. "I'll send a telegram to the staff in Austin to ready the house for our arrival."

"I wouldn't want to cause tongues to wag, Ava," he said, "and me staying under your papa's roof with you is surely going to get back to the gossips in Hartville."

"I guarantee the house will be filled to the rafters with students from the university anyway," she said. "I'm offering a spot in one of the smaller cottages on the property with Tiny as your roommate."

"I suppose that might work. So off with you." He glanced past her and caught Tiny's impassive gaze. "That is, if Miss Ava says so."

"She does." Ava linked arms with the ranch hand. "Come on, Tiny. Let's go shopping. I think you're in need of a new set of clothes if you're going to look presentable in Austin. That I don't mind Mr. Creed buying."

"Miss Ava, truly I don't want to—"

"Trust me, Tiny," Ezra interrupted. "Let her buy you whatever she thinks you need. Just keep a close eye on her while she's doing it."

"Yes, sir," he said without much enthusiasm.

They made plans to meet back for dinner before boarding the train, and then Ezra parted with them to head for the station. After purchasing tickets and sending a fellow back to the Triple C and Becker ranches to inform them of their change of plans, he found himself with time on his hands and decided to stroll down to the Ranger office.

There he found Branch studying his notebook and the captain going over what looked like arrest records. "I thought I'd find you two here," he said when the door closed behind him.

Both men rose, and the captain met him halfway to clasp his hand on Ezra's shoulder. "Figured you'd be off chasing a horse thief by now," Cap said.

"Train leaves in a while. I thought I'd come by and check in."

"Glad you did." The captain nodded to the desk where Branch looked up from his ledger. "I checked into this fellow Simon Temple. He's got no warrants, and he's not trying to hide what he's doing. That makes me doubt he's joined up with the Markhams."

"I agree, although there's always the possibility that they're getting smart and changing up how they operate."

"That's true." He paused. "I haven't heard back from my contacts in Austin, but if he's not known to them, then we've got a whole other situation on our hands."

"I'll pay a visit to the office there while I'm in town to see what they know about Temple."

The captain nodded while Branch seemed to be studying him in that silent way of his. "That's a good idea." He hesitated a moment. "There's more. Rumor is the Markham Gang has sent three of their men to watch for that horse of yours. Apparently, word is out that it's a fine animal."

"Fine, indeed." Ezra didn't add how long he'd searched for a descendant of his Comanche grandmother's horses to provide half the bloodline.

Apparently, somewhere along the way, he'd made inquiries to

the wrong person for the news to get back to the Markham Gang. Just who that person was would be yet another question that needed answering.

The captain shrugged. "I don't know if the gang has followed your suspect, but you'd best watch for them."

"Sure will." He gave a brisk nod. "Do we know which ones, Cap?"

"Roan Galway, Bass Tomkins, and Cherokee Sam. Best be watching for them even though they may or may not cause you trouble. Far as I'm concerned, any Markham Gang member still out roaming free is a man in need of putting behind bars."

"I agree. Even if those three aren't looking to steal my horse, I guarantee they'll want someone else's."

"Or anything else they can steal. Now tell me about this horse everyone wants. What exactly happened out at Becker Ranch with the Temple fellow?"

Branch met his gaze, seeming to dare him to admit to something. What that something was, Ezra had no idea.

"Short version is I bought a horse from Gus Becker. When I came to pick it up, another man had showed up and convinced Miss Becker he was the one Gus agreed to sell to."

"But he wasn't," the captain said in that understated way of his.

"No, he wasn't. I paid Gus weeks ago."

"Did Miss Becker know this?"

Ezra gave that a minute's thought. "No, she says she believed Mr. Temple when he told her the horse was his. He paid her fair and square, so she didn't think anything of it."

"So he paid her? And you're still calling it horse theft?" The captain gave him that look usually reserved for new recruits. "How do you figure that?"

"The horse was mine, bought and paid for. The fact that a man I've never heard of just rode up and then left with it doesn't settle well." He paused. "Temple will get his money back, but he paid for a horse that wasn't for sale and, according to Miss Becker, was extremely insistent that he buy it."

"As you said, it's a fine horse."

"Yes, that's true. But how does a stranger come to know about this fine horse when it was never up for sale other than the transaction between Gus and me?" Ezra shifted positions to lean against the doorframe. "That's a question I'd like Mr. Temple to answer."

The captain scratched his head and seemed deep in thought. Finally, he nodded. "And Ava can identify Temple?"

"She can."

"As can the ranch hands," Branch said evenly.

He looked past the captain to see Branch watching him closely. His expression gave nothing of his thoughts away, but Ezra had a good idea of what the seasoned Ranger was thinking.

"I've got one of them going with us. I figure two witnesses are better than one."

"Especially when one is newly widowed, and you used to be sweet on her," Cap said with a twitch of a grin.

"Water under the bridge." Ezra waved his hand. "This is all business."

"What's this I hear about water under a bridge?" Cap's wife Etta swept in with a smile on her face. "The Becker girl is back, you know. It'd be neighborly to give her a proper Hartville welcome, what with you two being old friends and all."

Ezra returned her grin. "Yes, I did have a chance to meet up with her, so you don't have to worry about that."

Etta shook her head. "I don't believe you understand my meaning. I'm sure she's missed our little town. Why don't you be a gentleman and keep her company? Maybe escort her around and help her get used to being back in Texas again?"

"Long as he doesn't let all that neighborly help get in the way of catching those Markham Gang members." He returned his attention to Ezra. "You say this trip is all business?"

"It is, sir."

"See that you keep it that way." Cap glanced back at Branch. "You got anything to add to that, Branch?"

Branch met Ezra's gaze, his expression solemn as always. "Nope. Said all I intend to on the subject."

The captain turned back around, his mustache twitching above his grin. "Well, all right, then. I guess there's nothing else to add to that, but I've got an errand I'd like you to run while you're in Austin."

"Sure, Cap. What is it?"

"Fellow named James Lacy is in charge of the law over there. Good man. I rode with him when he was a Ranger. You let him know me and my men are at his disposal if he needs us."

"You know they caught the Servant Girl Annihilator." Branch spoke without looking up from his work. "I doubt Lacy will be needing any backup."

"No, Branch," the captain said. "They're still looking for the man. Everyone they've brought up on charges has been acquitted."

"Well, that's because the real murderer is dead." Branch lifted his head. "Footprints taken at the scenes of each of the crimes showed the killer took his boots off so he could get in the houses without being heard."

"I read something about that," Ezra said. "They took casts of the footprints and made an estimate on the size of the man based on how heavy the victim was that he carried. Fascinating police work. I'd like to study it more."

"Yes, that's true." Branch raised a brow. "But what you probably didn't read was the killer only had four toes."

"No, I didn't know that," Ezra said. "That ought to make him easy to find when they catch him."

"I told you they already did. Remember that last murder where the police shot the man when he was fleeing from the scene?"

"That fellow lingered in the hospital close to twenty-four hours before he died, didn't he?"

Branch nodded. "Medical report says he had four toes."

"How'd you know this?" the captain asked.

"I read the report." He shrugged. "Interesting case. Thought I'd research it in my spare time. If you need any further proof, there hasn't been another murder since that man died, and it's been what? Five or six months?"

Cap nodded. "Yes, it has. I hope you're right, then. I wouldn't like to think the man who was capable of doing what he did is still out there."

Another nod and Branch went back to his notebook. Ezra reached to shake hands with the captain. "I'll pass your message on to Chief Lacy. Want me to tell him to stop looking for that murderer, Branch?"

The Ranger ignored him.

Cap chuckled. "You ought not tease him. Like as not he's right, you know."

Ezra found Branch peering up at him once more. "He usually is."

"Keep in touch," the captain said, shaking Ezra's hand, "and let me know if you need me to send backup."

Ezra very nearly took the captain up on that offer when he saw the amount of luggage Ava somehow managed to collect during the short time she was away from him. Though she acted as though there was nothing peculiar about standing beside a mountain of items that weren't there just a short while ago, at least Tiny looked contrite.

He also looked quite dapper in his new suit of clothes and hat. "I kept her out of trouble," was all he could offer as he strained to lift a trunk.

"What is in here?" Ezra asked as he threw the last bag on the porter's cart. "And how long do you think you're going to be gone? I told you I'd have you back by tomorrow."

"I know you did," she said sweetly, "but I had an idea that as long as I'm in Austin, I may as well enjoy myself for a few days."

"A few days? This looks like enough to see you to Europe and back." Once the words were out, Ezra immediately wanted to reel them back in.

Tiny's pained expression worsened. "I tried to talk sense into her. Mr. Henry's not going to like this at all."

Ava's smile was radiant, but Ezra recognized the flash of irritation in her eyes. "And I have reminded Tiny that while Henry might be his boss, he is not mine."

Tiny gave Ezra a *what-can-I-do* look.

The conductor gave notice the train was boarding. "That's all fine and good, Ava," Ezra said, "just as long as you remember that while you're with me, I'm in charge."

"I fail to see how that applies to me," she said imperiously.

"Right now, you're just a pretty girl on a shopping trip, but the minute you climb onto that train, you are a witness in a Ranger investigation. Do you understand the difference?"

She looked up at him with a grin on her lovely face. "I'm sure you're about to explain the difference."

He stifled a smile. "My investigation, my control. That's the short version. What that means for you and your fellow witness is that as long as you're with me, I am the boss of you."

Her smile fell. "I don't think I like the sound of that, Ezra."

"I'm sure you don't. But that's how it works. Next time you're in charge, I'll do what you say. But today it's the other way around. You're either a witness who's going with me or a woman who's got to find a way to get all her fancy purchases back home to the ranch house. Which is it, Ava?"

While Ava took her time making up her mind, Tiny apparently

had no such issue with who was in control of the situation. He nodded toward Ezra with the expression of a man who liked knowing what his job was and to whom he'd be answering.

"I'd be proud to help with a Ranger investigation," he told Ezra as he tugged at the collar of his new shirt. "Unless Miss Ava needs me to escort her back to the ranch. Then I'll be begging off of coming along with you."

"That's fair." Ezra returned his attention to the feisty female. "Ava?"

CHAPTER 5

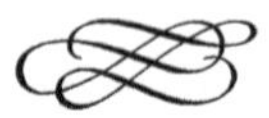

Ezra Creed had just called her pretty right there in front of Tiny, the train conductor, and whoever else might be listening. Something like that shouldn't matter to a woman of her age and experience, but it did.

It mattered more than it ought to.

"Ava?" the subject of her thoughts said. "The train will be leaving soon. Will you be on it or did Tiny get all prettied up in his new suit of clothes just to follow you back to the ranch and get teased?"

Ezra Creed said she was pretty.

That thought followed Ava up onto the train, floating just a step behind as the conductor led her to her seat. She gave the older man a smile and then settled down to await her companions.

The plan to escape to Austin had come quite suddenly while perusing frocks at the mercantile. In Hartville, she'd always be looked at askance as the woman who fled, wed, and then returned a widow.

A few would bother to find out the details and offer support. Many would not.

Truth be told, she'd been looking for a way out of Hartville since she took off on Gus's favorite pony at the age of seven. She'd been heading for the big city then, declaring it a place where she could be someone other than Ava Becker, daughter and sister of two of the most stubborn men on the planet.

Not much had changed in fifteen years. She was still running from living under the constant supervision of stubborn men. Only now, she could add one more man to the list.

She looked up at the man himself, the Texas Ranger with the slow smile, a long, lean profile, and those haunting Comanche eyes that missed nothing. Somewhere between irritation and infatuation, Ava had realized there was something special about Ezra Creed.

The older she got, the more she was certain of it.

Her view of the Ranger was suddenly blocked by Tiny, who pressed past him to take the seat next to her. "Just doing my job," he said to Ezra.

Ezra grinned as he easily folded his lanky frame onto the seat across from her. "I'm sure her daddy will appreciate the effort."

When the Ranger spared her a glance, Ava rolled her eyes. She'd come all the way from Prussia alone. Surely, these two realized she could take a simple train ride to Austin without a bodyguard and a lawman.

And yet it was nice to have two men standing between her and danger. During her time abroad, very few had cared where she went or with whom she traveled. She liked to think her late husband, had he lived longer, might have at least held enough fondness for her to consider her safety, but she would never know.

"So, Ranger," Tiny said. "This horse we're going to fetch...what makes it so special? I mean, it's fine horseflesh. Saw it from a colt grown to now, but what specifically makes it worth all this trouble?"

Ezra's expression went contemplative. A moment later, his focus returned.

"It all goes back to a paint pony and a family story," he said. "My Comanche grandmother rode that horse until the day she was taken up in the removal that took the Comanche from their lands. I'm sure there was more to it than what she told me as a child, but when she was snatched up, the men who took her took all the livestock too. She tried to stay with her family but got lost in all the commotion."

Tiny shook his head. "Just awful," he said softly.

"My grandmother marched along and did what she was told, but all the time, she planned her escape. One night, she slipped past the guards and took off on foot. Wouldn't you know it, but she got maybe a mile down the road when she heard someone coming after her."

Ava had never heard this story. Despite her intention to ignore both of them the entire trip, she leaned in so as not to miss a word.

"So my granny, she hid behind first one tree and then another. She even waded out into a stream to hide her tracks. That might have worked, too"—Ezra paused to shift his attention from Tiny to Ava—"except for the snake. Cottonmouth. Bit her twice before she killed it."

She gasped in spite of herself. "Oh, Ezra," she said softly. "No."

"Last thing she remembered was burying that head so it wouldn't hurt anyone else." Another pause. "She woke up under a quilt on a fine cotton mattress with more than a week of her life gone. Turns out the man who'd been chasing her was a guard who'd been so sickened by what he saw on the trail that he was running from it too. He brought her to his mama because she knew the healing arts. It was a brave thing that man did because that's the first place anyone would have looked for him."

Tiny let out a low breath. "Well, how about that?"

Ezra nodded. "The man who saved my grandmother fell in

love with her, and they were married. And you asked about the horse?" At Tiny's nod, Ezra continued. "Turns out the horse my grandfather randomly chose for his escape was the very horse that had been taken from my grandmother."

"Oh," Ava said softly. "That's such a beautiful story."

Tiny nodded.

"It is." Ezra shifted positions. "Which is why when I heard there was one descendant of that horse on my uncle's land, I tried to buy the stallion, but my uncle refused. He said we could bring one of Gus's mares to breed. The result was that paint."

"I know we all took a liking to that pony," Tiny said, "but can't you just breed the mare again and get another one?"

"Barn fire," he said, his eyes downcast. "Lost that stallion and a half dozen more."

"And now the only remaining offspring is gone too." Guilt stabbed at her.

"That's awful, Ranger," Tiny said, a tremor in his voice.

Ava reached across the short distance between them to briefly touch his hand. He looked up, their gazes colliding. "I'm so sorry. I just didn't realize..."

She shook her head. Not realizing was no excuse.

In her hurry to prevent a meeting with Ezra, Ava had allowed herself to be convinced of Mr. Temple's story. But who was Simon Temple, and why did he care so much about this horse?

When she asked this question of Ezra, he shrugged. "That's what I've been trying to figure out. Much as I think that horse is priceless, a good percentage of the value is sentimental."

Tiny nodded. "That does make sense, except what if that fellow wasn't after this horse specifically? What if he just wanted on the Becker Ranch for some reason?"

"Any idea what that reason might be?" Ezra's gaze fixed on Tiny.

"Well," he said slowly, "I don't know. To see something else he's interested in? Or maybe to find out if there was anything to steal?"

"It's possible." He shrugged as he shifted his attention to Ava. "I'll have to think on that some more. In the meantime, Ava, do you have a theory?"

"I do, actually." She clasped her hands in her lap. "I think when you find the horse, we'll all be happy."

"Sarcasm?" He gave her a sideways look.

"Truth. Your story deserves a happy ending, Ezra."

"There was a time I thought that was going to happen." He reached up to the medal at his neck.

"It still can."

Ezra held her gaze. "We're not talking about horses anymore, are we?"

Her heart lurched. Somehow Ava managed to tear her attention away from the handsome Ranger. "Tiny, would you mind giving us a minute?"

The overattentive bodyguard surprised her by pausing just long enough to give Ezra a look. "I'll just be right over there," he said as he indicated an empty seat nearby.

The train was two-thirds full of passengers, many of whom were from Hartville. Those who didn't dare study them openly peered at them over open but unread newspapers or beyond their knitting needles or fussy children.

Ava lifted her chin and ignored them all. Let the gossips gossip—that's what Mama used to say. It had been so much easier in theory, but now that she had to put it into practice, she found it most difficult, especially when she'd heard them referring to her as *the countess* or *her highness.*

Even more difficult was her proximity to the Ranger as he slid over to the seat next to her.

She exhaled a breath she didn't realize she was holding and looked up at Ezra. "We were interrupted before we could finish an important conversation. I wonder if you'd like to resume our discussion about what happened the night we were supposed to meet up at the tree."

Ava kept her gaze diverted but managed to see his wince out of the corner of her eye. Her breath caught as she waited for Ezra's response.

"I've been thinking about that," the Ranger said slowly. "Maybe it's just as well we just let that topic go."

~

Coward.

Ezra looked away. Never once had he ever thought of himself as cowardly. Until now.

He'd faced down a half-dozen desperadoes with their guns pointed at him and won, but that paled in comparison to allowing Ava Becker to tell him to take a hike. But looking into those beautiful eyes and admitting anything about the past or, for that matter, the future, terrified him.

However, Ava Becker, or whatever her name was legally, was well worth facing his fear. He took a deep breath and let it out slowly, planning just the right words to say to let her know that losing her had torn his heart out and finding her again had given him hope that he might become whole again.

Ava slid him a sideways look. "Yes, you're right. The past should stay in the past."

His heart sank. Somehow Ezra managed a nod as he moved back to his place across from Ava and pretended interest in the scenery passing outside the window.

What happened after that, he could barely say. At some point, Tiny returned. Food was offered, but he declined, as did Ava. And then, finally, they arrived in Austin.

As the train screeched to a stop, Tiny reached over to nudge

Ezra. "We're gonna get that horse of yours back, Ranger. I promise it, you hear?"

Ezra managed a nod.

"Then cheer up." Tiny patted Ezra on the arm. "I never made a promise I didn't keep."

Ava nodded. "That's true. He promised to watch over me, and look where that's got us."

A chaperone we didn't need, after all, Ezra almost said. "You're right," he replied instead.

And if these two wanted to believe his sadness came from the potential loss of his horse, then so be it. He certainly wouldn't be the one to admit they were wrong.

Then Ava reached for his hand and grasped it as they walked off the train. Her eyes spoke of a friendship that had taken root as children and grown into something more.

Ezra looked again, and whatever he'd seen was now gone. Or had he actually seen it at all?

Without pausing to contemplate the answer to that question, Ezra helped Ava off the train and onto the platform. Tiny hovered close by, a worried look on his face.

"What's wrong?" Ezra asked as the big man looked around nervously.

"They never caught that man who was killing those women," he said. "Said in the papers he might work at the train station. So if he's coming for Miss Ava here, I need to be ready. Don't see anyone who looks like a killer, right off, though. Do you, Ranger?"

At that moment, the only one he'd pick out of a crowd as looking as if he were up to no good was Tiny. So he shrugged. "Could be anyone. They rarely look like you think they would."

"There you are," someone called over the noise. "Don't you try to run from me. I've been waiting for you."

Ezra turned toward the sound as a dressed-up dandy in a

bowler hat parted the crowd as he stalked toward them. "Tiny, hang on to Miss Ava, would you?"

The ranch hand shook his head. "Let me handle him."

"I'd rather you didn't. I'm the law here. Now stand between Ava and that fellow."

"You know," Ava said, "I do have a say here and—"

"I'm sorry, Miss Ava." Tiny hauled her behind him, effectively silencing any protest she might want to make.

With one hand on his weapon and his badge in full sight, Ezra faced the fellow straight on. "Nobody's running from you," he said evenly.

The dandy must have spied his badge, or maybe it was his gun that caused the fellow to stutter to a halt. Either way, the expression on his face swiftly went from outrage to something a whole lot more docile.

"Hey now, you're a Ranger." He held his palms up. "I have no beef with you. It's your traveling companions, or rather those folks I assume are with you, that I am here to confront."

The man craned his neck as if attempting to look past Ezra. Fortunately, Ezra's superior height and Tiny's large frame prevented the man from seeing Ava.

"And who exactly would you be?"

"I am Simon Temple, Esquire. The thieving woman who took my money is the one I wish to have a strong and spirited discussion with."

Ezra offered the beginnings of a grin that held no humor. "Now, isn't that something? You see, we came here to have a strong and spirited discussion with you. Tiny, is this the man you saw leave with the paint?"

"It is, Ranger," he said, "but I take strong exception to how he's spoken about Miss Ava. This Temple fellow needs to make that right."

"I'll do no such thing." Simon Temple raised his nose in the air. "I'm the one who has been travailed upon, and I will have justice."

"Look here..." Ava darted around Tiny to poke the dandy with her pointer finger. "You will not dare disparage my name by calling me a thief, do you understand? You convinced me to sell you a horse knowing you had absolutely no right to own it. If there's a thief in our midst, sir, it is you. And if anyone needs justice in this matter, it is—"

"Not here, Ava." Ezra's trigger finger twitched. In his experience, provoking an angry man was never a good idea. Doing it in a crowded train station, even worse.

Apparently, Ava was not to be silenced. "You heard what he said. The accusations he made are intolerable."

Ezra spared Tiny a quick glance. "Take her out to the sidewalk so Mr. Temple and I can speak in peace, please." He looked down at Ava. "My investigation," he told her, his voice firm. "Do as I say."

Although she appeared to consider arguing, Ava narrowed her eyes and walked away. Head held high, she left Tiny to scramble after her.

"All right, Mr. Temple," Ezra said slowly when he returned his attention to the dandy. "I'm a patient man, but I will not stand for what you've just said about Miss Becker."

"I only speak the truth, Ranger."

Temple reached into his pocket, and Ezra drew his revolver. Even though Temple only retrieved a handkerchief and began to dab at his temples, Ezra kept the revolver at the ready. He fixed the man with a glare he generally reserved for the worst of the worst. Temple glanced down at the revolver and then slowly returned his gaze to Ezra's face.

"I speak the truth."

"Unless you've got proof of what you say, you'll be needing to apologize to me and, if I can calm her down enough to allow you into her presence, to Miss Becker. You just nod if you understand. Got that?"

Though it appeared to pain him, Simon Temple slowly nodded.

"All right. Let's you and me go find a place where we can speak in private." He nodded in the opposite direction from where Ava and Tiny had gone. "That'll suit just fine," he said as he took a step toward the door.

"Wait a minute." Temple reached out to stop Ezra's progress by grabbing his arm.

Instinct caused Ezra to whirl around and pin the man to the ground. A moment later, Simon Temple was blinking up at the barrel of a loaded revolver and the crowd in the train station had dispersed.

"Look, I meant no harm." Temple once again showed his empty palms. "I thought perhaps we could speak at my law office. It is just across the street there."

"What's the meaning of this?" a man shouted as footsteps hurried toward them.

Ezra glanced over at a uniformed police officer. "Texas Ranger," he said as he nodded to the badge pinned to his lapel. "This man is in my custody."

"Take him in," Ava said from a spot somewhere behind Ezra. "He has made nefarious accusations."

Ezra shook his head as Ava stepped into his line of sight. "I told you to stay with Tiny."

She gestured to her right. "There's Tiny, so I am with him." She paused, looking only slightly uncertain. "Of a sort."

"All of you," the police officer said, "take this elsewhere before an innocent is harmed."

"This innocent has been harmed," the dandy said as he climbed to his feet. "I wish to lodge a complaint against that woman." He pointed to Ava. "For horse thievery."

The officer looked amused. "Can't imagine a reason for it. Ranger, I'm going to have to ask you to take your prisoner out of the train station. Will you be needing any assistance?"

He gestured toward Tiny. "My associate and I can handle him, but I do thank you."

The officer gave a curt nod. "If you change your mind, I'll be close by and can lock him up if need be."

"You heard the man," Ezra said to Simon Temple. "Now, if you're as smart as I believe you think you are, you won't make any more moves like you did a few minutes ago."

"Just let the officer arrest him." Ava moved to stand beside him. "And don't you dare tell Tiny to take me away. I only went with him because I thought it was a good idea. Now that I've seen what this man is capable of, I do not think it's such a good idea for you to be alone with him. So," she said slowly, "exactly where is your office, Mr. Temple? We can discuss this either there or at the jail."

Simon Temple sent an incredulous look in Ezra's direction.

Ezra answered it with a shrug. "You probably ought to answer her. In my experience, she's much more dangerous than either of us."

CHAPTER 6

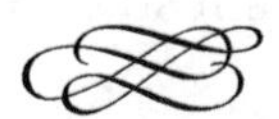

While Tiny escorted Mr. Temple across the street to a law office tucked into a row of brick buildings that made up a corner of Austin's busy downtown, Ava stood her ground. "You were almost shot, Ezra."

"Hardly." He looked down at her in that infuriating way he sometimes had. "I'm the only one with a gun."

"That's not exactly true." She glanced down at the specially made skirt pocket that held a small Derringer pistol she'd purchased upon her return to Texas.

"Ava Becker," he said with a tone she couldn't help but think held some measure of pride. "Really?"

She shrugged. "Yes, really. The pistol is smaller than what I used to use, but I'm still a better shot than you and can help should you need backup."

His laughter filled the space between them, and then he stilled. "It's still my investigation, Ava. Don't forget that."

"I have a feeling you're not going to let me."

Ezra's grin disappeared. "Listen...if I'm worried about you, I cannot focus on whatever danger I'm facing. So when I say I'm the one making the rules and you're the one following them, it's for good reason."

She frowned. "I do see your point, but I don't have to like it."

"No, you don't." Ezra offered his arm. "As long as you listen and obey, we'll get along fine."

"Listen and obey, is it?" It was her turn to laugh as she allowed him to lead her out of the train station and across the street. "Oh, Ezra, I'll do my best."

They paused at the door beneath a sign that proclaimed this to be the office of Simon Temple. Ezra opened the door and looked inside then stepped back and indicated for Ava to enter.

They found Mr. Temple sitting in a chair in the corner with Tiny looming over him as if he might jump should the lawyer make a wrong move. Ezra moved past Tiny to seat himself at Mr. Temple's desk. Ava remained near the door just in case she was called upon to provide the backup she promised.

"All right, Mr. Temple," Ezra said in that slow drawl of his, "let's get down to business. Where is the horse?"

Mr. Temple sat up straighter and cast a glance over at Ava before returning his attention to Ezra. "That is quite the question. I would like to know that myself. I demand to be told where your men took it." He looked over at Ava. "Or rather, *her* men."

"I have no idea to whom you are referring," Ava said, indignant. "But I advise you to tell the Ranger the truth about where you've hidden the horse."

Mr. Temple ignored her to continue staring at Ezra.

"How did you get here so quickly, Mr. Temple?" Ezra asked. "Fellow at the livery in Hartville had you leaving in the early hours of this morning."

"And indeed I did," he said. "Had I not been waylaid by her men, I'd still be on the trail. Instead, I was fortunate enough to escape them and stop a train in hopes of having them caught."

"Impossible." Ava frowned. "Our train made no such stops."

Ezra shot her a look that let her know he did not appreciate her adding to the conversation. Stifling the childish urge to make a face at him, she merely stared back in return.

"No, it did not, but the early train from Houston did," Mr. Temple said. "I'd made excellent time along the trail, so I was able to arrive and send a telegram to your sheriff in Hartville. He responded with the one you see on the desk in front of you, Ranger."

Ezra looked down, shuffled a few papers, and then picked up a scrap to read. A moment later, he looked up. "Appears you're telling the truth," he said to Mr. Temple before looking at Tiny. "Stand down but remain close to him."

Tiny nodded and moved a step away to lean against a windowsill. Though his stance was relaxed, his gaze never left the lawyer.

"Tell me about these men." Ezra gestured with one hand. "What can you remember about them?"

Mr. Temple gave a detailed description of three men, then spared Ava a disgusted look. "I'm sure what I've left out your pretty companion can add."

"My pretty companion had nothing to do with those men stealing that horse," Ezra snapped. "The three men you've just described sound like Roan Galway, Bass Tomkins, and Cherokee Sam."

"So you know them," he said with a smile. "Good, then go and get my horse back."

"Well, now, just like that?" Ezra laughed. "The Irishman, Roan, is the best horse thief in the business, and Cherokee Sam is as well. Sam's good with a knife and a gun and is wanted in Indian Territory. And Sam's buddy Tomkins—he's a preacher's son, but you'd never know it. He wears double the guns and shoots like he has nothing to lose."

"How do you know all that, Ranger?" Tiny frowned. "I've never heard of none of them, and I've lived in Hartville all my life."

"That's because you're not charged with putting the Markham Gang out of business."

"Oh my," Mr. Temple said. "It appears I am lucky to have escaped them."

"Few do, Mr. Temple." He shifted positions and seemed to be thinking about something. Then he stood up and reached for his hat. "Tiny, keep an eye on these two. I'll be back directly."

"Oh no, you don't," she said as she grasped his arm when he tried to walk past her. "Wherever you go, I go." Ezra looked about to protest when Ava shook her head. "I caused this problem. It's the least I can do to go along with you and see if I can help fix it."

"All right," he said slowly. "But on one condition."

"That I remember it's your investigation."

"Exactly." Ezra looked over his shoulder. "One more question, Temple. Why that particular horse?"

For the first time since Simon Temple accosted them in the train station, he refused to speak. Ezra shook his head. "Never mind. Tiny, keep him right where he's sitting, will you? Use any means."

"Sure will, Ranger," Tiny called as the door shut behind them.

Ava looked up at Ezra as they stepped onto the sidewalk. "'Use any means'? What are you suspecting?"

"I think he's connected to the theft. The likelihood he could convince a train to stop for him and beat us back here, then come looking for us when our train arrives is very low. That those three from the Markham Gang would let him go after they supposedly stole his horse—even more unlikely."

Ezra guided her down the sidewalk, then helped her to cross the street. The number of wagons and buggies traversing the street was more than double what Hartville would have in a day. The crowd reminded her a little of Berlin, although the buildings around them and the clothes they wore were decidedly Texan.

"Why not just bring him to the sheriff and let him handle it?" Ava asked when they'd made their way safely to the other side of the road.

"I could," he said, "but once the law takes custody of him, my horse is forgotten. They'll want Markham's men, and they won't care how they get them." He paused. "I know that sounds selfish, but that's just a fact."

The afternoon sun shone across Ezra's tanned features, his black hair lifting at the edges to accommodate the slight breeze that slid past.

"Not selfish at all," she said as he paused in front of the telegraph office.

"I'll just be a minute. I want to let Cap know what's going on."

Ava nodded. "I'll just wait at the milliner's next door then. I saw a darling hat I would love to try on."

"Just what you need is another box to haul back to Hartville." He shook his head. "Speaking of boxes, I didn't see to your trunks before we left the train station. I'll go do that when I'm done here."

"No need." She looked up at him with a smile. "I'm used to traveling alone. When you banished Tiny and me, I used that opportunity to find a porter to take my things to Papa's house near the university. I suspect the maids will have everything put away by now."

"Well, now. I am impressed, although I don't like hearing that you have gotten used to traveling alone. A woman like you ought to be used to having..."

"Having what?"

~

H*aving a man like me to travel with* was what he wanted to tell her.

"Never mind," Ezra said. "Go try on your hat, but be ready to go when I come for you. Much as I doubt Temple will try anything with Tiny standing guard, I don't want to chance it."

He made quick work of sending the telegram, then emerged onto the sidewalk to see Ava coming out of the milliner's shop. "Where are you going?" he demanded as he fell into step beside her.

"While I was trying on the hat, I saw a man go into Mr. Temple's law office. I thought perhaps I would investigate."

Ezra gave her a sideways look. "Without me?"

"Instinct. Though I admit, I wasn't thinking things through."

He allowed that statement to go unanswered. "What did the man look like?"

"Average height. Reddish curly hair from what I could see under his hat—oh, and a mustache." She paused as if recalling. "He was wearing a striped shirt and a suit of clothes that looked as if he'd ridden the trail in it for a while."

"Roan Galway," Ezra said as his pulse quickened. "And if I'm right, he's up to no good. Can I depend on you to go down the street to police headquarters and let them know I need backup?"

"I told you I would back you up."

"And I told *you*, I cannot be worrying about where you are and what's happening in front of me at the same time. If something were to happen to you, Ava, I..." Ezra took a deep breath and let it out slowly. "Look, go bring back a police officer. I'll check out what's going on over there from the alley behind the place while I wait for both of you to be backup."

Seemingly satisfied with the bargain, Ava hurried off toward the police station while Ezra opted for casually strolling down the block. When he was out of sight of the law office, he made two turns and ended up in the alley behind Temple's building.

Once he'd figured out which door led to the office, Ezra tested the knob and found it unlocked. Good to know, but like as not, the door hinges weren't oiled well enough for him to enter the building unannounced. The window, however, just might work.

He tugged on the sash, but the pane refused to budge. After retrieving his knife, Ezra managed to wedge the tip of the blade between the windowpane and the sill. Remarkably, the pane lifted slightly.

The sound of footsteps caught his attention and flattened him against the building behind a trio of rain barrels. "Someone here?" a man called.

Rather than respond, Ezra waited. If one of the Markham Gang was inside, it was likely at least one more would be watching the building.

When the footsteps were near enough, Ezra jumped out to tackle the trespasser. A glint of steel passed by his face as he rolled into the alley and took his attacker with him.

Though the man he fought was strong, Ezra was stronger. A moment later, he'd pinned a familiar face to the ground and pushed the man's weapon well out of reach.

"A knife's out of character for you, Tomkins." He grunted out as he continued to wrestle with the horse thief. "Seems like you like to shoot first."

Tomkins slithered from his grasp and climbed to his knees.

Ezra grabbed him and threw him back down on the ground, holding him there with a boot in his gut as he took away the man's double pistols. He managed to speak between quick breaths. "I'd guess you didn't shoot because you were figuring the man behind those barrels was friend and not foe."

"You're right about that, Ranger." Another man's voice rang out behind him. "Now step away from my friend there before I get trigger happy and forget that I might draw unwanted attention by shooting you."

Cherokee Sam. Ezra let out a long breath. "And if I'm willing to call your bluff?"

Sam's chuckle held no humor. "Then I'd have to shoot you. But think about it, Ranger. That pretty young thing you were flirting with across the street? We know where she lives. Her pa, he's a lecturer at the college. Talks about plants and such. But he's not home now, is he? Nor is her mama. Just her. Like as not anybody she employs at that house isn't willing to die saving her." He paused. "Not like you would."

Sam had him there. He'd take a bullet before he'd allow anyone to touch Ava Becker. Slowly, he lifted his hands and straightened.

Sam took the pistols he was holding and tucked them into his trousers, then nodded down at Bass. "Get up. We've got a Ranger to get rid of."

"Took you long enough," Bass Tomkins said as he crawled away from Ezra, his nose bleeding and dirt covering him. "I thought I was a goner."

Ezra faced down Cherokee Sam, ignoring the unarmed Tomkins for a moment. He needed a diversion, something that would cause these men to lose their focus.

Then it came to him. "Sam, how is it a man of the cloth can sire a son such as your friend there?"

"Oh, Ranger," Bass called. "The Lord, He helps those who help themselves, don't you know? I am just helping myself."

"That's not in the Bible. But then, Sam knows that, don't you? I bet you get tired of him saying things like that, what with your superior knowledge."

"You saying Sam's smarter than me?" Bass headed toward them, obviously intent on retribution.

"I'm saying a man who can't get the Bible right is probably a man who will mess up other things." He returned his attention to his captor, his plan for taking the weapon out of Sam's hand complete. "I hear people think that, Bass. That he's smarter than you."

Bass looked hurt. "Do you think so, Sam? Because I thought you and I was friends."

"We are. Now go check on Roan," Sam told him. "See if he's got things under control in there."

"Good idea." Ezra met Sam's gaze. "Send the weaker man in so as not to get shot if the police officers have arrived."

Bass paused, his hand on the doorknob. "Say what?"

Ezra nodded. "That's right, Tomkins. That pretty girl I was with has gone to fetch the law. And lest you think you ought to try and hurt her, she's a better shot than either of you. So..." He allowed Bass and Sam to consider what he'd said a moment. "Unless you're certain Roan's managed to overpower my man in there, who outweighs him by double, you just might be opening the door to a City of Austin police officer."

A moment's indecision flickered on Sam's face. Then he looked down at Ezra's neck.

"What's this?" He touched Ezra's necklace with the barrel of his pistol. "Why would a Ranger dare to wear this medal? There is meaning there that should not be defiled by a neck such as yours."

"I wear this medal because my Comanche grandmother put it around my neck on the occasion of my thirteenth birthday. It is a peace medal awarded to her by—"

"I know what it is," he snapped as he eyed Ezra carefully. "Your grandmother was Comanche?"

Ezra replied in the language of his grandmother's people. To his surprise, Sam took a step backward.

Seizing the opportunity, Ezra knocked the gun out of Sam's hand, then scrambled to retrieve it. Sam kicked at his hand, but

Ezra managed to snatch up the gun just as Sam pulled another weapon out and aimed it at him.

"Your call, Sam," Ezra said as he spied Bass watching them from the door. "Either send your man in to get shot, or the both of you give up. I guarantee the law is in there by now. I sure wouldn't want to be the man having to make that decision." He glanced past Sam to his accomplice. "You sure you trust him?"

"Go check," Sam told Bass.

"But what if he's right?" Bass protested. "You want me to get shot?"

"You want *me* to get shot?" Sam nodded toward Ezra.

"I do see your point."

The horse thief yanked on the doorknob and stepped inside. Meanwhile, Ezra kept his weapon pointed at Sam and his attention squarely on the gang member's eyes. Sam kept looking down at the peace medal.

"Still bothers you that I wear this?" Ezra said.

"Bothers me because my grandmother had one just like it."

"You're Cherokee," Ezra said. "And I assure you, I didn't steal this from your grandmother."

"Comanche," he corrected. "And I'm not accusing you of that. Last I saw, my pa was still wearing it."

Ezra tightened his grip on the gun as he realized Sam's grandmother and his must have come from the same tribe or, at the least, been in attendance at the same event where the medals were given. As soon as he considered it, Ezra shook off the idea.

"If you're Comanche, how'd you come to be called Cherokee Sam?"

He shrugged. "One Indian's the same as another to most people. Someone called me Cherokee, and it stuck."

So it was possible. Ezra let out a long breath, his hand still steady on the weapon he hoped he would not have to use.

"You don't have to make a living like this, Sam," Ezra said. "The

Comanche are proud and honest people. Go raise horses legally without taking from others."

Sam chuckled. "You going to give me horses to raise?"

"It appears I already have." His temper flared. "That paint was mine. I aim to get it back."

"That paint's sire was mine," Sam said. "The man who stole it from me claimed otherwise, but I owned that horse from the time it was a colt. It came from my people."

It was Ezra's turn to be shocked. "No," he said slowly. "It came from mine. My uncle owned that horse."

"It came from the Comanche." Sam stared him down. "Our people. And it is likely your uncle bought it from a thief."

"How would a thief know the lineage of that horse? It's not possible."

"It is if the thief was my own father." Sam appeared to be daring Ezra to speak. "Yes, my father was a horse thief, Ranger. One who would steal from his own kind."

"Then don't be like him, Sam. Don't do what he did."

A shot rang out, and Bass Tomkins stumbled out of the door, blood seeping from his left shoulder. "There's no law in there," he called. "But there's a woman with a gun who shoots better than any man I've met."

And then another shot rang out.

CHAPTER 7

"Ava!"

Ezra kicked Sam down and raced for the open door, caring nothing for the fact that the outlaw still held a gun in his hand. A bullet zinged past and lodged in the wooden barrel. Another flew over his head and broke a window on the second floor.

He felt a sting but ignored it, rushing inside the building with his gun drawn. The door shut behind him, leaving Ezra in darkness.

"Ava," he called as he felt his way forward by holding on to the wall with his free hand. "Where are you?"

No response.

Ezra stumbled, nearly falling over something in the darkened hallway. "Ava, answer me if you're here."

"I'm here," she said quietly as Ezra rounded the corner and into the bright sunshine of the lawyer's office. When his eyes adjusted, he found her seated behind the lawyer's desk in the empty room.

"I heard gunfire and thought you'd been shot." When she rose,

Ezra gathered her into his arms and held her tight as he looked over her head into the empty room. "Where are the others?"

"When the shooting began, Mr. Temple went running for the door. After Tiny made sure I wasn't hurt, he went after him."

"And the police?"

She looked away toward the front windows of the office. Outside, buggies and wagons traversed the wide thoroughfare, and people strolled past as if nothing had happened.

"I never made it inside the police station," Ava said so softly that he could barely hear her. "I was on my way down the sidewalk when two men passed me talking about Simon Temple. I remember how Mr. Temple said three men had robbed him, so I thought maybe these two—"

"Were in league with the Irishman," Ezra supplied.

"Yes. I know what you told me to do, but I thought it best to follow, just to see where they were going." She lifted her eyes to meet his gaze, and tears shimmered once more. "Then they came here, and I knew Tiny would be outnumbered, so there was no question of turning around and going for a police officer."

Ezra removed his handkerchief and gently dabbed at her tears. "Where is Galway?" he said as he handed the handkerchief to her.

She looked up at him, her lower lip quivering. "Do you mean that Irishman I saw coming in here when I was across the street?"

"Yes, that's the man."

Ava fell back into his arms, tears suddenly flowing. "I shot him. He didn't get up, but the other one did. He ran out the back door."

Ezra peeled her out of his arms and caused her to look up at him. "Didn't get up from where? I don't see anyone here. Tomkins came running out with a shoulder wound, but he was alone. Are you sure you shot Galway?"

She nodded in the direction of the back door, and Ezra thought of how he'd tripped over something in the darkened corridor. "Wait right here."

He tried to step away, but her fingers curled around his arm. "He aimed a gun at Tiny, and they were wrestling over it. I couldn't let him… He didn't get up."

"It's all right, Ava." He gathered her into his arms again. "You saved Tiny's life. Now let me go just a minute so I can make sure Galway isn't going to bother us anymore."

It wasn't Galway he was worried about. Any man who was stumbled over as he'd accidentally done in the corridor either wasn't alive or was close enough to gone that he didn't feel anything anymore. The other two, Bass Tomkins and Cherokee Sam, were the ones he was concerned about.

This time, Ava released him, though she kept her eyes on him until he disappeared into the corridor. With the door open and the light streaming in from the front office, Ezra could easily make out the unmoving body of Roan Galway lying face down on the floor.

He rolled the man over and then stood. There was no need to take a pulse. Ava's aim had been exact.

Ezra went to the back door and looked out in both directions. Neither Cherokee Sam nor Bass Tomkins was in sight.

"He didn't suffer." Ezra returned to Ava and held her gently. "If that's what you're wanting to know. And the other man you wounded was well enough to run. I saw that myself."

"I just want to know that Tiny is safe. And you."

"I'm safe," he whispered against her ear. "I am perfectly safe."

She wiggled out of his arms, and he saw the blood. The room seemed to tilt. "Ava…you've been shot."

"No, Ezra." Her eyes went wide. "You're the one who's been shot."

He looked down at his arm, and there was the stain of blood. A glance beneath his sleeve told Ezra it was nothing but a flesh wound. "I'll be fine. Let's go see about Tiny."

Ava gave him a skeptical look and refused to budge.

"Trust me. If it was anything but a scratch, I wouldn't ignore it. The last thing a Ranger needs is to lose an arm."

"Promise?"

"I promise." He nodded to the door. "Now, tell me which way they went."

A few minutes later, they passed in front of the police station, and Ezra paused. "We need to let the police know what happened at Temple's office."

Ezra ducked inside, bringing Ava with him.

A man of middle age with a slight build met them. "Ranger Creed?" He stuck his hand out to shake with Ezra. "Your captain told me I'd be getting a visit from you. Name is Lacy."

"Chief Lacy?" At his nod, Ezra continued. "The captain did ask me to stop in to see if we could assist you in any way with your current investigation."

"Ah, the Servant Girl Annihilator." He rocked back on his heels. "Though I'm grateful he hasn't struck for months, I would like very much to bring him to justice."

Ezra thought for a moment about offering Branch's theory that the police had indeed already caught the man. Given the urgency of the circumstances, he elected to save that for his next visit.

"Actually, sir, Miss Becker and I are here to report a crime that's just occurred down the street." At the chief's raised eyebrows, Ezra hurried to continue. "There was a shooting at Simon Temple's law office. One man down and one wounded."

"Two wounded," Ava added as she nodded toward the stain on Ezra's sleeve.

"It's just a scratch," Ezra told him. "But I'm worried about our friend. Last time Miss Becker saw him, he was chasing Mr. Temple to keep him from escaping."

"Why would Simon Temple seek to escape?" the chief asked.

"We believe he was in league with the three men involved in

the shooting. That would be Bass Tomkins, Cherokee Sam, and Roan Galway. Galway's the one down. Tomkins is wounded."

"So the Markham Gang is still in Austin, then? I'd been told they were confining their antics to the area around Hartville."

"They have been, but it appears someone brought them here. I have no idea why, but I sure would like the horse back that Temple took with him when he left Hartville."

"This friend of yours—would you describe him?"

When Ezra obliged, the chief nodded. "Well, now. That is interesting. Follow me."

He led them down a hall that led to an area filled with holding cells. All were empty except one.

"Tiny?" Ava said. "Why are you in jail?"

He rose to meet them. "The policeman arrested me for threatening that lawyer."

Chief Lacy stepped up to the bars and inserted a key, then turned it to allow Tiny to exit the cell. "For that, I do apologize. I'll have my men begin the search for Temple. He shouldn't be hard to find. The man's been an attorney here for quite some time."

"Long enough to get in league with the Markham Gang," Ezra said.

"Indeed," was the chief's brief response.

They walked out the front door together, and then the chief bade them goodbye but not before once again apologizing to Tiny. Ezra clasped his hand onto Tiny's shoulder. "Well done, my friend."

"Well done?" Tiny shook his head. "Temple got away."

"Ava was safe. You made sure of that."

"I tried." Tiny grimaced. "Until she pulled that gun out of her skirt pocket and told me to step back from that Irishman. I would've won the fight, but she was afraid he'd kill me."

"He probably would have," Ezra said. "He usually does."

Tiny's eyes widened for a moment, and then he nodded. "So what's the plan now?"

"My guess is, Temple is in trouble with the Markhams now, what with the attention he's drawn to them here in Austin. So he's either at the train station or the livery." Ezra looked up at Tiny. "Take the train station, but if you see him, find the officer on patrol and let him know. And try not to let Temple see you first."

"Yessir," Tiny said but seemed reluctant to leave.

"I'll keep Miss Ava close, all right?"

"All right." He offered Ava a smile. "Be sure and listen to what he says. It's his—"

"His investigation," she echoed. "Yes, I know, and I promise, I will."

Tiny offered her a smile and then returned his attention to Ezra. "Where do we want to meet in case any of us have information?"

"How about right here?" Ezra suggested.

Tiny nodded and headed off toward the train station while Ezra and Ava went to search the liveries. A short while later, they returned to find Tiny waiting.

"No sight of him," Tiny said.

"We had no luck either," Ava told him. "Nor did we see Ezra's horse." She sighed. "It's getting late. I suggest we take up the search again in the morning."

They walked in silence until they reached the Becker residence on Twelfth Street. The opulent home was scented by the hearty fare that maids were putting on the table as they arrived.

"Before you eat anything, Ezra, I must insist you get that scratch seen to."

Inhaling deeply, he let out a long breath. "You're a cruel woman, Ava. I'm starving and that smells delicious."

She called for a maid and instructed her to bring Will Becker's first aid kit. When the girl had gone, Ava gestured to a chair in the foyer. "Sit down and submit to treatment, Ranger, so you can eat."

Ezra did as he was told, and a few minutes later, the maid returned with a curious-looking box filled with plants and poultices. Ava made short work of slathering something that stunk on his injury, then wrapping a length of linen around it.

"I've never seen your pa use this out at the ranch." Tiny turned up his nose at Ezra.

"Well..." She closed the lid on the box and rose. "It's somewhat experimental. Papa uses this for instructional purposes."

Ezra jumped to his feet. "Ava Becker, are you experimenting on me?"

She grinned. "Absolutely. Now let's eat."

The food was excellent, but conversation was scarce. Finally, Ava rose and declared the meal at an end. "I've had the quarters nearest the house readied for you," she told them.

"About that, Miss Ava..." Tiny frowned. "I don't like it that you'll be in here and we'll be out there."

"We won't be." Ezra spoke firmly as he stood. "I'm sleeping against the front door. Tiny, you take the back."

"Yessir," he said as he ambled toward the back door.

"Wait a minute." Ava threw her hands out. "Don't I get a vote here?"

"No," Ezra said. "This is my investigation. See you in the morning."

CHAPTER 8

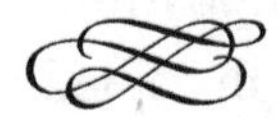

"See you in the morning?"

Ava huffed up the stairs, not exactly sure why Ezra's dismissive attitude bothered her. After all, it *was* his investigation.

Still, she felt so helpless soaking in lavender-scented bathwater and sinking into her soft feather bed when those two were sleeping downstairs in front of doors. After ringing for the maid, she paced.

"Are the men asleep yet?" she asked the maid.

Rather than give a direct response, the maid looked past her. "I believe they are settled, ma'am."

Ava stepped in front of the maid so she couldn't look away. "What aren't you telling me?"

She sighed. "I told Cook I couldn't be trusted not to let you know the men went out in search of those outlaws."

After she spoke, the maid's eyes widened. She pressed her fingers to her lips and fled the room.

Ava hurried to dress, irritation chasing her as she tiptoed downstairs. True enough, rather than seeing Ezra at the door, the fellow who usually tended the garden was snoring there. Edging her way toward the back of the house, she found the door guarded by the gardener's assistant. Unlike his boss, the assistant had left just enough space between his sleeping form and the back door for Ava to slip out into the night.

The gardens were quiet, the moon still hidden by the trees. Ava made her way around the side of the house to find the gate locked. Climbing over was impossible.

She looked around until she spied a ladder leaning against the side of the garden shed. Lugging it around to the fence, Ava easily climbed over.

Landing on the other side, however, was a little more difficult. Though the distance was only five or six feet, the spot she'd chosen presented an uneven surface.

Ava gripped the ladder and considered her options. She could go back inside and pretend she'd never left her room, or she could make herself useful by continuing to search for the criminals who'd invaded the law office.

The fact that she'd been the one to let Simon Temple leave with Ezra's horse propelled her over the wall. Though she was prepared for a hard landing, it did not happen.

Instead, she fell directly into Tiny's arms.

"Ranger's not going to be happy about this," he said against her ear.

"Put me down, please. And I know he won't, but I was hoping I could be of help."

"I wish you had stayed inside."

"Too late," she said as she struggled to gain her feet.

"No, he's right," another voice said. "You should have stayed inside."

She looked past Tiny to Simon Temple standing in the shadows, his gun drawn.

"Now that I have two bargaining chips instead of one, I suppose I should be happy. Maybe the Markhams will pay double for both of you." The lawyer gestured toward Tiny with his gun. "Put her down so she can walk."

Tiny leaned close. "Nod if you remembered that gun of yours."

Ava looked up into his eyes and nodded slowly.

"When I touch my nose, draw and shoot straight up. A distraction."

Mr. Temple approached. "What're you two gabbing about?" He poked Ava with his gun, urging them ahead of him into the shadows.

"Just trying to figure out how to get away from you," Ava said as Tiny gave her a warning look.

"That's funny." Temple grunted. "Now stop here. This is our buggy. Ranch hand, you'll do the driving, and Miss Becker, you'll sit with me."

"What makes you think I'm going to let you get away with that? You know the Ranger won't let you," Tiny said.

"Because Miss Becker wants to get the Ranger's horse back for him, and I'm going to take you to it."

"You said we were bargaining chips," Ava countered. "That doesn't sound like an offer to return the horse."

"The two are not mutually exclusive." He gestured to a buggy parked at the curb. "You're in first, ranch hand."

Tiny glowered at him. "Why should I drive you?"

Mr. Temple boosted Ava up into the buggy. "If you don't, I shoot Miss Becker. Or may I call you Ava?"

Ava ignored him while Tiny climbed into the driver's seat and took up the reins. Mr. Temple settled beside Ava, his gun still drawn and pointing her direction.

"You were quite clever in my office," he told Ava. "I've been wanting to shoot Roan Galway for years. The man is insufferable." He shrugged. "But he pays well."

"What does he pay you for, Mr. Temple?" Ava asked as casually as she could manage.

He laughed. "Whatever he needs done." The attorney paused. "Legally, of course. I do have a reputation to uphold."

It was Ava's turn to laugh. "You've just kidnapped the daughter of a University of Texas professor, Mr. Temple. You're responsible for a Ranger being shot. I think the time to brag about your reputation is long gone."

"I did not shoot a Ranger. And none of the rest of it can be proven."

"You caused Mr. Creed to be shot, and that's close enough. As for me, if you're suggesting I won't press charges, then you are sorely mistaken."

"Oh, I know you won't." He leaned forward to instruct Tiny to make a turn up ahead that led them out of the city and into the countryside. Finally, Mr. Temple sat back against the cushions. "You won't turn me in because you're going to tell the chief that I helped you get the Ranger's horse back."

She gave him a sideways look. "Why should I trust you? And if you mean us no harm, why the gun?"

"Would you have cooperated had I not taken you at gunpoint?"

"No," she said as Tiny shook his head.

"My point exactly." He called out more instructions to Tiny, this time taking them to a clearing where a small cabin sat beside the river. "Just over there, please," he told Tiny. "And remember, I do not want to shoot you, but I will if you make me."

"Just so we're clear," Ava said, "what's going to happen when we get to that cabin?"

"I'm going to have your ranch hand pull the buggy up into that shed there on the other side of the cabin. I've got the horse tied up nearby, but I won't tell you where until I conclude my business."

As Tiny turned the buggy toward the cabin, Ava spied two horses tied to a hitching post out front. "Looks like you've got company."

"Oh, I know," he said happily. "They're invited guests. Just stop here, ranch hand."

Tiny did as he was instructed and then climbed out. Mr. Temple remained seated.

"What now?" Tiny asked.

"Start running," he told Tiny as he aimed his weapon toward him.

Ava reached for her pistol and fired it into the air, giving Tiny a distraction that allowed him to duck beneath the buggy. The door of the cabin flew open, and two men spilled out.

"He's under the buggy," Mr. Temple called. "I've got the woman right here."

Ava was about to aim her gun at him when an arm wrapped around her waist and hauled her backward. As the world tilted, she stared up into Ezra Creed's beautiful brown eyes.

"Got her," Ezra said with a grunt, his voice disguised. He lifted his finger to his lips to indicate for her not to speak and then set her down behind the buggy where Mr. Temple could not see her.

"What? No," the lawyer said. "You were supposed to grab the ranch hand. I've got the—"

Something strangled off his voice. When Ava peered around the back of the buggy, she saw Tiny had him in a choke hold.

"We need him alive," Ezra told him. "We'll tie him up and keep an eye on him."

"There were two men in the cabin," Ava said. "Where are they? I don't want you hurt."

The police chief stepped into view and grinned. "That was me. We set a trap for this fellow thinking we'd get all three of the perpetrators. Unfortunately, we didn't think he'd be bringing you and Tiny."

"About that..." Ezra said tersely. "How is it you came to be riding with Temple tonight?"

"It's a long story." Ava sighed. "But we're fine. I'm fine. Thanks to Tiny."

Tiny beamed, loosening his grip on Temple only slightly, then his thick brows furrowed. "I tried to convince her to go back in the house, but he pulled a gun, and then I was afraid he'd shoot her."

Ezra clasped a hand on the ranch hand's shoulder. "You did a good job of fixing the problem this one caused."

"I suggest we discuss this inside," the chief said. "Unless I miss my guess, those two should be heading this way soon."

Tiny hauled the lawyer inside and bound him to a chair, then found a length of cloth to provide a gag. "I'm sorry about that," he told the lawyer, "but we can't have you calling out to those folks."

Ezra doused the lamp. "Ava, I want you over there." He indicated a spot on the floor beside the fireplace. "It's the least likely spot to take gunfire and the darkest corner in the room. I don't want you seen or shot."

She complied, then curled up to await whatever action was about to happen. "Say," she called out after a moment. "Did you know he's got your horse tied up nearby? At least that's what he claimed."

"That's not true," Ezra said. "We scoured the woods within a mile radius and found nothing."

"It was there," the lawyer managed to reply, though it came out muffled. "I've been robbed again."

"Shh," Ezra said as he stood in the shadows near the window. "A lone horseman is coming up from the east."

The chief took up a position beside Ezra, and Tiny went to the only other window in the cabin. A moment later, a horse whinnied, and the sound of a man's feet hitting the ground echoed in the silent cabin.

"Temple," someone called. "You in there?"

"Door's open," Ezra called, his voice once again disguised. "You alone?"

"Yeah, I'm alone."

The door opened slowly, and a slender man in dark clothing stepped inside. The chief slipped behind him to slam the door, and then Tiny lit a lamp.

"Bass Tomkins," Ezra said as he pressed his pistol to the criminal's gut. "I see you survived the bullet you got this afternoon. Want another one?"

His eyes went wide. "I do not. Where's Sam?"

"We were about to ask you that," the chief said. "He's supposed to be with you."

"No, he told me he was with Temple over there." He cast a sneer in the lawyer's direction. "Something about fetching that horse for the Ranger. I told him he was an idiot, but what do I know?"

"Not much, apparently," the chief said. "Tie him up, too," he told Tiny. "We will wait a while and see if we can catch his buddy."

Tiny did as he was told and then doused the lamp and returned to the window to watch. An hour later, the chief stepped away from the window.

"I don't think he's coming. What say you, Ranger? Do we content ourselves with two out of three?"

"For tonight, we do," Ezra agreed. "Tomorrow is another day."

"It is, indeed. Would you mind loaning me your friend here until I can get these two settled in the jailhouse? I'll send him back when they're behind bars."

"No need," Ezra told him. "Miss Becker and I can find our way back."

Tiny looked undecided. "You sure?" he said to Ezra.

"I'm sure. We'll be fine. I'm more worried about one of those two getting loose with only the chief to keep them in line. You take the buggy, and we'll share a horse. That way, Ava won't set off on her own."

He nodded and disappeared out the door with the lawyer in tow. "Any trouble and you shoot, got it, Creed?"

Ezra nodded. "Got it."

A few minutes later, they were alone in the cabin. Ava rose and dusted off her skirts. "All right, Ezra. What are you up to?"

"I don't know what you mean." He spoke in the tone he always used when he absolutely knew what she meant.

"Why would you send off those two when there's still a member of the Markham Gang at large and possibly right outside our doorstep?"

"Come with me," he told her as he led her outside.

The stars were bright overhead, a canopy of diamonds broken only by the silver light of the moon. The lone horse that awaited stomped as they walked toward it.

Ava stopped short, her breath catching in her throat. "Ezra," she said. "That's the paint."

He grinned. "It appears you're right."

"But it wasn't there when we rode up. I know that for certain."

"No," he said slowly as he climbed into the saddle and helped her up in front of him, "it wasn't."

Ezra flicked the reins and pointed the horse toward the trail where they'd come from earlier in the evening. They rode in silence for a few minutes, and then Ava could stand it no more.

"Are you going to tell me how you managed this?" she said as she tried to turn to face him.

"Nope," was his quick response. "Although if you turn around again, I just might kiss you."

"Kiss me?" She shook her head. "You wouldn't dare. Not after saying you had no feelings for me anymore."

"I never said that. I said we shouldn't talk about it. You agreed. Not that it matters because I was an idiot not to follow you to Germany and beg you to marry me instead. I like to think I might have if I'd known where you were."

Her heart lurched. "I wrote letters, Ezra," she said softly. "So many letters. I begged you to come for me, but I never heard from you."

"I never got them."

Ava turned to face him. "How is that possible?"

True to his word, Ezra gathered her into his arms and kissed her soundly. When she attempted to ask the question again, he repeated his kiss.

She let out a breathless little laugh. "So let me get this straight. All I have to do is question you, and you're going to kiss me?"

"Is that a complaint?"

"No," she said with a grin. "Just a question."

So he kissed her again.

Then he stopped the horse at the bend in the road where the river parted ways with the trail. "Ava," he said against her ear, "we missed our chance once. I don't want to miss it again."

"What are you suggesting?"

He kissed her with passion and promise, then grinned. "Marry me? Tonight?"

She shook her head. "How do you propose to manage that?"

"I'm sure we can find someone to marry us. I'll knock on every church door until a parson answers. But marry me, Ava. Tonight. Before something happens to stop us."

She reached up to touch the medal at his throat and then traced his jawline with her finger. "Yes, Ranger. I'll marry you."

"Tonight?"

"Tonight." Then she kissed him.

CHAPTER 9

Ava settled down on the log and watched as her husband of exactly one week joined her. "Papa and Mama return tomorrow. Are you worried?" she teased.

"It's a little late for worrying, don't you think?" He winked at her. "We're adults, we're married, and neither of your parents have any say in the matter."

"I thought Gus took it pretty well." Her brother had declared their joke not to be funny and then, when he was convinced of their seriousness, he had complained that they hadn't waited for him to be a witness to the festivities.

"Why wouldn't he?" Ezra tucked a strand of Ava's hair behind her ear. "Seems like just about everyone else knew we were in love before I did."

"Including my father." She leaned over to kiss her husband. "I wish we wouldn't have had all that time apart."

Ezra gathered her to him. "You were worth the wait."

A rustling sound caught their attention. Ezra rose, seemingly unsurprised.

Out of nowhere, a man emerged from the forest. He wore buckskins and braids and had moccasins on his feet.

"Wait here," Ezra told her as he went to speak to the fellow.

Though she could hear them as they spoke, the language was unfamiliar. Once they finished their conversation, the stranger shook hands with Ezra and then took a step toward Ava.

"Take care of this man," he told her. "Great honor rests with him."

She rose but stayed where she was. "I will." The man wore the same necklace as her husband. Something else was familiar about him, but she couldn't place it.

He nodded toward Ezra, who returned the gesture. Then the man disappeared once again into the forest.

"Who was that?" she asked when Ezra again settled on the log.

"That was the fellow who stole my horse."

She joined him on the log but swiveled to face him. "Explain, please?"

Ezra shrugged. "We had a bargain. My horse for his honor. He delivered the horse, and I allowed him to do what he needed to do before he turned himself in."

"I don't follow. What incentive does he have for turning himself in?"

"Honor. It exists even among thieves. The man who stole my horse asked to render justice against the man who stole his horse. Then he would turn himself in."

"I'm not sure I believe you."

He shrugged. "Remember that man I brought in right after we got back from our honeymoon in San Antonio?"

"The older fellow?"

Ezra nodded. "Well, he stole a horse first. That horse was the sire to mine. When the sire was lost in a barn fire, Sam there, he decided to get back the only link to his stolen horse by taking mine."

"All right..."

"The deal was justice. And honor." Ezra paused. "And just in case, I've had Tiny following him ever since I made the deal."

"So that's where he's been."

Ezra laughed. "He'll make a good lawman someday. Not sure he wants to be a Ranger, but if he decides to, I reckon Company B will get a good man."

Ava rested her hand on her husband's shoulder. "So if your horse thief doesn't turn himself in tonight?"

"Then Tiny will see he's arrested before he can leave town." He gathered her back into his arms. "Now where were we?"

"Not so fast, Ranger. Remember how you told me once that next time I was in charge of an investigation, you would do what I say?"

"I do," he said, "but I fail to see what anyone might be investigating out here in the middle of the woods."

She leaned forward to whisper in his ear. "Trust me."

Ezra grinned. "Am I about to regret this, Mrs. Creed?"

"Oh, I do hope you don't, Mr. Creed." Ava matched his smile and then drew his lips toward hers.

AUTHOR'S NOTE ON TEXAS HISTORY

I hope you have enjoyed your historical trip through one of my favorite places in the world—Texas. Because I am a historian at heart, I take the factual events of history very seriously. As a tenth-generation Texan, I wanted to honor one of my favorite places on the planet by getting the history right and not guessing. Any errors in this story are mine alone.

In addition to being a history nerd, I am also a novelist, so upon occasion, I have had to bend the facts slightly to allow my fictional characters to live, work, and fall in love in a "real" world. Here are a few true-to-life historical facts that have been woven into this tale:

In the 1840s, the Republic of Texas—yes, we were our own country from 1836 until 1845, when we became a state—issued almost 4.5 million acres of land grants. In 1842 alone, thousands of families from German, Dutch, Swiss, Danish, and Norwegian ancestry settled on these land grants. The most interesting of these stories is the true tale of German-born John Meusebach, son of Baron Gregor von Meusebach, who renounced his title of baron in order to start a new life as a landowner in Texas. Meusebach's story is fascinating, and his background was the inspiration for the character of Ava's Prussian-born father, William Becker.

From December 1884 until December 1885, a serial killer called the Servant Girl Annihilator stalked Austin, Texas. The killer took the lives of eight serving girls, each murder following the same pattern. Then, almost exactly one year later, the murders abruptly stopped. Theories range from the one that Ranger Branch Kilborn proposes, namely that the killer was shot by police and died, to others that attempt to associate these murders with the infamous Jack the Ripper killings. Whatever the true story, there are many theories, and the murderer has never been definitively named. Just as the captain states in my story, however, the police chief in Austin during this time was the real-life former Texas Ranger James Lucy.

ABOUT THE AUTHOR

Bestselling author Kathleen Y'Barbo is a multiple Carol Award and RITA nominee of more than sixty novels with almost two million copies in print in the US and abroad. She has been nominated for a Career Achievement Award as well as a Reader's Choice Award and is the winner of the 2014 Inspirational Romance of the Year by *Romantic Times* magazine. Kathleen is a paralegal, a proud military wife, and a tenth-generation Texan, who recently moved back to cheer on her beloved Texas Aggies. Connect with her through social media at www.kathleenybarbo.com.

Unless otherwise indicated, all Scripture quotations are taken from the Holy Bible, Kings James Version.

Cover design by: Wild Heart Books

SIMPLE INTEREST

SUSAN PAGE DAVIS

CHAPTER 1

O'Neal Brewster stood behind three other men in the teller's line. Payday was always the highlight of the month, and he always came to the bank as soon as he could with two purposes in mind. To make a deposit into his savings account, obviously, and—he hoped not so obviously—for a chance to talk to Augusta Ferris for a couple of minutes.

A lot of fellows were attracted to the pretty, red-haired teller. She was known to be a widow, but the rest of her personal life was a close-kept secret. It was almost a game to go into the bank and try to flirt with her. The woman might be sweet-faced and shapely, but she was also straitlaced and had a reputation for soundly rebuffing all comers.

But O'Neal thought the last time he'd made a deposit that he'd seen a wistfulness in her eyes, even as she told him, "Go on, now, Mr. Brewster. You're much too forward."

"It's the Irish in me," he'd replied, setting her up to make a joke about blarney, but she didn't even smile at his remark.

He sure wished he could get past that granite wall she put up in addition to the barred teller's cage. Someday maybe she'd smile and throw a good-natured barb back at him. When that happened, O'Neal was ready with an invitation to a fancy dinner at the Hartville Hotel. She couldn't turn down every single man forever, could she? More and more, he hoped he was the one she would quit freezing out.

Finally, the customers ahead of him moved on, and he found himself face-to-face with Augusta Ferris. The bodice of her medium-blue dress had buttons that looked like little blueberries. They were round and covered in the same cloth the dress was made from, and they matched her captivating eyes.

"Hello, Mr. Brewster," she said gravely.

"Howdy, Miz Ferris." O'Neal grinned, determined to make her smile today. "That's a mighty pretty dress you're wearing, ma'am."

"Thank you. Do you wish to make a deposit?"

"That I do." He stacked a twenty-dollar gold piece and five silver dollars on the counter between them, his usual monthly deposit. The rest he kept out for whatever he wanted to spend it on in the next thirty days.

She pulled the coins through the slot at the bottom of the window without looking at him. "And the usual bank check?"

"Yes, ma'am. Make it out to my mother, please." He sent ten dollars home to his widowed mother each month, out of the money he took to the bank.

"How are the Rangers doing?" she asked without looking up.

Now that was progress, real progress. She'd said something entirely unnecessary, and she'd asked about his personal life, to boot. That showed she'd been paying attention to him, yes sir.

"We're doing just fine." O'Neal leaned on the ledge outside her window. "Busted up a bunch of cattle rustlers last week, and foiled a bank robbery in Victoria."

"Thank you on behalf of all bankers."

She was clearly impressed. O'Neal grinned like a coon dog

with a ring-tail up a tree. "Say, Miz Ferris," he said as she pushed his mother's check out the slot, "I was wondering if—"

The bank's front door flew open so fast and hard, it hit the wall with a *thunk*. O'Neal glanced over his shoulder and jerked to attention, reaching for his gun.

"Hold it right there, Ranger." A masked man advanced toward him, a shotgun pointed squarely at O'Neal's chest.

~

Augusta caught her breath as five armed men with kerchiefs over their faces strode into the bank. The leader of the gang had his shotgun barrel scarcely a yard from O'Neal Brewster's shiny badge. The cheeky Irish Ranger had frozen with his revolver an inch out of his holster.

The other customers scurried up against the walls, eyes wide and hands rising to ear level. The other teller, Lawrence Taylor, ducked down below his window, and she heard the door to Mr. Palmer's private office open. Augusta followed Brewster's lead and sat stock still, staring at the man menacing the Texas Ranger. Were those retreating rustles behind her? Lawrence trying to get out the back door?

"Nice and easy," the robber said. "Lay it on the floor."

Brewster's jaw twitched, and Augusta caught a flash of steel in his eye. Giving up his gun was probably the hardest thing he could ever do. He held the robber's gaze, watching the other man's gray eyes, hard as granite, which showed above the bandana. A mole southwest of the robber's right eye made this hombre unmistakable if they met again.

"Put it down," the robber repeated.

She held her breath. Would Brewster follow his orders? Part of her hoped not, but she couldn't see how he could avoid obeying without causing some bloodshed. And she was right behind

Brewster, in the most likely line of fire for that lethal-looking shotgun.

Ranger Brewster drew the revolver out slowly, pointing it downward, and lowered it gently to the floor. Perhaps they'd leave it there, but that was wishful thinking.

The robber kept aiming at the Ranger and called, "Spyder, get over here."

Another masked man, this one tall and lean with light-blue eyes, hurried to his side.

"Git that gun."

The one called Spyder stooped to pick it up.

Brewster winced. Yes, this was a blow to him. The revolver looked like the Colt Peacemaker Augusta's dearly departed husband used to own. He'd probably spent a lot of his pay for it. He tensed and clenched his fist down at his side. Hopefully, he wouldn't do something foolish. If he was tempted to give Spyder a swift uppercut to the jaw, he'd best remember the other four armed men standing by. He and Augusta, not to mention the other bank customers, would no doubt get shot to pieces. Brewster had more than enough in his savings account to buy another gun, so one could hope he would put their lives ahead of his own wants.

Of course, if someone didn't interfere, by the time this bunch was finished, there wouldn't be enough left in the bank for him to buy a postage stamp, let alone a new gun. Anger bubbled inside her at the injustice to O'Neal Brewster and all the others who trusted the bank to keep their money safe.

"Awright, now git over there against the wall." The first man waved his gun a little, herding Brewster with the other customers. He stood against the side wall with three cowboys, two women, Mr. Mortenson, who owned the mercantile next door, and one of the railroad depot employees. Brewster was the only lawman in the bunch.

Augusta glanced toward Lawrence's seat, but he was gone. Had he gotten out to alert the local sheriff to the trouble? Hopefully, Sheriff Watson was in town today. His office was only two doors down, and he was back on the job after recovering from an injury last winter. Maybe he'd seen the outlaws ride up.

The Ranger captain, Hugh Sterling, was a good man, too, but his place was clear down at the other end of the street, and he couldn't help if he didn't know the gang was in Hartville.

She studied Brewster's face. He was calculating, all right. She'd bet his mind was percolating like a coffeepot on a hot fire. Maybe he had a derringer stuck down his boot. Still, five to one. She sent up a quick prayer, echoing one of the many Psalms she had memorized. *Plead my cause, O Lord, with them that strive with me: fight against them that fight against me.*

The one who seemed to be the leader left Spyder in charge of the hostages and moved out of her line of vision. Maybe Brewster could do something now.

"Hey, now, Missy."

She jumped and whirled around. A sinister man with long black hair and bronzed skin stood right beside her. He'd found the door that led back into the offices and the vault. He held his revolver not a yard from Augusta's face. She felt suddenly faint, as though her spine had melted and her head was floating. She wanted to look around at O'Neal Brewster, but she didn't dare move.

"Let's have everything out of your cash drawer," the robber said.

Augusta faced forward and opened her drawer. Unless she was mistaken, that robber was an Indian, but there wasn't anything to keep an Indian from joining a gang of white desperados. The skin of another man was dark like black coffee. The life of crime offered opportunity to all.

She took the stack of bills and handful of coins she'd collected that morning out of her drawer, including Brewster's deposit. The man who'd demanded the money had a sugar sack ready, and she dropped it inside.

"Might as well put that ring in there, too," he said.

"What—that's my wedding ring!" She looked up into his dark eyes.

"It's gold."

Her fingers trembled as she pulled it off over her knuckle and dropped it into his sack.

"Take it easy, Ranger."

She looked up through her window. Spyder, the man covering Brewster with his shotgun, was scowling at him. Had Brewster started to make a move?

Two more of them went past her chair, and from the direction of the office, she heard Mr. Palmer sputtering in outrage.

"Do we need some dynamite?" one of the outlaws asked.

"Not if this gentleman wants to live," said another.

Poor Mr. Palmer. They were threatening him so he'd open the vault. Hopefully, he would do it and not try any heroics. The money wasn't worth his life. And if the bandits decided to dynamite the vault door, the whole bank could collapse on them. She prayed they wouldn't do that. Then she revised her prayer, asking only that no one be hurt.

"Let's go, ma'am." The robber beside her motioned with his revolver.

She rose slowly. He seemed to indicate that he wanted her to go toward the vault. She didn't want to go out of Brewster's line of sight and lose contact with him.

"Move it," the robber barked.

She cast a final bleak glance toward Ranger Brewster. What good could he do? Even so, she hoped.

~

O'Neal clenched his fists. One of the gang—he was sure this was the Markham Gang—was ordering Mrs. Ferris out of her chair. Where was he taking her? O'Neal couldn't let them hurt her. The gaze she threw him was one of anguish. Was she pleading for his help? He was the only man she looked to for aid. The outlaw who held her at gunpoint had long black hair and eyes like obsidian. O'Neal was pretty sure he was Cherokee Sam. He'd been known to run with Markham before.

More than anything, O'Neal wished he could get Mrs. Ferris away from the robbers, but all he could do was stand there with his hands high. He would never live down this humiliation, but that wasn't as bad as seeing her hauled off. If they harmed Augusta Ferris in any way, he would have their hides. He vowed inwardly to hunt them down if it was the last thing he did.

All of the robbers but the one aiming his gun at O'Neal went into the back. It sounded like they were arguing. He couldn't hear anything out of Mrs. Ferris or the banker. He did hear one of them ask, "Do we need Spyder back here?"

"Nah, I'll just blow it."

That must be Arch Russell, the gunpowder man of the Markham Gang, with his hard gray eyes and telltale mole. O'Neal also recognized the dark-skinned man, Bass Tomkins, but he didn't think Cass Markham himself was with them today. For some reason, Russell was bossing this escapade, and he could be just as ruthless as Cass.

Out front in the street, a commotion arose, and Spyder looked toward the door, still pointing his shotgun at O'Neal.

"You all right in there?" yelled Sheriff Watson.

O'Neal sprang. He and Spyder went down with a thud that knocked the breath out of them both. O'Neal clutched the hand that held the gun and slammed the masked man's wrist against the floor over and over. The shotgun went off, and glass shattered. The women against the wall shrieked. Pieces of plaster fell from the ceiling.

One more slam of his wrist, and the robber dropped the gun just as the front door burst open and Watson charged in with a deputy and Gordy, the bartender from the Bluebonnet, behind him. Gordy wielded a shotgun, probably the one he kept under the bar, and Watson and the deputy had their six-shooters out.

"They went out the back," O'Neal yelled to Watson.

The deputy came to secure Spyder with handcuffs. O'Neal grabbed the robber's revolver and tore for the door to the inner rooms. He found his way past the tellers' stations, down a hallway, and around the corner. The vault stood wide open, but nobody was there now. He charged past it to the back door and out into the glaring sun.

He counted six horses through the dust cloud their hooves threw up. But they were too far away for him to catch on foot, and Mrs. Ferris's blue skirts fluttered in the wind of their speed as they galloped south. O'Neal was a good shot, but with a handgun at this distance, he didn't dare risk shooting. Augusta's life was worth more than a little glory, and he couldn't stop them all.

Six horses. One of them had to belong to Spyder, the man he'd taken down. That meant they'd had a sixth man out here holding their mounts, and O'Neal had walked right into their trap.

Watson came around the corner of the bank and pulled up next to O'Neal. "They're gone?"

"Yeah. It's got to be the Markham Gang."

"Think so?"

"I saw Arch Russell's mole, and I recognized his voice. Bass Tomkins and Cherokee Sam were with them, too, and unless I'm mistaken, that fella inside is Spyder Jackson."

"We've got him. I sent for Captain Sterling." Watson stowed his six-shooter.

"He's away. Went with a couple of the Rangers into Austin."

"Too bad. It's a good thing Mrs. Mortenson was alert. She ran to my office and said she'd seen some armed men ride up and head for the bank, and her husband was inside. At least nobody's hurt. How many are there?"

"Five now. Five robbers and Augusta Ferris." The woman he had to get back unharmed.

CHAPTER 2

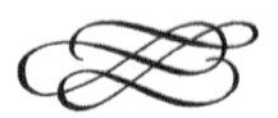

Augusta clung to the saddle horn and tensed her legs around the brown horse's barrel. She could ride a docile horse, but she hadn't done so in a long while. And this steed was tearing along like a locomotive. Trees and fence posts whipped by so fast, she felt dizzy.

The worst part was the man sitting behind her. She hadn't been this close to a man since her husband died three years ago, and she didn't like it, at least not with this particular man. Now, someone like Ranger Brewster might have been easier to accept as a riding partner, but even with someone she liked, this was close quarters.

She sent up silent prayers continually. So far as she knew, no one had been hurt in the robbery, and she offered her thanks for that. But these men had stolen all the cash from the vault and the tellers' drawers. A verse from her favorite Psalm, number 37, came to her mind.

The wicked borroweth and payeth not again: but the righteous sheweth mercy, and giveth.

She prayed that O'Neal Brewster and the other Texas Rangers

would get the money back. Her second request was that they could do it without any of them being killed. Her third plea was that she would escape from the outlaws and get safely home.

Augusta was not in the habit of waiting to be rescued. She'd been on her own since her husband was killed in a carriage accident back in Cincinnati. She had no one to take care of her now, but she'd done fairly well looking after herself, thank you. She wasn't going to let these hoodlums get away with kidnapping her out of the bank in the peaceful little town of Hartville.

True, Hartville was not as tame as Cincinnati, but it wasn't generally what she would call a wild frontier town either. Mostly, it was populated by ranchers and merchants. She rented two rooms from another widow and enjoyed her quiet life as a bank teller. Until today.

The band's leader had forced her to go with them, and he had made her, at gunpoint, climb onto his horse. He had swung up behind her and was now careening out of town with his comrades. She didn't like the way his arm was clamped about her waist. She pried at his fingers to make him loosen his hold, but he only laughed and held her tighter against him.

If she were the one sitting behind the saddle, she'd have slipped off over the horse's hindquarters in an instant, but his position made that impossible—which was probably why he'd put her in front of him.

The other four outlaws galloped ahead or beside them, and they'd brought along an extra horse. After thinking about it, she realized that horse belonged to the man they'd left behind in the bank—the one who had held O'Neal Brewster and the other customers at gunpoint.

She did hope Ranger Brewster was safe. She'd always liked the jaunty young man, though she would never admit it to him or anyone else in Hartville. Things had happened very quickly back there, but judging by the noise as the outlaws led her toward the back door, Brewster might have disarmed one of the robbers.

The outlaw's hand tightened on her stomach, sliding upward in a most disconcerting manner. Augusta threw her head back against him, hoping she would break his nose. The thud that resulted was satisfying until he cursed loudly in her ear and punched her in the belly. Her breath flew out of her, and she doubled over, gasping.

"Just sit still." He growled and added a name most unsuitable in decent company. She couldn't do anything *but* sit still for several minutes as she tried to catch her breath and decide just how badly the ruffian had bruised her.

That morning as she'd walked to the bank, she had thanked the Lord for such a bright, sunny day. But now that same sun beat down on them relentlessly as they veered off across the plains, making her most uncomfortable. In fact, with the rough man holding her so improperly close, rivulets of perspiration trickled down her sides. No doubt the bodice of her good dress would be stained.

Unfortunately, the robber was perspiring too. Her nose told her that, even though the breeze wafted most of his odor away from her.

When they were well out of town, they made their way down to a ford and paused to let their horses drink. The men yanked off their bandannas and crowed to each other over their success.

"How much you reckon we got?" one of them asked the leader.

"Plenty. We don't want to stop to count it yet. There'll be a posse after us. We've got to keep moving."

"We taking the high road?" another man asked. He was solid-looking, very muscular, and the way he eyed Augusta made her stomach shrivel. His crooked nose bespoke some past brawling.

"That's right," the leader said. "We can throw 'em off in those hills."

Augusta furtively studied their faces. She was certain at least two of them were among the faces she'd seen on the *wanted* posters last month. Mr. Palmer got them every now and then from the marshal—thieves to watch out for. If one of them came in the bank, they were supposed to tell the boss at once, and he would go out the back door and fetch Sheriff Watson. That plan had failed miserably today. They'd charged into the bank in force, with one man at the back door, before anyone could give an alarm. Not even an armed Texas Ranger in the lobby had been able to help them.

The biggest man raked his eyes over Augusta, where she sat on the horse. "Why'd you bring her along, anyway?"

"Because he could," said the one who looked like a prize fighter with a coarse laugh.

Augusta shivered.

The leader glared at him. "No, Dusty. Because sometimes a hostage is useful."

Augusta squirmed and tried to turn far enough to look at him. "Please, this arrangement is most unsatisfactory. If I must go with you, couldn't I ride that extra horse?"

"That's Spyder's horse," the leader said. "I'm not taking no chances of you gettin' away. He's also my insurance in case the posse gets too close or my nag goes lame."

That made sense to Augusta in a practical but selfish way. *The righteous man regards the life of his beast, but the tender mercies of the wicked are cruel.* Proverbs 12:10. One of his cohorts had been captured, and he was taking advantage of the other man's misfortune.

She wasn't going to give in so easily. "May I get down to drink? I'm very uncomfortable."

He hefted an old army canteen and shoved it at her. "Here. I'm not lettin' you down."

She drank from it but not too much. Heaven knew when he'd allow her privacy to tend to her personal needs. She shoved the stopper back in place. After giving him the canteen, she started working at one of the buttons on the sleeve of her bodice. It was the only thing she could think of that she might be able to leave behind without it being noticed. One of her cuff buttons was slightly loose. She scraped it over the saddle horn several times. To her satisfaction, one of the threads gave, and she let it hang there, loose but still attached.

To his band, the leader yelled, "Let's move out!"

The man on the next horse, the large sandy-haired one called Dusty, said, "If you're so all-fired uncomfortable, ma'am, you could shed that wool jacket you're wearing."

The other men hooted, and Augusta, despite her determination to stay calm, felt her face go scarlet. Precious few garments lay underneath the ensemble's bodice.

"Insolent man." If his horse were two feet closer, she'd have slapped him.

"You heard the lady," the leader drawled. "Quit bein' insolent. Now, let's ride." He urged his mount forward, and they splashed across the ford at a trot.

The horse reached the opposite bank and stretched its neck out, lunging up the incline. The outlaw's only reaction was to squeeze her hard against his chest with one arm and reach around with his other hand to grasp the saddle horn, which would have been reasonable if Augusta's hand hadn't already been glued to it.

She looked down at his dirty hand, with a scab on the back and broken nails. She shuddered.

As the horse labored up the stream bank, she pulled the button off her sleeve and let it fall. Her captor didn't appear to suspect a thing. She only hoped the fabric-covered disk wasn't so small the lawmen who came after them would miss it. Because they had to follow, didn't they? She sent up another prayer.

When they reached flat ground, the man pummeled the horse with his heels, and they were off at a gallop. She tried to form another prayer in her mind, but all she could come up with was, *Lord, what are You thinking? I can't ride off into the wilderness with these brutes!*

~

'Neal sent a quick telegram to the sheriff in Austin.

HARTVILLE BANK ROBBED-*Stop*-HOSTAGE-*Stop*-ALERT STERLING-*Stop*-FOLLOW-OB.

To Sheriff Watson, he gave careful instructions.

"I'll put out the word for a posse," Watson said.

O'Neal frowned. "It might be better to let the Rangers handle it. We've been trying to catch this gang for months. Just make sure you tell Captain Sterling I'm headed south and I'll leave sign for him."

"Got it. But, Brewster…it's Mrs. Ferris."

"I know."

"Half the men in town will want to go after her."

No doubt he was right, but O'Neal couldn't see letting fifty incompetent civilians get in the crossfire. "I'll leave it up to you, but I think we can handle it. If Sterling doesn't get here within a couple of hours, you might reconsider. If you do get up a posse, tell Chisholm Hart."

"He's away," Watson said.

"Oh, that's right." Chisholm Hart had turned in his badge, so he could retire and live a peaceful ranching life, but they could count on him if they needed him. But Chisholm and his wife, Caro, had gone off to buy cattle. And a dozen other Rangers had ridden to break a mine strike in the hill country. Hopefully, they were finished and headed home, or Captain Sterling wouldn't be able to raise many to help out.

A few from O'Neal's unit—Company B of the Frontier Battalion—should be in or near Hartville. He'd have to trust Watson to alert them. "Tell the captain. He can round up a few Rangers, I'm sure."

As they talked, O'Neal strode from the telegraph office to where he'd left his blue roan hitched in front of the bank, and the sheriff walked beside him.

"Did Palmer tell you how much they got away with?" O'Neal unlooped Chester's reins from the hitching rail.

"Nearly six thousand."

O'Neal shook his head. "Could have been worse, I guess."

"It's the end of the month—payroll time at the ranches."

"Yeah." O'Neal took a quick look in his saddlebags. He had a little jerky but not much else for food. His plan had been to restock after making his deposit. He debated stopping at the general store but rejected the idea. He had plenty of ammunition that would fit the revolver he'd confiscated from Spyder Jackson, and every minute might mean the difference for Augusta.

He tightened the cinch on Chester's saddle and put his foot in the stirrup.

"If you'll just wait—" the sheriff began.

"Can't do that." He swung onto the horse's back and turned Chester south, along the route the outlaws had taken. He pushed the roan into a gallop, determined to reach all three of his goals—to get the bank's money back, to rescue Augusta Ferris, and to live down the humiliation of being in a bank while it was robbed and not being able to stop it.

The trail was easy to follow at first. About a mile out of Hartville, they left the road and took off on a wagon track that paralleled the river. It led to a ford that was a lot closer than the bridge wagons used. The gang probably crossed the water there. O'Neal knew the trail well and kept Chester moving at a good pace. When he reached the ford, he stopped. They had definitely crossed here. The dirt on the descent from the bank was churned up, and he found a boot print close to the water's edge. They may have watered their horses here, though that seemed a bit risky.

He let Chester lower his head and take a few sips from the stream, then he pulled up on the reins and made the gelding carry him over the river. The water was low, only about eighteen inches in the deepest part of the channel. On the other side, many hoof-prints showed where the outlaws and probably dozens of other horses had recently crossed.

He was about to spur Chester forward when something caught his eye. Something small and unnaturally blue on the muddy slope. "Whoa, Chester."

The horse stopped at the top of the bank and snorted a couple of times.

"Take it easy." O'Neal leaped down and crouched at the spot where he'd seen the glimpse of color. He picked it up carefully and smiled. Not a marble, not a blueberry, not a smashed blossom or an odd stone. He held in his hand a round, cloth-covered button with a steel shank. It was the color of Augusta Ferris's eyes. More important, it was the color of the dress she had worn to the bank that morning.

~

Augusta never stopped praying or thinking. She had to get away from this man, but how could she when they galloped steadily on toward some unknown destination? He held her too tightly for her to bail over the side. Maybe she could make the horse buck or something. She was willing to take that chance, but how? Oh, for a hatpin!

She hadn't had a chance to bring a thing with her. How long did they intend to keep her? She prayed she would be safely home by nightfall. But if not ... she didn't like her options.

They kept on for what seemed like hours. The sun was high overhead, and Augusta's stomach rumbled. Were they going to ride all the way to Mexico? She stuck her elbows back, hard.

"Oof! What are you doing, woman?" the man behind her shouted in her ear.

"Sorry. I had a cramp."

A few minutes later, she did it again.

He swore, and she flinched.

"Quit it, woman."

Augusta gulped. "I'm sure you would be more comfortable if I rode that other horse."

"Oh, that's what you're up to," he said.

"You can keep a lead rope on it, if you're worried I'll run for it."

Their horse had slowed to a trot, and the rider ahead of them, who was leading the horse Augusta coveted, turned and yelled, "You comin', Arch?"

Arch. First name or last? She tried to remember the *wanted* posters. Had she seen that name on one?

Oh, of course. Arch Russell, the explosives man. A chill passed over her, despite the heat. Cass Markham was the leader of the most notorious gang in these parts, and Russell was part of the gang. But Cass Markham didn't seem to be with this bunch. Why not? Still, she was sure. That mole...she ought to have recognized Russell before.

"Please," she gasped. "This is most uncomfortable."

"Hold on, Dusty," Arch called. He pulled back on the reins, and the horse stopped.

Dusty gave a loud whistle, and the other riders halted and circled back to them. Meanwhile, Arch slid off the horse.

"Giddown."

Augusta had never been so thankful to feel the solid earth beneath her feet, though she staggered when she tried to stand.

Arch took a short length of rope from his saddlebags. "Hold out yer hands."

That wasn't part of her plan, but she had to obey with him looming over her. She held both hands out in front of her, and he roughly forced them together.

"What are we doin'?" asked Dusty.

"I'm takin' Spyder's horse, and she can ride this one. Take your lariat and get ready to tie her in the saddle."

Another of the outlaws, a huge, bearded man, rode closer. "We're wastin' time."

"Shut up," Arch said.

Augusta turned her wrists, hoping she could gain a little slack in the line he was tying.

He roughly squeezed her forearms together and pulled the dozen coils of rope tight around them, and she inhaled sharply.

"You'll cut off my circulation."

He eyed her keenly for a moment and then loosened the rope a bit, but not nearly as much as she'd have liked. Finally, he tied the knot, high up her forearms, where she couldn't reach it with her fingers.

"All right, get up there."

She just stared at him.

He sighed, picked her up bodily, and tossed her in the saddle. She clutched desperately with her calves and hooked her tied forearms over the saddle horn to keep from pitching off the far side.

"How dare you?" She glared at him.

He let out a laugh. She supposed she deserved it. He dared lots of things a gentleman would never do—everything from robbing banks to kidnapping innocent citizens. Touching a woman's leg would mean nothing to him, but it shocked her to her core. Oh, for a Texas Ranger to defend her! A man like O'Neal Brewster might flirt and tease a little, but he would never behave so brazenly.

Suddenly, she realized the other man, Dusty, had tied a knot around her high shoe top on the right side and was threading the rope through the stirrup. He passed it under the horse's belly to Arch, who threaded it through the left stirrup and looped it around that ankle a couple of times. Then he pulled the long shank of rope up and tied her bound hands securely to the horn.

"You—you can't," she sputtered. "You'll kill me."

"No, ma'am," Arch said. "I'm keeping you from killing the both of us."

"We're just tying you on so you can't fall off," Dusty said. "You'll be safe."

Augusta didn't dare speak. She was frightened, but much stronger than her fear, rage filled her. She would get away from these thugs. She would.

The wicked plotteth against the just, and gnasheth upon him with his teeth. The Lord shall laugh at him; for he seeth that his day is coming. Psalm 37:12–13.

Yes. Your day is coming, Arch Russell. Lord, just don't let it take too long.

She looked behind them. Where was that dashing Ranger, anyway? Surely, they'd left a trail O'Neal Brewster could follow, even if he missed the small clue she'd tried to leave him.

"One more thing, Arch." The man with coppery skin approached with a grimy bandanna in his hand.

"Right." Arch looked up at her. "Bend down here."

She glared at him, but would refusing do any good?

"I can reach," the biggest man said.

Arch nodded. "Do it, Curly."

He was uncommonly large, and he did manage to tie the smelly bandanna securely over her eyes. With her arms and legs tied down, Augusta couldn't struggle. She was afraid to try to scold the outlaw for fear the filthy cloth would get in her mouth. She could only pray that the horse didn't fall with her strapped to it.

"Can you see anything?" Arch asked.

She shook her head.

"All right, let's move."

Any time, now, Lord. As Psalm 35 says, Let them be as chaff before the wind: and let the angel of the Lord chase them. Today, Lord, if it's not too much trouble.

CHAPTER 3

"We're not going to take her to the hideout, are you?" one of the men asked peevishly. Augusta couldn't see him, but it might be Dusty's voice.

"Why not? Chances are, she can cook."

"But Arch," said a man on her other side, "we can't let her see the hideout. Soon's you let her go, she'll tell the Rangers."

"Who says I'm gonna let her go?" Arch growled.

Her stomach clenched, worse than it had when he'd sat behind her and squeezed her.

"Not a good idea." That voice was more mature—maybe the man she was sure was an Indian.

Augusta swallowed hard. "I'm not much of a cook."

Arch grunted, but nobody stopped to untie her.

"If you let me go, I'll go straight home and not tell anyone where you are."

A couple of the men laughed outright at that.

"We ain't going to be there too long, anyway," one of them said.

What did that mean? Were they headed for a temporary camp?

They kept jogging along. Her seat was getting sore, and she'd surely walk bowlegged after sitting all day on a stock saddle.

Arch sent one man he called Bass back along their trail to see if anyone was following. After about a half hour, he rode up alongside the leader.

"I didn't see no one," he reported. "If anyone's on our trail, they ain't close."

"Good," Arch said. "Let's keep moving."

"Don't you think this would be a good time to dump the little lady?" one of the others asked, maybe the one leading Augusta's horse.

Arch didn't answer right away.

"More trouble than she's worth," another man said.

The blood rushed to Augusta's cheeks, which was silly. Why should she be upset if they thought that? She had a much better chance of going free if they saw her as a liability. Unless they decided to kill her, of course.

"I'll think on it," Arch said. "Let's ride."

Augusta's wrists chafed where the coils of rope bit into them. Since she was now trussed up, she was unable to shed any more buttons. She tried to stay alert and take notice of sounds and smells.

Altogether, they crossed a total of four streams, though one seemed little more than a trickle. Willow trees hugged the bank of one. Before they'd blindfolded her, she had noticed a couple of odd rock formations, and a place where wildflowers had carpeted a hillside in orange, yellow, and red blossoms. Under other circumstances, she would have stopped to admire the colored patches undulating in the wind. After they covered her eyes, she smelled sage once, strong in the summer sun, but she wasn't sure that would help.

An hour later, some of the men galloped ahead, whooping. Her horse neighed and strained against the lead rope.

"What is it?" she asked, clutching for anything to hold on to.

"We're here, missy." The horses stopped, and she could feel men working at the ropes that bound her to the saddle.

As soon as her hands were free, she yanked off the blindfold and threw it on the ground.

"Take it easy." Dusty pushed on her right foot so he could work the rope out through the stirrup.

The pressure gave way as he pulled the rope off, and she kicked free of both stirrups. Her legs were sore, especially her knees, where they'd been confined in one unnatural position for hours.

"All right. Slide down." Arch, on the left side, grabbed her calf.

Augusta swung her leg as far as she could, which wasn't far, and kicked him in the chest.

The tall, gray-eyed man flew back against his own horse, which snorted and shied sideways. The outlaw recovered and stood glaring up at her. "I was trying to help you."

"I don't need your help. Keep your hands off me."

Arch held both hands up in a gesture of surrender. "All right, long as you don't try nothing funny. Get down, and I'll show you where the supplies are."

"Supplies?"

"Sure. We're all hungry."

"I told you, I'm not much of a cook."

He ignored that comment and gestured toward the door.

"Pa!"

Augusta turned toward the shout and was shocked to see a boy charging toward Arch Russell. He hugged the outlaw fiercely around the waist.

"Easy, now, Lane," Arch said. "Take this lady's horse to the corral for me."

The boy gave her an appraising glance and grabbed the lead rope. He hurried off with the horse.

"You have your families with you?" she asked.

Arch only grunted and shoved her toward the door.

The hideout was an abandoned shack. No one could call it a house. Someone had probably tried to start a ranch out here and given up, leaving behind this pitiful hovel when they pulled up stakes. Or maybe the outlaws had driven out the owner and taken over his cabin.

Augusta was allowed a few minutes in the makeshift outhouse while the dark-skinned man, the one called Bass, was stationed only a few feet away. If she hadn't been desperate, she would have refused to use the crude facility.

Next, she was taken to the kitchen, where they obviously expected her to cook for them, despite what she had said. Apparently, they'd been consuming marginally edible offerings which they took turns preparing.

Augusta frowned at Dusty, who was detailed to watch her while she got supper. "Who cooked your supper last night?"

"Curly."

"Curly wasn't a good cook?" she asked.

"It's not that, ma'am. It's just, we figured you might be a better hand in the kitchen than we are."

"Oh, you did, did you? You assumed that any woman can cook better than any man."

"Well ... "

"Of course, they can," snarled Arch, who sat on a bench at the small rickety table, cleaning his revolver.

"I beg your pardon," Augusta said, as if she was truly sorry to have made such an error. "And how long have you gentlemen been eating each other's inferior cooking?"

"Maggie cooks for us all sometimes," Dusty said.

"But Maggie ain't here," Arch added testily.

Augusta looked from one to the other. "Who's Maggie?"

"Never you mind." Arch stood and holstered his gun. "Dusty, shut yer trap and just keep watch." He stomped out the door.

The other men were outside, probably tending their horses or counting their loot, but whatever they were up to, they seemed confident that they had escaped punishment for today's escapade. No posse had made itself known so far, and the sun was sinking fast.

"It was Spyder's turn tonight," Dusty said.

She whirled to look at him. "Oh, and he's the man who was caught at the bank?"

"That's right. Spyder usually cooks rice and beans."

"Was he good at it?"

"He warn't no better than any of the rest of us," Dusty admitted.

"Then why did you have him cook for you?"

"Well, he warn't no worse either."

There was some sense to that, she supposed. "Well, you don't have any eggs or milk." She poked about the bench that held their meager groceries. "What do you expect me to prepare?"

Dusty frowned. "Shoot, I knew we shoulda stopped and picked up some stuff in town before we went over to the bank."

Apparently, she wasn't dealing with the smartest outlaw gang. But that might be good. The dumber they were, the easier it would be to get away, right? Arch, however, seemed a calculating man, and she'd gotten the impression that Cherokee Sam, as they called the Indian, might be mean, but he wasn't stupid.

She put a kettle of dry beans to soak and pulled out flour, lard, salt, and baking powder. She could probably make something that passed for biscuits with water to moisten the dough. Of course, if she cooked better than Spyder and the others did, they might decide she was worth keeping and set a closer watch on her.

What could she do that would give her a chance to escape? She could get creative with the meal. Hungry as they were, they would eat whatever she cooked. Too much salt? Or too much baking powder? Which one would give them a worse bellyache? Probably the leavening.

Dusty sat down in a corner and commenced whittling. She took that as a positive development. He wasn't watching her every second. She worked steadily for an hour, then asked for another visit to the privy.

She tried to use every second she had outdoors to learn more about her situation. She didn't see how she could get a horse, saddle, and bridle without being caught. Maybe after dark, but hopefully, she wouldn't be here when the sun set.

When she came out of the privy, she eyed the track they'd followed in. The hideout was isolated, far off the regular roads and miles from any habitation. She'd need a good head start if she was going to set out on foot. In the distance, hills loomed. She remembered riding up and down inclines on the horse, but she couldn't be certain they had come over those hills. Being blindfolded might have exaggerated the sensations in her mind.

Augusta tried to recall the route. Sage, stream, long stretches of jogging overland, the place where they'd blindfolded her, and before that, flowers, rocks, stream, willows...

She'd overheard a few telling comments on the ride in. Even though she wore the blindfold, that didn't mean she was deaf. They'd come to a spot where they'd left a lookout. That was on a steep upgrade, and she'd had to lean forward to keep her weight centered. And Arch had mentioned a snare when they'd left the Indian man, Cherokee Sam, to stand watch. Going down the other side of the hill, someone else had said something about a trap not being sprung. They'd taken that to mean no one had disturbed their hideout while they were away.

She sighed. Did she really stand a chance of rescuing herself? For the first time, she admitted she was utterly alone in this mess.

Of course, the heavenly Father would not forsake her. But as for the Rangers...

When had she stopped thinking O'Neal Brewster and his cohorts would rescue her and started planning a solo escape? She was just being realistic, wasn't she?

"Let's not dawdle." Dusty poked her with his gun barrel. Grimly, she went back to the sweltering shack.

~

O'Neal was getting close to their hideout. He could feel it. The trail had become faint when the gang had ridden over a rocky hill and down the other side, but he'd picked them up again when they joined a dirt track heading southwest. He'd watched carefully for another button or some other token from Augusta's wardrobe, but he hadn't found anything else like that. Even so, he was sure he was on the right track. The horses' hoof-prints looked right. Two of them had shoes on their front hooves, but not behind. Another was missing a couple of horseshoe nails, and unless O'Neal was mistaken, he'd lose that shoe before long.

He was coming into another piece of rugged terrain, and he slowed Chester to a walk and took out a piece of jerky to chew on while he rode. They'd have a lookout, of that he was certain.

Ahead, a wisp of smoke rose from behind a knoll. O'Neal dismounted and led Chester behind a clump of stunted trees. He tied up his horse and peered through the branches, analyzing what he saw. Could be a homesteader's cabin, but he doubted it. Those same horses had cut off across the hillside, forsaking the trail. Unless his intuition was all wrong today, the outlaw gang had holed up in the spot where that smoke was coming from.

He scoured the skyline among the trees and bushes for a look-out. If he was up there, watching for pursuers on his back trail, where would he be sitting? Near the top of the hill, a couple of large rocks pushed up out of the soil. Most likely, he'd stay behind one of them and watch over the top. He kept his eyes glued to those boulders while he chewed.

Not for a good twenty minutes was he rewarded. The movement was so slight, he almost dismissed it as a twitch of his tired eyes. But no, there it was again. He studied the ground and the plume of smoke that had grown more businesslike, in relation to the lookout's perch. Getting the drop on that hombre would be nigh impossible. But he might could work his way around slowly from one side, where the hillside was rougher and had more cover.

He wriggled back through the bushes to where he'd left Chester and decided the horse was impossible to see from the lookout's vantage point.

"Sorry, boy, I'm going to leave you here a while."

O'Neal always carried scraps of paper and a pencil in his gear, at the captain's insistence. He wrote his intentions down and folded the note. If one of the outlaws found it, he was a gone goose. He stuck it in the saddlebag.

"Now, you behave." He stroked Chester's withers. The roan had been good to him for the last year and a half, and he always tried to return the kindness. "I won't leave you here forever, but it might be a few hours."

~

At last, the beans were cooked to tenderness, or near enough. Augusta ate a small piece of bacon and the biscuit she'd made from dough she pinched off before adding the extra baking powder. That would hold her until she got back to civilization or was caught and punished. As she worked, she whispered one of the Lord's promises from Psalm 34. "'The angel of the Lord encampeth round about those who fear him, and delivereth them.'"

She walked over to Bass, the dark-skinned man, who had spelled Dusty at guarding her an hour ago. He had left off his whittling and appeared to be dozing. If he were the only outlaw, she could waltz out of this place with no problems.

"Hey," she said loudly, about six inches from his ear.

Bass jumped, fumbled for his gun, and sat up blinking. "Yeah?"

"Time to eat. Tell your friends."

She went back to the box stove and picked up the kettle of beans, using a rag for a potholder. She had thought about putting a few pebbles in the beans, but she hadn't found a chance to go out and gather any. Instead, she stirred in a handful of uncooked beans.

As she set the kettle on the table, Dusty, Arch, Bass, and Curly came through the door, with the boy, Lane, tagging along. None of them looked as though they had washed.

Arch sat down at the head of the table. "Dusty, you relieve Sam after you eat."

"It ain't my turn," Dusty said. "Send Lane up there."

Arch scowled at him. "No, I ain't sendin' the boy by himself when we're likely to get a visit from that Ranger outfit tonight."

"Well, I ain't doin' it till it's my turn," Dusty said.

"I can do it, Pa," Lane offered.

"I said no." Arch frowned at the boy.

"I'll take it if'n you don't want to go up there tonight, Arch," Bass said quietly. "Jes' send somebody up at midnight so's I can get some sleep before we ride out."

Clearly, seniority gave Arch privileges. He probably didn't stand watch alone very often. Did they miss Spyder? Maybe it was his turn. Nobody mentioned him.

"These biscuits look funny." Curly scowled at the misshapen lumps of over-leavened dough.

"They taste funny too." Dusty made a sour face. "What'd you put in 'em?"

"Just the usual stuff." Augusta shrugged. "Maybe your flour's gone bad."

Curly tapped his biscuit on the edge of his plate, and it thudded.

Arch swore and took a mouthful of beans. Those at least seemed edible. When he'd swallowed, he said, "Hush up and eat, Curly."

Curly took a bite of his biscuit and shuddered. "Maybe you snatched the wrong woman, Arch."

"Yeah." Dusty grunted. "We ought to have grabbed that lady what runs the boardinghouse."

"We didn't take her to be our cook," Arch said.

"Good thing," Bass muttered.

"Then why did you take her?" Dusty cocked his head.

"Insurance. In case that Ranger or the sheriff chased us." Arch speared a piece of bacon with his fork.

Dusty shoveled a spoonful of beans into his mouth and spit it out on the floor. "I think I broke a tooth."

"We got clean away, Arch," Bass said. "Maybe we should let her go now."

"No, she'd tell 'em where we are." Curly scowled at him.

"Besides, you'll have to cook if she goes," Arch added. "We ain't got Spyder now, in case you didn't notice."

"I noticed," Dusty said glumly. He took a bite of his biscuit and spit the wad out on his plate. "Maybe that'd be better'n this. That woman's tryin' to pizen us."

Arch swung around and glared at Augusta. "Well? You tryin' to kill us all?"

"No." Augusta threw her hands up. "A simple mistake. I'm sorry."

Dusty rubbed his jaw. "I'll just bet you are."

Bass looked up for a moment. “Maybe we should just get rid of her, Arch. You know.”

Augusta found it hard to inhale. Was he talking about killing her?

Arch fixed her with a hard look. “I’m not one to tolerate pranks, or to hang on to people who don’t serve my purpose. You understand?”

She nodded, her throat so tight she couldn’t utter a word.

“You’d best do better next time.” Arch attacked his beans and left his biscuit alone.

Augusta didn’t like the sound of that either. Next time? That meant he intended her to cook another meal for them. Was he planning to keep her indefinitely? Had he really planned to bring her all the way to the hideout? She had expected them to let her go before they got too far from Hartville. But they’d blindfolded her so she couldn’t see their path. Why did they bother if they were keeping her?

She was going to have to get out of here, that was for sure. At least none of these no-goods had tried to manhandle her yet, other than Arch picking her up and plopping her on the horse. But she didn’t want to stick around and find out what would happen once the sun went down.

Where was Brewster, anyhow? Four or five hours ago, she’d have sworn he’d be right along to rescue her, but not so. That snappy Ranger may be sightly, but so far, he’d proved a big disappointment in the derring-do department.

Dusty swore and clapped a hand to his jaw. No doubt he’d chomped down on one of the uncooked beans.

She’d have to be clever, and she’d have to be quick. They’d talked about traps and snares on the way in. If she waited for darkness, she’d no doubt stumble into one and wind up hanging by her heels from some cottonwood. No, she had to leave soon, while there were still a couple hours of daylight left.

Curly took a scoop of beans and started to chew. He stopped and glared at her. Standing slowly, the big man moved away from the table. After a long moment, he swallowed and yelled, "What on earth did you do, woman?"

"I..." Augusta gulped. "I didn't think I'd put enough in the pot, so I put in some more at the last minute. I guess they didn't simmer long enough?"

Curly swung around, his angry face toward Arch. "If you don't get rid of her tonight, I will."

CHAPTER 4

"Take it easy, Curly." Arch lifted his biscuit, eyed it with resignation, and laid it down again with a sigh. "All right. It's not in our best interest to take her along when we ride out in the morning. Take her back to the road and head her toward Hartville. But blindfold her until you get out there. I don't want her seeing how we get in here."

"Gladly." Curly tossed his spoon on the table and strode toward her. "Come on, you she-wolf. Let's go."

"Dusty," Arch said as the big man hustled Augusta toward the door, "you were supposed to be watching her. Now, you see if you can fix something edible for us."

Outside the crooked doorway, Curly grabbed Augusta's arm and steered her around the house to the corral.

"Use that saddle." He pointed to one sitting on the top fence rail.

"What horse do I use?" Augusta looked apprehensively toward the half-dozen animals milling around in the pen.

"The same one you rode in on. I'll bring him over."

Five minutes later, Augusta was still struggling with the cinch strap. She knew how to tie the knot, but she just couldn't get the leather strap to cooperate and slide tight, holding the girth against the horse's middle.

"Get out of the way," Curly snarled. He brought a knee up sharply, hitting the horse in the belly. The poor dun's breath whooshed out, and Curly hauled the strap tight. It took him all of ten seconds to bridle the beast and put a lariat over his head.

Augusta reached for the left stirrup, determined to mount quickly before Curly had a chance to put his hands on her.

"Wait a second," he said.

She turned her head, and her insides squeezed. He was going to put that smelly bandanna over her face again. She stood still, telling herself to stay calm. *Many are the afflictions of the righteous, but the Lord delivereth him out of them all.* Psalm 34:19.

Curly folded up the bandanna and stood behind her. To her surprise, he was gentler this time than he had been earlier in the day, tying it securely but not too tight. "Can you see?"

"No."

Before she realized what was happening, he lifted her bodily, and she was once more on the horse's back.

Augusta was not a woman to use profanity, but if she were, she would have blasted him right then. She heard leather creak and gentle hoofbeats as her horse began to move. At least he hadn't tied her to the saddle.

~

O'Neal crept along the hillside, trying to stay behind rocks and shrubs as much as he could. He'd worked his way east, away from the lookout point, keeping off the trail but near the base of the hill. Right now, he couldn't see the two boulders where he was sure the watchman lurked. He crouched and scurried to the next clump of juniper.

He thought he heard voices—or were his ears playing tricks on him? The muffled neigh of a horse came to him, but he was sure it wasn't Chester. It sounded as though it came from the hilltop.

Cautiously, he peered over the top of the bush. He thought he glimpsed the edge of one of the boulders in the distance. And if he could see those rocks, the lookout might be able to see him. It would get dark soon. Maybe he should wait. But no, every minute might count, with Mrs. Ferris in the outlaws' hands. He scrunched down and surveyed the hillside, looking for his next cover.

A clump of juniper spread a couple of feet high above the earth five yards away. He waited, listening. No voices. No whinnying. Was that thump-thump his heartbeat or the echo of slow hoofbeats?

He glanced toward the hilltop and ran for the juniper, hitting the ground behind it on his stomach. He lay panting for a few seconds, thinking about what he'd seen in that glance—a rider silhouetted against the darkening sky, leading a second horse over the crest of the hill, away from the lookout point.

What did it mean? Had they switched out the guard? What was the extra horse for?

He huddled behind the shrub, uncertain what to do. One thing was becoming clear to him. The outlaws had a trail that led over the top of the hill. Probably their hideout was on the other side. Could he get to it by going a longer route around the hillside? Maybe it was possible, and he could avoid the lookout that way. It might be hard to do in the dark, though, and the light was fading fast.

Some sort of noise reached his ears—like some animal scrabbling around on the debris from a rock slide. Had the lookout seen him? Maybe he was coming down to confront him, but that seemed odd. O'Neal looked ahead for more cover, heading around the base of the slope and away from the outlaws' trail.

Some kind of dried vine was half buried beneath the rocks

from a slide about five yards away. Maybe he could pull that out and use it like a rope. It might come in handy when he made his move to retrieve Mrs. Ferris. Beyond it was a jumble of good-sized rocks he could hide behind.

He went down on all fours and started toward the vine.

"It's a trap!"

Startled, O'Neal rocked back on his feet and crouched there, looking around. He'd heard a voice, no question about it, and it had an almost musical quality to it, but he didn't think it was an angel.

"Don't touch the vine."

He homed in on it then. The words came from the shadow of a mesquite up the slope. The sun had disappeared behind the high ground, and twilight was setting in. He stared at the mesquite. The shadow stirred, and a faint glimmer of blue touched the dark bulk beneath it.

O'Neal pulled in a sharp breath and hissed, "Miz Ferris?"

CHAPTER 5

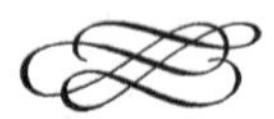

"Hush," she said. "I'll come to you."

He watched in disbelief as the woman moved from the shadow and plodded toward him, stepping whenever she could on a rock. She was trying not to leave a trail. O'Neal had guessed she was smart, or she wouldn't have a job at the bank, but this revelation nearly knocked his boots off. She wasn't screaming, she wasn't crying, she wasn't begging for some man to come rescue her. Instead, she was walking away from the outlaw camp under her own power, and she had the presence of mind to do it without leaving tracks.

She also steered clear of the vine he'd been watching.

When she got close enough, he grabbed her wrist and pulled her down behind his juniper clump.

"What on earth? How did you get away from them?"

"I cooked their supper."

"Huh?"

She grinned. "I warned them I'm not much of a cook. At least, I wasn't today. I gave them some pretty awful biscuits and beans that weren't cooked through, hoping they'd decide I wasn't worth keeping."

O'Neal stared at her. "They might have killed you. Those men are ruthless."

She nodded. "I knew it was risky, but I didn't know what else to do. Hours went by, and I didn't see any sign of you Rangers coming to help me out." She squinted toward the roadway. "Are there more of you out here?"

He gritted his teeth. "Not yet. I left word for the captain. And Sheriff Watson was talking about getting up a posse when I left, but I haven't seen or heard any sign of them yet."

"You came after me all by yourself?"

"Well, yeah."

She gazed at him in the near-darkness. What did she see?

"Thank you," she said softly. "I prayed to God to help me get away from them. And I prayed for you and your lot."

"So they just let you walk out the door?"

She shook her head. "They blindfolded me and put me on a horse. One of the bandits took me up there." She pointed up the hill.

"I figured the path to their hideout went over the hilltop," O'Neal said.

"I think it does. But they kept me blindfolded on the way here, too, so I couldn't see the path and tell anyone about it."

"But we're not far from the hideout now, are we?"

"No. Curly—that's the biggest one of them—he took me up there to where they have a sentry posted in the rocks. It was all uphill, and not too far from their shack. He let me go from there. He took off my blindfold and pointed me downhill. He said, 'There's a road down there. When you get to it, turn left. It will take you east, toward Hartville.' How far away from town are we, anyhow? We rode for hours coming out here."

"Yeah, I reckon it's thirty miles or so." O'Neal couldn't quite figure her out. "So they really let you go, and they're not coming after you?"

"That's right—at least, unless they find out you're here." She turned her head and looked up the hill. "There's a guard up there. One of the other men was supposed to relieve him after he finished his supper. Not Curly. He just wanted to get rid of me real bad, so Arch let him turn me loose. He's not the smartest man in the bunch, that Curly, but he can be mean."

O'Neal pointed beyond the juniper bushes. "The lookout's yonder about a hundred yards. I stayed low so he wouldn't see me. I was trying to work around to where I could cross the ridge and sneak up on their hideout without the lookout seein' me." He shrugged. "Guess I don't need to do that now. Let's get down to where my horse is. If they find out I'm out here, neither one of us will be safe."

"I heard them talking about traps and snares," she said. "Curly pointed one out to me, to make sure I didn't step in it. They'd have to rescue me if I did that, and he just wanted to be rid of me. That vine poking out of the rocks is likely one of them."

O'Neal squinted at the vine again. "You may be right about that, Miz Ferris."

She looked up at him. "Since we're in this together, my name is Augusta."

He smiled. "All right, then. I'm O'Neal. I can get you safely back to Hartville. I expect we'll meet my captain on the way, or else Sheriff Watson's posse."

"Go back?" Augusta frowned at him. "I'm not going back until I figure out how to get my wedding ring away from them."

"What? No. No, you can't. It wouldn't be safe for you to try to outwit the bandits again."

"I'll be careful."

"No, ma'am. You were mighty blessed to have gotten away from their hideout in one piece." All his caution and planning were for nothing, it seemed. He'd set out to rescue her and catch the robbers.

"I mean it," she said. "I've got a personal score to settle. Those swine stole my wedding ring. And I wouldn't mind going back to town with the bank's money either."

O'Neal thought about it for half a minute. If he couldn't get the rescue part right, would he be able to recover the loot without bungling?

Not likely, but she sure was determined. It wouldn't be so bad to face Captain Sterling with the bank's money in hand.

Slowly, he smiled. "All right, then, Gussie, let's go get 'em."

Her eyes sparked, and for a second, he thought she would light into him for calling her that. Instead, she cocked her head to one side.

"I'm with you, O. Do you have a plan?"

He almost burst out laughing, but mindful of the lookout, he stifled it. "My first thoughts were to make sure you were safe. I guess I can cross that off the list."

"Maybe not safe, exactly," she said, "but at least I'm no longer a hostage."

"Right. Now, where's the money?"

"They had it in the shack, last I knew."

He nodded and squinted a her. "And they think you're hoofing it back to Hartville."

"Yes. Unless their lookout's been watching for me on the road and thinks it funny he hasn't seen me yet. Do you suppose he's got a good view of it from up there?"

"There's one stretch he's probably watching pretty close. But it is dark, and something might have distracted him."

"We can hope," Augusta said.

"I guess this is better than having them all out here looking for you." O'Neal rubbed his scratchy chin. "Maybe we'd best pull back a little and let them think you got clean away. We can find a place to talk over what we'll do."

"Where's your horse?" she asked.

"Back a half mile or so, off the road. I scouted the place where I thought the lookout was watching, and I was careful not to let my horse be seen."

"Good thinking, O."

He grinned. "You're having the time of your life, aren't you, Gussie?"

She sobered. "Well, I admit at first, I was pretty scared. But then I remembered I've got God and the Texas Rangers on my side, so I quit moaning and started thinking of how I could make the best of this little jaunt."

"And what were your conclusions?"

"Getting out was the first thing to consider. I wasn't at all sure they'd release me, not after they put the blindfold on me. And then, after I'd seen the hideout, Arch Russell was talking like he'd kill me sooner than let me go."

"I'm rather surprised they didn't."

She was quiet for a moment. "I'd sure like to take that money back to Mr. Palmer, and I'd like almost as much to give those hoodlums their comeuppance."

O'Neal nodded. That pretty much dovetailed with his thoughts. And to carry them out with a spunky and beautiful woman at his side might just be the highlight of his week. Year. Lifetime. But he wouldn't endanger Augusta again, not if he could help it.

Even if they could get past the lookout, they would need a plan if there were several able-bodied men in their hideout. Somehow, they'd have to get Arch Russell and the others away from that money. But if they stayed where they were, they might be discovered, and if Sheriff Watson or Captain Sterling came this far along the road, the lookout would see and hear them, for sure.

"Let's go back to my horse," he whispered and parted the juniper branches. The hillside and the roadway below looked clear. He seized her hand. "Keep low and keep close, Gussie. I think I can get us off this hill without them seeing us."

The gathering darkness was a big help. It hid their flight, and yet it hid obstacles as well. O'Neal led the way, trying not to roll any stones with his feet. When he caught his toe on one and splatted on his face, he managed to go down without crying out—only a thud and a rattle as a pebble skittering down the slope gave him away. Cautiously, he raised his head. His knee hurt.

Augusta knelt by his side and placed her hand on his back. "Are you all right?"

"Yeah." He couldn't help noticing her hand was warm through his flannel shirt.

"Can you walk?"

He pushed himself upward and stifled a groan. He tested his left leg, putting some weight on it, and sucked in a breath.

"Is it your ankle?" Augusta whispered.

"My knee."

"Here, lean on me, O. I got you."

She pushed up against his left side and lifted his arm. O'Neal raised it and curved it about her shoulders.

"That's it," she said. "Which way?"

He limped along, steering her down the hill, and when they reached the base, he turned her northeast.

"We need to cross the road quick and stay under cover," he said.

"You said your horse was a half mile from here. Think you can make it?" Even Augusta was panting now.

"I have to," he said.

"I could get the horse and bring him to you."

"I suspect he'd put up a fuss if a stranger tried to take him."

"Hmm." The stars were coming out now, and a quarter moon

poked over the eastern horizon. "We'd best get across the trail and let you rest a bit," she said.

O'Neal tried to read her face in the dim light. She was, if anything, prettier now than when she sat primly counting out silver dollars at the bank. Something about the moonlight—wasn't there a poem like that? Moonlight becomes you, or some such folderol? O'Neal never had much use for poets.

"Not here," he said, nodding toward the roadway. "There's a place farther down where there's more bushes. It will be safer to cross there."

She nodded soberly, eyeing the pale expanse of the road. "Yes, you're right. It's too open here. Anyone up on the hill could see us."

"Let's go. We can't waste time." O'Neal grimaced as he hopped along beside her. Augusta's shoulder fit snugly under his arm, and he tried not to think about how soft and comely she was.

They reached the place he'd mentioned, where bushes on the other side of the trail threw moon shadows onto the roadway.

"Go, or rest first?" Augusta whispered.

"Go."

He hobbled as quickly as he could, struggling not to gasp each time his knee wrenched. As soon as they gained cover on the other side, she paused.

"You'd better rest."

O'Neal shook his head. "If I sit down now, I may not be able to get up again."

She looked along the roadway and up at the hillside they'd left, muttering under her breath.

"What's that, Gussie?" O'Neal asked.

"'Deliver me, O Lord, from mine enemies: I flee unto thee to hide me.'"

"Oh." He frowned, bending over to rub his sore knee. "Is that in the Good Book?"

"Psalm 143, O. It seemed appropriate."

He nodded. "I guess you don't like me calling you Gussie."

"What makes you say that?"

He smiled, and she smiled back at him in the moonlight. "Just guessin'."

"I do prefer Augusta."

"Augusta it is."

"And do you prefer O'Neal?"

"Frankly, I don't care what you call me, so long as you're still talking to me when we get home."

She considered that for a moment, then said gravely, "Well, you've acted a gentleman so far. Tell me—you do trust in the Lord, don't you?"

"Yes, ma'am. 'Course, in a situation like this, I mostly believe He helps them that helps themselves. But I think you believe that, too, or you'd still be back in that shack."

"That's true."

"All right." He squared his shoulders. "Shall we help ourselves get to the horse, or would it be better to strike out for the hideout from here?"

"I'm not sure how far you'd get on that knee."

O'Neal had rubbed it continuously while they talked. He straightened and lifted his foot off the ground. To steady himself, he placed his hand on her shoulder, then he swung his leg back and forth, bending the knee a little. "That's not so bad."

"You don't want to overdo it."

"Let's get the horse."

"Can he carry us both?" she asked.

"Sure. Maybe we can ride him around the bottom of this hill and come at the hideout from the side."

"I like that idea," Augusta said. "I doubt they've got a guard near the house. They'll be depending on that lookout up on the hill."

"Let's go." O'Neal clamped his arm about her shoulders. He limped beside her, putting less weight on her now. Amazingly, the more he moved, the less his knee hurt. "It's better. Not perfect, but better."

"Good." She strode along with him at his pace.

"Almost there," O'Neal said after about fifteen minutes. He gave a soft whistle, and a gentle nicker answered him.

"Good boy," he said, rounding a large rock. The roan horse looked black in the moonlight, sleek as greased lightning. O'Neal reached out to stroke his muzzle. "Chester, this here's Miz Ferris, but you can call her Augusta."

She laughed. "Pleased to meet you, Chester." She stroked the gelding's nose and looked up at O'Neal.

"How many of them are in the hideout?" he asked.

"Well, there were four at the supper table, and a boy."

"A boy?" O'Neal frowned.

"Yes. I think he's a child of one of the outlaws."

"Really?" It was the first O'Neal had heard about a kid traveling with the Markham Gang.

"Add the lookout," Augusta said, "and that's five men. Five is all I've seen, other than the one who held his shotgun on you at the bank."

"He's safe in jail. So the ones who came into Hartville are the only ones here? Cass Markham isn't around?"

"I didn't see him. They did mention him once."

"What about his sister, Maggie?"

"Oh, so *that's* who Maggie is. She's not here either."

"Well, who've they got? I recognized Arch Russell, and you said the big man is Curly?"

"Yes, for sure."

O'Neal frowned. "That'd be Curly LaFever, then. A lot of muscle, and he's got a hot temper."

"You've got him pegged. There's an Indian they call Sam. He was the lookout when you got here."

"Cherokee Sam." O'Neal nodded. "Is Bass Tomkins with him—black man? They're pals."

"He's there. He's the one that was going to take the next watch. And there's a young man called Dusty, a fair-looking fellow."

"Yeah, Dusty Dabou. I know who he is. That's it?"

"I think so."

"Tell me about the layout in the shack."

Augusta told him succinctly about the room in the rundown cabin, the corral, and the outhouse. "I don't think we're more than a mile from their place," she said. "Curly brought me up to the hilltop on a horse, but as I said, it didn't take that long."

O'Neal looked out toward the road, but all was quiet. If Captain Sterling or the sheriff was coming, they were sure taking their sweet time.

"Guess we'd better get a move on. Let's see if we can ride up close to the shack." He turned to Chester.

"How do you suggest we mount?" Augusta's voice had a wary tinge. Had she ever ridden double with a man before her jaunt with the outlaws? Probably being hauled off by Arch Russell was no treat for a fastidious lady.

"Reckon I'd better get on first...in case my knee gives out." That would allow her to climb on behind the saddle without prolonged contact too.

"All right. Tell me if I can help."

He tightened the saddle girth. Bending his leg enough to get his foot in the stirrup brought searing pain to his knee. He stood for a few seconds with his foot up there, trying to get a breath that didn't hurt.

"Maybe—and I hate to ask this of a lady—but maybe I could use a little boost, ma'am."

"Of course. On three?"

"One. Two." He pulled in a deep breath. "Three."

He hauled himself up mostly with his arms. Good old Chester stood rock still while he flailed. Augusta pulled upward on his belt, pushing her other against his thigh. To be honest, her timid efforts didn't help much, but she was such a reserved lady, she probably would be too embarrassed to really give him a shove where it would count.

He managed to right himself and took a deep breath, kicking the stirrup off.

"All right, take my hand and put your foot in the stirrup. When you jump, I'll help pull you up behind me. Just latch on and don't go off the other side."

She gulped. "All right, if you say so, O."

It took her several tries to get her left foot into the stirrup. O'Neal kept his leg forward of the leather, and at last, she got it. She lifted her hand to him.

He reached across with his right hand and grasped her wrist. "One, two, three."

She understood perfectly this time and jumped up on three, swinging her right leg over the horse's rump. Chester nickered as she settled her billowing skirts.

"Easy, boy." O'Neal stroked Chester's neck. "Good old fella. It won't be far."

For a hundred yards, he eased the horse along parallel to the road, but the footing got rougher as they went. Augusta seemed to be searching for her balance, weaving a little from one side to the other as Chester picked his way. One of her hands sneaked around O'Neal's waist and held him just above his belt. Maybe he could get used to that. Too bad they weren't out for a moonlight picnic.

"How you doin', ma'am?" he asked.

"Shh!" Augusta hissed in his ear.

CHAPTER 6

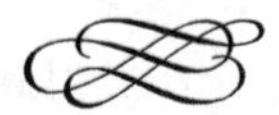

Augusta held her breath. O'Neal pulled the horse to a halt and turned his face toward the faint sound. Someone was riding along the road but not from Hartville. Maybe one of the outlaws had taken the route she and O'Neal planned to take in reverse, to see if she'd reached the road and was headed home.

He didn't say a word but guided his horse away from the trail and toward some rocks farther off the track. Once there, he turned Chester to face the road. Maybe that would make them as small a lump of blackness as possible—like another boulder, only bigger than most. The gelding's head, mane, and tail were glossy black, but his body, a mixture of black and white hairs, might show up as gray in the moonlight if the rider saw it from the right angle.

"Hush now, Chester," O'Neal whispered, stroking the horse's withers.

Chester's chin rose, and Augusta feared he would let out a whinny.

"Don't do it, boy," O'Neal whispered. "Don't even think it."

Two horses trotted past, their riders intent on the road and the bushes and rocks that bordered it. Augusta hid her face in the back of O'Neal's shirt.

"Come on," one of the men said, so clearly she had to peek over O'Neal's shoulder to see how close they were. The two mounts broke into a lope and were soon out of sight down the road.

Chester shook his head and pawed the ground once.

"Good boy," O'Neal said softly. "Let 'em go. You don't wanna hang around with the likes of them."

Augusta realized she was still holding him around his middle and squeezing a little tighter than before. In fact, she was using both hands. Highly improper.

Before she could loosen her grip, his warm hand patted hers, as gently as he patted Chester. "It's all right, Gussie. They didn't see us."

She exhaled heavily. "Thank heaven. You have a very well-behaved horse."

"Yes, I do. Did you recognize those fellas?"

"I can't be sure." She couldn't tell him she'd closed her eyes and hid her face in his back, but then he probably knew that.

"One of them was quite large," he said.

"It might have been Curly, I suppose. But I don't know why Arch would send him out again. He was the one who took me up the hill and let me go."

"Maybe it was someone else, not men from the gang," O'Neal said softly.

"But wouldn't any honest people traveling this time of night move along faster?"

"Seems like it."

His hand still covered hers. Augusta loosened her hold, reluctant to do so but a little embarrassed that she'd shown her anxiety by squeezing the man. She hoped he didn't take that the wrong way and think she was making improper advances.

~

Augusta pulled her hands away from his, which was kind of too bad. If only O'Neal dared put Chester into a trot so she'd have to hang on tighter, but then the outlaws might hear them. He made the horse move along slowly, but the ground was getting rougher, with more rocks and less grass. Hopefully, they were far enough past the base of the hill that the lookout wouldn't see them.

They were in a tight spot, but even so, O'Neal grinned as he headed Chester slowly and quietly back toward the road. Augusta had a lot more spunk than he'd given her credit for, and it sure did feel nice when she leaned her head against him, trying to hide. He put Chester on the road and took the risk of pushing him into a jog. Sure enough, her hands slipped around him again, and her arms tightened. That was better.

When he could, he eased off the road again, into some sparse trees, toward where his best guess told him the hideout lay. Augusta kept quiet, never uttering a word. How much effort did it take her to keep the cool evening breeze flowing between them? She wasn't going to snuggle up to him for anything. He couldn't quit smiling.

He came to the edge of the trees and stopped Chester so he could look out into the clearing ahead. After a moment, he turned his head and said quietly, "I think I see a ridgepole."

Augusta squirmed and wiggled, craning her neck to see. O'Neal turned Chester sideways so she could view the scene.

"Yes," she whispered. "I think that's it. I see a bit of white. That's one of the horses in their corral. One of them rode a pinto."

O'Neal remembered seeing it. He made out the white spot she'd noticed, and it moved a little. A horse snuffled in the distance.

"I wonder if they're all in the cabin." He walked Chester

forward a few steps, and the shack's lit window came into view. He stopped the horse and listened. That might be voices, but the slight breeze that swayed the branches above them camouflaged the quiet sounds. He pushed Chester on a little farther.

An unmistakable laugh broke out, followed by a steadier murmur of voices. O'Neal tightened the reins, and Chester stood at the edge of the woods, swishing his tail.

"Too bad they didn't let me take that horse they had me on," Augusta whispered.

"Yeah." But O'Neal wasn't really sorry. If their plans went well, she could ride back to town on one of the gang's horses. If not...well, he'd always have the memory of her arms around him. "I wonder how many of them are inside."

"We could count the horses in the corral."

"I'm not sure we want to get that close. The horses might get upset and start making noise."

"I suppose you're right." She shifted behind him. "What do you want to do?"

"I'm thinking on it. We need a way to get them outside, away from the money long enough for us to grab it."

"Well, I was thinking," she said softly, so close to his ear that her breath tickled him. "They talked about traps and snares."

"We're lucky we didn't get into one."

"Yes. Psalm 35 says, 'For without cause have they hid for me their net in a pit, which without cause they have digged for my soul. Let destruction come upon him at unawares; and let his net that he hath hid catch himself: into that very destruction let him fall.'"

"Now, that gives me an idea." O'Neal took her hand where it rested lightly on his waist and gave it a squeeze. "Suppose we get them out of their hideout and booby-trap it? Give them some surprises for when they come home?"

Augusta didn't pull her hand away. It kind of made him

wonder if she didn't like to feel his warm hand on hers, the same way he did. He turned toward her, and she leaned away a little. It was dark, and he couldn't see her face as clearly as he'd like. She looked down, not into his eyes. Was she blushing? She could be as red as Spyder Jackson's bandanna right about now, and he wouldn't know it.

"I like that," she said. "Maybe we can find the money first and get it out of the shack."

"You think they'll just leave it in there?"

"I don't know."

"Tell me about the inside again."

"It's one big room. I was only in there a few hours, but there are bunks on both sides and a small box stove on the back wall. The only window is farther along that same wall with the stovepipe."

"Just the one door?"

"Yes, but a man could fit through the window if he had to. Well, maybe not Curly. He's pretty stout."

"Good, good." O'Neal mulled it over. "Let's leave Chester here. I don't want their horses getting excited when they smell a newcomer."

He held her left arm firmly, and Augusta slid off on the near side of the horse. O'Neal lowered himself to the ground and sucked in a sharp breath as pain shot through his knee, like a boning knife. He stood for a moment, holding on to the saddle and waiting for the stars to quit swimming.

"How's the knee?" she asked softly.

"Not great. I shouldn't have kept my foot in the stirrup."

She touched his sleeve. "Maybe it will feel better once you move around a little."

"Let's hope."

~

He leaned on her as they walked slowly to the edge of the trees. Augusta liked the firm pressure of his arm across her shoulders. It wasn't a cold night, but the warmth radiating from him was comforting, like a crazy quilt stitched by loving hands.

Muffled voices came from inside the shack. Once, a burst of laughter rang out.

"Maybe they're counting the money," Augusta said.

"More likely, playing cards. Did they have some liquor along?"

"I saw Curly take a bottle out of his saddlebag."

They listened, but they couldn't make out what the men were saying.

"Want me to sneak up to the door and see how many of them are inside?" Augusta whispered.

"I don't want you going alone." He sounded genuinely concerned about her. "I'll go take a look at things." He dropped his arm and took a tentative step. He stopped and scrunched his eyes shut, breathing carefully in and out. He was hurting—that was one thing for certain.

"Lean on me, O. We need to move if we're going to do this." Augusta put her arm around him in a most brazen manner.

They approached the cabin cautiously, and when they were close, a line of light became visible at the bottom of the door.

"Think they're all in there?" O'Neal asked.

"All but Cherokee Sam. He's up at the lookout's nest. Him or Bass."

"I wish we could see inside."

Augusta stood beside him, eyeing the slice of lantern light in silence for a few seconds. "Maybe they left the window open out back," she whispered.

"Let's go by way of the corral, slow and easy. Maybe we can get around back and take a peek in the window."

A minute later, they were leaning on the fence. A couple of the horses snuffled, and one came over and nuzzled Augusta's sleeve.

"Six horses. What do you think, O?"

"I think they're our best bet to get them out of the cabin. If we turn the horses loose, when they all go out to catch them, we can slip inside for the money."

"Worth a try," she said. "I wish we could get one of these horses for me."

"We don't want to wait too long. If things work out, we'll snitch you a horse later. If not, well, I reckon Chester will take us both home."

"I'm with you. Let's go."

O'Neal gazed down at her. The moonlight highlighted the rugged planes of his face. "They should have let you go once they got out of town."

"Yes. But Arch, the leader, said I was his insurance in case they were followed." She looked up at him. "What happened to Spyder, anyway? I didn't see, but I heard gunfire."

"The sheriff arrested him."

"Was anyone hurt?"

"Nope."

She studied his face for a long moment. "You tackled Spyder, didn't you?"

"Yes, ma'am."

She grinned. "I knew it."

"Did you, now?" He slid his arm around her shoulders again, and she slipped hers around his waist.

"Ready?" she asked. "If they're all in there, I'll let the horses out. Think they'll hear and come out to see?"

"Maybe. I could fire my gun once. That would get their attention. But I don't want you that close when they come outside."

"I should be the one to chase the horses out of the corral. You can't move fast with your knee hurt like that."

O'Neal shook his head. "I'll think on it."

~

Augusta's arm tightened around his waist. Maybe it was just a reflex, but O'Neal squeezed her shoulder a tiny bit to see if he got a reaction. Her smile didn't falter, bringing about a new rush of protectiveness and appreciation for her. "I didn't want Arch haulin' you off, to say nothing of the bank's money."

"I'm obliged for the sentiment," she whispered. "And that you put feet to it and came after me."

It was nice standing there in the warm evening, chatting with a pretty woman, but they'd better do something fast, or they'd lose their chance.

"Come on." He tugged her toward the side of the shack. The truth was, his knee had limbered up, and he could have walked just fine on his own now, but he didn't want to let go of her. It struck him that an attitude like that could make him less cautious and cause them both a heap of grief, so as soon as they reached the corner, he took his arm down. She let go of him, too, leaving a cold spot around his middle.

O'Neal peeked around the corner of the building at the back outside wall. About halfway down, the stovepipe stuck out and poked skyward, belching smoke. A couple of yards beyond it, a square of light spilled out onto the rock face behind the shack.

He turned to Augusta and leaned close to her ear. "Stay here while I get a look."

She grasped his head and pulled him lower so she could whisper to him. "You take care they don't see you."

"Yeah." It sure was nice being so close to her, but he put all thoughts of kissing her firmly out of his mind. If all went well, he could think about that later. Maybe. No, for sure. He frowned and looked at the window again.

Augusta tugged on his sleeve, and he bent down again. "I'll be praying, O."

That wouldn't hurt, but he wasn't convinced it would make everything turn out all right. Sometimes God had things turn out differently than men could foresee. He patted her shoulder and sneaked to the wall. He tiptoed along it, his revolver in hand. All he needed was to have a lookout come around the corner at the other end of the wall.

After ducking around the stovepipe, he stopped beside the window. It didn't have glass in it. It was just a rectangular hole with a shutter hanging down below it. He could hear the men's voices clearly now.

"I'll raise you two." That voice was deep and growly.

"An' I'll see your raise." More amiable.

O'Neal cautiously peeked past the window frame. He ducked back with the impression of three men sitting around a rough table and another sprawled on a bunk. A slender boy stood near the stove. Good thing his back had been turned to the window, or he'd have seen O'Neal when he took his reconnoiter.

He hesitated and decided not to chance another look. He tiptoed back to Augusta, wrapped his arm firmly around her waist, and pulled her toward the corral. Close to her ear, he said, "You're right. Three of 'em's playing poker, and one's lyin' down. The kid's in there too. Not sure what he's doing. Making coffee, maybe. Something near the stove."

"That's Lane."

O'Neal sighed. "I'd been thinking we could set fire to the shack, but with that kid in there..."

"We couldn't do that, O! Not with a boy's life at stake."

"That's what I figure. I guess the horses are our only chance. I don't suppose you can handle a revolver?"

She drew back her shoulders. "I most certainly can. Mr. Ferris insisted I learn."

He held out his revolver. “Here. Take the gun and get across the clearing. I want you at least a hundred yards from the cabin when I drive the horses out. After they start running, you fire off one shot. Only one.”

“Right. How do we get back together?”

“If they all tear after the horses, meet me at the door. If they don’t, then you stay put. I don’t want you getting in the middle of that gang again.”

“You won’t have your weapon.”

He didn’t like that either. “I’ve got my knife.”

She let out a long breath. “I guess it’s the best we can do.”

He cocked his head to one side. “If you got a better idea, I’m listening.”

“No. Sorry. I didn’t mean to impugn your strategy.”

He blinked. “Right.” He seized her hand and wrapped it around the revolver’s butt. “Get going. I’ll give you three minutes.”

“What if we get in there, and we can’t find the money?”

“No time to worry about that. Let’s just get them out of the way. If they don’t all go, I don’t know what we’ll do.”

“We’ll have to improvise.”

O’Neal nodded. “Go. And once you find a spot to hide, it wouldn’t hurt to pray again.”

She smiled. “I can pray while I run. And I’ll find a good rock.” She clutched the fabric of his sleeve. “There’s one thing.”

“Yeah?”

For a moment, she held his gaze in the moonlight. “We don’t want to kill anyone, O.”

He nodded slowly. “Unless we have to.”

“Fair enough. Because I don’t want to lose you now.”

Did she mean that she needed him to make the plan a success, or that she cared about him and that he should use deadly force if he needed to, in order to survive and return to her? He wished he knew, but either way, he wasn't going to let a gang of scum get the best of him.

He squeezed her hand. "Go."

She strode quickly across the clearing in front of the shack. Her steps sounded loud to him, but nothing changed from inside the shack. The crack of light still shone under the door, and the droning voices maintained their sporadic conversation as the poker game continued.

When he couldn't see Augusta any longer, O'Neal started counting. When he'd got to a hundred, he'd waited long enough. He turned to the corral gate and lifted the loop of rope that held it closed over the top of the post.

Glancing up at the sky, he whispered, "All right, Lord. Give us a chance here."

He propped the gate wide open. The horses milled about, whickering. One pawed the ground. He didn't want to yell—not yet, anyway. Not until he was sure he could scatter them. The spotted horse came over and nipped at his arm.

"Come on, now." He shoved it toward the open gate. The paint moseyed through it, and O'Neal stepped farther into the pen. He slapped a dark horse on the hindquarters and blocked another from circling around him. "Get, now!" He was about to remove his gun belt and use it as a whip when a sorrel let out a whinny and charged past him, toward the opening. The other horses followed, fleeing from the stranger and stretching their legs out as they bounded into freedom. Their hoofbeats thundered across the night. The voices in the cabin had stilled.

A gunshot rang out, and the door of the shack was yanked open.

O'Neal dove between the rails at the back of the corral fence.

CHAPTER 7

The gun's report startled Augusta, even though she knew it was coming. The small herd of horses streamed across the clearing, their hooves drumming the ground. She had positioned herself behind a large rock near some mesquite, and she could see the front of the shack as well as the spot where the corral was, though she couldn't make out the fence.

The door of the shack swung open, and a big man was silhouetted in the frame. He swore and yelled, "The horses are loose!"

He dove back inside for a moment, and a scramble followed. Augusta crouched behind her rock and clung to it, trembling. At least none of the horses had run toward her. But what if they ran to where Chester was tied up in the trees? And where was O'Neal?

She heard someone—Arch, maybe—shout, "Dusty, you stay here with Lane."

Her heart plummeted. So much for getting them all out of the shack to round up their mounts. Dusty Dabou was a man she didn't want to face again. And they were leaving Lane behind, too, as Arch, Curly, and one other man charged out into the night and stood listening and staring around them.

"This way!" Arch led them at a run toward the hill path.

Augusta ducked low, but she thought the third man was Bass, not Cherokee Sam. She hadn't seen the Indian's long hair, and the compact figure looked more like Bass Tomkins.

She waited only a few seconds, until she surmised they were out of earshot of her footsteps, then she bolted for the far side of the shack.

In the light that spilled out through the rough window hole, she saw movement and pulled back behind the corner. Her heart hammering, she inched forward and peeked around at the back of the shack.

O'Neal!

She scurried toward him as quietly as she could.

He met her midway and put his hands on her shoulders. He leaned close, and her heart pounded.

"Dabou's in there with the boy," he whispered.

She nodded.

"I think I can drop Dabou from the window. You sneak around to the front and be ready to hold the boy down until I get there."

"All right." She tried not to let his words unnerve her. She held the revolver toward him, and he took it. "You be careful."

"I will."

"'Many are the afflictions of the righteous, but the Lord delivereth him out of them all.'"

O'Neal blinked. "I'm guessing that's a psalm."

"Number 34, verse 19."

He nodded. Instead of going into immediate action, he hesitated, then touched her cheek. "Augusta, if it doesn't go right..."

"What?" She looked up at him, but the shadows were too deep here under the eaves, and she couldn't see his eyes.

"I'm probably crazy to let you do this," O'Neal said.

"We'll be fine."

He brushed her lips softly with his, and her stomach lurched.

"Godspeed." He pulled away, leaving her shivering. He was halfway to the window already.

She peeked around the corner, then tiptoed toward the front.

~

O'Neal crouched and edged over to the window, praying without words as he went. He stood cautiously and peered inside, keeping his face as far to the edge as he could. The window ledge was as high as his chest.

He'd been on the other side of the frame the last time he looked in, and now he couldn't see anyone at first glance. He sidled over a little and caught sight of a pair of boots, crossed at the end of a pair of long legs. Dusty still sat on the bench, drinking coffee, his back to the window, and his revolver lay on the table beside him.

The bad part was that Lane, the boy, stood in the open doorway with his back to the room, gazing out into the night.

It seemed like an hour had passed since Augusta had left him. Had she reached the front wall? He didn't want to wait until the boy caught sight of her. Still, he didn't want to shoot an unarmed man in the back. O'Neal hesitated and trained his revolver on a spot between Dusty's shoulder blades.

"Nobody out here," Lane said, turning away from the door.

Afraid the boy would see him and cry out, O'Neal ducked down below the window frame. He made himself count to ten silently before moving again.

"Hey," Lane said.

"What?"

O'Neal rose just enough to peek over the window ledge.

Lane was gesturing toward the open doorway. Dusty shoved the bench back with his legs as he stood and reached for his revolver.

Augusta! He couldn't leave her exposed like that.

Before O'Neal could act, Lane leaped out the door and off the steps. Dusty ran outside. O'Neal almost fired at him, but any gunfire would surely bring back the rest of the gang. They couldn't have gotten too far away by now. He ran for the front of the cabin.

As he rounded the corner, he heard a thunk and scrabbling noises. He kept back to give him time to assess things.

Augusta appeared to be wrestling with the boy on the ground on the near side of the stoop. Dusty stood a few feet away, watching and moving his revolver around as though trying to find a good angle for a clean shot.

O'Neal stepped out from behind the wall and took quick aim. As he moved, Dusty looked his way. The line of his gun arm changed as he swung the revolver in O'Neal's direction.

No help for it. O'Neal's gun roared, and a spark flashed near Dusty's hand. O'Neal jumped back behind the corner as soon as he'd fired. Once his heart started beating again, lickety-split, he decided he wasn't injured. But he wasn't sure he'd hit Dusty, and he'd lost his advantage. And Gussie was in deep trouble.

His own shot was probably not true, due to Dusty's movement. Their gunfire would no doubt bring the rest of the outlaws back. O'Neal's nerves didn't usually bother him when he was in a tight spot, but knowing Augusta was out there with a bloodthirsty outlaw may have put him a little off kilter. He had to look and see what happened.

No more gunshots followed, so he cautiously took a peek around the corner. The two brawling figures still struggled on the ground. A flurry of skirts rose as they rolled over, and Augusta said, "Stop it, Lane. Stop."

Dusty was farther away now, which O'Neal took as a good sign. His bullet must have hit him and knocked him backward. The stocky man was slowly picking himself up and looking around. No gleam of metal showed in his hand.

O'Neal ran out from his cover and yelled, "Hold it right there, Dusty. Don't move."

The outlaw's revolver lay on the ground ten feet from Dusty, and O'Neal ran over and picked it up. Still aiming his own gun at the fallen outlaw, he stuck the second one in his holster and walked sideways toward Augusta and Lane.

"Give it up, boy," he said sternly.

Lane was sitting on Augusta now, pummeling her with his fists. O'Neal grabbed the boy's collar with his free hand and jerked him backward. He tossed Lane a couple of yards toward Dusty, and the boy sprawled in the grass.

"You all right, Gussie?" O'Neal asked.

Augusta sat up, panting and clutching her hand to her jaw. "I'll live, but that boy's feisty."

O'Neal risked a quick glance at her. Augusta seemed a little shaky and disoriented.

"Come here, Lane," Dusty said.

O'Neal jerked his attention back to them. "No, kid, you stay put."

To his dismay, Lane scrambled on all fours toward Dusty. Before he could say another word, Dusty had grabbed the boy around the waist and crunched him up against his middle. O'Neal's blood froze when a blade flashed in Dusty's right hand. He held the knife close to Lane's neck.

In the light that spilled from the cabin door, O'Neal noticed a stain darkening the side of Dusty's plaid shirt. So he was right—his shot hadn't missed entirely. Too bad it hadn't finished the job. He should have fired again when he had the chance. He was just too polite—maybe Augusta's influence.

The boy struggled in Dusty's arms, and he tightened his hold. "Quit, kid! Just stay still or I'll hurt you. You understand?"

Lane made a little sound in his throat, then nodded and went limp in the outlaw's grasp.

"Let the boy go," O'Neal shouted.

"Oh, no," Dabou replied. "You're not taking the kid."

"Lane shouldn't be with you blackguards," Augusta said, her voice surprisingly strong.

Dabou laughed. "We let you go once, lady. You shouldn't have come back, and you're not getting this kid. Now get out of here."

O'Neal swallowed hard. Lane was a foot shorter than the outlaw. O'Neal could hit Dusty in the head without harming the boy. Unless Dusty made another quick move. Maybe it was best to give Augusta half her list of wishes.

"Go get the money," he said in a low voice.

She stared at him for a moment.

"In the shack," he said. "See if you can find it. Be quick."

She drew a swift breath and dashed inside.

Dusty stared after her, then jerked Lane backward, toward the corral. "Come on, kid. Let's make ourselves scarce."

"You stay put," O'Neal growled.

"Why should I?" Dusty pulled Lane farther away. His knife stayed within slashing distance of the boy's throat.

"I can get you anytime I want," O'Neal said, not sure if it was true. "You run for it, and you're history."

He didn't dare take his eyes off Dusty long enough to see if Augusta was successful, but the noises from inside the cabin told him she was tearing the bedding off the bunks.

"Y'all right, Gussie?" he called.

"I'm fine, O."

"Let the kid go, Dabou," O'Neal said.

"Not going to happen," Dusty replied.

"Come on, you don't want the boy to get hurt."

"I don't care about this kid." Dusty took another step backward, hauling Lane with him, and grimaced. The wound was hurting him, and he wouldn't get far.

"Arch Russell will care if you let him get hurt," O'Neal said. "He'll fill you full of holes."

Dusty scowled at him. "All I got to do is stay alive till Arch and the rest get back here, which should be any second."

Unfortunately, he just might be right. O'Neal listened hard and thought he heard distant hoofbeats. They'd found at least some of the horses. "Gussie, you got that money?"

Dusty moved so fast, O'Neal barely had time to think. He almost pulled the trigger, but it was dark, and he truly did not want to hurt the child. He also didn't want to fire his gun again, with Arch and the other outlaws drawing closer. Dabou rolled under the bottom rail of the corral fence, taking the boy with him.

Augusta appeared in the cabin doorway, holding a sack. "I think I got it all." She looked around. "Where's Dusty and Lane?"

"Running for cover."

A faint rustling sound came from the direction of the woods beyond the corral, then the boy shouted, "My pa will kill you. Both of you!"

Best to get out while they had a chance. "Let's move!"

"I hear horses." She grabbed his hand.

O'Neal pulled her around the corner of the cabin as the hoof-beats grew louder. "Run!"

~

Augusta might well smother, or else her corset strings would break. O'Neal wouldn't let her slow down for a second as they fled the shack and stumbled through the woods. He barely faltered. His knee must be doing better.

At last he pulled her beneath the branches of a pine tree.

"Get your breath."

She couldn't speak, but she did as he said, trying to take in slow, big breaths. O'Neal stood with his head cocked and his revolver raised, listening. In the distance, hoofbeats and shouts continued, and her heart tripped.

"Are we near Chester?" She gasped out the question.

"About halfway. I took you farther from the cabin first, then we circled around. I didn't want to run into them."

She pulled in another breath and made herself exhale slowly.

"That kid hit you pretty hard, did he?" O'Neal asked.

"Not too bad. I'll probably have bruises tomorrow. But I hate to leave the boy with them. Dusty would have slit the poor child's throat if you'd tried to get closer to him." She felt the back of her head, where she'd whacked it against a rock when Lane jumped on her and pushed her to the ground. A tender lump loomed beneath her hair.

"I'm sorry," O'Neal said. "I shoulda come up with a better plan. I was stupid to let you go around front like that."

"You thought you'd get Dusty with your first shot."

"Yeah. Unfortunately, Lane spotted you before I let him have it. I didn't want to shoot him in the back, but I should've just let loose on him."

"Well, it's over now," she said.

He sighed.

"Think they'll follow us?" Her voice shook.

"They'll try. They don't seem to have hit our trail yet, but we'd best get going. Here, give me the sack." He took the bag of money from her and tucked it under his arm. "You said you can shoot. Here." O'Neal put his revolver in her hand and pulled a second one from his holster. Dusty's gun. He took her hand firmly. "Come on. It's not too far now."

Her chest still burned a little from running earlier, and her ribs screamed for freedom from her corset. Worst of all was the throbbing pain in her head, but she mentioned none of it. She just held on to O'Neal's strong, warm hand and flitted with him from tree to tree. When they broke into the open, they ran from rock to rock and from scrub pine to mesquite. Finally, they crossed the road.

Chester waited patiently. O'Neal managed to stuff the sack into his saddlebag and tightened the girth. He hefted himself into the saddle and reached for Augusta. She didn't think she could swing up behind him without dropping the revolver she carried, so she placed it in his hand.

"Oh." He had holstered his revolver, and he stuck Dusty's into his belt. "Come on, then."

She grabbed his wrist and jumped. O'Neal gave her the leverage and the extra boost she needed, and she landed behind the saddle in a tangle of skirts. Chester snuffled and sidestepped.

"You on?" O'Neal asked, and she smiled.

"I'm here, O. Let's get the lead out."

"I think speed's more important than quiet at this point," he said, and he headed Chester out to the packed-dirt road.

As soon as they hit the byway, the horse leaped into a gallop. Augusta shifted to one side and started to slide. "Help!"

O'Neal's strong hand on the other side pulled her up. "Hang on," he shouted.

She wrapped her arms around his waist and buried her face in the back of his cotton shirt, not caring what he thought of her shameless behavior.

They rounded a bend, and a wordless, bloodcurdling cry sounded off to the side and high above them.

She gasped. "That's Cherokee."

"Easy. He's up in the lookout post," O'Neal said. "We've still got a good chance."

Were those hoofbeats behind them? O'Neal pushed Chester without mercy. The big roan snorted and galloped on. After a long time, she raised her head and dared to look back. The road stretched flat and white behind them in the light of the half moon. As far as she could see, it was empty.

"Did they give up?" she yelled.

"Doubt it."

A minute later, he slowed Chester and guided him off the road. Augusta held on tighter as she jostled around. When they reached a big clump of brush, O'Neal pushed the horse behind it and stopped him.

"What is it?" she asked.

"Listen."

Augusta held her breath. Over her pounding heart, she heard hoofbeats.

"What do we do?"

"Just wait. It's all we can do," O'Neal said.

A single horse tore past them, toward Hartville.

"Is it one of them?" she whispered.

"I couldn't tell. But we'll stay off the road for a while."

They went slowly, with O'Neal maneuvering the horse between obstacles and trying to choose soft ground by the moonlight so Chester's hoofbeats wouldn't ring out, announcing their presence.

After half an hour, they drew near the roadway again, and O'Neal stopped the roan.

"What now?" she asked.

"There was only one horse. I'm thinking it might not have been one of the gang. Probably somebody trying to make good time is all."

"Then where are they? Would we have missed them while we were out, away from the road?"

"I don't think so. We weren't that far from it. If five or six horses had passed, we'd have known it. Come on, Chester. Let's get you some better footing."

He urged the horse back onto the road and put him into a trot. Augusta lurched sideways and clawed at O'Neal's shirt in her effort to stay on. When the gelding switched to a smooth lope, she relaxed. She could sit this gait all night if she had to.

After a long stretch, O'Neal brought Chester down to a walk, then stopped him altogether. They turned around so they faced their back trail. Chester's flanks heaved beneath Augusta's calves as he huffed big breaths in and out.

"I can't hear anything," she said.

"Me either. Maybe they figure they'll run into a posse if they chase us too far toward town. We're probably safe now."

"They'd do better to pack up and make tracks for Mexico, or wherever they usually hide out." She loosened her iron grip on his stomach a bit, marveling at how hard his muscles were.

"I don't know where Cass Markham and his sister were. They must be off on another spree." He turned the horse toward home. "Come on, Chester, let's keep moving. You'll get a nice bucket of oats and a long rest when we get back to Hartville."

"I hated leaving that child with those desperados." Despite the hatred in Lane's eyes. She slid her hands around O'Neal again and held on lightly.

"There's nothing we can do about it right now." O'Neal patted her hands where they clasped his middle. "I'll tell the captain so's we all watch out for the kid when we go after them again. It'd be a shame if he got hurt. But it makes it harder for us to get at them if we have to be careful."

"Yes, but you must do everything you can to ensure that boy's safety."

"We'll do our best."

O'Neal let the roan walk. The horse must be tired with his double burden.

"I could walk beside you for a while, to lighten Chester's load," Augusta said.

"No, I want you on board in case someone comes along behind us, but I'll let him take it easy. I really think we've outrun them."

"I'm surprised Dusty isn't out to get you now."

O'Neal sighed. "He was hurtin' some. I expect they're thinking about saving their own necks more than they are about catching us."

"What about the money?" she asked. "They went to a lot of trouble to get it the first time."

"Well, there is that."

They rode along in the darkness. No one else traveled that stretch of road that night. Was anyone else awake in all of Texas? Back East, she would catch a lot of criticism if she stayed out all night with a man she wasn't related to.

Her stay with the outlaw gang seemed like a nightmare, but if she'd wakened from it, she had now stumbled into a sweet dream that she didn't want to leave. An unending ride with O'Neal Brewster, who had turned out to be much more genteel and honorable than she'd imagined, and no one could scold her for touching him.

Exhausted, she pillowed her head against his sturdy, warm back and closed her eyes. She might be more comfortable if she were home, tucked in her own bed under the bedspread her mama crocheted, but she didn't care. She would rather be here, in the back of beyond, with her arms around the Texas Ranger she loved.

That thought almost jerked her from her drowsiness, but she was too tired to argue with herself over whether or not she loved O'Neal Brewster. She might never again have an excuse to hug a man so stalwart and steady, and she wasn't going to fret over the propriety of it.

CHAPTER 8

O'Neal sensed how tired his horse was. Chester faltered with every step as they approached the stream. They were only two miles out of town, but the poor roan needed a rest.

"Whoa, fella." He didn't even have to pull back on the reins. Chester came to a halt in the middle of the road and lowered his head.

Augusta stirred. "Where are we?"

"Nearly to that stream where you dropped your button for me. I thought we'd get down and give Chester a rest."

She found his hand and held tight as she slid down to the ground. O'Neal swung his leg over and eased gently to earth, testing his knee as he landed. He'd kept his left foot free of the stirrup once they'd gotten out of the lookout's range of view, and it didn't feel as cramped and painful as it had earlier. Just a little soreness remained.

"How's the knee?" Augusta seemed to have the ability to read his mind.

"Better." He grasped the reins and clucked to Chester. "Come on, old boy. You must smell the water. You deserve a good, long drink."

They walked together to the bank. O'Neal let the reins slip through his hand to give Chester as much length as possible, and the horse lunged down the two-foot bank. O'Neal followed, wincing as his knee protested mildly. Letting the horse stand pastern-deep in the stream and slurp up water, he turned to find Augusta still on the bank.

"Come on down, Gussie."

"I'm so tired, I'm afraid I might tumble down and land at your feet in a heap."

He chuckled and reached out his hand to her. She leaned forward and grasped it, then edged carefully down to stand beside him.

"We'll nearly home," he said. "You want a drink?"

"I'll wait."

He stooped upstream of Chester, holding the end of the reins, and scooped up a handful of water. "That's good, and it's cool. I'll get you some," he told her as he stood.

Bending to drink would be awkward for a lady in full skirts, he supposed. He took his canteen from the saddle and filled it, then walked over and offered it to her.

"Thanks." She tipped it up and took a long drink.

"Augusta, I apologize for putting you in danger back there."

"It wasn't your fault. I insisted on getting the money back."

O'Neal shook his head. "I should have said no and taken you straight home."

"I would have gone back alone."

He eyed her and decided she would have. "You're some woman."

She laughed. "What does that mean?"

"It means...it means I admire you more every time you open your mouth. And every time the moonlight catches your face."

"Mr. Brewster..."

"What? You been calling me 'O' all night. Sunup's coming and we're going to get formal?"

Did her cheeks flush? Or maybe it was just the subtleties of the soft lighting.

He stepped toward her. "I mean that, Augusta. I admire you a heap."

Her lips twitched. "I thought you were cheeky when you'd come into the bank and pay me outrageous compliments."

"I was just bein' honest, ma'am."

"Now who's formal?"

He couldn't help it. He dropped Chester's reins and reached for her. Augusta came into his arms in a fluid motion, as if they'd rehearsed it. He folded her close and warm against him and lowered his lips to hers. He might just melt into a puddle and become part of the stream. Chester nickered, but O'Neal ignored him and lengthened the kiss. Gussie didn't seem to mind a bit.

The click of a cocking pistol jerked them apart.

~

Augusta gasped, and O'Neal reached for his revolver.

"Just hold it right there," Dusty Dabou said from where he stood on the bank above them. "I got you covered, Ranger. Now, toss my gun up here."

O'Neal's brain whirled. How could he turn the tables on Dabou? Because he wasn't going to let him get that money back. Of course, he had Augusta's well-being to consider. She was in danger again, and he wasn't going to let Dabou harm her this time.

"Where's the kid?" he asked.

"With his pa, where he oughta be. Toss me that gun. Now. Nice and easy."

"Yeah." O'Neal moved his left hand to the revolver in his belt and slowly slid it out. "Where's the rest of your boys?"

"They lit out."

"They left you to come after us all alone? That doesn't sound like Arch Russell." O'Neal feared the other four outlaws might appear at any moment on the stream bank.

"I'll meet up with them, but Arch told me to get that money back, or I'm out. So you see, it ain't personal. It's a necessity."

"You must be hurtin', Dabou."

"Shut yer mouth and throw me the gun."

O'Neal took a step toward him, hoping to put himself between Dusty and Augusta. If he hadn't let the reins go, he could have pulled Chester around to shield her.

"Stop right there," Dabou shouted. "Don't come any closer. Just throw it."

"I never was much good at playing catch," O'Neal said regretfully, "but here goes."

Using his left hand, he tossed the revolver as hard as he could toward Dabou's head and at the same moment went for his own gun with his right hand. The revolver he hurled fell short, landing at Dabou's feet, but it was all the distraction O'Neal needed. He let loose two quick shots.

The outlaw jerked and stood motionless for a second, then plummeted down the bank. O'Neal pushed Augusta out of the way, and Chester shrieked and sidestepped. Dusty landed right in front of O'Neal, half in the water. The gun he'd held was submerged, but O'Neal leaned down and plucked it from the stream. Dusty didn't appear to be breathing.

He looked around at Augusta. She had turned away, and she held her hands clamped tightly over her ears. She stood up to her ankles in water in the sluggish channel. Chester had splashed away from the sound. He was now a few yards downstream, where he once more plunged his nose in for a drink.

"You all right?" O'Neal asked Augusta.

She didn't respond.

He waded out a couple of steps and touched her shoulder. "Hey. You all right?"

She lowered her hands and nodded. "Yes. Are you?"

He smiled and holstered his revolver. "I sure am. Now, where were we?"

He reached out to draw Augusta toward him, but she held up a hand in protest. "O'Neal."

"Yes, ma'am?"

"Don't you think you should secure the horses so that we can both ride into town? The way things look, we might both be walking."

He glanced downstream. Chester took a few more steps, his reins trailing in the water, snatching a mouthful of grass now and then from the bank. And Dusty must have a mount somewhere near the back trail. If they wanted to make use of it, they'd have to find it.

"You're right. Sorry." He hurried off after Chester, his boots splashing in the shallow stream.

When he returned to the spot where Dusty had fallen, Augusta was already up the bank.

"Take care," O'Neal called. "He might have been lying."

"I see the horse," she replied from above. "I'll get it."

O'Neal paused to reload his own trusty Colt and put the other two guns in the saddlebag that wasn't full of money.

Augusta appeared at the edge of the bank, leading a large dark horse. "I got him, and I didn't see any sign of the rest of the gang."

"Hold on." O'Neal stooped and hefted the outlaw's body. It was all he could do to lift the muscular form and hoist it onto his shoulder. "All right, bring him down here."

Instead of leading Dusty's mount, Augusta sprang into the

saddle and guided the horse down to the stream. O'Neal stood there for a moment, gazing at her.

"What?" Augusta asked.

"I was going to lay him over the saddle."

"Oh." She frowned. "As I see it, O, we have two options—leave Dusty here for the sheriff to bring in, or let Dusty have one horse and we take the other."

All O'Neal knew was that Dusty Dabou was getting heavier by the second. He turned around and lumbered to Chester's near side. The horse whickered and sidestepped.

"Hold still." O'Neal pushed and heaved until Dabou's body lay across his saddle. The other horse couldn't be as tired as Chester —although, after lifting Dabou's body, O'Neal wasn't sure but what Dusty weighed as much as him and Augusta together.

He was trying to think of a way to secure the body so it wouldn't slide off Chester's back on the ride into Hartville when he heard hoofbeats. Anxiety surged, and he pulled out his Colt, turning toward the back-trail side of the stream.

Augusta spoke from atop the large horse. "It's coming from Hartville way."

She was right. Had the gang gone past them during their escape? "Get down! Stay behind the horse."

He dropped Chester's reins and splashed to the other side and up the bank. As he gained the higher ground, the hoofbeats drummed clearly. Several horses approached rapidly. There was no cover other than the stream bank, and no time to move the horses up- or downstream.

O'Neal glanced behind him. Dawn was upon them. The two horses stood in the water, with Dusty draped over Chester's saddle. He could just see the top of Augusta's red hair over the other horse's back. When he turned back toward town, he made out half a dozen horses loping toward him.

For just an instant, he wondered if he should dive down

toward the horses, but then the rising sun's rays glinted on a badge, and he recognized the form in the lead.

"Thank You, Lord." He holstered his revolver and called, "It's all right, Gussie. It's Sheriff Watson."

He held up both hands and walked out to meet the posse. Watson pulled his horse to a halt, and the others bunched up around him.

"Took you long enough," O'Neal said.

"We hoped Captain Sterling would get back," Watson said. "After sunset, we decided we might as well wait until first light. I'm mighty glad to see you in one piece, Brewster. Where's the gang?"

"Gone." O'Neal sized up the posse. The sheriff had chosen well. "I've got what's left of Dusty Dabou. He's down yonder. Mrs. Ferris is guardin' him."

Watson's eyes widened. "You've got Mrs. Ferris?"

"Good job, O'Neal," said Chisholm Hart, a retired Ranger.

O'Neal let out a big breath, able to let his guard down at last. "Thanks. Oh, and we've got the money too."

~

One of the Hart brothers led Chester with his grisly burden. Augusta was more than agreeable to have O'Neal join her on Dusty's big horse for the last two miles to Hartville.

He'd transferred the money to the horse they rode and given the two guns he'd taken from Dusty to the sheriff. Watson wanted to hear all about their adventure, and Augusta let O'Neal tell it. He didn't embellish it too badly, and she was cast as the heroine. She didn't cling to him as she had during their moonlit flight, but she did keep her hands lightly on his waist. She sat up as straight as she could, making sure the men accompanying them could see daylight between her and O'Neal.

As they rode down Main Street, dozens of people came out of their houses and businesses to see the posse's return.

"Well, that was mighty quick, Sheriff," said Mr. Mortenson from the mercantile.

"Yup," Watson said. "Ranger Brewster had things well under control."

The posse broke up, and most of the men headed for the mercantile to tell the tale. O'Neal stopped the horse before the bank and handed Augusta down. Mr. Palmer, Lawrence Taylor, and a couple other employees waited on the steps, staring at them.

Augusta took stock of herself. She'd torn her skirt, but that wasn't serious and could be easily mended. Her hat was long gone, her hair a pinless mess. She no doubt had some bruises from her tussle with Lane. But all in all, she'd done all right during the last twenty-four hours.

O'Neal dismounted and looped the reins over the hitching rail. "Morning, Mr. Palmer."

The banker rushed down the steps and clasped Augusta's hands. "Mrs. Ferris! I'm so glad to see you returned safely. We were all appalled at what happened to you."

Augusta smiled. "Well, you can quit that right now, Mr. Palmer. I'm fine, thanks to this upstanding Texas Ranger."

O'Neal came from the horse's side carrying the sack the outlaws had put the money in. "I believe I have something that belongs to you."

He handed it to Mr. Palmer. The banker stood staring down at it, his mouth hanging open.

"And you've recovered the money as well?"

O'Neal shrugged. "We hoped we could bring in the whole Markham Gang, but that's the best we could do. That and one outlaw killed."

"I assure you, Mr. Brewster, this is plenty. I don't know how to thank you. Of course, Mrs. Ferris was our main concern."

Augusta smiled. He probably meant it—or at least, he thought he did. But the loss of the bank's money would have weighed him down horribly.

"Welcome back, Mrs. Ferris," Lawrence said.

She nodded at him. He'd tried to flirt with her once, and she'd put him in his place. Since then, he'd treated her with exaggerated courtesy.

"Won't you come inside?" Mr. Palmer asked her.

Augusta let out a sigh. "If it's all the same to you, sir, I'd like to go home and clean up and take a nap."

"Of course. You needn't even think of coming in to work today. I only thought you might like to be present when we counted the money."

"Take Ranger Brewster with you."

O'Neal winked at her. "I'd be happy to assist. Thank you for a pleasant excursion, Mrs. Ferris."

Augusta laughed and turned toward her boardinghouse, her heart soaring. Would she see O'Neal again before next month's payday? She hoped so.

Her landlady was ecstatic to see her return relatively unscathed and put water on at once to heat for a bath. Augusta trudged up the stairs to her room and looked in her mirror.

"Horrors!" She sat down and reached for her hairbrush.

~

O'Neal had sat on the horse for hours. He was content to stand in a corner and watch Mr. Palmer and his head teller count out the recovered money.

"Ninety-one, ninety-two, ninety-three," Lawrence Taylor said as he laid the bills down. "That makes two thousand, four hundred and ninety-three."

"And I've got a hundred forty-seven dollars and thirty-five

cents in coin." Mr. Palmer smiled at O'Neal. "It appears we've lost less than fifty dollars all told, Mr. Brewster. The outlaws probably pocketed a bit, or else lost some on their way out of town. I'm very pleased."

"Glad to hear it." Fifty dollars might not seem like much to the banker, but it was more than a month's pay for O'Neal. Nothing to sneeze at.

Taylor upended the sack and shook it. "Oops, what's this?"

Instead of another coin, a gold ring rolled out and spun on the desktop. They all stared at it for a moment.

"I believe I know where that belongs," O'Neal said. "With your permission, I'll return it to the owner."

"Certainly." Mr. Palmer picked up the ring and handed it to him.

"All right, gents, I'll talk to you later."

Mr. Palmer and Lawrence rose.

"Thank you, Brewster." Mr. Palmer shook his hand. "Do come by later today. The bank would like to give you a reward for recovering so much of the money so quickly. And for rescuing Mrs. Ferris, of course."

O'Neal smiled. "Well, I'm not sure how much rescuing I did. If it's all the same to you, I'd like that reward to go to Mrs. Ferris. She fought those outlaws as hard as I did."

"Well, all right," Mr. Palmer said.

"Thank you, sir." O'Neal walked out into the sunshine and held the plain gold ring up to examine it. He tucked the band in his pocket and walked across to the mercantile.

Twenty minutes later, he knocked on the door of the boardinghouse. The landlady opened it. Mrs. Gower was a widow, about fifty, and plain. She looked at him and seemed to go all flustered.

"Why, it's Ranger Brewster, isn't it?"

"Yes, ma'am."

"Mrs. Ferris told me how gallant you were to bring her back to town safely. Such an awful time she had of it!"

"Yes, ma'am. I wondered if I might see her."

"See her?" The landlady looked over her shoulder, then back at him. "Well, I suppose so, but her water's not even hot yet. I'm sure she'd like to freshen up before she… Perhaps you could come back in an hour or two."

"If it's all the same to you, ma'am, I'd like to see her now. I already know what she looks like after being out all night."

That didn't sound quite right, and the landlady pulled back with a frown. "Really."

"Sorry, ma'am. What I mean is, they recovered a piece of her property from the robbery over at the bank, and I told Mr. Palmer I'd bring it to Mrs. Ferris."

"Oh. I see. Well, come in, then. I suppose I can tell her you're here. But if she doesn't want to entertain company right now—"

"Then I'll make myself scarce."

She led him reluctantly to her parlor, and O'Neal paced while she went up to give her boarder the news. He could only take four steps from the horsehair sofa to the window and back, and he did that fourteen times before Augusta appeared in the doorway.

O'Neal caught his breath. Her red hair was down about her shoulders but brushed to glossy smoothness. She'd changed her dress. If he recalled correctly, the other one would need washing and a few stitches, but this green one looked fine on her.

"Well, O. What brings you around here?" She walked in and sat on the sofa.

O'Neal seated himself in one of the wingchairs and gazed at her. "I, uh, brought you back this." He took out her wedding band. "It was in the bottom of the sack of money."

She let out a little sigh and smiled at him. "Thank you so much." When he placed it in her hand, her fingers touched his, and he was reminded of how she'd hugged him while they rode through the night.

"Of course, I'd had it in mind to buy you a new one."

She blinked at him. "You did? A replacement?"

"No, ma'am. Not exactly." He held her gaze. He could tell the exact moment she caught his drift, because her cheeks went pink, and she lowered her eyelashes.

O'Neal hopped slick as a whistle across to the sofa. He sat beside her and reached for her hands.

"Augusta, I've been thinking for some time that you were exactly the right woman for me, and our adventure together convinced me beyond doubt. And so, I went over to Tatienne's Jewelry Company and bought this, hoping maybe you'd wear it instead of the one Mr. Ferris gave you." He reached into his other pocket and drew out the ring he'd just purchased—gold with three small diamond chips glinting in a channel setting. At least that was what Mr. Tatienne called it. "I'm sure Mr. Ferris was a fine man," he added quickly, "but—well, I'm asking you to marry me, Gussie."

Her lips twitched as she gazed down at the ring. "This is very unexpected, O."

"Is it? I'm sorry. What would I have to do to make you expect it?"

She looked up at him, and slowly, a smile crossed her face. "Maybe kiss me again."

O'Neal was no slouch when it came to taking orders. He performed Augusta's wishes so well that Mrs. Gower was quite scandalized when she came to the doorway a moment later. She cleared her throat loudly.

"Excuse me," she said when the two jumped apart. "Captain Sterling is here, and I told him you were in the parlor."

Hugh Sterling strode in past the landlady, the dust of the trail still in his beard.

O'Neal jumped up. "Cap. Good to see you."

"Same here." They shook hands, and Sterling shot a glance at Augusta. "Mrs. Ferris. I'm glad to see you looking so well. I heard you two had quite an outing." Amusement tinged his voice, and O'Neal felt his own face redden.

"We got the money back," he said.

Sterling laughed. "So I'm told. Don't let me disturb you. I only wanted to check in with you."

"I'm afraid the gang got away again," O'Neal said. "All but Spyder Jackson and Dusty Dabou, that is. Spyder's in Sheriff Watson's jail, and Dabou's over to the undertaker's gettin' fitted for a coffin."

Sterling nodded. "Not bad, considering you were on your own. Come on over to my house later, Brewster. We'll talk about it. We need to stop that gang, once and for all."

"I agree."

Augusta stood. "Be sure you tell him about the child."

"Child?" Captain Sterling's eyebrows shot up.

"They had a boy with them," Augusta said.

"Seems Arch Russell's towing his kid around," O'Neal explained.

"How old?"

O'Neal shrugged. "Maybe ten or so. He beat up on Mrs. Ferris while I was dealing with Dabou."

"Yes, and he packs quite a wallop." Augusta rubbed her chin and frowned. "That boy shouldn't be with those desperados. He's picking up their habits, I'm afraid."

"Something to take into consideration when we go after them." Sterling cuffed O'Neal on the shoulder. "Plan to eat lunch with us. I'll tell Etta to expect you. Ma'am." He nodded at Augusta and turned on his heel. He ducked past the landlady, who cringed away from him in the doorway, and went out.

"Well," Mrs. Gower said. "I believe that bathwater might be

about ready." She clapped a hand to her mouth and fled toward the kitchen.

O'Neal eyed Augusta inquisitively. "Bathwater, eh?"

Augusta's face went so scarlet, it clashed with her hair. "I fear I'm in need of it. But, er, as to the topic we were discussing earlier..."

"Yes, ma'am?" O'Neal said softly.

She held out her clenched hand and opened it, palm up, revealing the glittering new wedding band. His heart pounded. Would he have to return it to the jeweler's? That would be embarrassing, not to mention disheartening. He'd let his hopes soar. Maybe he should have bided his time and done some more courting before declaring himself.

Her blue eyes were solemn, and he couldn't read her thoughts. It would be a relief just to know, one way or the other.

"This ring is lovely," she said. "I believe I would like to wear it."

O'Neal allowed himself to breathe. "Yes, ma'am. When would you like to commence wearing it?"

"I think I'll let you make the arrangements, O. But...soon."

"That sounds fine. Real fine." He pulled her into his arms for another kiss.

The End

ABOUT THE AUTHOR

Susan Page Davis is the author of more than 100 novels. She writes romantic suspense, historical romance, and mystery. She is a Maine native now living in Kentucky, and a member of American Christian Fiction Writers. Her books have won several awards including the Carol Award for her novel The Prisoners Wife; the Faith, Hope, and Love Inspirational Readers' Choice Award for The Prisoner's Wife and The Lumberjack's Lady (Maine Brides series); and the Will Rogers Medallion Award for her novels Captive Trail (Texas Trails series, 2012), The Rancher's Legacy (Homeward Trails series, 2022), and The Outlaw Takes a Bride (2016). Visit her website at https://susanpagedavis.com

Cover design by: Wild Heart Books

PARTNERS IN CRIME

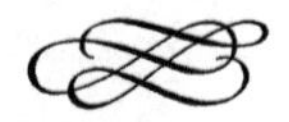

VICKIE MCDONOUGH

CHAPTER 1

October 1886

"Run, Laurel. Run!"

Walking as fast as she dared—slightly more than was proper—Laurel Underwood quickened her pace again. She gasped when a sharp pain stabbed her left side but kept moving.

"Hurry!" June Dawson slowed her speedy pace, then glided in a tight circle around to Laurel's side. She looped her arm through Laurel's. "You'd better move quicker, or you'll be late."

"A lady never runs." She double-stepped to keep up with her longer-legged friend, then turned to the side to avoid plowing into Mr. and Mrs. Harper. She reached for a post in front of the apothecary, hoping to slow her determined friend, but she missed it. June dragged her forward.

"You sound like your mother. Look! There's the judging tent."

Ignoring the curious glances from others attending the Bexar County Fair, Laurel trotted next to June. There was no swaying her best friend once she'd set her mind to something. Finally, June slowed her pace as they entered the crowded tent.

Squinting in the dimmer lighting of the large pavilion, Laurel worked to slow her breathing to normal. She followed June, weaving through the crowd toward the front, where she was to meet her parents near the stage. Excitement bubbled inside her. If things went as she hoped today, she'd be recognized as a silversmith in her own right and no longer reside in her father's shadow. But the competition was steep. Silver workers from all over San Antonio and the neighboring counties had entered wares to be judged. She could only hope her silver-plated butler's tray with the fancy scroll etching and intricate pattern would win.

"Excuse me. We have a competitor here." June squeezed through the crowd, tugging Laurel with her.

"Sorry. Excuse me." Laurel flashed a smile at a scowling man, and his expression softened.

"There are your parents and Bella. And Peter's with them." June finally slowed, casting a sideways glance at her. She leaned closer. "I still don't know what you see in him."

Laurel caught her younger sister's eye, biting back a grin as Bella rolled light-blue eyes that matched her own. Then her gaze shifted to Peter's. His frown, which parroted her father's, proved both men were unhappy with her late arrival.

Her mother reached for her arm and pulled Laurel beside her. "Fix your hair, dear. You don't want to go onstage looking like a scamp. You're twenty years old now and should act like a lady, not a hoyden."

"Yes, Mother." She tucked the loose tendrils of hair back, pulled free a pin, and stabbed them into place. She glanced at June, noting her friend's casual gaze at the top of the tent. Of course, June wouldn't look at her after causing her to get a scolding.

Laurel scanned the stage. Three tables covered in black cloths held the twelve gleaming entries in the silversmith contest. Her serving tray, as well as two others, had been placed in stands so the crowd could view them better. She checked out her competitors' entries once again. Most of the pieces were nearly flawless, but to one with a sharp eye like she'd developed from working in her father's store since she was twelve, a minute difference in quality could be seen when viewed up close.

"The competition sure looks tough this year," her father stated. "I examined each of our competitors' entries, and I firmly believe we have a more than fair chance of winning at least one award." He puffed out his chest and lifted his chin as several men walked to the center of the stage.

Laurel knew her father fully expected to win first place for the third year in a row. Last year had been the first he'd allowed her to enter, and she'd been delighted with her third-place ribbon. It hung from the side of the frame in which she'd put her beautiful hand-inscribed certificate. She loved the swirls and loops of the pretty calligraphy, and the lavender and soft yellow flowers surrounded by light-green leaves in the corners. Whoever had created it was an artist in his or her own right. Laurel crossed her fingers and took a steadying breath. Perhaps she'd win second place this year.

"All right, ladies and gentlemen, let's quiet down." A man spread his hands and flapped them until the din of the tent hushed. "I'm Ralph Meriwether, head judge, and it's time to announce the winners of the silversmith competition. As you can see, we had a number of fine entries. Judging was difficult, but several magnificent pieces stood out from the others. Emmett Taylor will announce the winners."

A thin man dressed in a pinstriped suit, wearing wire-framed glasses, joined Mr. Meriwether at the center of the stage. He glanced out at the crowd and smiled. "Afternoon. I'm going to thrill a few of you, although I'm sorry that more will be disappointed than not. But today is a day to honor the best of the best."

"Aw, get on with it," a man in the back hollered.

Mr. Taylor scowled. "Yes, very well." He glanced down at the certificates in his hand. "The third-place winner of the silversmith competition, with his sugar and creamer set, is Albert Zuniga."

Cheers erupted throughout the crowd as a man dressed in overalls and a faded red shirt made his way up front. June squeezed Laurel's hand, her brown eyes hopeful.

Should she be relieved or saddened? Was there a chance she could have placed second? Her father would certainly win again. Few men were as skillful at etching and design.

Mr. Zuniga made a short speech, then took his white ribbon and certificate and left the stage.

"All right, now." Mr. Taylor looked out at the crowd again, and his gaze landed on Laurel—or was it her father? Her heart pounded. Surely, someone hadn't beaten him. The coffeepot he'd created was exquisite.

"The second-place winner, with an engraved coffee server, is David Underwood. Mr. Underwood has been our first-place winner the past two years."

Rather than cheers, murmuring spread throughout the tent. She thought it a bit rude to rub in the fact that her father had won in the past but not this year. He trudged up the stairs, the droop of his shoulders revealing his dismay.

"Excuse me, Mrs. Underwood." Peter slipped past her mother to Laurel's side. "Maybe you beat him."

She shook her head. "I doubt it." Her mind raced through the images of their competitors' entries. Whose had been better than her father's?

After a muttered *thank you*, her father trod down the steps, then strode back to stand beside her mother and Peter, not even bothering to look at his award. Disappointment clouded his expression. She felt bad for him, knowing how much he valued being the best in the county. Her mother tugged the certificate from his hand, and the red ribbon fluttered to the floor. Peter bent and picked it up, then handed it back.

"Now for our winner—the best of this year's competitors. I have to admit, this came as quite a surprise. For the first time ever in the history of this competition, a woman has won."

June and Bella squealed.

"Laurel Underwood, would you please come onstage?"

Laurel gasped, as did most of those present, then applause broke out. Bella cheered, bouncing on her toes, until Mother halted her.

June clutched Laurel's arm and squeezed. "You won! You won!"

Numb with shock and heart pounding like a mallet on metal, Laurel didn't dare look at her father but forced her feet to move forward. She'd wanted to win so badly, but now she felt awful for besting him. At least the winning trophy would still be displayed in their store.

"Congratulations, Miss Underwood." Mr. Meriwether passed a shiny gold cup to her, which had her name etched on a matching plate attached to the wooden base.

"Thank you very much."

"Well done, Miss Underwood." Mr. Taylor handed her a certificate and a blue ribbon. "Is there anything you'd like to say?"

"I. . .um. . ." She hated how her voice wobbled and wished she'd planned a speech, but she'd never expected to win. "I want to thank my father, David Underwood, for teaching me his trade, and my mother for encouraging me through the early years when I often wanted to give up." She held up her trophy. "This award is for them." Applause echoed through the pavilion. She smiled at Mr. Taylor to let him know she was finished.

"I'm going to fetch your winning tray. Would you please

remain onstage for a moment for a photograph with Mr. Meriwether and me?"

"Of course." Laurel dared a glance at her family. Everyone smiled except her father. Was he not the least bit happy for her? After a moment, his scowl softened, and he gave a slight nod. Relief washed through her.

The photograph was taken, as well as another with the three finalists, then she and her father left the stage. Soon the awards for the best jewelry designs would be announced.

Mother, Bella, and June surrounded her as soon as her feet left the bottom step. Congratulations and hugs were abundant. Peter kissed her hand. Father was talking to several men and didn't look her way.

"Let me see your trophy," Bella cried as she plucked it from Laurel's hands. "Wow! My sister is the best silversmith in the county. Imagine that."

"All your hard work paid off." Her mother smiled as she caressed Laurel's cheek. "I'm so glad that you kept at it and didn't give up when things were difficult."

Peter cleared his throat and reached for Laurel. "You and I must go out and celebrate. And none of this fair food. We'll dine at the Menger Hotel."

"You can't leave yet, Laurel." Bella squeezed in front of Peter, folding her hands under her chin and pleading with her eyes. "The embroidery awards are to be given out at four. You have to be here—just in case *I* win something."

Laurel smiled, brushing her hand down her sister's arm. "I wouldn't miss it for anything."

Mother snapped open her fan, attached to her wrist with a pink ribbon that matched her dress. She waved it in front of her face. "I simply must get out of this stifling tent."

"Would you like to go view the quilts?" Bella asked. "I know you enjoy looking at them."

"That would be nice, but first, let's find some refreshment." She started forward, then paused and looked at Peter. "Experience tells me that Mr. Underwood and I will be quite tired after such a busy day. Why don't you and Laurel dine on your own this evening—with June or Bella as chaperone, of course."

Peter nodded. "Certainly, ma'am. Thank you for allowing your daughter to accompany me."

"I have a hankering for some apple cider." Bella walked away with Mother.

June slid up beside Laurel. "Do you want to get a drink and then go see the quilts with them? I'm parched."

Laurel glanced up at Peter. Did he wish to spend time with her? They weren't officially courting, but she suspected he would approach her father about that before long. He held up his hands. "I have no interest in seeing bed coverings. I'll stay here with your father. Perhaps we'll go have a look at the new steam engine on display."

"You're sure?"

He nodded. "Run along with your friend. I'll meet you after the sewing judging, outside of the tent."

"Let's go." June stood on her tiptoes, looking toward the exit. "Your mother and Bella are almost out of sight."

"See you later, Peter."

Outside the tent, June shook her head. "I don't understand what you see in Peter Newton. He's so stuffy—and he told you to run along as if you were a youngster."

"June! How can you say that?"

She shrugged. "Because he is—and he did."

"He's not stuffy, he's...reserved."

"If you say so. Look! There they are, by that vendor stand."

Laurel followed her friend at a more sedate speed than earlier. Bella had said something similar about Peter. Yes, he wasn't the most exciting man in Texas, but he was the owner of the *San*

Antonio Journal, one of the most popular newspapers in town, and he was smart. She wouldn't call him handsome, but he was steady. He was ten years older than she, but that meant he was firmly established in his work and well settled. Dependable.

She sighed. Were steady and dependable good enough reasons to consider allowing a man to court her? There was a part of her that wished he were more fun—that he could make her smile. All he liked talking about was business.

Ah well, she was getting her cart before her horses. Peter hadn't asked to court her yet. She was surprised her mother had suggested they dine without her and Father, since she thought Peter was a bit old for her.

"This is too delightful a place for such a serious expression, especially for someone who just won a first-place trophy." Bella took the gold trophy and set it on the table where her mother was already sipping lemonade, then handed Laurel a cup. "Stop thinking about Peter and enjoy yourself."

She took a sip of apple cider and wrinkled her nose. "It's tart. And how did you know what I was thinking about?" Laurel sat across from her mother.

"Because the only time you scowl is when you're etching or thinking of that man."

"So true." June sat on Laurel's left.

Laurel sipped the refreshing drink and pondered her sister's comment. Did she frown when she thought of Peter? He had been coming around for several months. She admired his business skills and his knowledge in so many different areas. Although he was a serious man and didn't exactly make her heart sing, he would be a good provider. She tightened her lips. That made him sound quite a lot like her father.

Bella narrowed her eyes and wagged her finger toward Laurel's forehead.

Was she frowning again? More importantly—why did thinking about Peter make her frown?

~

The sunlight from the front window of the store glistened on the shiny silver tray in Laurel's hands. It was similar to the tray she'd won the gold cup for but a bit larger and had an ivy pattern rather than a rose one. She studied each curve, swirl, and leaf, hoping to not find a mistake.

A shadow darkened the tray, and Laurel glanced up to see June.

Her friend smiled. "I think that's your best one so far—even better than the tray that won you first place in the county fair last month. Why, you've even surpassed your father's skill."

"You're too kind. And you're prone to hyperbole." She softened her words with a smile while rubbing a fingerprint off the tray with a velvet cloth.

"I'm not exaggerating. Why, even the *San Antonio Express* stated that your skill was equal to or greater than your father's."

"He wasn't too happy to read that. Made me work all the harder."

June tucked down her collar, which the wind had just blown up. "Is he still upset that he didn't win?"

"I wouldn't say he's upset. He's proud of me, but I do think he believes he should have won first place."

"Good thing it's the judges' opinions that matter and not his."

"Shh...you don't want him to hear you."

June sobered and looked around. "I thought he was gone to lunch. That's why I came at this time."

"He is, but you never know when he might return."

"True. I do think you should reconsider entering the Texas

State Fair in Dallas next October. I imagine it's too late to enter this year, unless you hurried. It's not until the end of the month."

Laurel set the tray on her worktable. "Thank you for your kind thought, but I've had enough competition for the year."

"I suppose it makes things more difficult with your pa. I never understood why he's so hard on you."

"I think he still resents that I wasn't born a son."

"That's hardly your fault."

"I know." Laurel sighed.

June picked up a teapot and studied it. "How was your dinner with Peter?"

"Fine. The food was delicious. I was too full to finish my pie, but Bella happily ate it along with her own."

"She didn't!"

Laurel smiled and nodded. "Mother would have been horrified had she been there."

"What did Peter do?"

"Nothing, other than scowl at her."

"He's perfected that action." June chuckled.

A man and woman entered the store, walking toward Laurel. June stepped aside and waved. "See you later."

Laurel smiled at her friend and then the customers. "How may I help you?"

"We'd like to look at your silverware. Our niece is getting married next month, and my wife believes a set would make a nice gift for her."

"It most certainly would." Laurel guided them to the area where they displayed half a dozen silverware place settings they'd received from other vendors. "Many women seem to like the floral pattern setting."

After a half hour of deliberating on which pattern to buy, the couple finally made their choice. They paid and left with excited smiles on their faces.

When her father returned, Laurel grabbed a quick lunch at home, then returned to the store. The afternoon sped by as she helped several other customers and worked on her tray.

Her father cleared his throat, turning in his chair, which was behind hers. "The sun will be setting before too long. You should go on home and help your mother with supper preparations."

"Oh?" Laurel glanced at the clock on the fireplace mantel. "I didn't realize it was getting so late. I'll put away my tools and head out."

Ten minutes later, her father locked the door behind her after telling her that he'd be home in half an hour. Laurel ducked through the alley between her father's store and the millinery. A doctor's office sat behind their store with an apothecary across the alley from it. Laurel glanced up the alley at one of the twin bell towers on the Cathedral of San Fernando, two blocks away. The tall tower blocked the descending sun, casting a shadow across the alley.

She loved the old cathedral, a popular site for visitors to San Antonio. It had played a role in the Battle of the Alamo when Mexican General Santa Anna had hoisted a flag of no quarter from the tower, marking the beginning of the siege.

A man she didn't recognize entered the alley. Laurel slowed her pace. He tipped his hat, smiled, and made a wide berth around her. She relaxed and pushed her feet forward.

A rustling sounded behind her. She glanced over her shoulder as a bag dropped onto her head. Rough arms grabbed her. "Don't make a sound, or your pa will be dead."

CHAPTER 2

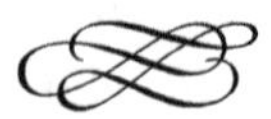

Micah McCullough grumbled under his breath as he tossed a pile of foul-smelling clothes out of the tiny cabin. Maggie Markham had ordered him and the Russell boy to clean it out, even though no one had used the place in the weeks he'd been working undercover at the Markhams' hideout.

By now, he should've learned where Cass Markham, leader of the gang, had gone, but no one was talking about him. So for now, Micah would bide his time. Then, once all three of the Markhams were in camp, he'd get word to Captain Sterling, and the raid they'd been planning would commence. But first, he needed to get the boy out of harm's way. He blew out a loud breath, frustrated that things were moving so slowly.

"It won't do no good to fuss." Lane Russell, the only kid at the Markhams' camp, shook his head. "Everyone does whatever Maggie says. Most of 'em are scared of her more than Cass."

That had been obvious from the first day he arrived at the camp, two-and-a-half weeks ago. He valued and respected women, but diabolic ones like Maggie Markham could make even a Texas Ranger want to shoot her. He steered clear of her whenever possible, because he didn't like the way she looked at him. Did she suspect he wasn't who he claimed to be? He dreaded to think what would happen to him if the gang learned he was a Texas Ranger. He'd drawn this assignment because he wasn't from the area and was less likely to be recognized by a member of the Markham Gang.

It irked him how Maggie hollered the last name the gang knew him by in her screechy voice. "Burns, muck the stalls. Burns, clean the rifles. Burns, clean up that outbuilding." He'd like to throw the old witch in a jail cell and drop the key down a well. And maybe one day he'd do just that.

"I don't let Maggie get to me. You shouldn't neither. Just do what she says, and you'll be aw right." Lane struggled to push open the cabin's only window, which was higher than he was tall. He was a bit on the scrawny side for a boy of thirteen, but he did his best to pull his share of the work.

"Let me get that." Micah crossed the room.

"I can do it." The boy grunted, and the small window creaked open.

"Good job!"

Lane's dark-blue eyes lit up at the rare praise. His battered hat, most likely a reject from a gang member who stole a new one, smashed his scruffy black bangs into his eyes. The back of his hair hung just past his collar. The boy only came up to Micah's chest.

Arch Russell was the lad's pa, but he sure didn't take to fathering well. Most of the time, he ignored his son, unless he was ordering him to fetch something or yelling at him. Maybe that was a good thing, though. He'd sure hate for Lane to become a powder monkey like his pa. Most men who handled dynamite regularly didn't live as long as Russell had.

Lane removed his slouch hat, flipped the hair from his eyes, then slapped the hat back on. "How'd you come to join the gang? We ain't had no one new in a coon's age."

"Being in the right spot at the right time, I reckon." Micah shoved the small table against a wall. "I was playing poker in a saloon when a ruckus occurred. Saved the life of the bartender, and it just so happened that Willie was there. Guess the man was his friend—or something. Willie got to talkin' with me after the commotion died down and offered me a job." The kid didn't need to know he'd been scoping out that particular saloon because he heard that Willie frequented it when he was in the area.

"I reckon I oughta sweep this dump." Lane grabbed the sad-looking broom that leaned against one corner of the six-foot by eight-foot cabin.

Micah took the straw mattress outside to empty and air out. Later, once the stink had lessened, he or the boy could restuff it with fresh hay. Back inside, he righted the only chair in the room and shoved it against the tiny table. He brushed the dust and debris off the top since Lane hadn't swept yet. "Do you have any idea what the Markhams have planned for this cabin? Seems odd it sat for so long with no one claiming it." Most of the outlaws slept in two small cabins, with the third being the cook and dining house. The Markhams shared a clapboard house that had seen better days. The location the Markhams had picked for their home base lay in a valley surrounded by hills, a bit closer to Hartville than San Antonio.

"I heard tell they's plannin' to keep someone in here."

"What do you mean?"

Lane shrugged. "I ain't privy to no more news than you are, 'less I happen to overhear somethin'." The boy's stomach growled.

Micah reached into his back pocket and handed Lane a piece of jerky he'd taken from his saddlebags this morning.

"Golly. Thanks, Burns!"

"Call me Micah."

"Aw right." He shoved the half jerky into his mouth as if he hadn't eaten in days.

Poor thing. Lane generally was the last one to get to his food, and oft' times, there wasn't much left. Micah had started trying to get in at the front of the line when he could and take a bit extra for the boy. He didn't like seeing children go hungry. He'd never experienced that since his ma always put plenty of tasty food on the table.

Lane started sweeping in the back corner. "'Bout done in here."

"Yup. I'll go finish the straw tick." Outside, he snatched up the mattress, slit the frayed threads holding it together, then dumped it a fair distance from the cabin. He hung the tick on the end of a broken branch and looked around.

How long would he have to work undercover before Cass arrived? All of the gang members were here, except for Willie and Spyder Jackson—a man who'd been in jail when Micah first came to the camp. They left two days ago, so Cass must be traveling alone—unless the three of them met up somewhere.

Smacking the mattress with a large branch, he created a cloud of dust equal to the haze of his confusion. Most times, he was decisive, but this time, there were too many variables to make a quick decision. Maybe he ought to just grab the kid and go. Then once Lane was stashed somewhere safe, he and the Rangers could return for the gang. Capturing Maggie would be quite a prize, but if he could confer with Captain Sterling, he knew what the man would say. Cass was the leader—and it was worth the wait to capture him—and Willie too.

All this waiting was giving his gut a permanent ache. Was he making the right choice by tarrying? What if more of them left? The Rangers could lose their chance. He blew out a loud breath. *Give me patience, Lord.*

"Burns! You and that boy get on back up here and help peel potatoes."

~

Laurel's head buzzed, and she felt as if her body was constantly moving. Where was she?

Suddenly, she stiffened. She was on a horse, her hands were tied together, and someone's arm was wrapped around her waist! She grabbed at the arm, but it only tightened.

"Easy there, missy." Foul-smelling breath wafted over her shoulder, nearly gagging her. "Behave and nothing will happen to you."

But something already had. Someone had sneaked up behind her in the alley and covered her face and given her something that made her pass out. The hood was gone now, but she couldn't see much since the sun had set—only a trail before them and another man on horseback, illuminated by the soft moonlight.

She shivered, not only from the chill of the evening but also from worry. What could these men want with her? Did they think they could extract a ransom from her father? She feared they would be disappointed.

And if they were, what would happen to her then? She swallowed the lump that suddenly built in her throat. Her father could be a difficult man, but would he refuse to ransom her? He had worked hard to provide a decent life for Bella and her and their mother, and to build a successful business. They might not be rich, but they had never gone without either.

If only Father were more affectionate. She supposed he loved her, in his own way, but she couldn't remember him ever telling her. And her poor mother. What would she do when Laurel didn't return home tonight?

The thought of the pain her mother and Bella would endure caused her eyes to sting. She blinked away the tears, not wanting to give these scoundrels who stole her the satisfaction of seeing her cry.

They rounded a curve in the trail, then started an uphill climb.

Though she tried to avoid it, Laurel couldn't help leaning back against the man holding her.

The continual rocking made her head ache—or perhaps it was whatever they'd used to cause her to pass out. Had she not been dead to the world, she would have fought and screamed until someone had come to her aid.

How had they been able to get her out of town without anyone seeing? What did they have planned for her?

She couldn't stop trembling at all the awful thoughts bombarding her mind.

"It ain't much farther. Sorry you're cold."

The man had misinterpreted her shivering. It was the unknown that chilled her.

Half an hour later, the man in front twisted around in his saddle. "You'd best hood her again. We'll be there soon."

"It's so dark, she cain't see nuthin'."

"*Hmpf.* Don't say I didn't tell ya if Maggie hollers at ya."

Who was Maggie? And what did she have to do with these rough men? Maybe the woman would help her. But if the man in front was scared of her, she didn't hold out much hope that Maggie would be of assistance.

Laurel's eyes closed as the remnants of whatever the men drugged her with made her sleepy. She yawned, wishing she were home in her own bed, all snug and warm. Would she ever see her home again? Her parents? Bella?

Her chin quivered, but again, she stiffened her resolve to not cry. Maybe things weren't as dire as they seemed. But how could they not be? *Please, God, help me.*

They rode over several more hills, then crested another one, and a wide valley spread before them. The lights of several buildings glimmered ahead. A town? Surely, someone there would help her. If only she could get free.

Ten minutes later, they pulled up in front of a dilapidated

shack. The man holding her dismounted, then pulled her off. Laurel's leg gave way, but he held her up. The other man slid off his horse and stared at her.

Fear like she'd never known slithered up her spine and made her limbs weak. Fingers of light stretched through cracks in the door, tracing the face of one of her captors. He was tall and thin with a small moustache. The other man stepped into a slice of light. Laurel winced at the ugly scar marring the otherwise handsome man's cheek.

He scowled at the man with the moustache. "Quit gawkin' at her and get the door, Spyder."

The thin man grumbled a bit but did as ordered. He grabbed her arm, hauling her forward. She struggled to keep up with his long legs. He pushed the door open, shoved her inside the tiny cabin, then took a look around and turned. He marched out the door, slamming it shut behind him.

Laurel's heart pounded as she stared at the closed door. Was it locked? Or was that spider man standing guard on the outside? The way he ogled her made the hair on her arms stand on end.

She turned and studied her prison. It was small—rustic—but fairly clean. She shuffled over to the single, high window, stood on her tiptoes, and tried to peer out, but all she saw was her reflection.

She limped over to the bed and flopped down, her legs still unsteady from riding astride for so long. If only she hadn't been unconscious, she might have an idea of how far they'd traveled or what direction they'd gone after leaving town.

Her hands remained tied, and she pressed them to her stomach as it grumbled.

No one who cared knew where she was. How would she ever be able to get out of this predicament?

She sniffled, losing the battle of her tears. "God, help me. Please."

CHAPTER 3

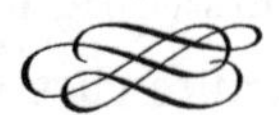

Micah watched Lane leave with a plate of food for the captive who'd arrived last night while he was on guard duty. He shoveled in the last bite of his oatmeal, then swigged down his coffee, stood, and stretched as if it were any other morning.

Willie had returned last night. Now he was spewing orders for the day. As usual, Micah had been assigned to groom the horses and clean out the stalls, with Lane's assistance.

Willie had grabbed a biscuit and headed back to the main house. The other men would linger as long as they could get away with it before doing any work. At camp, there wasn't a whole lot for the men to do. Having guarded the prisoner all night, Spyder Jackson was back in his cabin, trying to catch up on his sleep, while Bass Tomkins and Cherokee Sam started a game of poker. Micah set his mug and plate on the pile in the cupboard and glanced around. No one was looking at him.

"Guess I'd better get to work. Those horses won't groom themselves." Micah chuckled as if that mental picture was humorous. He grabbed his hat off the peg near the door, tugged on his duster, and headed out. No one else paid him much attention so long as he did what he was told.

He surveyed the quiet yard. With Curly LaFever and Arch Russell on guard duty, no one was about. He glanced at the big house. It would be the perfect time to sneak up on the Markhams and see if he could overhear something about Cass's whereabouts. But this morning, he had something more important to do. Lane had told him he'd been tasked to care for the prisoner that Willie and Spyder had stashed in the old cabin. He aimed to find out who the man was and why he'd been taken.

Most likely, Willie hoped to get a ransom in exchange for their captive. Unless maybe the prisoner happened to work at a bank and knew the combination of the safe. If so, the man wasn't in for a pleasant time here. Now, on top of saving the kid, Micah needed to help the prisoner escape before he was harmed.

He jogged toward the cabin and caught up with Lane just as the boy reached it. "Hey, let me feed our guest."

Lane narrowed his eyes. "Why? If Willie finds out, I'll be in for a world of hurt."

"I won't tell him if you won't."

"What's in it for me?"

Micah rubbed his unshaven jaw. "What if I clean all the stalls today? That way you can start on the dishes before the food hardens on them."

Lane studied him for a moment as if trying to determine his motive, then passed him the tray of food. "Deal." He turned to leave.

"Hey, wait. I need the key."

The boy skidded to a halt. "Oh. Yeah." He tugged it from his pocket and stared at it. "You'd better give it back to me so I can return it to Willie."

"Right. Good idea."

Lane continued to hold it. "You sure you won't tell?"

"Haven't you learned you can trust me yet?"

The boy's expression softened. "I'll allow that ye're nicer to me than most, but I ain't known ya all that long."

"You remind me of my little brother, Jimmy. I haven't seen him in years, and I miss him."

Lane grinned. "I do?"

"Yeah. I reckon Jimmy is older now, but he was about your age when I left home. What are you? Eleven?"

Lane lifted his dirty chin. "I'm thirteen now."

"Ah, well. Guess you'll be gettin' whiskers before long."

A strange expression flittered across the boy's face before he rubbed the area above his upper lip. His face was always dirty. "How old was you when you got yours?"

Micah gazed upward, thinking. "I don't rightly remember. Somewhere between thirteen and fifteen, I reckon."

"You like beards? Ain't they itchy?"

"Most times, I prefer to be clean shaven because beards do itch. But colder weather's coming." And the facial hair helped him blend in with the scruffy gang members.

Lane must have decided to trust him because he handed him the key. "Make sure you muck all the stalls. I'll start on the grooming, then do the dishes." He rubbed the back of his neck. "Just don't take too long here, 'cause I don't want to have'ta do *all* the groomin'."

Micah nodded. He watched the boy head out, then unlocked the door. He pushed it open with his foot and glanced around the empty cabin. His gaze came to rest on the cot. His mouth dropped open at the canopy of yellow hair cascading down the side and pooling onto the floor.

A woman? The Markhams had kidnapped a woman?

~

Laurel rolled over. A brilliant ray of sunlight burst through the open door, straight into her eyes. She yawned, then bolted upright as a shadow broke the plane of light. A man was in the cabin!

Though she still wore her dress, she tugged the scratchy blanket up to her chin and stared at him. He was better looking than the men who'd kidnapped and locked her up, but that hardly mattered.

He held up his hand. "I mean you no harm, miss. Just brought your breakfast."

"I'm not hungry." She struggled to sit and then stand. Untangling her skirts with her wrists bound was not an easy task.

He entered the cabin and set the tray on the table. "I reckon you've had quite a scare. I don't know why you're here, but you need to eat when you can. Food is sometimes scarce out here." His gaze skimmed her, then focused on her midsection, making her wish she could fold her arms across her bodice.

Frowning, he bent down, reached into his boot, and drew out a knife. Laurel sucked in a sharp breath and backed up, her calves bumping the cot.

The man held up one hand. "Don't be afraid, ma'am. I only meant to cut the ropes off."

She stared at him for a long moment, wanting to trust him, but at the same time, she was more frightened than she could ever remember being—except for last night. Finally, she nodded.

He stepped forward and sawed the ropes until they fell to the ground. Then he quickly backed away. "Try not to stir up a fuss, and you should be all right."

Should be? He wasn't sure? He evidently wasn't the person making the decisions around here—wherever here was. At least his blue eyes were much kinder than the other men's had been, and he didn't leer at her. He genuinely looked concerned about her welfare.

He returned to the doorway and leaned against the jamb. "Do you have any idea why you were taken?"

Laurel shook her head. "No. None."

"What's your name?"

"Laurel Underwood."

"You from Hartville?"

"San Antonio."

The blue chambray shirt brought out the color of his eyes, with denim pants and dusty brown boots completing his outfit. His worn slouch hat had been pushed back, revealing a nicely tanned face. She guessed him to be an inch or two over six feet and five or six years older than she. While his build was a bit lither than the men who'd taken her, she didn't doubt that he could hold his own in a fight.

There was something about this man that begged her to trust him. He bore an air of authority, even though he'd led her to believe he wasn't one of the men in charge. But she didn't dare trust him.

"I'm Micah Burns, by the way."

"So you have no idea why I'm here either?"

"Nope." He rubbed his scruffy jaw. "Who's your pa?"

"David Underwood."

"I don't recognize the name. What does he do?"

Laurel pushed her hair over her shoulder. "He's a silversmith."

"Hmm... I reckon the Markhams figured they could ransom you."

She gasped. "The Markhams took me?" They were the most heinous outlaws in the area. She'd read how the Texas Rangers had captured or killed some of the gang, but the ringleaders—Cass and Maggie—were still on the run, committing crimes wherever they went.

She swallowed the lump in her throat. Would her father be more likely to pay a ransom if he knew the awful Markham Gang had her?

The man took a step closer. "Try not to worry overly much, miss."

"How can I not?" She hated the shrill tone of her voice, but she couldn't control it.

He glanced behind him, then took another step toward her. "I probably shouldn't say this, but I will do all I can to keep you safe."

"How? You don't even know why I'm here."

"True, but try to trust me. Just do what you're asked. And if you believe in God, I suggest you pray."

"I have been—most of the night."

"That's good." He nodded. "I've got to go now. Is there anything else I can do for you?"

She glanced around the room before she shifted her gaze to the washstand. "I would appreciate some fresh water, if there's any to be had."

He nodded and walked to the washstand, grabbed the pitcher, then strode out. He closed and locked the door behind him.

Laurel stared at the door, surprised that she felt bereft at the man's leaving. Bereft wasn't something she'd ever experienced before last night. She'd often wished her father would state that he loved her, but she'd never lacked for her mother's affection.

Feeling forsaken that the outlaw left was foolishness. Perhaps he was merely trying to get on her good side so he could seek favors from her—favors she would refuse with every ounce of her strength. She shuddered at the thought.

She crossed the tiny room to the table, sat, and stared at the sad-looking meal. She lifted a biscuit to her mouth and nibbled the edge. At least it wasn't rock hard, but it made her thirsty. She gulped down the last bit of water she'd poured last night into the only glass in the cabin. She forced a bite of the lumpy oatmeal down her throat, but one was all she could manage.

A short while later, she heard someone fumbling with the key. She jumped up from the chair, praying Micah had returned and that it wasn't one of the men she'd met last night.

A rough-looking woman with her hair pulled in a bun so tight her features looked stretched backward and a tall, nicely dressed man with dark hair and a handlebar mustache entered, nearly filling the small area. They stared at her for a long moment, making her want to run to the bed and hide under the stinky blanket.

The woman glanced sideways at the man. "You're sure Willie did the right thing by taking her and not the father?"

The man nodded. If not for his hard expression and their location, Laurel might have considered him handsome. "She's the one that placed first in the county fair, not her pa."

The fair? What could that have to do with her being *here*?

The woman blew out a breath. "Well, she's the one that's here, so she'll have to do."

The man fiddled with the fob of his watch as he studied Laurel. "Tell me, Miss Underwood, what materials do you need in order to make plates for printing twenty-dollar bills?"

CHAPTER 4

Micah ran the brush down the shoulder of Curly LaFever's black gelding. He always tried to give this mount some extra care, considering how hard his owner treated him. Curly often lost his temper, and the poor horse endured the brunt of it if he was nearby at the time.

His thoughts galloped back to the woman in the cabin. She was lovely—and young. When he first saw her, he'd thought Willie had brought in a lady of the night to entertain the men, but there was no mistaking the woman's innocence. He couldn't shake the memory of her pale-yellow hair—the color of evening primrose—cascading like a waterfall off the side of the bed. The confusion and fear in her pretty blue eyes gutted him. He wanted to throw her over his horse and get her out of here, but he couldn't. Not yet, anyway.

Other than for a ransom, he couldn't figure out why Cass wanted her. How was he going to keep such a pretty gal safe from the gang and still maintain his cover? He couldn't watch over her night and day. *I could use some help here, Lord.*

She must be so frightened. He gritted his teeth, his anger with the leaders of the gang growing. The horse he was grooming grunted and sidestepped, then swung his head around and nipped at Micah's duster. He patted the beast, regretting that his train of thought had frustrated him enough that his treatment of the gelding was harsher than normal. He ran his hand along the black's hindquarters. "Sorry, boy. I'll be gentler."

He finished with Curly's horse and turned him out to pasture. As he walked back to the barn, Lane strode toward him, scowling. He slung his arm around the kid as they headed into the barn, and the boy stiffened. "What's wrong, buddy?"

Lane shrugged out of his grasp. He sure didn't like being touched, probably because he'd been hit by angry gang members before.

"I don't like that they took that gal. She seems real nice." Lane shook his head.

"I wish I knew what they had planned for her." Micah backed the nondescript bay gelding he'd been using for his mount while undercover out of his stall.

Lane grabbed a brush and went to work on Maggie's mare. "I took back the lady's water and overheard Cass saying something about making money plates. He had me follow him up to their house to get paper for the lady. She's s'posed to be making some kind of list."

Micah's hand paused. Miss Underwood had said her pa was a silversmith, but why would Cass Markham think the man's daughter could make counterfeit plates? It was the perfect scam, if she could do it. The Markhams could print all the money they needed and not have to risk their lives robbing banks and other places of business.

"Cass thinks she can because she won some kind of prize at a county fair."

If only Micah could have talked with the captive a bit more, but when he'd seen the Markhams head to her cabin, he'd hurriedly found Lane and passed the pitcher and pot to him so the boy wouldn't get in trouble for not tending to his duties.

He returned the brush to the tack room and took a comb off the shelf, then attacked the bay's tangled tail. How long would it take Miss Underwood to make plates? She'd need a whole bunch of supplies, as well as access to a heat source. Gathering all those items would take time, since they couldn't all be bought in the same town or suspicions might be aroused.

And how would they print the money? The gang would most likely have to steal a printing machine, and those things were heavy. It would be near impossible to take one and get away without leaving some kind of trail. Cass's plan sure wasn't very practical, but it was brilliant if they could accomplish it. Micah would make sure they didn't.

If Miss Underwood was a silversmith like her pa, why didn't Cass have her make a mold for pouring gold or silver coins instead of paper money? Though perhaps the gold or silver would be hard to come by unless they melted down some of the jewelry they'd stolen. Still, most folks would rather have a double eagle gold piece than twenty dollars in paper money. Even though government-backed paper bills had been printed for over twenty years, many people still had memories of when banks printed them, and when the bank shut down, the dollars were worthless.

Micah swatted a mosquito on his arm. It looked as though Miss Underwood would be here for a long time, which might work to his favor. The longer she was here, the more the Markhams should relax their guard.

Several scenarios traipsed through his mind as he led his horse to the pasture. Two men were usually on guard duty at all times, since there were only two easy entries into the valley on the north and south ends. The east end boasted a thick forest up a steep hill, while the west end had a sharp drop-off along the Sabinal River.

They were closer to Hartville than San Antonio. If he could get away with Miss Underwood, his best bet would be to head to Hartville, where Captain Sterling was stationed. Since Miss Underwood was from San Antonio, the gang would expect her to head there if she got away, and that's most likely the direction they'd take to find her.

But if he helped her flee, would he lose the chance to capture the Markhams? These weeks spent undercover might be wasted. Well, not completely wasted—if he helped her escape and got Lane out of the line of fire.

He blew out a sigh. As much as he wanted to capture the gang, he couldn't allow innocents to suffer. Laurel and Lane needed to be his priority.

"That's some heavy breathing you're doing over there. What'cha thinkin' about?"

"Lots of stuff." Micah started grooming the last horse's mane, brushing out the tangles at the end first. "Do you ever wish you lived somewhere else?"

Lane was silent for a while. "Yeah." He peeked over the back of Maggie's mare, glanced at the barn opening, and then back at Micah. "Don't tell no one, but I'd like to go to school. 'Cept I reckon I'm gettin' too old now."

"You're never too old to learn." Micah leaned his arms across the roan's back and relaxed. He enjoyed the barn far better than being in the stuffy cabin with men who preferred thieving and gambling to maintaining proper hygiene. The scent of leather, hay, and horses was far more appealing, as was being with the quiet, soft-spoken boy.

"What would you like to learn?"

Lane shrugged and then walked around to the front of the horse. "I'd like to learn to read mostly."

"Why?"

"Long time ago when I was little, I remember my ma telling

me and my brother that a person that could read could do about anything."

"Where's your ma? Your brother?" Arch Russell was Lane's pa, but this was the first he'd heard that the kid had other relatives. Maybe if his mother was still alive, Micah could help him get away from here and back to her.

Lane frowned. "They're dead. Ma died trying to birth another baby—at least, that's what Pa said. Mikey had been sick and passed a day later. Pa burned the cabin with their bodies in it. Didn't even give them a proper buryin'. I'd been staying with my grandpa, who'd broke his leg, otherwise, I might've taken sick and died too."

"I'm real sorry to hear that, kid."

Lane shrugged. "It was a long time ago, back when we lived in Colorado and Pa worked powder at a mine. They didn't have many kids there and no school, so I never gotta go to one."

Micah thought back to how he'd hated school. Not because he didn't like learning but because he wanted to be outside. His dream had always been to be a Ranger like his pa and maybe raise stock horses later on. At the time, he hadn't thought schooling would help him much. Now he knew different. He'd learned to read and cipher, but he wished he'd paid better attention.

Maybe he could put some of his learning to use. "Would you like me to teach you to read?"

Lane's blue eyes widened, filling with hope, before he narrowed them. "You really can? And how come you'd wanna help me?" He kicked up a cloud of dust. "What would you want in return?"

Micah's heart clenched. How sad that the boy couldn't accept a gift without thinking he had an ulterior motive. "I do know how, and I'm willing to help because I like you, and I want to."

"You wouldn't expect me to muck the stalls by myself every day, would ya?"

"Nope."

"Groom all the horses alone?"

"Nope."

Lane's eyes brightened again. "Truly, you would teach me?"

"As long as we can find the time."

Lane returned to grooming. "Uh. . .what if I came out to sit with you when you're on guard duty sometime?"

Micah nodded. "That could work, if we keep it a secret. Neither of us wants to face Maggie's wrath for not doing our jobs. We can probably sneak in some learnin' time while we're grooming—like right now."

"Now? But we ain't got no pen or paper."

"Don't need it." Micah left the stall, smoothed an area of the dirt floor with his boot, then squatted. He used his index finger to spell out Lane's name.

The boy leaned down. "What's that?"

"Your name." Micah studied Lane as his expression brightened.

"Mine?" he said with awe in his voice. "How come the first letter's bigger than the others?"

"It's called a capital letter. All names start with one." He went on to explain the names of the four letters, then had Lane copy them in the dirt below where he'd written. A warm feeling—one he rarely felt these days—saturated his insides.

When he left here, he was taking the boy with him—if there was any way he could get him to go. Lane had a good heart and a gentleness about him. Micah couldn't leave him to grow up into an outlaw like the kid's father.

"Hear that?" Lane gawked at the barn's entrance. "A rider's comin'."

A horse stopped in front of the barn and a man dismounted. Micah's heart leapt like a thoroughbred off a starting line.

Cass had finally arrived.

~

Laurel blinked, confused by the question the tall man asked. "Money plates? I have no idea."

The woman narrowed her eyes. "Well, you'd better figure out what you need and how to make the plates. Your life depends on it."

Laurel ducked her head, heart sinking. How was she to make something when she had no idea how to do it? She'd never made a plate for printing money and didn't even know where to start. She'd have to stall somehow. Perhaps if she delayed long enough, someone would come to her rescue.

"I...um...I'll try to come up with a list."

"That's more like it." The woman spun and left the cabin.

Something thudded outside, and a boy walked in carrying the pitcher Micah had left with. He glanced up at the man, crossed the room, and set the container on the washstand, then rushed back to the door.

"Hold up, boy. Come up to the house with me."

The kid shot a look at her, then nodded. "Yes, sir...um...Mr. Markham."

Laurel held back a gasp as they exited. The man shut the door, and the lock clicked. That must have been Cass and Maggie Markham. He'd said Willie had been the one to steal her from San Antonio, which meant all three of the Markhams were here.

She'd landed in the den of the most notorious outlaws in Texas. What was she going to do? If only she had a way to contact the Texas Rangers for help.

Laurel turned and studied the window she'd tried to look out of last night. It was small, but if she could get up high enough, she might be able to squeeze through if she removed some of her petticoats.

She dragged the chair across the floor, positioning it under the window, and stepped up and peered out. All she could see were trees and the edge of a rooftop. A woodpecker tapped at a spot on the nearest trunk, then hopped sidewise and rat-a-tatted again. A wall of trees blocked her from seeing anything else. Disappointment made her eyes sting.

At a noise outside the door, she jumped down and slid the chair back. She stood beside it, heart throbbing, as the door opened. The kid again. He looked at her, then at the window, and one side of his mouth quirked up.

"That window is nailed shut. Cass made me and Micah do it 'fore you got here." He laid several pieces of paper on the table, along with a stubby pencil. "That all you gonna eat?"

She nodded.

"The food here ain't all that appetizing, but it's better than some I've had." He snatched the biscuit and shoved it in his pocket, ignoring how it crumbled.

Laurel glanced at the open door. She could possibly make it there and shut the boy in the cabin, but what then? She had no idea where she was or how to get home. And there were countless outlaws outside these walls.

The youth seemed to be lingering. He was several inches shorter than her, with dark, shaggy hair and a very dirty face. "Thank you for the water. Would you like to wash off?"

He stared at her as if she'd gone loco. "Uh…no, ma'am." He grabbed her tray before backing out of the room, closing and securing the door.

No sound other than birds chirping filled the room. She should probably be thankful to be alone, considering the company she'd recently had.

The boy had looked as though he wanted something from her. But what? And why had he been so opposed to washing? Micah had looked clean, except his face had been unshaven. He must have scraped his whiskers off recently, though, for the stubble to be so short.

Many men these days wore beards, but she was always attracted more to the clean-shaven ones. That was something she liked about Peter. He was fastidious about the way he looked, even when working. Was he worried for her safety? Had he gone out searching for her? Would she ever see him again?

CHAPTER 5

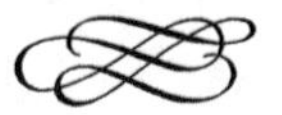

The next morning, Micah slipped out of the dining cabin before Lane exited with the food tray for Miss Underwood. He headed toward her cabin, staying out of view of anyone who might leave after him, and waited there. Lane soon ambled toward him, brow furrowed. Micah assumed he was concentrating on not spilling the coffee on the rocky trail, but someone could have said something to upset the boy. In spite of the gang's rough treatment, most days, Lane handled their gruffness fairly well. Too bad Arch Russell didn't take up for his child more often.

Micah made a shuffling noise with his boots so as not to scare the boy.

Lane glanced up, quirking a smile. "I'm guessin' you want to serve the pretty lady her meal again. You got eyes for her?"

Micah shrugged, fixing an embarrassed grin on his face. It was best Lane thought that than knew the truth. He liked the kid a lot, but he wasn't sure how far he could trust him.

"What'll you do for me if'n I let you take it to her?"

"What do you want?"

Lane glanced at Micah's gun belt.

"I'm not giving you my gun."

"I know that, but would you teach me to shoot?"

Micah studied the kid. He probably needed to know that sooner or later, but he would prefer it were much later. "Have you asked your pa to show you how?"

"He says he don't got time, but he mostly doesn't do nuthin' 'cept sleep, clean his gun, and do guard duty when we're in camp."

"How about I give you an extra reading lesson today?"

Lane's eyes widened. "Really?"

"Yep. We can work on one in the barn, and we'll figure a second time later this afternoon."

Lane handed him the tray and then fished around in his pocket until he pulled out the key. "Just don't let that gal slip past ya, and make sure you get the door locked. I don't wanna get in trouble with the Markhams."

"I don't want you to get in trouble either." Micah held the tray with one hand and squeezed Lane's skinny shoulder. "You can trust me, kid. I've got your back."

One of the few genuine smiles he'd seen from Lane illuminated the boy's face. His teeth were straight and white, although his lashes looked a bit long for a male. There were times like this when Micah thought the poor kid had a feminine look about him, but that'd go away once he got whiskers and some muscles.

"Thanks, Micah. I reckon I'll start on the groomin'."

"I'll be there shortly."

He watched Lane scurry off, his step lighter today than normal. Was the poor kid so starved for affection that Micah's simple comment had encouraged him?

Shaking his head, his anger fired at thinking how rough the gang members were with Lane. He'd even wondered why the Markhams allowed the kid to be here, but someone had to do the grunt work, and having the boy was better than having a woman here—a woman the men might fight over.

Hopefully, Cass's stern warning to leave Miss Underwood alone would keep the men away. It was a good thing most of them hadn't seen how pretty she was, or some might be tempted to ignore Cass's threat. But after the gang leader had stated that anyone bothering her would end up with a bullet in each knee and then staked out Indian style to die a slow, painful death, the men would not likely come sniffing around. They knew Cass meant what he said.

Micah hurried to the door. It was best he got his business with her over quickly. He rapped twice on the door, undid the lock, and stepped inside. Miss Underwood stood next to the small table, her pretty hair braided in a thick plait that hung over one shoulder. She watched him with a mixture of caution and curiousness.

"Morning, Miss Underwood. I brought your breakfast. Mind if I set it on the table?"

"Um...no. Go ahead." She took a step back, then folded her hands in front of her.

Micah set the tray down and quickly scanned the list of supplies she'd made—engraving tools, pens, ink, drawing paper, moveable print type and trays, a printing press. Good luck getting that last item into the valley. More than likely, the Markhams had a printer on the payroll who'd tend to the task of making the counterfeit bills.

He needed to cut the head off this snake of an idea before any money was printed. They had time before the danger to Miss Underwood increased. He highly doubted Cass Markham would let her go free even if she managed to make the plates. She knew what several of the gang members looked like. And that meant she was a danger to them.

Micah forced the troubling thoughts away, hoping to encourage Miss Underwood for a short while. "How are you managing—under the circumstances?"

Her gaze flicked up to his before flittering away like a butterfly. "All right, I suppose."

He took in her rumpled clothing. She'd slept in them two days already. Maggie was aware of Miss Underwood's presence and should have thought about her needing a change of clothing. He would ask...except he wasn't supposed to know anything specific about the captive. He'd have to say something to Lane, although it might even seem odd for the boy to inquire.

Maybe he should sneak into the house and get some clothes for her. He shook his head. Dumb idea. What if he got caught? He'd purposely worked to maintain a low profile and not get too close to the Markhams because they were savvy folk and might figure out he wasn't what he pretended to be.

If something happened to him, Miss Underwood would have no chance of escape.

~

Several expressions played across the man's face. His eyes held a kindness she hadn't expected to find in her captors. He seemed genuinely concerned for her wellbeing. But she couldn't afford to hope he might help her. He was a member of the Markham Gang, after all.

She glanced at the open door and took a small step sideways. He was so engrossed in his thoughts, he didn't seem to notice. She swung her skirt left and right, casually sliding her feet to the left again.

"You'd best stop doing that, miss."

Her gaze jerked to his, and up this close, she could see that his eyes weren't just blue, but more of a bluish-green—a very lovely shade. His brow lifted as she continued staring at him. Heat warmed her cheeks, and she broke his gaze.

She had no business being attracted to a kind, handsome

outlaw with overly long brown hair and eyes the color of the ocean. Dare she try to make him become sweet on her in hope of him helping her escape?

She shook her head at the foolish thought and walked over to the table. "How did you end up in this gang, if I may be so bold to ask?"

His gaze locked with hers again. Her chest tightened, making it hard to breathe, and her stomach churned. No man had ever affected her in such a manner, not even Peter. She broke their gaze, shamed by her reaction. He was an outlaw. A thief. Possibly a killer.

"I need to go. Is there anything you need? Anything I can do for you?"

She glanced down at her hopelessly wrinkled lavender dress, which now looked gray. If only she had a change of clothing, but she couldn't ask him for that. Laurel shook her head.

He pivoted, grabbed her water pitcher, and then strode out.

The door banged shut. She sighed and walked over to stare at her meal of lumpy porridge, two slices of bacon, and an odd-shaped biscuit that looked as if it had been thrown at someone's head. She sighed and sat. None of it was appetizing, but she had to keep up her strength if she was going to escape.

She reached for the spoon, then paused. Had Micah locked the door? She'd heard it shut but hadn't heard the click of the lock. Rising, she tiptoed to the door. She held her breath and tugged. The door gave way.

~

Angered at himself for being attracted to Miss Underwood, which would only complicate things, Micah stalked back to the cabin. Water sloshed over the side of the pitcher, so he forced himself to slow down. He wanted Miss Underwood to have as much as she needed, since he wasn't sure how often Lane fetched it.

He'd been gone longer than he'd expected. Bass Tomkins and Cherokee Sam had been talking by the water pump and seemed in no hurry to move along. Lane hadn't been in the barn, so he couldn't get him to finish the task.

Thinking he'd be right back, he'd left the door unlocked. Had Miss Underwood noticed?

Concern niggled at him like a poison ivy rash. He needed to hurry back, but if he rushed, he'd spill a good amount of the water. Next time, he'd get the water from the well and haul it in a bucket to the cabin.

Micah lifted his gaze from the pitcher as a shadow darkened his path. He froze, water spilling over the top of the pitcher and onto his boots. He nodded. "Willie."

Cass's younger brother narrowed his gaze, the scar on his cheek puckering. "What're you doin', Burns?"

Micah's mind raced. Had Willie been to the cabin? Seen the door unlocked? If he had, he'd be livid, so he must want something else.

Micah wouldn't let the kid get in trouble for doing him a favor. He faked a sheepish expression. "Lane...uh." He rubbed his jaw. "Well, he's...got the backdoor trots. I'm just helping him out."

Willie smirked. "We'll be lucky if'n we all don't have the runs since Curly's cooking today." He chuckled. "Get on with it then, and finish your work in the barn."

Micah nodded again, then let out a loud exhale as he wandered down the path to the cabin. He rounded the corner, and all breath left him.

The door was open.

CHAPTER 6

A branch smacked Laurel in the face as she raced away from the cabin. Heart pounding, she paused a moment, holding her hand to her stinging cheek as she surveyed her surroundings. The wooded area could have been just about anywhere.

She struggled to remember which direction the gang members had been riding when she'd come to. Was it west? Which way should she go now? Which way was home?

In the distance, birds sang a cheerful tune, and sunlight dappled the ground, creating a setting that would be pleasant if not for the fact that a heinous outlaw gang would soon be on her trail. She looked all around before heading uphill. It would slow her pace, but maybe once she was atop, she'd be able to recognize her surroundings.

At least the gang would have to chase after her on foot, since a horse couldn't manage the thick forest. Bushes clawed at her skirts, slowing her down. Rocks bit into her balmorals.

Behind her, the sound of something big charging through the trees made her increase her pace. She glanced over her shoulder, then her foot snagged, and she flew through the air, landing hard on the ground.

With no time to catch her breath, she struggled to rise, but her foot caught in her petticoat, thwarting her efforts. A man pushed through the trees—Micah. Tears burned her eyes at the thought of what he might do to her.

He knelt beside her with a concerned expression. "Are you all right?"

She blinked, confused by his kindness when she'd expected harsh treatment. "Um...yes. I merely got tangled in my skirts."

Frowning, he reached his hand toward her face but then pulled it back. "You've got a scratch on your cheek."

"I'm not surprised." She pressed her hand over the spot the branch had hit.

"Are you hurt anywhere else?"

She shook her head.

He reached out his hand. "Let me help you."

She gazed into his eyes, daring to risk his ire. "If you want to help, let me go."

Frowning, Micah flicked his gaze up the hill. "I am helping. There's a guard on top of the rise. He's been given orders to shoot if you happen to escape."

Laurel's mouth opened, but nothing came out. He could be bluffing, but from his serious expression, she doubted it.

His gaze captured hers, and she found it difficult to look away. "We need to get you back to the cabin before someone finds out you're gone. Lane has been tasked with your care, and if you run off, he's the one who'll suffer."

Her heart skipped a beat. As much as she longed to get away, she didn't want that poor boy to be harmed. But how could she go back to that awful place?

Micah pursed his lips, then blew out a loud breath. "I will help you escape. Later. But right now, we must return to the cabin."

Hope rose within her but quickly plummeted. "Why would you want to help me? You're part of the Markham Gang."

He stared at her for a long moment. She broke his gaze and rearranged her skirts so that her ankle was covered.

"Things aren't always what they seem. That's all I can tell you."

She wrinkled her brow. What did he mean by that?

He grabbed her hand. "C'mon. Get up."

She rose as he tugged on her hand, wincing at the pain in her ankle.

"What's wrong?"

"Nothing."

"Something is, or you wouldn't be grimacing."

She sighed. "I might have twisted my ankle when I tripped."

"Try leaning on me." He reached out, then paused. "May I put my arm around you to help you walk?"

She studied him for a moment. Something in his gaze begged her to trust him. But dare she? They were alone in the woods, and he had the strength to overpower her if he desired, although he truly seemed to want to get her back quickly. Was it his concern for Lane that motivated him? She thought of the boy being punished for her escape attempt and nodded.

Very gently, he placed his arm around her waist. "Now, lean on me as you take a step."

With no other choice, she leaned against his strong body, and he took most of her weight. With the anxiety of her escape, she hadn't noticed the chill in the air until she pressed against his warm side.

"Put your arm around my waist if it helps."

Walking while leaning against him was difficult, so she boldly did as he requested. In another time and place, she could see June smiling at her for her brazen behavior.

They soon managed a step-hop rhythm. Laurel's heart pounded, not from the exertion, but because she'd never been so close to a man. She doubted there was a speck of fat on Micah's solid body. He supported her weight easily with no strain that she could tell.

He was a strong man, well-spoken and mannerly, so he'd had some education. He could probably do anything he set his mind to, so what had motivated him to become an outlaw?

She thought back to what he said about Lane, and something bothered her. "Why would Lane get in trouble for my escape, and not you? You've brought me about the same number of meals as Lane."

When he didn't answer, she glanced up to see his jaw clenched tight. He didn't look at her but continued on.

At the edge of the tree line, he paused and looked around. Suddenly, he scooped her up in his arms. She yelped. He hurried to the edge of the cabin, then peered around the side. After a moment, he turned the corner and carried her inside, then he carefully set her on the bed.

"I should probably have a look at your ankle."

She raised her eyes to him. "That would be highly improper."

The man had the gall to crack a smile. "Then you should check it, although you might not be able to get your balmorals back on afterward."

He knew the name of her laced boots? And he'd offered to help her escape. The quiet man was an enigma. "Are you going to answer my question about why you've brought half of my meals if Lane is in charge of me?"

He schooled his expression. "I have my reasons. You should elevate your foot to help get any swelling to go down. Keep working on that list for the Markhams." He captured her gaze. "And don't mention to anyone that I said I'd help you get away from here—not even Lane."

She nodded.

He headed out the door. Right before he closed it, he stared at her for a long moment, making her heartbeat stampede. He tipped his hat, and then he shut the door and locked it.

She laid back, staring at the ceiling. With one long look from Micah, her heart had started dancing. How odd was that? Surely, she couldn't be attracted to an outlaw.

And why had her heart never reacted in such a way whenever Peter was near?

~

Maggie Markham scanned the list of supplies, then turned her stern gaze on Laurel. "You're sure that's all you'll need? I can't be sending my men back to town every day for some piddling thing you forgot."

Laurel twisted her hands. "Um... well...I've never made a plate before, so I can't be certain, but I believe that's everything."

Maggie stared at her as she had the list. Her lips pursed. "You need something else to wear. What happened to that dress?"

Stalling, Laurel glanced down at her sad-looking gown. She couldn't tell the woman that she'd ruined it by attempting to escape. "I...um...guess it snagged on the wood walls while I was sleeping."

"You wear it to bed?"

Laurel shrugged. "I never know when a man might walk in, so I haven't removed it since I got here."

Maggie nodded, although her expression remained hard. "It isn't always easy living with a passel of men. I'll see that you get something to change into."

"Thank you."

The older woman narrowed her eyes. "Don't thank me. I'm only doing it because I want you to finish your job."

She whisked out, leaving Laurel alone to ponder the strange woman. Maybe there was a smidgeon of compassion in Maggie

Markham, although she sure hadn't shown any, except for the offer of clothing.

Ah well, she'd never understand outlaws. Micah had returned her to this cabin, but he'd also said he'd help her escape. Even if he did, would she ever be safe as long as the Markhams were free?

They knew where she lived, and if she got away, what was to stop them from kidnapping her again? Or taking her father and forcing him to make the plates? He was probably better skilled to that task than she since he was a far more experienced silversmith. And what if the gang took Bella? Laurel splayed her hand over her chest, which ached at the dreadful thought. She would do almost anything to protect her sister.

Needing a change of view from the drab cabin, she dragged the chair to the window, climbed up in spite of the pain it caused her ankle, and stared out. Whoever had installed the window must have been quite tall.

Laurel sucked in a sharp breath. A painted bunting landed on a branch near the cabin. Its head flicked in different directions. The colorful bird with a red belly and chartreuse back and bright blue head looked as if it had flown through a rainbow. What a rare treat to see one. Then suddenly, as if hearing a warning, it flew away. If only she could fly away too.

The leaves had taken on the color of autumn—orange, yellow, and brown. Green still lingered in some of the leaves closer to the trunk.

Her prayers for safety and escape winged upward. She always felt closer to God when outside in the world He had created. She missed taking her morning coffee on the front porch of her family home on warm days.

A thump near the cabin's door made her heart leap. She climbed down and quickly moved the chair back to the table and sat.

Lane stumbled through the doorway, barely avoiding dropping her lunch.

Laurel rose and went to him. “What’s wrong?”

He slid past her, set the tray on the table, and flopped onto the chair. Grabbing his belly, he leaned over, moaning. “Ohh...I think I’m dying.”

CHAPTER 7

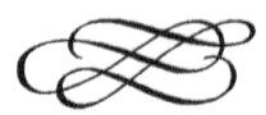

Micah sat in a tree, watching the back of the Markhams' house. No one had moved in the past half hour except for Bass, who rode out on some unknown task about twenty minutes ago. The only black man in the gang was the son of a preacher. Micah gritted his teeth each time Bass quoted Holy Scripture out of context to justify his bad habits. Being a God-fearing man, Micah despised Bass's false usage of God's Holy Word.

He prayed for Bass and the other members of the gang, especially Lane. Something had been wrong with the kid yesterday, and he seemed worse today. He'd been hunched over during breakfast and had set aside his barely touched meal and headed to the privy. Hopefully, whatever the kid had passed quickly, because he didn't like seeing Lane hurting.

With a final thorough look around, Micah dropped out of the tree. He stood behind the trunk for a long moment, then dashed to the bushy shrub that sat on the west side of the house. A window right above him had been raised. He listened for any sounds from inside, but when all remained quiet, he rose and peered in.

Once his eyes had adjusted to the dim interior, he realized he was looking into the parlor. He'd often wondered what Cass, Maggie, and Willie did in their house all day. Were they taking an early-afternoon siesta right now?

Muffled voices came his way, then silhouettes of Cass and Willie. He ducked down, keeping close to the window so he could hear.

"I did what you asked, Cass, but I still think it was a mistake to grab that gal. The law won't take it lightly, and folks are bound to be lookin' for her."

"More than likely, they won't search this far from San Antone."

"But what if they do?"

A chair screeched as someone dragged it across the floor.

"Then we'll deal with them like we always do. I sent Bass out to scout around and see if anyone was getting close."

"Good idea," Willie said.

Things grew quiet for a moment. Micah longed to rise up and look inside again, but chances were strong one of the men would see him.

"C'mon, Cass. When're we goin' to ride out and rob something? Bank? Train? It don't matter. I'm goin' stir-crazy just sittin' here."

"It's best you stay here for a time. We can't afford for you to land in jail again. You might not get out this time. Try reading a book. You might learn something."

Micah heard a thud and imagined Willie kicking something as he often did when growing impatient.

"You know I don't like readin'. It didn't take to me like it did you and Maggie."

"Well, find something to do and quit your bellyaching. We're staying close to home for now, whether you like it or not."

Willie grumbled something under his breath that Micah couldn't make out. "Guess I'll go see if I can stir up a card game."

Micah ducked down farther, making sure to stay behind the

thickest part of the bush. He just hoped Willie went out the front door and not the back, which would lead the man right past him.

When the front door banged, he blew out a relieved breath. Watching his step to avoid anything that would make noise, he crept away.

It was good that the gang wouldn't be doing any nasty business in the near future, but that meant Cass was counting on Miss Underwood to come through with the counterfeiting plates.

The Markham Gang had been hitting towns pretty regularly the past six months. It wasn't too often they'd go several weeks without pulling some kind of heist. If Cass was putting all his eggs in one basket with Miss Underwood, what would happen to her if she failed?

He strode into the barn, his mouth twisted to one side. There was only one thing Cass would do—get rid of her.

Micah leaned against one of the stall gates, removed his hat, and ran his fingers through his hair. He couldn't allow that to happen.

Miss Underwood was sweet and innocent. She didn't deserve to be held prisoner. The Markhams and the rest of their gang were the ones who needed to be rounded up and locked away for good.

But Miss Underwood should be set free. She tried to be so brave. Something stirred in his gut. He liked her. He was even attracted to her, but what did it matter?

Now that he knew the Markhams had no plans for a robbery in the near future, he had to figure out how to get Miss Underwood and Lane away from here without being seen. Once he had them safely stashed somewhere, he'd report to Captain Sterling and bring in a crew to capture the gang, once and for all.

~

"Dying?" Surely not. Had someone punched Lane in the stomach to make him feel so bad he thought he was mortally wounded? Could he have some kind of internal illness that caused the pain?

Laurel crossed the room and rested her hand on his back, wincing as she realized how thin he was. His loose clothing had hid that fact from her. Ire rose up within her—something she'd only felt the few times some rowdy boys had bullied Belle. "What happened? Did someone hurt you?"

Lane shook his head. "No one did nothin'."

Someone ought to have taught the boy to use better language, but there was probably a lot of truth in the fact that *no one did nothin'*. Judging by the way Lane looked, no one had taken an interest in the poor boy in a long while. Well, she certainly would.

She lifted her skirt and knelt in front of him to see his eyes. His old hat flopped down, covering his forehead, but up close, his long lashes gave him a delicate appearance. He would die for sure if she told him that. "Tell me what you're feeling."

"My stomach—down low—has been hurting since yesterday mornin'. Hurtin' bad. Like somethin's broke inside. All I feel like doin' is curling up in a ball on my bunk."

"Is anyone else having the same symptoms?"

He shook his head. "Don't think so."

"Well, that rules out eating something that disagreed with you."

She ran her hand up and down Lane's back. Sadly, the boy's face was covered in dirt like a street urchin she'd once seen in Houston. He needed a good scrubbing. He needed someone to care for him. "Is it just your stomach, or is something else wrong?"

Lane lifted his head, and the tears in his eyes and pale face startled her. "I—I can't stop the bleeding."

"What?" She ran her gaze all over his body but failed to see a bandage. "Where are you bleeding?"

A faint blush rose on his cheeks. He looked down and shook his head. His floppy hat once again hid his face.

Laurel understood his reluctance to tell her. After all, they'd just met, and she was the gang's captive. "Have you talked to your father?"

The boy jerked his head up, his eyes wide with something that looked like fear. "I did, but he just said my ma had the same thing. She passed on when I was three. Am I g–gonna die too?"

What a dreadful thing to tell a child. "Do you, by chance, know what she died of?"

"Birthin' my sister is what Pa said the few times he mentioned it."

"Well, you certainly don't have that." Laurel smiled, hoping to lighten the mood, then she gently squeezed Lane's arm. "Tell me where you're bleeding. Please. I can't help you if you don't."

Lane stood and shook his head.

His mother had the same thing.

Surely not. It couldn't be. Laurel stood, studying the youth's face. How had she not noticed before now? "Lane, you're a girl, aren't you?"

"No!" Lane backed up against the table, her gaze ricocheting off the walls and not once on Laurel. The poor child looked as if he'd—she'd—been shot. "How do you know that?" she screeched. "Pa's the only one that does, and he ain't been down here, so I know he didn't say nothin'."

"I figured it out."

Lane looked horrified and glanced down. "Am I gonna die? Tell me straight."

Laurel smiled. "No. Of course not."

"Then what's wrong with me? Why won't it stop?"

"It will in a day or two. What's happening is that you're becoming a woman."

Face the color of Laurel's petticoat, Lane slid like liquid into the chair. "But I can't."

Chuckling softly, Laurel removed Lane's hat and brushed the hair off her face. "Honey, there's nothing you can do to stop it. I'm amazed you've hidden the fact that you're a female all this time. Before long, though, you won't be able to."

"Why not?"

"Because your figure will grow more womanly." Laurel gestured at her own curves.

Lane shot up. "But I don't want it to."

Laurel rested her hands on the girl's shoulders. "It's out of your hands, sweetie." She explained the way of a girl becoming a woman and all it entailed, half fearing Lane would faint on her at any moment, but she didn't. Then she told her what to do about it.

"Pa is gonna kill me."

"No, he won't. He knew this would happen eventually. You need to talk to him in private and see if you have a relative you can live with."

"I don't. He'd've never brought me here, if'n I had."

"Well then, it's my guess that your days here are numbered. There's no way you can stay with this awful group of men. You shouldn't have been here in the first place, but now, things are different." She feathered Lane's hair back, wondering again why she hadn't noticed the girl's feminine features. Now the dirt and sloppy clothes made sense.

She handed Lane's hat back, quickly formulating a plan. "I'd like you to think about coming home with me when I leave here."

CHAPTER 8

At dinnertime, two days after Laurel learned Lane's secret, Micah followed the girl inside the cabin. Lane carried Laurel's food tray, while Micah toted a large crate. Laurel glanced at the bowl of stew and a biscuit and held back a sigh. She certainly hoped the stew was fresh and not the same batch she'd had the past two nights.

Micah thunked the crate on the table.

She peered at the crate with its dark-blue fabric on top. "What's that?"

"A rare gift from Maggie." He lifted up the blue skirt, revealing a shirtwaist and some ladies' unmentionables, with something metallic below them. Micah dropped the fabric as if it had burned his fingers. His ears turned as red as she imagined her cheeks were.

Lane chuckled. "It ain't nothin' but some clothes and tools."

Raising her eyebrows, Laurel focused her gaze on the girl. "I'm glad to see you're finally feeling better."

"I reckon I somewhat am." Lane flicked her blue eyes at Micah, then ducked her head. Did she fear Laurel would reveal her secret after promising not to? Most likely, Lane wasn't used to dealing with people who actually kept their word.

"I'd better get back to work. You'll lock up?" Lane held out the key to Micah.

"Of course. Meet you at the barn shortly."

Lane nodded then hurried out. What would happen to the girl if Laurel couldn't get her away from here?

Micah cleared his throat, drawing her gaze again. He looked mighty handsome in the black shirt and jeans, although he more resembled an outlaw than when he wore blue. Oddly, the dark color of his shirt emphasized his pretty eyes even more. Today, they looked a bit greener than blue, just like the ocean, ever changing colors.

"If...um...you..." Shifting from foot to foot, he dug his finger into his collar along his throat and tugged, his ears reddening again.

She cocked her head, curious as to what had made him so antsy. "If I what?"

"Well, since. . ....uh...Maggie sent you some fresh duds"—he waved his hand at the crate—"I can...um...fetch the washtub. That is, if you want to take a bath." He studied the floor as Lane had, not daring to look at her.

And for that she was grateful. She was mortified by the subject matter, even though there was nothing she'd like more at the moment, except to return home. "That would be wonderful if it's not too much trouble."

Micah's warm smile sent tingles racing through her. My, but he was a nice-looking man. But more important to her, he was kind and thoughtful. Not at all what she expected in an outlaw, especially one who was part of the Markham Gang.

"There's just one thing, though." And oh, what a thing to ask! But she had to know. "How do I...um...keep someone from"—she waved her hand at the door—"walking in before I'm done?"

"Ah, I understand your concern." He rubbed his jaw, which sported a dark shadow of whiskers, and she had to force herself not to stare.

He looked at the door and then the table. "Since the door opens inward like most, you could put the chair under the handle to keep folks out until you're done."

"That's a good idea." She glanced over at the window. Too bad it didn't have a curtain.

"Would you like me to cover that with something?"

She smiled, and his gaze collided with hers. They stood locked together by an invisible cord. Her throat tightened, and her heart pounded. No man had ever evoked such a strong reaction in her before. Hands sweating, she found herself staring at the floor. "That would be very nice, if it isn't a problem. I don't want you to get in trouble on my account."

"No trouble at all. You'd better eat while the food's still lukewarm. I'll fetch the tub." He spun and headed for the door.

"Thank you."

He paused at the entrance but didn't look at her. "It's a good thing most of those men don't know how pretty you are."

He slammed the door and locked it. She stared at the barrier between her and freedom, very thankful indeed that the gang members didn't know much about her. It seemed she wasn't the only one who could keep a secret.

"Thank you for sending two champions to watch over me, Lord."

~

Micah had to get her away from here. He wasn't sure how Willie and Spyder had managed to keep their traps shut about how beautiful Miss Underwood was, but they had because otherwise, there would have been all kinds of talk about her and men sneaking down for a peek—or something more heinous.

Cass must have threatened Willie and Spyder good and hard after they brought her here. And the gang leader was quite adept at making threats because he wasn't afraid to follow through.

Micah's prayers for Laurel's protection had surely helped too.

What he sure hadn't counted on, though, was being so attracted to her. A Ranger tried to keep things from getting personal with the people he encountered. Caring deeply caused him to take chances he might not otherwise, which could be deadly, not just for him but also for those he was helping. It made his job much harder, and to date, he'd been successful at keeping a safe distance, especially from marriageable women. But an innocent blue-eyed blonde with a big heart and concern for Lane had knocked him clean out of the saddle.

Her safety and well-being were more important to him than anything he could think of. How had she gotten under his skin so fast? And what was he going to do about it?

"Burns!"

He glanced up to see Willie striding toward him.

Micah slowed his steps. "How can I help you?"

"Last time I rode Apache, he limped the last mile or two. Check him out and see what's wrong."

"Yes, sir. Probably picked up a stone."

"I hope that's all. He's a good horse. I'd hate to have to put him down."

Micah gritted his teeth and worked hard to not look angry. When a man's horse was limping, he should get off and check out the offending leg and hoof. Then he should walk rather than torture his mount. "I'll check him over real good. Just got to do one quick job first."

Willie narrowed his eyes. "What's that?"

Micah didn't let the outlaw bully him. "Your sister sent some clean clothes for that gal you brought here, and now I've gotta fetch her a tub and water for her to clean up with."

A smirk twisted Willie's face. "I'll take it, and then I might stay and watch."

Micah's fist tightened. He'd like to knock the man clear to the San Antonio jail, but he couldn't. Not yet, anyway. "I doubt your brother would approve of that."

Willie snorted a derisive laugh. "Maybe I just won't tell him."

"You'd be playin' with fire, I imagine, but it's your life." Micah tightened his fist, aching to plow it into the scoundrel's jaw.

"I know, but she's sure a looker." He rubbed the back of his neck and glanced at the house the siblings stayed in. "Still, no gal's worth gettin' shot or strung up for." He rubbed his neck as if feeling the rope burns.

The man had an appointment with a hangman's noose somewhere in his near future. Somehow Willie had managed to escape jail each time he'd been captured, but his days were numbered—a very short number if he laid a hand on Laurel.

"Gotta go draw that bathwater." Although happy to help Miss Underwood, Micah worked hard to sound a bit peeved at the added task. Rather than play chummy with Willie, he'd like nothing more than to pummel the man, throw him belly down on the back of a horse, and haul him to jail. "Don't worry about me telling anyone about that gal. I know how to keep a secret."

Willie eyed him hard, as if determining whether or not he could believe him. Micah met him gaze for gaze, something he doubted the man was used to. Willie nodded, then scowled again. "See that you don't. Stop your lollygaggin', Burns, and get busy."

"Yes, sir." He'd sure be glad to see the last of the Markham siblings. One boss was bad enough, but three was downright confusing at times.

He headed to his cabin to get the round metal water tub a few of the men preferred to bathe in. Those that didn't mind cool water usually took a dunk in the creek every month or so or when they were headed to town for a night with the ladies. There were a few like Curly who rarely ever took a bath. He avoided the cranky, foul-smelling man as much as possible.

Micah grabbed the tub, carrying it on his left shoulder while hauling a bucket of water in his right hand. If only he could bless Laurel with a *warm* bath, but he couldn't afford to take too much time away from his assigned chores—and now tending Willie's horse.

Given what she'd been through, she probably wouldn't mind the cold water. It was a fine thing to feel clean. His mother had drilled into him that a decent man oughta be clean whenever possible. She didn't like the odor of horse or cattle in the house, especially while eating a meal.

He was never allowed to come to the table without washing first, and he'd always taken a weekly bath. Back then, the task had annoyed him, but not now.

Over a month had passed since he'd seen his parents, and he needed to visit them when he was done here.

Laurel was probably missing her family something awful. If only there was more he could do for her.

One thing was for certain—he had to get her to safety before she was found out. Bored men were cantankerous, and these men were especially dangerous.

Why had God allowed Laurel to be dropped in such a snake pit?

CHAPTER 9

Laurel stared at the array of tools—her own engraving tools—laid out on the table. Someone must have broken into her father's shop and stolen them. Had they also taken the lovely silver wares on display on the shelves and in the windows that she and her father had worked so hard to craft? How would the business recover from such a loss?

Had they harmed her father? She gasped, splaying her hand over her chest. "Lord, please. No."

And what about Bella and her mother? Ma must be distraught over her being missing for nearly a week. Was anyone searching for her? Had they given up when they couldn't find her?

She had no idea how far she'd ridden with the outlaws, mainly because of whatever they'd given her to make her sleep. There wasn't a lot west of San Antonio. Just some big ranches and a few small towns, spread out here and there. Had they gone east, she might be near Fredericksburg. She'd spent the night there on her way to her grandmother's home and had loved the quaint town with its German influence. If she were near there, the kind townsfolk would help her. If only she could escape.

But if they'd ridden west—her heart leapt at her sudden thought. Surely, they had not ridden so far that she was in Mexico.

A peace washed over her. She couldn't be in Mexico since this area was still hilly with quite a few tall trees. What she'd heard about Mexico was that it was far drier than where she was, with mostly smaller trees. She couldn't allow herself to think of being a captive in a foreign country. The thought was unbearably frightening.

She needed a diversion from her rampaging thoughts. Rising, she crossed the room and rummaged through the remaining items in the crate. While there were a few sheets of paper and pen and ink and a twenty-dollar bill, there was nothing to make a plate from nor any items for printing the counterfeit money.

How could she make a plate without a stove to melt metal? Perhaps she could do it in the small fireplace. She dropped a hammer she'd unknowingly picked up, making a thud. Was she seriously considering making the plates? Could she, even if she wanted to?

She paced the cabin, considering her options. Memories of reading a chapter in a book about currency and how it was made filtered through her mind. The article stated that numerous people were responsible for making a currency plate, not one single person. Each had a special task, such as creating the portrait, lettering, or the fancy floral design usually found around the main image. That way, no one could recreate a set of plates on their own. What the Markhams wanted her to do was nigh on impossible.

But if she didn't comply, she might die. She didn't fear death, but the pain of it was cause for concern. And it wasn't so much her own life she feared for since she believed in God and knew she'd go to heaven when she died, but what about her family? It would be a simple thing for the gang to grab Bella just as they had her.

Perhaps they'd already harmed her father when they broke into the store.

As she paced, she prayed. For her family. For Lane. And for someone to rescue her.

Micah continually popped into her thoughts, so she prayed for him too. "Lord, Micah seems to be a good-hearted man. He's been kind to me and has genuinely tried to help. Change his heart so that he no longer wants to be an outlaw before he becomes hardened like Cass Markham. Before it's too late."

Something banged against the front of the cabin, making her jump. Micah entered with a bucket of water in tow, which he placed on the table. Then he disappeared out the door for a moment and returned with a washtub. She stared at the metal container. How was she to bathe in that?

He set it near the door, casting her a shy glance. Then he dumped the water in. "I'll be right back with some more."

He closed and locked the door.

She walked over and stared down. As a child, she remembered bathing with Bella on the porch of their first home during the summer in a similar tub. The bathing tub at home was long and narrow, allowing her to stretch out, although it, too, had to be filled by hand. At least at home, the water was heated. But she wouldn't fuss. Even cold water would be a blessing at this point.

Micah returned with two more buckets, a man's shirt, and a hammer and nails. She stood by the table, watching him hang the shirt over the window. "That was a thoughtful thing to do."

He shrugged, then quickly left again, as if her comment embarrassed him. If only she could figure him out. He seemed too kind and considerate to be a criminal.

Did he fancy her? Was that why he was so nice? Her heartbeat sped up. In another time and place, she could see herself caring for Micah.

Peter had taken her to supper and graced her with his presence, but he'd never done something for her as sweet as Micah hanging the shirt over the window. She missed the sunlight, but she could bathe at a more relaxed pace now.

She sat in the chair and removed her balmorals, making sure her skirts covered her feet. For the first time since she'd arrived, excitement raced through her.

~

Laurel sighed over the bowl of brown beans Lane placed on the table. How did the Markhams stand eating the same fare night after night? Beans or stew. Or stew or beans.

"Don't waste your time wishing for somethin' different. This is about as good as it gets unless someone shoots a deer or steals a cow." Lane studied her. "You smell nice."

Laurel smiled. "Thank you. That bath refreshed me."

Lane frowned. "I don't like taking baths."

"I can understand why, given your circumstances."

The girl scratched the top of her ear. "What does that mean?"

"Just that I can see why you're uncomfortable bathing when there are so many men nearby who might discover your secret."

"Oh." She narrowed her eyes. "You didn't tell Micah, did you?"

Laurel rested her hand on Lane's shoulder. "Of course not. I promised that I wouldn't tell anyone, and I haven't. Your well-being depends on that secret."

The girl relaxed, leaning against the wall. She seemed in no hurry to leave today. "Ain't you gonna eat?"

Laurel sat. "I'd rather talk to you."

"Truly?" Lane looked at her with wonder in her eyes.

"Yes. So tell me...is Lane your real name?"

She shrugged, staring at the floor again. "Pa said I'm not s'posed to tell no one."

"I already know your big secret, so I think I've proven you can trust me."

Lane studied her face, then nodded slightly. "My given name is Elaine, like my grandma's."

"That's a very lovely name. Do you have a middle one?"

She twisted her lips and rolled her eyes. "Penelope."

Laurel smiled. "Why, that's a perfectly nice name for a girl."

"A bit too fancy, if you ask me."

"You could always go by Penny. I had a friend by that name when I was young, but she moved away."

"Nah. Pa already says I ain't worth a plugged nickel. A penny is worth even less than a nickel."

Laurel wished she could give the man a piece of her mind. "Don't listen to him. You've been such a blessing to me. I don't know what I would have done without you to talk to and to help me."

"You mean that?"

Laurel nodded. "Most certainly." She picked up her lumpy cornbread. She probably should choke it down since she never knew what she'd be served next. "Have you eaten?"

"Don't like beans."

"What about cornbread? Would you like mine?"

Lane eyed the offering in Laurel's hand. "You're sure ya don't want it?"

"I don't. Help yourself."

Lane snagged the gift and shoved one corner in her mouth. Laurel's heart ached for the girl. She needed a mother's affection and training in how a girl should act and speak. Perhaps Laurel could be the person who taught her. What would her parents say if she returned home with Lane in tow? One thing for sure—the child would need a bath.

"I was serious when I said you should come home with me."

Lane halted her next bite halfway to her face and peered at

Laurel over the cornbread. "Why would you want me to come? You got parents, don't 'cha? They wouldn't want me."

"I do have parents, but I'm perfectly old enough to live on my own. And I have a job." Her father didn't pay her anywhere near what she should be earning as a silversmith. Was her small income truly enough for two to live on? Doubtful that Father would want Lane to live with them, although her mother and Bella would adore the urchin.

"Please consider it."

"But you ain't likely gettin' out of here, not unless you make those plates."

From Lane's expression, she knew what the girl left unsaid. Even if she made the plates, she might never see her home or family again. "I believe in God, and He won't allow me to die here unless it's His will."

Lane shook her head and pushed the last bite into her mouth. "God don't know what the Markhams are like," she said, blowing crumbs into the air.

Laurel reached for Lane's hand, and the girl stiffened but didn't pull away. "Honey, God knows every single person on earth, and He loves each of them. He even knows about you, and He cares for you. Maybe that's why He sent me here."

A myriad of expressions raced across Lane's face, settling on something that resembled awe. "You really think God sent you here? Why?"

"It's quite possible. If I had to become a captive so I could tell you about God's love and show you that there are people like me who care, then it was worth it."

Lane stared at her with disbelief, but a sheen glistened in her eyes. She blinked hard and jumped up. "I should go."

"Lane! Where are ya, boy?" The harsh voice from outside sent Lane running to the door.

She stepped outside. “Right here. I brung that lady her supper.”

“Get back to camp. You’re spendin’ too much time down here.”

“Ow! Don’t hit me, Willie! I’m goin’.”

Laurel raced to the door and yanked on it, but it wouldn’t budge. “Please, Lord. Protect Lane.”

“I’ll hit ya if I want to.”

A loud smack sounded, followed by a squeal, then all was quiet.

Laurel wanted to cry out to Lane, but that might only get her in more trouble. All she could do was pray. “God, watch over Lane. Send Micah to help.”

CHAPTER 10

The light of a three-quarter moon illuminated the trail as Micah made his way back to camp after spending over four hours on guard duty. Yesterday he'd gone hunting, hoping to find a route out on the east side of the valley. He could have made it out on his own, but the rocky hills would be difficult for a woman in skirts to maneuver, especially at night. At least he'd gained a few claps on the shoulder when he returned with a deer to validate the time he'd been gone.

Tonight, he'd scouted the southern part of the valley for hours while pretending to keep watch. He'd come to the conclusion that there were only two ways out that Laurel could manage. And both were guarded, unless a man fell asleep on the job.

He had no choice but to take out the guard if they were going to make their escape. And the sooner the better. Several of the men had been complaining about not getting to visit saloon gals. He doubted Willie would cross his brother and let something slip about Laurel and how pretty she was, but how long before Spyder spilled the beans?

He had to get her out of here—soon.

An owl called in the distance, and a chorus of crickets and tree frogs joined in. The comfortable breeze touched his face as it swished the leaves overhead. Occasionally, nights this far south in October could be chilly, but this autumn's weather had been fairly mild. At least Laurel shouldn't be overly cold on their ride out, unless the weather changed between now and then.

His boots skidded on rocks as he strode down the hill closest to camp. He'd probably get in trouble for leaving his post without someone taking his place if he got caught, but something in his gut told him he needed to get to camp. Besides that, Spyder should have relieved him over half an hour ago. Where was the man? Sleeping or caught up in a late-night card game?

Micah slowed his steps as he neared the cabin where Laurel was being kept. No light shone under the door. He started to move past the cabin when a scratching sound made him pause. He listened carefully, trying to determine if it was an animal or just the wind. There it was again—coming from the back of the cabin.

Micah quietly leaned his rifle against the front of the shack, pulled out his gun, and tiptoed past the western side. He peered around the corner to the back, his heart jolting at the sight of Spyder standing on a crate, using a knife as he attempted to pry open the window.

The man was known to have extra-sharp hearing and had proven that in his job as an expert safecracker, but he must be intently concentrating on his task to not hear Micah's approach. "You're supposed to be on guard duty."

Spyder jumped so badly the crate tilted, sending him flying backward, landing in the knee-high grass. The knife was still stuck in the window frame. Spyder leapt up. "What're you doing here? You're s'posed to be up the hill."

"No. That's where *you* are supposed to be. You're late. And now I know why."

"Listen." Spyder licked his lips and glanced at the window. "You don't know what's in there."

"Actually, I do. And I know what Cass threatened to do to anyone who bothered her."

"How do you know about her?"

"Found out by accident, but that doesn't matter. You need to get on guard duty."

"Now, listen here—" Spyder took a step toward Micah but halted when he lifted his gun. The crook rubbed his jaw. "We could share her, and no one would be the wiser. She's a purty little thing."

Micah ground down hard on his back teeth to keep from shooting the vile man. "You may be willing to risk your life for a few moments of pleasure, but I'm not. You'd best get on up the hill before the law sneaks in and finds us."

"I don't answer to you, Burns."

Micah took a step toward Spyder. "How about I just go tell Cass what you're up to?"

Spyder frowned and yanked his knife from the window. Micah kept a close eye on him so he didn't end up skewered. Spyder turned and bent down, retrieving his hat from the grass. "Fine, but I'm tellin' you now that you'd better watch your back."

The man stomped off, grumbling. Micah stared after him until the outlaw blended into the shadows and disappeared.

He holstered his gun and retrieved his rifle. He started to walk away, then paused and knocked on the door. "Miss Underwood?"

"W–Who's there?" Laurel's shaky voice called out.

"It's me, Micah," he whispered loudly. "Do whatever you have to in order to leave. We're getting out of here."

"Tonight?"

"Yup. I'll be back as soon as I make sure everyone is asleep. Be ready to ride."

"I will. And t–thank you."

Striding back to camp, he wrestled with what to do about Lane. He didn't like the idea of leaving the kid behind, but dare he risk Laurel's chance of escape to see if Lane would go with him?

His gut kept nagging him as he neared the cabins. He needed to check on Lane for some reason. Turning his feet in that direction, he studied the area for signs of activity. With it being past midnight, the lanterns were out in all of the cabins as they generally were by the time he'd finished his guard shift.

Micah opened the door to the cabin Lane shared with his pa, Spyder Jackson, and Curly LaFever. A shaft of moonlight peeking through the bare window illuminated the small area. Both Curly and Arch slept in their beds, snoring as loud as a cattle stampede.

A moan drew his gaze to Lane. Micah tiptoed in. Was the kid having a nightmare?

Another moan, more pathetic than the first, pulled him closer. "Psst. Lane."

The boy opened his eyes and blinked several times. "Micah?"

"Yeah. You having a bad dream?"

"Naw. My arm hurts. Bad."

Micah knelt beside the bed. "What happened to it?"

"Uh...nuthin'."

He touched Lane's left arm, and the boy hissed. "That doesn't sound like nothing. Can you come out to the barn and let me look at it?"

"No. I cain't move."

Micah laid his rifle against the bedframe. "Then I'll carry you. I aim to look at that arm."

Arch Russell stirred. "Shut up over there."

Micah froze. Did the man know his son was injured? "Something's wrong with Lane."

"Give 'im some whiskey so he'll hush up. I'm sick of hearin' his whining." Arch rolled over and started snoring again.

"C'mon, Lane."

He reached out to lift the boy, but Lane sat up, groaning and holding his arm against his chest. "I'll walk."

Micah held Lane's right arm and helped him stand. He'd never noticed how puny the kid's muscles were before, and it pinched his heart.

In the barn, Micah turned up a lantern. "Go ahead and take off your shirt so I can get a good look at that arm."

Lane's eyes widened. "I can just roll up my sleeve."

"That's fine." Micah moved the lantern closer, setting it on a nearby crate.

A sheen of sweat glistened on Lane's forehead, and tearstains had created trails down the boy's filthy face. Anger surged through him. Arch Russell didn't deserve to be a father.

He knelt next to Lane and helped roll up the sleeve.

"Ow. I can't stand the pain," Lane cried.

Micah sucked in a breath as he stared at the bruised and swollen arm. The bump in Lane's lower arm told him what he needed to know. It was broken. "Who did this to you?"

Tears ran down Lane's cheeks. "Willie."

He'd like to pummel the man. Gritting his teeth, Micah rose and carried the lantern to the tack room. He looked around for something to bind Lane's arm to his chest. The ride to a doctor would be horribly painful for the kid. Seeing nothing, he strode back and removed his shirt.

"What're you doin'?" Lane looked up with tear-filled eyes. In the three weeks Micah had known him, he'd never seen the boy cry, no matter what the others said or did to him.

"I've got to bind your arm. I'm taking you to a doctor."

"Doctor? I cain't leave."

Micah stooped down, hands on his thighs, and looked the kid in the eye. "Your arm's busted. If I don't get you to a doctor, it won't heal right, and you may never be able to use it again."

Lane's face paled under the layer of grime. "Pa will kill me if I leave."

"You deserve better than him, Lane. My folks will be happy to take you in. You would have the chance to live a regular life. Go to school if you want."

Lane stared at him. "You'd take me to your own home?"

Micah smiled. "I would. You'd be more than welcomed."

After a long moment, Lane nodded.

Micah shot into action, saddling two horses. He couldn't risk returning to his cabin to get his clothing and the few things he'd brought with him. Laurel and Lane were all that mattered.

~

Getting free of the confining cabin brought Laurel unspeakable relief, but fear that the Markhams would catch and possibly harm them kept her from enjoying her fledgling freedom. And her worry over Lane had her biting her fingernails—a bad habit her mother made her quit years ago.

She prayed with each step the horse took. Prayed she wouldn't fall off. Prayed the outlaws wouldn't notice they were missing until morning. Prayed for Lane. The girl rode in front of Micah, who kept his arm around her. Thankfully, Lane had fallen asleep for part of the ride, easing her pain.

Songbirds serenaded them. The sun rose on their left in beautiful shades of pinkish-vermillion. That meant they were headed south. But were they going toward San Antonio or away from it? She'd been too frightened and too focused on staying in the saddle to ask. The hours passed slowly as they mostly walked the horses to keep from jarring Lane.

They had ridden through the night seeing little, but as dawn crept closer, they'd quietly ridden past several houses. Few had shown signs of activity, although they had seen numerous herds of grazing cattle and horses. A roadrunner had even dared to dart across their path.

They continued on, and just as the sun peeked over the horizon, they crested yet another hill. Laurel sucked in a breath at the sight before her. An incredible two-story stone mansion with a tower that would rival any in San Antonio's wealthiest neighborhood rose up before her. "What is this place?"

"El Regalo. Home of a friend."

Did that mean another outlaw owned this amazing place? Had she misplaced her trust in Micah?

Several men watched them as they rode up, hands near their guns. A man with a rifle strode forward, but as he neared them, he shifted his weapon so that it pointed down. He nodded. "Good to see you again, Ranger."

"You too, Gage." Micah nodded. "Is Austin here?"

"Up at the house."

"Thanks." Micah glanced at Laurel. "Can you ride a bit more?"

Ranger? Though her arms and legs ached, she nodded and followed him toward the house. So was *Ranger* Micah's real surname...or Burns? And what was this place?

As they neared the house, a tall, dark-haired man walked out, holding a steaming mug. Coffee. Laurel's stomach growled. She'd love a decent cup after drinking sludge for days. The man set the mug on the porch railing and trotted down the steps. "Howdy, Ranger. What brings you down our way?"

"Trouble. Got a kid with a broken arm. Let's get him inside, and I'll tell you everything."

The man let out a shrill whistle, making Laurel jump. A man on horseback galloped toward them from the barn area.

"Go fetch Travis."

"Sure, boss." The rider turned his horse and raced off.

The man walked up to Micah's horse and held out his arms. Micah lifted Lane off the horse and handed her to him. Lane groaned and attempted to get free, then collapsed against the stranger. Micah dismounted and turned to Laurel. "Let me help you down." He reached up, and Laurel allowed him to help her. When her feet touched the ground, her legs gave way, and she sagged against him. "Steady, now."

"Just give me a moment."

"I'll get this youngster settled in Houston's old room. It's at the front of the house on the left."

"We'll be right there," Micah called over his shoulder, then stared into her eyes. "How are you doing?"

Her heart thundered at his nearness and the genuine concern in his gaze. "Sore, but I'll live. Who is that man?"

"His name is Stephen Austin Hart. He's the eldest of seven brothers who own much of the land we rode across the past few hours. His brother, Travis, is a doctor."

If Travis was a doctor, chances were Mr. Hart wasn't an outlaw. "So is your last name Ranger or Burns?"

A smile quirked Micah's lips, drawing her gaze to them. Her breathing suddenly became strained.

"Actually, neither." He released one of her arms, reached into his pocket, and pulled out something silver—a star with TEXAS RANGER inscribed around the outer circle and COMPANY B in the center of the star. "My real name is Micah McCullough, and I'm a Texas Ranger."

Laurel's mouth dropped open. "A Ranger? Not an outlaw?"

"I was working undercover."

"And I ruined all your hard work."

Micah tucked a strand of hair behind her ear. "Not completely. But you were a surprise I sure didn't plan for. A very pleasant surprise."

She ducked her head, unable to hold his intense stare any longer. Her insides tingled with a delightful sensation. She actually thought for a moment that he might kiss her. Her stomach chose that unfortunate moment to grumble.

Micah chuckled. "Let's see if the Harts will share their breakfast."

Mortified and still a bit stunned by his revelation, she allowed him to escort her up the stairs. A Texas Ranger. The concept was as difficult to grasp as liquid silver. She'd had a feeling he wasn't a bad man, and she'd been right. Part of her hated to see her time at the cabin end because she didn't know if she'd ever see Micah McCullough again once she returned home.

And that bothered her.

A lot.

CHAPTER 11

Micah and the seven men who'd ridden with him dismounted a half mile from the Markhams' camp. He'd been gone less than twenty hours, and he'd prayed most of the way here that the gang would still be at the camp and not out searching for Laurel, Lane, and him.

He surveyed the well-armed group. If these highly capable men couldn't capture or finish off the Markham Gang, he didn't know that anyone could. Captain Sterling had sent four Rangers to take down the gang. Branch Kilborn, a man Micah trusted with his life, was second in command of Ranger Company B and in charge of today's mission. Branch's shadow—his dog Jack—sat at his side. Jesse Rawlings, a reliable man with a scruffy beard, was Branch's good friend and an expert with a knife. Ezra Creed showed his Comanche heritage in his dark hair and eyes, and he was a man to be counted on. He didn't know Griff Sommer, the rookie of the squad, as well as he did the others, but the man was dependable and a good shot.

They tied off the horses in a copse of Texas pistachio and oak trees. Each man pulled out his weapons and rechecked his ammunition.

The four Hart brothers who had accompanied them—Austin, Crockett, Travis, and Chisholm, a former Ranger—followed suit. Each man was good with a rifle, and all the Hart brothers were thought highly of.

Part of him was glad they'd come, but another part felt uneasy. Each brother was a husband and father, and he'd hate for something to happen to one of them. But then several of the Rangers were also married now. At least having the doctor with them could be a good thing, if anyone took a bullet today.

The sun was setting low in the sky. They'd have just enough light to see well but plenty of shadows to hide in.

Branch gave a soft, quick whistle. "Gather 'round." The men huddled around him. "We went over the layout of the camp back in Hartville, but let's cover it again." Branch looked at Micah and nodded.

Micah grabbed a stick and stooped down, drawing a map in the dirt. "This trail leads up and to the right. It's probably safe to ignore the cabin on the trail to the left, since that's where Miss Underwood was held. The main camp is about two hundred yards on the right." He tapped the stick on the biggest square. "This is the Markhams' house. And these two cabins are where the men sleep. That's the cookhouse. Barn."

"Good." Branch lifted his hat and pushed his long hair back, then reset it. "Jesse, Griff, and I will cover the main house. Micah and Ezra, take the first two cabins, and you Hart men split and take the cookhouse and barn."

"Don't forget that two men are generally on duty, here and here." Micah jabbed the stick at the north and south ends of the valley. "The south guard shouldn't be trouble for at least ten minutes after the shooting starts. Jesse and I can take out the one near here, if you want to give us a head start. I figure Jesse can take him out with his knife if I can't get close enough to knock him out."

Branch inhaled a loud breath and nodded. "Ten minutes enough?"

"Should be."

"Go on, then. We'll scout the area to make sure there aren't any surprises. Meet back here."

Jesse followed close on Micah's tail as he quietly made his way up the hill where he'd previously stood guard. By his best guess, Curly should be on duty.

At the top, he surveyed the relatively flat area for several minutes. One large boulder gave the outlaws cover when they needed it, but it also created a high point, good for keeping watch of anyone entering the valley.

Even though he and the Rangers had come up through the trees as far as they could, a man with a sharp eye could have spotted them. He was counting on Curly, who'd been known to fall asleep while on duty, to not notice them. So far, so good.

Jesse crawled up beside him. "See anyone?" he whispered.

Micah shook his head and pointed at the boulder. His gut twisted. Had the gang abandoned camp after he left? "Should be right there. Someone could be sittin' in the shade on the far side. Let's sneak over there. You go right. I'll go around on the left. Try to take him alive—and quietly."

Jesse nodded. They crept forward, eyes searching in all directions. At the boulder, they split. Micah tiptoed around the massive rock, but all he saw was Jesse. Micah pushed his hat brim up with the barrel of his gun. "I don't like this. I sure hope they haven't lit out."

"Let's get back down."

A few minutes later, Micah told Branch about the missing guard.

Branch pursed his lips. "Let's storm the camp. There may still be some of the gang there."

Micah prayed there would be. The Rangers needed to stop these criminals from their rampant thieving and murdering. Too many innocent people had died.

They split up as planned. Micah and Ezra headed to the cabin he'd lived in for three long weeks. Once all the men were in place, a loud yell rang out. All the men cried out in unison and stormed their targets. With Ezra watching the window, Micah kicked open the door. Dust motes floated in the sunlight, but not a soul was present.

He whistled to Ezra. Shots rang out near the barn. Micah and Ezra charged the second cabin just as Arch Russell opened the door. Micah lifted his gun, but Ezra got a shot off first. Lane's father grabbed his chest, fired a shot that went wild, then collapsed.

The shooting ended too soon for them to have gotten the whole gang. Micah had a sick feeling in his gut.

Austin Hart peered out the barn door, waving his rifle at Micah. "We got two as they were about to ride out. Bass Tomkins is shot, but he'll live. Cherokee Sam is dead."

"Ezra got Arch Russell. Are y'all all right?"

"Yep." Austin grinned.

A shout from the big house drew their gaze. Branch stood on the small porch. "The Markhams have cleared out. Not much left here. Do a good search of the area before we head back."

"There's no sign of Curly LaFever or Spyder Jackson, either," Micah shouted.

"They weren't in the barn," Austin hollered. "There are only three horses left, so they've probably hightailed it to somewhere else." Austin gave Branch his report on Tomkins and Cherokee Sam.

Travis and Chisholm Hart exited the barn with their guns on

Bass and walked toward the porch, while Crockett led out two horses. The best Micah could tell, Bass only had a shoulder wound. The men began gathering at the house.

Micah checked Arch Russell for a pulse, but the man had passed. At least he hadn't been the one to kill him. But how was he going to tell Lane that his pa was dead?

~

Laurel paced the front porch of the Harts' home, searching once again for Micah. He'd left shortly after eating breakfast, and he'd been gone for hours. He left to go to Hartville, a town named after the Hart family. He'd said his commanding officer was stationed there, and they'd heard from one of the ranch hands that a group of Rangers and Hart brothers had gone after the Markham Gang. Was Micah all right?

"Pacing a hole in the porch won't bring them back any sooner." Rebekah Hart smiled and patted the porch swing. "Come sit with me."

"I swing, Mama." Two-year-old Betsy lifted her arms, and Rebekah pulled her onto the swing.

"There's room for all three of us."

Laurel sat beside them. "It's so peaceful here. I have to say, I don't miss the busyness of San Antone, although I do miss my family."

"You'll see them soon enough, I'm sure. Once the Markhams are caught, it will be safe for you to return home."

"I hope so."

"You don't sound totally convinced."

"I'll be safe if the Markhams are captured, but I'm not sure how my parents will feel about taking Lane in. Father can be a hard man at times."

"She's welcome to stay here. Even though there's four years

between them, my Janey is quite taken with her. She can't stop talking about how the girl was raised in an outlaw camp."

"I hope Lane can overcome her past. I'm worried she'll want to return to her father, even though he didn't seem to care for her very well."

"That's normal, but I've seen how she dotes on your affection. Just give her some time. I bet she'll adjust easily enough."

Betsy scooted to the front of the swing. "Down, pwease." Rebekah helped her daughter to the floor. The dark-haired girl trotted over to a small table with two chairs and sat.

"She's adorable."

"Thank you, but she's quite the challenge at times."

"I hope to have a family one day."

A knowing smile tilted Rebekah's lips. "You seem quite smitten with the Ranger."

Laurel's heart leapt at the mention of Micah. "I just barely met him."

"That doesn't matter. I was attracted to Austin almost from the beginning, and he was engaged to my sister at the time."

Laurel's eyes widened. "Truly?"

"Yes. Things didn't work out between Jenny and him because God had other plans."

"What happened to your sister?"

"She's a happily married mother of two, living in Dallas now. I don't see her often, but I'm so glad she finally settled down. She was quite a wild thing for many years."

"She sounds a bit like my little sister, Bella. Although I'd call her feisty rather than wild."

"Sisters. What would we do without them?" Rebekah chuckled. She drew in a breath, then turned to look at Laurel. "I don't want to horn in where I'm not wanted, but I almost lost Austin before we got together. I'd hate for that to happen to you. If you have any feelings for Micah, I encourage you to talk to him. Don't let him get away. He's a good, honorable man."

"I'll consider what you've said. Thank you." Laurel didn't know what she felt for Micah—she just couldn't get him out of her mind. It dawned on her that she hadn't once thought of Peter since arriving at the Hart ranch. "I should probably check on Lane. . .um, *E*-laine. Maybe she's feeling well enough to come sit outside."

In the room where Elaine was staying, Janey sat on the bed next to her, reading. Laurel watched until Janey slammed the book shut.

Elaine glanced up and smiled. Laurel stepped into the room. "How are you feeling?"

"Better."

Janey slid off the bed. "I'm going to see if I can find us a snack."

Elaine's eyes were dulled by the strong medicine Dr. Hart had given her after setting her arm, but that was far better than seeing them narrowed in pain. She yawned.

"I was wondering if you'd feel up to sitting on the porch for a bit?"

Elaine shook her head. "Maybe later. I'm not exactly dressed for that now." Her pale cheeks brightened with a blush.

Laurel hadn't noticed until then that she was wearing a nightgown. "All right. You probably should rest, anyway. That ride here was quite an ordeal for you."

"Is Micah back yet?"

Laurel shook her head. "No, sweetie."

The girl picked at the edge of the sheet. "What's gonna happen to me?"

Laurel sat on the side of the bed and took Elaine's hand. "I think that's up to you. Micah told me he offered to take you to his parents' home, and you know I want you to come back to San Antonio with me. Mrs. Hart even mentioned you'd be welcome here, if you wanted to stay."

"I don't know what to do. Pa wasn't a good father like Mr. Hart is to his young'uns, but I kinda miss 'im."

Laurel squeezed her hand. "That's natural. My father is a hard man, but I miss him too."

"You do?"

She nodded.

"What if they don't want me?"

Brushing Elaine's hair out of her eyes, Laurel smiled. "Then we'll get our own place."

Frowning, the girl looked up. "But what about Micah?" She dropped her gaze and picked at the sheet again. "Couldn't we live together—be a family?"

Laurel sucked in a breath. It was the very thing she'd dreamed of last night. "I don't know. Micah's job takes him all over the state. It would be hard for him to settle in one place."

"Oh. It was a bad idea, anyway."

"No, it wasn't. But Micah has a say in it, and he's not here now." And she had no idea how he felt about her.

Stephen, Austin and Rebekah's oldest son, and Seth, their five-year-old, darted into the room. "Riders are coming," they said in unison.

CHAPTER 12

"Papa's home," Betsy squealed as Laurel rushed to the front porch of the Harts' home. The little girl tottered down the steps, stopping on the last one.

"Stay there, Betsy." Rebekah rose from the swing.

"I will, Mama."

Austin and one of his brothers accompanied a buggy up the lane to the house. A pretty woman, who looked a few years older than her mother, glanced her way and smiled. Laurel searched the trail behind them, but there was no sign of Micah. Disappointment washed through her. Was he all right?

Austin dismounted as Rebekah hurried down the stairs, grabbed Betsy's hand, and greeted her husband. Austin lifted up his daughter. Rebekah gave him a quick hug and kiss, then turned to her guest. "It's nice to see you again, Mrs. Sterling. What brings you out here today?"

Austin's brother—what was his name?—assisted Mrs. Sterling from the buggy.

"Captain Sterling told me about Miss Underwood's horrible ordeal, and I came to see if there was anything I could do. Oh, and as you can see"—she fluttered her hand in the air—"the Rangers and Hart men have returned. None of our men were harmed, and several of the bandits were killed and one was apprehended."

"Thank you for reporting that to us. Come inside, and we'll have tea to celebrate their success." Rebekah took the woman's arm and led her up the stairs, stopping in front of Laurel. "This is Etta Sterling, wife of Captain Sterling, who is in command of the Ranger company Micah is a part of." She turned to face the older woman. "And this is Laurel Underwood."

Mrs. Sterling smiled. "I imagine you can expect Ranger McCullough to return before too long. There are reports to be filed, of course. I can see why our Micah is so intrigued with you, my dear."

Her heart bucked at the thought of seeing Micah again. Laurel shot a peek at Rebekah, who merely smiled. "Your Micah? Are you two related?"

"Not by blood, but all the young men under my husband's command are like sons to me."

"I'm sure they don't mind your looking after them."

Mrs. Sterling chuckled. "Not overly much, especially when there's food involved."

"Speaking of refreshment, shall we go to the dining room?" Rebekah escorted them to the fancy room then excused herself.

"This place never fails to impress me." Mrs. Sterling ran her hand over one of the large wooden chairs that had the name *James Bowie Hart* carved on it. Each brother and his wife had a matching chair. A long, gleaming wood table sat in the center of the room.

Laurel stared up at the large portrait of Victoria Hart, mother of the seven brothers. "I've never seen anything quite like this place. Everything here is so...magnificent."

"That's true. The Harts never did anything halfway. Where do you hail from, dear?" Mrs. Sterling paused in front of one of the large windows.

"San Antonio." Laurel wrung her hands. "I really must get to town and send word that I'm safe. My family must be worried sick."

The kind woman patted her shoulder. "I'm sure they are too. We should have done that this morning, but the men left in such a rush."

"It is unfortunate those awful Markham siblings and one man from the gang escaped."

Laurel drew in a sharp breath. The Markhams were still free? She wouldn't be able to go home, after all.

Rebekah returned, carrying a fancy silver tray with a teapot, cups, and cookies. She set it on the end of the table. "Ignore the names on the chairs and sit where you like—well, except for GW's. We don't sit there."

Mrs. Sterling lifted her hands. "I should probably wash after driving that buggy."

"I'm sorry. I should have thought of that. Follow me please." Rebekah left the room for a moment, then returned and rushed over to Laurel. "I have to tell you that Mrs. Sterling is a notorious matchmaker. Be careful what you say to her, or she'll have you and Micah in front of a preacher by day's end."

Laurel's eyes widened at Rebekah's proclamation. Why did that not sound so bad?

~

Things were quiet at El Regalo as Micah rode up to the big house. He dismounted. A man he didn't recognize walked out of the barn, toward him.

"Can I see to your horse, Ranger?"

He nodded. "Thanks, but I'm not sure how long I'll be here."

"No problem. Just let me know when you need him, and I'll get him ready to ride."

Eager to see Laurel again, Micah strode up to the house and knocked.

Austin answered, a wide grin pulling at his lips. "You Rangers always show up at mealtime."

"We get mighty tired of campfire food. I think I could eat a whole cow by myself."

In the wide entryway, Austin stopped. "I probably should warn you that Etta Sterling stopped by today."

"She did?"

"Of course. There's a new woman in town. You and Branch are the only two Rangers not married, and she aims to see you are."

Micah swallowed the lump that suddenly appeared in his throat.

Austin chuckled. "Don't look so worried. Marriage to the right woman is a fine thing—a godly thing."

"I reckon. Being a Ranger, I never thought much about settling down." A gale of laughter echoed through the house, drawing Micah's gaze across the hall. Was that Laurel?

"Until now?"

"What?" His gaze shot back to Austin's, and he grimaced. "Does it show that much?"

Grinning, Austin clapped him on the shoulder. "You look like a man in love."

Micah groaned. "It kinda snuck up on me."

"Love has a way of doing that. I suggest you take that pretty lady for a walk this evening and have a talk with her. This may sound funny coming from another man, but I doubt you'll be sorry for sharing your heart with her. Rebekah said Laurel's been worried sick about you."

Micah grinned. That was certainly good news. He was pretty sure what his own heart was saying, but he had no idea if Laurel felt anything for him.

He followed Austin into the huge dining room, and his gaze

shot straight to Laurel's. Her lips tipped up at something Janey said, then she peered over the girl's head, spying him. Her widening smile took his breath away. His crazy heart pounded so hard, his Ranger badge was probably shaking.

Yep, they definitely needed to talk.

~

With a borrowed shawl wrapped around her shoulders, Laurel walked alongside Micah behind the Harts' home. Excitement battled shyness. She barely knew this man, and yet he made her heart sing. He'd saved her from a wretched fate—maybe even saved her life. More than that, though, he was a good man—one she believed she could trust.

Micah stopped and stared into the distance toward a pasture filled with horses. He rubbed his jaw, then turned toward her. "I've never been a big talker, but I find myself at a complete loss of words right now."

Her heart dipped. Did that mean he felt nothing for her? Proper rules of society said a man should lead things in a relationship, so she kept quiet.

The breeze whipping the shawl made the tall grass dance around them. A hawk cried overhead, and in the distance a horse whinnied. The scene was so peaceful compared to busy San Antonio.

Micah turned to her and cleared his throat. "I never expected to meet someone like you."

"Someone like me?"

His lips turned up in a crooked smile. "Yeah. There you were, kidnapped and trapped by a vicious gang, but your main concern was for Lane. How is he, by the way?"

"Getting better. Just needs some rest, especially since the pain medicine Doc Travis gave causes sleepiness." They needed to talk about Lane, but at the moment, she only wanted to talk about *them*.

"Good." Micah reached down and took her hand. "All my life, I wanted to be a Texas Ranger like my pa. I never thought I'd be anything else, but recently that desire has changed."

"It has?"

"Yeah. I have strong feelings for you, Laurel. I realize we haven't known one another for long, but if you're willing, I'd like to spend time with you and see how things go."

She couldn't hold back her smile. "I'd like that too."

Micah's shoulders relaxed, and his expression brightened. "You would?"

"Yes." She nodded. "Very much."

"So then, what do we do?"

Laurel shrugged. "I don't know. With the Markhams still loose, I'm hesitant to return home."

"You could go home with me, to my parents' ranch near Austin. They'd love you and Lane."

Laurel lifted her brows. "That wouldn't be proper."

"Oh, hey, I forgot. I sent a telegram earlier to let your folks know you were safe. I imagine they'll come here to make sure."

Happiness flooded her so much that she almost hugged him. "Thank you for doing that. I've been concerned about them."

He touched the end of his slouch hat. "Happy to help, ma'am."

Grinning, she gave him a playful shove. He grabbed her hands and pulled them to his chest, staring down so intently that her mouth went dry. She couldn't break his gaze. After a moment, he dipped his head, his lips passing an inch from hers.

Laurel's heart thundered. She'd never been kissed before. Peter hadn't once tried, and she'd never really wanted him to. What she felt for Micah was so much deeper—stronger. It was as if God Himself had put them in one another's path. She pushed up on her tiptoes and closed the distance between them. Delicious sensations raced through her as their lips met.

Micah wrapped his arms around her, pulling her close. Joy unlike anything she'd ever felt before overwhelmed her.

A shot rang out. Micah jerked away from her. He groaned but then dove toward her, knocking her to the ground. She couldn't breathe with his heavy weight trapping her.

More shots were fired. One hit the ground just inches from her shoulder.

"Stay down." Micah lifted his head, and a shot zipped past his hat.

God, help us. Protect Micah. Had the Markhams found her again?

"I told you that you'd be sorry for crossing me, Burns." Harsh laughter rang out from the field on her left. "And now you've double-crossed the whole gang. You'll pay for that."

"Sounds like Spyder Jackson," Micah whispered.

Fast footsteps sounded on the porch behind them. Two shots fired. "McCullough!"

Micah used his gun to lift his hat up. "Here."

Another shot rang out, and his hat flew through the air. Micah ducked. He rolled off of Laurel but stuck to her side, his face next to hers. The length of his body shielded her from the gunman. His hand held her cheek close to his. In that moment, she knew she loved him.

Shots blasted from the direction of the house. Bullets zinged over their heads, then all was quiet. Someone ran past them and soon shouted, "We got him!"

Sweet relief made Laurel weak, and she laid back. Micah blew out a loud breath.

Another person jogged through the grass, stopping next to them. Austin. "Y'all hurt?"

"I got winged." Micah stared at Laurel. "Are you all right?"

"Bruised, but that's— Wait! What do you mean, you got winged?"

He glanced at his upper arm. Her gaze followed, and she gasped at the sight of blood.

"It's safe to get up now...if you want to." Austin chuckled.

Micah pushed off the ground, then lifted his good hand to Austin, who tugged him up the rest of the way. Then Micah reached out for Laurel and helped her stand. His gaze ran down her body. "You sure you're not hurt?"

"I'm fine, but we need to get you inside."

"Not until I see who was shooting at us."

Crockett stood over a body about fifty feet away. Laurel watched as Micah and Austin walked over.

"You know him?" Austin asked.

Micah nodded. "Just as I thought—Spyder Jackson. I crossed him the night we made our escape. He told me then to watch my back."

"So he's part of the gang?" Crockett asked.

"Yep."

"Go on in and get your arm tended," Austin said. "Crockett and I will see to the body."

"I'm obliged."

"Micah!"

He glanced up to see Lane running toward him—in a dress. His mouth dropped open as he struggled to wrap his mind around that fact.

Lane halted a few feet away, eyes wide. Her broken arm was strung up in a sling. "You're bleeding."

"You're...uh...wearing a...dress."

Lane grinned. "Laurel didn't tell you my secret, I reckon."

Micah lifted his gaze as the woman he was falling with love with walked toward him, grinning.

"Surprise!" Laurel's blue eyes twinkled. "And *her* real name is *E*-laine."

"No kidding." Micah chuckled. "I never suspected that." Some Ranger he was.

Lane shrugged. "It ain't so bad wearing a dress. Don't know how I'm gonna ride, though."

"In a buggy." Laurel gave her a no-nonsense look that said, *don't argue.*

Lane lifted a pleading gaze to Micah.

He raised his hands as in surrender. "Don't look to me for help."

Austin chuckled. "Not even married, and he's already deferring to his lady."

Lane gasped. "Are you two gettin' married?"

Micah gently looped Laurel's arm around his wounded one, then wrapped his other arm around Elaine's shoulders. He needed to tell Lane about his—her—father, but he had a feeling the kid would take it all right. He and Laurel would make sure she was. And marrying Laurel sounded like the perfect thing to do. "Time will tell, but I'd say the prospects are mighty good."

ABOUT THE AUTHOR

Bestselling author Vickie McDonough grew up wanting to marry a rancher, but instead married a computer geek who is scared of horses. She now lives out her dreams in her fictional stories about ranchers, cowboys, lawmen, and others living in the Old West. Vickie is the award-winning author of more than forty published books and novellas. Her novels include the fun and feisty Texas Boardinghouse Brides series and the Land Rush Dreams series. Vickie has been married forty-one years to Robert. They have four grown sons, one of whom is married, and a precocious ten-year-old granddaughter. When she's not writing, Vickie enjoys reading, antiquing, watching movies, and traveling. To learn more about Vickie's books or to sign up for her newsletter, visit her website: www.vickiemcdonough.com.

Cover design by: Wild Heart Books

GUARD YOUR HEART

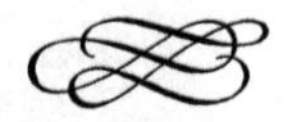

ERICA VETSCH

CHAPTER 1

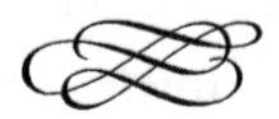

Hartville, Texas
December 2, 1886

Constance Spanner loved her older sister, but all too often, she wanted to put a gag on her.

"The Christmas Eve Charity Ball is coming, and he still hasn't asked me to accompany him." Clarice's wail could be heard in every corner of the dress shop, even back in Constance's workroom. Constance clipped a length of ribbon and began sewing it along the brim of the hat she was creating, trying to blot out her sister's histrionics.

Clarice leaned against the doorframe to the workroom, a fistful of lace in one hand and a tape measure in the other. "That man will be the everlasting death of me."

Since Constance's arrival in Hartville the week before, her sister had bragged, bemoaned, and besieged her with news of one Harley P. Burton, Attorney-at-Law and longtime beau. If the man didn't have an office just across the street, with his name clearly painted on the sign over the door, Constance would believe her sister had made up her suitor, since Constance had yet to see Harley P. Burton in person. But she'd heard more than enough to sour her on the subject.

"If only he wasn't away at that trial in San Antonio." Clarice sighed, and Constance half expected her to put the back of her hand against her forehead in heartfelt dramatic fashion. Clarice had always been overly emotive, and Constance was reminded once again why she had always resisted Clarice's repeated demands over the years that her baby sister leave Shreveport and join her in Hartville.

If only she could go back. But Shreveport was no longer an option...not unless she wanted to be arrested. "Ouch!" Constance dropped the hat and ribbon, putting her finger into her mouth. The third time today she'd pricked a digit.

The bell over the door jangled, and Clarice straightened as if she was the one who had been poked with a needle. Composing herself, she put on a broad smile and headed around the corner to the front of the store. "Hello, what can I do for yo—" Her sister's voice broke off abruptly.

"Ma'am." A deep voice, the likes of which were rarely heard in the female-dominated establishment, cut through the air.

"Sir." Clarice's tone was clipped and disapproving. "I do not allow dogs in my store. Kindly put him outside."

"I won't be here long." The gravelly voice brooked no argument. "He promises not to hike his leg on anything."

"Really, sir, there is no need to be crass." A huge sniff, and Constance could picture her sister's best prunes-and-persimmons expression.

"Just saying it like it is."

Constance snickered, stood, and peered around the workroom door. Anyone who would stand up to her sister's pinch-mouthed demands deserved at least a look. A tall, lean man with a heavy beard stood between the bolts of calico and the rack of lace samples. The femininity of the surroundings seemed to accentuate his manliness, though Constance had a feeling he would stand out in any company.

She couldn't tell the color of his eyes, not at this distance. But they glittered under the shadow of his hat brim. At his side, a large dog plopped his rump down, tongue lolling, one ear cocked, one drooping over. There was some shepherd in there, and maybe some hound dog. The rest was a mystery. Whatever he was made of, he came across as quite friendly, his tail brushing the polished pine floor.

"A gentleman would at least remove his hat." Her sister crossed her arms, the handful of lace dangling down her side.

Slowly, the man eased his hat off, revealing nearly shoulder-length black hair and hot, dark eyes. "If I remember correctly, the first time we met, you informed me that I was no gentleman. And the second."

Constance could well imagine that. Clarice wasn't one to mince words or hold her tongue. What had the man done to anger her sister?

The dog spied Constance lurking in the workshop doorway and stood, tail wagging. His nails clicked as he crossed the shop floor, coming to stand in front of her, nudging her hand for a pat.

She obliged, stroking his soft fur, rubbing the hollows behind his ears. He gave a long, slow blink.

"You're in trouble now, ma'am."

Constance had been so enamored of the dog, she hadn't heard the approach of the stranger. She jerked her hand from the dog's head, afraid she'd transgressed by petting him. As she brought her gaze up, it traveled over the man's high boots, long legs, sidearm, broad chest...and stopped cold at the silver badge pinned to his left breast pocket. Her mouth went dry, and her heart rate kicked up like a runaway team.

Had Pasquale's father sent the law after her? All the way to the middle of Texas? How had he found her? She never should've come here, but what other option was there? She'd never mentioned where her sister lived, had she?

"Now that you've patted him, he's going to pester you every time he sees you." The man bent and slapped the dog's side, raising a puff of dust. "Jack's a sucker for pretty girls."

A ripple of pleasure went through her. This lawman thought she was pretty? This close, she saw his eyes were a deep, chocolaty brown. He smelled of sunshine, leather, and something very... male. She'd never been so aware of a man before.

"Is there something we can do for you, sir?" Glancing at the badge again, she noted the inscription. "I mean, Ranger." The dog nudged her again, and she stroked his head.

"Branch. Branch Kilborn." He looked her over, from her upswept hair to her coal-black leather shoes. "I don't think we've met."

She stopped patting the dog long enough to hold out her hand. "Constance Spanner. I've just newly arrived in Hartville. Clarice is my sister."

Ranger Kilborn looked from her to Clarice, his brows rising a fraction. He quickly smothered the expression, but Constance knew what he was thinking. The two women looked nothing alike. Clarice was tall, big-boned, and buxom, with luxurious brown hair and hazel eyes, while Constance was of average height, slender, with unruly flaxen curls that were forever escaping their pins, and blue eyes.

Clarice was almost old enough to be Constance's mother, what with the fifteen-year age gap. And she was certainly bossy enough, though her sister meant well. Add to that the fact that they were really only half sisters, and the differences became understandable.

"Nice to meet you, ma'am." He clasped her hand in a firm grip, and warmth spread up her arm. She withdrew her fingers, resisting the urge to put them behind her back in a fist to preserve the feel of his touch. What was wrong with her? She had never reacted to a man this way, not even Pasquale, and she'd been engaged to him.

"Are you in town for long?" He asked the question not as if he were interested in her personally, but rather as if he was making mental notes about the residents of Hartville. Very much a peace officer.

"I'm not sure. Clarice has invited me to join her in the business, and for now, I'm helping her on the millinery side of things." She waved her hand to the open workshop door where hat-making supplies strewed the bench.

The tall Ranger's gaze bounced off her handiwork, and he shrugged. "What I don't know about women's fripperies would fill several books, but those seem like a waste of time. Won't keep the sun or rain off you, and they look like a good wind would blow them to Galveston."

Constance's hands fisted at her sides. Of course, he didn't appreciate her talents. It was no more than she'd come to expect from any man. Though why she should care at all when she'd only just met him and would likely not encounter him in the course of her work was beyond her understanding at the moment. She bit back a sharp reply. Perhaps he thought she should only make slab-sided sunbonnets?

"You certainly don't mince words, do you?"

"No ma'am. I believe in honesty." He looked about to say more when Clarice butted in.

"What is it you want?" She tapped her foot. "We have work to do."

Constance blinked at her sister's brusqueness.

Branch turned to Clarice. "The boss sent me to make the rounds of the businesses here in town to remind folks to take extra care. Lock your doors when you aren't here. And don't keep cash here overnight. The Mortenson's Mercantile got broken into last night, and the robbers cleaned out the till." He hung his hat on the butt of his gun, resting most of his weight on one leg, his eyes never lighting on one place for too long.

Constance hadn't met the Mortensons yet, but she felt for them. "Do you know who did it?"

He nodded, digging in his shirt pocket. "It was the Markhams." Opening his palm, he revealed a large silver coin with a bullet hole dead center. "They left this so we'd be sure to know it was them."

Clarice sniffed, crossing her arms and tapping her foot again. "I have to say, I am disappointed, and I know I'm not alone. Here we've had an entire company of Rangers stationed in Hartville with the sole job of ridding this state of one outlaw gang, and in a year, you've made no progress. Cass Markham is robbing and terrorizing as much as he ever did, and you Rangers seem more interested in getting married than protecting the citizens who pay your wages."

Branch Kilborn straightened to his full height, his expression hardening and his eyes boring into Clarice to the point where she began to fidget and color rose in her face. Constance bit the inside of her lower lip to keep from giggling. Here was one man who wasn't intimidated by her outspoken sibling.

"Ma'am, you're entitled to your opinion, to be sure, but before you go spouting off, you might want to check your facts." He tilted his head back to draw his hair off his face. "We've arrested more than a few of Markham's Gang, and we've killed the ones that resisted arrest. And not every Ranger in the troop has matrimony on the mind, I can assure you." He jabbed his chest with his thumb, leaving no doubt that he wasn't interested in marriage. "We'll get the rest of the gang, but until we do, lock your doors and deposit your receipts in the bank at night." He replaced his hat and snapped his fingers, and the dog bounded to his side.

Touching his fingertip to the brim of his hat, he nodded to Constance. “Ma’am.”

The bell over the door tinkled, and a trio of ladies entered, chattering and clutching parcels. Ranger Kilborn stopped midstride.

“Oh, Branch,” one of the ladies simpered, fluttering over and putting her lace-gloved hand on his arm. “You’re the last person I expected to see here.”

“Miss Palmer.” His lips seemed tight, as if he were speaking through clenched teeth.

“I hope you’re anticipating our supper tonight as much as I am. In fact, I’ve stopped in to see if Miss Spanner has a hat that will go with my new dress.”

So the Ranger not interested in matrimony had a dinner date with a syrupy blonde? And evidently one who would be wearing one of her “good for nothing” hats, to boot. Constance covered her smile with her hand.

“I won’t keep you.” He lifted Miss Palmer’s hand from his arm. “Don’t forget what I said, Miss Spanner.” He spoke to Clarice, but his glance flicked to Constance and held her gaze for a long moment. With a small shake, he broke the stare, snapped his fingers for the dog again, and ducked through the door.

One of Miss Palmer’s companions fanned herself. “I declare, Veronica, you’re a brave woman. I swear that man is half wolf.”

Veronica Palmer sniffed and put her pert little chin in the air. “I’ll tame him soon enough.”

Constance wished her luck. Branch Kilborn might be fine to look at, and he might exude masculinity, strength, and a touch of that wildness the ladies spoke of, but Constance didn’t trust her judgment about men anymore. Look what had happened the last time she had let a man turn her head.

She’d become involved in a scandal that made her wary of the law.

~

That evening, Branch Kilborn stood on the boardwalk outside the Hartville Hotel, staring at the door, gearing himself up to go inside.

Dinner with Veronica Palmer?

How had he allowed himself to be cornered in this particular box canyon?

Hugh and Etta, that was how. They were pleased as parade marshals at how their efforts to get most of the Rangers in the troop married off had worked out. Branch shook his head. He was the last holdout, and by sugar, he was going to stay that way. Marriage changed a man too much, divided his loyalties and attention. He had no time for that kind of foolishness.

The law was mistress enough for any man. If a Ranger wasn't totally dedicated to the job, he lost focus and found trouble.

Look at how being married had changed the other six in the troop. They all had houses, property, families, livestock, furniture, bills at the mercantile, and so much more to weigh them down. They were forever talking about their wives, thinking about them, pining for them when they were apart.

It was like they were hardly men anymore, shackled as they were to their womenfolk.

Branch had only himself to look after, and that was just the way he liked it. He could fit everything he owned in his saddlebags, be packed and out the door in two minutes. His gun, his saddle, his horse, and his dog—those were the essentials. He wouldn't give up his freedom for any woman.

He motioned to Jack and put his hand on the doorknob. Best to get this evening over with, then he'd make it plain to Hugh and Etta that he wasn't having any more of their matchmaking games.

Jack nosed his leg and edged past him into the hotel lobby. The shepherd mix, now around three, was just hitting his prime, and he'd come a long way in his training as a tracker. Branch preferred his company to just about any person he'd ever met. People talked too much, made too many demands.

He chose action over gabbing—another reason to steer clear of females. They were talk, talk, talk all the time, and they seemed to expect a man to pay attention to every word and have an opinion about everything. It could flat wear a man out. And it seemed most of the time, a woman never said what she really meant. He was just supposed to know, or guess, what was on her mind. Who had time for that?

Conversation and the sound of cutlery on china came from the dining room on his left, and he nodded to the desk clerk before rounding the screen that separated the restaurant from the hotel.

At least he'd been able to get out of actually picking Miss Palmer up at her house and escorting her to the hotel. Hugh and Etta had done that chore for him while he stopped by the telegraph office to check for news on the Markham Gang.

Hugh spotted him and rose, waving him over. Branch had to weave through diners clear to the far side of the room. He had hoped their table would be in one of the alcoves, but no, it sat full square in front of one of the big windows where everyone inside and out could see them.

"Evening, Branch." Hugh shot a look at Branch's head.

With a guilty nod, Branch removed his hat, jerking his chin to toss his hair back. Etta was forever after him to cut it, but he liked it long. It was a sign of his freedom, a mark of his untamed ways. He'd turn in his badge before he'd cut his hair.

Branch edged his chair a few inches away from the others. Manners said he shouldn't turn it around and straddle it at the end of the table away from his dinner companion, but the temptation was strong.

"Good evening, Miss Palmer."

"Branch, I thought you'd never get here." Veronica fluttered her lashes at him. "I've been looking forward to this all week." She had to tilt her head back to see him because her hat had a swooping brim that dipped into her line of vision.

The outlandish headgear had him remembering the younger Miss Spanner, whom he'd met that afternoon. She'd bristled like a barrel cactus when he'd commented on the uselessness of her hat creations, but she'd tried to cover it up. She'd seemed a bit nervous when she'd spied his badge, but he was used to women being a bit nervous around him.

Branch took the seat next to Veronica, hanging his hat on the corner of his chair and adjusting his sidearm so it didn't knock against anything.

Jack snuffled around and got onto his belly, squirming until he could curl up under Branch's chair. He'd done that ever since he was a pup and didn't seem to realize that he was too big to be comfortable under the rungs anymore.

Veronica scowled as though she'd just guzzled spoiled milk. "A dog? In a restaurant? Surely, he should stay outside?" Every time she moved, a cloud of expensive-smelling scent wafted over Branch. Had she doused herself in perfume? The fruity smell clogged in his nose and throat, and he fought a sneeze.

Etta spread her napkin and smiled. "Jack goes everywhere with Branch."

Jack's tail thumped the floor at the sound of his name, and Branch reached down to scrub the dog's ears. "You don't have to worry about the dog, Miss Palmer. He won't cause any trouble. If I left him outside, he'd be barking and blocking the door trying to get in."

The waitress, Tillie, bustled over, red hair flying, apron wrinkled, but a smile on her large freckled face. "Evening, folks. What can I get you?"

Branch shrugged and looked to Hugh, who ordered for the table. He didn't care much what he ate, as long as it was filling.

"I love your dress, Veronica. Did you make it yourself?" Etta asked.

"Oh no." Miss Palmer laughed, sounding a bit like a yipping coyote to Branch's way of thinking. "I'm hopeless with a needle. I have my clothes made for me, either in San Antonio when I can talk Daddy into making the trip, or by Miss Spanner when I can't."

Daddy. Did grown women call their fathers "Daddy"? Branch glanced at the dress, which he had to admit fit Miss Palmer well in all the right places to garner a fellow's attention. Her clothing allowance from her "daddy" would probably bankrupt Branch in a month.

The food arrived, steak and potatoes and beans. Branch's steak was just as he liked it, charred just short of burnt and tough enough to sole a boot.

Etta surveyed the table, and the minute Tillie left, she smiled at Branch. "Would you say grace, please?"

Branch's gut clenched. He hated praying out loud, especially in front of anyone he didn't know well. Etta knew this, but true to her nature, she was forever pushing him to "expand his horizons," as she put it. And he couldn't very well refuse. So he fell back on the Selkirk Grace, the one his father always said, a connection to his Scots roots and Robbie Burns, his father's favorite poet.

"Some hae meat and canna eat,
And some wad eat that want it,
But we hae meat and we can eat,
Sae let the Lord be Thanket!"

The Scots burr rolled off his tongue as he mimicked the accent he'd heard all his life. As he raised his head, Hugh smothered a smile, and Etta pursed her lips. A glance at Miss Palmer revealed a puzzled expression as she looked from one to another under her lashes. Finally, realizing that was all there was to the prayer, she lifted her chin.

Branch looked away, wishing he were anywhere else, when his eye was caught by a commotion at the entry.

The elder Miss Spanner swept into the room, wearing a hat even less practical than Miss Palmer's, clutching the arm of the town's lawyer, Harley P. Burton. She paused in the doorway, as if to be certain as many people as possible noticed her, before heading toward the table next to the one where Branch sat.

"I heard Harley got back this afternoon. He looks none the worse for his trip." Hugh picked up his knife and fork. "Evening, Harley. Miss Spanner."

"Captain. Mrs. Sterling." Harley ran his hand down his silk patterned vest. "Kilborn. Miss Palmer. Good to see you all."

He held out a chair for the dressmaker, and Branch flinched. He hadn't even noticed that the younger Miss Spanner was joining her sister and the lawyer. Her eyes, the color of a bluebird's wing, took in their table, the Sterlings, Miss Palmer, and finally lighted on him. Branch felt as if he'd been poked hard in the chest.

She was as pretty as he remembered. Not that he spent much time thinking about those things. But he wasn't blind, and it was his job to notice people. Harley held her chair for her, and she seated herself, more gracefully than her sister had.

Miss Palmer touched his arm, and he broke his look with Constance Spanner, only then realizing he had been staring.

"As I was saying, I spent a summer in Newport, and it was delightful. So many parties and beautiful homes. Coming home was a bit of a letdown. Nothing in Hartville can compare to the summer cottages of Newport. Unless it's El Regalo. Have you been out to the Seven Heart, Branch?"

Miss Palmer said his name as if they had been close friends for years, as though she was...caressing it or something. Branch shifted in his seat, all too aware that those at the next table could hear everything she said.

"Yes, ma'am." When he'd first arrived in Hartville, he'd met Bowie Hart and found a friend. Friends didn't come easily to Branch, but in Bowie, he found a kindred spirit. And Bowie had helped him hone Jack's tracking skills.

Hugh speared a piece of steak. "Branch, what did you find at the telegraph station? Any word?"

"Yep, but you're not going to like it." Branch drew the yellow paper from his vest pocket and passed it over. Hugh unfolded the page, scanned the contents, and grimaced. "The governor wants this ended, and soon."

Which was putting things mildly. The state leader wasn't any more satisfied with the results of their efforts to catch Cass Markham than the dressmaker. Ten outlaws killed or captured, with only four more on the loose, but it wasn't the successes folks remembered.

And it galled Branch too. For eleven months, Cass, Maggie, and Willie Markham had eluded capture. It had gone well beyond just a job for Branch. It was now a personal mission. Cass was mocking them, daring them to catch him, and thus far, they hadn't proven up to the task.

Branch ate doggedly, half listening to Veronica Palmer regale them with stories of her trip back East, which he gathered had occurred more than a decade ago, though she spoke as if it was only yesterday. Probably the highlight of her life. Did the woman ever stop talking?

All the while, he was aware of the party at the next table. Miss Spanner held court there, describing the minutiae of her life while Burton had been out of town. Constance sat quietly, eating little and saying less, but she watched—her dinner companions, out the window behind Branch, and the diners.

"You've said hardly a word, Branch." Veronica touched his arm again. "Aren't you having a nice time?"

Though he prided himself on always telling the truth, he couldn't very well in this instance, could he? That he'd rather be anywhere but here listening to her yammer about places he'd never been and didn't want to go?

"Yes, ma'am."

"Oh, now, that will never do. You must call me Veronica. After all, we're well beyond the formal stage now." She leaned into his arm, pressing against him in a way that made his heart kick up a notch and his skin crawl all at the same time.

His eyes met Constance's, and his collar tightened. Her gaze held no judgment, but he felt embarrassed all the same. The two women couldn't be more different. Veronica Palmer talked too loudly, flashed her father's wealth, and made sure everyone noticed her...and therefore him. Constance seemed to do nothing to draw attention to herself, and if anything looked as if she, too, would rather be somewhere else.

Jesse Rawlings came into the restaurant, making a straight line for their table. Great, just what Branch needed. When the boys found out he'd been at dinner with a single female, there would be no end to the ribbing. This was all Etta's fault, inviting Veronica to dinner right in front of him and giving him no way to escape. He should've gone against everything his ma had taught him and just been rude. Then he wouldn't be here now.

"Hey, Branch, glad I found you. Gage O'Reilly rode in with word that someone was camped out near Bowie Hart's place on the Sabinal. He only saw them from a distance, but he thought one of them looked like he might be Willie Markham. Said the man had a red mark under his right eye and wore a wideawake."

Branch reached for his hat and snapped his fingers for Jack to get out from under his chair. Relief coursed through him at this turn of events, both that someone reliable had made the report, and that he had a reason to leave the table. "How long ago did he see these fellows?" Markham sightings were common, though they seldom turned out to be true...unless a crime had occurred. Here was their chance to get ahead of Cass for once.

"Couple of hours at the most. I told him he was smart not to try to get any closer, and he said he had no more reason to want to die than the next man." Jesse touched the knife he kept strapped up his shirt sleeve.

"You're leaving?" Veronica's voice pierced the room, and all the diners went quiet.

"Duty calls, ma'am. I'm sure Hugh and Etta will see you home." He drew his fingers through his hair to smooth it back and settled his hat firmly on his head, trying not to convey his relief at escaping her company.

As he followed Jesse from the restaurant, he passed Constance, and she looked up at him with those big blue eyes, her lips pressed together in what, if he didn't know better, he might interpret as a bit of concern, as if she wanted him to be careful.

Stupid notion. He didn't know her, she didn't know him, and she couldn't possibly care about any danger he might be riding into.

He'd spent too much time in feminine company today. Time to get his mind back on the business at hand—finding and capturing Cass Markham.

CHAPTER 2

Constance was definitely a third wheel at this dinner. The change that had come over Clarice when Harley P. Burton had stepped through the dress shop doorway had to be seen to be believed. She went from starchy spinster to saucy simpleton in a trice. Here she sat, hanging on every word the lawyer said, touching his arm, batting her lashes. It was enough to make a person ill.

"I can't tell you how good it is to be home." Harley tucked his napkin deeper into his collar. He'd finished his supper and ordered dessert for them all—sour cream and raisin pie.

Constance didn't like sour cream and raisin pie, but she didn't want to appear ungracious. Checking the regulator clock on the wall, she toyed with her fork. When could she decently plead tiredness and let her sister and her beau be alone?

Not that she had wanted to come with them tonight at all. How embarrassing to be the dowdy sister who tagged along on a date. But they had insisted.

Laughter trilled from the next table, and Constance gritted her teeth. Veronica Palmer was practically drooling over Ranger

Kilborn. She hung on his arm to the point where he couldn't even eat his meal. That had to be good for his ego, if not his hunger. Didn't all men love a woman who fawned over them?

Constance jabbed the piece of pie the waitress set before her, savaging the crust. Why did she care? She had no claim on Branch Kilborn or anyone else, and she wanted none. Men were nothing but trouble every hour of the day. Look at where caring for someone had gotten her. And look at her sister, practically panting after Harley P. Burton for over a decade, but never getting him to the point of a proposal. How long were they going to be stuck in this courting phase, anyway? Constance would've demanded Harley make his intentions known, or she would've cut her losses and moved on. As she had with Pasquale...though that hadn't been voluntary on her part, but rather a necessity.

A bearded young man wearing a sidearm brushed past her and stopped at Branch Kilborn's side.

"Hey, Branch, glad I found you. Gage O'Reilly rode in with word that someone was camped out near Bowie Hart's place on the Sabinal. He only saw them from a distance, but he thought one of them looked like he might be Willie Markham. Said the man had a red mark under his right eye and wore a wideawake."

And just like that, Branch was on his feet and headed for the door, leaving an outraged Veronica calling out in his wake.

Harley excused himself for a moment and went to where the older couple and Veronica sat. He spoke for a few minutes in low tones, and with the other conversations swirling around the dining room, Constance couldn't make out his words.

When he returned, he shook his head. "That Markham Gang is a menace." He nodded to Constance. "That's the reason I was out of town for so long. I was appointed legal council for gang member Spyder Jackson, but his trial was over in San Antonio. It lasted for only two days, and he was found guilty, but I had to be there when they executed him, so I was gone for almost two weeks. I'll be glad when the rest of the gang is rounded up and incarcerated or hung."

"So you had to defend this man? What was his crime?" Constance poked at her slice of pie once more. All the interest had gone out of the dining room.

"Kidnapping, counterfeiting, horse thieving, stage robbing, rustling, you name it. If there's a crime to be done in the West, Spyder Jackson has done it. They arrested him for bank robbery here in Hart County, but he was wanted on murder charges over in San Antonio, so they extradited him to Bexar County."

He pronounced it "bear" county, with a Texas twang, and Constance reddened a bit. On her trip here from Shreveport, she'd mistakenly called it "Bex-ar: and been corrected by a stuffy old woman on the train.

"Still, most all the gang has been rounded up. Though the principals still elude the law. Cass Markham and his two younger siblings, Maggie and Willie. There might be one or two others still on the loose, but the Rangers have made things tough for the Markhams, picking them off by ones and twos over the last year. And they'll get the rest of them, I have no doubt." Harley scraped his pie plate with the edge of his fork, sending a shiver up Constance's spine.

She dabbed her lips with her napkin, having eaten none of the pie but having mangled it beyond recognition. "I believe I'll head over to the shop. I have a bit more work to do on the hat for Reverend Longley's wife, and I'd like to finish it up tonight in time to deliver it in the morning."

Clarice frowned. "I don't like the thought of you being in the shop alone at night. You remember what that Ranger said." She turned to Harley. "Ranger Kilborn marched into the store as big as life today and told us Mortenson's got robbed last night. He said we should keep the doors locked and not too much in the till. And not only that, but he brought his dog into the shop with him."

Constance didn't know what outraged her sister more, the robbery or the canine. She scooted back her chair and stood. "Not to worry, Clarice. I'll lock the door behind me. You can't see my workroom from the street, so no one will even know I'm there. Anyway"—she smiled at her sister—"you and Harley deserve a bit of time to yourselves. Goodnight."

Before they could protest further, she departed, drawing her shawl around her shoulders, thankful for its warmth. Stopping at the front desk, she pulled a few coins from her purse and left them with the desk clerk to pay for her meal and a little something extra for their waitress, Tillie.

That would have to be the end of her extravagance for a while, though. She was down to her last few dollars, and until she got paid for the hats she had made, she would need to be cautious with her funds.

Remembering Branch's warning, she locked the door to the dress shop behind herself and carefully made her way through the store. "Ouch!" She stopped to rub her knee, leaning against the counter she'd collided with. She should've lit a lamp. It would take her some time before she would be able to navigate the store in the dark the way she had been able to go through the carriage works and her office back home.

A pang struck her heart, but she shook her head. "None of that, my girl. You will not pine for that life, or that man."

She felt the glass knob on her workroom door, cool and faceted under her palm. The hinges squealed as she swung the door open, and she winced. Making a mental note to oil them in the morning, she felt for the top drawer where she kept the matches.

A sulfurous tang filled the air as she struck a match. Soon she had the room warmly lit, the glass lamps and bright reflectors dispelling the dark.

She put her hands on her hips, surveying the little work space, all her own. In the week she'd been in Hartville, she'd arranged the contents three times to get it just so.

Her little kingdom. Just what she needed to soothe the ache around her heart. A place where she could be creative without criticism, work without anyone peering over her shoulder. Clarice was happy to have her here and was already talking about making her a full partner in the shop.

Constance had been able to put her off for the time being. It was too soon to talk of anything permanent. She had spent the last four years as a secretary in a big carriage works in Shreveport, and that had ended badly. She needed time to heal and decide what it was she wanted.

Her evening's project lay on the workbench, half finished and looking a bit of a mess at the moment. Mrs. Longley had asked for a rouche-lined bonnet in the poke style, opting for verdigris fabric to bring out the green flecks in her hazel eyes.

Constance had selected a lovely charmeuse of the perfect shade, but the silky fabric was difficult to work with. Pulling her stool up to the bench, she picked up her needle and thread and began tucking and pin-stitching the lining to the inside of the brim.

No sounds came from the street in front of the store, though the back door of the hotel to the north slammed. Constance had found it difficult to get to sleep since her arrival in Hartville and finally pinned it down to things being too quiet. Her boarding-house room in Shreveport had overlooked one of the busiest streets in town, and there was always a hum of noise, even well after dark. At her sister's house, two blocks off the main thoroughfare, nothing could be heard but crickets and the wind in the trees.

"What you should get is a dog." She said the words aloud to dispel her sense of unease. But thoughts of a dog only reminded her of Branch Kilborn's friendly mutt, Jack. The Ranger had not only brought the animal into the dress shop today, but he'd allowed the dog to follow him into the restaurant and lie under his chair.

Constance giggled, remembering the outraged look on Veronica Palmer's face. If Veronica thought she would tame the Ranger, it was going to take more than simpering and fluttering and flattery, and it was going to take longer than one evening.

She worked on, losing track of the time as she neared completion of her project. Holding the bonnet up, she turned it in the lamplight. Now to add the ribbon ties, and she would be done. She looked at the small clock on the workbench, surprised to see the hands nearing midnight. Clarice would not approve. Still, Constance didn't like leaving a job unfinished. Just a few minutes more wouldn't make a big difference, not when she was already so late.

Something thumped the back wall of the dress shop, and Constance jumped, dropping the bonnet onto the workbench and knocking her spool of thread to the floor. What was that?

A scraping, banging sound came next, and a rattling of the back door's knob. Constance froze. Was it the robbers Branch had warned them about? Her breath stuck in her throat. What should she do? Should she call out, make some noise so they would know someone was here? Would that drive them off, or would that make them investigate?

She doused the two lamps and immediately regretted it when darkness pressed in around her. The smell of smoke and kerosene filled the air as the wicks glowed orange and then faded. Constance stood in the center of the room, the door open into the small hallway. If she went out and to the left, she would be in the shop, and if she went out and to the right, she would be at the back door.

And if she stood where she was, maybe whoever it was would just go away.

Then she heard a gasp, and a whimper, scuffling sounds. Was that a woman? Or a child? Someone in distress?

Constance was moving before she thought. She darted into the hallway, wincing when she nudged the workroom door and the hinges squeaked. She went to her right and crouched beneath the window in the back door. Her sister had hung a shirred-lace panel over the glass, and Constance raised herself up a few inches and drew the lace aside.

A figure crouched over something crumpled on the ground, about fifteen yards from the back of the dress shop. Though the moon had risen, it cast deep shadows, and Constance couldn't make out any details. Then the back door of the hotel opened again, lighting the alleyway behind the shop. The man straightened, his face briefly illuminated.

Constance had only an instant before the man leaped away from whatever was on the ground and disappeared around the corner of the closest building. Water splatted the dirt, and the hotel door slammed shut once more.

With fingers chilled through, she turned the key in the lock and eased the door open. Gaze darting everywhere, alert for trouble, she dashed across the alleyway to the mound on the ground. When she reached her objective, she knelt, atremble.

It was a woman, skirts tangled, hair a shawl of brown across her face.

"Miss?" Constance shook her shoulder, but she expected no response and got none. The woman's head lay at an odd angle, her eyes staring through the tangle of hair, a trickle of blood coming from the corner of her mouth.

She was dead.

~

Branch clenched and relaxed his fists, waiting for Jesse to finish questioning the drummer. Their ride out to Bowie Hart's place had been a washout. There were signs of a campfire, but nothing else. The only information they gleaned was that it appeared to be a single rider, not a gang, who had stopped for a day or so along the river.

When they'd returned to town, there had been a note closed into the Ranger office front door. Ed from over at the depot reporting that a traveling salesman had gotten off the train tonight claiming that he'd seen Cass Markham in Uvalde outside the bank. They'd tracked down the man at Miss Ruthy's Saloon. But the interview was proving fruitless because the man was quickly on his way to being falling-down drunk.

Branch consulted the small notebook he carried. "You're saying a man matching Cass Markham's description was on the street outside the First Bank of Texas in Uvalde at ten o'clock this morning?"

"Yep." The drummer, Walter Coffey, tie loose around his neck, suit coat open, and collar unbuttoned, threw back his whiskey and tapped the bar for a refill. "Looked just like his...pit'cher on the... wanted poster." A shout rose from the faro table, and poker chips and glasses clinked. The place was jumping, and cigar smoke hung in a hazy cloud near the ceiling. Branch glanced at the door. If only he could head out into the clear air.

Jack sat on Branch's boot, leaning against his leg, looking up as if to say, "When can we get out of here?"

Soon, I hope. Branch rubbed the dog's head.

"Why didn't you alert the sheriff in Uvalde?" Jesse asked.

"If I had done that, I wudda mished my train." Coffey drained his shot glass again, his eyes unfocused. "Can't mish my appointments with the good"—he smothered a belch— "merchants of Hartville."

"What is it you're selling?" Jesse asked.

Hopefully, headache powders because the man was going to have a blue-ribbon-winning hangover in the morning.

"Haber...dashery." He toed the bulky case on the floor beside him. "The finest in men's accessories." He reached out to poke Branch in the chest, but Branch leaned back, causing the man to miss. "Say, you could use a bit of sprucing up. I have the best... starched collars, pershonal...linens..." He blinked and swallowed. "And shaving equipment, which, if you will pardon me for saying so...you could shuuure ushe."

Branch flipped the notebook closed. The man was too drunk to hit the ground with a hat. "C'mon, Jack." He headed toward the door, having to weave around a rowdy bunch of cowboys. Jack trotted at his side, and Jesse traveled in his wake. They had just reached the entrance when Giles Brown, Hartville's resident carpenter, entered, pushing aside the batwing doors.

He put his hand on Branch's arm, and Jack let out a low growl. The woodworker jerked his hand back, eyeing the dog. "No offense. I been looking for you. You better come." He kept his voice low so as not to attract attention.

"What is it?" Branch followed him out onto the street, taking his first deep breath in too long.

"There's been a killing."

Branch stopped walking. "What?" He hadn't heard a gunshot, though the saloon had been so noisy, a cannon could've gone off in the next building and gone unnoticed. "Where?"

"Behind the dress shop. A woman's been murdered."

Branch's heart kicked like a mustang, and he took off for the dress shop. He was halfway down the street before he realized he had immediately thought of Constance. He'd only met her the one time and seen her once after that, and she was the first person he thought of?

Ducking into the alley between *The Hartville Herald* and the dress shop, he came upon a group of folks gathered around a figure on the ground.

"Stand back." Perfect. More than a dozen folks trampling the scene. "Get back, folks." Branch shouldered his way through to the victim, not wanting to see the hat maker...or her sister, for that matter, but doing what the job required.

Jesse came behind him, guiding people back.

Branch took a lantern from Big Joe, the livery stable owner, and squatted beside the body. His first thought was relief. The woman had brown hair. It couldn't be Constance. Constance had golden hair.

Still, he shouldn't be so relieved. This was someone's daughter, someone's sister, maybe? Someone's wife or mother? He brushed the hair off her face.

This part of the job never got any easier.

"Anybody know who she is?"

Big Joe bent at the waist, planting his massive hands on his knees. "Why, it's Mollie Olson."

Branch shook his head, looking up at Big Joe. "Who?"

"She was one of the girls who worked at Miss Ruthy's. Used to be a real nice kid. Once upon a time, she worked for Doc Hart, cleaning his office and showing people in. Her pa had a place a few miles south of town, but he never made much of it. Died a few years back. That's when Mollie took up the sportin' life, I guess." Joe scrubbed his hand down his face, his eyes wide in the lantern light. "Poor kid. Never had no breaks."

A working girl murder. That complicated things. It was a dangerous profession, and the suspect pool had just grown very large.

"Jesse, get these onlookers back. Clear the alley. Start asking questions, see if anyone saw anything. Giles"—Branch searched for the carpenter—"better go get the undertaker, and send someone for Doc Hart too. I want him to examine the body."

"I'm here." Dr. Travis Hart approached, his black bag gripped in his fist. "Is it true? Is it Mollie?"

Branch held the lantern over the woman, and Dr. Hart nodded, his face sad.

"I tried so hard to get her out of that life. Why wouldn't she listen to me?" The anguish in his voice had the onlookers backing up, whispering behind their hands.

"I know it's hard, Doc, but I need you to focus. The sooner I get some answers, the sooner we can catch who did this." Branch scanned the crowd. Sometimes it paid to see who showed up to watch.

One familiar figure strode toward him, working his way through the growing number of spectators. "What do you have, Branch?" Hugh Sterling rested one hand on his sidearm, smoothing his moustache with the other.

"Sporting girl. Broken neck. She's still warm, so it happened not too long ago."

"This should be the local sheriff's jurisdiction, but since he's laid up, I suppose it's up to us." Hugh sighed.

The doctor bent over the body for a moment and then called for a blanket so some men could carry her over to his office.

"With so many folks milling around, there's no trail to follow, nothing to put Jack on the scent of." Branch smacked his notebook into his hand and stuffed it into his pocket. "I guess we'll have to see if the doc can tell us anything from examining the corpse."

Jesse nudged Branch's elbow. "Might not be necessary. I found us a witness. She heard the killing take place, but I haven't questioned her yet. She said she only wanted to talk to you."

Hugh's head snapped up, and Branch sharpened his focus. "Me? Who is it?"

"Miss Spanner."

Branch put his hand on Jesse's shoulder. "Which one?"

Something in his tone caught Jesse's attention, and he raised his eyebrows. "Um, the pretty one?"

Rolling his eyes, Branch shook his head. "Why didn't she give a statement to you?"

"She seems awful shook up about it all. Not that you can blame her—a murder happening right outside her door. I asked her what she knew, but she wouldn't say. She just wanted to speak to you." Jesse grinned. "Wonder what that's about."

Branch shrugged. "Probably because I met her earlier today when Hugh had us warning the shopkeepers." He felt in his hip pocket for his notebook and pencil. "Where is she, and what was she doing out and about this late?"

"She's in the dress shop. And I don't know. As I said, she wouldn't talk to me."

"Go see what she has to say," Hugh said. "We'll finish here and come find you."

Branch nodded, but he wished Constance Spanner had asked for anyone else but him. He wasn't entirely comfortable around women, and women shaken up by violence were apt to be skittish.

He opened the back door to the dress shop, easing inside with Jack. "Miss Spanner?"

Light came from the workroom doorway, and he closed the door behind himself.

"In here." Her voice sounded small.

She sat next to her workbench, the surface still strewn with ribbons and furbelows.

"Ma'am, Jesse said you wanted to speak to me."

Her hand trembled as she brushed back a spiraling curl, and for a ridiculous moment, Branch wondered if it was as soft and silky as it looked. She wrapped her arms across her middle as if she was cold, though Branch felt the room was plenty warm.

"I saw him." The words were barely a whisper.

Her blue eyes were wide as a child's as she stared into space, and Branch had an odd wanting to put his arms around her and tell her it would be all right. Which was utter nonsense. He'd never entertained such a foolish notion in his life before. What was it about this woman?

To stay his wayward thoughts, he squatted in front of her, catching her gaze and holding it. "Tell me what happened. Start at the beginning."

He looked steadily into her eyes, keeping his tone firm, willing her to concentrate. She seemed to gather herself, her features tightening.

"I was finishing up an order when I heard a noise at the back door." Succinctly, she led him up to the moment she pulled aside the lace curtain. "He sounded like the man I overheard you speaking of at the restaurant. The wideawake brim on his hat, tall, young..." Her throat worked, and she gripped her hands in her lap. "He had a scar under his right eye. Thick and red, as though it hadn't been there long."

Willie Markham. It had to be him.

CHAPTER 3

Constance jabbed the pin into the pincushion on her workbench and shoved back her chair. She checked the hat she had been working on once more before settling it into a tissue paper nest inside the striped hatbox. *Spanner's* in gold lettering decorated the top. Clarice never did anything by halves, and that included her signature packaging.

"I tell you, it was the most dreadful thing. A murder, not twenty feet from our back door." Her sister's words filled the shop. "I can still scarcely believe it."

This had to stop. It had been the same all week. Every customer who came in was regaled with everything Clarice Spanner knew about the killing and the culprit. Constance regretted telling her anything, though Clarice had insisted on being present when Constance went over her story again with the Rangers when they came back to question her.

It was bad enough to have to relive that night over and over in her head, but to have to listen to it secondhand every few minutes was worse. Even Mr. Barth from *The Hartville Herald* had been by looking for a story while Constance had been out of the shop. Clarice had given him enough to fill the entire front page.

Constance pinned on her own hat, a brown velvet affair with a grosgrain bow in the back, and picked up her reticule and the hatbox, stepping out of the workroom and down the short hall to the showroom.

Veronica Palmer sat in one of the pink upholstered chairs reserved for waiting clients, sipping a cup of tea. "It's just awful. I'm glad the Rangers caught the killer quickly. Stupid man, hiding in the baggage room at the depot. I suppose he was trying to hop the first train out of town. He'd have been better off stealing a horse from the livery and running. And I heard he was pie-eyed drunk too!"

Constance had been required to go to the jail and identify the man as the one she saw that night. He had been smug and defiant, raking his gaze over her, leering. A shiver went through her at the memory. How thankful she'd been that Branch had been there, and that a wall of iron bars separated her from Willie Markham.

Clarice picked up her teacup. "There's quite a crowd around the jailhouse, trying to get a look at him. And I heard there are as many as five Rangers posted as guards at any one time." She was dining on her favorite food—rich gossip.

"I know. It's just been impossible. I haven't even seen Branch to talk to him, he's been so busy." Veronica pursed her lips in a pout. "I had that man hanging on my every word at dinner the other night, and then, *bang*, he had to leave."

Constance cleared her throat. "Pardon me. Clarice, I am going to deliver an order to Mrs. Mortenson. Is there anything you need at the mercantile?"

Clarice looked up as if surprised at her appearance. "I forgot you were back there. You're so quiet. No, there's nothing I need, though if you run into Ardith Dagg, tell her she can come pick up her new dress. I finished it this morning."

When had her sister found the time, what with informing all and sundry of the murder? Constance let herself out of the dress shop, hurrying past *The Hartville Herald* offices, trying to ignore the front page the editor had placed in the front window declaring, *Willie Markham Arrested for Murder of Local Woman—Eyewitness to Appear at Trial.*

Two ladies stopped at the window, and Constance had to tuck the hatbox close to get around them. She didn't intend to eavesdrop, but she couldn't help overhearing their comments.

"I think Clarice Spanner is right. The place is overrun with Texas Rangers, but a murder happened practically under their noses and they didn't stop it." The taller of the two jerked her chin.

"Oh, Hattie, how could they have prevented this? After all, the victim was a saloon girl." The shorter juggled her packages. "I thought you liked all the Rangers. You've certainly spent enough time mooning over them."

"Edith Partridge, I hereby rescind every nice thing I said about them. I know when they hit town, I was the first to hope they were the answers to the prayers of many a maiden of Hartville. And so it's proven, with all of them finding brides, but now that Branch Kilborn is the only one left, no thanks you."

Constance halted at the mention of Branch.

"But he's so handsome."

"So is a cougar, but that doesn't mean I want one near me." Hattie shuddered. "A woman would be a fool to fall for a man like Branch Kilborn. He's completely undomesticated."

"Still, it takes a hard man to catch hard men, and I for one," Edith declared, "am glad he's here. Without him, Willie Markham would still be running free, terrorizing and killing. And maybe the next time, it would be decent folks, not just some sporting woman from one of the brothels."

Mollie Olson. That poor woman. Regardless of her occupation, she deserved to be remembered with dignity. As for the two women's opinions of Branch Kilborn...they weren't wrong. He was handsome, but there was an aura of danger about him, something that fascinated Constance but made her wary all the same.

Odd to feel both safe and at risk when she was near him. Still, it wouldn't matter since they would have little to do with one another, surely.

A crowd of about twenty men stood in front of the jailhouse, just as Veronica Palmer had claimed, and Constance frowned. Her destination, Mortenson's Mercantile, lay on the far side of the jail.

"Bring him on out here! We'll show him how swift Texas justice can be!" a man shouted from the back of the group.

"Yeah, I've got a brand-new rope with his name on it." Folks jostled and yelled, raising their fists. Constance got bumped, forcing her to stagger to keep her feet.

"You bring him out, or we'll come in after him," someone threatened.

Constance could feel the menace from the men pressing ever closer to the jail. The door swung open, and someone came out.

"You boys need to stand down."

A shiver went up her spine, and she stood on tiptoe to see over the crowd. She knew that voice. Constance edged sideways to get a better view.

Branch Kilborn stood at the door, his rifle held crossways in his arms. He closed the jail door behind himself and leaned against it. The older Ranger, Captain Sterling, stood at Branch's elbow, his hand resting on his sidearm.

The captain's eyes bored into the assembly. "Go about your business, gentlemen. We've got things under control. The circuit judge will be here soon, and we'll have us a nice, fair trial, and most likely, not long afterwards, a first-class hanging." The captain ran his thumb along the left side of his moustache. "We're doing this by the book, and that means no lynch mob. I'd hate to have to arrest anyone today, and I know none of you want to be sharing jail space with the likes of Willie Markham."

"How do we know you can hold him this time? He's busted out of jail before."

"Don't you worry. Willie Markham's guarded around the clock, and he'll stand trial in the courthouse over yonder. After that, it will be up to the judge and jury to decide his fate."

Branch hadn't said another word, just looked from one face to the next, leaving no one in doubt as to his intentions regarding a lynch mob. The men he stared at backed up a step or two and stared at the ground, shuffling their feet. When his eyes finally met Constance's, they stopped, holding her look for a long moment.

Constance was the first to turn away, needing to breathe after the intensity in his expression. She hurried to the mercantile, clutching the hatbox as the crowd behind her dispersed. It seemed as if she could feel Branch's eyes on her the entire way.

By the time she returned to the dress shop, the jail door was closed and nobody blocked the boardwalk. Her sister stood in front of the shelf of poplins, her tape measure dangling around her neck, her pincushion tied to her wrist, chatting with a customer.

"And there he was, right in the light from the hotel's back door, standing over the body. It's enough to make the blood freeze in your veins." Clarice clutched her hand to her chest.

The woman listened raptly, her dark eyes glittering. There was a...hardness...to her features that sent a frisson of unease through Constance. She looked calculating.

Stop that. Next thing you know, you'll have an attack of the vapors. Constance went through to her workroom and hung up her hat. The woman was probably a very nice person, and there was no need to act like a timid cat.

"I'm new in town. Do you have a recommendation for where I

should stay? Is there a boardinghouse that takes women traveling alone?"

Constance lingered in her workroom, half listening as Clarice gave her opinion of the various lodging establishments in town. "I have a house, thank goodness, over on Pecan. The only yard with a proper picket fence on the whole street. My Harley helped me buy it, saw to all the legal work. He's the town lawyer, you know. Has his offices right across the street there. He's the one who will be prosecuting that ruffian Willie Markham. Why, that murder happened right outside the back door here. Can you imagine? I'm so grateful that another of that viscous Markham Gang is behind bars."

With a shudder, Constance pinched the bridge of her nose, wishing Clarice would stop talking about the killing to every person who walked through the door. The scene outside the jail had shaken Constance more than she wanted to admit. In the back of her mind, she had known that being a Ranger, or being any kind of a peace officer, was a dangerous business, but to see it firsthand... She had no doubt that if those men had rushed the jail, Branch would've stood his ground and either been forced to kill someone or been killed. He would not have willingly turned his prisoner over to a lynch mob.

A woman would be a fool to let herself care for a man who could be shot at any moment of the day.

Late that evening, Constance rolled over in her bed, tugging the patchwork quilt one way and then another, unable to get comfortable. Her mind wouldn't slow down, hopping from one thought to another. No, that wasn't true. She kept returning to Branch. Which was confusing. She barely knew the man, and hadn't she vowed less than a month ago that she would never let her head be turned by another handsome male?

Branch couldn't be more different from Pasquale. Her former fiancé had been civilized, suave, and sophisticated.

And a complete rat.

Under that dashing façade had been nothing but rottenness.

So what might be lurking beneath Branch's rough-hewn façade? He projected an aura of leashed power, of strength, of... aloneness. In spite of his blunt manners, he exuded integrity and honesty. You would take him as he was, or not at all.

Stop it. Go to sleep, you ninny. Even if you were looking for love—which you are most definitely not!*—Branch Kilborn would never look your way.*

Constance bunched her pillow and slammed her eyes shut, determined that she would fall asleep.

She must've dozed off, because a crash awakened her. Bolting upright in her bed, her heart slammed into her throat.

Something thudded against the bedroom wall, and a scream ripped through the air, quickly muffled.

Swinging her feet over the side of the bed, her nightgown tangled with the sheets, and she nearly fell. Grasping the edge of her bedside table, she kicked free of the bedding and hurried to the door.

Opening it a crack, she spied lantern light flickering in her sister's bedroom doorway. A large figure in a wide-brimmed hat stood in the opening, facing away from Constance.

"If you testify at that trial, I'll come back and do worse. Do you understand?"

Several quick slaps, and a sob that could only be Clarice. Constance cast about her room for a weapon of some sort, but nothing came to hand. Finally, she snatched up her black silk umbrella, the one with the steel ferrule and heavy handle.

Her umbrella at the ready, she opened her door. The big man whirled, his gun drawn, a bandana covering the lower half of his face. A jolt of fear shot through her. His eyes glittered in the lantern light. "Well, what have we here?" The rasp of his voice grated across her skin, and she became very aware that she was standing in her nightgown.

"Who's there, Curly?" a male voice called from her sister's room.

"A girl."

"I told you to check the house. Get her in here!" The voice thundered, and the man with the gun snatched at Constance's arm, dragging her into Clarice's bedroom. Her sister huddled on the bed, bleeding from a cut lip, her eye swelling. She held her arms across her ribs, eyes shut tight, sobbing.

Constance struggled against the big man's grip, swinging her umbrella and whacking him on the head. He yelped, let go of her arm, and grabbed the parasol as she arched back to hit him again.

"Knock it off." He growled, jerking the umbrella from her hand and slinging it into the corner of the room. He swung again and backhanded her across the cheek, sending her crashing into the doorframe. Pain shot through her head and the right side of her body where she impacted the wall, and her knees wobbled.

"Enough."

Constance froze at the sound of a woman's voice.

She stood in the corner of the bedroom, observing what the men were doing but not taking part. She, too, wore a bandana over half her face, but Constance recognized those eyes. It was the woman who had come into the store today asking about rooms for rent.

The big man resumed his place in the doorway, trapping Constance in the room. The second man leaned menacingly over Clarice, fisting his hand into her hair and jerking her head back. "You hear me? You testify at that trial, and we'll come back and kill you." He shoved her head back, cracking it against the headboard. Clarice's tear-filled eyes rolled upward, and she sagged onto the mattress, knocked senseless.

"Why don't we just kill 'em now and be done with it?" The one called Curly snarled.

"Too much killing. Bad enough Willie killed that saloon girl. We start murdering regular women, none of our friends will hide us. All Pa's contacts will disown us. We'll be out of business quicker than you can shoot."

Then the man turned to Constance.

"I don't know who you are, but you tell her when she wakes up. Tell her not to testify. You hear me?"

Cheek still throbbing, eyes watering with the pain, Constance nodded. Somehow these people had confused her with her sister, had thought Clarice was the one who had witnessed the killing and would be called upon to tell what she saw in court.

The woman in the corner strode past Constance, and the big man with the wild eyes scrambled to get out of her way. She didn't look at Constance, acting as if she wasn't even there. The man who had been hurting her sister paused, assessing Constance, and then he winked, chucking her under the chin like a child. She recoiled from his touch, and he laughed.

With a slam of the front door, they were gone.

~

Pounding on the front door had Branch hopping up from the desk where he had been poring over his notebooks from eleven months of chasing and capturing Markham Gang members. Jack's nails clicked as he trotted to the door, lowering his head and letting out a whine.

Branch unholstered his gun and drew aside the blind hanging in the window of the front door. Griff stood on the boardwalk, and Branch unlocked the door and let him in. "What's happened?" Hopefully, not another murder. The town would ignite. Things were tense enough at the moment, and several of the townsfolk were just looking for something to set them off.

Griff jerked his head. "Captain Sterling needs you. There's been a dust up at the Spanner house. A break-in. Clarice Spanner got roughed up. Don't know about her sister." He reached down to pat Jack.

Branch was out the door and jogging up the street when he remembered that he didn't know where the Spanner sisters lived. He stopped, and Griff came up behind him. "Pecan Street. House with the picket fence. Tell the captain I'm heading back to guard duty at the jail."

What could've happened now? In nearly a year in Hartville, Branch hadn't encountered the dressmaker more than a handful of times...none of which had been particularly pleasant...but in the last week, he found himself crossing her trail over and over.

And thinking about the sister way too much.

When Branch turned onto Pecan, the house was lit up, and the front door stood open. Jack didn't wait for an invitation, trotting through the gate as if he owned the place. Branch followed more slowly, noting the broken lock on the door. His gut muscles tightened, and his hand went to his sidearm as he walked into the front room.

The parlor was crammed with furniture and little tables and shelves of bric-a-brac. An overstuffed settee, glass-globed lamps, fussy lace on the backs and arms of the chairs. The place reeked of spinster.

Voices came from down the hall, and he headed that way. Hugh stood in a bedroom doorway, and Branch nudged him. "What happened?" He leaned to get a better view of the room, looking for Constance.

She sat on the far side of a bed, her yellow hair tumbled down her back. Something in his chest eased and tightened all at the same time. She was all right.

And mighty pretty.

Her sister lay in the bed, and Doc Hart bent over her.

Hugh jerked his head toward the back of the house. "Let's talk in the kitchen."

Constance rose and came with them, her housecoat tied around her waist, but her feet bare. She looked younger, more vulnerable, than Branch remembered, her eyes wide, face pale.

He spotted the reddening bruise on her cheekbone. "Somebody tell me what's going on here."

Hugh went to the stove and pulled a coffeepot toward the front. "Miss Spanner, tell Branch what you told me."

She gripped her upper arms as if she was chilled, her eyes downcast as she described the three intruders. When she mentioned a woman, Branch's eyes collided with Hugh's, and the captain nodded.

"They must've thought Clarice was their witness. She's done nothing but talk about the murder all week with everyone who came into the store, including that woman who was here tonight. I recognized her voice, and her eyes. She was in the store today asking questions." Constance's voice sounded small. "This is my fault. Poor Clarice. They beat her terribly. They said if she testified, they'd come back and kill her. Though they meant me, of course."

"It had to be Markham. Cass and Maggie, from the sounds of it. And the big guy, he had to be Curly LaFever. They were all right here." Branch's hands fisted. Witness intimidation. That sounded about right for what Markham would do. He couldn't get to Willie in the jail, so he was going to sabotage the trial. "We should fan out, see if we can pick up a trail." Branch snapped his fingers, and Jack's ears perked up.

"We'll do that. But I have another task in mind for you, Branch." Hugh took coffee cups from their hooks under the cupboard. "I'm putting you in charge of the Spanner sisters' protection. Until the trial, you don't leave their side."

Branch made it a point never to argue with his commanding officer, but this was too much. Babysit witnesses when his quarry was so near? Though he wanted to protest the assignment, he wouldn't do so in front of Constance.

"Constance!" The wail came from down the hall. She raised her chin, looked long at Branch, and then hurried from the room to answer her sister's call.

"I know." Hugh sipped his coffee. "I know you'd rather be beating the bushes looking for Cass and Maggie, but here's the thing. You're the best suited to protect her. The boys and I can scout around for Markham and guard the jail, but I think it would be better to get Constance out of town until the trial. You can pick up and go right now in the middle of the night, and you don't have to worry about anyone else. You can focus on the job."

"What you're saying is, I'm still single, and the rest of the boys are married or close to it. I knew this would happen. Rangering and women don't mix." He held up his hand. "Don't start, Hugh. The boys have been distracted every which way by women since we started this manhunt. Otherwise, it wouldn't have taken us nearly a year to whittle the Markham Gang down to just three left on the loose."

A commotion came from the front of the house, and Jack left to investigate. When Branch and Hugh got to the bedroom door, a disheveled Harley Burton had burst into the room. His nightshirt had been stuffed half into his trousers, and long strands of his combed-over hair ran amok on his head.

"Oh, my dearest. Clarice, are you badly hurt? I came as soon as I heard." He knelt beside the bed, pushing Doc Hart out of the way and clasping Miss Spanner's hand to his chest. "Oh, my dearest, I nearly lost you. I'm beside myself. Please, say you will marry me and never leave me again."

Everyone in the room froze. It was common knowledge around Hartville that Clarice Spanner had been after Harley Burton for more than a decade without bringing him to the point of a proposal.

Constance raised her hand to cover her mouth, and Doc Hart stopped stuffing instruments and bandages into his bag. Even Jack plopped onto his rear, his head cocked to the side.

"What did you say?" Clarice winced as she straightened against her pillows, pressing her hand against her ribs.

"Marry me, dearest Clarice." Harley looked like a hail-struck calf.

Branch half turned away, not wanting to see the pair in a clinch declaring their eternal love.

"No."

"No?"

Everyone in the room but Branch said the word aloud.

Clarice Spanner, her hair in a brown-and-gray braid lying like a shotgun on her shoulder, crossed her arms and shook her head. One eye was nearly swollen shut, her lip had been split open, and she moved as if she'd busted a couple of ribs. "Harley P. Burton, how dare you come barging into my bedroom in the middle of the night declaring your intentions to finally marry me when I'm lying in bed looking like I went ten rounds with a prize fighter? I'm cut and bruised, and I'm in my nightgown, and this is the time you choose to propose?"

Her indignation would've stripped wallpaper. Harley gulped and eased back a few inches.

"Well, I'm not having it," she continued. "You will wait until the proper time, when I am healed up, when I'm feeling better and wearing my best dress. You'll take me out for a romantic dinner and drive, and you'll bring some flowers and a ring, by sugar. You'll not do me out of a proper proposal by being a dramatic ninny."

Harley gaped like a landed trout. Clarice looked righteous, even in her battered state, and Branch didn't envy Harley a bit.

"Doc, can Miss Clarice be moved?" Hugh broke the silence. "We don't want them staying here at their house alone."

Doc Hart snapped his bag shut. "I'd like to take Clarice out to El Regalo. Perla can look after her, and the place is always busy with ranch hands."

Hugh nodded. "Miss Constance, pack a bag for yourself and one for your sister. We'll see you out to El Regalo while it's still dark."

Constance shook her head. "There isn't any need. We can stay here. Just put out the word that the witness won't testify. Get it in the paper. I have no intention of putting Clarice in further danger. You'll have to convict that man without my help."

What could Branch do? His instincts told him to toss her over his shoulder and get her out of town, and then try to talk some sense into her. Her face told him she would not appreciate being coerced.

Doc Hart solved the problem, at least temporarily. "I'm taking Clarice to El Regalo where she can be safe and looked after. Gather what you need, and if one or more of you gentlemen would like to accompany us, I'm sure we'd appreciate it." He nodded to Branch. "Clarice has had quite a traumatic experience, and she needs rest and attention if she's to recover fully. Harley, I'm sure she would appreciate if you called on her tomorrow or the next day." At this, Clarice beamed, and Constance's shoulders drooped. She opened a bureau drawer and began assembling belongings to take along.

Branch had to hand it to Doc. He was one smart fella when it came to dealing with women.

CHAPTER 4

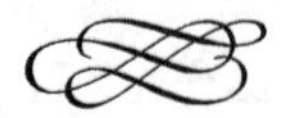

Constance woke early on Sunday morning, staring at the plaster medallion on the ceiling as sunlight crept over the horizon. Her sister lay in the next bed, breathing deeply. Slipping from between the sheets, Constance dressed quickly and quietly, not wanting to rouse her sister.

Moving her right arm and shoulder made her wince, and when she looked in the beveled glass mirror, she grimaced and touched the bruise swelling on her cheekbone.

Clarice let out a moan as she turned over in bed. "Oh, I hurt everywhere."

Constance went to her sister's side. "Is there anything I can do for you?"

"Yes. Tell me you won't testify." She let out a sniffle, and Constance reached for the handkerchief on the bedside table and put it in her sister's hand. "Promise me." She'd begged the same thing over and over last night before finally falling asleep.

"I told Branch I wouldn't testify. I won't put you in further danger." And she wouldn't. If she had kept her mouth shut, not given Clarice so many of the details, her sister wouldn't have been able to spill them to all and sundry. Or if Constance had somehow been able to impress upon Clarice that she shouldn't talk so much...but that was water over the dam. Her only concern now was not putting Clarice in further danger.

Someone tapped on the door, and Constance went to open it. The housekeeper who had shown them to their room last night stood in the hallway with a tray.

"I have brought you breakfast." Her lined face smiled gently. Behind her, a younger woman carried another tray. And behind her, Branch sat in a chair just outside the door. Had he been there all night? Guarding them?

Constance blushed for some odd reason when their eyes met. She'd never had anyone be so protective of her.

Not that it was personal, of course. It was his job. And from what she had gathered, he took his job very seriously.

She stepped back to allow the housekeeper into the room, and Branch brought his chair legs down and stood. "When you're ready, we need to talk." He adjusted his gun belt. "Downstairs. Alone."

His expression brooked no argument, though she wished she didn't have to face him. He would try to talk her into testifying, and she would have to resist. Her sister's life was at stake, not to mention her own. If it was just her, she might risk it, but she couldn't do that to Clarice.

As they finished their breakfast, the sound of horses' hooves on the drive had her peering out the window, anxiety tensing her neck muscles.

"Dr. Hart is here." She forced herself to relax. "And he's brought Harley with him."

"Oh, dear. Help me. I must look a fright." Clarice began to fuss. "Don't let them in until I'm ready."

By the time she let the doctor in, Constance was exhausted. Worry sapped her energy, and the late night and restless sleep began to wear on her. But Dr. Hart had good news for them. He didn't feel Clarice had broken any ribs, just bruised them badly. The swelling had begun to go down in her face, and in a couple of weeks' time, she should be as good as new.

Constance walked Dr. Hart downstairs, allowing Harley into the room to see Clarice.

"I'd like to speak with you for a moment," Dr. Hart said. "Come into the office, and I'll take a look at that eye of yours."

"I'm fine, really. Just a bit of a bruise."

"Let me look, anyway. Satisfy my doctor curiosity." He guided her into a high-ceilinged room dominated by a massive desk and bookshelves. "This is where my father and Austin run the Seven Heart empire." He chuckled. "At least, they run it as much as they can with seven ranches and seven bosses." He told her briefly about how, more than a dozen years before, his father had laid down an ultimatum that all his sons must marry within the calendar year or be disinherited. "And we did too. Every last one of us."

He guided her to a leather chair that creaked when she sat, and he took the chair opposite her, turning her face to the light from the windows to examine her eye. "I heard you tell the Rangers last night that you weren't going to testify against Willie Markham."

She stiffened, but he smiled. "I'm not going to try to argue you into changing your mind. I just wanted to tell you a story. You see, I knew Mollie Olson, the woman who was killed. I've known her since she was a child. When she was about fifteen, I gave her a job at my office, cleaning, organizing, showing patients in." He smiled, but his eyes were sad. "She was a bright little thing, always talking, always wanting to learn. She dreamed of going to college one day, becoming, as she put it, 'a real nurse.'"

Constance twisted her fingers in her lap. "What happened?"

"Life, I suppose. Annie—that's my wife—and I wanted to

adopt her, take her into our home, but her father, who was a lazy, mean man, refused to let her go. We offered to pay for her to go to nursing school and to employ her when she finished, but she wouldn't accept. When her father died and left two siblings for her to support, she quit working for me and went to Miss Ruthy's instead. She was a grown woman and said she could make more money there than she would make working for me, though I tried, and my wife tried several times, to get her out of that lifestyle."

"What happened to her siblings?"

"They're grown now. The brother works for the railroad, and the sister lives in San Antonio. But even when they left home, Mollie wouldn't quit. Said she had ruined her reputation and nobody would have her as a nurse now. She felt trapped, I'm sure, by her choices and her lack of choices." He rubbed his hand down his face. "Whatever she was, she didn't deserve to be killed. And her killer doesn't deserve to go free, to possibly kill again. If there's no justice for Mollie, then there is no justice for our society, for Hartville. Her story deserves to be told. She deserves justice."

Guilt pressed hard on Constance, but uncertainty too. "But what about what those men did? What about what they threatened? How can I testify and put Clarice in danger?"

Dr. Hart leaned forward and took her hand, pressing her fingers, asking her without words to look him in the eye. "You've been put into the care and keeping of Branch Kilborn and the Texas Rangers. I'd back his play any day of the week. You can trust him. Trust him to keep you safe, and trust him to deal with the Markhams."

Trust. She had little trust these days for any man, not after what Pasquale had done to her. But did she have any other choice but to put her safekeeping into the hands of Branch Kilborn?

Branch knocked on the half-open door and came in. "Miss Spanner, we need to talk."

He'd rolled up his sleeves, exposing his forearms, and his gun rode low on his hip. Everything about him spoke of capability and strength. "I think we should leave El Regalo. Your sister should stay here, but I'd like to get you out. There are too many people in and out of this place, and GW tells me the entire clan will be coming for Sunday dinner." He looked to Dr. Hart, who nodded.

"Sunday tradition. There are more than fifty of us, if everyone comes."

"That's too many. I'm taking Constance out of here. I'll hide her away until the morning of the trial. Hugh will post someone, probably Whit, here at El Regalo to watch over Miss Clarice. And I want it spread far and wide that Miss Clarice is refusing to testify. Which won't matter, since she's not a witness, anyway. But Markham thinks she is, and I'd just as soon have him feeling like he accomplished his mission by roughing her up."

"You're assuming I'll still testify?" Constance stood, and Dr. Hart rose as well, the epitome of good manners.

Branch shrugged. "If you do or if you don't, it's still my job to protect you."

He made it sound as if he didn't care one way or the other, but she sensed that he did.

All Dr. Hart had said about Mollie tumbled around in her mind, as well as the fear and anger and violation she felt at those people breaking into her house and attacking her and her sister. She would have to live the rest of her life knowing she had been a coward...again. Instead of staying and fighting for the truth, she would have run away again.

Well, not this time.

"Very well. I will testify, if you can assure me my sister will be safe." She straightened her shoulders.

"She'll be guarded around the clock," he promised. "Pack light. Enough for four days."

"Where are we going?"

"You'll see when we get there. I'll go saddle the horses." He reached out and shook Dr. Hart's hand. "Thanks for the hospitality last night. Tell your pa for me. And if anyone needs to reach us, Bowie could probably figure out where we are."

Constance thanked the doctor as well and braced herself to go upstairs and tell Clarice she was leaving.

~

She hadn't been on a horse very often—that was for certain. Branch grated at the slow pace, but he couldn't push her too fast. She was barely perched in the saddle as it was. What should've been a two-hour trip had taken nearly half a day. He feared their slow pace left them vulnerable to being seen, but short of tossing her across the saddle in front of him and racing for cover, there wasn't much he could do about it. His mount, Charger, was fed up with the pokey ambling and chomped at the bit, tossing his head and swishing his tail, begging to break into a canter.

Women slowed a man down, for sure. At least it was only one woman this time, though. If he had been forced to bring the elder Miss Spanner along on this little junket, he would've been sorely tempted to hogtie and gag her just to get a little peace. The scene she had put on at El Regalo when she'd heard her sister was not only going to testify, but that she was leaving the ranch house accompanied by only one man had practically lifted the rafters off the mansion.

Poor old Harley. He was a glutton for punishment. What he saw in that woman was beyond Branch's understanding. Still, to each his own, and Branch's own was steering clear of females whenever possible. Which made this current assignment frustrating. Was Hugh up to his old matchmaking tricks? Aided and abetted by Etta? Well, if that was so, their hopes were to be dashed. Branch was a lone wolf, and that was how it was going to stay.

Constance straightened her back, her lips pressed together, shifting her weight slightly in the saddle. She winced, and Branch shook his head slightly. She was going to be sore tomorrow.

Though he had to give her credit. She hadn't voiced a word of complaint, not even when he told her she would have to ride astride and could only take one valise. Though she looked like a little hothouse flower, she hadn't whined, and she'd come down the stairs with a single bag.

Jack zigzagged through the brush, nose down, tail wagging. Branch watched the dog because Jack would be the first to know if someone was in the area. Ahead of them, a winding line of trees rose, indicating the river. They were getting close now.

At the smell of water, Charger raised his head and hurried his pace. In a slight bend of the Sabinal, a weathered cabin and corral sat, silent.

"This is the place."

Constance's eyes widened, and she tucked her lower lip behind her upper teeth.

He shrugged. It wasn't exactly the Menger Hotel over in San Antonio, he would admit. In fact, you could fit the cabin and corral into the Menger lobby and still have room left over.

"It isn't fancy, but it's secluded." He tried not to sound defensive about the state of the place. It wasn't his job to pamper her. It was his job to protect her and get her to that trial in four days' time.

"However did you know about this place?"

"I was thinking about buying it. Bowie Hart and I brought the dogs out here on a hunting trip this fall. When GW divided up the Seven Heart, this was on Bowie's land, and he said he'd sell it to me if I was interested."

They drew up at the shack, and Branch swung down, pulling the reins over Charger's head. A cool breeze kicked up a bit of dust, and Constance huddled into her cloak, both hands fisted on the saddle horn.

"You can get down. We aren't going any farther."

"I'm not sure I can..." She trailed off with a blush.

He frowned, chastising himself for not realizing her distress. Two strides had him at her side, reaching up and taking her from the saddle. She held onto his forearms, and he kept hold of her waist until he was certain she was steady. Her head came only to his chin, and he looked down on her, smelling sunshine and flowers. He took a step back.

"You can go on into the cabin. I'll take care of the horses and bring in the supplies."

Jack went with her, and Branch shook his head. The dog rarely left his side, and here he was besotted. Branch led the horses down into the trees to the river bank to water them, then tied them there, away from the corral. He didn't want to chance someone noticing the horses and perhaps investigating the cabin. When he had finished these chores, he carried his bedroll and saddlebags and her valise inside the cabin.

Dust motes floated in the air, and Constance stood in the center of the single small room surveying her lodgings. A pair of bunks stood in one corner, a cook stove opposite, and in the center, a rough-hewn table with a couple benches. That was it, aside from one cupboard that held basic cooking utensils. She looked as out of place as a crystal goblet in a chuck wagon cupboard.

He slung the saddlebags on the table, and she jumped. "You don't have to worry. I'll be sleeping outside. You'll have the house to yourself."

She nodded as if she didn't really hear him and approached the bunk. With a grimace, she picked up the wool blanket, and the movement stirred more dust. Firming up her chin in a way that reminded him of Etta Sterling tucking into a task, she dropped the blanket and put her hands on her hips. "We have plenty to do before nightfall. I'll need firewood and lots of water."

Hours later, the room had been swept and scrubbed, and Branch had hauled enough water from the river to float an ark—or at least it felt that way. Why did women always want to spit-polish everything? He finally sagged onto one of the benches. "Enough. You could about eat off that floor now. Speaking of eating, let's get some grub. My belly thinks my throat's been cut."

She went to the front door and tossed the contents of the scrub pail out onto the dirt with a splat. "Why do you want to buy this place?"

It was the first she'd spoken to him in a couple hours other than to order him to bring more water.

He shrugged, unbuckling the straps on his saddlebags where GW's housekeeper Perla had stowed some provisions. "I liked the look of the place. Good water nearby, good grazing."

"So you plan to settle down here?"

"No, I don't plan to settle down. But I'll have to retire somewhere if I live that long." The idea of settling down was absurd. He hadn't had a home since his parents were killed by Indians. He was as free as a prairie wind, nothing to tie him down. Nothing to distract him from his mission.

She dried her hands on her apron. What woman brought an apron along when she was hiding from outlaws? Females were a mystery every minute of the day.

"Then why buy a house? And I assume some land? Are you going to get married or quit the Rangers?"

"I would never quit the Rangers. I was put on this earth to do one thing—get justice for those who can't get it for themselves. That's why I won't ever settle down or get married. Being married divides a man's attention, makes him lose focus. When a man joins the Rangers, he makes a promise to be there for the citizens of Texas whenever they need him, wherever they need him."

She blinked at his vehemence, but he was warming to his topic. "I've been to my share of weddings the last few months, what with the matrimony bug biting nearly the entire troop, and I listened to the vows they make. They promised to love, honor, and cherish their bride, to put her next to God in importance, to spend their lives caring for her and treasuring her. But what happens when duty calls?"

He stood and went to the window. "They go, because it's their job, but more than half the time, their minds and hearts are focused on what they left behind. My uncle, who took me in after my parents were killed, he used to talk about how married soldiers during the war weren't hardly worth the effort, always pining for hearth and home. Marriage turns fighting men into milksops."

Turning around to lean against the sill, he crossed his arms.

"Really?" Skepticism dripped from the single word. "What about all those men in your company? Jesse Rawlings? Whit Murray? Griff Sommer and the rest? Are they all milksops? Has marriage ruined them?"

"It sure seems like it sometimes. Some of them waltzed around like sky pilots for weeks. All they can talk about was their girls, about how life is so much better for them now they're hitched, about how great it is to have someone to love and to come home to." He rolled his eyes. "None of them have been married long enough to tell just how bad it will affect them, but every last one of them fell harder than a blacksmith's hammer."

"What about Captain Sterling? He's been married a long time, and he seems quite dedicated to his job. His wife hasn't ruined him for being a peace officer." Her chin lifted in triumph.

He shook his head. "Etta Sterling is the exception that proves the rule. She's as tough as an old boot, can shoot like a sniper, ride like a Comanche, and run a Ranger company like a cavalry drill sergeant. She goes everywhere with Hugh, makes camp, travels through all weather. He knows he can count on her to stand beside him in trouble."

"And your fellow Rangers' wives cannot be counted upon to stand beside their husbands in times of trouble?"

Why was it a woman always tried to twist a fellow into knots? "A bank teller, a silversmith, a jewelry store owner, a widow with a kid, a former working girl, and a European princess of some sort? They couldn't wait to latch onto a man. Just which one of them do you think will be able to reload the weapons while her husband is holding off an Indian attack, or which one will be able to cut a bullet out of a wounded Ranger while the troop is pinned down by outlaws? Nope, they'll just stay home, having babies and diverting their husbands' attentions and loyalties until one day when he gets killed because he was daydreaming about the little wife and children instead of paying attention to his job."

She lowered her chin and looked at him out of the tops of her eyes, the way a woman did when she was pitying a man and not believing a word he said. "You really believe that, don't you? That marrying weakens a man. And that every woman is looking to latch onto a man and drag him down?"

"Well, aren't you? Looking to get married, I mean?" He felt better turning the attention back onto her.

"No. I am *never* getting married."

"Why not?"

She shrugged and looked away. "Let's just say that the specimens to which I have been exposed have discouraged me from pursuing matrimony."

There was another woman tactic. Get pushed into a corner and come out talking like a Harvard professor. "Women say that, and then, when the right fellow crosses their trail, they pounce."

"Not this woman. Not after what I've been through. I might have to trust a man with my safety right now, but I will never trust another man with my heart. I've learned the hard way that a man can turn on you quicker than that!" She snapped her fingers, and Jack bolted upright.

So she'd been hurt by someone. That explained the guardedness he'd felt from her.

Well, fine.

Good.

That meant he was safe from one female at least.

Though the pain in her eyes made him want to find whoever it was who had let her down so badly and pound him into pulp.

CHAPTER 5

Four days. Four long days of watching and waiting and laying low. Branch had nothing to do but tend the horses, fill the water bucket from time to time, and read his notebook, and the inactivity was driving him mad. Not that Constance was difficult to be with, but knowing Cass and Maggie and Curly were still at large and most likely plotting something grated on him.

"What is that?" Constance asked.

"Notes."

She sighed. "If anyone is looking to get information out of you, they're going to have a sticky time of it. I'm bored. We've done nothing but sit here day after day watching the wind blow through the grass. I'm ready to grab any reading material you might have. What kind of notes?"

"They're notes on the Markham Gang. What we know, what we suspect, who we've captured, who's been killed." Branch licked the end of his pencil, a habit Etta detested, and began a new list of questions.

Where was security around Willie Markham most vulnerable?

When would Constance most likely be called to testify?

How soon after a conviction would the judge set the hanging?

"Why do you take notes like that?"

"A couple of reasons." He didn't look up. "First, it helps me think, to organize my thoughts. And second, I'm allowed to bring it into the witness box with me if I am called to testify. Sometimes we don't try an outlaw until months or even years after he committed the crime, depending on how long it takes us to apprehend him. Memories get fuzzy, facts get lost. If I write things down as I go, I can refer back to it and make sure I'm telling the truth."

"That's very smart. Do all the Rangers have notebooks?"

"Some. Not all." He shrugged, flipping the book shut and stuffing it and his pencil into his pocket. The quality of the light had changed, and darkness would fall soon. Time to check the horses before spreading his bedroll out on the porch boards again. Tomorrow, they would head back into town. The circuit judge should be arriving on the afternoon train, and he would want all the witnesses and lawyers and such to be in Hartville and ready to start the trial first thing the following morning.

He got to his feet, but before he could step out on the porch, Jack growled, the hair rising on the back of his neck. Branch grabbed Constance's arm and pushed her onto the bunk, pressing his finger to his lips and pointing for her to stay put.

Drawing his sidearm, he crossed quietly to the window and put his hand on the back of Jack's neck. The dog quieted, but his ears were up and his dark eyes intent on the opening.

A gunshot and the window glass exploding sounded simultaneously, and Branch ducked, turning away from the window. "Get down." Another shot screamed through the open front doorway and hit the water bucket, sending a gout of water skyward and a gush across the floor.

Branch steeled himself, leaped across the opening, and

slammed the front door. His momentum carried him to the corner where his bedroll and rifle were propped up.

Constance had slipped off the side of the bunk and crouched beside it, her face white. "Who is it?" she whispered.

"Has to be the Markhams or someone they hired. Question is, how did they know we were here?" Branch checked the load on his Winchester, slung his saddlebags over his shoulder, and dared another peek out the corner of the window. Was there just one shooter? Or were they surrounded?

The cabin was miles from anywhere, so they couldn't expect outside help. If there was only one man out there, they had a chance. It would be full dark soon, and perhaps they could slip away down to the river where the horses were tied.

Jack crouched in front of Constance, head and tail low, eyes shifting from Branch to the door and back again.

"Kilborn! You come out of there real slow, and maybe I'll kill you quick instead of dragging this out. Boss said you gotta die, so that's what you're gonna do, but I'll be merciful if you surrender now. You don't, and it'll go hard for you and that gal."

Branch set his teeth. Curly LaFever.

Curly was both a plus and a minus. A plus because he hadn't had an original thought in his entire life. Cass Markham did the thinking for Curly, and Curly didn't make a move without spelled-out directions. Outwitting him was possible. On the minus side, once Curly was given an order, he carried it out with the relentlessness of the obsessed. He would keep coming until he was successful or dead.

Thus far, he'd been pretty successful.

"You coming out?" Curly yelled. "You was hard to find, until I grabbed one of them little Mexican gals that works up at the big ranch house. She heard you say Bowie Hart would know where you was, so I been scouting for days all over Bowie's land."

Branch searched for the location of the voice. The one drawback to the cabin was that brush grew almost up to the front door. There were dozens of places to hide...which gave Branch hope. If they could get to the brush, they could use it for cover too. But how to wait out Curly until full dark...?

Something thwacked the side of the cabin, and something else landed on the shake-shingle roof. The smell of smoke told Branch they wouldn't have long.

Firebrands. Curly planned to burn them out.

"I gave you a chance, Ranger. Now it's too late."

Branch ran across the cabin in a crouch, dragging his saddlebags and clutching his rifle. He thrust the saddlebags into Constance's arms. "You're in charge of these. Don't lose them. We have to get out of here." Smoke gusted under the front door. Curly had thrown a firebrand onto the porch, and the flames were licking the tinder-dry wood, blocking the way out.

Jack whined.

"He's probably covering the back door by now, but we have to go out that way." Branch's eyes began to sting, and near the ceiling, a gray-white cloud of smoke grew thicker. Another thump hit the roof, rolled a bit, and halted. "Curly won't stop until the place is a bonfire."

"If he's covering the back, how are we going to get out?"

"C'mon!" Branch grabbed her wrist, tugging her toward the back door, keeping low. He waited for a billow of smoke to roll off the roof, eyeing the closest cover. At least the rear exit faced the river. If they could make it to the horses, they had a fighting chance.

A thick blanket of smoke gusted down, and he jerked the door open, keeping hold of Constance's wrist, running low for the scrub about thirty yards from the back stoop.

He'd give her credit—she kept up, though she did falter and cry out at one point when Curly started shooting. Branch returned one shot, not taking the time to aim, hoping it would at least force Curly to duck and buy them some precious time to get to cover.

Jack darted into the mesquite bramble. Branch crashed into the brush after him, burrowing a hole. Constance followed. He darted a look over his shoulder, dropping her wrist and putting his finger to his lips.

"Stay close."

She nodded, her eyes tense.

Jack raised his nose, sniffing the air, and Branch put his hand on the dog's neck. "You stay close too."

They worked farther into the brush, skirting open areas, going carefully, stopping to listen often. Curly must be doing the same because he fired no more shots. The smell of smoke hung in the air, and for a while, the roar of the fire covered other sounds. Branch only hoped the flames wouldn't spread beyond the house and devour the surrounding thickets.

The horses were to their right, down the bank near the water. Branch worked his way toward them, checking briefly from time to time to make sure Constance was still on his heels. If he didn't have her with him, he would've gone on the offensive, swinging around and trying to get behind Curly, but he couldn't, hampered as he was with a woman. And didn't that go to show what he'd been saying? Females held a fellow back, made him have to consider them and their safety first.

Every minute, meant darkness was falling, which gave them better cover but also made it harder to move through the brush. Branch skidded down the steep bank toward the river, and Constance came after him, letting out a little cry as her feet slipped and she landed hard.

"Sorry." Her voice sounded strained, which he supposed was understandable. She had to be scared out of her wits. Branch himself felt calm and cool, the way he always did when things got dangerous. His mind was clear and focused without a shred of fear.

He turned to the right along the river. The horses should be just around the next bend.

But they weren't. At first, he thought he'd misjudged the location, but then he saw the severed ropes hanging from the trees where he'd tethered Charger and the horse he'd borrowed from the Seven Heart for Constance.

Curly had gotten here first. And if he knew where the horses were, he would know where Branch would head if he escaped the cabin.

A bullet thwacked the tree next to him, sending splinters and bark flying. Branch hit the dirt and rolled away, coming up on his belly, rifle aimed at where he'd seen a muzzle flash. He pumped three shots in that direction before jumping to his feet and darting through the trees. Curly could track him by muzzle flash just as easily, and he didn't want to stay in a place he'd fired from for long.

He found cover behind another big willow tree, looking back to see where Constance was. She'd huddled behind a tree of her own, still clutching the saddlebags. Her hair had snagged on something and pulled lose from its hairpins, hanging over her shoulders like a tangled shawl. Crouched as she was, her arms around her knees, she looked small and fragile.

He had to get her out of here. Curly was somewhere ahead of them, and the river was to their backs. The horses were loose, but finding them in the dark would be impossible.

As quietly as he could, he edged around until he could reach Constance. He took her hand, icy cold, and she gripped his fingers. Pressing his lips against her ear to speak as softly as possible, he whispered, "Come. Quiet now."

Her hair smelled like flowers.

He found a place where the willows grew right up to and hung over the water, drawing her into the hanging limbs. "Take off your shoes, stuff them in the saddlebags, and follow me." He yanked off his boots, tied them together with his belt, and hung them around his neck. "We're going wading."

Though wading hardly covered it. The winter had been unusually wet, and where the Sabinal should be a trickle at this time of year, it now came up to his waist. There wasn't much current, but the bottom was sandy and boggy. Jack paddled by, his nose in the air. The dog reached the far side first and clambered out. He shook himself from nose to tail, sending water flying.

Branch kept Constance's hand in his, feeling his way. When they made the east bank, he sat down to pull on his boots while she did the same. The night air chilled his skin. She had to be freezing. They'd fled the cabin without grabbing his coat or her cloak...not even his bedroll.

But she still had the saddlebags. The woman had some serious grit. He couldn't help but admire her.

"C'mon. Let's put some distance on the cabin." The light of the flames had died down some, but an orange-yellow glow still hovered on the far bank.

It was a long, miserable night. Branch led them up the far bank of the Sabinal and out into the brush. Once daylight came, they could work their way around, following the river, and get to Bowie's place. But blundering around in the dark was a quick way to twist an ankle or alert Curly to their presence.

He found a little draw. The rocky side walls shielded them from some of the wind, but it was still cold.

"We'll rest here until daylight."

She sank to the ground, letting the saddlebags plop into the dirt. "Do you have a knife?"

"What?" Branch leaned against the chest-high rock wall, facing away from her, his rifle at the ready, looking for anything in the moonlight that might resemble a determined outlaw.

"I asked if you have a knife."

"Of course, I have a knife." He didn't look at her, keeping his attention on their surroundings.

"Can I borrow it, please?"

"What do you need a knife for?"

"I want to cut some of my petticoat." She said this as if she was at the mercantile ordering a length of ribbon for one of those fancy hats she made.

"Why would you do that?"

"Because I've been shot, and I need a bandage."

~

Branch was kneeling in the dirt at her side before she could drop a hanky. "Where are you hit? Why didn't you say something?"

"There wasn't time."

He began patting her down.

"Ouch!" She gasped. "It's my arm."

"You're bleeding." He probed the back of her upper left arm.

"That's why I need the bandage." She tried to keep her voice calm, but now that she'd admitted to the injury, the pain seemed to intensify. Ever since they left the cabin, she'd been biting her lip, holding her tongue, not wanting to acknowledge what had happened to her, how scared she was, or how much pain she was in.

He muttered under his breath, drawing a wicked-looking knife from a sheath inside his boot. The blade gleamed in the moonlight, and she drew back.

"I'm going to have to cut your sleeve off."

"Can't we just bind it up and wait for Dr. Hart to look at it when we get back to town?"

"I have to see if the bullet is still in there. You don't want blood poisoning, do you?"

She could think of fewer things she wanted less.

The knife sliced through the fabric as if cutting tissue paper. A match scratched and flared, illuminating Branch's face as he looked at her wound. She almost sighed with relief that he didn't look worried. It couldn't be too bad, then.

"Looks as though the bullet went through, but it's still bleeding pretty good. When did this happen?" He folded the cut-off sleeve into a pad and pressed it against the wound, making her wince.

"When we ran out the back door, in the smoke." She spoke through gritted teeth.

"Here, hold this on. Hard." He pressed her hand against the pad. "Pull your skirt up to your knee so I can see the edge of your petticoat."

Heat surged through her cheeks, but he acted as if nothing untoward was happening, sheering off the bottom ruffle of her best petticoat in one swipe of that wicked-looking knife. Jack burrowed into her side, putting his big head on her lap and looking up at her with his huge brown eyes.

When Branch moved her hand away from the wound, she stroked Jack's head. "How did you come to have a dog like Jack?" She asked to keep her mind off the pain shooting from her fingertips to her hairline as he wound the makeshift bandage around her upper arm.

"We were bivouacked up on the Brazos, trailing a bunch of rustlers, and he wandered near camp. Maybe about six weeks old, nearly starved. Etta fed him some bread and gravy, and when we bedded down, he crawled into my bedroll." Branch shrugged as he tied off the ends of the bandage. "I tried to give him to Etta a couple of times, but she wouldn't take him. Said he'd chosen me and I was stuck with him. I carried him tucked into my coat at first, then he rode in my saddlebags, and then he was big enough to trot along with us."

He reached out and roughed the dog's ears. "He's a bit of a

nuisance, but he's got his uses. I want you to try to get some sleep. As soon as there's some light, we're going to have to be on the move."

She was tired, and thirsty, and in pain, and scared...but keeping in mind his thoughts about how women distracted and slowed a man down, she voiced none of what she was feeling. *Be like Etta Sterling. What would Etta Sterling do?*

To hear Branch tell it, she would grab a gun, use her superhuman night vision, and track down the outlaw stalking them, dragging him back to camp hogtied. Then she'd make the perfect Ranger dinner of beef and beans, and have the dishes washed and the guns cleaned and polished all before the sun rose.

You're losing your mind. Go to sleep, Constance.

It felt as if she'd only closed her eyes for a moment when Branch was waking her up. Every bone ached, and the cold had made her muscles stiff. When she tried to move her injured arm, it hurt so badly, she wanted to cry. Her head felt stuffed with cotton wool, and her tongue stuck to the roof of her mouth.

"We've got to go. Here." He pressed something hard and knobby into her hand. "Eat this, and don't let Jack take it from you. He's had some already."

In the light from the not-quite-risen sun, she saw he'd given her a piece of beef jerky. Her stomach roiled. She didn't like jerky.

"Come on. We need to go. I wish I had known you were wounded last night. You've left a blood trail that even your sister could follow."

His comment stung. He acted as if she should be as seasoned as Kit Carson when it came to this evade and pursue lark. He could've asked if she was hurt.

No doubt Etta Sterling would've known to bind up her own wound without stopping or leaving a trace.

Stop it, Constance. She's a nice lady. She can't help it if Branch has put her up on a pedestal as some sort of paragon. I don't know why you care what he thinks, anyway. It isn't as if you have any interest in him.

After that, she didn't think about much of anything except putting one foot in front of the other.

She had no idea where they were or how long they'd been going when Branch stopped, called for Jack who was nosing through the brush ahead, and knelt beside the dog.

"What are you doing?" Constance cradled her injured arm against her middle.

"We need some help. Without a horse, we're still hours away from Bowie's place. You're about to collapse. There's a spot ahead there"—he pointed—"where we can wait for reinforcements, or at the very least, I can hold off an attack if Curly comes at us."

Constance shaded her eyes and spied a jagged outcropping of sand-colored rocks. "How are we going to get help?"

Sunlight flashed off something in his hand. His badge. "I'm going to send Jack." Slipping the pin through one of the holes on Jack's collar, he secured it, tugging it a bit to make sure it was fast. "Jack, where's Hugh?"

The dog's ears perked up, and his tail began to wag.

Branch dug in his saddlebag, unfolding a piece of burlap. He drew out a red bandana and held it out for Jack to sniff. The dog took a whiff, and a shiver ran through his body. "Find him, Jack. Go get Hugh."

With a low woof, the dog took off as if he'd been shot from a rifle, disappearing into the brush.

"Will he find him?"

Branch shrugged. "We've been working on it, teaching him to return to the office when he's given Hugh's scent. That's Hugh's bandana. So far, we've only tried it in town, but Jack's smart. And when Hugh sees Jack without me, he'll know we're in trouble. Not to mention the badge. Hugh had them made for us, with our names on the back. If any of us get into a tight spot, we're supposed to send the badge."

They were steps away from the rocks when a bullet screamed by and ricocheted off the crag ahead, chipping off bits. Branch dragged her into a crouch, pushing her ahead of him, trying to shield her from behind as many more shots came. Her lungs were bursting by the time they reached cover.

"Stay down." Branch knelt behind a pile of rocks that half concealed the entrance to the crevasse he'd shoved them into. Setting his hat aside, he flicked his hair out of his eyes and studied the area where the shots had come from. "Definitely more than just Curly now. This could be our chance to take down Cass Markham for good." He sounded determined, even eager, for the fight to start.

Constance wedged herself into the back of the small overhang.

Branch tossed the saddlebags her way. "There's a bandolier in there with rifle shells and a bag with bullets for my pistol. I can hold them off here for a while, but I'm going to need you to reload for me." He glanced at her over his shoulder. "Have you ever loaded a gun before?"

She shook her head. Her heart pounded so loud, his voice sounded as though it was coming from far away. "Show me."

He went through the steps, and Constance nodded that she understood.

Which was just as well because over the next half an hour, she loaded the rifle twice and the pistol once. The noise of gunfire was appalling, and with each blast from the rifle, it felt as if the concussion hit her in the chest.

"They're working their way in closer, spreading out." Branch swiped his arm across his forehead.

"How long before Hugh and the others might come?" Constance thumbed another round into the rifle. "Do you have more bullets?"

With a tug, he jerked his gun belt and holster from his waist. “What you have and these.” He pointed to the bullets in the loops on the belt without looking at her. “I figure we can hold out here for another hour or two.”

He went still, his eyes sharpening. Slowly, he raised his rifle, resting it on the rock ledge in front of him. “Gotcha.”

Constance held her breath, waiting for the explosion, and even though she knew it was coming, she jerked.

A howl went up from a distance, and Branch nodded. “That’s one.”

For a long time, nothing happened, no gunshots, no noise. Constance’s body hurt with tension, and she battled lightheadedness. Her stomach growled, but worse than that, she was so thirsty, she could only think of how much she wanted...needed...water. They’d had nothing to drink since leaving the river last night.

But she wouldn’t complain. There was nothing Branch could do about the problem. At the moment, he had his hands full. And if he could stand it, she could too.

Captain Sterling and Jesse Rawlings found them at dusk. Jesse led Branch’s horse, and Jack raced into the little cave, lapping Constance’s face as she hugged him with her good arm.

“Evening, Branch. Miss Spanner.” Hugh touched his hat brim. “How are you this evening?”

Jesse and Branch went to scout around, and Captain Sterling squatted beside Constance and offered her his canteen. She tried to be ladylike but finally gave it up, guzzling the water with all the finesse of a draft horse.

“Go easy. You don’t want to upset your tummy.” He checked under the edge of her bandage. “Looks like you’ve had yourself quite a time.”

“Did Jack find you?”

“Actually, Charger found us first. Griff spotted him running down the main street of Hartville this morning, trailing his lead rope and breathing fire. It was all we could do to catch him. But I knew if Branch had been separated from Charger, there was trouble. We headed out toward Bowie Hart's place to see if he knew where you might be, since Branch didn't tell anyone. Then Jack jumped out of the bushes and scared the life out of us. He led us here."

Branch came in, squatted, and leaned on his rifle. He took out his notebook and pencil and made a line. "Curly LaFever's dead. There were two more with him, but they escaped. From the tracks, one of them was Cass, and I suspect the other was Maggie."

Hugh nodded. "We brought two spare mounts. Charger for you, and a livery horse for Miss Spanner here. Load the body on the livery horse, and one of us can take Miss Spanner up with us for the ride back to town."

"I'll take her." Branch pushed himself upright. He looked down at her.

Constance became aware of her bedraggled appearance. Her hair hung in hanks down her back. Her dress was a sight—torn, dirty, and wrinkled. Her sister wouldn't recognize it as the custom piece it had been. She tried to reach up to smooth her hair, but her arm hurt too much. Still, what did her appearance matter? They were alive. Shaking her head, she let Branch help her to her feet, holding her waist as she walked out of their hiding place.

Jesse came, leading the horses. Across the back of one, an enormous blanket-wrapped bundle had been tied, hands dangling on one side, boots sticking out the other.

Curly LaFever.

She shuddered, and Branch's arm tightened around her.

"He can't hurt you now. Not you or anyone else."

She nodded, pressing her lips together.

Branch's horse snorted and pawed the ground, but when Branch spoke to him, running his hand along the crest of his neck under his mane, the animal quieted and allowed Branch to swing aboard. Jesse waited to lift Constance up into Branch's arms.

Those strong arms went around her, tucking her into his chest, careful of her injury. He pressed her head into his shoulder. "Try to rest. I won't let you fall."

The last thing she remembered before she fell asleep was how protected and safe she felt. Which was odd since her life had been one long dangerous event since she'd met Branch Kilborn.

CHAPTER 6

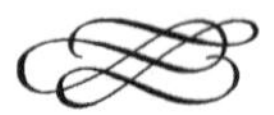

Hartville turned into a circus overnight. Newspapermen, bigwigs, and gawkers packed the town. All of Texas, it seemed, wanted to be on hand when one of the Markham family was finally made to answer for his crimes. Even the governor was in town, taking over the entire top floor of the Hartville Hotel for his entourage.

No fewer than three Texas Rangers guarded Constance at all times. They'd decided the Ranger office was the safest place for her, so she'd been given a bed in the barracks upstairs, had food brought to her, and kept under lock and key.

"You don't have to worry about a thing, my dear." Harley Burton had stopped by, going over his notes once more. "Just answer the questions honestly. The trial should only last two days at the most, and then this will all be over."

Her sister had visited as well, bringing sympathy and a steamer trunk of clothes and personal items, more than Constance would ever need.

Clarice also sported a shiny new engagement ring, Harley having come up trumps in the romance department, it seemed.

Her sister's bruises were fading, and she'd strategically covered the worst of them with face powder.

Her sister had remonstrated, cried, berated, and cajoled, trying to convince Constance not to testify, not to put herself at risk like this, but in the end, she had resigned herself to the idea. The fact that Harley had promised to marry Clarice the minute the trial was over and take her on a trip to New York City away from danger had mollified her somewhat. She was insisting that Constance go with them.

As if she would. Go on her sister's honeymoon with her? But what would happen to her after she testified? Cass and Maggie Markham were still out there, still a danger to her. Would they return to exact their revenge once the trial was over? Hugh had told her not to worry about that until after the trial, but how could she not?

Of Branch she had seen very little. She knew he took the night watch guarding her because every evening, Jack trotted up the stairs to sleep on the rug beside her bed. During the day, visible from the window where she watched the street below, Branch sat in a chair in front of the jail, his rifle across his lap and his dog by his side.

Not that she spent all day watching him or anything.

Her arm was sore but healing. The bandage she wore didn't even show under the sleeve of her dress. Dr. Hart had fixed her up well and had assured her she would be fine in a couple of weeks.

And the waiting continued. Captain Sterling reported that the judge had arrived in town. Etta brought the news that Willie Markham's lawyer had come as well, a man named Eustace Fowler.

"He's wily. Hugh has testified in a trial where he was the council for the defense, and it was brutal." Etta's brows came down. "Pompous little man. Looks like a gnome and fights like a

Viking. However, your account is solid, and there isn't much he can do to rough you up on the stand. Nothing to worry about."

Nothing but some killers who didn't want her in the courtroom at all.

But now the trial was finally here.

And so was Branch.

The sight of him walking into the barracks that had been both her safe haven and her prison for the past two days made her heart flutter. His eyes were sharp, his gun was low on his hip, and his badge caught the light. He looked competent, fearless, and determined.

"It's time." He studied her. At Harley's direction, she'd chosen a sober navy dress and simple hairstyle. The lawyer wanted her to appear serious and reliable. Did Branch see serious and reliable?

Harley came in behind Branch, his attaché case in his hand. "My dear, I am headed over to the courthouse. Ranger Kilborn and his men will escort you. There will be a place reserved for you behind the prosecution's table."

She nodded, her mouth dry.

Griff Sommer and Micah McCullough formed the rest of her bodyguard as they walked the short distance to the courthouse. Jack pressed close to her side, eyes watchful. The boardwalks were filled with onlookers who hadn't been able to get into the courtroom. They gave way before the armed guards, but their eyes followed her.

Why did it seem she was the prisoner?

Branch didn't waste time out in the street, hurrying her into the courthouse and up the stairs to the second floor.

Hugh Sterling met them at the courtroom door and held it open. "Thank you, my dear. This will be over soon." He pressed Constance's hand and gave her a quick smile.

Then she was in her seat, mauling her handkerchief, flanked by Branch on one side and Micah on the other in the front row when the judge came in and the bailiff called for order. Jack lay at her feet, and not even the bailiff had the courage to tell Branch to remove him from the courtroom.

The jury filed in, and the accused was brought to the defendant's table in shackles. Ezra Creed removed the handcuffs and sat in the row behind Willie Markham and his defense council, Eustace Fowler.

Constance scanned the jury for any faces she knew. Giles Brown, the woodworker. Austin Hart and two of his brothers, Hays and Bowie, Mr. Chambers, who drove the stagecoach, Mr. Yost from the Everything Store, and Big Joe, the livery owner. The others she didn't know, but they all looked grimly from the jury box.

Micah leaned over and whispered, "I didn't think they were going to be able to fill the box. A lot of the men they called had to be recused because they'd had a run-in with the Markhams in the past. Mr. Palmer from over at the bank, Mike Mortenson from the mercantile, even Harry Bales, the lookout at the saloon where the victim worked, all wanted to be on the jury but couldn't."

Branch said nothing, but his reassuring bulk, his shoulder just touching hers, brought comfort. She avoided looking across the way to the defense table.

When she was finally called to testify, her knees were shaking so badly, she wondered if she could make it to the stand. Branch got to his feet, held her elbow, and walked her to the gate. His steady brown eyes bore down into hers, and she raised her chin a fraction.

"You can do this." He squeezed her elbow and released her.

The courtroom was so quiet, her footsteps sounded loud on the polished floor.

The bailiff swore her in, and for the first time since the night of the murder, she met the gaze of Willie Markham. He stared back at her, his eyes like two coals burning hot. The scar under his eye stood out, a reddish-purple reminder of the hard life he'd lived.

Harley walked her through the evening in question, from their dinner at the Hartville Hotel to her decision to go to work at the dress shop instead of going home. As she relived the events, her fingers closed around her handkerchief. She locked eyes with Branch, refusing to look at anyone else, drawing strength from his calm certainty.

"The man looked up, and that's when I saw his face."

"Is that man in the courtroom today?" Harley asked.

"He is."

"Would you point to him?"

She raised her hand and indicated Willie Markham. He glared back at her, hatred rolling off him in waves, and she was left in no doubt that he was more than capable of killing a woman. Fear spiraled down her spine and settled in her middle, and she broke their eye contact, swiveling her gaze back to Branch.

Branch gave a single nod, and she drew courage, a sense of calm washing over her. She had done it.

"No further questions, Your Honor." Harley resumed his seat.

When Constance began to rise, the judge, The Honorable Winslow Yaley, stopped her. "Just a moment, miss. There's still the cross-examination. Counselor?" He inclined his head to Mr. Fowler.

"Yes, Your Honor. Just a few questions." Mr. Fowler, with silver hair and a fussy rusty-brown suit, appeared harmless, pink-cheeked, a dumpling of a man. He removed his glasses and cleaned them on his lapel. "Miss Spanner, you say you clearly saw my client in the alley behind your dress shop?" His voice was mild, conversational, but keeping in mind what Etta had said about how wily he was, she kept her answers short.

"Yes."

"What time was this?"

"Nearly midnight." Her stomach muscles were taut, and she had to force herself to breathe normally.

"Would it surprise you to know I stood on the back stoop of the dress shop last night at midnight?"

Harley half rose. "Objection. Relevancy?"

"Your Honor, I'm merely trying to establish the conditions under which the witness claims to have seen a crime."

"Overruled. For now."

"Miss Spanner, would it also surprise you to know that at midnight, in the alley behind the dress shop, it is impossible to discern any specific features due to the darkness and shadows?"

Her tension eased a bit. "Yes."

His eyebrows rose. "Yes?"

"Yes, unless, of course, someone from the hotel adjacent to the alley opens the back door and light spills into the alley. And when that light also spills across the face of the man leaning over a woman's body, and he looks up at the noise, it is quite easy to identify his face." She smoothed her hands along her skirts. "It was especially helpful that the man wore a wideawake-style brim on his hat, so not even his hat shielded his face."

A stir went through the courtroom, and Harley smothered a grin. Constance sat straighter. Surely, Mr. Fowler would stop his questions now.

But the little lawyer wasn't finished yet. He returned to his table and picked up a piece of paper. "Miss Spanner, you are from Shreveport, Louisiana, correct?"

"Once upon a time. I'm from Hartville now." A thread of worry hitched up her spine and prickled her scalp.

"Is it true that when you lived in Shreveport, you worked at the LeBeque Carriage Works as a secretary to the owner?"

Her mouth went dry. "Yes." She forced the word out. Where was he going with this? She looked to Harley, who stood.

"Objection, Your Honor. How is the witness's past employment germane to this case?"

"Your Honor, I am attempting to establish the credibility of this witness. I am holding in my hand an inquiry from the police in Caddo Parish, Louisiana. Miss Spanner is wanted for questioning in the matter of missing company funds."

A gasp went through the room, and heat flamed through Constance's cheeks. So Pasquale was holding firm, spreading his lies about her. All expression had been wiped from Branch's face, and he crossed his arms, staring at her. He, who stood for justice, for law and order, who saw everything in black and white. Surely, he wouldn't believe Pasquale's lies too?

"It's not true. I didn't steal anything." Her voice trembled, backed with so many emotions—anger, frustration, fear, but not guilt. She wasn't guilty—she just couldn't prove it.

The judge banged the gavel as noise rippled around her. "Order. Quiet."

"I charge that as a probable embezzler, Miss Spanner's testimony is tainted at best. How can we trust her word?" He tossed the paper onto the judge's bench. "I have no further questions."

Mr. Fowler stalked back to his seat in high disgust, and the judge gave Harley a moment for redirect, but he appeared flummoxed. After stammering for a moment or two, he sat back down.

Constance was excused from the stand. She went through the gate, hearing the whispers, seeing the looks, though she tried not to. She didn't stop at the row where she'd been sitting but kept walking, down the aisle and out the door. She couldn't look at Branch.

Clicks behind her and shuffling, but with tears blurring her eyes, she forged ahead through the crowd, only wanting to get away. Humiliation burned through her. Once again, she had no defense against the lies Pasquale had told about her to hide his own thievery.

A hand grabbed her arm. She tried to shake it off, but the grip was too firm.

"You little fool. Where do you think you're going?" Branch pulled her up tight against his side, his voice a growl in her ear.

"Let me go. I've done what you wanted. I testified."

"And look what it got us. You're wanted for theft? A criminal?" He strode along the boardwalk. Jack trotted at her side, and when she glanced over her shoulder, Griff and Micah were there, faces grim.

Branch took her to the Ranger office, unlocked the door, and nudged her inside. He pressed the key into Griff's hand. "She stays here and nobody goes in, right?"

"Right."

"Micah, you're on the back door."

Her hands fisted. "I am not your prisoner. I have to pack my bags and leave."

He paused at the door. "Sounds like that's typical for you. Running away. But I can't let you go. You're wanted for questioning in a crime. Here you'll stay." He slammed the door.

He'd left without Jack, who whined and pressed against her leg.

~

Branch headed back to the trial, his mind a jumble.

This was what letting a woman get under your skin did for you. He'd actually begun to admire Constance Spanner, to think maybe his fellow Rangers had it right, that you could have a woman in your life and not let it affect your job.

What fiction.

The one time he let his head be turned and the woman wound up to be a criminal. He was only glad none of his comrades knew how close he'd come to making a fool of himself.

Branch entered the courtroom and stood along the back wall through the closing arguments and the judge's instructions to the jury, but he heard nothing. The twelve men filed out to the jury room, and Branch checked his watch. Nearly four o'clock. Would the jury return a quick verdict, or would Fowler's trapping of Constance on the stand gum up the works?

The crowd seemed to think a quick verdict was coming, because no one gave up their seats. Branch waited to escort Willie back to the jail when the time came, certain sensible men like the Hart brothers would not turn a killer loose.

The crowd was right. In less than ten minutes, the bailiff led the jury back into the courtroom. Branch searched each jury member's face, but they gave nothing away.

The judge resumed the bench, and the bailiff took a slip of paper from Austin Hart, the jury foreman, and passed it to the judge. His Honor read the paper.

"Gentlemen of the jury, you have reached a verdict?"

"We have." Austin stood.

"Will the defendant please rise?"

Ezra Creed, who had taken the seat beside Willie Markham in case of trouble, put his hand under Willie's arm and tugged him to his feet.

"In the issue of *Texas vs. William J. Markham*, charged with the murder of one Mollie Olson, do you find the defendant guilty or not guilty?" the judge asked.

"We find the defendant guilty."

A charge zipped through the crowded rows, followed by a low hum of whispers.

The judge tapped his gavel. "Mr. Markham, in light of the jury's verdict and the lack of remorse on your part or mitigating circumstances, I sentence you to hang by the neck until dead. This hanging will take place three days from now on Monday, December twentieth, at ten a.m. Until that time, you are remanded into the custody of the Texas Rangers in the Hartville County Jail. May God have mercy on your soul." He banged the gavel one last time and disappeared into his chambers.

Branch worked his way through the onlookers as Ezra put handcuffs on the prisoner. He and Whit Murray flanked Willie, and they hustled him out a side door to avoid the crush.

Getting him to the jail wasn't easy, with reporters jostling them and angry townsfolk hurling insults at Willie. Branch followed him into the cell, took off the cuffs, and locked him in. Outside, cheers and yells came through the thick walls.

Willie eased himself down onto the bunk, still wearing his new suit.

"You want to talk to anyone? I can send someone for Pastor Longley." Branch tossed the cuffs through the doorway to the cells, and Ezra caught them, putting them in the sheriff's desk.

"I won't need no preacher." Willie lay back on the bunk, lacing his fingers behind his head and staring at the ceiling.

Branch hooked his thumbs through his belt loops. "You're going to meet your Maker in a few days, and you need to get right with Him."

"I ain't gonna die on Monday. Leastways not by hanging."

"The judge says different."

"Don't matter. Cass and Maggie are still out there, and we made a pact a long time ago that none of us would ever let the other be executed. There's no glory in that. We aim to go out someday like Sam Bass...shooting. Cass and Maggie will be hatching a plan to spring me. They've busted me out of jail three other times, and they'll come through for me now too. And if Cass can kill a few Rangers in the bargain, he'll be mighty pleased."

Branch shook his head. "If you change your mind about the preacher, let me know."

He closed the door to the cells and locked it. "Ezra, go find Hugh and ask him to come to the jail, then relieve O'Neal. He's on patrol. Keep an ear to the ground, see if you can detect anything Cass and Maggie Markham might be cooking up. Willie seems to think they're going to help him escape."

"Will do. Think they'll try to harm Miss Spanner now that the trial's over?"

"No telling. Micah and Griff are with her, so she's safe enough, short of bringing her here to the jail." Which maybe they should do, since she had been accused of thievery in open court. And hadn't she tried to hightail it out of there? She'd run from Shreveport, and she'd tried to run from here. In his mind, only those guilty of something ran.

Hugh came in a few minutes later, taking off his hat and dropping it on a peg by the door. "Everything secure?"

Branch nodded. "Gonna be a long seventy-two hours. Ezra's patrolling. Just relieved O'Neal. Whit came with us from the jail, and he peeled off to join Jesse. They're going to keep an eye on Harley and the dressmaker."

"What about Constance?" Hugh perched on the corner of the desk.

"Micah and Griff are guarding her down at the office. She's as safe as we can make her short of hauling her down here to the jail." He scrubbed the back of his neck. "Which we probably should do. Sounds like the police in Shreveport would appreciate it."

"What are you talking about?"

"You heard Fowler in court. Wanted for questioning because money is missing from where she worked."

"Etta thought you might be getting sweet on Miss Constance." Hugh's mustache twitched. "Looks like she was right."

Branch pushed up from the desk. "That's loco. Where'd you get that idea, anyway?"

"If you weren't, then why would you care so much about what you think she might've done?"

"Because I'm a lawman. I'm about justice."

"Really? You're about justice? If that's so, what happened to innocent until proven guilty? You're all in a bother, acting like judge and jury on poor Miss Constance without even hearing her side of things. Wanted for questioning isn't the same as guilty. What if she's just a witness to something that happened, same as she was here? If we had known she had seen the murder, but we hadn't been able to talk to her, we would have sent out word that she was wanted for questioning in this case. That wouldn't have meant we thought she did the killing, would it? I think you care about her, but you're scared, so when the opportunity presented itself, you jumped to a conclusion that felt safe."

Slowly, Branch lowered himself into the chair. Had he misjudged her? Jumped to conclusions? And him, scared?

"But she ran. And if I hadn't stopped her, she'd be running now. Anyway, what does it matter? I'm not *sweet* on her." He spit the word out, giving it the ridiculous emphasis it required. No, he wasn't sweet on Constance Spanner. He might've been in danger of feeling something for her, something that might've gone a lot deeper than *sweet*, but he'd squashed that nonsense. "Rangering and women don't mix."

"So you've said for years, all evidence to the contrary." Hugh slipped a bullet out of his gun belt and used the point to clean under his fingernails. "I've been married for more than twenty-five years, and though I'm the one to say it, I think I've been a better than average Ranger."

"That's different. Etta's special."

"That she is, and though I think she's one of a kind, she's also one of a type. She's the type of woman who stands by her man in trouble, who doesn't complain, and who cares about the people around her. She's the same type as Evelyn, Violet, Sara, Ava, Augusta, Laurel, and I suspect, Constance Spanner. You've set up some sort of ideal, the perfect woman, but nobody could meet that standard. Etta's not perfect, but she's the perfect gal for me. Constance isn't perfect, either, but I have a feeling that if you pursued her, she'd be the perfect one for you too."

Branch shook his head. "I am not looking for a woman." When would everyone realize that and leave him alone?

"You might not be looking, but one might've found you."

"We sound like a pair of old women. Change the subject before I fall asleep from boredom. Willie's sure Cass and Maggie will try to bust him out of here before Monday. Let's stop talking about females and talk about how we're going to handle the guarding and the hanging."

"Fine, I just don't want you looking back someday and regretting that you let that gal get away."

CHAPTER 7

The trouble with guard duty was that it left a fellow too much time to think. Branch couldn't get Hugh's words out of his head, nor Constance's denial on the stand that she was guilty of anything. Time went slowly, and he found himself standing to the side of the window in the jail so he could look down the street to the Ranger office where she was being guarded.

Constance.

How had she gotten under his skin so quickly? With those big blue eyes, those kiss-me lips, and a walk that made it hard for a man to look anywhere else.

Tough enough not to complain after she'd been wounded, cool enough in a fight to keep loading weapons, brave enough to stand up in open court and accuse a murderer, even though she'd been threatened, chased, and shot at.

If it wasn't for the thing in Shreveport, he might've thought she was downright perfect.

He shook his head. He had better things to think about.

Hammers pounded as Giles Brown directed builders in the construction of the scaffolding for the execution. Branch had to admit, Texas justice was swift once it was sure it had its man. Three days between the trial and the hanging.

Hugh came by, and they worked out which Ranger would be where when it came time for justice to be dispenesd.

"I think we should enlist some help." Branch found himself reaching down to pat Jack, forgetting again that the dog had abandoned him for Constance. "I suggest getting some of the Hart brothers to join us. They're all reliable, and they can shoot."

Hugh agreed, and word was sent.

Branch stayed at the jail nearly the entire weekend, leaving only to send a telegram and then hurrying back to guard the prisoner.

The morning of the hanging, five days before Christmas, the town was quiet, as if holding its breath.

As the clock ticked toward ten, the tension thickened. Crowds gathered around both the jail and the courthouse where the hanging would take place. If Willie was to be believed, Cass and Maggie were planning something, but Rangers patrolled the town. Etta had gathered all the Rangers' wives and girls and brought them to the office where the Hart brothers guarded them and Constance, and everyone in the Ranger company was as ready as they could be.

Branch took the keys to Willie's cell. "Time to go, Willie."

The young man eased himself up off the bunk, his face pale. As the hours had trickled by, his confidence in his siblings appeared to wane. He sweated now, and his eyes showed a lot of white.

"You sure you don't want to talk to the preacher?"

He shook his head.

"Let's go, then." Branch put on the shackles, and Ezra opened the jail door.

The walk to the scaffold seemed to take forever, but it was only two blocks from the jail to the courthouse lawn. Branch estimated a couple thousand people had gathered for the spectacle, and it made him sad. The end of a man's life wasn't something to be celebrated. It might be necessary sometimes, but never enjoyed.

His fellow Rangers formed a cordon to keep people back as they mounted the steps to the platform. Pastor Longley stood up there, along with the man the judge had appointed as executioner.

"Any last words, Willie?"

Branch stepped back as the executioner edged forward to put the noose around Willie's neck. Before he could, a shot rang out, and the short man rocked back, hitting the railing.

Screams filled the air, and Willie laughed. "I told you, Ranger! They're coming for me!"

Branch had his gun out, scanning the crowd as people ran, falling, pushing, shouting. Whit and Griff were moving folks out of the way, trying to get to the platform. O'Neal, who had been tasked with protecting the governor, had that man by the arm, towing him out of the fray. A man with his hat pulled down low was fighting against the crowd, his gun drawn. He raised the gun and fired.

Heat seared Branch's thigh, and his leg buckled. He snapped off a shot at the man, but Branch couldn't fire because there were too many fleeing citizens in the way.

Another shot came from a different tangent.

Willie's laughter cut off abruptly with a gurgle, and he sank to his knees, shock coloring his features. "Maggie? You shot me?"

Branch steadied his weapon, waited for an opportunity, and shot at the man rushing toward him while his fellow Rangers—Griff and Jesse and Ezra—all fired at the woman coming in from the side with her gun blazing.

Cass also kept on coming, firing again and again. He almost made it to the stairs before Branch shot him in the chest, sending him tumbling back down in a cloud of dust and gun smoke.

It was over in less than a minute. Branch swept the area with his gun, searching for more shooters, hanging onto the railing by one arm, unable to support his weight on his injured leg. Beside him, Willie lay face down, not moving. The executioner stirred, moaning, and Pastor Longley crawled over to give him aid.

Cass sprawled in the dirt, his gun still clutched in his hand, but he would never fire it again.

And Maggie...Jesse bent over her, then stood, hands on hips. He looked up at Branch and shook his head.

Branch holstered his gun, his hand shaking. He had the ridiculous urge to pull out his notebook and cross out three more names. The job was finished.

~

Constance excused herself from the women in the Ranger office and went upstairs to the barracks where she'd been housed for the past several days. Jack came with her, and she sat on the edge of the bed, hugging his furry head in her lap. The day of the hanging had come, and even now Branch and the others were out there in the crowd, seeing justice carried out.

Etta Sterling had brought all the Ranger wives and fiancées to the office. "To be company for you, my dear, and not have to deal with the crush outside."

But Constance wasn't up for company. She was too raw inside.

Branch had somehow managed to slip past her defenses, rough-hewn and blunt as he was, and steal her affections.

No, that wasn't entirely true. He hadn't stolen anything. She'd flat out given her heart to him.

He, who had propounded on the subject of never getting married, never giving up that much control in his life, that much freedom, had managed through his wild brand of chivalry to make her feel safe, protected, cherished, and even admired. He was capable, direct, fiercely loyal to those he considered his family—

his fellow Rangers and the Sterlings—and handsome enough to stop traffic on a busy street.

But in one moment on the witness stand, it had all come unraveled.

Branch Kilborn thought she was a thief.

Pasquale had ruined her life once, accusing her of stealing money from his father's company. Pasquale, the man who had promised to love her forever and begged her to be his wife, even though his father didn't approve of him marrying a mere secretary.

When the accountant had come to audit the company books, thousands of dollars were missing, and Pasquale had pointed the finger at her. She hadn't taken the money, hadn't even considered stealing from her employer. She had no explanation of where the funds had gone.

The police chief wouldn't press charges without proof, but Pasquale's father, Jacques LeBeque, had fired her on the spot. Pasquale had demanded his ring back, and she had gone away in shock and humiliation. Hoping to escape the shame, hoping to build a new future devoid of men and the trouble they cause, and what had happened? Branch Kilborn strode right into her life.

And right out of it, too, if his accusatory look was any indication.

A bang from down the street drifted up, then the sound of screams and running feet. Constance jumped up from the bed and raced to the window.

More shots, more screams. What was happening? Had the Markhams come to free their brother? Or had they come for her to get their revenge?

Where was Branch?

In her heart, she knew he would be in the thick of the danger, whatever it was.

Scores of people ran down the street past the Ranger office.

She spied O'Neal Brewster pushing the governor through the front door of the Hartville Hotel.

The shooting stopped, but her pulse refused to calm. For the longest time, nothing seemed to happen, and then she saw him. Hugh and Jesse flanked him, his arms across their shoulders, head hanging, hair obscuring his face.

And blood saturating his right pants leg.

Constance didn't know how she got downstairs so quickly. She might've flown. Beating Austin Hart to the door, she flung it open and raced out into the street, Jack on her heels. "Branch, what happened?"

His head came up, his teeth clenched.

"Might need a bandage."

"Go get a bunk ready." Hugh started toward the office again. "We'll take him upstairs."

Reluctant to leave him, Constance returned to the barracks.

Etta was already giving orders. "Stoke up that stove, Evelyn. Augusta, fetch Dr. Hart if he's available. There might be more wounded out there that he needs to tend first. Laurel, bring some water and put it on the boil."

Constance raced up the stairs to pull back the blankets on the bed she'd been using. Hugh and Jesse weren't far behind, with Branch hanging silent between them. Jack circled, head down, whining.

They got Branch onto the bed, and Jesse had his knife out, cutting Branch's pant leg while Hugh tugged off his boots.

Etta edged in with a basin of water and some towels. "Will someone tell me what happened?"

Constance hovered around the fringe, trying not to get in anyone's way but wanting to help if she could. Branch's face was drawn so tight, his hands gripping the sheets.

Hugh took off his hat and ran his fingers through his hair. "Cass and Maggie Markham came out of nowhere, shooting up the place. At first, I thought they were trying to spring Willie, but Maggie aimed right at him and shot him dead."

Etta looked up sharply, her hands pressing a towel to the wound in Branch's thigh. "What? Why would she do that?"

"Pact." Branch forced the word out, eyes closed. "Willie said they had a pact never to let one of them be executed. Said there was no glory in that. They wanted to go down shooting and take some Rangers with them."

Etta motioned for Constance. "Keep pressure on this wound. Hugh, were any other Rangers hurt?"

"No, but Doc Hart will be busy with the hangman. He took a bullet to the chest."

Constance pressed the towel onto the wound, wincing when Branch grimaced. "I'm sorry."

His eyes opened. "You're safe now. All the Markhams are dead."

She nodded, pressing her lips together. What did that matter if Branch was hurt?

Etta returned with a box, sitting on the side of the bed.

Branch grunted. "Not the Remedy Box."

"Hush, you. The doc's busy, and we can't wait for him to get here. You're bleeding all over a perfectly good set of bedsheets." Etta opened the box to reveal medical supplies. "Here."

She put a dowel sideways into Branch's mouth, and he bit down.

"Constance, move around to the other side of the bed and hold his hand."

Hugh and Jesse stepped away, and Etta went to work. Constance prayed. Prayed that Etta's hands would be steady, prayed that the wound wasn't as bad as it looked, and prayed that she wouldn't pass out. Branch gripped her hand, looking into her eyes, face rigid with pain as Etta worked.

The Lord heard her prayer, even as a commotion began downstairs and she recognized her sister's voice. Hugh left and things quieted down on the ground floor.

When Etta finished, she washed her hands and took the dowel, holding it up to admire the teeth marks Branch had left. "The bullet's out, and I've wrapped the wound tight. The doctor can decide if it needs stitches, but for now, Constance, you stay with him. Don't let him move around too much. And don't look so worried. He's as tough as a railroad spike. He'll be fine."

When they were alone, she reached out with her free hand and brushed the hair off his brow. "Is there anything I can do for you?"

He studied her for a long time, not saying anything, and then said, "You can forgive me for being a horse's patoot."

"What?"

"It galls me to say it, but..." He shifted on the bed, his forehead furrowed. "Constance Spanner, you're making me loco. One minute, I know what I'm about, what I want, what I've always said, and the next minute, I'm tossing it all aside because I can't stop thinking about you."

Her heart jerked like a horse hitting the end of a lasso.

"I can't believe I'm going to say this, but I think..." He stopped, closing his eyes, wincing. "I'm in love." The words came out as if they tasted badly, and Constance couldn't help it.

She laughed.

He loved her.

"What's so funny?" he growled.

"Is it so terrible, to be in love?"

"Do you have any idea the noise I'm going to hear from the boys? Not to mention the smug look on Etta's face?" His hand caressed hers, his actions contradicting the harshness of his tone.

Constance sobered. "But what about the things that were said about me at the trial?"

"That's what I was apologizing for. For doubting you. I jumped to the conclusion that you must be guilty. I don't know what happened back there in Shreveport, but I would stake my last two bits on you being innocent."

Her heart soared. He believed her, taking it on faith that she was innocent. She paused. "You heard Etta, right? You know you're not dying?"

A chuckle forced its way up his chest. "You think I'm saying this because it's some dying declaration?" He shook his head on the pillow. "I'm doing my best to propose to you, and it would help if you could stop giggling for a minute." His fierce glare sent another ripple of laughter through her.

"What is it about us Spanner women that inspires the men we love to propose to us in the most unlikely fashion? Harley finally popped the question when Clarice had just suffered a beating, and now you, when you've been shot."

"You aren't going to make me buy a new suit and pick you some flowers, are you? Moonlight and a carriage ride and all that?"

"Are you sure?" She put her hand against his cheek. His came up to cover hers, and he lowered it to his chest, pressing her fingers against his shirt front.

He took a deep breath. "I finally found a woman who can load a rifle during a gunfight, who doesn't complain when she's been shot, who doesn't faint or fuss when she has to help dig a bullet out of her man, who can camp out in a cabin in the middle of the brush country without complaining...the perfect Ranger's wife. I don't think I should let her get away."

Constance closed her eyes. The perfect Ranger's wife. Like a stand-in Etta Sterling.

"But," he continued, "she's also pretty as a sunrise, with eyes the color of bluebird wings, and she smells like flowers. She makes my heart beat faster, and she makes me forget every foolish thing I ever thought or said about falling in love."

His hand came up to the back of her neck, and he drew her forward slowly, staring into her eyes. He stopped her when her lips hovered an inch from his, giving her plenty of time to pull away…

But she didn't, lowering her lips to his, sealing all she felt for him with a kiss that promised so much more.

As she retreated a few inches, a smile touched his lips. "You make me forget I'm shot."

"It's really over. The Markham Gang is done?"

He reached into his shirt pocket and pulled out the notebook and a stub of pencil. "Cass, Willie, and Maggie. Cross them off the list."

She took the pencil, opening the little leather book. On the first left-hand page, more than a dozen names, some with an *X* beside them, some crossed through. Captured or killed. Soberly, she drew a line through the three names at the top of the list.

She thumbed through the pages of close, neat writing, her eye landing here and there on events and arrests and information… until she stopped at her own name.

Constance Spanner, witness, Mollie Olson murder.

Protection order by Capt. Sterling. Branch Kilborn custody.

Injured. Testified. Continued Protection.

Shreveport?

Just Marry Her.

Constance wrote under her name. *She said yes. Happily ever after.* And signed her name with a flourish.

EPILOGUE

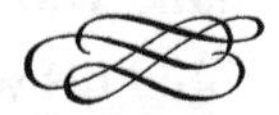

New Year's Day, 1887

"Now that you're an old married man, what are you going to do?" Griff asked, putting his arm around Evelyn and grinning at Branch. Company B of the Frontier Battalion of the Texas Rangers had taken over the private dining room of the Hartville Hotel once again, though their numbers had grown.

Branch shrugged. He'd been married for a whole week, and he couldn't for the life of him think why he'd ever been against the idea. "Guess we've all earned a bit of time off. Constance and I are headed to Shreveport to clear up a few things." He nudged Jack off his foot.

Hugh, at the head of the table, reached into his pocket and pulled out a yellow paper. Everyone grew quiet. "Actually, Griff ran by the telegraph office for me. I spoke with the governor about your situation, and he sent a special investigator to Shreveport." He unfolded the telegram. "According to this, the missing money has been found, and two men, Jacques and Pasquale LeBeque, have been arrested. Seems they were stealing the company money themselves, and when it was discovered, they blamed Miss Spanne—" He stopped and smiled. "Excuse me, Mrs. Kilborn...for the theft."

Constance gripped Branch's leg—his uninjured leg—under the table, and he covered her hand with his.

"That's great news." Jesse lifted his water glass in a little salute.

"I have some other information that affects you all." Hugh rose, setting the telegram beside Branch's plate. "After more years than I care to remember of serving the people of Texas, I've decided to retire from the Texas Rangers."

All levity went out of the room. The men looked from one to another, waiting.

"Etta and I like it here in Hartville, and with Sheriff Watson not recovering the way he had hoped, I've been approached about taking on his job and settling down here. Which means..." He sucked in a long breath. "You'll need a new captain. I've spoken with the governor, and he is very pleased with your work here this last year. He's recommending that you stay on with Hartville as your headquarters, and that Branch become the new company captain."

Hugh slapped him on the shoulder, as he sat there, dumbfounded at this turn of events. Constance leaned against him, and he squeezed her hand harder.

"I propose a toast." Micah stood, and everyone followed suit. "To your happy retirement, to our new company captain, and to the Texas Rangers."

They all raised their glasses, but before they could drink, a knock sounded on the door.

A dusty cowboy barged in. "They stole my cattle. Cut my fence and ran off more than three hundred head of stock."

Branch set his glass down, planted a firm kiss on Constance's mouth, and reached for his hat. He grinned when the other Rangers followed suit, even down to kissing their wives. Wincing a bit on his sore leg but not giving in to the desire to limp, he led his company out the door, ready to tackle their next assignment.

ABOUT THE AUTHOR

Best-selling, award-winning author **Erica Vetsch** loves Jesus, history, romance, and sports. When she's not writing fiction, she's planning her next trip to a history museum. You can connect with her at her website, www.ericavetsch.com and you can find her on Facebook at **The Inspirational Regency Readers Group** where she spends way too much time!

Cover design by: Wild Heart Books

Did you enjoy this book? We hope so!

Would you take a quick minute to leave a review where you purchased the book?

It doesn't have to be long. Just a sentence or two telling what you liked about the story!

Receive a FREE ebook and get updates when new Wild Heart books release: https://wildheartbooks.org/newsletter

Want more?

If you love historical romance, check out the other Wild Heart books!

The Bartered Bride by Erica Vetch

A rebellious suffragette and a steadfast sailor—tied by duty, divided by secrets, and tempted by a love that changes everything.

A born sailor, Jonathan Kennebrae thrives in his role running his grandfather's shipping enterprise. That is until his grandfather delivers a crippling ultimatum—Jonathan will marry Melissa Brooke or lose his inheritance and everything he's worked for. Though Jonathan finds himself drawn to Melissa, he can't help feeling his intended may not be who she appears to be.

Melissa Brooke is tired of being voiceless. She's been the perfect daughter all her life, doing what she's told for the good of the family. Except she has a secret. Melissa lives a double life, teaching literacy to struggling immigrant women and fighting for the suffragette movement. If she goes through with the wedding, she'll be forced to abandon her life's work. Yet refusing the union could cost her any chance at an inheritance to fund her cause. To make matters worse, she can't deny the tender feelings blooming between her and her fiancé.

~

Murmur in the Mud Caves by Kathleen Denly

He came to cook for ranch hands, not three single women.

Gideon Swift, a visually impaired Civil War Veteran, responds to an ad for a ranch cook in the Southern California desert mountains. He wants nothing more than to forget his past and stay in the kitchen where he can do no harm. But when he arrives to find his employer murdered, the ranch turned to ashes, and three young women struggling to survive in the unforgiving Borrego Desert, he must decide whether his presence protects them or places them in greater danger.

Bridget "Biddie" Davidson finally receives word from her older sister who disappeared with their brother and pa eighteen years prior, but the news is not good. Determined to help her family, Biddie sets out for a remote desert ranch with her adopted father and best friend. Nothing she finds there is as she expected, including the man who came to cook for the shambles of a ranch.

When tragedy strikes, the danger threatens not only her plans to help her sister, but her own dreams for the future—with the man who's stolen her heart.

~

The Bandit's Redemption

A holdup gone wrong, a reluctant outlaw, and the captive she's sworn to guard.

Life in the American West hasn't been easy for French refugee Lorraine Durand. She has precious few connections and longs to return to her native land. So when the man who rescued her from a Parisian uprising following the Franco-Prussian War persuades her to help him with a deadly holdup, she reluctantly agrees. Despite his promises otherwise, the gang kidnaps a man, forcing Lorraine to grapple with the fallout of her choices even as she is drawn to the captive she's meant to guard.

Jesse Alexander must survive. If not for himself, then for the troubled sister he left behind in Los Angeles. At the mercy of his captors, he carefully works to earn Lorraine's trust, hoping he can easily subdue her when the time comes. But as they navigate the treacherous wilderness and he searches for his opportunity to escape, he realizes there may be more to her than he first believed.